CHARLOTTE TURNER was born in London in 1749. As a result of her father's reckless spending, she was required to marry very early, at the age of 15, Benjamin Smith, the violent son of a wealthy merchant. They had twelve children. Her husband was eventually incarcerated for debt, and she joined him in debtor's prison. Her first publication, a book of poetry entitled *Elegiac Sonnets*, was published while she lived there in 1784. After release from the prison, the couple moved around trying to avoid Smith's creditors; she finally left him in 1787.

Smith settled near Chichester and her first novel, *Emmeline*, was published very successfully in 1788. It was followed by nine more, as well as essays, children's books and further poetry. She grew increasingly radical, and embraced the growing movement for the rights of women, as well as the huge political changes that accompanied the American War of Independence and the French Revolution.

A legal dispute over her father's will, starving her of funds, had been churning through the chancery system for many years, since his death in 1776. It was not settled in her lifetime. Having hitherto earnt enough through her writing to support herself and her children, changing times saw her star waning and income decreasing. By 1803 she was living in poverty. She died at the age of 57 in 1806.

EMMELINE

THE ORPHAN OF THE CASTLE

WALMER CLASSICS

already published

TOBIAS SMOLLETT
The Adventures of Roderick Random (1748)

CHARLOTTE SMITH
Emmeline (1788)

EMMELINE

THE ORPHAN OF THE CASTLE

by

CHARLOTTE SMITH

Walmer Classics

SANDNESS
MICHAEL WALMER
2023

Emmeline first published in four volumes 1788

This edition first published 2023

by

Michael Walmer
North House
Melby
Sandness
Shetland ZE2 9PL

ISBN 978-0-6457519-0-1 paperback

The publisher gratefully acknowledges the assistance of Robert Heatley in the typesetting process for this volume

TO MY CHILDREN

O'erwhelm'd with sorrow — and sustaining long
'The proud man's contumely, the oppressor's wrong,'
Languid despondency, and vain regret,
Must my exhausted spirit struggle yet?
Yes! robb'd myself of all that Fortune gave,
Of every hope — but shelter in the grave;
Still shall the plaintive lyre essay its powers,
And dress the cave of Care, with Fancy's flowers;
Maternal love, the fiend Despair withstand,
Still animate the heart and guide the hand.
May you, dear objects of my tender care!
Escape the evils, I was born to bear:
Round my devoted head, while tempests roll,
Yet there — 'where I have treasured up my soul,'
May the soft rays of dawning hope impart
Reviving patience to my fainting heart;
And, when its sharp anxieties shall cease,
May I be conscious, in the realms of peace,
That every tear which swells my children's eyes,
From evils past, not present sorrows, rise.
Then, with some friend who loves to share your pain,
(For 'tis my boast, that still such friends remain,)
By filial grief, and fond remembrance prest,
You'll seek the spot where all my miseries rest,
Recall my hapless days in sad review,
The long calamities I bore for you,

And, with an happier fate, resolve to prove
How well ye merited your mother's love!

VOLUME I

CHAPTER I

IN a remote part of the county of Pembroke, is an old building, formerly of great strength, and inhabited for centuries by the ancient family of Mowbray; to the sole remaining branch of which it still belonged, tho' it was, at the time this history commences, inhabited only by servants; and the greater part of it was gone to decay. A few rooms only had been occasionally repaired to accommodate the proprietor, when he found it necessary to come thither to receive his rents, or to inspect the condition of the estate; which however happened so seldom, that during the twelve years he had been master of it, he had only once visited the castle for a few days. The business that related to the property round it (which was very considerable) was conducted by a steward grown grey in the service of the family, and by an attorney from London, who came to hold the courts. And an old housekeeper, a servant who waited on her, the steward, and a labourer who was kept to look after his horse and work in that part of the garden which yet bore the vestige of cultivation, were now all its inhabitants; except a little girl, of whom the housekeeper had the care, and who was believed to be the natural daughter of that elder brother, by whose death Lord Montreville, the present possessor, became entitled to the estate.

This nobleman, while yet a younger son, was (by the partiality of his mother, who had been an heiress, and that of some other female relations) master of a property nearly equal to what he inherited by the death of his brother, Mr. Mowbray.

He had been originally designed for the law; but in consequence of being entitled to the large estate which had been his mother's, and heir, by will, to all her opulent family, he had quitted that profession, and at the age of about four and twenty, had married Lady Eleonore Delamere, by whom he had a son and two daughters.

The illustrious family from which Lady Eleonore descended, became extinct in the male line by the premature death of her two brothers; and her Ladyship becoming sole heiress, her husband took the name of Delamere; and obtaining one of the titles of the lady's father, was, at his death, created Viscount Montreville. Mr. Mowbray died before he was thirty, in Italy; and Lord Montreville, on taking possession of Mowbray Castle, found there his infant daughter.

Her mother had died soon after her birth; and she had been sent from France, where she was born, and put under the care of Mrs. Carey, the housekeeper, who was tenderly attached to her, having been the attendant of Mr. Mowbray from his earliest infancy.

Lord Montreville suffered her to remain in the situation in which he found her, and to go by the name of

Mowbray: he allowed for the trifling charge of her board and necessary cloaths in the steward's account, the examination of which was for some years the only circumstance that reminded him of the existence of the unfortunate orphan.

With no other notice from her father's family, Emmeline had attained her twelfth year; an age at which she would have been left in the most profound ignorance, if her uncommon understanding, and unwearied application, had not supplied the deficiency of her instructors, and conquered the disadvantages of her situation.

Mrs. Carey could indeed read with tolerable fluency, and write an hand hardly legible: and Mr. Williamson, the old steward, had been formerly a good penman, and was still a proficient in accounts. Both were anxious to give their little charge all the instruction they could: but without the quickness and attention she shewed to whatever they attempted to teach, such preceptors could have done little.

Emmeline had a kind of intuitive knowledge; and comprehended every thing with a facility that soon left her instructors behind her. The precarious and neglected situation in which she lived, troubled not the innocent Emmeline. Having never experienced any other, she felt no uneasiness at her present lot; and on the future she was not yet old enough to reflect.

Mrs. Carey was to her in place of the mother she had never known; and the old steward, she was accustomed to call father. The death of this venerable servant was the first sorrow Emmeline ever felt: returning late one evening, in the winter, from a neighbouring town, he attempted to cross a ford, where the waters being extremely out, he was carried down by the rapidity of the current. His horse was drowned; and tho' he was himself rescued from the flood by some peasants who knew him, and carried to the castle, he was so much bruised, and had suffered so much from cold, that he was taken up speechless, and continued so for the few hours he survived the accident.

Mrs. Carey, who had lived in the same house with him near forty years, felt the sincerest concern at his death; with which it was necessary for her immediately to acquaint Lord Montreville.

His Lordship directed his attorney in London to replace him with another; to whom Mrs. Carey, with an aching heart, delivered the keys of the steward's room and drawers.

Her health, which was before declining, received a rude shock from the melancholy death of Mr. Williamson; and she and her little ward had soon the mortification of seeing he was forgotten by all but themselves.

Frequent and severe attacks of the gout now made daily ravages in the constitution of Mrs. Carey; and her illness recurred so often, that Emmeline, now almost fourteen, began to reflect on what she should do, if Mrs. Carey died: and these reflections occasionally gave her pain. But she was not yet of an age to consider deeply, or to dwell long on gloomy subjects. Her mind, however, gradually expanded, and her judgment improved: for among the deserted rooms of this once noble edifice, was a library, which had been well furnished with the books of those ages in which they had been collected. Many of them were in black letter; and so injured by time, that the most indefatigable antiquary could have made nothing of them.

From these, Emmeline turned in despair to some others of more modern appearance; which, tho' they also had suffered from the dampness of the room, and in some parts were almost effaced with mould, were yet generally legible. Among them, were Spenser and Milton, two or three volumes of the Spectator, an old edition of Shakespeare, and an odd volume or two of Pope.

These, together with some tracts of devotion, which she knew would be very acceptable to Mrs. Carey, she cleaned by degrees from the dust with which they were covered, and removed into the housekeeper's room: where the village carpenter accommodated her with a shelf, on which, with great pride of heart, she placed her new acquisitions.

The dismantled windows, and broken floor of the library, prevented her continuing there long together: but she frequently renewed her search, and with infinite pains examined all the piles of books, some of which lay tumbled in heaps on the floor, others promiscuously placed on the shelves, where the swallow, the sparrow, and the daw, had found habitations for many years: for as the present proprietor had determined to lay out no more than was absolutely necessary to keep one end of the castle habitable, the library, which was in the most deserted part of it, was in a ruinous state, and had long been entirely forsaken.

Emmeline, however, by her unwearied researches, nearly completed several sets of books, in which instruction and amusement were happily blended. From them she acquired a taste for poetry, and the more ornamental parts of literature; as well as the grounds of that elegant and useful knowledge, which, if it rendered not her life happier, enabled her to support, with the dignity of conscious worth, those undeserved evils with which many of her years were embittered.

Mrs. Carey, now far advanced in life, found her infirmities daily increase. She was often incapable of leaving her chamber for many weeks; during which Emmeline attended her with the solicitude and affection of a daughter; scorned not to perform the most humble offices that contributed to her relief; and sat by her whole days, or watched her whole nights, with the tenderest and most unwearied assiduity.

On those evenings in summer, when her attendance could for a few hours be dispensed with, she delighted to wander among the rocks that formed the bold and magnificent boundary of the ocean, which spread its immense expanse of water within half a mile of the castle. Simply dressed, and with no other protection than Providence, she often rambled several miles into the country, visiting the remote huts of the shepherds, among the wildest mountains.

During the life of Mrs. Mowbray, a small stipend had been annually allowed for the use of the poor: this had not yet been withdrawn; and it now passed thro' the hands of Mrs. Carey, whose enquiries into the immediate necessities of the cottagers in the neighbourhood of the castle, devolved to Emmeline, when she was herself unable to make them.

The ignorant rustics, who had seen Emmeline grow up among them from her earliest infancy, and who now beheld her with the compassion as well as the beauty of an angel, administering to their necessities and alleviating their misfortunes, looked upon her as a superior being, and throughout the country she was almost adored.

Perfectly unconscious of those attractions which now began to charm every other eye, Emmeline had entered her sixteenth year; and the progress of her understanding was equal to the improvement of her person; which, tho' she was not perfectly handsome, could not be beheld at first without pleasure, and which the more it was seen became more interesting and engaging.

Her figure was elegant and graceful; somewhat exceeding the middling height. Her eyes were blue; and her hair brown. Her features not very regular; yet there was a sweetness in her countenance, when she smiled, more charming than the effect of the most regular features could have given. Her countenance, open and ingenuous, expressed every emotion of her mind: it had assumed rather a pensive cast; and tho' it occasionally was lighted up by vivacity, had been lately frequently overclouded; when the sufferings of her only friend called forth all the generous sympathy of her nature.

And now the first severe misfortune she had known was about to overtake her. Early in the spring of that year, which was the sixteenth from her birth, Mrs. Carey had felt an attack of the gout, which however was short; and her health seemed for some time afterwards more settled than it had been for many months. She was one evening preparing to go down to the village, leaning on the arm of Emmeline, when she suddenly complained of an acute pain in her head, and fell back into a chair. The affrighted girl called for assistance, and endeavoured by every means in her power to recover her, but it was impossible; the gout had seized her head; and casting on Emmeline a look which seemed to express all she felt at leaving her thus desolate and friendless, her venerable friend, after a short struggle, breathed her last.

What should Emmeline now do? In this distress (the first she had ever known) how should she act? She saw, in the lifeless corps before her, the person on whom she had, from her first recollection, been accustomed to rely; who had provided for all her wants, and prevented every care for herself. And now she was left to perform for this dear friend the last sad offices, and knew not what would hereafter be her own lot.

In strong and excellent understandings there is, in every period of life, a force which distress enables them to exert, and which prevents their sinking under the pressure of those evils which overwhelm and subdue minds more feeble and unequal.

The spirits of Emmeline were yet unbroken by affliction, and her understanding was of the first rank. She possessed this native firmness in a degree very unusual to her age and sex. Instead therefore of giving way to tears and exclamations she considered how she should best perform all she now could do for her deceased friend; and having seen every proper care taken of her remains, and given orders for every thing relative to them, with the solemn serenity of settled sorrow, she retired to her room, where she began to reflect on her irreparable loss, and the melancholy situation in which she was left; which she never had courage to consider closely till it was actually before her.

Painful indeed were the thoughts that now crouded on her mind; encreasing the anguish of her spirit for her recent misfortune. She considered herself as a being belonging to nobody; as having no right to claim the protection of any one; no power to procure for herself the necessities of life. On the steward Maloney she had long looked with disgust, from the assured and forward manner in which he thought proper to treat her. The freedom of his behaviour, which she could with difficulty repress while Mrs. Carey lived, might now, she feared, approach to more insulting familiarity; to be exposed to which, entirely in his power, and without any female companion, filled her with the most alarming apprehensions: and the more her mind dwelt on that circumstance the more she was terrified at the prospect before her; insomuch, that she would immediately have quitted the house — But whither could she go?

By abruptly leaving the asylum Lord Montreville had hitherto allowed her, she feared she might forfeit all claim to his future protection: and, unknown as she was to the principal inhabitants of the country, who were few, and their houses at a great distance, she could hardly hope to be received by any of them.

She had therefore no choice left but to remain at the castle till she heard from Lord Montreville: and she determined to acquaint his Lordship of the death of Mrs. Carey, and desire to receive his commands as to herself.

Fatigued and oppressed, she retired to bed, but not to sleep. The image of her expiring protectress was still before her eyes; and if exhausted nature forced her to give way to a momentary forgetfulness, she soon started from her imperfect slumber, and fancied she heard the voice of Mrs. Carey, calling on her for help; and her last groan still vibrated in her ears — while the stillness of the night, interrupted only by the cries of the owls which haunted the ruins, added to the gloomy and mournful sensations of her mind.

At length however the sun arose — the surrounding objects lost the horror that darkness and silence had lent them — and Emmeline fell into a short but refreshing repose.

CHAPTER II

AS soon as Emmeline arose the next morning, she addressed the following letter to Lord Montreville.

'My Lord,

In the utmost affliction, I address myself to your Lordship, to acquaint you with the death of Mrs. Carey, after an illness of a very few moments: by which unhappy event I have lost a friend who has indeed been a mother to me; and am now left at the castle, ignorant of your Lordship's pleasure as to my future residence.

You will, my Lord, I doubt not, recollect that it is, at my time of life, improper for me to reside here with Mr. Maloney; and if it be your Lordship's intention for me to continue here, I hope you will have the goodness to send down some proper person to fill the place of the worthy woman I have lost.

On your Lordship's humanity and consideration I depend for an early answer: in which hope I have the honour to remain,

your Lordship's
dutiful and most humble servant,
EMMELINE MOWBRAY.'

Mowbray Castle,
21st May.

The same post carried a letter from Mr. Maloney, informing Lord Montreville of the housekeeper's death, and desiring directions about *Miss,* as he elegantly termed Emmeline.

To these letters no answers were returned for upwards of a fortnight: during which melancholy interval, Emmeline followed to the grave the remains of the friend of her infancy, and took a last farewell of the only person who seemed interested for her welfare. Then returning with streaming eyes to her own room, she threw herself on the bed, and gave way to a torrent of tears; for her spirits were overcome by the mournful scene to which she had just been a witness, and by the heavy forebodings of future sorrow which oppressed her heart.

The troublesome civilities of the steward Maloney, she soon found the difficulty of evading. Fearful of offending him from whom she could not escape; yet unable to keep up an intercourse of civility with a man who would interpret it into an encouragement of his presumptuous attentions, she was compelled to make use of an artifice; and to plead ill health as an excuse for not dining as usual in the steward's room: and indeed her uneasiness and grief were such as hardly made it a pretence.

After many days of anxious expectation, the following letter arrived from the house-steward of Lord

Montreville; as on such an occasion his Lordship did not think it necessary to write himself.

Berkley-square, June 17, 17—

'Miss,

My Lord orders me to acquaint you, that in consequence of yours of the 21st ult. informing his Lordship of the old housekeeper's, Mrs. Carey's, decease, he has directed Mrs. Grant, his Lordship's town housekeeper, to look out for another; and Mrs. Grant has agreed with a gentlewoman accordingly, who will be down at the castle forthwith. My Lord is gone to Essex; but has directed me to let Mr. Maloney know, that he is to furnish you with all things needful same as before. By my Lord's command, from, Miss,

your very humble servant, RICHARD MADDOX.'

While Emmeline waited the expected arrival of the person to whose care she was now to be consigned, the sister of Mrs. Carey, who was the only relation she had, sent a nephew of her husband's to take possession of what effects had belonged to her; in doing which, a will was found, in which she bequeathed fifty pounds as a testimony of her tender affection to 'Miss Emmeline Mowbray, the daughter of her late dear master;' together with all the contents of a small chest of drawers, which stood in her room. The rest of her property, which consisted of her cloaths and about two hundred pounds, which she had saved in service, became her sister's, and were delivered by Maloney to the young man commissioned to receive them.

In the drawers given to her, Emmeline found some fine linen and laces, which had belonged to her mother; and two little silk boxes covered with nuns' embroidery, which seemed not to have been opened for many years.

Emmeline saw that they were filled with letters: some of them in a hand which she had been shewn as her father's. But she left them uninspected, and fastened up the caskets; her mind being yet too much affected with her loss to be able to examine any thing which brought to her recollection the fond solicitude of her departed friend.

The cold and mechanical terms in which the steward's letter was written, encreased all her uneasy fears as to her future prospects.

Lord Montreville seemed to feel no kindness for her; nor to give any consideration to her forlorn and comfortless situation. The officious freedoms of Maloney encreased so much, that she was obliged to confine herself almost entirely to her own room to avoid him; and she determined, that if after the arrival of the companion she expected, he continued to besiege her with so much impertinent familiarity, she would quit the house, tho' compelled to accept the meanest service for a subsistence.

After a fortnight of expectation, notice was received at the castle, that Mrs. Garnet, the housekeeper, was arrived at the market town. The labourer, with an horse, was dispatched for her, and towards evening she made her entry.

To Emmeline, who had from her earliest remembrance been accustomed only to the plainest dress, and the most simple and sober manners, the figure and deportment of this woman appeared equally extraordinary.

She wore a travelling dress of tawdry-coloured silk, trimmed with bright green ribbands; and her head was covered with an immense black silk hat, from which depended many yellow streamers; while the plumage, with which it was plentifully adorned, hung dripping over her face, from the effects of a thunder shower thro' which she had passed. Her hair, tho' carefully curled and powdered on her leaving London, had been also greatly deranged in her journey, and descended, in knotty tufts of a dirty yellow, over her cheeks and forehead; adding to the vulgar ferocity of a harsh countenance and a coarse complexion. Her figure was uncommonly tall and honey; and her voice so discordant and shrill, as to pierce the ear with the most unpleasant sensation, and compleat the disagreeable idea her person impressed.

Emmeline saw her enter, handed by the officious Maloney; and repressing her astonishment, she arose, and attempted to speak to her: but the contrast between the dirty, tawdry, and disgusting figure before her, and the sober plainness and neat simplicity of her lost friend, struck so forcibly on her imagination, that she burst into tears, and was altogether unable to command her emotion.

The steward having with great gallantry handed in the newly arrived lady, she thus began:

'Oh! Lord a marcy on me! — to be shore I be got here at last! But indeed if I had known whereabout I was a coming to, 'tis not a double the wagers as should a hired me. Lord! why what a ramshakel mild place it is! — and then such a monstrous long way from London! I suppose, Sir,' (to Maloney) 'as you be the steward; and you Miss, I reckon, be the young Miss as I be to have the care on. Why to be sure I didn't much expect to see a christian face in such an out of the way place. I don't b'leve I shall stay; howsomdever do let me have **some** tea; and do you, Miss, shew me whereabout I be to sleep.'

Emmeline, struggling with her dislike, or at least desirous of concealing it, did not venture to trust her voice with an answer; for her heart was too full; but stepping to the door, she called to the female servant, and ordered her to shew the lady her room. She had herself been used to share that appropriated to Mrs. Carey; but she now resolved to remove her bed into an apartment in one of the turrets of the castle, which was the only unoccupied room not wholly exposed to the weather.

This little room had been sashed by Mrs. Mowbray on account of the beautiful prospect it commanded between the hills, where suddenly sinking to the South West, they made way through a long narrow valley, fringed with copses, for a small but rapid river; which hurrying among immense stones, and pieces of rock that seemed to have been torn from the mountains by its violence, rushed into the sea at the distance of a mile from the castle.

This room, now for many years neglected, was much out of repair, but still habitable; and tho' it was at a great distance from the rooms yet occupied, Emmeline chose rather to take up her abode in it, than partake of the apartment which was now to belong to Mrs. Garnet: and she found reason to applaud herself for this determination when she heard the exclamation Mrs. Garnet made on entering it —

'Lord! why 'tis but a shabbyish place; and here is two beds I see. But that won't suit me I asshore you. I chuses to have a room to myself, if it be ever so.'

'Be not in any pain on that account, Madam,' said Emmeline, who had now collected her thoughts; 'it is my intention to remove my bed, and I have directed a person to do it immediately.'

She then returned into the steward's room, where Maloney thus addressed her —

'Sarvent again, pretty Miss! Pray how d'ye like our new housekeeper? A smartish piece of goods upon my word for Pembrokeshire; quite a London lady, eh, Miss?'

'It is impossible for me, Sir, to judge of her yet.'

'Why ay, Miss, as you justly observes, 'tis full early to know what people be; but I hope we shall find her quite the thing; and if so be as she's but good tempered, and agreeable, and the like, why I warrant we shall pass this here summer as pleasant as any thing can be. And now my dear Miss, perhaps, may'nt be so shy and distant, as she have got another woman body to keep her company.'

This eloquent harangue was interrupted by the return of Mrs. Garnet, full of anxiety for her tea; and in the bustle created by the desire of the maid and Maloney to accommodate her, Emmeline retired to her new apartment, where she was obliged to attend to the removal of her bed and other things; and excusing herself, under the pretence of fatigue, from returning to the steward's room, she passed some time in melancholy recollection and more melancholy anticipation, and then retired to rest.

Some days passed in murmurs on the part of Mrs. Garnet, and in silence on that of Emmeline; who, as soon as she had finished her short repasts, always went to her own room.

After a few weeks, she discovered that the lady grew every day more reconciled to her situation; and from the pleasures she apparently took in the gallantries of Maloney, and his constant assiduities to her, the innocent

Emmeline supposed there was really an attachment forming between them, which would certainly deliver her from the displeasing attentions of the steward.

Occupied almost entirely by her books, of which she every day became more enamoured, she never willingly broke in upon a tête à tête which she fancied was equally agreeable to all parties; and she saw with satisfaction that they regretted not her absence.

But the motives of Maloney's attention were misunderstood. Insensible as such a man must be supposed to the charms of the elegant and self-cultivated mind of Emmeline, her personal beauty had made a deep impression on his heart; and he had formed a design of marrying her, before the death of Mrs. Carey, to whom he had once or twice mentioned something like a hint of his wishes: but she had received all his discourse on that topic with so much coldness, and ever so carefully avoided any conversation that might again lead to it, that he had been deterred from entirely explaining himself. Now, however, he thought the time was arrived, when he might make a more successful application; for he never doubted but that Mrs. Garnet would obtain, over the tender and ingenuous mind of Emmeline, an influence as great as had been possessed by Mrs. Carey.

Nor did he apprehend that a friendless orphan, without fortune or connections, would want much persuasion to marry a young man of handsome figure (as he conceived himself to be,) who was established in a profitable place, and had some dependance of his own.

The distance which Emmeline had always obliged him to observe, he imputed to the timidity of her nature; which he hoped would be lessened by the free and familiar manners of her present companion, whose conversation was very unlike what she had before been accustomed to hear from Mrs. Carey.

Impressed with these ideas, he paid his court most assiduously to the housekeeper, who put down all his compliments to the account of her own attractions; and was extremely pleased with her conquest; which she exhausted all her eloquence and all her wardrobe to secure.

CHAPTER III

IN this situation were the inhabitants of Mowbray castle; when, in the beginning of July, orders were received from Lord Montreville to set workmen immediately about repairing the whole end of the castle which was yet habitable; as his son, Mr. Delamere, intended to come down early in the Autumn, to shoot, for some weeks, in Wales. His Lordship added, that it was possible he might himself be there also for a few weeks; and therefore directed several bed-chambers to be repaired, for which he would send down furniture from London.

No time was lost in obeying these directions. Workmen were immediately procured, and the utmost expedition used to put the place in a situation to receive its master: while Emmeline, who foresaw that the arrival of Lord Montreville would probably occasion some change in regard to herself, and who thought that every change must be for the better, beheld these preparations with pleasure.

All had been ready some weeks, and the time fixed for Mr. Delamere's journey elapsed, but he had yet given no notice of his arrival.

At length, towards the middle of September, they were one evening alarmed by the noise of horses on the ascent to the castle.

Emmeline retired to her own room, fearful of she knew not what; while Mrs. Garnet and Maloney flew eagerly to the door; where a French valet, and an English groom with a led horse, presented themselves, and were ushered into the old kitchen; the dimensions of which, blackened as it was with the smoke of ages, and provided with the immense utensils of ancient hospitality, failed not to amaze them both.

The Frenchman expressed his wonder and dislike by several grimaces; and then addressing himself to Mrs. Garnet, exclaimed —

'Peste! Milor croit'il qu'on peut subsister dans cette espece d'enfer? Montré moi les apartements de Monsieur.'

'Oh, your name is Mounseer, is it?' answered she — 'Aye, I thought so — What would you please to have, Mounseer?'

'Diable!' cried the distressed valet; 'voici une femme aussi sauvage que le lieu qu'elle habite. Com, com, you Jean Groom, speak littel to dis voman pour moi.'

With the help of John, who had been some time used to his mode of explaining himself, Mrs. Garnet understood that Mounseer desired to be shewn the apartments, destined for his master, which he assiduously assisted in preparing; and then seeing the women busied in following his directions, he attempted to return to his companion; but by missing a turning which should have carried him to the kitchen, he was bewildered among the long galleries and obscure passages of the castle, and after several efforts, could neither find his way back to the women, nor into the kitchen; but continued to blunder about till the encreasing gloom, which approaching night threw over the arched and obscure apartments, through windows dim with painted glass, filled him with apprehension and dismay, and he believed he should wander there the whole night; in which fear he began to make a strange noise for assistance, to which nobody attended, for indeed nobody for some time heard him. His terror encreasing, he continued to traverse one of the passages, when a door at the corner of it opened, and Emmeline came out.

The man, whose imagination was by this time filled with ideas of spectres, flew back at her sudden appearance, and added the contortions of fear to his otherwise grotesque appearance, in a travelling jacket of white cloth, laced, and his hair in papillotes.

Emmeline, immediately comprehending that it was one of Mr. Delamere's servants, enquired what he wanted; and the man, reassured by her voice and figure, which there was yet light enough to discern, approached her, and endeavoured to explain that he had lost himself; in a language, which, though Emmeline did not understand, she knew to be French.

She walked with him therefore to the gallery which opened to the great stair-case, from whence he could hardly mistake his way; where having pointed it to him, she turned back towards her own room.

But Millefleur, who had now had an opportunity to contemplate the person of his conductress, was not disposed so easily to part with her.

By the extreme simplicity of her dress, he believed her to be only some fair villager, or an assistant to the housekeeper; and therefore without ceremony he began in broken English to protest his admiration, and seized her hand with an impertinent freedom extremely shocking to Emmeline.

She snatched it from him; and flying hastily back through those passages which all his courage did not suffice to make him attempt exploring again, she regained her turret, the door of which she instantly locked and bolted; then breathless with fear and anger, she reflected on the strange and unpleasant scene she had passed through, and felt greatly humbled, to find that she was now likely to be exposed to the insolent familiarity of servants, from which she knew not whether the presence of the master would protect her.

While she suffered the anguish these thoughts brought with them, Millefleur travelled back to the kitchen; where he began an oration in his own language on the beauty of the young woman he had met with.

Neither Mrs. Garnet nor Maloney understood what he was saying; but John, who had been in France, and knew a good deal of the language, told them that he had seen a very pretty girl, in whose praise he was holding forth.

'Why, Lord,' exclaimed Mrs. Garnet, 'tis our Miss as Mounseer means; I had a quite forgot the child; I'll go call her; but howsomdever Mounseer won't be able to get a word out of her; if she's a beauty I asshore you 'tis a dumb beauty.'

Maloney, by no means pleased with Millefleur's discovery, would willingly have prevented the housekeeper's complaisance; but not knowing how to do it, he was obliged to let her ascend to Emmeline, whose door she found locked.

'Miss! Miss!' cried she, rapping loudly, 'you must come down.' 'Is my Lord or Mr. Delamere arrived?' enquired Emmeline. 'No,' replied Mrs. Garnet, 'neither of em be'nt come yet; but here's my Lord's waley de sham, and another servant, and you'll come down to tea to be sure.'

'No,' said Emmeline, 'you must excuse me, Mrs. Garnet. I am not very well; and if I were, should decline appearing to these people, with whom, perhaps, it may not be my Lord's design that I should associate.'

'People!' exclaimed Mrs. Garnet; 'as to people, I do suppose that for all one of them is a Frenchman, they be as good as other folks; and if I am agreeable to let them drink tea in my room, sure you, Miss, mid'nt be so squeamish. But do as you please; for my part I shan't court beauties.

So saying, the angry housekeeper descended to her companions, to whom she complained of the pride and ill manners of Miss; while Maloney rejoiced at a reserve so favourable to the hopes he entertained.

Emmeline determined to remain as much as possible in her own room, 'till Lord Montreville or Mr. Delamere came, and then to solicit her removal.

She therefore continued positively to refuse to appear to the party below; and ordered the maid servant to bring her dinner into her own room, which she never quitted 'till towards evening, to pursue her usual walks.

On the third afternoon subsequent to the arrival of Mr. Delamere's avant-couriers, Emmeline went down to the sea side, and seating herself on a fragment of rock, fixed her eyes insensibly on the restless waves that broke at her feet. The low murmurs of the tide retiring on the sands;

the sighing of the wind among the rocks which hung over her head, cloathed with long grass and marine plants; the noise of the sea fowl going to their nests among the cliffs; threw her into a profound reverie.

She forgot awhile all her apprehended misfortunes, a sort of stupor took possession of her senses, and she no longer remembered how the time had passed there, which already exceeded two hours; though the moon, yet in its encrease, was arisen, and threw a long line of radience on the water.

Thus lost in indistinct reflections, she was unconscious of the surrounding objects, when the hasty tread of somebody on the pebbles behind her, made her suddenly recollect herself; and though accustomed to be so much alone, she started in some alarm in remembering the late hour, and the solitary place where she was.

A man approached her, in whom with satisfaction she recollected a young peasant of the village, who was frequently employed in messages from the castle.

'Miss Emmy,' said the lad, 'you are wanted at home; for there is my Lord his own self, and the young Lord, and more gentlefolks come; so Madam Garnet sent me to look for you all about.'

Emmeline, hurried by this intelligence, walked hastily away with the young villager, and soon arrived at the castle.

The wind had blown her beautiful hair about her face, and the glow of her cheeks was heightened by exercise and apprehension. A more lovely figure than she now appeared could hardly be imagined. She had no time to reflect on the interview; but hastened immediately into the parlour where Lord Montreville was sitting with his son; Mr. Fitz-Edward, who was a young officer, his friend, distantly related to the family; and Mr. Headly, a man celebrated for his knowledge of rural improvements, whom Lord Montreville had brought down to have his opinion of the possibility of rendering Mowbray Castle a residence fit for his family for a few months in the year.

Lord Montreville was about five and forty years old. His general character was respectable. He had acquitted himself with honor in the senate; and in his private life had shewn great regularity and good conduct. But he had basked perpetually in the sunshine of prosperity; and his feelings, not naturally very acute, were blunted by having never suffered in his own person any uneasiness which might have taught him sensibility for that of others.

To this cause it was probably owing, that he never reflected on the impropriety of receiving his niece before strangers; and that he ordered Emmeline to be introduced into the room where they were all sitting together.

Having once seen Emmeline a child of five or six years old; he still formed an idea of her as a child; and adverted not to the change that almost nine years had made in her person and manners; it was therefore with some degree of surprize, that instead of the child he expected, he saw a tall, elegant young woman, whose air, though timidity was the most conspicuous in it, had yet much of dignity and grace, and in whose face he saw the features of his brother, softened into feminine beauty.

The apathy which prosperity had taught him, gave way for a moment to his surprize at the enchanting figure of his niece.

He arose, and approached her. — 'Miss Mowbray! how amazingly you are grown! I am glad to see you.' He took her hand; while Emmeline, trembling and blushing, endeavoured to recollect herself, and said —

'I thank you, my Lord, and I am happy in having an opportunity of paying my respects to your Lordship.'

He led her to a seat, and again repeated his wonder to find her so much grown.

Delamere, who had been standing at the fire conversing with Fitz-Edward, now advanced, and desired his father to introduce him; which ceremony being passed, he drew a chair close to that in which Emmeline was placed; and fixing his eyes on her face with a look of admiration and enquiry that extremely abashed her, he seemed to be examining the beauties of that lovely and interesting countenance which had so immediately dazzled and surprized him.

Fitz-Edward, a young soldier, related to the family of Lady Montreville, was almost constantly the companion of Delamere, and had expectations that the interest Lord Montreville possessed would be exerted to advance him in his profession. His manner was very insinuating, and his person uncommonly elegant. He affected to be a judge as well as an admirer of beauty, and seemed to behold with approbation the fair inhabitant of the castle; who, with heightened blushes, and averted looks, waited in silence 'till Lord Montreville should again address her, which he at length did.

'I was sorry, Miss Mowbray, to hear of the death of old Carey.' The tears started into the eyes of Emmeline.

'She was an excellent servant, and served the family faithfully many years.'

Poor Emmeline felt the tears fall on her bosom.

'But however she was old; and had been, I suppose, long infirm. I hope the person who now fills her place has supplied it to your satisfaction?'

'Ye—s, yes, my lord;' inarticulately sobbed Emmeline, quite overcome by the mention of her old friend.

'I dare say she does,' resumed his Lordship; 'for Grant, of whom Lady Montreville has a very high opinion, assured her Ladyship she was well recommended.'

Emmeline now found her emotion very painful; she therefore rose to go, and curtseying to Lord Montreville, tried to wish him good night.

'A good night to you, Miss Mowbray,' said he, rising. Delamere started from his chair; and taking her hand, desired to have the honour of conducting her to her room. But this was a gallantry his father by no means approved. 'No, Frederic,' said he, taking himself the hand he held, 'you will give *me* leave to see Miss Mowbray to the door.' He led her thither, and then bowing, wished her again good night.

Emmeline hurried to her room; where she endeavoured to recollect her dissipated spirits, and to consider in what way it would be proper for her to address Lord Montreville the next day, to urge her request of a removal from the castle.

Mrs. Carey had a sister who resided at Swansea in Glamorganshire; where her husband had a little place in the excise, and where she had a small house, part of which she had been accustomed to let to those who frequented the place for the benefit of sea-bathing.

She was old, and without any family of her own; and Emmeline, to whom she was the more agreeable as being the sister of Mrs. Carey, thought she might reside with her with propriety and comfort, if Lord Montreville would allow her a small annual stipend for her cloaths and board.

While she was considering in what manner to address herself to his Lordship the next day, the gentlemen were talking of the perfections of the nymph of the castle; by which name Delamere toasted her at supper.

Lord Montreville, who did not seem particularly delighted with the praise his son so warmly bestowed, said —

'Why surely, Frederic, you are uncommonly eloquent on behalf of your Welch cousin.'

'Faith, my Lord,' answered Delamere, 'I like her so well that I think it's a little unlucky I did not come alone. My Welch cousin is the very thing for a tête â tête.'

'Yes,' said Lord Montreville, carelessly, 'she is really grown a good fine young woman. Don't you think so, George?' addressing himself to Fitz-Edward.

'I do indeed, my Lord,' answered he; 'and here's Mr. Headly, tho' an old married man, absolutely petrified with admiration.'

'Upon my soul, Headly,' continued Delamere, 'I already begin to see great capabilities about this venerable mansion. I think I shall take to it, as my father offers it me; especially as I suppose Miss Emmeline is to be included in the inventory.'

'Come, come, Frederic,' said Lord Montreville, gravely, 'no light conversation on the subject of Miss Mowbray. She is under my care; and I must have her treated with propriety.'

His Lordship immediately changed the discourse, and soon after complaining of being fatigued, retired to his chamber.

CHAPTER IV

LORD Montreville, whose first object was his son, had observed, with some alarm, the immediate impression he seemed to have received from the beauty of Emmeline.

The next day, he made some farther remarks on his attention to her when they met at dinner, which gave him still more uneasiness; and he accused himself of great indiscretion in having thrown an object, whose loveliness he could not help acknowledging, in the way of Delamere, whose ardent and impetuous temper he knew so well. This gave his behaviour to Emmeline an air of coldness, and even of displeasure, which prevented her summoning courage to speak to him in the morning of the day after his arrival: and the evening afforded her no opportunity; for Lord Montreville, determined to keep her as much as possible out of the sight of Delamere, did not send for her down to supper, and had privately resolved to remove her as soon as possible to some other residence.

Thus his apprehensions lest his son should form an attachment prejudicial to his ambitious views, produced in his Lordship's mind a resolution in regard to placing more properly his orphan niece, which no consideration, had it related merely to herself, would probably have effected.

At supper, Delamere enquired eagerly for his 'lovely cousin.' To which Lord Montreville drily answered, 'that she did not, he believed, sup below.'

But the manner of this enquiry, and the anxious looks Delamere directed towards the door, together with his repeated questions, increased all Lord Montreville's fears.

He went to bed out of humour rather with himself than his son; and rising early the next morning, enquired for Miss Mowbray.

Miss Mowbray was walked out as was her custom, very early, no one knew whither.

He learned also that Mr. Delamere was gone out with his gun without Fitz-Edward; who not being very fond of field sports, had agreed to join him at a later hour.

He immediately fancied that Delamere and Emmeline might meet; and the pain such a suspicion brought with it, was by him, who had hardly ever felt an hour's uneasiness, considered as so great an evil, that he determined to put an end to it as soon as possible.

After an hasty breakfast in his own room, he summoned Maloney to attend him, and went over the accounts of the estates entrusted to him, with the state of which his Lordship declared himself well contented. And not knowing to whom else he could apply, to enquire for a situation for Emmeline, he told Maloney, that as Miss Mowbray was now of an age to require some alteration in her mode of life, he was desirous of finding her a reputable house in some town in Wales, where she might lodge and board.

Maloney, encouraged by being thus consulted by his Lord, ventured, with many bows, blushes, and stammering apologies, to disclose to Lord Montreville his partiality to Miss Mowbray.

And this communication he so contrived to word, that his Lordship had no doubt of Emmeline's having allowed him to make it.

Lord Montreville listened therefore in silence, and without any marks of disapprobation, to the account Maloney proceeded to give of his prospects and property.

While he was doing so, family pride made a faint struggle in his Lordship's breast on behalf of his deserted ward. He felt some pain in determining, that a creature boasting a portion of the Mowbray blood, should sink into the wife of a man of such inferior birth as Maloney.

But when the advantages of so easily providing for her were recollected; when he considered that Maloney would be happy to take her with a few hundred pounds, and that all apprehensions in regard to his son would by that means for ever be at an end; avarice and ambition, two passions which too much influenced Lord Montreville, joined to persuade him of the propriety of the match; and became infinitely too powerful to let him listen to his regard to the memory of his brother or his pity for his deserted ward.

He thought, that as the existence of Emmeline was hardly known beyond the walls of the castle, he should incur no censure from the world if he consigned her to that obscurity to which the disadvantages of her birth seemed originally to have condemned her.

These reflections arose while Maloney, charmed to find himself listened to, was proceeding in his discourse.

Lord Montreville, tho' too much used to the manners of politicians to be able to give a direct answer, at length put an end to it, by telling him he would consider of what he had said, and talk to him farther in a few days.

In the mean time his Lordship desired that no part of their conversation might transpire.

Maloney, transported at a reception which seemed to prognosticate the completion of his wishes, retired elated with his prospects; and Lord Montreville summoning Mr. Headly to attend him, mounted his horse to survey the ground on which he meditated improvements round the castle.

The cold and almost stern civility of Lord Montreville, for the little time Emmeline had seen him, had created despondence and uneasiness in her bosom.

She fancied he disliked her, unoffending as she was, and would take the first opportunity of shaking her off: — an idea which, together with the awe she could not help feeling in his presence, made her determine as much as possible to avoid it, 'till he should give her a proper opportunity to speak to him, or 'till she could acquire courage to seek it.

At seven in the morning, she arose, after an uneasy night, and having taken an early breakfast, betook herself to her usual walk, carrying with her a book.

The sun was hot, and she went to a wood which partly cloathed an high hill near the boundary of the estate, where, intent only on her own sorrows, she could not beguile them by attending to the fictitious and improbable calamities of the heroine of a novel, which Mrs. Garnet (probably forgetting to restore it to the library of some former mistress,) had brought down among her cloaths, and which had been seized by Emmeline as something new, at least to her.

But her mind, overwhelmed with its own anxiety, refused its attention: and tired with her walk, she sat down on a tree that had been felled, reflecting on what had passed since Lord Montreville's arrival, and considering how she might most effectually interest him in her behalf.

Delamere, attended by a servant, had gone upon the hills in pursuit of his game; and having had great success for some hours, he came down about eleven o'clock into the woods, to avoid the excessive heat, which was uncommon for the season.

The noise he made in brushing through the underwood with his gun, and rustling among the fading leaves, alarmed her.

He stepped over the timber, and seating himself by her, seized her hands.

'Oh! my charming cousin,' he cried, 'I think myself one of the most fortunate fellows on earth, thus to meet you.'

Emmeline would have risen.

'Oh! no,' continued he, 'indeed you do not go, 'till we have had a little conversation.'

'I cannot stay, indeed Sir,' said Emmeline — 'I must immediately go home.'

'By no means; I cannot part with you. — Come, come, sit down and hear what I have to say.'

It was to no purpose to resist. The impetuous vehemence of Delamere was too much for the timid civility of Emmeline; and not believing that any thing more than common conversation or a few unmeaning compliments would pass, she sat down with as much composure as she could command.

But Delamere, who was really captivated at the first, and who now thought her more beautiful than he had done in their former interviews, hesitated not to pour forth the most extravagant professions of admiration, in a style so unequivocal, that Emmeline, believing he meant to insult her, burst into a passion of tears, and besought him, in a tremulous and broken voice, not to be so cruel as to affront her, but to suffer her to return home.

Delamere could not see her terror without being affected. He protested, that so far from meaning to give her pain, he should think himself too happy if she would allow him to dedicate his whole life to her service.

Poor Emmeline, however, continued to weep, and to beseech him to let her go; to which, as her distress arose almost to agony, he at length consented: and taking her arm within his, he said he would walk home with her himself.

To this Emmeline in vain objected. To escape was impossible. To prevail on him to leave her equally so. She was therefore compelled to follow him. Which she did with reluctance; while he still continued to profess to her the most violent and serious attachment. They proceeded in this manner along the nearest path to the castle, which lay principally among copses that fringed the banks of the river. They had just passed through the last, and entered the meadows which lay immediately under the castle walls, when Lord Montreville and Headly, on horseback, appeared from a woody lane just before them.

At the noise of horses so near them, Emmeline looked up, and seeing Lord Montreville, again struggled, but without success, to disengage her hand.

Delamere continued to walk on, and his Lordship soon came up to them. He checked his horse, and said, somewhat sternly, 'So, Sir, where have you been?'

Delamere, without the least hesitation, answered — 'Shooting, my Lord, the early part of the morning; and since that, making love to my cousin, who was so good as to sit and wait for me under a tree.'

'For mercy's sake, Mr. Delamere,' cried Emmeline, 'consider what you say.'

'Waiting for you under a tree!' cried Lord Montreville, in amazement. 'Do Miss Mowbray be so good as to return home. — And you, Frederic, will, I suppose, be back by dinner time.'

'Yes,' answered Delamere, 'when I have conducted my cousin home, I shall go out again, perhaps, for an hour before dinner.'

He was then walking on, without noticing the stern and displeased looks of his father, or the terror of poor Emmeline, who saw too evidently that Lord Montreville was extremely angry.

His Lordship, after a moment's pause, dismounted, gave his horse to a servant, and joined them, telling Delamere he had some business with Miss Mowbray, and would therefore walk with her towards the castle himself.

Delamere kissed her hand gayly, and assuring his father that for the first time in his life he felt an inclination to take his business off his hands, he beckoned to his servant to follow with his dogs, and then leaping over the hedge that separated the meadow from the hollow lane, he disappeared.

Emmeline, trembling with apprehension, walked with faultering steps by the side of Lord Montreville, who for some time was silent. He at length said — 'Your having been brought up in retirement, Miss Mowbray, has, perhaps, prevented your being acquainted with the decorums of the world, and the reserve which a young woman should ever strictly maintain. You have done a very improper thing in meeting my son; and I must desire that while you are at the castle, no such appointments may take place in future.'

Tho' she saw, from the first moment of his meeting them, that he had conceived this idea, and was confirmed in it by Delamere's speech; yet she was so much shocked and hurt by the address, that as she attempted to answer, her voice failed her.

The tears, however, which streamed from her eyes, having a little relieved her, she endeavoured to assure his Lordship, that till she met Mr. Delamere in the wood that morning, she did not know even of his having left the castle.

'And how happened you to be where he found you, Miss Mowbray?'

'I went thither, my Lord, with a book which I was eager to finish.'

'Oh! I remember that Maloney told me you was a great reader; and from some other discourse he held relative to you, I own I was the more surprized at your indiscretion in regard to my son.'

They were by this time arrived at the castle, and Lord Montreville desired Emmeline to follow him into the parlour, where they both sat down.

His Lordship renewed the discourse.

'This morning Maloney has been talking to me about you; and from what he said, I concluded you had formed with him engagements which should have prevented you from listening to the boyish and improper conversation of Mr. Delamere.'

'Engagements with Mr. Maloney, my Lord? Surely he could never assert that I have ever formed engagements with him?'

'Why not absolutely so. — I think he did not say that. But I understood that you was by no means averse to his informing me of his attachment, and was willing, if my consent was obtained, to become his wife. Perhaps he has no very great advantages; yet considering your situation, which is, you know, entirely dependent, I really think you do perfectly right in designing to accept of the establishment he offers you.'

'To become the wife of Maloney! — to accept of the establishment *he* offers me! I am humbled, I am lost indeed! No, my Lord! unhappy as I am, I can *claim* nothing, it is true; but if the support of an unfortunate orphan, thrown by Providence into your care, is too troublesome, suffer me to be myself a servant; and believe I have a mind, which tho' it will not recoil from any situation where I can earn my bread by honest labour, is infinitely superior to any advantages such a man as Maloney can offer me!'

She wept too much to be able to proceed; and sat, overwhelmed with grief and mortification, while Lord Montreville continued to speak.

'Why distress yourself in this manner, Miss Mowbray? I cannot see any thing which ought to offend you, if Maloney *has* misrepresented the matter, and if he has not, your extraordinary emotion must look like a consciousness of having altered your mind.

'Your motive for doing so cannot be mistaken; but let me speak to you explicitly. — To Mr. Delamere, *my* son, the heir to a title and estate which makes him a desirable match for the daughters of the first houses in the kingdom, *you* can have no pretensions; therefore never do yourself so much prejudice as to let your mind glance that way.

'Maloney tells me he has some property, and still better expectations. He is established here in an excellent place; and should he marry you, it shall be still more advantageous. You are (I am sorry to be obliged to repeat it) without any dependance, but on my favour. You will therefore do wisely to embrace a situation in which that favour may be most effectually exerted on your behalf.

'As you have undoubtedly encouraged Maloney, the aversion you now pretend towards him, is artifice or coquetry. Consider before you decide, consider thoroughly what is your situation and what your expectations; and recollect, that as my son now means to be very frequently at Mowbray Castle, *you* cannot remain with propriety but as the wife of Maloney.'

'Neither as the wife of Maloney, nor as Emmeline Mowbray, will I stay, my Lord, another day!' answered she, assuming more spirit than she had yet shewn. 'I wished for an interview to entreat your Lordship would allow me to go to some place less improper for my abode than Mowbray Castle has long been.'

'And whither would you go, Miss Mowbray?'

'On that, my Lord, I wished to consult you. But since it is perhaps a matter unworthy your attention; since it seems to signify little what becomes of me; I must determine to hazard going to Mrs. Watkins's, who will probably give me an asylum at least 'till I can find some one who will receive me, or some means of providing for myself the necessaries of life.'

'You then positively reject the overtures of Maloney?'

'Positively, my Lord — and for ever! I beg it may not be mentioned to me again!'

'And who is Mrs. Watkins?'

'The sister of Mrs. Carey, my Lord.'

'Where does she live?'

'At Swansea in Glamorganshire; where she is accustomed to take in boarders. She would, I believe, receive me.'

After a moment's consideration, Lord Montreville said, 'that perhaps may do, since you absolutely refuse the other plan; I would have you therefore prepare to go thither; but I must insist on no more morning interviews with Mr. Delamere, and that whither you are going may be kept unknown to him. But tell me,' continued he, 'what I am to say to poor Maloney?'

'That you are astonished at his insolence in daring to lift his eyes to a person bearing the name of Mowbray; and shocked at his falsehood in presuming to assert that I ever encouraged his impertinent pretensions!'

This effort of spirit exhausted all the courage Emmeline had been able to raise. She arose, and attempted to reach the door; but overcome by the violence of her agitation, was obliged to sit down in a chair near it.

She could no longer restrain the tears which were extorted from her by the mortifying scene she had passed through; and her deep sighs, which seemed ready to burst her heart, excited the compassion of Lord Montreville; who, where his ambition was not in question, was not void of humanity. The violent and artless sorrow of a beautiful young woman, whose fate seemed to be in his power, affected him.

He took her hand with kindness, and told her 'he was sorry to have said any thing that appeared harsh.'

His Lordship added, 'that he would have her write to Mrs. Watkins; that a servant should be sent with the letter; and that on condition of her concealing her abode from Delamere, she should be supplied with an annual income equal to all her wants.'

Then hearing Delamere's gun, which he always discharged before entering the house, he hastened Emmeline away, desiring she would remain in her own apartment; where every thing necessary should be sent to her.

CHAPTER V

DELAMERE and Fitz-Edward soon after entered the parlour where Lord Montreville remained. He received his son with a coldness to which, tho' little accustomed to it, Delamere paid no attention.

Despotic as this beloved son had always been in the family, he felt not the least apprehension that he had really offended his father; or feeling it, knew that his displeasure would be so short liv'd that it was not worth any concern.

'Here, Fitz-Edward,' said he — 'here is my father angry with me for making love to my cousin Emmy. Faith, Sir,' (turning to Lord Montreville,) 'I think I have the most reason to be angry at being brought into such dangerous company; tho' your Lordship well knows how devilishly susceptible I am, and that ever since I was ten years old I have been dying for some nymph or other.'

'I know that you are a strange inconsiderate boy,' answered Lord Montreville, very gravely; — 'but I must beg, Frederic, to hear no more idle raillery on the subject of Miss Mowbray.'

To this, Delamere gave some slight answer; and the discourse was led by his Lordship to some other topic.

Fitz-Edward, who was about five years older than Delamere, concealed, under the appearance of candour and non-chalance, the libertinism of his character. He had entered very young into the army; the younger son of an Irish peer; and had contracted his loose morals by being thrown too early into the world; for his heart was not originally bad.

With a very handsome person, he had the most insinuating manners, and an address so truly that of a man of fashion, as immediately prejudiced in his favour those by whom he wished to be thought well of. Where he desired to please, he seldom failed of pleasing extremely; and his conversation was, in the general commerce of the world, elegant and attractive.

Delamere was very fond of his company; and Lord Montreville encouraged the intimacy: for of whatever fashionable vices Fitz-Edward was guilty, he contrived, by a sort of sentimental hypocrisy, to prevent their being known to, or at least offensive to those, whose good opinion it was his interest to cultivate.

Delamere was of a character very opposite. Accustomed from his infancy to the most boundless indulgences, he never formed a wish, the gratification of which he expected to be denied: and if such a disappointment happened, he gave way to an impetuosity of disposition that he had never been taught to restrain, and which gave an appearance of ferocity to a temper not otherwise bad.

He was generous, candid, and humane; and possessed many other good qualities, but the defects of his education had obscured them.

Lady Montreville, who beheld in her only son the last male heir of a very ancient and illustrious house, and who hoped to see all its glories revive in him, could never be prevailed upon to part with him. He had therefore a tutor in the house; and his parents themselves accompanied him abroad. And the weakness of Lady Montreville in regard to her son, encreased rather than diminished with his encreasing years.

Her fondness was gratified in seeing the perfections of his person, (which was a very fine one) while to the imperfections of his temper she was entirely blind.

His father was equally fond of him; and looked up to the accumulated titles and united fortunes of his own and his wife's families, as the point where all his ambitious views would attain their consummation.

To watch over the conduct of this only son, seemed now to be the sole business of his Lordship's life: and 'till now, he had no reason to fear that his solicitude for his final establishment would be attended with so little effect. Except a few youthful indiscretions, which were overlooked or forgiven, Delamere had shewn no inclinations that seemed inimical to his father's views; and Lord Montreville hoped that his present passion for Emmeline would be forgotten as easily as many other transient attachments which his youth, and warmth of temper, had led him into.

At dinner, Delamere enquired 'whether his charming cousin was always to remain a prisoner in her own room?'

To which Lord Montreville answered, 'that it had been her custom; and as there was no lady with them, it was better she should continue it.'

He then changed the discourse; and contrived to keep Delamere in sight the whole afternoon; and by that means prevented any further enquiries after Emmeline; who now, entirely confined to her turret, impatiently awaited the return of the messenger who had been sent to Swansea.

Delamere, in the mean time, had lingered frequently about the housekeeper's room, in hopes of seeing Emmeline; but she never appeared.

He applied to Mrs. Garnet for intelligence of her: but she had received orders from Lord Montreville not to satisfy his enquiries. He employed his servants therefore to discover where she was usually to be found, and by their means was at length informed in what part of the castle her apartment lay; and that there was a design actually on foot to send her away, but whither he could not learn.

The answer brought from Mrs. Watkins, by the man who had been sent to Swansea, expressed her readiness to take the boarder offered her.

This intelligence Lord Montreville communicated himself to Emmeline; who received it with such artless satisfaction, that his Lordship, who had before doubted whether some degree of coquetry was not concealed under the apparent ingenuous innocence of his niece, now believed he had judged too hastily.

It remained to be considered how she could be conveyed from Mowbray Castle without the knowledge of Delamere. She was herself ignorant of every thing beyond its walls, and could therefore be of no use in the consultation. His Lordship had, however, entrusted Fitz-Edward with his uneasiness about Delamere; at which the former only laughed; and said he by no means believed that any serious consequences were to be apprehended: that it was mere badinage; of which he was sure Delamere would think no more after they left Mowbray Castle; and that it was not a matter which his Lordship should allow to make him uneasy.

Lord Montreville however, who thought he could not too soon remedy his own indiscretion in introducing Emmeline to his son, determined to embrace the opportunity of putting an end to any future correspondence between them: he therefore insisted on a promise of secresy from Fitz-Edward; and had recourse to Headly, who from a frequent residence among the great was the most accommodating and obsequious of their servants.

As he was about to leave the castle in a few days, he offered his services to convey Miss Mowbray from thence, in a chaise of which he was master. This proposal was eagerly accepted by Lord Montreville. And enjoining Mr. Headly also to secresy, it was fixed that their journey should begin the next morning save one.

Emmeline had notice of this arrangement, which she received with the liveliest joy. She immediately set about such preparations as were necessary for her journey, in which she employed that and the remaining day; which had been destined by Lord Montreville to visit another estate that he possessed, at the distance of about twelve miles; whither Delamere and the whole party accompanied him.

Delamere had discovered, by his servants, that to remove Emmeline was in agitation; and he determined to see her again in spite of his father's precaution (which in fact only served to encrease his desire of declaring his sentiments); but he had no idea that she was to depart so soon, and therefore was content to go with his father, at his particular request.

It was late in the evening preceding that on which Emmeline was to leave the castle, before they returned to it; and she was still busied in providing for her journey; in doing which, she was obliged to open one of the caskets left her by Mrs. Carey. It contained miniatures of her father and her mother, which had been drawn at Paris before her birth; and several letters written by Mrs. Mowbray, her grandmother, to her mother, in consequence of the fatal step she had taken in quitting the protection of that lady, who had brought her up, to accompany Mr. Mowbray abroad.

These, Emmeline had never yet seen; nor had she now courage entirely to peruse them. The little she read, however, filled her heart with the most painful sensations and her eyes with tears.

While she was employed in her little arrangements, time passed insensibly away. She heard the hollow sound of shutting the great doors at the other end of the castle, as was usual before the servants retired for the night; but attentive only to what was at present her greatest concern, (making room for some favourite books in the box she meant to take with her,) she heeded not the hour.

A total silence had long reigned in the castle, and her almost extinguished candle told her it was time to take some repose, when, as she was preparing to do so, she thought she heard a rustling, and indistinct footsteps in the passage near her room.

She started — listened — but all was again profoundly silent; and she supposed it had been only one of those unaccountable noises which she had been used to hear along the dreary avenues of the castle. She began anew to unpin her hair, when a second time the same noise in the passage alarmed her. She listened again; and while she continued attentive, the great clock struck two.

Amazed to find it so late, her terror encreased; yet she endeavoured to reason herself out of it, and to believe that it was the effect of fancy: she heard it no more; and had almost determined to go out into the passage to satisfy herself that her fears were groundless, when just as she approached the door, the whispers were renewed; she saw the lock move, and heard a violent push against it.

The door, however, was locked. Which was no sooner perceived by the assailant, than a violent effort with his foot forced the rusty decayed work to give way, and Mr. Delamere burst into the room!

Emmeline was infinitely too much terrified to speak: nor could her trembling limbs support her. She sat down; — the colour forsook her cheeks; — and she was not sensible that Delamere had thrown himself at her feet, and was pouring forth the most vehement and incoherent expressions that frantic passion could dictate.

Recovering her recollection, she beheld Delamere kneeling before her, holding her hands in his; and Millefleur standing behind him with a candle. She attempted to speak; but the words died away on her lips: while Delamere, shocked at the situation into which he had thrown her, protested that he meant her not the smallest offence; but that having learnt, by means of his valet, that she was to go the next morning, and that his father intended to keep him ignorant of her future destiny, he could not bear to reflect that he might lose her for ever; and had therefore taken the only means in his power to speak to her, in hopes of engaging her pity, for which he would hazard every thing.

'Leave me, Sir! leave me!' said Emmeline, in a voice scarcely articulate. 'Leave me instantly, or I will alarm the house!'

'That is almost impossible!' replied Delamere; 'but I will not terrify you more than I have done already. No, Emmeline, I wish not to alarm you, and will quit you instantly if you will tell me that wheresoever you are, you will permit me to see you; and will remember me with pity and regard! My father shall not — cannot controul my conduct; nor shall all the power on earth prevent my following you, if you will yourself permit me. Tell me, Emmeline, —tell me you will not forget me!'

'As what, Sir, should I remember you, but as my persecutor? as one who has injured me beyond reparation by your wild and cruel conduct; and who has now dared to insult me by a most unparallelled outrage. — Leave me, Sir! I repeat to you that you must instantly quit the room!'

She arose, and walked with tottering steps to the end of it. Delamere followed her. She turned; and came towards the door, which was still open, and then recollected, that as she knew the passages of the castle, which she was convinced neither Delamere or his servant did, she might possibly escape, and find Lord Montreville's room, which she knew to be at the end of the East Gallery.

Delamere was a few steps behind her when she reached the door; which hastily throwing quite open, she ran lightly thro' the passage, which was very long and dark.

He pursued her, imploring her to hear him but a moment; and the Frenchman as hastily followed his master with the candle. But at the end of the passage, a flight of broken steps led to a brick hall, which opened on other stair-cases and galleries.

A gust of wind blew out the candle; and Emmeline, gliding down the steps, turned to the right, and opening a heavy nailed door, which led by a narrow stairs to the East gallery, she let it fall after her.

Delamere, now in total darkness, tried in vain to follow the sound. He listened — but no longer heard the footsteps of the trembling fugitive; and cursing his fate, and the stupidity of Millefleur, he endeavoured to find his way back to Emmeline's room, where he thought a candle was still burning. But his attempt was vain. He walked round the hall only to puzzle himself; for the door by which he had entered it, he could not regain.

In the mean time Emmeline, breathless with fear, had reached the gallery, and feeling her way 'till she came as she supposed to the door of the room where Lord Montreville slept, she tapped lightly at it.

A man's voice asked who it was?

'It is I, my Lord,' cried Emmeline, hardly able to make herself heard. — 'Mr. Delamere pursues me.'

Somebody opened the door. — But there was no light; and Emmeline retiring a step from it, the person again asked who it was?

'It is Emmeline,' replied she; who now first recollected that the voice was not that of Lord Montreville. — She flew therefore towards the next door, with exclamations of encreased terror; but Lord Montreville, who was now awakened, appeared at it with a lamp in his hand; and Emmeline, in answer to his question of what is the matter? endeavoured to say that she was pursued by Mr. Delamere; but fear had so entirely overcome her, that she could only sigh out his name; and gasping like a dying person, sat down on a bench which was near the door.

Fitz-Edward, who was the person she had first spoken to, had by this time dressed himself, and came to her with a glass of water out of his room; while Lord Montreville, hearing his son's name so inarticulately pronounced, and seeing the speechless affright in which Emmeline sat before him, conceived the most alarming apprehensions, and believed that his son was either dead or dying.

With great difficulty he summoned up courage enough, again to beg for heaven's sake she would tell him what had occasioned her to leave her room at such an hour?

She again exclaimed, 'it is Mr. Delamere, my Lord!'

'What of Mr. Delamere? — what of my son?' cried he, with infinite agitation.

'Save me from him my Lord!' answered Emmeline, a little recovered by the water she had drank.

'Where is he then?' said his Lordship.

'I know not,' replied Emmeline; 'but he came to my room with his servant, and I flew hither to implore your protection.'

Fitz-Edward intreated Lord Montreville to be more calm, and to give Miss Mowbray time to recollect herself. He offered to go in search of Delamere; but his Lordship was in too much anxiety to be satisfied with any enquiries but his own.

He therefore said he would go down himself; but Emmeline catching his hand, entreated him not to leave her.

At this moment the voices of Delamere and his man were heard echoing through the whole side of the castle; for wearied with their fruitless attempts to escape, they both called for lights in no very gentle tone.

Lord Montreville easily distinguished from whence the noise came; and followed by Emmeline, whom Fitz-Edward supported, he descended into the brick hall from whence Emmeline had effected her escape, where he found Delamere trembling with passion, and Millefleur with fear.

Lord Montreville could not conceal his anger and resentment. —

'How comes it, Sir,' he cried addressing himself to his son, 'that you dare thus to insult a person who is under my protection? What excess of madness and folly has tempted you to violate the retirement of Miss Mowbray?'

'I mean not, my Lord,' answered Delamere, 'to attempt a concealment of my sentiments. I love Miss Mowbray; passionately love her; and scorn to dissimulate. I know you had a design to send her from hence; clandestinely to send her; and I determined that she should not go 'till I had declared my attachment to her, which I found you endeavoured assiduously to prevent. You may certainly remove her from hence; but I protest to you, that wherever she is, there I will endeavour to see her, in spite of the universe.

Lord Montreville now felt all the force of the error he had committed in that boundless indulgence to which he had accustomed his son. In the first instance of any consequence in which their wishes differed, he saw him ready to throw off the restraint of paternal authority, and daring to avow his resolution to act as he pleased.

This mortifying reflection arose in his mind, while, with a look of mingled anger and amazement, he beheld Delamere, who having ordered Millefleur to light his candle, snatched it from him, and hastily retired.

Emmeline, who had stood trembling the whole time behind Lord Montreville, besought him to ring up the housekeeper, and direct her to stay with her for the rest of the night; for she declared she would on no account remain in her own room alone.

His Lordship recommending her to the care of Fitz-Edward, went himself in search of the housekeeper; and Emmeline refusing to seek a more commodious apartment, sat down in one of the windows of the hall to wait his return.

Fitz-Edward, to whom she had yet hardly spoken, now entertained her with a profusion of compliments, almost as warm as those she had heard from Delamere; but her spirits, quite exhausted by the terror which had so lately possessed them, could no longer support her; she was unable to give an answer of common civility, and was very glad to see Lord Montreville return with Mrs. Garnet; who, extremely discomposed at being disturbed and obliged to appear in her night-cap, followed her, grumbling, into her room; where, as Emmeline refused to go to it herself, she took possession of her bed, and soon falling into a profound sleep, left its melancholy owner to her sad reflections.

She had not been many minutes indulging them, and wishing for the return of light, before somebody was again at the door. Emmeline still apprehending Delamere, stepped to it; and was astonished to see Lord Montreville himself.

He entered the room; and told her, that as his son knew of her journey in the morning, he would probably try some means to prevent it, or at least to trace out her abode; that it was therefore absolutely necessary for her to be ready by day break or before, for which he had prepared Mr. Headly; who was up, and getting ready to set out as soon as there was light enough to make it safe.

Emmeline, who thought she could not be gone too soon, now hastily finished the remainder of her packing; and having dressed herself for the journey, which notwithstanding her sleepless night she rejoiced to find so near, she waited with impatience ‘till Mr. Headly summoned her to go.

CHAPTER VI

THE sun no sooner appeared above the horizon, than her conductor was ready with his one-horse chair: and Emmeline being seated in it, and her little baggage adjusted, she left the door of the castle; where Maloney, who saw his favourite hopes vanish as he feared for ever, stood with a rueful countenance to behold her departure.

However desirous she was of quitting a residence which had long been uneasy to her, and which was now become so extremely improper, such is the force of early habit, that she could not bid it adieu without being greatly affected.

There she had passed her earliest infancy, and had known, in that period of unconscious happiness, many delightful hours which would return no more.

It was endeared to her by the memory of that good friend who had supplied to her the place of a parent; from whom alone she had ever heard the soothing voice of maternal solicitude. And as she passed by the village church, which had been formerly the chapel of the monastery, and joined the castle walls, she. turned her eyes, filled with tears, towards the spot where the remains of Mrs. Carey were deposited, and sighed deeply; a thousand tender and painful recollections crouding on her heart.

As she left the village, several women and children, who had heard she was going that day, were already waiting to bid her farewell; considering her as the last of that family, by whom they had been employed when in health, and relieved when in sickness; they lamented her departure as their greatest misfortune.

The present possessor of the castle bore not the name of Mowbray, and was not at all interested for the peasantry, among whom he was a stranger; they therefore, in losing Emmeline, seemed to lose the last of the race of their ancient benefactors.

Emmeline, affected by their simple expressions of regret, returned their good wishes with tears; and as soon as the chaise drove out of the village, again fixed her eyes on the habitation she had quitted.

Its venerable towers rising above the wood in which it was almost embosomed, made one of the most magnificent features of a landscape, which now appeared in sight.

The road lay along the side of what would in England be called a mountain; at its feet rolled the rapid stream that washed the castle walls, foaming over fragments of rock; and bounded by a wood of oak and pine; among which the ruins of the monastery, once an appendage to the castle, reared its broken arches; and marked by grey and mouldering walls, and mounds covered with slight vegetation, it was traced to its connection with the castle itself, still frowning in gothic magnificence; and stretching over several acres of ground: the citadel, which was totally in ruins and covered with ivy, crowning the whole. Farther to the West, beyond a bold and rocky shore, appeared the sea; and to the East, a chain of mountains which seemed to meet the clouds; while on the other side, a rich and beautiful vale, now variegated with the mellowed tints of the declining year, spread its enclosures, 'till it was lost again among the blue and barren hills.

Headly declaimed eloquently on the charms of the prospect, which gradually unveiled itself as the autumnal mist disappeared. But Emmeline, tho' ever alive to the beauties of nature, was too much occupied by her own melancholy reflections to attend to the animadversions of her companion.

She saw nothing but the castle, of which she believed she was now taking an eternal adieu; and her looks were fixed on it, 'till the road winding down the hill on the other side, concealed it from her sight.

Headly imputed her sadness to a very different cause than that of an early and long attachment to a particular spot. He supposed that regret at being obliged to leave Delamere, to whose passion he could not believe her insensible, occasioned the melancholy that overwhelmed her. He spoke to her of him, and affected to lament the uneasiness which so violent and ungovernable a temper in an only son, might occasion to his family. He then talked of the two young ladies, his sisters, whom he described as the finest young women in the country, and as highly accomplished. Emmeline sighed at the comparison between *their* situation and her own.

After some hours travelling through roads which made it very fatigueing, they arrived at a little obscure house of entertainment, and after some refreshment, continued their journey unmolested.

Delamere arose early, and calling for Millefleur, enquired at what hour Miss Mowbray was to go. On hearing that she had left the castle more than an hour, his rage and vexation broke through all the respect he owed his father; who being acquainted by his valet of his resolution immediately to follow the chaise, entered the room. He remonstrated with him at first with great warmth; but Delamere, irritated by contradiction, obstinately adhered to his resolution of immediately pursuing the travellers.

Lord Montreville, finding that opposition rather encreased than remedied the violence of his son's passionate sallies, determined to try what persuasion would do; and Delamere, whose temper was insensible to the threats of anger, yielded to remonstrance when softened by paternal affection; and consented to forego his intention if Lord Montreville would tell him where Emmeline was gone.

His Lordship, who probably thought this one of those instances in which falsehood is excuseable if not meritorious, told him, with affected reluctance, that she was gone to board at Bridgenorth, with Mrs. Watkins, the sister of old Carey.

As this account was extremely probable, Delamere readily believed it; and having with some difficulty been prevailed upon to pass his word that he would not immediately take any steps to see her, tranquility was for the present restored to the castle.

Emmeline in the mean time, after a long and weary journey, arrived at Swansea. Mrs. Watkins, who expected her, received her in a little but very neat habitation, which consisted of a small room by way of parlour, not unlike the cabin of a packet boat, and a bedchamber over it of the same dimensions. Of these apartments, Emmeline took possession. Her conductor took leave of her; and she now wished to be able to form some opinion of her new hostess; whose countenance, which extremely resembled that of Mrs. Carey, had immediately prejudiced her in her favour.

Being assured by Lord Montreville of every liberal payment for the board and lodging of Miss Mowbray, she received her with a degree of civility almost oppressive: but Emmeline, who soon found that she possessed none of that warmth of heart and lively interest in the happiness of others which so much endeared to her the memory of her former friend, was very glad when after a few days the good woman returned with her usual avidity to the regulation of her domestic matters, and suffered Emmeline to enjoy that solitude which she knew so well how to employ.

Delamere, still lingering at the castle, where he seemed to stay for no other reason than because he had there seen Emmeline, was pensive, restless, and absent; and Lord Montreville saw with great alarm that this impression was less likely to be effaced by time and absence than he had supposed.

Fitz-Edward, obliged to go to Ireland to his regiment for some time, had taken leave of them; and the impatience of Lord Montreville to return to town was encreased by repeated letters from his wife.

Delamere however still evaded it; hoping that his father would set out without him, and that he should by that means have an opportunity of going to Bridgenorth, where he determined to solicit Emmeline to consent to a Scottish expedition, and persuaded himself he should not meet a refusal.

At length Lady Montreville, yet more alarmed at the delay, directed her eldest daughter to write to his Lordship, and to give such an account of her health as should immediately oblige the father and son to return.

Delamere, after such a letter, could not refuse to depart; and comforting himself that he might be able soon to escape from the observation of his family, and put his project in execution, he consented to begin his journey. He determined, however, to write to Miss Mowbray, and to desire her to direct her answer under cover to a friend in London.

He did so; and addressed it to her at Mrs. Watkins's, at Bridgenorth: but soon after his arrival in town, the letter was returned to the place from which it was dated; having been opened at the office in consequence of no such person as Miss Mowbray or Mrs. Watkins being to be found there.

Delamere saw he had been deceived; but to complain was fruitless: he had therefore no hope of discovering where Emmeline was, but by lying in wait for some accidental intelligence.

The family usually passed the Christmas recess at their seat in Norfolk; whither Delamere, who at first tried to avoid being of the party, at length agreed to accompany them, on condition of his being allowed to perform an engagement he had made with Mr. Percival for a fortnight. Part of this time he determined to employ in seeing Headly, who did not live above thirty miles from thence; hoping from him to obtain intelligence of Emmeline's abode. And that no suspicion might remain on the mind of his father, he affected to reassume his usual gaiety, and was to all appearance as volatile and dissipated as ever.

While the family were in Norfolk, their acquaintance was warmly renewed with that of Sir Francis Devereaux, who was lately returned from a residence on the Continent, whither he had been to compleat the education of his two daughters, heiresses to his fortune, on the embellishment of whose persons and manners all the modern elegancies of education had been lavished.

They were rather pretty women; and of a family almost as ancient and illustrious as that of Mr. Delamere. Their fortunes were to be immense; and either of them would have been a wife for Delamere, the choice of whom would greatly have gratified the families on both sides.

Infinite pains were taken to bring the young people frequently together; and both the ladies seemed to allow that Delamere was a conquest worthy their ambition.

As he never refused to entertain them with every appearance of gallantry and vivacity, Lord Montreville flattered himself that at length Emmeline was forgotten; and ventured to propose to his son, a marriage with whichever of the Miss Devereuxs he should prefer.

To which, Delamere, who had long foreseen the proposal, answered coldly, 'that he was not inclined to marry at all; or if he did, it should not be one of those over-educated puppets.'

So far were their acquisitions from having made any impression on his heart, that the frivolous turn of their minds, the studied ornaments of their persons, and the affected refinement of their manners, made him only recollect with more passionate admiration, that native elegance of person and mind which he had seen only in the Orphan of Mowbray Castle.

CHAPTER VII

THERE was, in the person and manner of Emmeline, something so interesting, that those who were little accustomed to attach themselves to any one, were insensibly disposed to love her, and to become solicitous for her welfare.

Even the insensibility with which long and uninterrupted prosperity had encased the heart of Lord Montreville, was not entirely proof against her attractive powers; and when he no longer apprehended the effect of her encreasing charms on his son, he suffered himself to feel a degree of pity and even of affection for her.

He therefore heard with pleasure that she was contented in her present situation; and was convinced she had kept her word in not giving any intelligence of her residence to Delamere. To shew his approbation of her conduct, he directed a person in town to send her down a small collection of books; some materials for drawing; and other trifles which he thought would be acceptable.

Emmeline, charmed with such acquisitions, felt the most lively gratitude for her benefactor; and having fitted up her little cabin extremely to her satisfaction, she found, in the occupation these presents afforded her, all that she wished, to engage her attention; and gratify her taste.

Sensible of the defects of her education, she applied incessantly to her books; for of every useful and ornamental feminine employment she had long since made herself mistress without any instruction.

She endeavoured to cultivate a genius for drawing, which she inherited from her father; but for want of knowing a few general rules, what she produced had more of elegance and neatness than correctness and knowledge.

She knew nothing of the science of music; but her voice was soft and sweet, and her ear exquisite. The simple songs, therefore, she had acquired by it, she sung with a pathos which made more impression on her hearers than those studied graces learned by long application, which excite wonder rather than pleasure.

Time, thus occupied, passed lightly away; Spring arrived almost imperceptibly, and brought again weather which enabled Emmeline to reassume her walks along the shore or among the rocks, and to indulge that contemplative turn of mind which she had acquired in the solitude of Mowbray Castle.

It was on a beautiful morning of the month of April, that, taking a book with her as usual, she went down to the sea side, and sat reading for some hours; when, just as she was about to return home, she saw a lovely little boy, about five years old, wandering towards the place where she was, picking up shells and sea weeds, and appearing to be so deeply engaged in his infantine pursuit, that he did not see her 'till she spoke to him.

'Whose sweet little boy are you, my love?' said she.

The child looked at her with surprize.

'I am my mamma's boy,' said he, 'and so is Henry,' pointing towards another who now approached, and who seemed hardly a year younger.

The second running up to his brother, caught his hand, and they both walked away together, looking behind at the strange lady with some degree of alarm.

Their dress convinced Emmeline that they belonged to a stranger; and as they seemed to have nobody with them, she was under some apprehension for their safety, and therefore arose to follow them, when on turning round the point of a rock whose projection had concealed the shore to the left, she saw a lady walking slowly before her, whom the two little boys had now rejoined. In her hand she held a little girl, who seemed only learning to walk; and she was followed by a nursery maid, who held in her arms another, yet an infant at the breast.

The stranger, near whom Emmeline was obliged to pass, curtseyed to her as she went by. And if Emmeline was surprized at the early appearance of company at a time when she knew it to be so unusual, the stranger was much more so at the uncommon elegance of her form and manner: she was almost tempted to believe the fable of the sea nymphs, and to fancy her one of them.

Emmeline, on regaining her apartment, heard from the hostess, whom she found with another neighbour, that the lady she had seen arrived the evening before, and had taken lodgings at the house of the latter, with an intention of staying a great part of the summer.

The next day Emmeline again met the stranger; who accosting the fair orphan with all that ease which characterises the address of those who have lived much in good company, they soon entered into conversation, and Emmeline almost as soon discovered that her new acquaintance possessed an understanding as excellent as her person and address were captivating.

She appeared to be not more than five or six and twenty: but her person seemed to have suffered from sorrow that diminution of its charms, which time could not yet have effected. Her complexion was faded and wan; her eyes had lost their lustre; and a pensive and languid expression sat on her countenance.

After the first conversation, the two ladies found they liked each other so well, that they met by agreement every day. Emmeline generally went early to the lodgings of Mrs. Stafford, and stayed the whole day with her; charmed to have found in her new friend, one who could supply to her all the deficiencies of her former instructors.

To a very superior understanding, Mrs. Stafford added the advantages of a polished education, and all that ease of manner, which the commerce of fashion can supply. She had read a great deal; and her mind, originally elegant and refined, was highly cultivated, and embellished with all the knowledge that could be acquired from the best authors in the modern languages. Her disposition seemed to have been naturally chearful; for a ray of vivacity would frequently light up her countenance; and a lively and agreeable conversation call forth all its animated gaiety. But it seldom lasted long. Some settled uneasiness lay lurking in her heart; and when it recurred forcibly to her, as it frequently did in the midst of the most interesting discourse, a cloud of sorrow obscured the brilliancy of her countenance and language, and she became pensive, silent, and absent.

Emmeline observed this with concern; but was not yet intimate enough with her to enquire or discover the cause.

Sometimes, when she was herself occupied in drawing, or some other pursuit in which Mrs. Stafford delighted to instruct her, she saw that her friend, believing herself unobserved, gave way to all the melancholy that oppressed her heart; and as her children were playing round her, she would gaze mournfully on them 'till the tears streamed down her cheeks.

By degrees the utmost confidence took place between them on every subject but one: Mrs. Stafford never dwelt on the cause, whatever it was, which occasioned her to be so frequently uneasy; nor did she ever complain of being so: but she listened with the warmest interest to the little tale Emmeline had to relate, and told her in return as much of her own history as she thought it necessary for her to know.

Emmeline found that she was not a widow, as she had at first supposed; for she spoke sometimes of her husband, and said she expected him at Swansea. She had been married at a very early age; and they now generally resided at an house which Mr. Stafford's father, who was still living, had purchased for them in Dorsetshire.

'I came hither,' she said, 'thus early in the year, at Mr. Stafford's request, who is fond of improvements and alterations, and who intends this summer to add considerably to our house; which is already too large, I think, for our present fortune. I was glad to get away from the confusion of workmen, to which I have an aversion; and anxious to let Charles and Henry, who had the measles in the Autumn and who have been frequently ill since, have a long course of sea-bathing. I might indeed have gone to Weymouth or some nearer place; but I wish to avoid general company, which I could not have done where I am sure of meeting so many of my acquaintance. I rejoice now at my preference of Swansea, since it has been the means of my knowing you, my dear Emmeline.'

'And I, Madam,' returned Emmeline, 'have reason to consider the concurrence of circumstances that brought you here as the most fortunate for me. Yet I own to you, that the charm of such society is accompanied with great pain, in anticipating the hour when I must again return to that solitude I have 'till now considered as my greatest enjoyment.'

'Ah! my dear girl!' replied Mrs. Stafford, 'check in its first appearance a propensity which I see you frequently betray, to anticipate displeasing or unfortunate events. When you have lived a few years longer, you will, I fear, learn, that every day has evils enough of its own, and that it is well for us we know nothing of those which are yet to come. I speak from experience; for I, when not older than you now are, had a perpetual tendency to fancy future calamities, and embittered by that means many of those hours which would otherwise have been really happy. Yet has not my presentiments, tho' most of them have been unhappily verified, enabled me to avoid one of those thorns with which my path has been thickly strewn.'

Emmeline hoped now to hear what hand had strewn them.

Mrs. Stafford, sighing deeply, fell into a reverie; and continuing long silent, Emmeline could not resolve to renew a conversation so evidently painful to her.

It was now six weeks since she had first seen Mrs. Stafford, and the hours had passed in a series of felicity of which she had 'till then formed no idea.

Mrs. Stafford, delighted with the lively attachment of her young friend, was charmed to find herself capable of adorning her ingenuous and tender mind with all that knowlege which books or the world had qualified her to impart.

They read together every day: Emmeline, under the tuition of her charming preceptress, had made some progress in French and Italian; and she was amazed at her own success in drawing since she had received from Mrs. Stafford rules of which she was before ignorant.

As the summer advanced, a few stragglers came in, and it was no longer wonderful to see a stranger. But Mrs. Stafford and Miss Mowbray, perfectly satisfied with each other, sought not to enlarge their society. They sometimes held short conversations with the transient visitants of the place, but more usually avoided those walks where it was likely they should meet them.

Early one morning, they were returning from the bathing place together, muffled up in their morning dresses. They had seen at a distance two gentlemen, whom they did not particularly notice; and Emmeline, leaning on the arm of her friend, was again anticipating all she should suffer when the hour came which would separate them, and recollecting the different company and conversation to which she had been condemned from the death of Mrs. Carey to her quitting Mowbray Castle —

'You have not only taught me, my dear Mrs. Stafford,' said she, 'to dread more than ever being thrown back into such company; but you have also made me fear that I shall never relish the general conversation of the world. As I disliked the manners of an inferior description of people when I first knew them, because they did not resemble those of the dear good woman who brought me up; so I shall undoubtedly be disappointed and dissatisfied with the generality of those acquaintance I may meet with; for I am afraid there are as few Mrs. Staffords in your rank of life as there were Mrs. Careys in hers. However, there is no great likelihood, I believe, at present, of my being convinced how little they resemble you; for it is not probable I shall be taken from hence.'

'Perhaps,' answered Mrs. Stafford, 'you might be permitted to stay some months next winter with me. I shall pass the whole of it in the country; the greatest part of it probably alone; and such a companion would assist in charming away many of those hours, which now, tho' I have more resources than most people, sometimes are heavy and melancholy. My children are not yet old enough to be my companions; and I know not how it is, but I have often more pain than pleasure in being with them. When I remember, or when I feel, how little happiness there is in the world, I tremble for their future destiny; and in the excess of affection, regret having introduced them into a scene of so much pain as I have hitherto found it. But tell me, Emmeline, do you think if I apply to Lord Montreville he will allow you to pass some time with me?'

'Dear Madam,' said Emmeline, eagerly, 'what happiness do you offer me! Lord Montreville would certainly think me highly honoured by such an invitation.'

'Shall I answer for Lord Montreville,' said a voice behind them, 'as his immediate representative?'

Emmeline started; and turning quickly, beheld Mr. Delamere and Fitz-Edward.

Delamere caught her hands in his.

'Have I then found you, my lovely cousin?' cried he. — 'Oh! happiness unexpected!'

He was proceeding with even more than his usual vehemence; but Fitz-Edward thought it necessary to stop him.

'You promised, Frederic, before I consented to come with you, that you would desist from these extravagant flights. Come, I beg Miss Mowbray may be permitted to speak to her other acquaintance; and that she will do us both the honour to introduce us to her friend.'

Emmeline had lost all courage and recollection on the appearance of Delamere. Mrs. Stafford saw her distress; and assuming a cold and distant manner, she said — 'Miss Mowbray, I apprehend from what this gentleman has said, that he has a message to you from Lord Montreville.'

'Has my Lord, Sir,' said Emmeline to Delamere, — 'has my Lord Montreville been so good as to honour me with any commands?'

'Cruel girl!' answered he; 'you know too well that my father is not acquainted with my being here.'

'Then you certainly ought not to be here,' said Emmeline, coolly; 'and you must excuse me, Sir, if I beg the favor of you not to detain me, nor attempt to renew a conversation so very improper, indeed so cruelly injurious to me.'

Mrs. Stafford had Emmeline's arm within her own, from the commencement of this conversation; and she now walked hastily on with her.

Delamere followed them, intreating to be heard; and Fitz-Edward, addressing himself on the other side to Mrs. Stafford, besought her in a half whisper to allow his friend only a few moments to explain himself to Miss Mowbray.

Now, Sir, I must be excused,' answered she — 'If Miss Mowbray does me the honour to consult me, I shall certainly advise her against commiting such an indiscretion as listening to Mr. Delamere.'

Ah! Madam!' said the colonel, throwing into his eyes and manner all that insinuation of which he was so perfect a master, 'is it possible, that with a countenance where softness and compassion seem to invite the unhappy to trust you with their sorrows, you have a cruel and unfeeling heart? Lay by for a moment your barbarous prudence, in favour of my unfortunate friend; upon my honour, nothing but the conviction that his life was at stake, would have induced me to accompany him hither; and I pledge myself for the propriety of his conduct. He only begs to be forgiven by Miss Mowbray for his improper treatment of her at Mowbray Castle; to be assured she is in health and safety; and to hear that she does not hate him for all the uneasiness he has given her; and having done so, he promises to return to his family. Upon my soul,' continued he, laying his hand upon his breast, 'I know not what would have been the consequence, had I not consented to assist him in deceiving his family and coming hither: but I have reason to think he would have made some wild attempt to secure to himself more frequent interviews with Miss

Mowbray; and that a total disappointment of the project he had formed for seeing her, would have been attended with a violence of passion arising even to phrenzy. — Madness or death would perhaps have been the event.'

Mrs. Stafford turned her eyes on Fitz-Edward, with a look sufficiently expressive of incredulity — 'Does a modern man of fashion pretend to talk of madness and death? You certainly imagine, Sir, that you are speaking to some romantic inhabitant of a Welch provincial town, whose ideas are drawn from a circulating library, and confirmed by the conversation of the captain in quarters.'

'Ah, madam,' said he, 'I know not to whom I have the honour of addressing myself,' (though he knew perfectly well); 'but I feel too certainly that madness and death would be preferable to the misery such coldness and cruelty as yours would inflict on me, was it my misfortune to love as violently as Delamere; and indeed I tremble, lest in endeavouring to assist my friend I have endangered myself.'

Of this speech, Mrs. Stafford, who believed he did not know her, took very little notice; and turning towards Emmeline, who had in the mean time been listening in trembling apprehension to the ardent declarations of Delamere, said it was time to return home.

Delamere, without attending to her hint, renewed his importunities for her friendship and interest with Miss Mowbray; to which, as soon as he would allow her to answer, she said very gravely — 'Sir, as Miss Mowbray seems so much alarmed at your pursuing her hither, and as you must be yourself sensible of its extreme impropriety, I hope you will not lengthen an interview which can only produce uneasiness for you both.'

'Let us go home, for heaven's sake!' whispered Emmeline. 'They are determined, you see, to follow us,' replied her friend; 'we will however go.'

By this time they were near the door; and Mrs. Stafford wishing the two gentlemen a good morning; was hurrying with Emmeline into the house; but Fitz-Edward took hold of her arm.

'One word, only, madam, and we will intrude upon you no farther at present: say that you will suffer us to see you again to-morrow.' Not if I can help it, be assured, Sir.'

'Then, madam,' said Delamere, 'you must allow me to finish now what I have to say to Miss Mowbray.'

'Good heaven! Sir,' exclaimed Emmeline, 'why will you thus persist in distressing me? You are perhaps known to Mrs. Watkins; your name will be at least known to her; and intelligence of your being here will be instantly sent to Lord Montreville.'

Emmeline, by no means aware that this speech implied a desire of concealment, the motives of which might appear highly flattering to Delamere, was soon made sensible of its import by his answer.

'Enough, my adorable Emmeline!' cried he eagerly, 'if I am worthy of a thought of that sort, I am less wretched than I believed myself. I will not now insist on a longer audience; but to-morrow I must see you again. — Your amiable friend here will intercede for me. — I must not be refused; and will wish you a good day before you can form so cruel a resolution.'

So saying, he bowed to Mrs. Stafford, kissed Emmeline's hand, and departed with Fitz-Edward from the door.

CHAPTER VIII

THE two fair friends no sooner entered the house, than Emmeline threw herself into a chair, and burst into tears.

'Ah! my dear madam,' said she, sobbing, 'what will now become of me? Lord Montreville will believe I have corresponded with his son; he will withdraw all favour and confidence from me; and I shall be undone!

'Do not thus distress yourself,' said Mrs. Stafford, tenderly taking her hand — 'I hope the rash and cruel conduct of this young man will not have the consequences you apprehend. Lord Montreville, from your former conduct, will easily credit your not having encouraged this visit.'

'Ah! my dear Mrs. Stafford,' replied Emmeline, 'you do not know Lord Montreville. He hastily formed a notion that I made an appointment with Mr. Delamere at Mowbray Castle, when I had not even seen him above once; and though, from my eagerness to leave it, I believe he afterwards thought he had been too hasty, yet so strong was that first impression, that the slightest circumstance would, I know, renew it as forcibly as ever: for he has one of those tempers, which having once entertained an idea of a person's conduct or character, never really alters it, though they see the most convincing evidence of its fallacy. Having once supposed I favoured the addresses of Mr. Delamere, as you know he did, at Mowbray Castle, the present visit will convince him he was right, and that I am the most artful as well as the most ungrateful of beings.'

Mrs. Stafford hesitated a moment, and then said, 'I see all the evil you apprehend. To convince Lord Montreville of your ignorance of Delamere's design, and your total rejection of his clandestine addresses, suppose I were to write to him? He must be prejudiced and uncandid indeed, if after such information he is not convinced of your innocence.'

To this proposal, Emmeline consented, with assurances of the liveliest gratitude; and Mrs. Stafford returning to her lodgings, wrote the following letter to Lord Montreville:

Swansea, June 20.

'My Lord,

'A short abode at this place, has given me the pleasure of knowing Miss Mowbray, to whose worth and prudence I am happy to bear testimony. At the request of this amiable young woman, I am now to address your Lordship with information that Mr. Delamere came hither yesterday with Mr. Fitz-Edward, and has again renewed those addresses to Miss Mowbray which she knows to be so disagreeable to your Lordship, and which cannot but be extremely prejudicial to her. Circumstanced as she is at this place, she cannot entirely avoid him; but she hopes your Lordship will be convinced how truly she laments the pain this improper conduct of Mr. Delamere will give you, and she loses not a moment in beseeching you to write to him, or otherwise to interfere, in prevailing on him to quit Swansea; and to prevent his continuing to distress her by a pursuit so unwelcome to you, and so injurious to her honour and repose.

I have the honour to be,
my Lord,
your Lordship's
most obedient servant,
C. STAFFORD.'

This letter being extremely approved of by Emmeline, was put into the next day's post; and the two ladies set out for their walk at a very early hour, flattering themselves they should return before Delamere and Fitz-Edward (who was lately raised to the rank of lieutenant-colonel) were abroad. But in this they deceived themselves. They were again overtaken by their importunate pursuers, who had now agreed to vary the mode of their attack. Fitz-Edward, who knew the power of his insidious eloquence over the female heart, undertook to plead for his friend to Emmeline, while Delamere was to try to interest Mrs. Stafford, and engage her good offices on his behalf.

They no sooner joined the ladies, than Delamere said to the latter — 'After the discouraging reception of yesterday, nothing but being persuaded that your heart will refuse to confirm the rigour you think yourself obliged to adopt, could make me venture, Madam, to solicit your favour with Miss Mowbray. I now warmly implore it; and surely' —

'Can you believe, Sir,' said Mrs. Stafford, interrupting him, 'that I shall ever influence Miss Mowbray to listen to you; knowing, as I do, the aversion of your family to your entertaining any honourable views? and having reason to believe you have yourself formed those that are very different?'

'You have no reason to believe so, Madam,' interrupted Delamere in his turn; 'and must wilfully mistake me, as an excuse for your cold and unkind manner of treating me. By heaven! I love Emmeline with a passion as pure as it is violent; and if she would but consent to it, will marry her in opposition to all the world. Assist me then, dear and amiable Mrs. Stafford! assist me to conquer the unreasonable prejudice she has conceived against a secret marriage!'

'Never, Sir, will I counsel Miss Mowbray to accept such a proposal! never will I advise her to unite herself with one whose family disdain to receive her! and by clandestinely stealing into it, either disturb its peace, or undergo the humiliation of living the wife of a man who dares not own her!'

'And who, Madam, has said that I dare not own her? Does not the same blood run in our veins? Is she not worthy, from her personal merit, of a throne if I had a throne to offer her? And do you suppose I mean to sacrifice the happiness of my whole life to the narrow policy or selfish ambition of my father?'

'Wait then, Sir, 'till time shall produce some alteration in your favour. Emmeline is yet very young, too young indeed to marry. Perhaps, when Lord and Lady

Montreville are convinced that she only can make you happy, they may consent to your union.'

'You little know, Madam, the hopelessness of such an expectation. Were it possible that any arguments, any motives could engage my father to forego all the projects of aggrandizing his family by splendid and rich alliances, my mother will, I know, ever be inexorable. She will not hear the name of Emmeline. Last winter she incessantly persecuted me with proposals of marriage, and is now bent upon persuading me to engage my hand to Miss Otley, a relation of her own, who possesses indeed an immense fortune, and is of rank; but who of all women living would make me the most miserable. The fatigueing arguments I have heard about this match, and the fruitless and incessant solicitude of my mother, convince me I cannot, for both our sakes, too soon put an end to it.'

Mrs. Stafford, notwithstanding the vehement plausibility of Delamere, still declined giving to Emmeline such advice as he wished to engage her to offer; and tho' aware of all the advantages such a marriage would procure her friend, she would not influence her to a determination her heart could not approve.

While Delamere therefore was pleading vainly to her, Fitz-Edward was exhausting in his discourse with Emmeline, all that rhetoric on behalf of his friend, which had already succeeded so frequently for himself. Tho' he had given way to Delamere's eagerness, and had accompanied him in pursuit of Miss Mowbray, after a few feeble arguments against it, he never intended to encourage him in his resolution of marrying her; which he thought a boyish and romantic plan, and one, of which he would probably be weary before it could be executed. But as it was a military maxim, that in love and war all stratagems are allowable, he failed not to lay as much stress on the honourable intentions of Delamere, as if he had really meant to assist in carrying them into effect.

Emmeline heard him in silence: or when an answer of some kind seemed to be extorted from her, she told him that she referred herself entirely to Mrs. Stafford, and would not even speak upon the subject but before her, and as she should dictate.

In this way several meetings passed between Delamere, the colonel, and the two ladies; for unless the latter had wholly confined themselves, there was no possible way of avoiding the importunate assiduity of the gentlemen. Fitz-Edward had a servant who was an adept in such commissions, and who was kept constantly on the watch; so that they were traced and followed, in spite of all their endeavours to avoid it.

Mrs. Stafford, however, persuaded Emmeline to be less uneasy at it, as she assured her she would never leave her; and that there could be no misrepresentation of her conduct while they were together.

Every day they expected some consequence from Mrs. Stafford's letter to Lord Montreville; but for ten days, though they had heard nothing, they satisfied themselves with conjectures.

Ten days more insensibly passed by; and they began to think it very extraordinary that his Lordship should give no attention to an affair, which only a few months before seemed to have occasioned him so much serious alarm.

In this interval, Delamere saw Emmeline every day; and Fitz-Edward, on behalf of his friend's views, attached himself to Mrs. Stafford with an attention as marked and as warm as that of Delamere towards Miss Mowbray.

He was well aware of the power a woman of her understanding must have over an heart like Emmeline's; so new to the world, so ingenuous, and so much inclined to indulge all the delicious enthusiasm of early friendship.

He had had a slight acquaintance with Mrs. Stafford when she was first married; and knew enough of her husband to be informed of the source of that dejection, which, through all her endeavours to conceal it, frequently appeared; and having lived always among those who consider attachments to married women as allowable gallantries, and having had but too much success among them, Fitz-Edward thought he could take advantage of Mrs. Stafford's situation, to entangle her in a connection which would make her more indulgent to the weakness of her friend for Delamere.

But such was the awful, yet simple dignity of her manner, and so sacred the purity of unaffected virtue, that he dared not hazard offending her; while aware of the tendency of his flattering and incessant assiduity, she was always watchful to prevent any diminution of the respect she had a right to exact; and without affecting to shun his society, which was extremely agreeable, she never suffered him to assume, in his conversation with her, those freedoms which often made him admired by others; nor allowed him to avow that libertinism of principle which she lamented that he possessed.

Fitz-Edward, who had at first undertaken to entertain her merely with a view of favouring Delamere's conversation with Emmeline, almost imperceptibly found that it had charms on his own account. He could not be insensible of the graces of a mind so highly cultivated;

and he felt his admiration mingled with a reverence and esteem of which he had never before been sensible: but his vanity was piqued at the coldness with which she received his studied and delicate adulation; and, for the first time in his life, he was obliged to acknowledge to himself; that there might be a woman whose mind was superior to its influence.

Not being disposed very tranquilly to submit to this mortifying conviction, he became more anxious to secure that partiality from Mrs. Stafford, which, since he found it so hard to acquire, became necessary to his happiness; and, in the hope of obtaining it, he would probably long have persisted, had not his attention been soon afterwards diverted to another object.

It wanted only a few days of a month since Mrs. Stafford's letter was dispatched to Lord Montreville. But the carelessness of the servant who was left in charge of the house in Berkley-square was the only reason of his not noticing it.

Immediately after the birth-day, his Lordship had quitted London on a visit to a nobleman in Buckinghamshire, whither his son had attended him, and where they parted. Delamere, under pretence of seeing his friend Percival, really went into Berkshire; and Lord Montreville, having insisted on Delamere's joining him at the house of Lady Mary Otley, beyond Durham, where Lady Montreville and her two daughters were already gone, set out himself for that place, where they intended to pass the months of July and August. He had many friends to visit on the road; and when his Lordship arrived there, he found all his letters had, instead of following him as he had directed, been sent immediately thither; and instead of finding his son, or an account of his intended arrival, he had the mortification of reading Mrs. Stafford's information.

Delamere had, indeed, passed a few days with Mr. Percival, and had written to his father from thence; but he had also seen Headly, from whom he had extorted the secret of Emmeline's residence.

Fitz-Edward, to whose sister Mr. Percival was lately married, had joined Delamere at the house of his brother-in-law: and Delamere persisting in his resolution of seeing Emmeline, had, without much difficulty, prevailed on Fitz-Edward, (who had some weeks on his hands before he was to join his regiment in Ireland, and who had no aversion to any plan that looked like an intrigue) to accompany him.

They contrived to gain Mr. Percival: and Delamere, by inclosing letters to him, which were forwarded to his father as if he had been still there, imagined that he had prevented all probability of discovery. Could he have persuaded Emmeline to a Scottish marriage, (which he very firmly believed he should) he intended as soon as they were married, to have taken her to the house of Lady Mary Otley, and to have presented her to his father, his mother, his sisters, and Lady Mary and her daughter, who were also his relations, as his wife.

Lord Montreville, on reading Mrs. Stafford's letter, shut himself up in his own apartment to consider what was to be done.

He knew Delamere too well to believe that writing, or the agency of any other person, would have on him the least effect.

He was convinced therefore he must go himself; yet to return immediately, without giving Lady Montreville some very good reason, was impossible; nor could he think of any that would content her, but the truth. Though he would very willingly have concealed from her what had happened, he was obliged to send for her, and communicate to her the intelligence received from Mrs. Stafford.

Her Ladyship, whose pride was, if possible, more than adequate for her high blood, and whose passions were as strong as her reason was feeble, received this information with all those expressions of rage and contempt which Lord Montreville had foreseen.

Though the conduct of Emmeline was such as all her prejudice could not misunderstand, she loaded her with harsh and injurious appellations, and blamed his Lordship for having fostered a little reptile, who was now likely to disgrace and ruin the family to which she pretended to belong. She protested, that if Delamere dared to harbour so degrading an idea as that of marrying her, she would blot him for ever from her affection, and if possible from her memory.

Lord Montreville was obliged to wait 'till the violence of her first emotion had subsided, before he ventured to propose going himself to recall Delamere. To this proposal, however, her Ladyship agreed; and when she became a little cooler, consented readily to conceal, if possible, from Lady Mary Otley, the reason of Lord Montreville's abrupt departure, which was fixed for the next day; for the knowledge of it could not have any good effect on the sentiments of Lady Mary and her daughter; the former of whom was at present as anxious as Lady Montreville for an union of their families.

After some farther reflection, Lord Montreville thought that as Delamere was extremely fond of his youngest sister, her influence might be of great use in detaching him from his pursuit. It was therefore settled that she should accompany his Lordship; making the most plausible story they could, to account for a departure so unexpected; and leaving Lady Montreville and Miss Delamere as pledges of their intended return, Lord Montreville and his daughter Augusta set out post for London, in their way to Swansea.

CHAPTER IX

EMMELINE had, for some days, complained of a slight disposition; and being somewhat better, had determined to walk out in the evening; but having rather favoured and indulged her illness, as it gave her a pretext for avoiding Delamere, whose long and vehement assiduities began to give great uneasiness to both the ladies, she still answered to their enquiries that she was too ill to leave her room, and in consequence of this message, she and Mrs. Stafford, who came to sit with her, soon afterwards saw the Colonel and Delamere ride by as if for their evening airing. They kissed their hands as they passed; and as soon as the ladies believed them quite out of sight, and had observed the way they had gone, Emmeline, who had confined herself three days to her room, and who languished for air, proposed a short walk the opposite way, to which Mrs. Stafford consented; and as soon as the heat was a little abated, they set out, and enjoyed a comfortable and quiet walk for near an hour; from which they were returning when they saw Delamere and Fitz-Edward riding towards them.

They dismounted, and giving their horses to their servants, joined them; Delamere reproaching Emmeline for the artifice she had used, yet congratulating himself on seeing her again. But his eyes eagerly running over her person, betrayed his extreme anxiety and concern at observing her pale and languid looks, and the lassitude of her whole frame.

Fitz-Edward, in a whisper, made the same remarks on her appearance to Mrs. Stafford; who answered, 'that if Mr. Delamere persisted in pursuing her, she did not doubt but that it would end in her going into a decline.'

'Say rather,' answered Fitz-Edward artfully, 'that the interesting langour on the charming countenance of your friend, arises from the sensibility of her heart. She cannot surely see Delamere, dying for her as he is, without feeling some disposition to answer a passion so ardent and sincere: I know it is impossible she should. It is only your Stoic prudence, your cold and unfeeling bosom, which can arm itself against all the enthusiasm of love, all the tenderness of friendship. Miss Mowbray's heart is made of softer materials; and were it not for the inhuman reserve you have taught her, poor Delamere had long since met a more suitable return to an attachment, of which, almost any other woman would glory in being the object.'

There was something in this speech particularly displeasing to Mrs. Stafford; who answered, 'that he could not pay her a compliment more gratifying, than when he told her she had been the means of saving Miss Mowbray from indiscretion; though she was well convinced, that her own excellent understanding, and purity of heart, made any monitor unnecessary.'

'However,' continued she, 'if you think that *my* influence has prevented her entering into all the wild projects of Mr. Delamere, continue to believe, that while I am with her the same influence will invariably be exerted to the same purpose.'

Delamere and Emmeline, who were a few paces before them while this dialogue was passing, were now met by Parkinson, the colonel's servant, who addressing himself to Delamere, told him that Lord Montreville and one of the young ladies were that moment alighted from their carriage at the inn, and had sent to his lodgings to enquire for him.

Mrs. Stafford advancing, heard the intelligence, and looked anxiously at Emmeline, who turned paler than death at the thoughts of Lord Montreville.

Delamere was alternately red and pale. He hesitated, and tried to flatter himself that Parkinson was mistaken; while Fitz-Edward, who found he should be awkwardly situated between the father and son, silently meditated his defence.

Mrs. Stafford, who saw Emmeline ready to sink with the apprehension of being seen walking with Delamere, intreated the gentlemen to leave them and go to Lord Montreville; which she at length prevailed on them to do; Delamere pressing Emmeline's hand to his lips, and protesting, with a vehemence of manner particularly his own, that no power on earth should oblige him to relinquish her.

Mrs. Stafford got the trembling Emmeline home as well as she could; where she endeavoured to strengthen her resolution and restore her spirits, by representing to her the perfect rectitude with which she had acted.

But poor Delamere, who had no such consolatory reflections, felt very uneasy, and would willingly have avoided the immediate explanation which he saw must now take place with his father.

He determined, however, to temporize no longer; but being absolutely fixed in his resolution of marrying Emmeline, to tell his father so, and to meet all the effects of his anger at once.

In this disposition, he desired Fitz-Edward to leave him; and he entered alone the parlour of the inn where Lord Montreville waited for him. His countenance expressed a mixture of anger and confusion; while that of his Lordship betrayed yet sterner symptoms of the state of his mind.

Augusta Delamere, her eyes red with weeping, and her voice faultering through agitation, arose, and met her brother half-way.

'My dear brother!' said she, taking his hand.

He kissed her cheek; and bowing to his father, sat down.

'I have taken the trouble to come hither, Sir,' said Lord Montreville, 'in consequence of having received information of the wicked and unworthy pursuit in which you have engaged. I command you, upon your duty, instantly to return with me, and renounce for ever the scandalous project of seducing an innocent young woman, whom *you* ought rather to respect and whom *I* will protect.'

'I intend ever to do both, Sir; and when she is my wife, you will be released from the task of protecting her, and will only have to love her as much as her merit deserves. Be assured, my Lord, I have no such designs against the honour of Miss Mowbray as you impute to me. It is my determined and unalterable intention to marry her. Would to God your Lordship would conquer the unreasonable prejudice which you have conceived against the only union which will secure the happiness of your son, and endeavour to reconcile my mother to a marriage on which I am resolved.'

Having pronounced these words in a resolute tone, he arose from his seat, bowed slightly to his father, and waving his hand to his sister, as if to prevent her following him, he walked indignantly out of the room.

Lord Montreville made no effort to stop him. But the recollection of the fatal indulgence with which he had been brought up recurred forcibly to his Lordship's mind; and he felt his anger against his son half subdued by the reproaches he had to make himself. The very sight of this darling son, was so gratifying, that he almost forgot his errors when he beheld him.

After a moment's pause, Lord Montreville said to his daughter, 'You see, Augusta, the disposition your brother is in. Violent measures will, I fear, only make him desperate. We must try what can be done by Miss Mowbray herself, who will undoubtedly consent to elude his pursuit, and time may perhaps detach him from it entirely. For this purpose, I would have *you* see Emmeline to-morrow early; and having talked to her, we can consider on what to determine. Tonight, try to recover your fatigue.'

'Let me go tonight, Sir,' said his daughter. — 'It is not yet more than eight o'clock, and I am sensible of no fatigue that should prevent my seeing the young lady immediately.'

Lord Montreville assenting, Miss Delamere, attended by a servant, walked to the house of Mrs. Watkins.

The door was opened by the good woman herself; and on enquiry for Miss Mowbray, she desired the lady to walk in, and sit down in her little room, while she went up to let Miss know. — 'For I can't tell,' said she, (folding up a stocking she was knitting) 'whether she be well enough to see a strange gentlewoman. She have been but poorly for this week; and to night, after she came from walking, she was in such a taking, poor thing, we thought she'd a had a fit; and so Madam Stafford, who is just gone, bid her she should lie down a little and keep quiet.'

This account, added to the disquiet of the fair mediatrix; who fancied the heart of Emmeline could hardly fail of being of Delamere's party, and that uneasiness at his father's arrival occasioned the agitation of her spirits which Mrs. Watkins described.

Mrs. Watkins returned immediately, saying that Miss Emmy would be down in a moment.

Emmeline instantly guessed who it was, by the description of the young Lady and the livery of the servant who attended her: and now, with a beating heart and uncertain step, she entered the room.

Miss Delamere had been prepared to see a very beautiful person: but the fair figure whom she now beheld, though less dazlingly handsome than she expected, was yet more interesting and attractive than she would have appeared in the highest bloom of luxuriant beauty. Her late illness had robbed her cheeks of that tender bloom they usually boasted; timidity and apprehension deprived her of much of the native dignity of her manner; yet there was something in her face and deportment that instantly prejudiced Miss Delamere in her favour, and made her acknowledge that her brother's passion had at least personal charms for its excuse.

A silent curtsey passed between the two ladies — and both being seated, Miss Delamere began. —

'I believe, Miss Mowbray, you know that my father, Lord Montreville, in consequence of a letter received from Mrs. Stafford, who is, he understands, a friend of yours, arrived here this morning.'

'The letter, madam, was written at my particular request; that my Lord did not notice it sooner, has, believe me, given me great concern.'

'I do sincerely believe it; and every body must applaud your conduct in this affair. My father was, by accident, prevented receiving the letter for some weeks: as soon as it reached him, we set out, and he has now sent me to you, my dear cousin (for be assured I am delighted with the relationship) to consult with you on what we ought to do.'

Emmeline, consoled yet affected by this considerate speech, found herself relieved by tears.

'Though I am unable, madam,' said she, recovering herself, 'to advise, be assured I am ready to do whatever you and Lord Montreville shall dictate, to put an end to the projects your brother so perseveringly attempts. Ah! Miss Delamere; my situation is singularly distressing. It demands all your pity; all your father's protection!'

'You have, you shall have both, my dear Emmeline! as well as our admiration for your noble and heroic conduct; and I beg you will not, by being thus uneasy, injure your health and depress your spirits.'

This and many other consoling speeches, delivered in the persuasive voice of friendly sympathy, almost restored Emmeline to her usual composure; and after being together near an hour, Miss Delamere took her leave, charmed with her new acquaintance, and convinced that she would continue to act with the most exact obedience to the wishes of Lord Montreville.

CHAPTER X

LORD Montreville, on hearing from his daughter what had passed between her and Emmeline, was disposed to hope, that since she was so willing to assist in terminating for ever the views of Delamere, they should be able to prevail on him to relinquish them.

While Miss Delamere was with Emmeline, his Lordship had himself waited on Mrs. Stafford, to whom he thought himself obliged.

He thanked her for the letter with which she had favoured him; and said, 'that having heard of the great regard with which she honoured Miss Mowbray, he waited on her to beg her advice in the present difficult circumstance. Since Mr. Delamere has pursued her hither,' said his Lordship, 'she cannot remain here; but to find a situation that will be proper for her, and concealed from him, I own appears so difficult, that I know not on what to determine.'

'My Lord,' answered Mrs. Stafford, 'I intended to have asked your Lordship's permission to have been favoured with Miss Mowbray's company for some months; and still hope to be indulged with it when I return home. But could I go thither now, which I cannot, (my house not being in a condition to receive me,) it would be impossible to prevent Mr. Delamere's knowledge of her abode, if she was with me. But surely Mr. Delamere will leave this place with you, and will not oblige Miss Mowbray to quit her home to avoid him.'

'Ah, madam!' answered Lord Montreville, 'you do not yet know my son. The impetuosity of his temper, which has never been restrained, it is now out of my power to check; whatever he determines on he will execute, and I have too much reason to fear that opposition only serves to strengthen his resolution. While Emmeline is here, it will be impossible to prevail on him to quit the place: and though her behaviour has hitherto been irreproachable and meritorious, how can I flatter myself that so young a woman will continue steadily to refuse a marriage, which would not only relieve her at once from the difficulties and dependance of her situation, but raise her to an elevated rank, and a splendid fortune.'

'To which,' said Mrs. Stafford, 'she would do honour. I do not, however, presume to offer my opinion to your Lordship. You have, undoubtedly, very strong reasons for your opposition to Mr. Delamere's wishes: and his affluent fortune and future rank certainly give him a right to expect both the one and the other in whoever he shall marry. But a more lovely person, a better heart, a more pure and elegant mind, he will no where meet with. Miss Mowbray will reflect as much credit as she can borrow, on any family to which she may be allied.'

'I acknowledge, madam, that Miss Mowbray is a very amiable young woman; but she never can be the wife of my son; and you I am sure are too considerate to give any encouragement to so impossible an idea.'

After some farther conversation, Mrs. Stafford promised to endeavour to recollect a proper situation for Miss Mowbray, where she might be secured from the importunities of Delamere; and his Lordship took his leave.

By six o'clock the next morning, Delamere was at Mrs. Watkins's door; and nobody being visible but the maid servant, he entered the parlour, and told her he wanted to speak with Miss Mowbray; but would wait until she arose.

The maid told her mistress, who immediately descended; and Delamere, who was known to her as a young Lord who was in love with Miss Emmy, was courteously invited to her own parlour, and she offered to go up with any message he should be pleased to send.

He begged she would only say to Miss Mowbray that a gentleman desired to speak to her on business of consequence.

But the good woman, who thought she could do more justice to her employer, told Emmeline, who was dressing herself, that 'the handsome young Lord, as used to walk every night with her and Madam Stafford, was below, and wanted to speak to her directly.'

At this information, Emmeline was extremely alarmed. She considered herself as particularly bound by what had passed the evening before between her and Augusta Delamere, to avoid her brother; and such an interview as he now demanded must have an appearance to Lord Montreville of which she could not bear to think. She desired Mrs. Watkins, therefore, to let the gentleman know that she was not well, and could not see any body.

'Why, Lord, Miss!' exclaimed the officious landlady, 'what can you mean now by that? What! go for to refuse seeing such an handsome young man, who is a Lord, and the like of that? I am sure it is so foolish, that I shan't carry no such message.'

'Send Betty with it then,' answered Emmeline coldly; let her inform the gentleman I cannot be seen.'

'Well,' said Mrs. Watkins, as she descended, 'it is strange nonsense, to my fancy; but some folks never knows what they would be at.'

She then returned to the parlour, and very reluctantly delivered the answer to Mr. Delamere; who asked if Emmeline was really ill?

'Ill,' said the complaisant hostess, 'I see nothing that ails her: last night, indeed, she was in a desperate taking, and we had much ado to hinder her from going into a fit; but to day I am sure she looks as if she was as well as ever.'

Delamere asked for a pen and ink, with which she immediately furnished him; and as she officiously offered to get him some breakfast, he accepted it to gain time. While it was preparing he sent up to Emmeline the following note:

'I came hither to entreat only one quarter of an hour's conversation, which you cruelly deny me! You determine then, Emmeline, to drive me to despair!

'You may certainly still refuse to see me; but you cannot oblige me to quit this place, or to lose sight of your abode. My father will, therefore, gain nothing by his ill-judged journey hither.

'But if you will allow me the interview I solicit, and after it still continue to desire my absence, I will give you my promise to go from hence to-morrow.

F. DELAMERE.'

The maid was sent up with this billet to Emmeline; who, after a moment's consideration, determined to send it to Miss Delamere, and to tell her, in an envelope, how she was situated.

Having enclosed it therefore, and desired the maid to go with it without saying whither she was going, she bid her, as she went through the house, deliver to Mr. Delamere another note, which was as follows:

'Sir,

'Your request of an interview, I think myself obliged on every account to refuse. I am extremely sorry you determine to persevere in offering me proposals, to which, though they do me a very high and undeserved honour, I never ought to listen; and excuse me if I add, that I never will.

EMMELINE MOWBRAY.'

Emmeline had not before so positively expressed her rejection of Delamere's addresses. The peremptory stile, therefore, of this billet, added to his extreme vexation at being overtaken by his father, and the little hope that seemed to remain for him any way, operated altogether on his rash and passionate disposition, and seemed to affect him with a temporary phrenzy. He stamped about the room, dashed his head against the wainscot, and seizing Mrs. Watkins by the arm, swore, with the most frightful vehemence, that he would see Miss Mowbray though death were in the way.

The woman concluding he was mad, screamed out to her husband, who descending from his chamber in astonishment, put himself between his wife and the stranger, demanding his business?

'Alack-a-day!' cried Mrs. Watkins, ' 'tis the young Lord. He is gone mad, to be sure, for the love of Miss up stairs!'

Emmeline, who in so small a house could not avoid hearing all that passed, now thought it better to go down; for she knew enough of Delamere to fear that the effects of his fit of passion might be very serious; and was certain that nothing could be more improper than so much confusion.

She therefore descended the stairs, with trembling feet, and entered Mrs. Watkins' parlour; where she saw Delamere, his eyes flashing fire and his hands clenched, storming round the room, while Watkins followed him, and bowing in his awkward way, 'begged his Honour would only please to be pacified.'

There was something so terrifying in the wild looks of the young man, that Emmeline having only half opened the door, retreated again from it, and was hastening away. But Delamere had seen her; and darting out after her, caught her before she could escape out of the passage, and she was compelled to return into the room with him; where, on condition of his being more composed, she agreed to sit down and listen to him.

Watkins and his wife having left the room, Delamere again renewed his solicitations for a Scottish expedition. 'However averse,' said he, 'my father and mother may at present be to our marriage, I know they will be immediately reconciled when it is irrevocable. But if you continue to harden your heart against me, of what advantage will it be to them? Their ambition will still suffer; for I here swear by all that is sacred, that then I never will marry at all; and by my dying without posterity, their views will for ever be abortive, and their projects disappointed.'

To this, and every other argument Delamere used, Emmeline answered, 'that having determined never to accept of his hand, situated as she at present was, nothing should induce her to break through a determination which alone could secure her the approbation of her own heart.'

He then asked her, 'whether if the consent of Lord and Lady Montreville could be obtained, she would continue averse to him?'

This question she evaded, by saying, 'that it was to no purpose to consider how she should act in an event so unlikely to happen.'

He then again exerted all the eloquence which love rather than reason lent him. But Emmeline combated his arguments with those of rectitude and honour, by which she was resolutely bent to abide.

This steadiness, originating from principles he could not controvert or deny, seemed, while it shewed him all its hopelessness, to give new force to his passion. He became again almost frantic, and was anew acting the part of a madman, when Mrs. Stafford and Miss Delamere entered the house, and enquiring for Miss Mowbray, were shewn into the room where she was with Delamere; who, almost exhausted by the violence of those emotions he had so boundlessly indulged, had now thrown himself into a chair, with his head leaning against the wainscot; his hair was dishevelled, his eyes swoln, and his countenance expressed so much passionate sorrow, that Augusta Delamere, extremely shocked, feared to speak to him; while Emmeline, on the opposite side of the room, sat with her handkerchief to her eyes; and as soon as she saw Mrs. Stafford, she threw herself into her arms and sobbed aloud.

Delamere looked at Mrs. Stafford and his sister, but spoke to neither; till Augusta approaching him, would have taken his hand; but he turned from her.

'Oh, Frederic!' cried she, 'I beseech you to consider the consequence of all this.'

'I consider nothing!' said he, starting up and going to the window. His sister followed him.

'Go, go,' said he, turning angrily from her — 'Go, leave me, leave me! assist Lord Montreville to destroy his only son! go, and be a party in the cruel policy that will make you and Fanny heiresses!'

The poor girl, who really loved her brother better than any thing on earth, was quite overwhelmed by this speech; and her tears now flowed as fast as those of Emmeline, who continued to weep on the bosom of Mrs. Stafford.

Delamere looked at them both with a stern and angry countenance; then suddenly catching his sister by the hand, which he eagerly grasped, he said, in a low but resolute voice — 'Tears, Augusta, are of no use. Do not lament me, but try to help me. I am now going out for the whole day; for I will not see my father only to repeat to him what I have already said. Before I return, see what you can do towards persuading him to consent to my marriage with Miss Mowbray; for be assured that if he does not, the next meeting, in which I expect his answer, will be the last we shall have.'

He then snatched up his hat, and disengaging himself from his sister, who attempted to detain him, he went hastily out of the house; leaving Mrs. Stafford, Miss Mowbray, and his sister, under great uneasiness and alarm.

They thought it necessary immediately to inform Lord Montreville of the whole conversation, and Miss Delamere dispatched a note to Fitz-Edward, desiring him to attend to the motions of his friend.

Fitz-Edward was at breakfast with Lord Montreville; who took the first opportunity of their being alone, to reproach him with some severity for what he had done.

The Colonel heard him with great serenity; and then began to justify himself, by assuring his Lordship that he had accompanied Delamere only in hopes of being able to detach him from his pursuit, and because he thought it preferable to his being left wholly to himself. He declared that he meant to have given Lord Montreville information, if there had appeared the least probability of Delamere's marriage; but that being perfectly convinced, from the character of Emmeline, that there was nothing to apprehend, he had every day hoped his friend would have quitted a project in which there seemed not the least likelihood of success, and would have returned to his family cured of his passion.

Though this was not all strictly true, Fitz-Edward possessed a sort of plausible and insinuating eloquence, which hardly ever failed of removing every impression, however strong, against him; and Lord Montreville was conversing with him with his usual confidence and friendship, when the note from Miss Delamere was brought in.

His Lordship, ever anxious for his son, gazed eagerly at it while Fitz-Edward read it; and trembling, asked from whom it came?

Fitz-Edward put it into his hand; and having ran it over in breathless terror, his Lordship hurried out, directing all his servants to go several ways in search of Delamere; while he entreated Fitz-Edward to run to whatever place he was likely to be in; and went himself to Mrs. Stafford's lodging, who was by this time returned home.

What he heard from her of the scene of the morning, contributed to encrease his alarm. The image of his son in all the wildness of ungovernable passion, shook his nerves so much, that he seemed ready to faint, yet unable to move to enquire where he was. As he could attend to nothing else, Mrs. Stafford told him how anxiously she had thought of a situation for Emmeline, and that she believed she had at length found one that would do, 'if,' said she, 'your Lordship cannot prevail on him to quit Swansea, which I think you had better attempt, though from the scene of this morning I own I despair of it more than ever.

'The person with whom I hope to be able to place Miss Mowbray is Mrs. Ashwood, the sister of Mr. Stafford. She has been two years a widow, with three children, and resides at a village near London. She has a very good fortune; and would be happy to have with her such a companion as Miss Mowbray, 'till I am so fortunate as to be enabled to take her myself. As her connections and acquaintance lie in a different set of people, and in a remote part of the country from those of Mr. Delamere, it is improbable, that with the precautions we shall take, he will ever discover her residence.'

Lord Montreville expressed his sense of Mrs. Stafford's kindness in the warmest terms. He assured her that he should never forget the friendly part she had taken, and that if ever it was in his power to shew his gratitude by being so happy as to have the ability to serve her or her family, he should consider it as the most fortunate event of his life.

Mrs. Stafford heard this as matter of course; and would have felt great compassion for Lord Montreville, whose state of mind was truly deplorable, but she reflected that he had really been the author of his own misery: first, by bringing up his son in a manner that had given such boundless scope to his passions; and now, by refusing to gratify him in marrying a young woman, who was, in the eye of unprejudiced reason, so perfectly unexceptionable. She advised him to try once more to prevail on his son to leave Swansea with him; and he left her to enquire whether Fitz-Edward had yet found Delamere, whose absence gave him the most cruel uneasiness.

Fitz-Edward, after a long search, had overtaken Delamere on an unfrequented common, about a mile from the town, where he was walking with a quick pace; and seeing Fitz-Edward, endeavoured to escape him. But when he found he could not avoid him, he turned fiercely towards him — 'Why do you follow me, Sir? Is it not enough that you have broken through the ties of honour and friendship in betraying me to my father? must you still persecute me with your insidious friendship?'

Fitz-Edward heard him with great coolness; and without much difficulty convinced him that Miss

Mowbray herself had given the information to Lord Montreville by means of Mrs. Stafford.

This conviction, while it added to the pain and mortification of Delamere, greatly reconciled him to Fitz-Edward, whom he had before suspected; and after a long conversation, which Fitz-Edward so managed as to regain some degree of power over the passions of his impetuous friend, he persuaded him to go and dine with Lord Montreville; having first undertaken for his Lordship that nothing should be said on the subject which occupied the thoughts of the father; on which condition only the son consented to meet him.

CHAPTER XI

NOTWITHSTANDING the steadiness Emmeline had hitherto shewn in rejecting the clandestine addresses of Delamere, he still hoped they would succeed. A degree of vanity, pardonable in a young man possessing so many advantages of person and fortune, made him trust to those advantages, and to his unwearied assiduity, to conquer her reluctance. He determined therefore to persevere; and did not imagine it was likely he could again lose sight of her by a stratagem; against which he was now on his guard.

As he fancied Lord Montreville and his sister designed to carry her with them when they went, he kept a constant eye on their motions, and set his own servant, and Fitz-Edward's valet, to watch the servants of Lord Montreville.

Fitz-Edward, who had been so near losing the confidence of both the father and son, found it expedient to observe a neutrality, which it required all his address to support; being constantly appealed to by them both.

Lord Montreville, he advised to adhere to moderate measures and gentle persuasions, and to trust to Emmeline's own strength of mind and good conduct; while to Delamere he recommended dissimulation; and advised him to quit Swansea at present, which would prevent Emmeline's being removed from thence, and leave it in his power at any time to see her again.

Lord Montreville, on cooler reflection, was by no means satisfied with Fitz-Edward. To encourage his son's project, and even to accompany him in it, in the vain hope of detaching him from Emmeline before an irrevocable engagement could be formed, seemed to be at least very blameable; and if he had seen the connection likely to take place on a less honourable footing, his conduct was more immoral, if not so impolitic.

Either way, Lord Montreville felt it so displeasing, that he determined not to trust Fitz-Edward in what he now meditated, which was, to remove Emmeline from Swansea before he and his daughter quitted it, and to place her with the sister of Mr. Stafford; who being now arrived, had engaged to obtain his sister's concurrence with their plan.

A female council therefore was held on the means of Emmeline's removal; and it was settled that a post-chaise should, on the night fixed, be in waiting at the distance of half a mile from the town; where Emmeline should meet it; and that a servant of Mr. Stafford should accompany her to London, who was from thence to return to his master's house in Dorsetshire.

This arrangement being made three days after the arrival of Lord Montreville, and his faithful old valet being employed to procure the chaise, the hour arrived when poor Emmeline was again to abandon her little home, where she had passed many tranquil and some delightful days; and where she was to bid adieu to her two beloved friends, uncertain when she should see them again.

Her friendship for Mrs. Stafford was enlivened by the warmest gratitude. To her she owed the acquisition of much useful knowledge, as well as instruction in those elegant accomplishments to which she was naturally so much attached, but which she had no former opportunity of acquiring. The charms of her conversation, the purity of her heart, and the softness of her temper, made her altogether a character which could not be known without being beloved; and Emmeline, whose heart was open to all the enchanting impressions of early friendship, loved her with the truest affection. The little she had seen of Augusta Delamere, had given that young lady the second place in her heart. They were of the same age, within a few weeks. Augusta Delamere extremely resembled the Mowbray family: and there was, in figure and voice, a very striking similitude between her and Emmeline Mowbray.

Lady Montreville, passionately attached to her son, as the heir and representative of her family, and partial to her eldest daughter for her great resemblance to herself, seemed on them to have exhausted all her maternal tenderness, and to have felt for Augusta but a very inferior share of affection.

Of the haughty and supercilious manners which made Lady Montreville feared and disliked, she had communicated no portion to her younger daughter; and if she had acquired something of the family pride, her good sense, and the sweetness of her temper, had so much corrected it, that it was by no means displeasing.

Elegantly formed as she was, and with a face, which, tho' less fair than that of Emmeline was almost as interesting, her mother had yet always expressed a disapprobation of her person; and she had therefore herself conceived an indifferent opinion of it; and being taught to consider herself inferior in every thing to her elder sister, she never fancied she was superior to others; nor, though highly accomplished, and particularly skilled in music, did she ever obtrude her acquisitions on her friends, or anxiously seek opportunities of displaying them.

Her heart was benevolent and tender; and her affection for her brother, the first of its passions. She could never discover that he had a fault; and the error in regard to Emmeline, which his father so much dreaded, appeared to his sister a virtue.

She was deeply read in novels, (almost the only reading that young women of fashion are taught to engage in); and having from them acquired many of her ideas, she imagined that Delamere and Emmeline were born for each other; though she dared not appear to encourage hopes so totally opposite to those of her family, she found, after she had once seen and conversed with Emmeline, that she never could warmly oppose an union which she was convinced would make her brother happy.

She fancied that Emmeline could not be insensible to Delamere's love; she even believed she saw many symptoms of regard for him in her manner, and that she made the most heroic sacrifice of her love to her duty, when she resigned him: a sacrifice which heightened, almost to enthusiasm, the pity and esteem felt for her by Augusta Delamere; and though they had known each other only a few days, a sisterly affection had taken place between them.

But from these two friends, so tenderly and justly beloved, Emmeline was now to depart, and to be thrown among strangers, where it was improbable she would meet with any who would supply the loss of them. Her duty however demanded this painful effort; and she determined to execute it with courage and resolution.

Delamere was so perpetually about his father, that it was judged improper for him to hold any private conference with Emmeline, lest something should be suspected.

His Lordship therefore sent her by Mrs. Stafford a bank note of fifty pounds; with his thanks for the propriety of her conduct, and an assurance, that while she continued to merit his protection, he should consider her as his daughter, and take care to supply her with money, and every thing else she might wish for. He desired she would not write; lest her hand should be known, and her abode traced; but said, that in a few weeks he would see her himself, and wished her all possible health and happiness.

On the night of her departure, instead of retiring to rest at the usual hour, Emmeline dressed herself in a travelling dress, and passed some melancholy hours waiting for the signal of her departure.

At half past two in the morning, every thing being profoundly quiet, she saw, from her window, her two friends, who had declared they would not leave her 'till they saw her in the chaise.

She took with her only a small parcel of linen, Mrs. Stafford having engaged to forward the rest to an address agreed upon; and softly descending the stairs for fear of alarming Mrs. Watkins, she opened the door; and each of her friends taking an arm, they passed over two fields, into a lane where the chaise was waiting with the servant who was to go with her.

The tears had streamed from her eyes during the little walk, and she was unable to speak. The servant now opened the chaise door and let down the step; and Emmeline kissing the hand of Mrs. Stafford, and then that of Augusta Delamere, went hastily into it — 'God bless you both!' said she, in a faint and inarticulate voice. The servant shut the door, mounted a post horse, and the chaise was in an instant out of sight; while the two ladies, who at any other time would have been alarmed at being obliged to take so late a walk, thought not of themselves; but full of concern for poor Emmeline, went back in tears; and Miss Delamere, who had agreed to remain the rest of that night at the lodgings of Mrs. Stafford, retired not to rest, but to weep for the departure of her friend and the distress of her brother.

Emmeline, thus separated from every body she loved, pursued her journey melancholy and repining.

The first hour, she wept bitterly, and accused her destiny of caprice and cruelty. But tho' to the unfortunate passion of Delamere she owed all the inconvenience she had lately experienced, she could not resolve to hate him; but found a degree of pity and regard perpetually mingled itself with his idea in her heart. Yet she was not in love; and had rather the friendship of a sister for him than any wish to be his wife.

Had there been no impediments to their union, she would have married him, rather to make him happy than because she thought it would make herself so; but she would have seen him married to another, and have rejoiced at it, if he had found felicity.

An attachment like his, which had resisted long absence, and was undiminished by insuperable difficulties, could hardly fail of having its effect on the tender and susceptible mind of Emmeline. But whatever affection she felt, it by no means arose to what a romantic girl would have perhaps fancied it; and she was much more unhappy at quitting the dear Augusta than at the uncertainty she was in whether she should ever again see Delamere.

The parting was extremely embittered by the prohibition she had received in regard to writing to her. But painful as it was, she determined to forbear; and steadily to adhere to that line of duty, however difficult to practice, that only could secure the peace of her mind, by the acquittal of her conscience; which, as she had learned from Mrs. Stafford, as well as from her own experience, short as it was, could alone support her in every trial to which she might be exposed.

She reflected on her present situation, compared to what it would have been had she been prevailed upon to become the wife of Delamere against the consent of his family.

Splendid as his fortune was, and high as his rank would raise her above her present lot of life, she thought that neither would reconcile her to the painful circumstance of carrying uneasiness and contention into his family; of being thrown from them with contempt, as the disgrace of their rank and the ruin of their hopes; and of living in perpetual apprehension lest the subsiding fondness of her husband should render her the object of his repentance and regret.

The regard she was sensible of for Delamere did not make her blind to his faults; and she saw, with pain, that the ungovernable violence of his temper frequently obscured all his good qualities, and gave his character an appearance of ferocity, which offered no very flattering prospect to whosoever should be his wife.

By thus reasoning with herself, she soon became more calm, and more reconciled to that destiny which seemed not to design her for Delamere.

She met with no remarkable occurrence in her journey; and on the evening of the third day arrived in town; where the servant who attended her was ordered to dismiss the chaise, and to procure her an hackney coach, in which she proceeded to the house of Mrs. Ashwood.

This residence, situated in a populous village three miles from London, bore the appearance of wealth and prosperity. The iron gate, which gave entrance into a large court, was opened by a servant in a laced livery, to whom Emmeline delivered the letter she had brought from Mrs. Stafford, and after a moment's waiting the lady herself came out to receive her.

Emmeline, by the splendour of her dress, concluded she had left a large company: but being ushered into a parlour, found she had been drinking tea alone; of which, or of any other refreshment, Miss Mowbray was desired to partake.

Her reception of her visitor was perfectly cordial; and Emmeline soon recovering her easy and composed manner, Mrs. Ashwood seemed very much pleased with her guest; for there was in her countenance a passport to all hearts.

Mrs. Ashwood, tho' not in the bloom of life, and tho' she never had been handsome, was so unconscious of her personal disadvantages, that she imagined herself the object of admiration of one sex and of the imitation of the other. With the most perfect reliance on the graces of a figure which never struck any other person as being at all remarkable, she dressed with an exuberance of expence; and kept all the company her neighbourhood afforded.

Where her ruling passions, (the love of admiration and excessive vanity) did not interfere, she was sometimes generous and sometimes friendly. But her ideas of her own perfections, both of person and mind, far exceeding the truth, she had often the mortification to find that others by no means thought of them as she did; and then her good humour was far from invincible.

Though Emmeline soon found her conversation very inferior to what she had of late been accustomed to, she thought herself fortunate in having found an asylum, the mistress of which seemed desirous of making it agreeable; and to which she was introduced by the kindness of her beloved Mrs. Stafford.

But while serenity was returning to the bosom of Emmeline, that of poor Delamere was torn with the cruellest tempest. The morning after Emmeline's departure, Delamere, who expected no such thing, arose at his usual hour and rode out alone, as he had frequently done. As he passed her window, he looked up to it, and seeing it open, concluded she was in her room.

On his return, his father met him, and asked him to breakfast; but he designed to attend the tea-table of Mrs. Stafford, where he thought he should meet Emmeline, and therefore excused himself; and Lord Montreville, who wished the discovery to be delayed to as late an hour of the day as possible, let him go thither, where he breakfasted; and then proposed a walk to Mrs. Stafford, which he hoped would include a visit to Emmeline, or at least that Mrs. Stafford would not walk without her. She excused herself, however, on pretence of having letters to write; and Delamere went in search of Fitz-Edward, whom he could not find.

It was now noon, and he grew impatient at not having had even a glimpse of Emmeline the whole morning, when he met Fitz-Edward's man, and asked him hastily where his master was?

The man hesitated, and looked as if he had a secret which he contained with some uneasiness. 'Sir,' said he, 'have you seen Miss Mowbray to-day?'

' — why do you ask?'

'Because, Sir,' said the fellow, 'I shrewdly suspect that she went away from here last night. I can't tell your Honour why I thinks so; but you may soon know the truth on't.'

The ardent imagination of Delamere instantly caught fire. He took it for granted that Fitz-Edward had carried her off: and without staying to reflect a moment, he flew to the inn where his horses were, and ordered them to be saddled; then rushing into the room where his father and sister were sitting together, he exclaimed — 'she is gone, Sir — Emmeline is gone! — but I will soon overtake her; and the infamous villain who has torn her from me!'

Lord Montreville scorned to dissimulate. He answered, 'I know she is gone, and it was by my directions she went. You cannot overtake her; nor is it probable you will ever see her again. Endeavour therefore to recollect yourself, and do not forget what you owe to your family and yourself.'

Delamere attended but little of this remonstrance; but still prepossessed with the idea of Fitz-Edward's being gone with her, he swore perpetual vengeance against him, and that he would pursue him through the world.

With this resolution on his lips, and fury in his eyes, he quitted his father's apartment, and at the door met Fitz-Edward himself, coming to enquire after him.

He was somewhat ashamed of the hasty conclusion he had made, and was therefore more disposed to hear what Fitz-Edward had to say, who presently convinced him that he was entirely ignorant of the flight of Emmeline.

Delamere now insisted, that as a proof of his friendship he would instantly set out with him in pursuit of her.

Fitz-Edward knew not what to do; but however seemed to consent; and saying he would order his servant to get his horse, left him, and went to Lord Montreville, to whom he represented the impracticability of stopping Delamere.

His Lordship, almost certain that Emmeline was out of the possibility of his overtaking her, as she had now been gone thirteen hours, thought it better for Fitz-Edward, if he could not prevent his departure, to go with him: but he desired him to make as many artificial delays as possible.

Delamere, in the mean time, had been to Mrs. Stafford, and tried to force from her the secret of Emmeline's route. But she was inexorable; and proof against his phrenzy as well as his persuasion. She held him, however, as long as she could, in discourse. But when he found she only tried to make him lose time, he left her, in an agony of passion, and mounting his horse, while his trembling servants were ordered to follow him on pain of instant dismission, he rode out of the town without seeing his father, leaving a message for Fitz-Edward that he had taken the London road, and expected he would come after him instantly.

Lord Montreville intreated Fitz-Edward to lose not a moment; and bidding an hasty adieu to his Lordship, he ordered his horses to the door of Mrs. Stafford, where he took a formal leave of her and her husband, entreating permission to renew his acquaintance hereafter. Then getting on horseback, he made as much speed as possible after Delamere; whom with difficulty he overtook some miles forward on the London road.

This way Delamere had taken on conjecture only; but after proceeding some time, he had met a waggoner, whom he questioned. The man told him of a post chaise he had met at four o'clock in the morning; and encouraged by that to proceed, he soon heard from others enough to make him believe he was right.

The horses, however, at the end of forty miles, were too much fatigued to keep pace with Delamere's impatience. He was obliged to wait three hours before post horses could be found for himself and Fitz-Edward. His servants were obliged to remain yet longer; and the horses which were at length procured, were so lame and inadequate to the journey, that it was six hours before they reached the next stage; where the same difficulty occurred; and Delamere, between the fatigue of his body and anxiety of his mind, found himself compelled to take some rest.

The next day he still traced Emmeline from stage to stage, and imagined himself very near her: but the miserable horse on which he rode, being unable to execute his wish as to speed, and urged beyond his strength, fell with him in a stage about sixty miles from London; by which accident he received a contusion on his breast, and was bruised so much that Fitz-Edward insisted on his being blooded and put to bed; and then went to the apothecary of the village near which the accident happened, and procuring a phial of laudanum, infused it into the wine and water which Delamere drank, and by the artifice obtained for him the repose he otherwise would not have been prevailed on to take.

After having slept several hours, he desired to pursue his journey in a post chaise; but Fitz-Edward had taken care that none should be immediately to be had. By these delays only it was that Emmeline reached London some hours before him.

However, when he renewed his journey, he still continued to trace her from stage to stage, till the last postillion who drove her was found.

He said, that he was ordered to stop at the first stand of coaches, into one of which the lady went, and, with the servant behind, drove away; but the lad neither knew the number of the coach, or recollected the coachman, or did he remember whither the coach was ordered to go.

Delamere passed two days, questioning all the coachmen on the stand; and in consequence of information pretended to be given by some of them, he got into two or three quarrels by going to houses they pointed out to him. And after offering and giving rewards which only seemed to redouble his difficulties, he appeared to be farther than ever from any probability of finding the fair fugitive he so anxiously sought.

Lord Montreville and his daughter staid only two days at Swansea after his departure. They travelled in very indifferent spirits to London; where they found Delamere ill at the lodgings of Fitz-Edward in Hill-street.

Lord Montreville found there was nothing alarming in his son's indisposition; but could not persuade him to accompany him to Lady Mary Otley's.

His Lordship and Miss Augusta Delamere set out therefore for that place; leaving Delamere to the care of Fitz-Edward, who promised not to quit him 'till he had agreed either to go to the Norfolk estate or to Mr. Percival's.

Lord Montreville was tolerably satisfied that he could not discover Emmeline; and Delamere having for above a fortnight attended at all public places without seeing her, and having found every other effort to meet her fruitless, reluctantly agreed to go to his father's estate in Norfolk.

It was now almost the end of August; and Fitz-Edward, after seeing him part of the way, took his leave of him, and again went to attend his duty in the North of Ireland.

CHAPTER XII

WHILE Delamere, in the deepest despondence, which he could neither conquer or conceal, made a vain effort to divert his mind with those amusements for which he no longer had any relish, Emmeline, at her new residence, attracted the attention of many of Mrs. Ashwood's visitors.

A widow, in possession of an handsome jointure, and her children amply provided for, Mrs. Ashwood was believed to entertain no aversion to a second marriage: and her house being so near London, was frequented by a great number of single men; many of whom came there because it was a pleasant jaunt from the city, where most of them resided; and others, with hopes of amending their fortunes by an alliance with the lady herself.

These latter, however, were chiefly the younger sons of merchants; and though pleased with their flattery and assiduity, Mrs. Ashwood, who had an almost equal share of vanity and ambition, had yet given no very decided preference to any; for she imagined her personal attractions, of which she had a very high idea, added to the advantages of a good income, good expectations, and opulent connections, entitled her to marry into an higher line of life than that in which her father had first engaged her.

Her acquaintance, however, was yet very limited among persons of fashion; and it was not wholly without hopes of encreasing it that she had consented to receive Miss Mowbray, whose relationship to Lord Montreville would, she imagined, be the means of introducing her to his Lordship's notice and to that of his family.

Her civility and kindness to Emmeline were unbounded for some time. And as she was not easily convinced of her own want of beauty, she never apprehended that she ran some risk of becoming a foil, instead of the first figure, as she expected generally to be.

The extreme simplicity of Emmeline's appearance, who not withstanding the remonstrances of Mrs. Ashwood continued to dress nearly as she did in Wales; and her perfect ignorance of fashionable life and fashionable accomplishments, gave her, in the eyes of many of Mrs. Ashwood's visitors, the air of a dependant; and those who visited with a view to the fortune of the latter, carefully avoided every appearance of preference to Emmeline, and kept her friend in good humour with herself.

But there were, among those who frequented her house, some men of business; who being rather in middle life, and immensely rich, had no other views in going thither than to pass a few hours in the country, when their mercantile engagements prevented their leaving London entirely; and who loved pleasure better than any thing but money.

With one or two of these, Mrs. Ashwood and her father had at different times encouraged overtures of marriage. But they knew and enjoyed the pleasure their fortune and single state afforded them too well to give those indulgences up for the advantage of increasing their incomes, unless the object had possessed greater attractions than fell to the share of Mrs. Ashwood; and her father could not be prevailed upon to give her (at least while he lived) a sum of money large enough to tempt their avarice. These overtures therefore had ended in nothing more than an intercourse of civility.

But Emmeline no sooner appeared, than one of these gentlemen renewed his visits with more than his original assiduity.

The extreme beauty of her person, and the *naivete* of her manners, gave her, to him, the attractive charms of novelty; while the mystery there seemed to be about her, piqued his curiosity.

It was known that she was related to a noble family; but Mrs. Ashwood had been so earnestly entreated to conceal as much as possible her real history, lest Delamere should hear of and discover her, that she only told it to a few friends, and it had not yet reached the knowledge of Mr. Rochely, who had become the attendant of Mrs. Ashwood's tea table from the first introduction of Emmeline.

Mr. Rochely was nearer fifty than forty. His person, heavy and badly proportioned, was not relieved by his countenance, which was dull and ill-formed. His voice, monotonous and guttural, was fatiguing to the ear; and the singularity of his manners, as well as the oddness of his figure, often excited a degree of ridicule, which the respect his riches demanded could not always stifle.

With a person so ill calculated to inspire affection, he was very desirous of being a favourite with the ladies; and extremely sensible of their attractions. In the inferior ranks of life, his money had procured him many conquests, tho' he was by no means lavish of it; and much of the early part of his time had been passed in low amours; which did not, however, impede his progress to the great wealth he possessed. He had always intended to marry: but as he required many qualifications in a wife which are hardly ever united, he had hesitated till he had long been looked upon as an old bachelor.

He was determined to chuse beauty, but expected also fortune. He desired to marry a woman of family, yet feared the expensive turn of those brought up in high life; and had a great veneration for wit and accomplishments, but dreaded, lest in marrying a woman who possessed them, he would be liable to be governed by superior abilities, or be despised for the mediocrity of his own understanding.

With such ideas, his relations saw him perpetually pursuing some matrimonial project; but so easily frightened from his pursuit, that they relied on his succession with the most perfect confidence.

When first he beheld Emmeline, he was charmed with her person; her conversation, at once innocent and lively, impressed him with the most favourable ideas of her heart and understanding; and, brought up at a great distance from London, she had acquired no taste for expences, no rage for those amusements and dissipations which he so much apprehended in a wife.

When he came to Mrs. Ashwood's, (which was almost every afternoon) Emmeline, who was generally at work, or drawing in the dressing-room, never discomposed herself; but sat quietly to what she was doing; listening with the most patient complaisance to the long and uninteresting stories with which he endeavoured to entertain her; an attention which greatly contributed to win the heart of Rochely; and he was as much in love as so prudent a man could be, before he ventured to ask himself what he intended? or what was the family and what the fortune of the person who now occupied most of his time and a great portion of his thoughts?

Mrs. Ashwood, frequently engaged at the neighbouring card-tables, from which Emmeline almost always excused herself, often left her and Mr. Rochely to drink tea together; and when she was at home, would sometimes make her party in another room, where the subject of laughter with her own admirers, was the growing passion of the rich banker for the fair stranger.

Emmeline did not, when present, escape ridicule on this subject: but as she had not the least idea that a man so much older than herself had any intention of offering himself as an husband, she bore it with great tranquility, and continued to behave to Mr. Rochely with the attentive civility dictated by natural good breeding; while she heard, without any concern but on his account, the perpetual mirth and loud bursts of laughter which followed his compliments and attentions to her.

If he was absent a few days, the door of Mrs. Ashwood was crouded with servants and porters with game from Mr. Rochely. And his assiduities became at every visit more marked.

As it was now late in the autumn, Mrs. Ashwood was desirous of shewing Miss Mowbray some of those public places she had not yet seen; and Emmeline (not apprehending there was any reason to fear meeting Mr.

Delamere at a season when she knew field sports kept him altogether in the country) made no difficulty to accompany her.

Mr. Rochely no sooner heard a party to the play proposed, than he desired to join it; and Mrs. Ashwood, Miss Galton, (an intimate friend of hers), with Miss Mowbray, Mr. Hanbury, (one of Mrs. Ashwood's admirers) and Mr. Rochely, met at Drury-Lane Theatre; where Emmeline was extremely well entertained.

When the play was over, the box was filled with several of Mrs. Ashwood's acquaintance, who talked to *her,* while their eyes were fixed on her young friend; an observation that did not greatly lighten up her countenance.

The most conspicuous among these was a tall, thin, but extremely awkward figure, which in a most fashionable undress, and with a glass held to his eye, strided into the box, and bowing with a strange gesture to Mrs. Ashwood, exclaimed — 'Oh! my dear Mrs. A! — here I am! — returned from Spa only last night; and already at your feet. So here you are? and not yet enchained by that villainous fellow Hymen? You are a good soul, not to give yourself away while I was at Spa. I was horridly afraid, my dear widow! you would not have waited even to have given me a wedding favour.'

To this speech, as it required no answer, Mrs. Ashwood gave very little; for besides that she was not pleased with the matter, the manner delighted her still less. The speaker had, during the whole of it, leaned almost across the person who was next to him, to bring his glass nearly close to Emmeline's face.

Emmeline, extremely discomposed, drew back; and Mr. Rochely, who sat near her, putting away the glass softly with his hand, said very calmly to the leaning beau —

'Sir, is there any occasion to take an account of this lady's features?'

'Ah! my friend Rochely!' answered he familiarly, 'what are you the lady's Cicisbeo? as we say in Italy. Here is indeed beauty enough to draw you from the contemplation of three per cent. consols, India bonds, omnium, scrip, and douceurs? But prithee, my old friend, is this young lady your ward?

'My ward! no,' answered Rochely, 'how came you to think she was?'

Mr. Elkerton, who fancied he had vastly the advantage in point of wit, as well as of figure, over his antagonist, now desired to know, 'whether the lady was his niece? though if I had not recollected' said he, 'that you never was married, I should have taken her for your grand daughter.'

This sarcasm had, on the features of Rochely, all the effect the travelled man expected. But while he was preparing an answer, at which he was never very prompt, the coach was announced to be ready, and Emmeline, extremely weary of her situation, and disgusted even to impatience with her new acquaintance, hastily arose to go.

Elkerton offered to take her hand; which she drew from him without attempting to conceal her dislike; and accepting the arm of Rochely, followed Mrs. Ashwood; while Elkerton, determined not to lose sight of her seized the hand of Miss Galton, who being neither young, handsome, or rich, had been left to go out alone: they followed the rest of the party to the coach, where Mrs. Ashwood and Miss Mowbray were already seated, with Mr. Hanbury; who, as he resided with his mother in the village where Mrs. Ashwood lived, was to accompany them home.

The coach being full, seemed to preclude all possibility of Elkerton's admittance. But he was not so easily put off: and telling Mrs. Ashwood he intended to go home to sup with her, he stepped immediately in, and ordered his servant, who waited at the coach door with a flambeau, to direct his vis-a-vis to follow.

Rochely, who meant to have wished them a good night after seeing them to their carriage, was too much hurt by this happy essay of assurance not to resolve to counteract its consequences. Elkerton, though not a very young man, was near twenty years younger than Rochely; besides the income of his business (for he was in trade) he had a large independent fortune, of which he was extremely lavish; his equipages were splendid; his house most magnificently furnished; and his cloaths the most expensive that could be bought.

Rochely, whose ideas of elegance, manners, or taste, were not very refined, had no notion that the absurdity of Elkerton, or his disagreeable person, would prevent his being a very formidable rival. He therefore saw him with great pain accompany Emmeline home; and though he had formed no positive designs himself, he could not bear to suppose that another might form them with success.

Directing therefore his chariot to follow the coach, he was set down at the door a few minutes after Mrs. Ashwood and her party; where Emmeline, still more displeased with Elkerton, and having been teized by his impertinent admiration the whole way, looked as if she could have burst into tears.

Mrs. Ashwood, in a very ill humour, hardly attended to his flourishing speeches with common civility; he had therefore recourse to Miss Galton, to whom he was giving the history of his travels, which seemed to take up much of his thoughts.

Miss Galton, who by long dependance and repeated disappointments had acquired the qualifications necessary for a patient hearer, acquiesced in smiling silence to all his assertions; looked amazed in the right place; and heard, with great complacency, his wonderful success at cards, and the favour he was in with women of the first fashion at Spa.

The entrance of Mr. Rochely gave no interruption to his discourse. He bowed slightly to him without rising, and then went on, observing that he had now seen every part of Europe worth seeing, and meant, at least for some years, to remain in England; the ladies of which country he preferred to every other, and therefore intended taking a wife among them. Fortune was, he declared, to him no object; but he was determined to marry the handsomest woman he could meet with, for whom he was now looking out.

As he said this, he turned his eyes towards Emmeline; who affecting not to hear him, tho' he spoke in so loud a tone as to make it unavoidable, was talking in a low voice to Mr. Rochely.

Rochely placing himself close to her, had thrown his arm over the back of her chair; and leaning forward, attended to her with an expression in his countenance of something between apprehension and hope, that gave it the most grotesque look imaginable.

Mrs.. Ashwood, who had been entertained apart by Mr. Hanbury, now hurried over the supper; during which

Elkerton, still full of himself, engrossed almost all the conversation; gave a detail of the purchases he had made abroad, and the trouble he had to land them; interspersed with *bon mots* of French Marquises and German Barons, and witty remarks of an English Duke with whom he had crossed the water on his return. But whatever story he told, himself was still forwardest in the picture; his project of marrying an handsome wife was again repeated; and he told the party how charming a house he had bought in Kent, and how he had furnished his library.

Rochely, who lay in wait to revenge himself for all the mortifications he had suffered from him during the evening, took occasion to say, in his grave, cold manner, 'to be sure a man of your taste and erudition, Mr. Elkerton, cannot do without a library; but for my part, I think you will find no books can say so much to the purpose as those kept by your late father in Milk-street, Cheapside.'

Elkerton turned pale at this sneer; but forcing a smile of contempt, answered, 'You bankers have no ideas out of your computing-houses; and rich as ye are, will never be any thing but *des bourgeois les plus grossieres!* For my part I see no reason why — why a man's being in business, should prevent his enjoying the *elegancies* and *agrémens* of life, especially if he can *afford* it; as it is well known, I believe, even to *you,* Sir, *that I can.'*

'Oh! Sir,' replied Rochely, 'I know your late father was *reputed* to have died rich, and that no body has made a better *figure about town* than *you* have, ever since.'

'As to figure, Sir,' returned the other, it is true I like to have every thing about me *comme il faut.* And though I don't make fifty per cent. of money, as *some* gentlemen do in *your* way of business, I assure you, Sir, I do nothing that I cannot very well afford.'

Mrs. Ashwood, who thought it very likely a quarrel might ensue, here endeavoured to put an end to such very unpleasant discourse; and prevented Mr. Hanbury, who equally hated them both, from trying to irritate them farther, to which he maliciously inclined.

The hints, however, of fatigue, given by her and Miss Mowbray, obliged Mr. Rochely to ring that his chariot might be called, which had waited at the door; while Elkerton, who had a pair of beautiful pied horses in his vis-à-vis, desired to have them sent for from a neighbouring inn — 'for *I'* said he, rising and strutting round the room, 'never suffer *my* people or *my* horses to wait in the streets.'

He then leant over Emmeline's chair, and began in a court tone to renew his compliments. But she suddenly arose; and begging Mrs. Ashwood would give her leave to retire, wished Mr. Rochely and ladies a good night; and slightly curtseying to Elkerton, who was putting himself into the attitude for a speech and a bow, she tripped away.

Rochely, as soon as she was gone, hastened to his chariot; and Elkerton, whose people were in no haste to leave the ale-house, begged to sit down 'till they came.

Mrs. Ashwood had been the whole evening particularly out of humour; and being no longer able to command it, answered peevishly, 'that her house was much at his service, but that she was really so much fatigued she must retire — however,' said she, 'Miss Galton, you will be so good as to stay with Mr. Elkerton — good night to you, Sir!'

He was no sooner alone with Miss Galton, than he desired her, after a speech (which he endeavoured to season with as much flattery as it would bear) to tell him who Emmeline was?

'Upon my word, Sir,' answered she, 'it is more than I know. Her name is Mowbray; and she is somehow connected with the family of Lord Montreville; but *what* relation,' (sneeringly answered she) 'I really cannot pretend even to guess.'

'A relation of Lord Montreville!' cried Elkerton; 'why I knew his Lordship intimately when I was abroad three or four years ago. He was at Naples with his son, his lady, and two daughters; and I was domesticated, absolutely domesticated, among them. But pray what relation to them can this Miss Mowbray be?'

'Probably,' said Miss Galton, 'as you know his Lordship, you may know what connections and family he has. I suppose she may be his cousin — or his niece — or his —.'

Here she hesitated and smiled; and Elkerton, whose carriage was now at the door, and who had a clue which he thought would procure him all the information he wanted, took leave of Miss Galion; desiring her to tell Mrs. Ashwood that he should wait upon her again in a few days.

CHAPTER XIII

DELAMERE continued in Norfolk only a few weeks after his father and the family came thither. During that time, he appeared restless and dissatisfied; his former vivacity was quite lost; he shunned society; and passed almost all his time in the fields, under pretence of hunting or shooting, tho' the greatest satisfaction those amusements now afforded him was the opportunity they gave him of absenting himself from home. He seldom returned thither 'till six or seven o'clock; dined alone in his own apartment; and affected to be too much fatigued to be able to meet the party who assembled to cards in the evening.

Lady Mary Otley and her daughter, a widow lady of small fortune in the neighbourhood, with Lord and Lady Montreville and their eldest daughter, made up a party without him. Augusta Delamere had been left in their way from the North, with a relation of his Lordship's who lived near Scarborough, with whom she was to remain two months.

The party at Audley-Hall was soon encreased by Sir Richard Crofts and his eldest son, who came every autumn on a visit to Lord Montreville, and who was his most intimate friend.

Lord Montreville, during the short time he studied at the Temple, became acquainted with Sir Richard, then clerk to an attorney in the city; who, tho' there was a great difference in their rank, had contrived to gain the regard and esteem of his Lordship (then Mr. Frederic Mowbray) and was, when he came to his estate, entrusted with its management; a trust which he appeared to execute with such diligence and integrity, that he soon obtained the entire confidence of his patron; and by possessing great ductility and great activity, he was soon introduced into a higher line of life, and saw himself the companion and friend of those, to whom, at his setting out, he appeared only an humble retainer.

Born in Scotland, he boasted of his ancestry, tho' his immediate predecessors were known to be indigent and obscure; and tho' he had neither eminent talents, nor any other education than what he had acquired at a free-school in his native town, he had, by dint of a very common understanding, steadily applied to the pursuit of one point; and assisted by the friendship of Lord Montreville, acquired not only a considerable fortune, but a seat in Parliament and a great deal of political interest, together with the title of a Baronet.

He had less understanding than cunning; less honesty than industry; and tho' he knew how to talk warmly and plausibly of honour, justice, and integrity, he was generally contented only to talk of them, seldom so imprudent as to practice them when he could get place or profit by their sacrifice.

He had that sort of sagacity which enabled him to enter into the characters of those with whom he conversed: he knew how to humour their prejudices, and lay in wait for their foibles to turn them to his own advantage.

To his superiors, the cringing parasite; to those whom he thought his inferiors, proud, supercilious, and insulting; and his heart hardening as his prosperity encreased, he threw off, as much as he could, every connection that reminded him of the transactions of his early life, and affected to live only among the great, whose luxuries he could now reach, and whose manners he tried to imitate.

He had two sons by an early marriage with a woman of small fortune, who was fortunately dead; for had she lived, she would probably have been concealed, lest she should disgrace him.

To his sons, however, he had given that sort of education which was likely to fit them for places under government; and he had long secretly intended the eldest for one of the Miss Delameres.

Delamere, all warmth and openness himself, detested the narrow-minded and selfish father; and had shewn so much coolness towards the sons, that Sir Richard foresaw he would be a great impediment to his designs, and had therefore the strongest motive for trying to persuade Lord Montreville, that to send him on another tour to the Continent, would be the best means of curing him of what this deep politician termed 'a ridiculous and boyish whim, which his Lordship ought at all events to put an end to before it grew of a more dangerous consequence.'

Mr. Crofts, as he was no sportsman, passed his mornings in riding out with Miss Delamere and Miss Otley, or attending on the elder ladies in their airings:

while Delamere, who wished equally to shun Miss Otley, whom he determined never to marry, and Crofts, whom he despised and hated, lived almost alone, notwithstanding the entreaties of his father and the anger of his mother.

Her Ladyship, who had never any command over her passions, harrassed him, whenever they met, with sarcasms and reflections. Lady Mary, scorning to talk *to* a young man who was blind to the merits of her daughter, talked *at* him whenever she found an opportunity; and exclaimed against the disobedience, dissipation, and ill-breeding of modern young men: while Miss Otley affected a pretty disdain; and flirted violently with Mr. Crofts, as if to shew him that she was totally indifferent to his neglect.

The temper of Delamere was eager and irritable; and he bore the unpleasantness of this society, whenever he was forced to mix in it, with a sort of impatient contempt. But as he hourly found it more irksome, and the idea of Emmeline press every day more intensely on his heart, he determined, at the end of the third week, to go to London.

Not chusing to have any altercation with either Lord or Lady Montreville, he one evening ordered his man to have his horses ready at five o'clock the next day, saying he was to meet the fox-hounds at some distance from home; and having written a letter to his Lordship, in which he told him he was going to London for a fortnight, (which letter he left on the table in his dressing-room) he mounted his horse, and was soon in town; but instead of going to the house of his father in Berkley-square, he took lodgings in Pall-Mall.

Every night he frequented those public places which were yet open, in hopes of finding Emmeline; and his servant was constantly employed for the same purpose; but as he had no trace of her, all his enquiries were fruitless.

On the night that Emmeline was at the play, he had been at Covent-garden Theatre, and meant to have looked into the other house; but was detained by meeting a young foreigner from whom he had received civilities at Turin, 'till the house was empty. So narrowly did he miss finding her he so anxiously sought.

Elkerton, in looking about for the happy woman who was worthy the exalted situation of being his wife, had yet seen none whom he thought so likely to succeed to that honour as Miss Mowbray; and if she was, on enquiry, found to be as she was represented, (related to Lord Montreville) it would be so great an additional advantage, that he determined in that case to lay himself and his pied horses, his house in Kent, his library, and his fortune, all at her feet immediately. Nor did he once suffer himself to suspect that there was a woman on earth who could withstand such a torrent of good fortune.

In pursuance therefore of this resolution, he determined to make enquiry of Lord Montreville himself; of whom he had just known so much at Naples as to receive cards of invitation to Lady Montreville's *conversationes.*

There, he mingled with the croud; and was slightly noticed as an Englishman of fortune; smiled at for his affectation of company and manners, which seemed foreign to his original line of life; and then forgotten.

But Elkerton conceived this to be more than introduction enough; and dressing himself in what he thought *un disabille la plus imposante,* and with his servants in their morning liveries, he stopped at the door of Lord Montreville.

'Lord Montreville was not at home.'

'When was he expected?'

'It was uncertain: his Lordship was at Audley-hall, and might be in town in a fortnight; or might not come up till the meeting of Parliament.'

'And are all the family there?' enquired Elkerton of the porter. 'No, Sir; Mr. Delamere is in town.'

'And when can I see Mr. Delamere?'

The porter could not tell, as he did not live in Berkley-square. 'Where, then, is he?'

'At lodgings in Pall-Mall:' (for Delamere had left his direction with his father's servants.)

Elkerton therefore took the address with a pencil; and determined, without farther reflection, to drive thither.

It was about four o'clock, and in the middle of November, when Delamere had just returned to his lodgings, to dress before he met his foreign friend, and some other young men, to dine at a tavern in St. James's-street, when a loud rap at the door announced a visitor.

Millefleur having no orders to the contrary, and being dazzled with the splendour of Elkerton's equipage, let him in; and he was humming an Italian air out of tune, in Delamere's drawing-room, when the latter came out in his dressing-gown and slippers to receive him.

Delamere, on seeing the very odd figure and baboonish face of Elkerton, instead of that of somebody he knew, stopped short and made a grave bow.

Elkerton advancing towards him, bowed also profoundly, and said, 'I am charmed, Sir, with being permitted the honour of paying you my devoirs.'

Delamere concluded from his look and bow, as well as from a foreign accent, (which Elkerton had affected 'till it was become habitual) that the man was either a dancing master or a quack doctor, sent to him by some of his companions, who frequently exercised on each other such efforts of practical wit. He therefore being not without humour, bowed again more profoundly than before; and answered, 'that the honour was entirely his, tho' he did not know how he had deserved it.'

'I was so fortunate, Sir,' resumed Elkerton, 'so fortunate as to — have the honour — the happiness — of knowing Lord Montreville and Lady Montreville a few years ago at Naples.'

Delamere, still confirmed in his first idea, answered, 'very probably, Sir.'

'And, Sir,' continued Elkerton, 'I now waited upon *you*, as his Lordship is not in town.'

'Indeed, Sir, you are too obliging.'

'To ask, Sir, a question, which I hope will not be deemed — be deemed —' (a word did not immediately occur) 'be deemed — improper — intrusive — impertinent — inquisitive — presuming —'

'I dare say, Sir, nothing improper, intrusive, impertinent, inquisitive, or presuming, is to be apprehended from a gentleman of your appearance.'

Delamere expected something very ridiculous to follow this ridiculous introduction, and with some difficulty forbore laughing. Elkerton went on —

'It relates, Sir, to a Lady.'

'Pray, Sir, proceed. I am really impatient where a lady is concerned.'

'You are acquainted, Sir, with a lady of the name of Ashwood, who lives at Clapham?'

'No, really Sir, I am not so happy.'

'I fancy then, Sir, I have been misinformed, and beg pardon for the trouble I have presumed to give: but I understood that the young lady who lives with her was a relation of Lord Montreville.'

A ray of fire seemed to flash across the imagination of Delamere, and to inflame all his hopes. He blushed deeply, and his voice faultering with anxiety, he cried —

'What? — who, Sir? — a young lady? — what young lady?'

'Miss Mowbray, they tell me, is her name; and I understand, Sir — but I dare say from mistake — that she is of your family.'

Delamere could hardly breathe. He seemed as if he was in a dream, and dared not speak for fear of awaking.

Elkerton, led on by the questions Delamere at length summoned resolution to ask, proceeded to inform him of all he knew; how, where, and how often, he had seen Emmeline, and of his intentions to offer himself a candidate for her favour — 'for notwithstanding, Sir,' said he, 'that Mr. Rochely seems to be *fort avant en ses bon graces,* I think — I hope — I believe, that his fortune — (and yet his fortune does not perhaps so much exceed mine as many suppose) — his fortune will hardly turn the balance against *me;* especially if I have the sanction of Lord Montreville; to whom I suppose (as you seem to acknowledge some affinity between Miss Mowbray and his Lordship) it will be no harm if I apply.'

Thro' the mind of Delamere, a thousand confused ideas rapidly passed. He was divided between his joy at having found Emmeline, his vexation at knowing she was surrounded by rivals, and his fear that his father might, by the application of Elkerton to him, know that

Emmeline's abode was no longer a secret: and amidst these various sensations, he was able only to express his dislike of Elkerton, whose presumption in thinking of Emmeline appeared to cancel the casual obligation he owed to him for discovering her.

'Sir,' said he haughtily, as soon as he could a little recover his recollection, 'I am very well assured that Lord Montreville will not hear any proposals for Miss Mowbray. His Lordship has, in fact, no authority over her; and besides he is at present about to leave his house in Norfolk, and I know not when he will be in town; perhaps not the whole winter; he is now going to visit some friends, and it will be impossible you can have any access to him for some months. As to myself, you will excuse me; I am engaged to dine out.'

He rang the bell, and ordered the servant who entered to enquire for the gentleman's carriage. Then bowing coolly to him, he went into his dressing room, and left the mortified Elkerton to regret the little success of an attempt which he doubted not would have excited, in the hearts of all those related to Miss Mowbray, admiration at his generosity, and joy for the good fortune of Emmeline: for he concluded, by her being a companion to Mrs. Ashwood, that she had no fortune, or any dependance but on the bounty of Lord Montreville.

Delamere, whose ardent inclinations, whatever turn they took, were never to be a moment restrained, rang for his servants; and dispatching one of them with an excuse to his friends, he sent a second for an hackney-coach. Then ordering up a cold dinner, which he hardly staid to eat, he got into the coach, and directed it to be driven as fast as possible to Clapham Common; where he asked for the house of Mrs. Ashwood, and was presently at the door.

The servant had that moment opened the iron gate, to let out a person who had been to his mistress upon business. Delamere therefore enquiring if Miss Mowbray was at home, entered without ringing, and telling the servant that he had occasion to speak to Miss Mowbray only, the man answered, 'that she was alone in the dressing room.' Thither therefore he desired to be shewn; and without being announced, he entered the room.

Instead of finding her alone, he saw her sat at work by a little table, on which were two wax candles; and by her side, with his arm, as usual over the back of her chair, and gazing earnestly on her face, sat Mr. Rochely.

Emmeline did not look up when he came in, supposing it was the servant with tea. Delamere therefore was close to the table when she saw him. The work dropped from her hands; she grew pale, and trembled; but not being able to rise, she openly clasped her hands together, and said faintly, 'Oh! heaven! — Mr. Delamere!'

'Yes, Emmeline, it is Mr. Delamere! and what is there so extraordinary in that? I was told you were alone: may I beg the favour of a few minutes' conversation?'

Emmeline knew not what to reply. She saw him dart an angry and disdainful look at poor Rochely; who, alarmed by the entrance of a stranger that appeared on such a footing of familiarity, and who possessed the advantages of youth and a handsome person, had retreated slowly towards the fire, and now surveyed Delamere with scrutinizing and displeased looks; while Delamere said to Emmeline —'if you have no particular business with this gentleman, will you go into some other room, that I may speak to you on an affair of consequence?'

'Sit down' said Emmeline, recovering her surprize; 'sit down, and I will attend you presently. Tell me, how is your sister Augusta?'

'I know not. She is in Yorkshire.'

'And Lord Montreville?'

'Well, I believe. But what is all this to the purpose? can I not speak to you, but in the presence of a third person?'

Unequivocal as this hint was, Rochely seemed determined not to go, and Delamere as resolutely bent to affront him, if he did not.

Emmeline therefore, who knew not what else to do, was going to comply with his request of a private audience, when she was luckily relieved by the entrance of Mrs. Ashwood and the tea table.

Mrs. Ashwood, surprized at seeing a stranger, and a stranger whose appearance had more fashion than the generality of her visitors, was introduced to Mr. Delamere; a ceremony he would willingly have dispensed with; and having made his bow, and muttered something about having taken the liberty to call on his relation, he sat down by Emmeline, and in a whisper told her he must and would speak to her alone before he went.

Emmeline, to whose care the tea table was allotted when Miss Galton happened not to be at Mrs. Ashwood's, now excused herself under pretence of being obliged to make tea; and while it was passing, Mrs. Ashwood made two or three attempts to introduce general conversation; but it went no farther than a few insignificant sentences between her and Mr. Rochely.

Delamere, wholly engrossed by the tumultuous delight of having recovered Emmeline, and by contriving how to speak to her alone, thought nothing else worthy his attention; and sat looking at her with eyes so expressive of his love, that Rochely, who anxiously watched him, was convinced his solicitude was infinitely stronger than his relationship only would have produced.

He had at length learned, by constant attention to every hint and every circumstance that related to Emmeline, who she was; and had even got from Mrs. Ashwood a confused idea of Delamere's attachment to her, which the present scene at once elucidated.

Rochely saw in him not only a rival, but a rival so dangerous that all his hopes seemed to vanish at once. Unconscious, 'till then, how very indiscreetly he was in love, he was amazed at the pain he felt from this discovery; and with a most rueful countenance, sat silent and disconcerted.

Mrs. Ashwood, used to be flattered and attended to, was in no good humour with Mr. Delamere, who gave her so little of his notice: and never perhaps were a party more uncomfortable, 'till they were enlivened by the entrance of Miss Galton and Mr. Hanbury, with another gentleman.

They were hardly placed, and had their tea sent round, before a loud ring was heard, and the servant announced 'Mr. Elkerton.'

Mr. Elkerton came dancing into the room; and having spoken to Mrs. Ashwood and Emmeline, he slightly surveyed the company and sat down.

He was very near sighted, and affected to be still more so; and Delamere having drawn his chair out of the circle, sat almost behind Emmeline; while the portly citizen who had accompanied Mr. Hanbury sat forward, near the table; Delamere was therefore hardly seen.

Elkerton began to tell them how immoderately he was fatigued. 'I have been over the whole town,' said he, 'to-day. In the morning I was obliged to attend a boring appointment upon business relative to my estate in Kent; and to meet my tenants, who disagreed with my steward, and then, I went to call upon my old friend Delamere, Lord Montreville's son, in Pall-Mall; we passed a very chearful hour discoursing of former occurrences when we were together at Turin. Upon my word, he is a good sensible young man. We have renewed our intimacy; and he has insisted upon my going down with him to his father's house in Norfolk.'

Emmeline suspended her tea making, and looked astonished. Mrs. Ashwood seemed surprized.

But Delamere, who had at first felt inclined to be angry at the folly and forwardness of Elkerton, was now so struck with the ridicule of the circumstance, that he broke into a loud laugh.

The eyes of the company were turned towards *him,* and Elkerton with great indignation took his glass to survey who it was that had thus violated the rules of good breeding; but great was his dismay and astonishment, when he beheld the very Delamere, of whom he had spoken with so much assurance, rise up, and advancing towards him, make a grave bow. —

'Sir,' said Delamere, very solemnly, 'I cannot sufficiently express my gratitude for your good opinion of me; nor my happiness to hear you intend to honour me with a visit at Audley Hall. Upon my word you are *too* obliging, and I know not how I shall show my gratitude!'

The ironical tone in which this was delivered, and the discomposed looks of the distressed Elkerton, explained the matter to the whole company; and the laugh became general.

Elkerton, tho' not easily disconcerted, could not stand it. After a sort of apology to Delamere, he endeavoured to reassume his consequence. But he had been too severely mortified; and in a few minutes arose, and under pretence of being engaged to a rout in town, went away, nobody attempting to stop him.

Rochely, who hated Elkerton, could not forbear to triumph in this discomfiture. He spoke very severely of him as a forward, impertinent, silly fellow, who was dissipating his fortune.

The old citizen heartily joined in exclaiming against such apostates from the frugality of their ancestors. 'Sir,' said he to Rochely, 'we all know that *you are* a prudent man; and that cash at your house is, as it were, in the Bank. Sir, you do honour to the city; but as to that there Mr. Elkerton, one must be cautious; but for *my* part, I wonder how some people go on. To my certain knowledge his father didn't die so rich as was supposed — no — not by a many thousands. Sir, I remember him — (and I am not ashamed to say it, for every body knows *I* have got my money honestly, and that its all of my own getting) — but, Sir, I remember that man's father, and not a many years ago neither, carrying out parcels, and sweeping the shop for old Jonathan Huggins. You knew old Jonathan Huggins: he did not die, I think, 'till about the year forty-one or two. You remember him, to be sure?'

Rochely, ever tremblingly alive when his age was called in question, yet fearing to deny a fact which he apprehended the other would enter into a convincing detail to prove, answered that 'he slightly remembered him when he was quite a boy.'

But his evasion availed him nothing. The old citizen, Mr. Rugby, was now got upon his own ground; and most inhumanly for the feelings of poor Rochely, began to relate in whose mayoralty old Jonathan Huggins was sheriff, and when he was mayor; who he married, who married his daughters; and how he acquired an immense fortune, all by frugality at setting out; and how one of his daughters, who had married a Lord against the old man's will, had spent more in *one* night than his father did in a twelvemonth.

Delamere, who sat execrating both Jonathan Huggins and his historian, at length lost all patience; and said to Emmeline, in an half whisper, 'I can bear this no longer: leave these tedious old fools, and let me speak to you for two minutes only.'

Emmeline knew not how to refuse, without hazarding some extravagance on the part of Delamere. But as she did not like the appearance of leaving the room abruptly, she desired Mrs. Ashwood would give her permission to order candles in the parlour, as Mr. Delamere wished to speak with her alone.

As soon as the servant informed her they were ready, she went down: and Delamere followed her, having first wished Mrs. Ashwood a good night; who was too much displeased with the little attention he had shewn her, to ask him to supper, tho' she was very desirous of having a man of his fashion in the list of her acquaintance.

Delamere and Emmeline were no sooner alone, than he began to renew, with every argument he thought likely to move her, his entreaties for a private marriage. He swore that he neither could or would live without her, and that her refusal would drive him to some act of desperation.

Emmeline feared her resolution would give way; for the comparison between the people she had lately been among, and Delamere, was infinitely favourable to him. Such unabated love, in a man who might chuse among the fairest and most fortunate of women, was very seducing; and the advantages of being his wife, instead of continuing the precarious situation she was now in, would have determined at once a mind more attentive to pecuniary or selfish motives.

But Emmeline, unshaken by such considerations, was liable to err only from the softness of her heart.

Delamere unhappy — Delamere wearing out in hopeless solicitude the bloom of life, was the object she found it most difficult to contend with: and feeble would have been her defence, had she not considered herself as engaged in honour to Lord Montreville to refuse his son, and still more engaged to respect the peace of the family of her dear Augusta.

Strengthened by these reflections, she refused, tho' in the gentlest manner, to listen to such proposals; reproached him, tho' with more tenderness in her voice and manner than she had yet shewn, for having left Audley Hall without the concurrence of Lord Montreville; and entreated him to return, and try to forget her.

'Let me perish if I do!' eagerly answered Delamere. 'No, Emmeline; if you determine to push me to extremities, to you only will be the misery imputable, when my mistaken parents, in vain repentance, hang over the tomb of their only son, and see the last of his family in an early grave. It is in your power only to save me — You refuse — farewel, then — I wish no future regret may embitter your life, and that you may find consolation in being the wife of some one of those persons who are, I see, offering you all that riches can bestow. Farewel, lovely, inhuman girl! be happy if you can — after having sacrificed to a mistaken point of honour, the repose and the life of him who lived only to adore you.'

So saying, he suddenly opened the door, and was leaving the room. But Emmeline, who shuddered at the picture he had drawn of his despair, and saw such traces of its reality on his countenance, caught his arm.

'Stay! Mr. Delamere,' cried she, 'stay yet a moment!'

'For what purpose?' answered he, 'since you refuse to hear me?'

He turned back, however, into the room; and Emmeline, who fancied she saw him the victim of his unfortunate love, could no longer command her tears.

Delamere threw himself at her feet, and embraced her knees. 'Oh Emmeline!' cried he, weeping also, 'hear me for the last time. Either consent to be mine, or let me take an eternal adieu!'

'What would you have me do? good God! what is it you expect of me?'

'To go with me to Scotland to-morrow — to-night — directly!'

'Oh, no! no! — Does not Lord Montreville depend upon my honour? — can I betray a trust reposed in me?'

'Chimeras all; founded in tyranny on his part, and weakness on yours. *He* had no right to exact such a promise; *you* had no right to give it. But however, send to him again to say I have seen you — summons him hither to divide us — you may certainly do so if you please; but Lord Montreville will no longer have a son; at least England, nor Europe, will contain him no longer — I will go where my father shall hear no more of me.'

'Will it content you if I promise you *not* to write to Lord Montreville, nor to cause him to be written to, and to see you again?' 'When?'

'To-morrow — whenever you please.'

Delamere, catching at this faint ray of hope, promised, if she would allow him to come thither when he would, he would endeavour to be calm. He made her solemnly protest that she would neither write to Lord Montreville, or procure another to do it; and that she would not leave Mrs. Ashwood without letting him know when and whither she went; and if by any accident his father heard of his having found her, that she would enter into no new engagements to conceal herself from him.

Having procured from her these assurances, which he knew she would not violate, and having obtained her consent to see him early the next morning, he at her request agreed to take his leave; which he did with less pain than he had ever before felt at quitting her; carrying with him the delightful hope that he had made an impression on her heart, and secure of seeing her the next day, he went home comparatively happy.

Emmeline, who had wept excessively, was very unfit to return to the company; but she thought her not appearing again among them would be yet more singular. She therefore composed herself as well as she could; and after staying a few minutes to recollect her scattered spirits, she entered the room where they were at cards.

Rochely, who was playing at whist with Mrs. Ashwood, Mr. Rugby, and Mr. Hanbury, looked anxiously at her eyes; and presently losing all attention to what he was about, and forgetting his game, he played so extremely ill, that he lost the rubber.

The old cit, who had three half crowns depending, and who was a determined grumbler at cards, fell upon him without mercy; and said so many rude things, that Rochely could not help retorting; and it was with some difficulty Mrs. Ashwood prevented the grossest abuse being lavished from the enraged Rugby on the enamoured banker; who desiring to give his cards to Miss Galton, got up and ordered his carriage.

Emmeline sat near the fire, with her handkerchief in her hand, which was yet wet with tears.

Rochely, with a privilege he had been used to, and which Emmeline, from a man old enough to be her father, thought very inconsequential, took her hand and the handkerchief it held.

'So, Miss Mowbray,' said he, 'Mr. Delamere is your near relation?'

'Yes, Sir,' sighed Emmeline.

'No death, I hope?'

'No, Sir.'

'Whence then, these tears?'

Emmeline drew her hand away.

'What a strange young man this is, to make you cry. What has he been saying to you?'

'Nothing, Sir.'

'Ah! Miss Mowbray; such a lad as that is but an indifferent guardian; pray where does his father live?'

Miss Mowbray, not aware of the purpose of this enquiry, and glad of any thing that looked like common conversation, answered 'at Audley Hall, in Norfolk; and in Berkley-square.'

Some other questions, which seemed of no consequence, Rochely asked, and Emmeline answered; 'till hearing his carriage was at the door, he went away.

'I don't like your Mr. Delamere at all, Miss Mowbray,' said Mrs. Ashwood, as soon as the game ended. 'I never saw a prouder, more disagreeable young man in my life.'

Emmeline smiled faintly, and said she was sorry he did not please her.

'No, nor me either,' said Miss Galton. 'Such haughtiness indeed! — yet I was glad he mortified that puppy Elkerton.'

Emmeline, who found the two friends disposed to indulge their good nature at the expence of the company of the evening, complained of being fatigued, and asked for a glass of wine and water: which having drank, she retired to bed, leaving the lady of the house, who had invited Mr. Hanbury and his friend to supper, to enjoy more stories of Jonathan Huggins, and the pretty satyrical efforts of Miss Galton, who made her court most effectually by ridiculing and villifying all their acquaintance whenever it was in her power.

CHAPTER XIV

WHEN Rochely got home, he set about examining the state of his heart exactly as he would have examined the check book of one of his customers.

He found himself most miserably in love. But avarice said, Miss Mowbray had no fortune.

By what had passed in his bosom that evening, he had discovered that he should be wretched to see her married to another.

But avarice enquired how he could offer to marry a woman without a shilling?

Love, represented that her modest, reserved, and unambitious turn, would perhaps make her, in the end, a more profitable match than a woman educated in expence, who might dissipate more than she brought.

Avarice asked whether he could depend on modesty, reserve, and a retired turn, in a girl not yet eighteen?

After a long discussion, Love very unexpectedly put to flight the agent of Plutus, who had, with very little interruption, reigned despoticly over all his thoughts and actions for many years; and Rochely determined to write to Lord Montreville, to lay his circumstances before him, and make a formal proposal to marry Miss Mowbray.

In pursuance of this resolution, he composed, with great pains, (for he was remarkably slow in whatever he undertook) the following epistle. –

'My Lord,

'This serves to inform your Lordship, that I have seen Miss Mowbray, and like her well enough to be willing to marry her, if you, my Lord, have not any other views for her; and so to fortune, I will just give your Lordship a memorandum of mine.

'I have sixty thousand pounds in the stocks; viz. eighteen in the three per cent. consols. twenty in Bank stock: ten in East India stock; and twelve in South Sea annuities.

'I have about forty thousand on different mortgages; all good, as I will be ready at any time to shew you. I have houses worth about five more. And after the death of my mother, who is near eighty, I shall have an estate in Middlesex worth ten more. The income of my business is near three thousand pounds a year; and my whole income near ten thousand.

'My character, my Lord, is well known: and you will find, if we agree, that I shall not limit Miss Mowbray's settlement to the proportion of what your Lordship may please to give her, (for I suppose you will give her something) but to what she ought to have as my widow, if it should so happen that she survives me.

'I have reason to believe Miss Mowbray has no dislike to this proposal; and hope to hear from your Lordship thereon by return of post.

I am, my Lord,

your Lordship's very humble servant,
HUMPHREY ROCHELY.'

Lombard-street,
Nov. 20th. 17—.

This was going to the point at once. The letter arrived in due time at Audley-Hall; and was received by Lord Montreville with surprize and satisfaction. The hint of Miss Mowbray's approbation made him hope she was yet concealed from Delamere; and as he determined to give the earliest and strongest encouragement to this overture, from a man worth above a hundred thousand pounds, he called a council with Sir Richard Crofts, who knew Rochely, and who kept cash with him; and it was determined that Lord Montreville should go to town, not only to close at once with the opulent banker, but to get Delamere out of the way while the marriage was in agitation, which it would otherwise be impossible to conceal from him. To persuade him to another continental tour was what Sir Richard advised: and agreed to go to town with his Lordship, in order to assist in this arduous undertaking.

Lord Montreville, however, failed not immediately to answer the letter he had received from Mr. Rochely, in these terms —

'Sir,

This day's post brought me the honour of your letter.

If Miss Mowbray is as sensible as she ought to be, of so flattering a distinction, be assured it will be one of the most satisfactory events of my life to see her form a connection with a gentleman truly worthy and respectable.

To hasten the completion of an event so desirable, I fully intend being in town in a very few days; when I will, with your permission, wait on you in Lombard-street.

'I have the honour to be, with great esteem,

Sir,

your most devoted,

and most obedient servant,

MONTREVILLE.'

Audley-Hall, Nov. 23

The haughty Peer, who derived his blood from the most antient of the British Nobility, thus condescended to flatter opulence and to court the alliance of riches. Nor did he think any advances he could make, beneath him, when he hoped at once to marry his niece to advantage, and what was yet more material, put an invincible bar between her and his son.

While this correspondence, so inimical to Delamere's hopes, was passing between his father and Mr. Rochely, he was every hour with Emmeline; intoxicated with his passion, indulging the most delightful hopes, and forgetting every thing else in the world.

He had found it his interest to gain (by a little more attention, and some fine speeches about elegance and grace,) the good opinion of Mrs. Ashwood; who now declared she had been mistaken in her first idea of him, and that he was not only quite a man of fashion, but possessed an excellent understanding and very refined sentiments.

The sudden death of her father had obliged her to leave home some days before: but as soon as she was gone, Emmeline, who foresaw that Delamere would be constantly with her, sent for Miss Galton.

No remonstrance of hers could prevent his passing every day at the house, from breakfast 'till a late hour in the evening.

On the last of these days, he was there as usual; and it was past eight at night, when Emmeline, who had learned to play on the harp, by being present when Mrs. Ashwood received lessons on that instrument, was singing to Delamere a little simple air of which he was particularly fond, and into which she threw so much pathos, that lost in fond admiration, he 'hung over her, enamoured,' when she was interrupted by the entrance of a servant who said that a Lord, but he forgot the name, was below, and desired to speak with Miss Mowbray.

If Emmeline was alarmed at the sight of Lord Montreville at Swansea, when she had acted with the strictest attention to his wishes, she had now much more reason to be so, when she felt herself conscious of having given encouragement to Delamere, and had reason to fear her motives for doing so would be misbelieved or misunderstood.

Tho' the servant had forgotten his name, Emmeline doubted not but it was Lord Montreville; and she had hardly time to think how she should receive him, before his Lordship (who had impatiently followed the servant up stairs) entered the room.

Delamere, immovable behind Emmeline's chair, was the first object that struck him.

He had hoped that her residence was yet unknown to his son; and surprize, vexation, and anger, were marked in his countenance and attitude.

'Miss Mowbray!' (advancing towards her) 'is it thus you fulfil the promise you gave me? And you, Mr. Delamere

— do you still obstinately persist in this ridiculous, this unworthy attachment?'

'I left you, my Lord,' answered Delamere, 'without deceiving you as to my motives for doing so. I came in search of Miss Mowbray. By a fortunate accident I found her. I have never dissimulated; nor ever mean it in whatever relates to her. Nothing has prevented my making her irrevocably mine, but her too scrupulous adherence to a promise *she* ought never to have given, and which your *Lordship* ought never to have extorted.'

Emmeline, gentle as she was, had yet that proper spirit which conscious worth seldom fails of inspiring: and knowing that she had already sacrificed much to the respect she thought Lord Montreville entitled to, she was hurt at finding, from his angry and contemptuous tone, as well as words, that she was condemned unheard, and treated with harshness where she deserved only kindness and gratitude.

The courage of which her first surprize had deprived her, was restored by these sensations; and she said, with great coolness, yet with less timidity than usual, 'my Lord, I have yet done nothing in violation of the promise I gave you. But the moment your Lordship doubts my adherence to it, from that moment I consider it as dissolved.'

Delamere, encouraged by an answer so flattering to his hopes, now addressed himself to his father, who was by this time seated; and spoke so forcibly of his invincible attachment, and his determined purpose never to marry any other woman, that the resolution of Lord Montreville was shaken, and would perhaps have given way, if the violent and clamorous opposition of his wife on one hand, and the ambitious projects and artful advice of Sir

Richard Crofts on the other, had not occurred to him. He commanded himself so far as not to irritate Delamere farther, by reflections on the conduct of Emmeline, which he found would not be endured; and trying to stifle his feelings under the dissimulation of the courtier, he heard with patience all he had to urge. He even answered him with temper; made an apology to Emmeline for any expressions that might have given her offence; and at length threw into his manner a composure that elated Delamere to a degree of hope hitherto unfelt. He fancied that his father, weary of hopeless opposition, and convinced of the merit of Emmeline, would consent to his marriage: and his quick spirit seizing with avidity on an idea so flattering, converted into a confirmation of it, all Lord Montreville's discourse for the remainder of the visit: in which, by dissimulation on one part, and favourable expectations on the other, they both seemed to return to some degree of good humour.

Delamere agreed to go home with his father; and Lord Montreville having determined to return the next day to speak to Emmeline on the proposals of Rochely, they parted; his Lordship meditating as he went home how to prevent Delamere's interrupting the conference he wished to have on a subject which was so near his heart.

On his arrival at his own house, he found Sir Richard Crofts waiting for him, whom he detained to supper. Delamere, as soon as it was over, went to his lodgings; which Lord Montreville did not oppose, as he wished to be alone with Sir Richard; but he desired, that after that evening Delamere would return to his apartments in Berkley-square; which he partly promised to do.

Lord Montreville related to Sir Richard what had passed, and the uneasiness he was under to find that Delamere, far from relaxing in his determination, had openly renewed his addresses; and that Emmeline seemed much less disposed to sacrifice his wishes to those of his family, than he had yet found her.

Sir Richard, himself wholly insensible to the feelings of a father, discouraged in Lord Montreville every tendency to forgive or indulge this indiscreet passion. And equally incapable of the generous sentiments of a gentleman towards a woman, young, helpless, dependant, and unfortunate, he tried to harden the heart of Lord Montreville against his orphan niece, and advised him peremptorily to insist on her marrying Rochely immediately, or, as the alternative, to declare to her that from the moment of her refusal she must expect from him neither support or countenance.

This threat on one hand, and the affluence offered her by Rochely on the other, must, he thought, oblige her to embrace his proposals. The greatest difficulty seemed to be, to prevent Delamere's impetuosity from snatching her at once out of the power of his father, by an elopement; to which, if she preferred him to Rochely, it was very probable she might be driven by harsh measures to consent; and that Delamere must have in her heart a decided preference, there could be little doubt.

Lord Montreville was apprehensive that Delamere, who had, he found, for many days lived entirely at Mrs. Ashwood's, would be there before him in the morning, and preclude all possibility of a private conversation with Emmeline.

Fitz-Edward, who could, and from the duplicity of his character would perhaps have made a diversion in his favour, was not in town; and to both the Mr. Crofts Delamere had an antipathy, which he took very little pains to conceal; they therefore could not be employed to engage him.

In this difficulty, Sir Richard offered to go himself to Miss Mowbray, that Lord Montreville might be at liberty to detain his son; pretences for which could not be wanting.

His Lordship closed with this offer with pleasure; and felt himself relieved from a painful task. His heart, though greatly changed by a long course of good fortune, and by the habit of living among the great, was yet not quite lost to the feelings of nature.

His brother, than whom he was only a year younger, and whom he had loved thro' childhood and youth with singular attachment, was not wholly forgotten; and the softened likeness, in the countenance of Emmeline, to one whom he had so long been used to look up to with tenderness, frequently said as much for her to his affection, as her unprotected and helpless state did to his honour and his compassion. Nor, whatever pains he took to stifle his pity for his son, could he entirely reconcile to his own heart the part he was acting.

But of these feelings meritorious as they were, he was ashamed, and dared not avow them even to himself; while he was intimidated by the supercilious spirit and unconquerable pride of Lady Montreville, and tempted by the visions of encreasing splendour and accumulated riches which Sir Richard perpetually presented to his imagination, and which there was indeed but little doubt of realizing.

The Mowbray family were known to possess abilities. Those of the deceased Mr. Mowbray were remarkably great, tho' he had thrown away his time and health in a course of dissipation which had made them useless.

The talents of Lord Montreville, tho' less brilliant, were more solid. And now in the meridian of life, with powerful connections and extensive interest, he was courted to accept an eminent post in administration, with a promise of a Marquisate being restored to him, which had long lain dormant in his own family, and of the revival of which he was extremely ambitious.

To support such a dignity, his son's future fortune, ample as it must be, would not, he thought, be adequate; and could only be made so by his marrying Miss Otley or some woman of equal fortune.

This, therefore, was the weight which entirely over-balanced all his kindness for his niece, and confirmed his resolution to tear her from Delamere at whatever price.

CHAPTER XV

IT was much earlier than the usual hour for morning visits, when Sir Richard Crofts was at the door of Mrs. Ashwood.

Miss Mowbray had given no orders to be denied; and he was, on enquiring for her, shewn into the parlour.

As soon as the servant informed her a gentleman was below whom she found was not Delamere, she concluded it was Lord Montreville; and with a fearful and beating heart, went down.

She saw, with some surprize, a middle-aged man, of no very pleasant countenance and person, to whom she was an entire stranger; and concluding his business was with Mrs. Ashwood, she was about to retreat, when the gentleman advancing towards her, told her he waited on her, commissioned by Lord Montreville.

Emmeline sat down in silence, and Sir Richard began.

'Miss Mowbray, I have the honour to be connected with Lord Montreville, and entirely in his Lordship's confidence: you will please therefore to consider what I shall say to you as coming immediately, directly, and absolutely, from himself; and as his Lordship's decided, and unalterable, and irrevocable intentions.'

The abruptness of this speech shocked and distressed Emmeline. She grew very pale; but bowing slightly to the speaker, he went on.

'My Lord Montreville hopes and supposes, and is willing to believe, that you have not, in direct violation of your promise solemnly given, encouraged Mr. Delamere in the absurd, and impossible, and impracticable project of marrying you. But however that may have been, as it is his Lordship's firm resolution and determination never to suffer such a connection, you have, I suppose, too much sense not to see the mischief you must occasion, and bring on, and cause to yourself, by encouraging a giddy, and infatuated, and ignorant, and rash young man, to resist paternal authority.'

Emmeline was still silent.

'Now here is an opportunity of establishing yourself in affluence, and reputation, and fortune, beyond what your most sanguine hopes could offer you; and I am persuaded you will eagerly, and readily, and immediately embrace it. Lord Montreville insists upon it; the world expects it; and Mr. Delamere's family demand it of you.'

'Sir!' said Emmeline, astonished at the peremptory tone and strange purport of these words.

'It is my custom,' resumed Sir Richard, 'when I am upon business, to speak plainly, and straitly, and to the point. This then is what I have to propose — You are acquainted with Mr. Rochely, the great banker?'

'Yes, Sir.'

'He offers to my Lord Montreville to marry you; and to make settlements on you equal to what you might have claimed, had you a right to be considered as a daughter of the house of Mowbray. His real fortune is very great; his annual income superior to that of many of the nobility; and there *can* be no reason, indeed none will be allowed, or listened to, or heard of, why you should not eagerly, and instantly, and joyfully accept a proposal so infinitely superior to what you have any claim, or right, or pretence to.'

This was almost too much for poor Emmeline. Anger and disdain, which she found fast rising in her bosom, restrained her tears: but her eyes flashed indignantly on the unfeeling politician who thus so indelicately addressed her.

He would not give her time to speak; but seemed determined to overwhelm her imagination at once with the contrast he placed before her.

'If,' continued he, 'you will agree to become the wife of Mr. Rochely, as soon as settlements can be prepared, my Lord Montreville, of whose generosity, and greatness of mind, and liberality, too much cannot be said, offers to consider you as being really his niece; as being really a daughter of the Mowbray family; and, that being so considered, you may not be taken by any man portionless, he will, on the day of marriage, present, and settle on, and give you, three thousand pounds.

'Now, Miss Mowbray, consider, and weigh, and reflect on this well: and give me leave, in order that you may form a just judgment, to tell you the consequence of your refusal.'

'My Lord Montreville, who is not obliged to give you the least assistance, or support, or countenance, does by me declare, that if you are so weak (to call it by no harsher name) as to refuse this astonishing, and amazing, and singular good fortune, he shall consider you as throwing off all duty, and regard, and attention to him; and as one, with whose fate it will be no longer worth his while to embarrass, perplex, and concern himself. From that moment, therefore, you must drop the name of Mowbray, to which in fact you have no right, and take that of your mother, whatever it be; and you must never expect from my Lord Montreville, or the Mowbray-Delamere family, either countenance, or support, or protection.

'Now, Miss Mowbray, your answer. The proposition cannot admit of deliberation, or doubt, or hesitation, and my Lord expects it by me.'

The presence of mind which a very excellent understanding and very innocent heart gave to Emmeline, was never more requisite than on this occasion. The rude and peremptory manner of the speaker; the dreadful alternative of Rochely on one side, and indigence on the other, thus suddenly and unexpectedly brought before her; was altogether so overcoming, that she could not for a moment collect her spirits enough to speak at all. She sighed; but her agitation was too great for tears; and at length summoning all her courage, she replied —

'My Lord Montreville, Sir, would have been kinder, had he delivered himself his wishes and commands. Such, however, as I now receive them, they require no deliberation. I *will not* marry Mr. Rochely, tho' instead of the fortune you describe, he could offer me the world. — Lord Montreville *may* abandon me, but he *shall not* make me wretched. Tell him therefore, Sir,' (her spirit rose as she spoke) 'that the daughter of his brother, unhappy as she is, yet boasts that nobleness of mind which her father possessed, and disclaims the mercenary views of becoming, from pecuniary motives, the wife of a man whom she cannot either love or esteem. Tell him too, that if she had not inherited a strong sense of honour, of which at least her birth does not deprive her, she might now have been the wife of Mr. Delamere, and independant of his Lordship's authority; and it is improbable, that one who has sacrificed so much to integrity, should now be compelled by threats of indigence to the basest of all actions, that of selling her person and her happiness for a subsistence. I beg that *you,* Sir, who seem to have delivered Lord Montreville's message, with such scrupulous exactness, will take the trouble to be as precise in my answer; and that his Lordship will consider it as final.'

Having said this, with a firmness of voice and manner which resentment, as well as a noble pride, supplied; she arose, curtseyed composedly to Sir Richard, and went out of the room; leaving the unsuccessful ambassador astonished at that strength of mind, and dignity of manner, which he did not expect in so young a woman, and somewhat mortified, that his masculine eloquence, on which he was accustomed to pride himself, and which he thought generally unanswerable, had so entirely fallen short of the effect he expected.

Unwilling however to return to Lord Montreville without hopes of success, he thought he might obtain at least some information from Mrs. Ashwood of the likeliest means to move her untractable and high spirited friend. He therefore rang the bell, and desired to speak with that lady. But as she was not yet returned from the house of her father, where a family meeting was held to inspect his will, Sir Richard failed in attempting to secure her agency; and was obliged, however reluctantly, to depart.

Emmeline, whose command of herself was exerted with too much violence not to shake her whole frame with its effects, no sooner reached her own chamber than she found all her courage gone, and a violent passion of tears succeeded.

Her deep convulsive sighs reached the ears of Miss Galton; who entered the room, and began, in the common mode of consolation, first to enquire why she wept?

Emmeline answered only by weeping the more.

Miss Galton enquired if that gentleman was Lord Montreville.

Emmeline was unable to reply; and Miss Galton finding no gratification to her curiosity, which, mingled with envious malignity, had long been her ruling passion, was obliged to quit the unhappy Emmeline; which was indeed the only favour she could do her.

The whole morning had passed before Miss Mowbray was able to come down stairs, and when she did, her languor and dejection were excessive. Miss Galton only dined with her; if it might be called dining, for she eat nothing; but just as the cloth was removed, a coach stopped, and Mrs. Ashwood appeared, led by her brother, Mr. Stafford.

Emmeline, who had not very lately heard from her beloved friend, now eagerly enquired after her, and learned that the illness of one of her children had, together with her being far advanced in her pregnancy, prevented her coming to London with Mr. Stafford; who, tho' summoned thither immediately on his father's death, had only arrived the evening before; the messenger that went having missed him at his own house, and having been obliged to follow him into another county.

He delivered to Miss Mowbray a letter from Mrs. Stafford, with which Emmeline, eager to read it, retired —

'Trust me, Emmeline, no abatement in my tender regard, has occasioned my omitting to write to you: but anxiety of mind so great, as to deprive me of all power to attend to any thing but its immediate object. — Your poor little friend Harry, who looked so much recovered, and so full of health and spirits, when you left him at Swansea, was three weeks ago seized again with one of those fevers to which he has so repeatedly been liable, and for many days his life appeared to be in the most immediate danger. You know how far we are from a physician; and you know my anxiety for this first darling of my heart; judge then, my Emmeline, of the miserable hours I have known, between hope and fear, and the sleepless nights I have passed at the bed side of my suffering cherub; and in my present state I doubly feel all this anxiety and fatigue, and am very much otherwise than well. Of myself, however, I think not, since Harry is out of danger, and Dr. Farnaby thinks he will soon be entirely restored; but he is still so very weak, that I never quit him even a moment. The rest of my children are well; and all who are capable of recollection, remember and love you.

'And now, my dear Miss Mowbray, as the visitors who have been with me ever since my return from Swansea, are happily departed and no others expected, and as Mr. Stafford will be engaged in town almost all the winter, in consequence of his father's death, will you not come to me? *You* only can alleviate and share a thousand anxieties that prey on my spirits; *you* only can sweeten the hour of my confinement, which will happen in January; and before *you* only I can sigh at liberty and be forgiven.

'Ah! Emmeline — the death of Mr. Stafford's father, far from producing satisfaction as increasing our fortune, brings to me only regret and sorrow. He loved me with great affection; and I owe him a thousand obligations. The family will have reason to regret his loss; tho' infirmities of the latter part of his life were not much alleviated by their attendance or attention.

'Come to me, Emmeline, if possible; come, if you can, with Mr. Stafford; or if he is detained long in town, come without him. I will send my post-chaise to meet you at Basingstoke. Lord Montreville cannot object to it; and Delamere, whom you have never mentioned, has, I conclude, given way to the peremptory commands of his father, and has determined to forget my Emmeline.

'Is it then probable any one can forget her? I know not of what the volatile and thoughtless Delamere may be capable; but I know that of all things it would be the most impossible to her truly attached and affectionate,

C. STAFFORD.'

Woodfield, Nov. 30.

This letter gave great relief to the mind of the dejected Emmeline. That her first and dearest friend, opened at this painful crisis her consolatory bosom to receive and pity her; and that she should have the power to share her fatigue, and lessen the weight of her anxiety during the slow recovery of her child; seemed to be considerations which softened all the anguish she had endured during the day.

She was however too much disordered to go down to tea; and told Mrs. Ashwood, who civilly came up to enquire after her, that she had a violent pain in her head and would go to bed.

Mrs. Ashwood, full of her increased fortune, and busied in studying to make her deep mourning as becoming as possible, let her do as she would, and thought no more about her.

She had therefore time to meditate at leisure on her wayward fate: and some surprize that Delamere had not appeared the whole day, mingled itself with her reflections.

Poor Delamere was not to blame. Lord Montreville had sent him very early in the morning to desire to see him for five minutes on business of consequence.

Delamere, who from what had passed the evening before had indulged, during the night, the fondest dreams of happiness, obeyed the summons not without some hopes that he should hear all his favourable presages confirmed. When he came, however, his father, waving all discourse that related to Emmeline or himself, affected to consult him on a proposal he had received for his eldest sister, which the family were disposed to promote; and after detaining him as long as he could on this and on other subjects, he desired him to send to his lodgings for Millefleur, and to dress as expeditiously as possible, in order to accompany him to dine at Lord Dornock's, a Scottish nobleman, with whom his Lordship was deeply engaged in the depending negociation with Ministry; and who was at his seat, about nine miles from London.

Delamere reluctantly engaged in such a party. But however short his father's discourse fell of what he hoped, he yet determined to get the better of his repugnance and obey him; still flattering himself that Lord Montreville would lead to the subject nearest his heart, or that in the course of the day he should at least have an opportunity of introducing it.

They therefore set out together, on the most amicable terms, in Lord Montreville's coach. But as they had taken up on their way a gentleman who held a place under Lord Dornock, his presence prevented any conversation but on general subjects, during their short journey.

The dinner passed as such dinners generally do — too much in the secret to touch on politics, all such discourse was carefully avoided at the table of Lord Dornock.

In literature they had no resource; and therefore the conversation chiefly turned on the pleasure they were then enjoying — that of the luxuries of the table. They determined on the merits of the venison of the past season; settled what was the best way of preparing certain dishes; and whose domain produced the most exquisite materials for others. And on these topics a society of cooks could not have more learnedly descanted.

Delamere, not yet of an age to be initiated into the noble science of eating, and among whose ideas of happiness the delights of gratifying his palate had not yet been numbered, heard them with impatience and disgust.

He was obliged, however, to stay while the wines were criticised as eloquently as the meats had been; and to endure a long harangue from the master of the house on *cote roti* and *lacryma Christi;* and after the elder part of the company had adjusted their various merits and swallowed a sufficient quantity, the two noblemen retired to a private conference; and Delamere, obliged to move into a circle of insipid women, took refuge in cards, which he detested almost as much as the entertainment he had just quitted.

The hours, however slowly, wore away, and his patience was almost exhausted: soon after ten o'clock he ventured to send to his father, to know whether he was ready to return to town? but he received a message in reply, 'that he had determined to stay all night where he was.'

Vexed and angry, Delamere began to suspect that his father had some design in thus detaining him at a distance from Emmeline; and fired by indignation at this idea, equally scorning to submit to restraint or to be detained by finesse, he disengaged himself from the card table, fetched his hat, and without speaking to any body, walked to the next village, where he got into a post-chaise and was presently in London; but as it was almost twelve o'clock, he forbore to visit Emmeline that night.

CHAPTER XVI

AS soon as there was any probability of Emmeline's being visible the next morning, Delamere was at Clapham.

The servant of whom he enquired for her, told him, that Miss Mowbray had not yet rung her bell, and that as it was later than her usual hour, she was afraid it was owing to her being ill.

Alarmed at this intelligence, Delamere eagerly questioned her further; and learned that the preceding morning, a gentleman who had never been there before, had been to see Miss Mowbray, and had staid with her about three quarters of an hour, during which he had talked very loud; and that after he was gone, she had hastened to her own room, crying sadly, and had seemed very much vexed the whole day afterwards. That when she went to bed, which was early in the evening, she had sighed bitterly, and said she was not well. The servants, won by the sweetness and humanity with which Emmeline treated them, all seemed to consider her health and happiness as their own concern; and the girl who delivered this intelligence to Delamere, had been very much about her, and knowing her better, loved her more than the others.

Delamere could not doubt the truth of this account; yet he could not conjecture who the stranger could be, in whose power it was thus to distress Emmeline. But dreading lest some scheme was in agitation to take her from him, he sat in insupportable anxiety 'till she should summons the maid.

Her music book lay open on a *piano forte* in the breakfast parlour. A song which he had a few days before desired her to learn, as being one which particularly charmed him, seemed to have been just copied into it, and he fancied the notes and the writing were executed with more than her usual elegance. Under it was a little *porte feuille* of red morocco. Delamere took it up. It was untied; and two or three small tinted drawings fell out. He saw the likeness of Mrs. Stafford, done from memory; one yet more striking of his sister Augusta; and two or three unfinished resemblances of persons he did not know, touched with less spirit than the other two. A piece of silver paper doubled together enclosed another; he opened it — it was a drawing of himself, done with a pencil, and slightly tinged with a crayon; strikingly like; but it seemed unfinished, and somewhat effaced.

Though among so many other portraits, this could not be considered as a very flattering distinction, Delamere, on seeing it, was not master of his transports. He now believed Emmeline (whom he could never induce to own that her partiality for him exceeded the bounds of friendship) yet cherished in her heart a passion she would not avow.

While he was indulging these sanguine and delicious hopes, he heard a bell ring, and flew to enquire if it was that of Emmeline?

The maid, who crossed the hall to attend its summons, told him it was. He stepped softly up stairs behind the servant, and waited at the door of the chamber while she went in.

To the question, from the maid, 'how she did?' Emmeline answered, 'much better.'

'Mr. Delamere is here, Madam, and begs to know whether he may see you?'

Emmeline had expected him all the day before, and was not at all surprized at his coming now. But she knew not what she should say to him. To dissimulate was to her almost impossible; yet to tell him what had passed between her and Sir Richard Crofts was to create dissentions of the most alarming nature between him and his father; for she knew Delamere would immediately and warmly resent the harshness of Lord Montreville.

She could not however determine to avoid seeing Delamere; and she thought his Lordship was not entitled to much consideration, after the indelicate and needless shock he had given her, by employing the peremptory, insolent, and unfeeling Sir Richard Crofts.

After a moment's hesitation, she told Nanny to let Mr. Delamere know that as soon as she was dressed she would be with him in the parlour.

Delamere, who heard the message, stepped softly down stairs, replaced the drawings, and waited the entrance of Emmeline; who neither requiring or accustoming herself to borrow any advantage from art or ornament, was soon dressed in her usual simple undress.

But to give some appearance of truth to what she intended to alledge, a cold, in excuse for her swollen eyes and languid looks, she wrapt a gauze hood over her head, and tied a black ribband round her throat; for tho' she could not wholly conceal the truth from Delamere, she wished to prevent his seeing how much it had affected her.

When she entered the room, Delamere, who was at the door to meet her, was astonished at the alteration he saw in her countenance.

'You are ill, Emmeline?' said he, taking her hand.

'I am not quite well — I have a violent cold coming.'

'A cold?' eagerly answered Delamere, 'you have been crying — who was the person who called on you yesterday?'

It was now in vain to attempt concealment if she had intended it.

'He did not tell me his name, for our conversation was very short; but his servants told those of Mrs. Ashwood that his name is Sir Richard Crofts.'

'And what business could Sir Richard Crofts possibly have with you?'

Emmeline related the conversation with great fidelity and without comment.

Delamere had hardly patience to hear her out. He protested he would immediately go to Sir Richard Crofts, and not only force him to apologize for what had passed, but promise never again to interfere between Lord Montreville and his family.

From executing this violent measure, Emmeline by earnest entreaty diverted him. She had not yet recovered the shock given her by the unwelcome interview of the preceding day; and though she had a very excellent constitution, her sensibility of mind was so great, that when she suffered any poignant uneasiness, it immediately affected her frame. In the present state of her spirits, she could not hear Delamere's vehement and passionate exclamations without tears; and when he saw how much she was hurt, he commanded himself; spoke more calmly; and by a rapid transition from rage to tenderness, he wept also, and bathed her hands with his tears.

He was not without hopes that this last effort of Lord Montreville would effect a change in his favour; and he pleaded again for an elopement with the warmest eloquence of love.

But Emmeline, though she felt all the force of his arguments, had still the courage to resist them; and all he could obtain from her was a renewal of her former promise, neither to leave Mrs. Ashwood unknown to him or to conceal the place of her residence; to consent to see him wherever she should be, and positively to reject Mr. Rochely's offer.

In return, she expected from Delamere some concessions which nothing but the sight of her uneasiness would have induced him to grant. At length she persuaded him to promise that he would not insult Sir Richard Crofts, or commit any other rashness which might irritate Lord Montreville.

Nothing was a stronger proof of the deep root which his passion had taken in his heart, than the influence Emmeline had obtained over his ungovernable and violent spirit, hitherto unused to controul, and accustomed from his infancy to exert over his own family the most boundless despotism.

Emmeline, tranquillized and consoled by his promises, then entreated him to go; as the state of Mrs. Ashwood's family made visitors improper. In this, too, he obeyed her. And as soon as he was gone, Emmeline sat down to write to Mrs. Stafford, related briefly what had lately happened, and told her, that as soon as Lord Montreville could be induced to settle some yearly sum for her support, (which notwithstanding his threats she still thought he would do, on condition of her engaging never, without his consent, to marry Delamere,) she would set out for Woodfield.

Lord Montreville, absorbed in politics and in a negociation with ministry, had on the evening when he and his son were at Lord Dornock's, forgotten the impatient temper and particular situation of Delamere. His non appearance at supper occasioned an enquiry, and it was found he had left the house. It was too late for Lord Montreville to follow him that night, and would, indeed, have been useless; but early the next morning he was in Berkley-square, where he heard nothing of his son.

He received a letter from Sir Richard Crofts, relating the ill success of his embassy; but adding, that he would bring Rochely to his Lordship the next day, to consider together what was next to be done. A letter also soon after arrived from Lady Montreville, to let his Lordship know that herself and her daughter, with Lady Mary and Miss Otley, were coming to town the next evening.

Delamere, the tumult of whose spirits was too great immediately to subside, took, for the first time in his life, some pains to conquer their violence, in consideration of Emmeline.

He sent his servants to Berkley-square, to enquire among the domestics what had passed. He thence learned that his father had returned in the morning from Lord Dornock's in very ill humour, and that his mother was expected in town. An interview with either, would, he was conscious, only be the occasion of that dissention he had promised Emmeline to avoid. His mother, he knew, came to town determined to keep no terms with him; and that she would incessantly harrass him with reproaches or teize him with entreaties. He therefore determined to avoid entirely all conversation with both; and after a short reflection on the best means to do so, he ordered Millefleur to discharge the lodgings; told him and his other two servants that he was going out of town, and should not take either them or his horses; therefore would have them go to Berkley-square, and wait there his return. He bade his valet tell Lord Montreville that he should be absent ten days or a fortnight. Then ordering an hackney coach, he directed it to drive to Westminster Bridge, as if he meant there to take post: instead of which he dismissed it at the end of Bridge-street; and walking over to the Surry side, he presently provided himself with lodgings under the name of Mr. Oswald, a gentleman just come from Ireland; and all traces of Mr. Delamere were lost.

END OF THE FIRST VOLUME

VOLUME II

CHAPTER I

SIR Richard Crofts brought Mr. Rochely to Lord Montreville at the time appointed; and in consequence of the conversation then held, his Lordship was confirmed in his resolution of persisting in the plan Sir Richard had laid down to force Emmeline to accept the good fortune offered her. Lord Montreville had sent as soon as he got to town to Delamere's lodgings, whose servants said that he had slept there, but was then gone out. His Lordship concluded he was gone to Clapham; but as he could not remedy his uneasiness on that head, he was obliged to endure it. About twelve o'clock Delamere had arranged matters for his concealment; and about three, as Lord Montreville was dressing to go out, Millefleur, together with Delamere's footman and groom, came as they had been ordered to Berkley-square. This circumstance was no sooner related to Lord Montreville by his valet de chambre, than he ordered Millefleur to be sent up. The Frenchman related to his Lordship, that his master was certainly gone to Mr. Percival's; but Lord Montreville concluded he was gone to Scotland, and, in a tempest of anger and vexation, cursed the hour when he had listened to the advice of Sir Richard Crofts, the harshness of whose proceedings had, he imagined, precipitated the event he had so long dreaded. He was so entirely persuaded that his conjecture was the truth, that he first gave orders for a post-chaise and four to be ready directly; then recollecting that if he overtook his son he had no power to force him back, he thought it better to take with him some one who could influence Emmeline. His youngest daughter was still in Yorkshire; Mrs. Stafford he knew not where to find; but he supposed that Mrs. Ashwood, with whom she had lived some months, might have power to persuade her; and not knowing what else to do, indeed hardly knowing what he expected from the visit, he ordered his coachman to be as expeditious as possible in conveying him to the house of that lady.

Mrs. Ashwood, her brother, and four or five other persons related to the family, were at dinner. Lord Montreville entered the room; spoke to those he knew with as much civility as he could; but not seeing Emmeline among them, his apprehensions were confirmed. He desired they would not disturb themselves; and declined sharing their repast; but being unable to conceal his emotion till it was over, he said to Mrs. Ashwood — 'I am sorry, Madam, to trouble you on this unhappy business. I did hope you would have had the goodness at least to inform me of it. What can I do?' exclaimed he, breaking suddenly from his discourse and rising — 'Good God, what can I do?'

The company were silent, and amazed.

Mrs. Ashwood, however, said, 'I am sorry that any thing, my Lord, has disturbed your Lordship. I am sure I should have been happy, my Lord, could I have been of any service to your Lordship in whatever it is.'

'Disturbed!' cried he, striking his forehead with his hand, 'I am distracted! When did she go? How long has she been gone?'

'Who, my Lord?'

'Miss Mowbray — Emmeline — Oh! it will be impossible to overtake them!'

'Gone! my Lord?'

'Gone with Delamere — Gone to Scotland!'

'Miss Mowbray was however in the house not an hour ago,' said Miss Galton; 'I saw her myself go up the garden just as we sat down to dinner.'

'Then she went to meet him! — then they went together!' —exclaimed Lord Montreville, walking round the room.

An assertion so positive staggered every one. They rose from table in confusion.

'Let us go up,' said Mrs. Ashwood; 'I can hardly think it possible, my Lord, that Miss Mowbray is gone, unless your Lordship absolutely saw them.'

Yet Mrs. Ashwood remembered that Delamere had been there in the morning, and that Emmeline had dined early alone, and had remained by herself all the rest of the day, under pretence of sickness; and she began to believe that all this was done to give her time to elope with Delamere.

She went up stairs; and Lord Montreville, without knowing what he did, followed her. The stairs were carpetted; any one ascending was hardly heard; and Mrs. Ashwood suddenly throwing open the door of her chamber, Lord Montreville saw her, with her handkerchief held to her face, hanging over a packet of papers which lay on the table before her.

Emmeline did not immediately look up — an exclamation from Lord Montreville made her take her handkerchief from her eyes.

She arose; tried to conceal the sorrow visible in her countenance yet wet with tears, and assuming as much as she could her native ease and sweetness, she advanced towards his Lordship, who still stood at the door, amazed, and asked him if he would pardon her for desiring him to sit down in a bed-chamber; if not, she would wait on him below. She then went back to the table; threw the papers into the casket that was on it; and placing a chair between that and the fire, again asked him if he would do her the honour to sit down.

Lord Montreville did so, but said nothing. He was ashamed of his precipitancy; yet as Emmeline did not know it, he would not mention it; and was yet too full of the idea to speak of any thing else.

Mrs. Ashwood had left them — Emmeline continued silent.

Lord Montreville, after a long pause, at length said, with a stern and displeased countenance, 'I understand, Miss Mowbray, that my son was here this morning.'

'Yes, my Lord.'

'Pray, do you know where he now is?'

'I do not, indeed. Is he not at your Lordship's house?'

'No; I am told by his servants that he is gone to Mr. Percival's —But *you* —' (continued he, laying a strong emphasis on the word) '*you,* Miss Mowbray, are I dare say better informed of his intentions than any one else.'

'Upon my word, my Lord,' answered Emmeline, astonished, 'I do *not* know. He said nothing to me of an intention to go any where; on the contrary, he told me he should be here again to-morrow.'

'And is it possible you are ignorant of his having left London this morning, immediately after he returned from visiting you?'

'My Lord, I have never yet stooped to the meanness of a falsehood. Why should your Lordship now suppose me guilty of it? I repeat — and I hope you will do me the justice to believe me — upon my honour I do *not* know whither Mr. Delamere is gone — nor do I know that he has left London.'

Lord Montreville could not but believe her. But while his fears were relieved as to the elopement, they were awakened anew by the uncertainty of what was become of his son and what his motive could be for this sudden disappearance.

He thought however the present opportunity of speaking to Emmeline of his resolution was not to be neglected.

'However ignorant you may be, Miss Mowbray,' said he, 'of the reason of his having quitted his lodgings, you are not to learn that his motive for estranging himself from his family, and becoming a stranger to his father's house, originates in his inconsiderate attachment to you. Contrary to the assurances you gave me at Swansea, you have encouraged this attachment; and, as I understand from Sir Richard Crofts, you peremptorily and even rudely refuse the opportunity now offered you of establishing yourself in rank and affluence, which no other young woman would a moment hesitate to accept. Such a refusal cannot be owing to mere caprice; nor could it possibly happen had you not determined, in despite of every objection, and of bringing discord into my family, to listen to that infatuated and rash young man.'

'Your Lordship does not treat me with your usual candour. I have promised you, voluntarily promised you, not to marry Mr. Delamere without your Lordship's consent. To prevent his coming here was out of my power; but if I really aspired to the honour of which your Lordship thinks me ambitious, *what* has prevented me from engaging at once with Mr. Delamere? who has, I own to you, pressed me repeatedly to elope. My Lord, while I am treated with kindness and confidence, I can rely upon my own resolution to deserve it; *but* when your Lordship, on suspicion or misrepresentation, is induced to withdraw that kindness and confidence — why should *I* make a point of honour, where *you* no longer seem to expect it?'

The truth of this answer, as well as its spirit, at once hurt and irritated Lord Montreville.

Determined to separate Emmeline from his son, he was mortified to be forced to acknowledge in his own breast that she merited all his affection, and angry that she should be in the right when he wished to have found something to blame in her conduct. Pride and self-love seemed to resent that a little weak girl should pretend to a sense of rectitude, and a force of understanding greater than his own.

'Miss Mowbray,' said his Lordship sharply, 'I will be very explicit with you — either you consent to marry Mr. Rochely, whose affection does you so much honour, or expect from me no farther kindness.'

'Your Lordship knows,' answered Emmeline, 'that I have no friend on whom I have the least claim but you. If you abandon me — but, my Lord, ought you to do it? — I am indeed most friendless!'

She could no longer command her tears — sobs obliged her to cease speaking.

Lord Montreville thought her resolution would give way; and trying to divest himself of all feeling, with an effort truly political, he determined to press his point.

'It is in your power,' resumed he, 'not to place yourself above all fear of such desertion, but to engage my affection and that of my whole family. You will be in a situation of life which I should hardly refuse for one of the Miss Delameres. You will possess the most unbounded affluence, and a husband who adores you. A man unexceptionable in character; of a mature age; and whose immense fortune is every day encreasing. You will be considered by me, and by Lady Montreville, as a daughter of the house of Mowbray. The blemish of your birth will be wiped off and forgotten.'

Emmeline wept more than before.

And his Lordship continued, 'If you absurdly refuse an offer so infinitely above your expectations, I shall consider myself as having more than done my duty in putting it in your way; and that your folly and imprudence dissolve all obligation on my part. You must no longer call yourself Mowbray; and you must forget that you ever were allowed to be numbered among the relations of my family. Nor shall I think myself obliged in any manner to provide for a person, who in scorn of gratitude, prudence and reputation, throws from her an opportunity of providing for herself.'

Emmeline regained some degree of resolution. She looked up, her eyes streaming with tears, and said, 'Well, my Lord! to the lowest indigence I must then submit; for to marry Mr. Rochely is not in my power.'

'We will suppose for a moment,' resumed Lord Montreville, 'that you could realize the visionary hopes you have presumed to indulge of uniting yourself to Mr. Delamere. Dear as he is to me and his mother, we are determined from that moment to renounce him — never shall the rebellious son who has dared to disobey us, be again admitted to our presence! — never will we acknowledge as his wife, a person forced upon us and introduced into our family in despite of our commands, and in violation of duty, honour, and affection. *You* will be the occasion of his being loaded with the curses of both his parents, and of introducing misery and discord into his family. Can you yourself be happy under such circumstances? In point of fortune too you will find yourself deceived — while *we* live, Mr. Delamere can have but a very slender income; and of every thing in our power we shall certainly deprive him, both while we live, and at our decease. Consider well what I have said; and make use of your reason. Begin by giving up to me the ridiculous witness of a ridiculous and boyish passion, which must be no longer indulged; to keep a picture of Delamere is discreditable and indelicate — you will not refuse to relinquish it?'

He reached over the table, and took from among two or three loose papers, which yet lay before Emmeline, a little blue enamelled case, which he concluded contained a miniature of Delamere, of whom several had been drawn. Emmeline, absorbed in tears, did not oppose it. The spring of the case was defective. It opened in his hand; and presented to his view, not a portrait of his son, but of his brother, drawn when he was about twenty, and at a period when he was more than a brother — when he was the dearest friend Lord Montreville had on earth. A likeness so striking, which he had not seen for many years, had an immediate effect upon him.

His brother seemed to look at him mournfully. A melancholy cast about the eye-brows diminished the vivacity of the countenance, and the faded colour (for the picture had been painted seven and twenty years) gave it a look of languor and ill health; such perhaps as the original wore before his death, when a ruined constitution threatened him for some months, tho' his life terminated by a malignant fever in a few hours.

The poor distrest Emmeline was the only memorial left of him; and Lord Montreville felt her tears a reproach for his cruelty in thus threatening to abandon to her fate, the unhappy daughter of this once loved brother.

Sir Richard Crofts and Lady Montreville were not by, to intercept these sentiments of returning humanity. He found the tears fill his eyes as he gazed on the picture.

Emmeline, insensible of every thing, saw it not; and not conscious that he had taken it, the purport of his last words she believed to relate to a sketch she had herself made of Delamere. She was therefore surprized, when Lord Montreville arising, took her hand, and in a voice that witnessed the emotion of his soul, said — 'Come, my dear Emmeline, pardon me for thus distressing you, you shall *not* be compelled to marry Mr. Rochely if you have so great a dislike of him. You shall still have an adequate support; and I trust I shall have nothing to fear from your indiscretion in regard to Delamere.'

'Your Lordship,' answered Emmeline, without taking her handkerchief from her eyes, 'has never yet found me capable of falsehood: I will repeat, if you desire it, the promise I gave you — I will even take the most solemn oath you shall dictate, never to be the wife of Mr. Delamere, unless your Lordship and Lady Montreville consent.'

'I take your promise,' answered his Lordship, 'and shall rely firmly upon it. But Emmeline, you must go from hence for your own sake; your peace and reputation require it; Delamere must not frequent the house where you are: you must conceal from him the place of your abode.'

'My Lord, I will be ingenuous with you. To go from hence is what I intend, and with your Lordship's permission I will set out immediately for Mrs. Stafford's. But to conceal from Mr. Delamere where I am, is not in my power; for I have given him a solemn promise to see him if he desires it, wherever I shall be: and as I hope you depend on my honour, it must be equally sacred whether given to him or you. You will therefore not insist on my breaking this engagement, and I promise you again never to violate the other.'

With this compromise, Lord Montreville was obliged to be content. He entreated Emmeline to see Rochely again, and hear his offers. But she absolutely refused; assuring Lord Montreville that were his fortune infinitely greater, she would not marry him, tho' servitude should be the alternative.

His Lordship therefore forbore to press her farther. He desired, that if Delamere wrote to her, or saw her, she would let him know, which she readily agreed to; and he told her, that so long as she was single, and did nothing to disoblige him, he would pay her an hundred guineas a year in quarterly payments. He gave her a bank note of fifty pounds; and recommending it to her to go as soon as possible to Mrs. Stafford's, he kissed her cheek with an appearance of affection greater than he had yet shewn, and then went home to prepare for the reception of Lady Montreville, whose arrival he did not greatly wish for; dreading lest her violence and ill-temper should drive his son into some new extravagance. But as her will was not to be disputed, he submitted without remonstrance to the alteration of the plan he had proposed; which was, that his family should pass their Christmas in Norfolk, whither he intended to have returned.

The next day Delamere was again at Clapham, very early.

Emmeline, the additional agitation of whose mind had prevented her sleeping during the night, appeared more indisposed than she had done the day before.

Delamere, very much alarmed at her altered looks, anxiously enquired the cause? And without hesitation she told him simply all that had passed; the promise she had given to his father, to which she intended strictly to adhere, and the arrangement she had agreed to on condition of being persecuted no more on the score of Mr. Rochely.

It is impossible to describe the grief and indignation of Delamere, at hearing this relation. He saw all the hopes frustrated which he had been so long indulging; he saw between him and all he loved, a barrier which time only could remove; he dared not hope that Emmeline would ever be induced to break an engagement which she considered as binding; he dared not flatter himself with the most distant prospect of procuring the consent of Lord and Lady Montreville, and therefore by their deaths only could he obtain her; which if he had been unnatural enough to wish, was yet in all probability very distant; as Lord Montreville was not more than seven and forty, and of an excellent constitution; and Lady Montreville three years younger.

Passion and resentment for some moments stifled every other sentiment in the heart of Delamere. But the impediments that thus arose to his wishes were very far from diminishing their violence.

The more impossible his union with Emmeline seemed to be, the more ardently he desired it. The difficulties that might have checked, or conquered an inferior degree of passion, served only to strengthen his, and to render it insurmountable —

It was some moments before Emmeline could prevail upon him to listen to her. She then enquired why he had concealed himself from his father, and where he had been?

He answered, that he had avoided Lord Montreville, because, had he met him, he found himself incapable of commanding his temper and of forbearing to resent his sending Sir Richard Crofts to her, which he had promised her not to do. That therefore he had taken other lodgings in another part of the town, where he intended to remain.

Emmeline exhorted and implored him to return to Berkley-square. He positively refused. He refused also to tell her where he lodged. And complaining loudly of her cruelty and coldness, yet tenderly entreating her to take care of her health, he left her; having first procured permission to see her the next day, and every day till she set out for Woodfield.

When he was gone, Miss Mowbray wrote to Lord Montreville —

'My Lord,

'In pursuance of the word I passed to your Lordship, I have the honour to acquaint you that Mr. Delamere has just left me. I endeavoured to prevail on him to inform me where he lodges; but he refuses to give me the least information. If it be your Lordship's wish to see him, you will probably have an opportunity of doing it here, as he proposed being here to-morrow; but refused to name the hour, apprehending perhaps that you might meet him, as I did not conceal from him that I should acquaint you with my having seen him.

I have the honour to be,
my Lord,
your Lordship's
most obedient servant,
EMMELINE MOWBRAY.'

Clapham, Dec. 3.

Lord Montreville received this letter in her Ladyship's dressing-room. The servant who brought it in, said it came from Clapham; and Lady Montreville insisted on seeing its contents. She had been before acquainted with what had passed; and bestowed on her son the severest invectives for his obstinacy and folly. Poor Emmeline however, who was the cause of it, was the principal object of her resentment and disdain. Even this last instance of her rectitude, could not diminish the prejudice which embittered the mind of Lady Montreville against her. She lamented, whenever she designed to speak of her, that the laws of this country, unlike those of better regulated kingdoms, did not give people of fashion power to remove effectually those who interfered with their happiness, or were inimical to their views. 'If this little wretch,' said she, 'was in France, it would not be difficult to put an end to the trouble she has dared to give us. A *lettre de cachet* would cure the creature of her presumption, and place her where her art and affectation should not disturb the peace of families of high rank.'

Lord Montreville heard these invectives without reply, but not without pain.

Augusta Delamere, who arrived in Berkley-square the same morning that Lady Montreville did, felt still more hurt by her mother's determined hatred to Emmeline, whom she languished to see, and had never ceased to love.

Miss Delamere inheriting all the pride of her mother, and adding to it a sufficient share of vanity and affectation of her own, had taken a dislike to the persecuted Emmeline, if possible more inveterate than that of Lady Montreville. Tho' she had never seen her, she detested her; and exerted all her influence on her mother to prevent her being received into the family as her father's relation. Fitz-Edward had praised her as the most interesting woman he had ever seen. Miss Delamere had no aversion to Fitz-Edward; and tho' he had never seemed sensible of the honour she did him, she could not divest herself wholly of that partiality towards him, which made her heartily abhor any woman he seemed to admire. When to this cause of dislike was added, what she called the insolent presumption of the animal in daring to attempt inveigling *her* brother into the folly of marrying, she thought she might indulge all the rancour, envy, and malignity of her heart.

When Lady Montreville had read the letter, she threw it down on the table contemptuously.

'It requires no answer,' said she to the servant who waited.

The man left the room.

'Well, my Lord,' continued she, addressing herself to her husband, 'what do you intend to do about this unhappy, infatuated boy?'

'I really know not,' answered his Lordship.

'I will tell you then,' resumed she — 'Go to this girl, and let her know that you will abandon her pennyless; force her to accept the honour Mr. Rochely offers her; and, by shewing a little strength of mind and resolution, break these unworthy chains with which your own want of prudence has fettered your son.'

'It has already been tried, Madam, without success. Consider that if I am bound by no obligations to support this young person, I am also without any power over her. To force her to marry Mr. Rochely is impossible. I have however her promise that she will not enter into any clandestine engagement with Delamere.'

'Her promise!' exclaimed Lady Montreville. — 'And are you weak enough, my Lord, to trust the promise of an artful, designing creature, who seems to me to have already won over your Lordship to her party? What want of common sense is this! If you will not again speak to her, and that most decisively, I will do it myself! Send her to me! I will force her not only to tell me where Delamere has had the meanness to conceal himself, but also oblige her to relinquish the hopes she has the insolence to indulge.'

Miss Delamere, who wanted to see the wonderful creature that had turned her brother's head, and who was charmed to think she should see her humbled and mortified, promoted this plan as much as possible. Augusta, dreading her brother's violence, dared not, and Lord Montreville would not oppose it, as he believed her Ladyship's overwhelming rhetoric, to which he was himself frequently accustomed to give way, might produce on Emmeline the effect he had vainly attempted. He therefore asked Lady Montreville, whether she really wished to see Miss Mowbray, and when?

'I am engaged to-morrow,' answered she, 'all day. But however, as she is a sort of person whom it will be improper to admit at any other time, let her be here at ten o'clock in the morning. She may come up, before I breakfast, into my dressing-room.'

'Shall I send one of the carriages for her?' enquired his Lordship.

'By no means,' replied the Lady. 'They will be all wanted. Let her borrow a coach of the people she lives with. I suppose all city people now keep coaches. Or if she cannot do that, a hack may be had.' Then turning to her woman, who had just brought her her snuff-box, 'Brackley,' said she, 'don't forget to order the porter to admit a young woman who will be here to-morrow, at ten o'clock; tho' she may perhaps come in a hack.'

Lord Montreville, who grew every hour more uneasy at Delamere's absence, now set out in search of him himself. He called at Fitz-Edward's lodgings; but he was not yet come to town, tho' hourly expected. His Lordship then went to Clapham, where he hoped to meet his son; but instead of doing so, Emmeline put into his hands the following letter —

'I intended to have seen you again today; but the pain I felt after our interview yesterday, has so much disordered me, that it is better not to repeat it. Cruel Emmeline! — to gratify my father you throw me from you without remorse, without pity. I shall be the victim of his ambition, and of your false and mistaken ideas of honour.

'Ah! Emmeline! will the satisfaction that you fancy will arise from this chimerical honour make you amends for the loss of such an heart as mine! Yet think not I can withdraw it from you, cold and cruel as you are. Alas! it is no longer in my power. But my passions, the violence of which I cannot mitigate, prey on my frame, and will conduct to the grave, this unhappy son, who is to be sacrificed to the cursed politics of his family.

'I cannot see you, Emmeline, without a renewal of all those sensations which tear me to pieces, and which I know affect you, though you try to conceal it. For a day or two I will go into the country. *Remember your promise* not to remove any where but to Mrs. Stafford's; and let me know the day and hour when you set out. You plead to me, that your promise to my father is *sacred.* I expect that those you have passed to me shall be at least equally so. Farewel! till we meet again. You know that seeing you, and being permitted to love you, is all that renders supportable the existence of your unhappy

F.D.'

'This letter, my Lord,' said Emmeline, 'was delivered by a porter. I spoke to the man, and asked him from whence he brought it? He said from a coffee-house at Charing-cross.'

'Did you answer it?'

'No, my Lord,' said Emmeline, blushing; 'I think it required no answer.'

He then told her that Lady Montreville expected to see her the next day; and named the hour.

Emmeline, terrified as she was at the idea of such an interview, was forced to assure him she would be punctual to it; and his Lordship took an hasty leave, still hoping he might meet his son. He was hardly gone, before another porter brought to Emmeline a second letter: it was from Augusta Delamere.

'At length, my dear Emmeline, I am near you, and can tell you I still love you; tho' even that satisfaction I am forced to snatch unknown to my mother. Oh, Emmeline! I tremble for your situation to-morrow. The dislike that both my mother and sister have taken to you, is inconceivable; and I am afraid that you will have a great deal of rudeness and unkindness to encounter. I write this to prepare you for it; and hope that your conscious innocence, and the generosity with which you have acted, will support you. I have been taken to task most severely by my mother for my partiality to you; and my sister, in her contemptuous way, calls you my sweet sentimental friend. To be sure my brother's absence is a dreadful thing; and great allowances are to be made for my mother's vexation; tho' I own I do not see why it should prevent her being just. I will try to be in the room to-morrow, tho' perhaps I shall not be permitted. Don't say you have heard from me, for the world; but be assured I shall always love you as you deserve, and be most truly

your affectionate and faithful,

A. DELAMERE.'

Berkley-square, Dec. 5.

CHAPTER II

EMMELINE had the convenience of Mrs. Ashwood's carriage, who agreed to set her down in Berkley-square. She was herself sitting for her picture; and told Miss Mowbray she would send the chariot back for her when she got to the house of the painter.

Exactly at ten o'clock they arrived at the door of Lord Montreville; and Emmeline, who had been arguing herself into some degree of resolution as she went along, yet found her courage much less than she thought she should have occasion for; and with faultering steps and trembling nerves she went up stairs. The man who conducted her, told her that his Lady was not yet up, and desired her to wait in an anti-room, which was superbly furnished and covered with glasses, in which Emmeline had leisure to contemplate her pale and affrighted countenance.

The longer the interview was delayed the more dreadful it appeared. She dared not ask for Miss Augusta; yet at every noise she heard, hoped that amiable girl was coming to console and befriend her. But no Augusta appeared. A servant came in, mended the fire, and went down again;

then Miss Delamere's maid, under pretence of fetching something, took a survey of her in order to make a report to her mistress; and Emmeline found that she was an object of curiosity to the domesticks, who had heard from Millefleur, and from the other servants who had been at Swansea, that this was the young woman Mr. Delamere was dying for.

An hour and a half was now elapsed; and poor Emmeline, whose imagination had been busied the whole time in representing every form of insult and contempt with which she expected to be received, began to hope that Lady Montreville had altered her intention of seeing her.

At length, however, Mrs. Brackley, her Ladyship's woman, was heard speaking aloud to a footman — Walter, tell that young woman she may be admitted to see my Lady, and shew her up.

Walter delivered his message; and the trembling Emmeline with some difficulty followed him.

She entered the dressing-room. Her Ladyship, in a morning dress, sat at a table, on which was a salver with coffee. Her back was to the door, where stood Mrs. Brackley; who, as Emmeline, hesitating, seemed ready to shrink back, said, with a sort of condescending nod, 'There, you may go in, Miss.'

Emmeline entered; but did not advance.

Lady Montreville, without rising or speaking, turned her head, and looked at her with a scowling and disdainful countenance.

'Humph!' said she, looking at her eldest daughter, who sat by the fire with a newspaper in her hand — 'humph!' as much as to say, I see no such great beauty in this creature.

Miss Delamere, whose countenance wore a sort of disdainful sneer, smiled in answer to her mother's humph! and said, 'Would you have her sit down, Madam?'

'Aye,' said Lady Montreville, turning again her head towards Emmeline — 'You may sit down.'

There was a sofa near the door. Emmeline, hardly able to stand, went to it.

A silence ensued. Lady Montreville sipped her coffee; and Miss Delamere seemed intent upon the newspaper.

'So!' cried her Ladyship, 'my son has absented himself! Upon my word, Miss What-d'ye-call-it, (for Mowbray I don't allow that your name is) you have a great deal to answer for. Pray what amends can you ever hope to make to my Lord, and me, for the trouble you have been the cause of?'

'I sincerely lament it, Madam,' answered Emmeline, forcing herself to speak; 'and do assure you it has been on my part involuntary.'

'Oh, no doubt on't. Your wonderful beauty is the fatal cause. You have used no art, I dare say; no pretty finesse, learned from novels, to inveigle a silly boy to his undoing.'

'If I had been disposed, Madam, to take advantage of Mr. Delamere's unhappy partiality for me —'

'Oh dear! What you was coy? You knew your subject, no doubt, and now make a merit of what was merely a piece of art. I detest such demure hypocrites! Tell me, — why, if you are *not* disposed to take advantage of Mr. Delamere's folly, you do not accept the noble offer made you by this banker, or whatever he is, that my Lord says is worth above an hundred thousand pounds? The reason is evident. A little obscure creature, bred on the Welch mountains, and who was born nobody knows how, does not so easily refuse a man of fortune unless she has some other views.

You would like a handsome young man with a title! Yes! you would like to hide your own obscurity in the brilliant pedigree of one of the first families in Europe. But know, presumptuous girl, that the whole house shall perish ere it shall thus be contaminated — know' — She grew inarticulate with passion; pride and malignity seemed to choak her; and she stopped, as if to recover breath to give vent to her rage.

Miss Delamere took the opportunity to speak —

'Indeed, child,' said she, 'it is hurting yourself extremely; and I am really sorry you should be so deceived. *My* brother can never marry *you;* and as Lord Montreville has brought you up, under the notion of your belonging to a part of his family, we are really interested, my mother and I, in your not going into a bad course of life. If you do not marry this rich city-man, what do you think is to become of you?'

'My Lord Montreville has been so good as to assure me,' said Emmeline — her words were so faint, that they died away upon her lips.

'What does she say, Fanny?' asked Lady Montreville.

'Something of my father's having assured her, Madam.'

'Don't flatter yourself, girl,' resumed her Ladyship, 'don't deceive yourself. If you refuse to marry this man who offers to take you, not one shilling shall you ever receive from this family; determine therefore at once; send to the person in question; let him come here, and let an agreement for a settlement be directly signed between Lord Montreville and him. Lord Montreville will in that case give you a fortune. I will hear no objection! I *will* have the affair closed this morning! I *will* have it so!'

Lady Montreville, accustomed to undisputed power in her own family, expected from every body an acquiescence as blind as she found from her tradesmen and servants, who endured her ill-humour and gave way to her caprices. But she forgot that Emmeline was equally unaccustomed to her commands, and free from the necessity of obeying them. The gentlest and mildest temper will revolt against insolence and oppression: and the cruelty and unfeminine insults she had received, concluded by this peremptory way of forcing her into a marriage from which her whole soul recoiled, at length restored to her some portion of that proper spirit and presence of mind which had been frightened from her. Conscious that she deserved none of these ungenerous insults, and feeling herself superior to her who could cruelly and wantonly inflict them, she regained her courage.

'If your Ladyship has nothing more to say,' said she, rising, 'I shall have the honour to wish you a good morning; for I believe Mrs. Ashwood has been waiting for me some time.'

'Don't tell me of Mrs. Ashwood — but tell me where is my son? Where is Delamere?'

'I know not,' answered Emmeline. 'I have already told my Lord Montreville that I am entirely ignorant.'

'Nobody believes it!' said Miss Delamere.

'I am sorry for it,' replied Emmeline, coolly. 'If, however, I did know, it is not such treatment, Madam, that should compel me to give any information.' She then opened the door and walked down stairs. A footman met her, whom she desired to enquire for Mrs. Ashwood's carriage. Before the man could descend to obey her, a violent ringing was heard. The footman said it was his Lady's bell, and ran up to answer it; while Emmeline still descending, heard somebody softly calling her. She looked up, and saw Augusta Delamere leaning over the bannisters; she put her finger as if to prevent Emmeline's speaking, threw her a letter, and immediately disappeared.

The spirits of Emmeline were again greatly hurried by this transient view of her friend. She put the letter hastily into her pocket, and was got down into the hall, where she spoke to another footman to see for her carriage; but the man whom she had met on the stairs, now came to say his Lady must see her again. Emmeline answered that she had already made her friend wait, and must beg to be excused returning to her Ladyship this morning. The man however said, that he dared not disobey his Lady, nor call up the chariot.

Emmeline, alarmed at the idea of being detained, advanced towards the door, told the porter (who had not heard this dialogue,) to open it, and walked resolutely into the street.

The two footmen followed her to the door; but contented themselves with looking after her, without attempting to stop her.

'She is pretty enough, however,' said one to the other, 'to excuse our young Lord.'

'The devil's in't if she is not,' answered the other.

Emmeline heard this; and between vexation at their impertinence, and fear of their following her, she found her whole strength again forsake her.

She walked on however towards Charles-street, looking round for Mrs. Ashwood's carriage, but could not see it. She was totally unacquainted with the streets, where she had never been on foot before; but recollected that she might get an hackney-coach, which was the more necessary, as snow was falling fast, and her muslin cloaths were already wet almost through.

She was picking her way, still in some hopes of seeing the carriage, when an hackney-coach passed empty. Emmeline looked wishfully towards it. The man stopped, and asked if she wanted a coach? She answered yes, as eagerly as if she had been afraid of a disappointment; and hurrying into it, told the man to drive to Clapham.

Just as he was mounting the box, another hack passed, and a young officer who was in it looked earnestly into that where Emmeline sat; then calling to his driver to stop, he leaped out, and Emmeline saw Fitz-Edward at the door of her coach.

'Miss Mowbray!' said he — 'Is it possible! alone and in this equipage, in Berkley-square! Where is Delamere?'

Before Emmeline had time to answer him he had opened the coach door.

'It snows too much,' said he, 'for a comfortable conference, unless you will give me leave to sit by you; where are you going to?'

'To Clapham,' answered Emmeline.

'Oh! take me with you,' said he. 'I have a thousand things to say to you.'

He gave her no time to refuse: but flinging half a crown to the man who had driven him, he got into the coach which she was in, and ordered the man to shut the door and go where he had been directed.

Emmeline was vexed at this incident, as she was too uneasy to wish for the presence of any one, and impatient to open the letter in her pocket. But Fitz-Edward was not easily discouraged; and possessed, together with perfect good breeding, a fortunate sort of assurance with which nobody was ever long displeased.

He enquired after Mrs. Stafford with a degree of interest for which Emmeline felt inclined to love him. She related all she knew of her; and her eyes re-assumed their lustre, while she told him how soon she was likely to see her. He then renewed his questions about Delamere.

Emmeline could not dissemble; and indeed saw in this case no reason why she should. She therefore told him ingenuously all that had happened since they met at Swansea; most of which he already knew from Delamere. He watched her looks however while she was speaking; and by her blushes, her manner, and the softness of her eyes he thought he saw evidently enough that Delamere was no longer indifferent to her. Her indignation at the treatment she had just received from his mother and sister, dyed her cheeks with crimson while she related it; but when she returned to speak of Delamere, she forgot her anger, and seemed to feel only pity and tenderness.

Fitz-Edward, a most perfect judge of female hearts, made his observations on all this, with which he knew he should most effectually gratify his friend; and in his insinuating way he said all he could think of to encrease her compassion for her lover, and inflame her resentment against those who impeded a union, which he was pretty sure Emmeline now wished for, as well as Delamere.

CHAPTER III

WHEN they arrived at Clapham, Emmeline found Mrs. Ashwood was not yet returned. Fitz-Edward entreated her to sing to him; and either was, or pretended to be, in raptures at her improvement since they had met in the summer.

About half an hour after four, Mrs. Ashwood came in; and throwing open the parlour door, asked Emmeline, in no very sweet accent, 'Why she had given her the trouble to go in her carriage to Berkley-square, if she intended going home by any other conveyance?'

Mrs. Ashwood was subject to causeless fits of ill-humour, to which Emmeline was a good deal accustomed; and concluding she was now seized with some sudden discomposure of temper, mildly answered, 'That she supposed there had been a mistake; for that the chariot did not come for her at the appointed time.'

'Mistake!' replied the other lady, sharply; 'I don't know as to mistake; but if you had chosen it, you might have staid dinner with Lady Montreville.'

Emmeline, without seeming to attend to the asperity of the address, desired to introduce Colonel Fitz-Edward.

As this short dialogue had passed without Mrs. Ashwood's having entered the room, she had not seen the stranger, who now advanced towards her.

The title of Colonel, added to his military air and handsome figure, seemed to gain at once her favourable opinion; and her countenance losing the unpleasing expression of ill-temper, immediately put on its best smile, and an affectation of softness and complacency with which she frequently adorned it.

She seemed to consider the handsome young soldier as a conquest worthy all her ambition; and finding he was the most intimate friend of Delamere, had no apprehension that his admiration would be diverted by the youth and attractions of Emmeline.

Fitz-Edward presently understood her character; and with admirable adroitness acted the part of a man afraid of being too much charmed. He cast an arch look at Emmeline; then made to the Lady of the house some compliments so extravagant, that only the weakest vanity could prevent her seeing its ridicule. But Fitz-Edward, who found in a moment that nothing was too gross to be believed, fearlessly repeated the dose; and before dinner came in, she was in the best humour imaginable, and pressed him so earnestly to partake of it, that, after an apology for sitting down in his morning dishabille, he consented.

The same unlimited flattery was continued during dinner by Fitz-Edward, and received by the lady with the same avidity; and Emmeline, tho' half-angry with him for the pleasure he seemed to take in making Mrs. Ashwood absurd, could not help being amused with the scene.

Before their repast ended, she was so much charmed with her new acquaintance, and so much longed to shew him to her female friends, and her other admirers, that she could not forbear pressing him to stay to a card party, which she was to have in the evening.

He loved the ridiculous; and, influenced by a vanity as silly as that he delighted to expose, he took pleasure in shewing how extremely absurd he could make women appear, who were not on other occasions void of understanding. Tho' he had really business with Lord Montreville, who had left several messages at his lodgings desiring to see him, and was going thither when Emmeline met him, yet he accepted Mrs. Ashwood's invitation, on condition of being allowed to go home to dress.

He was no sooner gone than she flew to her toilet, and Emmeline to a second perusal of the letter she had received from Augusta Delamere.

'I am forbidden to see you, my dearest Emmeline; and perhaps may not have an opportunity of giving you this. My heart bleeds for you, my sweet friend. I fear my father will be prevailed upon wholly to abandon you. They are all inventing schemes to force you into a marriage with that odd-looking old Rochely. He has been here once or twice, and closetted with my father; and part of the scheme of to-day is, to persuade you to dine here with him. But I am almost sure you will not stay; for unless my mother can command herself more before you than she does when she is talking about you, I think you will be frightened away. I am certain, my dear Emmeline, from what I have heard, tho' they say but little before me, that no endeavours will be omitted to drive you to marry Rochely; and that they will persecute you every way, both by persuasions, and by distressing you. But be assured, that while Augusta Delamere has any thing, you shall share it. Indeed I love you, not only as if you were my sister, but, I think, better. Ah! why are there such unhappy impediments to your being really so? At present I foresee nothing but perplexity; and have no dependance but on you. I know you will act as you ought to do; and that you will at last prevail with Delamere to act right too. Whoever loves you, cannot long persist in doing ill; and surely it is very ill done, and very cruel, for Delamere to make us all so unhappy. I need not tell you to arm yourself with fortitude against the attacks that will be made upon you. You have more fortitude and resolution than I have. Situated as you have been, I know not what I should have done; but I fear it would not have been so worthy of praise as the noble and disinterested part you have acted; which, tho' unaccompanied with the thousand amiable qualities of heart and understanding you possess, would ever command the esteem and admiration of your faithful and affectionate

AUGUSTA DELAMERE.'

'Do not write to me till you hear from me again; as I should incur great displeasure if known to correspond with you.

A.D.'

Charmed as Emmeline was by the tender solicitude and affectionate simplicity of her beloved friend, the pleasure this letter gave her was very much abated by learning that the domestic infelicity of Lord Montreville's family fell particularly heavy on her. She now recollected what Mrs. Ashwood had said on her first entrance into the room, when she returned home; and concluded from thence that she had seen Lady Montreville, tho' her whole attention was so immediately engrossed by the Colonel, that she had no more named it. She therefore grew anxious to hear what had been said; and her own toilet being very soon over, she sent to desire admittance of that of Mrs. Ashwood; on receiving which, she attended her, and begged to know whether she had seen Lady Montreville, and what had passed?

Mrs. Ashwood was in so happy a disposition, that she hesitated not to oblige her; and while she finished the important business of accommodating a pile of black feathers, jet and crape, upon her head, 'the mockery of woe' which she did not even affect to feel, she gave Emmeline the following account, interlarded with directions to her woman.

'Why, my dear, you must know that when I got to Gainsborough's *[more to the left]* he had unluckily a frightful old judge, or a bishop, or some tedious old man with him, and I was forced to wait: I cannot tell what possessed me, but I entirely forgot that I was to send the chariot back for you. So the chariot *[put it a little forwarder]* staid. I thought the tiresome man, whoever he was, would never have gone; however he went at last *[raise the lower curl]* and then I *sot.* You cannot think how much the likeness is improved! So when I had done *[give me the scraper; here is some powder on my eye-brow]* I went away, thinking to call on you; but as I went by Butler's, I remembered that I wanted some pearl-coloured twist to finish the purse I am doing for Hanbury. I was almost an hour matching it. Well, then I thought as I was so near Frivolité's door, I might as well call and see whether she had put the trimming on the white bombazeen, as you know we agreed would be most the thing. There were a thousand people in the house; you know there is never any possibility of getting out of that creature's room under an hour.' [Oh! heaven! thought Emmeline, nor is there any end to the importance you affix to trifles which interest nobody else.] 'So, however, at last I got to Berkley-square, and stopped at the door. The man at the door said you was gone. I thought that very odd, and desired another servant go up and see, for I concluded it was some mistake. After a moment or two, the footman came down again, and said if I was the Lady Miss Mowbray lived with, his Lady desired I would walk up. Upon my word it is a noble house! When I got into the room, there was Lady Montreville and her daughters. Her Ladyship was extremely polite, indeed; and after some discourse, "Mrs. Ashwood," said she, "you know Miss Mowbray's situation: I assure you I sent for her to-day with no other view in the world but for her own good, and you know, *[dear me! here is a pimple on my chin that is quite hideous; give me a patch.]* you know that for her to refuse Mr. Rochely is being absolutely blind to her own interest; because you must suppose, Mrs. Ashwood, that she is only deceiving herself when she entertains any thoughts of my son; for that is a thing that never can happen, nor ever shall happen; and besides, to give my Lord and me all this trouble, is a very ungrateful return to us for having brought her up, and many other obligations she has received at our hands; and will be the ruin of herself; and the greatest perverseness in the world. You, Mrs. Ashwood, are, I hear, a very sensible woman *[where is the rouge box?]* and I dare say, now you know how agreeable it would be to me and my Lord to have Miss Emmeline come to her senses about Mr. Rochely, you will do your endeavours to persuade her to act reasonably; and then, tho' she has behaved very disrespectful and very ill, which is only to be forgiven on account of her knowing no better, I shall countenance her, and so will my Lord." This was, as near as I remember, Emmeline, what my Lady said to me. You know *[the milk of roses is almost out]* you know I could not refuse to tell her I would certainly talk to you. I was surprized to find her Ladyship so obliging and affable, as you had told me she is reckoned so very proud. She ordered her gentleman to give me a ticket for a rout and a supper her Ladyship gives on Tuesday three weeks; and she said, that as she did not doubt that you would discover your own interest by that time, I should take one for you. Look you, here it is.'

'I shall be in Dorsetshire, I hope, long before Tuesday se'nnight,' said Emmeline, laying the card coolly on the toilet. She found Mrs. Ashwood had nothing more material to say; and being apprehensive that she impeded the last finish which her dress and person required, she thanked her, and went back into her own room.

The eagerness and resolution with which Lady Montreville opposed her son's marriage, appeared from nothing more evidently, than from her thus endeavouring to solicit the assistance of Mrs. Ashwood, and humbling herself to use flattery and insinuation towards a person to whom it is probable nothing else could have induced her to speak. With persons in trade, or their connections, or even with gentlemen, unless of very ancient and honourable families, she seldom deigned to hold any communication; and if she had occasion to speak to them individually, it was generally under the appellation of 'Mr. or Mrs. I forget the name;' for to remember the particular distinctions of such inferior beings, was a task too heavy for Right Honourable intellects. When she spoke of such collectively, it was under the denomination of 'the people, or the folks.'

With that sort of condescension that seems to say, 'I will humble myself to your level,' and which is in fact more insolent than the most offensive haughtiness, her Ladyship had behaved to Mrs. Ashwood; who took it for extreme politeness, and was charmed on any terms to obtain admission to the house of a woman of such high fashion, and who was known to be so very nice in the choice of her company.

In return for so much favour, she had been lavish of her assurances that she would influence Miss Mowbray; and came home, fully determined to talk to her sharply; believing too, that to make her feel the present dependance and uncertainty of her situation by forcing her to bear a fit of ill-humour, might help to determine her to embrace the affluent fortune that would set her above it. This it was that occasioned her harsh address to Emmeline; which would have been followed by acrimonious reflections and rude remonstrances, under the denomination of 'necessary truths and friendly advice,' had not the presence of Fitz-Edward, and his subsequent enchanting conversation, driven all that Lady Montreville had said out of her mind, and left it open only to the delightful prospect which his compliments and praises afforded her.

The company assembled to cards at the usual hour. Rochely was among them; who had not seen Emmeline since the rejection of his proposal, with which Sir Richard Crofts was obliged to acquaint him, tho' he had softened the peremptory terms in which it had been given. H6 had this evening adorned himself in a superb suit of cut velvet of many colours, lined with sables; which tho' not in the very newest mode, had been reckoned very magnificent at several city assemblies; and he had put it on as well in honour of Lord Montreville, with whom he had dined, as in hopes of moving the perverse beauty for whom he languished. But so far was this display of clumsy affluence from having any effect on the hard heart of Emmeline, that it rather excited her mirth. And when with a grave and solemn aspect he advanced towards her, she felt herself so much disposed to laugh at his figure, that she was forced to avoid him, and took refuge at the table, round which the younger part of the company assembled to play.

Mrs. Ashwood had fixed Fitz-Edward to that where she herself presided; and where she sat triumphantly enjoying his high-seasoned flattery; while her female competitors, hearing he was the son of an Irish Earl, and within three of being a Peer himself, contemplated her supposed conquest with envy and vexation, which they could not conceal, and which greatly added to her satisfaction.

Several persons were invited to stay supper; among whom were Fitz-Edward and Rochely. About half an hour before the card-tables broke up, a servant brought a note to Emmeline, and told her that it required an answer. The hand was Delamere's.

'For two days I have forborne to see you, Emmeline, and have endeavoured to argue myself into a calmer state of mind; but it avails nothing; hopeless when with you, yet wretched without you, I see no end to my sufferings. I have been about the door all the evening; but find, by the carriages, that you are surrounded by fools and coxcombs. Ah! Emmeline! that time you owe only to me; those smiles to which only I have a right, are lavished on them; and I am left to darkness and despair.

'There is a door from the garden into the stable-yard, which opens into the fields. As I cannot come to the house (where I find there are people who would inform Lord

Montreville that I am still about London,) for pity's sake come down to that door and speak to me. I ask only *one* moment; surely you will not deny me so small a favour, and add to the anguish which consumes me. I write this from the neighbouring public-house, and wait your answer.

F. DELAMERE.'

Emmeline shuddered at this note. It was more incoherent than usual, and seemed to be written with a trembling and uncertain hand. She had left the card-table to read it, and was alone in the anti-room; where, while she hesitated over it, Rochely, whose eyes were ever in search of her, followed her. She saw him not: but wholly occupied by the purport of the note, he approached close to her unheeded.

'Are you determined, Miss Mowbray,' said he, 'to give me no other answer than you sent somewhat hastily to Lord Montreville, by my friend Sir Richard Crofts? May I ask, are you quite determined?'

'Quite, Sir!' replied she, starting, without considering and hardly knowing what she said; but feeling he was at that moment more odious to her than ever, she snatched away the hand he attempted to take, and flew out of the room like a lapwing.

The dismayed lover shook his head, surveyed his cut velvet in the glass, and stroaked his point ruffles, while he was trying to recollect his scattered ideas.

Emmeline, who had taken refuge in her bed-chamber, sat there in breathless uncertainty, and unable to determine what to do about Delamere. At length, she concluded on desiring Fitz-Edward to go down to him; but knew not how to speak to the colonel on such a subject before so many witnesses, nor did she like to send for him out of the room. She rung for a candle, and wrote on a slip of paper —

'Delamere is waiting at a door which opens into the fields, and insists upon speaking to me. Pray go down to him, and endeavour to prevail on him to return to his father. I can think of no other expedient to prevent his engaging in some rash and improper attempt; therefore I beseech you to go down.'

When she had written this, she knew not how to deliver it; and for the first time in her life had recourse to an expedient which bore the appearance of art and dissimulation. She did not chuse to send it to Fitz-Edward by a servant; but went down with it herself; and approaching the table where he was settling his winnings —

'Here, colonel,' she said, 'is the *charade* you desired me to write out for you.'

'Oh! read it colonel; pray read it;' cried Mrs. Ashwood, 'I doat upon a *charade* of all things in nature.'

He answered, that 'he would reserve it for a *bon bouche* after supper.' Then looking significantly at Emmeline, to say he understood and would oblige her, he strolled into the anti-room; Emmeline saying to him, as he passed her, that she would wait his return in the parlour below.

Fitz-Edward disappeared; and Emmeline, in hopes of escaping observation, joined the party of some young ladies who were playing at a large table, and affected to enter into their conversation. But she really knew nothing that was passing; and as soon as they rose on finishing their game, she escaped in the bustle, and ran down into the parlour, where in five or six minutes Fitz-Edward found her.

He wore a look of great concern; and laid down his hat as he came in, without seeming to know what he did.

'Have you seen Mr. Delamere, Sir?' said Emmeline.

'Seen him!' answered he; 'I have seen him; but to no manner of purpose; his intellects are certainly deranged; he raves like a madman, and absolutely refuses to leave the place till he has spoken with you.'

'Why will he not come in, then?' said Emmeline.

'Because,' said Fitz-Edward, 'Rochely is here, who will relate it to that meddling fellow, Sir Richard Crofts, and by that means it will get to his father. I said every thing likely to prevail on him to be more calm; but he will hear nothing. I know not what to do,' continued he, rising, and walking about the room. 'I am convinced he has something in his head of fatal consequence to himself. He protests he will stay all night where he is. In short he is in an absolute frenzy with the idea of Rochely's success and his own despair.'

'You frighten me to death,' said Emmeline. 'Tell me, colonel, what ought I to do?'

'Go to him,' returned Fitz-Edward; 'speak to him only a moment, and I am persuaded he will be calm. I will go with you; and then there can be nothing wrong in it.'

'I *will* go, then,' said she, rising and giving Fitz-Edward her hand, which trembled extremely.

'But it is very cold,' remarked he; 'had you not better take a cloak?'

'There is my long *pelisse* in the back parlour,' answered she.

Fitz-Edward fetched it, wrapt her in it, and led her down stairs; and by a garden door, they reached a sort of back stable-yard, where rubbish and stable-litter was usually thrown, and which opened into a bye-lane, where the garden-wall formed a sudden angle. Delamere received her with transport, which he tried to check; and reproached her for refusing to come down to him.

Seizing the opportunity, as soon as he would give her leave to speak, she very forcibly represented to him the distress of his family at his absence, and the particular uneasiness it inflicted on his sister Augusta.

'I knew not,' said Delamere, 'that she was come home.'

Emmeline told him she was, and related the purport of her letter, and again besought him to put an end to the uncertainty and anxiety of his family.

Delamere heard her with some impatience; and holding her hands in his, vehemently answered — 'It is to no purpose that my father either threatens or persuades me. He has long known my resolution; and the unhappiness which you so warmly describe arises solely from his and my mother's own unreasonable and capricious prejudice — prejudice founded in pride and avarice. I do not think myself accountable for distress to which they may so easily put an end. But as to Augusta, who really loves me, I will write to her to make her easy. Now Emmeline, since I have listened to you, and answered all you have to urge, hear my final determination — *If you* still continue firm in your chimerical and romantic obstinacy, which you call honour, *I* go from hence this evening, never to return — you condemn me to perpetual exile — you give me up to despair!'

He called aloud, and a post-chaise and four, which had been concealed by the projection of the wall, attended by two servants, drove round. 'There,' continued Delamere, 'there is the vehicle which I have prepared to carry me from hence. You know whether I easily relinquish a resolution once formed. If then you wish to save my father and mother from the anguish of repentance when there will be no remedy — if you desire to save from the frenzy of desperation the brother of your Augusta, and to snatch from the extremity of wretchedness the man who lives but to adore you, go with me — go with me to Scotland!'

Astonished and terrified at the impetuosity with which he pressed this unexpected proposal, Emmeline would have replied, but words were a moment wanting. Fitz-Edward taking advantage of her silence, used every argument which Delamere had omitted, to determine her.

'No! no!' cried she — 'never! never! I have passed my honour to Lord Montreville. It is sacred — I cannot, I will not forfeit it!'

'The time will come,' said Fitz-Edward, 'believe me it will, when Lord Montreville will not only be reconciled to you, but' —

'And what shall reconcile me to myself? Let me go back to the house, Mr. Delamere; or from this moment I shall consider you as having taken advantage of my unprotected state, and even of my indiscreet confidence, to offer me the grossest outrage. Let me go, Sir!' (struggling to get her hand from Fitz-Edward) 'Let me go! Mr. Delamere.'

'What! to be driven into the arms of Rochely? No, never, Emmeline! never! I *know I am not* indifferent to you. I feel that I cannot live without you; nay, by heaven I will not! But if I suffer this opportunity to escape, I deserve indeed to lose you.'

They all this while approached the chaise. Delamere had hired servants, whom he had instructed what to do. They were ready at the door of the carriage. Emmeline attempted in vain to retreat. Delamere threw his arms around her; and assisted by Fitz-Edward, lifted her into it with a sort of gentle violence. He leaped in after her, and the chaise was driven away instantly.

Fitz-Edward, to whom this scene was wholly unexpected, returned to the company he had left with Mrs. Ashwood.

He had not any notion of Delamere's design when he went to him, but heartily concurred in its execution; and tho' he did not believe Delamere intended to marry Emmeline, yet his morals were such, that he congratulated himself on the share he had had in putting her into his power, and went back with the air of a man vastly satisfied with the success of his exploit.

'Goodness! colonel,' exclaimed Mrs. Ashwood, 'supper has been waiting for you this half hour. Upon my word we began to suspect that you and Miss Mowbray were gone together. But pray where is she?'

'Miss Mowbray, Madam! I really have not been so happy as to be of her party.'

'Why, where in the world can she be?' continued Mrs. Ashwood. 'However, as the colonel is come we will go to supper. *[The company were standing round the table.]* I suppose Miss Mowbray will come presently; she has a pretty romantic notion of contemplation by moonlight.'

Supper, however, was almost over, and Miss Mowbray did not appear. Mrs. Ashwood, engaged wholly by the gallant colonel, thought not of her; but Rochely remarked that her absence was somewhat singular.

'So it is I declare,' said Miss Galton; 'do Mrs. Ashwood send to enquire for her again.'

The chambers, the drawing-room, dressing-room, closets, and garden were again searched. Miss Mowbray was not to be found! Mrs. Ashwood was alarmed — Rochely in dismay — and the whole company confusedly broke up; each retiring with their several conjectures on the sudden disappearance of the fair Emmeline.

CHAPTER IV

FOR some moments after Emmeline found herself in the chaise, astonishment and terror deprived her of speech and even of recollection. While Delamere, no longer able to command his transports at having at length as he hoped secured her, gave way to the wildest joy, and congratulated himself that he had thus forced her to break a promise which only injustice he said could have extorted, and only timidity and ill-grounded prejudice have induced her to keep.

'Do you then hope, Sir,' said Emmeline, 'that -I shall patiently become the victim of your rashness? Is this the respect you have sworn ever to observe towards me? Is this the protection you have so often told me I should find from you? and is it thus you intend to atone for all the insults of your family which you have so repeatedly protested you would never forgive? by inflicting a far greater insult; by ruining my character; by degrading me in my own eyes; and forcing me either to violate my word solemnly given to your father, or be looked upon as a lost and abandoned creature, undone by your inhuman art. I must now, indeed, seem to *deserve* your mother's anger, and the scorn of your sister; and must be supposed every way wretched and contemptible.'

A shower of tears fell from her eyes, and her heart seemed bursting with the pain these cruel reflections gave her.

Delamere, by all the soothing tenderness of persuasion, by all the rhetoric of ardent passion, tried to subdue her anger, and silence her scruples; but the more her mind dwelt on the circumstances of her situation, the more it recoiled from the necessity of entering under such compulsion into an indissoluble engagement. The rash violence of the measure which had put her in Delamere's power, while it convinced her of his passion, yet told her, that a man who would hazard every thing for his own gratification now, would hardly hereafter submit to any restraint; and that the bonds in which he was so eager to engage, would with equal violence be broken, when any new face should make a new impression, or when time had diminished the influence of those attractions that now enchanted him.

Formed of the softer elements, and with a mind calculated for select friendship and domestic felicity, rather than for the tumult of fashionable life and the parade of titled magnificence, Emmeline coveted not his rank, nor valued his riches. No woman perhaps can help having some regard for a man, who she knows ardently and sincerely loves her; and Emmeline had felt all that sort of weakness for Delamere; who in the bloom of life, with fortune, title, person and talents that might have commanded the loveliest and most affluent daughter of prosperity, had forsaken every thing for her, and even secluded himself from the companions of his former pleasures, and the indulgences his fortune and rank afforded him, to pass his youth in unsuccessful endeavours to obtain her.

The partiality this consideration gave her towards him, and the favourable comparison she was perpetually making between him and the men she had seen since her residence near London, had created in her bosom a sentiment warmer perhaps than friendship; yet it was not that violent love, which carrying every thing before it, leaves the mind no longer at liberty to see any fault in the beloved object, or any impropriety in whatever can secure its success, and which, scorning future consequences, risks every thing for its present indulgence.

Still artless and ingenuous as when she first left the remote castle where she had been brought up, Emmeline had not been able to conceal this affection from Delamere. Her eyes, her manner, the circumstance of the picture, and a thousand nameless inadvertences, had told it him repeatedly; but now, when he seemed to have taken an ungenerous advantage of that regard, it lost much of its force, and resentment and disdain succeeded.

Delamere tried to apease her by protestations of inviolable respect, of eternal esteem, and unalterable love. But there was something of triumph even in his humblest entreaties, that served but to encrease the anger Emmeline felt; and she told him that the only way to convince her he had for her those sentiments he pretended, was to carry her back immediately to Mrs. Ashwood's, or rather to Lord Montreville, there to acknowledge the attempt he had made, and that its failure had been solely owing to her determined adherence to her word.

Delamere, presuming on his ascendancy over her, attempted to interest her passions rather than tranquillize her reason. He represented to her how great would be her triumph when he presented her as his wife to the imperious Lady Montreville, who had treated her with so much unmerited scorn, and set her above the haughty Fanny Delamere, who had insulted her with fancied superiority.

But Emmeline had in her breast none of those passions that find their gratification in humbling an enemy. Too generous for revenge; too gentle for premeditated resentment; she saw these circumstances in a very different light, and felt that she should be rather mortified than elated by being forced into a family who wished to reject her.

Sir Richard Crofts, the object of Delamere's hatred and detestation, was the subject of those acrimonious reflections that his respect for his father and mother prevented his throwing on them. The influence of this man had, he said, made Lord Montreville deaf to the voice of nature, and forgetful of his own honour; while he was plunged into the dark and discreditable labyrinth of political intrigue, and acquired an habit of subterfuge and duplicity unworthy a nobleman, a gentleman, or a man.

Emmeline cared nothing about Sir Richard Crofts, and could not enter into the bitterness of his resentment towards him. Nothing he had yet been able to urge had shaken her resolution not to become his wife, even tho' he should oblige her to go with him into Scotland.

The ruder passions of anger and resentment had no influence over her mind. While he argued with warmth, or ran into reproaches, Emmeline found she had nothing to fear. But tho' he could not rouse her pride, or awaken her dislike against his family, but rather found them recoil on himself; he hoped in that sensibility of temper and that softness of heart to which he owed all the attention she had ever shewn him, he should find a sure resource. In her pity, an advocate for his fault — in her love, an inducement not only to forgive but to reward him.

And when he pleaded for compassion and forgiveness, the heart of Emmeline felt itself no longer invulnerable. But against this dangerous attack she endeavoured to fortify that sensible heart, but considering the probable event of her yielding to it.

'If I marry Delamere contrary to the consent of his family, who shall assure me that his violent and haughty spirit will bear without anguish and regret, that inferior and confined fortune to which his father's displeasure will condemn him? His love, too ardent perhaps to last, will decline; while the inconveniences of a narrow fortune will encrease; and I, who shall be the cause of these inconveniences, shall also be the victim. He will lament the infatuation which has estranged him from his family, and thrown him, for some years at least, out of the rank in which he has been used to appear; and recovered from the delirium of love, will behold with coldness, perhaps with hatred, her to whom he will impute his distresses. To whom can I then appeal? Not to my *own* heart, for it will condemn me for suffering myself to be precipitated into a measure against my judgment; nor to *his* family, who may answer, 'thy folly be upon thine own head;' and *I* have *no* father, *no* brother to console and receive me, if he should drive me from him as impetuously as now he would force me to be his. I shall be deprived even of the melancholy consolation of knowing I have not *deserved* the neglect which I fear I shall never be able to *bear*. But if my steady refusal now, induces him to return, it is possible that Lord Montreville, convinced at once of my adherence to the promise given him, and of the improbability of Delamere's desisting, may consent to receive me into his family; or if the inveterate prejudice of his wife still prevents his doing so, I shall surely regain his confidence and esteem. He will not refuse to consider me as his brother's daughter, and as such, he will enable me to pass my days in easy competence with Mrs. Stafford; a prospect infinitely preferable in my eyes to the splendid visions offered me by Delamere, if they cannot be realized but at the expence of truth and integrity.'

Confirmed in her determination by reflections like these, Emmeline was able to hear, without betraying any symptoms of the emotion she felt, the animated and passionate protestations of her lover. She assumed all the coldness and reserve which his headlong and inconsiderate attempt deserved. She told him that his want of respect and consideration had forfeited all the claim he might otherwise have had to her regard and esteem; that she certainly would quit him the moment she was able; and that tho' she might not be fortunate enough to do so before they reached Scotland, yet it would not be in his power to compel her to be his wife.

Delamere for some time imputed this language to sudden resentment; and again by the humblest submissions sought to obtain her forgiveness and to excite her pity. But having nearly exhausted her spirits by what she had already said, she gave very little reply to his entreaties. Her silence was however more expressive than her words. She took from him her hand, as often as he attempted to hold it, and would not suffer him to wipe away the tears that fell from her eyes; while to his arguments and persuasions she coldly answered, when she answered at all, '*that she was determined:*' and they arrived at Barnet before he had obtained the smallest concession in his favour.

Delamere had undertaken this enterprize rather in despair, than from any hope of its success, since he did not believe Emmeline would come out to him when he requested it; and had she been either alone, or only with Mrs. Ashwood, she certainly had not done it. Chance had befriended him in collecting a room full of company, and still more in sending Rochely among them. His abrupt approach while she read Delamere's note, had hurried her out of her usual presence of mind; and Fitz-Edward, whom mere accident had brought to Mrs. Ashwood's house, and whom she had taken with her in hopes of his influencing Delamere to return to his father, had contributed to her involuntary error.

CHAPTER V

DELAMERE had taken no precaution to secure horses on the road; and it was not till after waiting some hours that he procured four from Barnet. When they arrived there, it was past one o'clock; and Emmeline, who had gone thro' a very fatigueing day, and was now overcome with the terror and alarm of being thus hastily snatched away, could hardly sit up. She was without an hat; and having no change of cloaths, urged the inconvenience she must endure by being forced to go a long journey so situated. She wished to have stopped at the first stage; but Delamere thought, that in her present temper to hesitate was to lose her. He consented however to go for a moment into the house, where, while he gave a servant orders to go on to Hatfield to bespeak four horses, she drank a glass of water; and then Delamere intreating her to return to the chaise, she complied, for there was nobody visible at the inn but the maid and ostler; and she saw no likelihood of any assistance, had she applied for it.

They hastened with great expedition to Stevenage; but before they reached that place, Emmeline, who had ceased either to remonstrate or complain, was so entirely overwhelmed and exhausted, that she could no longer support herself.

His fears for her health now exceeded his fears for losing her, and he determined to stop for some hours; but when she made an effort to leave the chaise she was unable, and he was obliged to lift her out of it. He then ordered the female servants to be called up, recommended her to their care, and entreated her to go to bed for some hours.

Long darkness and excessive weeping had almost deprived her of sight; her whole frame was sinking under the fatigue she had undergone both of body and mind; and unable to struggle longer against it, she lay down in her cloaths, desiring one of the maids to sit by her.

Delamere came to the door of the room to enquire how she did. The woman told him what she had requested; and desiring they would obey her in every thing, and keep her as quiet as possible, he went not to repose himself, but to write to Fitz-Edward.

'Dear George,

'While my angelic Emmeline sleeps, I, who am too happy to sleep myself, write to desire you will go to Berkley-square and keep the good folks there from exposing themselves, or making a great bustle about what has happened, which they will soon know. As my Lord has long been prepossessed with the idea of a Scottish jaunt, it is very likely he may attempt to pursue us. Say what you will to put such plans out of his head. I shall be in London again, in a very short time. Farewell, dear George.

Yours, ever,

F.D.'

Emmeline in the mean time fell into a sleep, but it was broken and interrupted. Her spirits had been so thoroughly discomposed, that rest was driven from her. She dozed a moment; then suddenly started up, forgot where she was, and looked wildly round the room. An half-formed recollection of the events of the preceding day then seemed to recur, and she besought the maid who sat by her to go to Mr. Delamere and tell him she must be directly carried to Mrs. Stafford's; and having said this, and sighed deeply, she sunk again into short insensibility.

Thus past the remainder of the night; and before seven in the morning Delamere was at the door, impatient to know how she had rested.

The maid admitted him, and told him, in a low voice, that the Lady was in a quieter sleep than she had been the whole night. He softly approached the bed, and started in terror when he saw how ill she looked. Her cheek, robbed of its bloom, rested on her arm, which appeared more bloodless than her cheek; her hair, which had been dressed without powder, had escaped from the form in which it had been adjusted, and half concealed her face in disordered luxuriance; her lips were pale, and her respiration short and laborious. He stood gazing on her a moment, and then, shocked at these symptoms of indisposition his rapid imagination immediately magnified them all. He concluded she was dying; and in an agony of fear, which deprived him of every other idea, he took up in breathless apprehension her other hand, which lay on the quilt. It was hot, and dry; and her pulse seemed rather to flutter, than to beat against his pressure.

His moving her hand awakened her. She opened her eyes; but they had lost their lustre, and were turned mournfully towards him.

'Delamere,' said she, in a low and tremulous voice, 'Delamere, why is all this? I believe you have destroyed me; my head is so extremely painful. Oh! Delamere — this is cruel! — very cruel!'

'Let me go for advice,' cried he, eagerly. 'Wretch that I am, what will now become of me!'

He ran down stairs; and Emmeline making an effort to recover her recollection, tried to sit up; but her head was so giddy and confused that it was not till after several attempts she left the bed, even with the assistance of the servant. She then drank a glass of water; and desiring to have more air, would have gone to the window, but could only reach a chair near it, where she sat down, and throwing her arm on a table, rested her head upon it.

In a few moments Delamere returned up stairs. His wild looks, and quick, half-formed questions, explained what passed in his mind.

She told him faintly she was better.

'Shall I bring up a gentleman to see you who I am assured is able in his profession? I fear you are very ill.'

She answered, 'no!'

'Pray suffer him to come; he will give you something to relieve your head.'

'No!'

'Do not, Emmeline — do not, I conjure you, refuse me this favour?'

He took her hand; but when he found how feverish she was, he started away, crying — 'Oh! let him, let him come!'

He ran down stairs to fetch him, and returned instantly with the apothecary; a sensible, well-behaved man, of fifty, whose appearance indicated feeling and judgement. He approached Emmeline, who still sat with her head reclined on the table, and felt her pulse.

'Here is too much fever indeed, Sir,' said he; 'the young lady has been greatly hurried.'

'But what — what is to be done, Sir?' said Delamere, eagerly interrupting him.

'Quiet seems absolutely necessary. Pardon me, Sir; but unless I know your situation in regard to her, I cannot possibly advise.'

'Sir,' said Emmeline, who had been silent rather from inability to contend than from unconsciousness of what was passing round her — 'if you could prevail with Mr. Delamere to restore me to my friends' —

'Come with me, Sir,' cried Delamere; let me speak to you in another room.'

When they were alone, he conjured Mr. Lawson to tell him what he thought of the lady?

'Upon my word, Sir, she is in a very high fever, and it seems to be occasioned by extreme perturbation of spirits and great fatigue. Forgive, Sir, if I ask what particular circumstance has been the cause of the uneasiness under which she appears to labour? If it is any little love quarrel you cannot too soon adjust it.'

Delamere stopped his conjectures, by telling him who he was; and gave him in a few words the history of their expedition.

Mr. Lawson protested to him that if she was hurried on in her present state, it would be surprizing if she survived the journey.

'She shall stay here then,' replied Delamere, 'till she recovers her fatigue.'

'But, Sir,' enquired Mr. Lawson, 'after what you have told me of your father, have you no apprehension of a pursuit?'

His terror at Emmeline's immediate danger had obliterated for a moment every other fear. It now recurred with redoubled violence. He remembered that Rochely was at Mrs. Ashwood's on the evening of Emmeline's departure; and he knew that from him Sir Richard Crofts, and consequently Lord Montreville, would have immediate intelligence.

He struck his hands together, exclaiming, 'She will be every way lost! — lost irretrievably! If my father overtakes us, she will return with him, and I shall see her no more!'

He now gave way to such unbounded passion, walking about the room, and striking his forehead, that Lawson began to believe his intellects were as much deranged as the frame of the fair sufferer he had left. For some moments he attended to nothing; but Mr. Lawson, accustomed to make allowances for the diseases of the mind as well as those of the body, did not lose his patience; and at length persuaded him to be calmer, by representing that he wasted in fruitless exclamation the time which might be employed in providing against the apprehended evil.

'Good God! Sir,' cried he at length, 'what would you have me do?'

'What I would earnestly recommend, Sir, is, that you quiet the young lady's mind by telling her you will carry her whither she desires to go; and at present desist from this journey, which I really believe you cannot prosecute but at the hazard of her life; at present, farther agitation may, and probably will be fatal.'

'And so you advise me to let her stay till my father comes to tear her from me for ever! or carry her back by the same road, where it is probable he will meet me? Impossible! impossible! — but is she really so very ill?'

'Upon my life she is at this moment in a high fever. Why should I deceive you? Trust me, it would in my opinion be the height of inhumanity to carry her into Scotland in such a situation, *if* you love her' —

'*If* I love her, Sir!' cried Delamere, half frantic — 'talk not of *if* I love her! Merciful heaven! — you have no idea, Mr. Lawson, of what I suffer at this moment!'

'I have a perfect idea of your distress, Sir; and wish I knew how to relieve it. Give me a moment's time to consider; if indeed the young lady could' —

'What, Sir? speak! — think of something!

'Why I was thinking, that if she is better in a few hours, it might be possible for you to take her to Hertford, where she may remain a day or two, till she is able to go farther. There you would be no longer in danger of pursuit; and if she should grow worse, which when her mind is easier I hope will not happen, you will have excellent advice. Perhaps, when the hurry of her spirits subsides, she may, since this *has* happened, consent to pursue the journey to the North; or if not, you can from thence carry her to the friends she is so desirous of being with, and avoid the risk of meeting on the road those you are so anxious to shun.

Tho' Delamere could not think, without extreme reluctance, of relinquishing a scheme in which he had thought himself secure of success; yet, as there was no alternative but what would be so hazardous to the health of Emmeline, he was compelled to accede to any which had a probability of restoring it without putting her into the hands of his father.

Mr. Lawson told him it was only fifteen miles from Stevenage to Hertford — 'But how,' said he, 'will you, Sir, prevent your father's following you thither, if he should learn at this place that you are gone there?'

Delamere was wholly at a loss. But Mr. Lawson, who seemed to be sent by his good genius, said — 'We must get you from hence immediately, if Miss Mowbray is able to go. You shall pass here as my visitors. You shall directly go to my house, and there be supplied with horses from another inn. This will at least make it more difficult to trace your route; and if any enquiry should be made of me, I shall know what to say.'

Delamere, catching at any thing that promised to secure Emmeline from the pursuit of Lord Montreville, went to her to enquire whether she was well enough to walk to Mr. Lawson's house.

He found her trying to adjust her hair; but her hands trembled so much, it was with difficulty she could do it. He desired her to dismiss the maid who was in the room; then throwing himself on his knees before her, and taking her burning hands in his, he said — 'Arbitress of my destiny — my Emmeline! thou for whom only I exist! be tranquil — I beseech you be tranquil! Since you determine to abide by your cruel resolution, I will not, I dare not persist in asking you to break it. No, Emmeline! I come only to entreat that you would quiet your too delicate mind; and dispose of *me* as you please. Since you cannot resolve to be mine now, I will learn to submit — I will try to bear any thing but the seeing you unhappy, or losing you entirely! Tell me only that you pardon what is past, and you shall go to Mrs. Stafford's, or whithersoever you will.'

Emmeline beheld and heard him with astonishment. But at length comprehending that he repented of his wild attempt, and would go back, she said hastily, as she arose from her chair — 'Let us go, then, Delamere; let us instantly go. Thank God, your heart is changed! but every hour I continue with you, is an additional wound to my character and my peace.'

She attempted to reach her cloak, but could not; her strength forsook her; her head became more giddy; she staggered, and would have fallen, had not Delamere caught her in his arms, and supported her to the chair she had left.

'Hurry not yourself thus, my Emmeline,' cried he; 'in mercy to me try to compose yourself, and spare me the sight of all this terror, for which believe me you have no reason.'

He sat down by her; and drawing her gently towards him, her languid head reposed on his shoulder, and he contemplated, in silent anguish, the ravage which only a few hours severe anxiety had made on that beauteous and expressive countenance.

He called to the maid, who waited in the next room, and desired her to send up Mr. Lawson; before whose entrance a shower of tears, the first she had shed for some hours, a little relieved the full heart of Emmeline.

Mr. Lawson desired Delamere would not check her tears; and in a friendly and consolatory manner told her what Delamere proposed to do. Emmeline, after this explanation, was still more anxious to depart; but Mr. Lawson greatly doubted whether she was able.

'I can walk, indeed I can,' said she, 'if you will each lend me an arm.'

Mr. Lawson then gave her a few drops in a glass of water, which seemed to revive her; and Delamere wrapping her carefully in her cloak, they led her between them to a neat brick house in the town, where Mrs. Lawson, a matron-like and well-behaved woman, and her daughter, a genteel girl of twenty, who had been apprized of Emmeline's situation, received her with great kindness and respect.

Breakfast was prepared for her, but she could eat nothing. The heaviness of her eyes, her pallid countenance, and the tenseness across her temples, seemed to threaten the most alarming consequences. Mrs. Lawson endeavoured to persuade her to go to bed; but her eagerness to be gone from thence was so great, that she evidently encreased the difficulty by endeavouring to surmount it. She had indeed considered, that if Lord Montreville overtook them, which was not only possible but probable, all the merit of her conduct would be lost. — She would appear to be carried back, not by her strict adherence to her promise, but by the authority of his Lordship; and instead of the pride and credit of a laudable and virtuous action, would be liable to bear all the imputation of intentional guilt. This reflection, added to the sense she could not fail to have of her improper situation in being so long alone with Delamere under the appearance of having voluntarily gone off with him, made her so impatient to be gone, that she declined any repose however necessary; and Mr. Lawson thought there was less to be feared from indulging than from opposing her.

Lawson therefore went himself to hasten the horses; and while he was absent, Emmeline, who remained with his wife, expressed so much fear that Delamere might alter his intentions of returning, and so much uneasiness at the thought of being seen at another inn, in the disordered dress she now wore, with a young man of Delamere's appearance, that Mrs. Lawson was truly concerned for her, and communicated to Delamere the source of the extreme anxiety she appeared to suffer.

He came to her; and she gently reproached him for all the inconvenience and uneasiness he had brought upon her. Her soft complaints, and the distress pictured on her speaking face, he felt with a degree of anguish and self-reproach that made him happy to agree to a plan proposed by Mrs. Lawson, which was, that she should be accommodated with cloaths of Miss Lawson's, and that Miss Lawson herself should accompany her to Hertford.

This latter offer, Emmeline eagerly accepted; and Delamere, who saw how much it soothed and relieved her, did not object to it. She was therefore immediately equipped with a morning dress, and her agitation of mind seemed to subside; but changing her cloaths, trifling as the exertion was, fatigued her so much, that Mr. Lawson on his return looked very grave; and Delamere, who watched his looks as if his existence depended upon his opinion, was wild with apprehension. The chaises (for Delamere had ordered one for himself, that the ladies might suffer no inconvenience by being crouded) were ready, and Lawson recollecting that Emmeline would require a more quiet situation than an inn could afford, told her that he had a sister at Hertford who would receive her with pleasure, and accommodate her at her house as long as she would stay — 'And remember,' added he, 'that Lissy is to continue with you till you leave Hertford.'

Emmeline, extremely sensible of all she owed to this excellent man, could only sigh her thanks; and to shorten them, Mr. Lawson put her and his daughter into the travelling chaise which Delamere had bought for this expedition. Delamere followed in another; and between one and two o'clock they arrived at Hertford, and were set down at the door of an elegant house; where Mrs. Champness, the wife of a man of fortune, received her niece with great affection; and having heard in another room the history of the young lady she had with her, immediately gave orders to have a bed chamber prepared, and shewed the utmost solicitude for her accommodation.

Delamere, seeing her so well situated for the night, and happy to find she bore her short journey with less increase of fatigue than he apprehended, consented at her request to leave her, and went to the inn, where he dined, and soon afterwards returned to enquire after her.

Miss Lawson came down to him, and told him Miss Mowbray was in bed, and had taken a medicine Mr. Lawson had sent to compose her; but that it was yet impossible to say much of her situation. She told him he must by no means attempt to see her for the remaining part of the day, and begged he would himself try to take some repose: to which salutary advice Delamere at length consented; his haggard looks and exhausted spirits sufficiently testifying how much he wanted it.

CHAPTER VI

THE evening on which Emmeline had been so suddenly missing from the house of Mrs. Ashwood, Rochely had left it in as much anguish as his nature was capable of feeling.

He had not for many years so seriously thought of matrimony as since he had seen Miss Mowbray. Her beauty first attracted him: the natural civility of her manner was by him, who had frequently met only contempt and derision from the young and beautiful, construed into encouragement; and though his hopes had been greatly damped by his knowledge of Delamere's attachment to her, yet they were almost as quickly revived by the great encouragement to persevere, which he had received from Lord Montreville. He fancied that the barriers between her and Delamere being insurmountable, she could not fail of being dazzled by so splendid a fortune as he could himself offer her. That evening, she looked more than usually lovely, and he determined with new ardour to pursue her. But her disappearance put an end to all his brilliant visions; and convinced him that his wealth, on which he had so long been accustomed to value himself, had failed of procuring him the favour of the only woman with whom he was disposed to share it. He was too well convinced that Delamere had carried her off: and though deprived of all hope for himself, he was too angry at the good fortune of his rival to forbear an attempt to disturb him in its possession. He drove therefore from Clapham to the house of Sir Richard Crofts, where he had the mortification of hearing that Sir Richard was gone with Lord Montreville to the country house of Lord Dornock, and was not expected to return 'till the next day.

Rochely, aware that the only possible chance of preventing Delamere's marriage was by an immediate pursuit, was greatly chagrined at this unavoidable delay. He sat down, however, and with his usual laboured precision wrote to Sir Richard Crofts, informing him of what had happened. This was the operation of near an hour; and he then sent off a man on horseback with it, who arriving at Lord Dornock's about three in the morning, roused the family with some difficulty, and delivered to Sir Richard the intelligence, which was immediately conveyed to Lord Montreville; who having read Mr. Rochely's letter, could not flatter himself with any hope that this alarm might be as groundless as one he had before had on the same subject.

The disobedience of his son; the broken faith of Emmeline; and the rage, complaints, and reproaches of Lady Montreville, all arose together in his imagination; and anger, vexation, and regret, took possession of his heart.

He had recourse in this, as in all other emergencies, to Sir Richard Crofts, who advised him immediately to pursue them.

As soon therefore as the sleeping servants could be collected, and the carriage prepared, his Lordship and Sir Richard set out for London together. — Lord Montreville determining to follow the fugitives as expeditiously as possible, though he hoped but little success from the pursuit.

Such was his apprehension of the clamours and passions of his wife, that he could not determine to see her 'till he had at least done all that was possible to recover her son. He therefore wrote to her a short letter, stating briefly w t had happened, and giving her hopes that he should be able to overtake the parties before they were married. This he ordered to be delivered to her in the morning; and directed his servant to hasten to him with his travelling chaise and four post horses.

The man, however, who had the care of carriages, believing his Lord would stay out all night, had gone out also, and taken with him the keys.

By this delay, and the blunders of the affrighted servants, who in their haste only impeded each other, it was near nine o'clock before his Lordship and Sir Richard left London. At Barnet, they heard of the fugitives, and easily traced them from thence to Hatfield; after which believing all farther enquiries useless, they passed through Stevenage (having sent on before for horses,) without asking any questions which might have led them to discover that Delamere and Emmeline had gone from thence towards Hertford only an hour and an half before their arrival.

This was fortunate for the pursued; for an enquiry would probably have led to questions which Mr. Lawson would have found it very difficult to evade.

Lord Montreville, however, and Sir Richard, hurried on to Buckden; where being obliged to get out for some refreshment for themselves and their servants, his Lordship renewed the question — 'At what time did a young gentleman and lady' (describing Delamere and Emmeline) 'pass by?'

The people told him they remembered no such persons about the time he named.

Lord Montreville then applied at the other houses, and made several other enquiries; but received only a general assertion that no such persons had been that way within the last four and twenty hours, or even within a week.

Sir Richard Crofts, who piqued himself upon his sagacity, told his Lordship that stupidity, the love of falsehood, or Delamere's bribes, might occasion this failure of intelligence; but there could be no doubt of their being gratified with better information when they got to Stilton. To Stilton therefore they went, but heard exactly the same answers as they had done at the last stage.

Sir Richard was now again to seek for some plausible conjecture that might quiet the apprehensive anxiety of Lord Montreville, who guessed and dreaded he knew not what.

He now said, that as there could be no doubt of the young people's having gone *towards* Scotland, from the information they had obtained at Barnet and Hatfield, it was most likely that in the apprehension of a pursuit they had afterwards quitted the high road, and were advancing to the borders of Scotland across the country, which must considerably lengthen and impede their journey; therefore if they themselves proceeded directly to the town where these marriages are usually celebrated, the probability was that they should arrive before Delamere and Miss Mowbray; and by such a circumstance the connection would be as effectually prevented as it could be by their overtaking them on the road.

Lord Montreville, despairing of being able by any means to obstruct a marriage on which his son seemed to be so determined, and harrassed in mind as much as he was fatigued in body, suffered himself to be carried forward merely through inability to determine what he could do better; and though quite hopeless of its success, pursued his journey.

The innocent cause of all this trouble and anxiety remained in the mean time at the hospitable house of Mrs. Champness; where Miss Lawson attended her with all possible kindness and solicitude. It was indeed impossible to be with her without loving her; unless to an heart insensible, like that of Mrs. Ashwood, to all but her own ideal perfections; or steeled by pride, like that of Lady Montreville.

A night passed in quiet sleep had greatly restored her; and her fever, though not gone, was considerably abated. Every noise, however trifling, still made her start; her nerves were by no means restored to their tone, and her spirits continued to be greatly affected. The idea which seemed to press most painfully on her mind, was the blemish which the purity of her character must sustain by her being so long absent with Delamere — a blemish which she knew could hardly ever be removed but by her returning as his wife.

But to break her promise to Lord Montreville; a promise so solemnly given; and to be compelled into a marriage which, however advantageous and fortunate it would appear under other circumstances, would now bring with it a severe alloy of mortification in the displeasure of his family; was a measure which she could not determine to pursue.

Her resentment towards Delamere for what was passed was not yet enough subdued by his reluctant repentance, to reconcile her to the thoughts of putting herself again into his power. Yet she could not suppose he would suffer her to return to London alone, if she had courage to attempt it; or was she sure that when there, Mrs. Ashwood would receive her.

These reflections made her so restless and uneasy that she could not conceal their source from Miss Lawson; who, tho' possessed of a very good understanding, was too young and too little acquainted with the world to be able to advise her.

The handsome person and high rank of Delamere, and his violent love and concern for Emmeline, made her suppose it impossible that she could help returning it, or be long able to resist his importunity. She concluded therefore that finally it would be a match; and was impressed with a sentiment that amounted almost to veneration for Miss Mowbray, whom she considered as a prodigy of female virtue and resolution.

Delamere had been several times to speak to Miss Lawson; and he had pleaded the violence of his passion with so much effect, that the soft-hearted girl became his warm advocate with Emmeline, and represented his tenderness and his contrition, 'till she consented (as she was now able to sit up) to admit him.

On his entrance, he said something, he hardly knew what, to Emmeline. She held out her hand to him in token of forgiveness. He seized it eagerly, and pressed it to his heart, while he gazed on her face as if to enquire there what passed in hers.

'Remember, Delamere,' said she, 'remember I am content to forgive your late rash and absurd attempt, only on condition of your giving me the most positive assurance that you will carry me directly to Mrs. Stafford's, and there leave me.'

Hard as these terms appeared, after the hopes he had entertained on undertaking the journey, he was forced to submit; but it was evidently with reluctance.

'I do promise then,' said he, 'to take you to Mrs. Stafford's; but' —

'But what?' asked Emmeline.

'Do you not mean, when you are there, to exclude me for ever? — Mrs. Stafford is no friend of mine.'

'I have already told you, Mr. Delamere, that I will see you wherever I am, under certain restrictions: and tho' your late conduct might, and indeed ought to induce me to withdraw that promise, yet I now repeat it. But do not believe that I will therefore be persecuted as I have been; recollect that I have already been driven from Mowbray Castle, from Swansea, and from Mrs. Ashwood's, wholly on your account.'

'Your remedy, my Emmeline, is, to consent to inhabit a house of your own, and suffer me to be the first of your servants.'

The varying colour of her complexion, to which the emotions of her mind restored for a moment the faint tints of returning health, made Delamere hope that her resolution was shaken; and seizing with his usual vehemence on an idea so flattering, he was instantly on his knees before her imploring her consent to prosecute their journey, and intreating Miss Lawson's assistance, to move her inexorable friend.

Emmeline was too weak to bear an address of this sort. The feebleness of her frame ill seconded the resolution of her mind; which, notwithstanding the struggles of pity and regard for Delamere, which she could not entirely silence, was immoveably determined. Rallying therefore her spirits, and summoning her fortitude to answer him, she said — 'How *can* you, Sir, solicit a woman, whom you wish to make your wife, to break a promise so solemn as that I have given to your father? Could you hereafter have any dependance on one, who holds her integrity so lightly? and should you not with great reason suspect that with her, falsehood and deception might become habitual?'

'Not at all,' answered Delamere. 'Your promise to my father is nugatory; for it ought never to have been given. He took an unfair advantage of your candour and your timidity; and all that you said ought not to bind *you;* since it was extorted from you by *him* who had no right to make such conditions.'

'What! has a father no right to decide to whom he will entrust the happiness of his son, and the honour of his posterity? Alas! Delamere, you argue against yourself; you only convince me that I ought not to put the whole happiness of my life into the hands of a man, who will so readily break thro' his first duties. The same impatient, pardon me, if I say the same selfish spirit, which now urges you to set paternal authority at defiance, will perhaps hereafter impel you, with as little difficulty to quit a wife of whom you may be weary, for any other person whom caprice or novelty may dress in the perfections you now fancy I possess. Ah! Delamere! shall I have a right to expect tenderness faith from a man whom I have assisted in making his parents unhappy; and who has by my means embittered the evening of their lives to whom he owes his own? Do you think that a rebellious and unfeeling son is likely to make a good husband, a good father?'

'Death and madness!' cried Delamere, relapsing into all the violence of his nature — 'what do you mean by all this! Selfish! rebellious! unfeeling! — am I then *so* worthless, *so* detestable in your eyes?'

His extravagant expressions of passion always terrified Emmeline; but the paroxysm to which he now yielded, alarmed her less than it did Miss Lawson, who never having seen such frantic behaviour before, thought him really mad. She tremblingly besought him to sit down and be calm; while the pale countenance of Emmeline which she shewed him, convinced him he must subdue the violence of his transports, or hazard seeing her relapse into that alarming state which had forced him to relinquish his project. This observation restored his senses for a moment. — He besought her pardon, with tears; then again cursed his own folly, and seemed on the point of renouncing the contrition he had just assured her he felt. The scene lasted till Emmeline, quite overcome with it, grew so faint that she said she must go to bed; and then Delamere, again terrified at an idea which he had forgot but the moment before, consented to retire if she would again repeat her forgiveness.

She gave him her hand languidly, and in silence. He kissed it; and half in resentment, half in sorrow, left her, and returned to the inn, in a humour which equally unfitted him for society or solitude. Obliged, however, to remain in the latter, he brooded gloomily over his disappointment; and believing Emmeline's life no longer in danger, he fancied that his fears had magnified her illness. He again deprecated his folly for having consented to relinquish the prosecution of his journey, and for having agreed to carry her where he feared access to her would be rendered rare and difficult, by the inflexible prudence and watchful friendship of Mrs. Stafford. Sometimes he formed vague projects to deceive her, and carry her again towards Scotland; then relinquished them and formed others. He passed the night however nearly without sleep, and the morning found him still irresolute.

At eight o'clock, he went to the house of Mrs. Champness; and uneasiness was so visible, that Delamere was almost afraid of asking how Miss Mowbray did.

She told him that she had passed a restless and uncomfortable night, and that the conversation he had held the evening before had been the cause of an access of fever quite as high as the first attack; and, that tho' she tried to conquer her weakness, and affected ability to prosecute a journey for which she hourly grew more eager, it was easy to see that she was as unfit for it as ever. Miss Lawson added, that if in a few hours she was not better, she should send to Mr. Lawson to come from Stevenage to see her. This account renewed with extreme violence all the former terrors of Delamere, which a few hours before he had been trying to persuade himself were groundless.

He now reproached himself for his thoughtless cruelty; and Miss Lawson seized this opportunity to exhort him to be more cautious for the future, which he readily and warmly protested he would be. He promised never again to give way to such extravagant transports, and pressed to be admitted to see Emmeline; but Miss Lawson would by no means suffer him to see her 'till she was more recovered from the effects of his frenzy.

In the afternoon, he was allowed to drink tea in Emmeline's room, and expressed his sincere concern for his indiscretion of the evening before. He tried, by shewing a disposition to comply with all her wishes, to obliterate the memory of his former indiscretion. Emmeline was willing to forget the offence, and pardon the offender, on his renewing his promise to take her the next day towards London, on her route into Dorsetshire; if she should be well enough to undertake the journey.

The spirit and fortitude of Emmeline, fatal as they were to his hopes, commanded the respect, esteem, and almost the adoration of Delamere; while her gentleness and kindness oppressed his heart with fondness so extreme, that he was equally undone by the one and the other, and felt that it every hour became more and more impossible for him to live without her.

It was agreed, that as it would be impossible to reach Woodfield from Hertford, without stopping one night on the road, they would proceed thro' London to Staines the first day, and from thence go on early the next to the house of Mrs. Stafford.

After lingering with her as long as he could Delamere took his leave for the evening, determined to observe the promises he had made her, and never again to attempt to obtain her but by her own consent. When he made these resolves, he really intended to adhere to them; and was confirmed in his good resolutions when he the next morning found her ready to trust herself with him, calm, chearful, full of confidence in his promises, and of gentleness and kindness towards him.

Emmeline took an affectionate leave of her amiable acquaintance, Miss Lawson, whose uncommon kindness, on so short a knowledge of her, filled her heart with gratitude. She promised to write to her as soon as she got to Woodfield, and to return the cloaths she had borrowed, to which she secretly purposed adding some present, to testify her sense of the civilities she had received.

Delamere enclosed, in a letter which he sent by Miss Lawson to her father, a bank note, as an acknowledgment of his extraordinary kindness.

They quickly arrived in London; and as Emmeline still remained in the resolution of avoiding a return to Mrs. Ashwood, they changed horses in Piccadilly to go on.

Tho' by going to her former residence she might have escaped a longer continuation, and farther journey, with Delamere, of the impropriety of which she was very sensible; yet she declined it, because she knew that as her adventure might be explained several ways, Mrs. Ashwood and Miss Galton were very likely to put on it the construction least in her favour; and she was very unwilling to be exposed to their questions and comments, till she could, in concert with Mrs. Stafford, and with her advice, give such an account of the affair as would put it out of their power to indulge that malignity of remark at her expence of which she knew they were capable.

She therefore dispatched a servant to Mrs. Ashwood with a note for her cloaths, whom Delamere directed to rejoin them at Staines.

At that place they arrived early in the evening; and Emmeline, to whom Delamere had behaved with the utmost tenderness and respect, bore her journey without suffering any other inconvenience than some remaining languor, which was now more visible in her looks than in her spirits. Charmed with the thoughts of so soon seeing Mrs. Stafford, and feeling all that delight which a consciousness of rectitude inspires, she was more than usually chearful, and conversed with Delamere with all that enchanting frankness and sweetness which made her general conversation so desireable.

CHAPTER VII

AS they had an hour or two on their hands, which Emmeline wished to employ in something that might prevent Delamere from entertaining her on the only subject he was ever willing to talk of when they were together, she desired him to enquire for a book. He went out, and returned with some volumes of novels, which he had borrowed of the landlord's daughter; of which Emmeline read in some a page, and in others a chapter, but found nothing in any, that tempted her to go regularly through the whole.

While she was reading, Delamere, equally unable to occupy himself with any other object whether she was absent or present, sat looking at her over the table which was between them. After some time passed in this manner, their supper was brought in, and common conversation took place while it was passing. When it was removed, Emmeline returned again to the books, and took up one she had not before opened. — It was the second volume of the Sorrows of Werter. She laid it down again with a smile, saying — 'That will not do for me to-night.'

'What is it?' cried Delamere, taking it from her. — 'O, I have read it — and if *you* have, Emmeline, you might have learned the danger of trifling with violent and incurable passions. Tell me — could you ever be reconciled to yourself if you should be the cause of a catastrophe equally fatal?'

Still meaning to turn the conversation, she answered gaily — 'O, I fancy there is very little danger of that — you know the value of your existence too well to throw it inconsiderately away.'

'Do not be too certain of that, Emmeline. Without you, my life is no longer valuable — if indeed it be supportable; and should I ever be in the situation this melancholy tale describes, how do I know that my reason would be strong enough to preserve me from equal rashness. Beware, Miss Mowbray — beware of the consequence of finding an Albert at Woodfield.'

'It is very unlikely I should find *any* lover there. I assure you I desire none; nor have I any other wish than to pass the remainder of the winter tranquilly with my friend.'

'If then you really never wish to encourage another, and if you have any sensibility for the pain I feel from uncertainty, why will you not solemnly engage yourself to me, by a promise which cannot be broken but by mutual consent?'

'Because we are both too young to form such an engagement. — You are not yet quite one and twenty; a time of life in which it is impossible you can be a competent judge of what will make you really happy. I am more than two years younger; but short as has been my knowledge of the world, I have already seen two or three instances of marriages made in consequence of early engagements, which have proved so little fortunate that they have determined me never to try the experiment.

Should you bind yourself by this promise, which you now think would make you easy, and should you hereafter repent it, which I know to be far from improbable, pride, obstinacy, the shame of retracting your opinion, would perhaps concur to prevent your withdrawing it; and I should receive your hand while your heart might be attached to another. The chains which you had yourself put on, in opposition to the wishes of your family, you would, rather than own your error, rivet, tho' your inclination prompted you to break them; and we should then be both miserable. — No, Delamere — let us remain at liberty, and perhaps —'

'It is impossible, Madam!' cried Delamere, suddenly and vehemently interrupting her — 'It is absolutely impossible you could argue thus calmly, if you had any regard for me — Cold — cruel — insensible —unfeeling girl! Oh! fool, fool that I am, to persist in loving a woman without an heart, and to be unable to tear from my soul a passion that serves only to make me perpetually wretched. Cursed be the hour I first indulged it, and cursed the weakness of mind that cannot conquer it!'

This new instance of ungovernable temper, so contrary to the promises he had given her at Hertford, extremely provoked Emmeline, who answered very gravely —

'If you desire, Sir, to divest yourself of this unfortunate passion, the task is already half accomplished. Resolve, then, to conquer it wholly: restore me to that tranquility you have destroyed — vindicate my injured reputation, which your headlong ardour has blemished —give me back to the kindness and protection of your father — and determine to see me no more.'

This spirited and severe answer, immediately convinced Delamere he had gone too far. He had never before seen Emmeline so much piqued, and he hastened to appease her.

'Pardon me! — forgive me, Emmeline! I am not master of myself when I think of losing you! But you, who feel not any portion of the flame that devours me, can coolly argue, while my heart is torn in pieces; and deign not even to make any allowance for the unguarded sallies of unconquerable passion! — the phrenzy of almost hopeless love! Sometimes, when I think your coldness arises from determined and insurmountable indifference — perhaps from dislike — despair and fury possess me. Would you but say that you will live only for me — would you only promise that no future Rochely, none of the people you have seen or may see, shall influence you to forget me — I should, I think, be easier!'

'You have a better opinion of yourself, Mr. Delamere,' answered Emmeline, calmly, 'than to believe it probable. But be that as it may, I have told you that I will neither make or receive any promises of the nature you require. I have already suffered too much from your extravagant passion to put it farther in your power to distress me. But I shall be better able to reassume this conversation to-morrow — tonight I am fatigued; and it is time for us to separate.'

'And will you leave me, then, Emmeline? — leave me too in anger?'

'I am not angry, Mr. Delamere — here is my hand.'

'This hand,' exclaimed he, eagerly grasping it, 'which ought to have been mine! — Now, even now, that you are about to tear yourself from me, it should have been mine for ever! But I have relinquished my prize at the moment I might have secured it; and if I lose it entirely my own folly only will be the cause.'

'These violent transports may terrify me, but shall not alter my determination. Quit my hand, Mr. Delamere,' continued she, struggling to disengage it — 'I will not be detained.'

She rang the bell; and the waiter almost instantly entering, she took a candle and went to the apartment prepared for her: while Delamere, vexed to have commanded himself so little, and to be so unable to adhere to the good resolutions he had made, dared not attempt to prevent her.

He had now again to make his peace, but would not venture to take any steps towards it that night; and he retired to his own room, considering how he might remain near her after she got into Dorsetshire, and dreading the hour of even a temporary separation.

The next morning Emmeline, impatient to be gone, dressed herself early; and just as she was about to go down to hasten their breakfast and departure, she saw, from a window that looked into the yard of the inn, a phaeton and four enter it, remarkable for the profusion of expensive and ill-fancied ornaments with which both the carriage and harness were covered. In it were two gentlemen wrapped in great coats, as the weather was very severe; on whom Emmeline casting a transient glance, discovered that one of them was Elkerton.

She was a good deal alarmed at his arrival: for she had reason to fear, that this man, to whom she had a decided aversion, would see her, and know that she was travelling alone with Delamere. She saw him get out, and give directions for putting up his horses, telling the people who came out to attend him that he should breakfast and stay there some hours.

Since his unfortunate *rencontre* with Delamere at Mrs. Ashwood's, he had almost entirely relinquished the pursuit of Emmeline. He had never been able to shake off the ridicule his vanity had brought upon him, and therefore had forborne to enter the circle where it had happened. He had, however, seen Miss Mowbray once or twice in public, and she had been too generally admired not to interest his pride in keeping up the acquaintance, tho' she treated him always with coldness, and found it difficult to be barely civil. She knew that he was severely mortified by her indifference, and that in matters of scandal and gossiping no old woman could be a greater adept. When therefore personal pique was added to his natural love of anecdote, Emmeline apprehended so much from him, that she determined, if possible, to escape his sight.

To do this, however, was very difficult. She saw him and his companion take possession of a room that had windows looking into the yard through which she must of necessity pass, and where, when the post-chaise drew up, they must see whoever got into it. She wrapped herself up in her cloak, pulled her hat over her eyes, and holding up her handkerchief as if to guard her face from the cold, she passed unobserved to the room where Delamere was waiting breakfast.

The rememberance of his last night's behaviour was in some measure obliterated by the alarm she had felt at the sight of Elkerton. Delamere looked melancholy and dejected. Emmeline speaking to him with her usual sweetness, seemed to have forgotten the offence he had given her, and tried to restore his good humour as if she had been the aggressor: but he continued gloomy and pensive.

They began their breakfast, and conversed on different subjects.

'Did you observe,' said Emmeline, 'the phaeton which drove in just now?'

'No — what was there remarkable about it?'

'Nothing, but that one of the persons it contained was Elkerton, the poor man you made so absurd at Mrs. Ashwood's, when he boasted of knowing you. I hope I shall get away without his seeing me — I should extremely dislike meeting him.'

'Stupid dog! — why should you care whether you meet him or no?'

'Because he must think it so strange that I am here with you.'

'Let him — Of what consequence is it to us what such a puppy thinks? I cannot possibly care about it.'

'But *I* do, Mr. Delamere,' said Emmeline, somewhat gravely. —'You will recollect that I may be very much injured by the scandal such a man may circulate.'

'Well, well, my dear Emmeline — we will set out directly, and you will not meet him. — I will order the chaise.'

He went out for that purpose as soon as their breakfast ended; but a few paces from the door was accosted by Elkerton, who feeling himself in point of figure equal to speak to any man, addressed him with all the confident familiarity of an old acquaintance.

'Sir, your most obedient humble servant.'

'Your servant, Sir,' replied Delamere, brushing by him.

'Sir, I hope you and my Lord and Lady Montreville, have been well since I had last the honour of seeing you?'

'Since you oblige me, Sir, to acknowledge the acquaintance, I must remind you that our last meeting was attended with some circumstances which should make you not very desirous of recollecting it.'

'Oh, dear! very far from not wishing to remember it, I am always pleased with such agreeable badinage from my friends, and some how or other contrive to be even with them. Prithee, dear boy, whither are you going? — perhaps we are travelling the same road?'

'I hope not,' said Delamere, turning from him, and advancing towards the bar.

Elkerton, unabashed, followed him.

'If we are,' continued he, 'I think you shall take me into your post-chaise. I am going to pass a month with a friend in Hampshire; and Jackman, who loves driving, tho' he knows nothing of the matter, persuaded me to use an open carriage; but it is so cold, that I believe I shall let him enjoy it alone the rest of the way. Suppose we go together, if your destination is the Winchester road?'

Delamere was so provoked at this forwardness, that he found he should be unable to give a moderate answer. — He therefore turned away without giving any.

'Pray, Sir,' said the bar maid to Elkerton, 'who is that young gentleman?'

'Lord Montreville's son,' replied he; 'and one of the strangest fellows in the world. — Sometimes we are as intimate as brothers; and now you see he'll hardly speak to me.'

'Perhaps, Mr. Elkerton,' said the woman, smiling, 'the young gentleman may have very good reasons for not taking another companion in his post-chaise.'

Elkerton pressed her to explain herself.

'Why you must know,' said she, 'that there's a young lady with him; one of the prettiest young women I ever see. Last night, after they comed here, his walet was pretty near tipsey; so he come and sot down here, and told me how his master had hired him to go along with 'em to Scotland; but that before they got near half way, somehow or other 'twas settled for 'em to come back again. But don't say as I told you, Mr. Elkerton, for that would be as much as my place is worth.'

This intelligence awakened all the curiosity of Elkerton, together with some hopes of being able to revenge himself on Delamere for his contempt and rudeness.

'Egad!' cried he, 'I'll have a peep at this beauty, however.'

So saying, he strutted across the yard, and placed himself under the little piazza which made a covered communication between the rooms of the inn which were built round the yard, and along which they were obliged to pass to get into the chaise.

The room door opened — Delamere and Emmeline appeared at it.

'Draw up, postillions, as close as you can,' cried the waiter.

Delamere, holding Emmeline's hand, advanced; but on seeing Elkerton, she stepped back into the room.

'Come, come,' said Delamere — 'never concern yourself about that impertinent fellow.'

Elkerton, tho' he did not distinctly hear this speech, had caught a view of the person to whom it was addressed; and tho' her face was concealed, her height and air convinced him it was Miss Mowbray.

'How do you, Madam?' exclaimed he, bowing and advancing —'Miss Mowbray, I hope I have the happiness of seeing you well.'

'We are in haste, Sir,' said Delamere, leading Emmeline towards the chaise.

'Nay, my good friend,' returned Elkerton, 'allow me I beg to pay my respects to this lady, with whom I have the honour of being acquainted — Miss Mowbray, permit me —'

He would have taken the hand which was disengaged; but Emmeline shrunk from him, and stepped quickly into the chaise.

Elkerton still advanced, and leaning almost into it, he said — 'Your long journey, I hope, has not too much fatigued you.'

'By heaven!' exclaimed Delamere, 'this is too much! Sir, you are the most troublesome, insolent fool, I ever met with!'

So saying, he seized Elkerton by the collar, and twisting him suddenly round, threw him with great violence against one of the pillars of the piazza.

He then got into the chaise; and taking out of his pocket two or three cards, on which his address was written, he tossed them out of the window; saying, with a voice that struck terror into the overthrown knight on the ground — 'You know where to hear of me if you have any thing to say.'

The chaise now drove quickly away; while Delamere tried to reassure Emmeline, who was so much terrified by the suddenness of this scuffle, that she had hardly breath to reproach him for his impetuosity. He answered, that he had kept his temper too long with the meddling ideot, and that to have overlooked such impertinence without resentment was not in his nature. He tried to laugh off her apprehensions; and flattered by the anxiety she felt for his safety, all his gaiety and good humour seemed to return.

But Emmeline, extremely hurt to find that Elkerton was informed of the journey she had taken, and vexed that

Delamere had engaged in a quarrel, the event of which, if not personally dangerous to him, could not fail of being prejudicial to her, continued very low and uneasy the rest of their journey, reflecting on nothing with pleasure but on her approaching interview with Mrs. Stafford.

But this hoped-for happiness was soon converted into the most poignant uneasiness. On their arrival at Woodfield, Emmeline had the pain of hearing that Mrs. Stafford, who had two days before been delivered of a daughter, had continued dangerously ill ever since. The physicians who attended her had that day given them hopes that her illness might end favourably; but she was still in a situation so precarious that her attendants were in great alarm.

As she had anxiously expected Emmeline, and expressed much astonishment at not having heard from her the week before, which was that on which she had purposed to be with her, and as she still continued earnestly to enquire for news of Miss Mowbray, Mr. Stafford insisted on informing her she was arrived; and this intelligence seemd to give her pleasure. She desired Emmeline might come to her bed-side: but she was so weak, that she could only in a faint voice express her pleasure at the sight of her; and pressing her hand, begged she would not leave her.

It was impossible Emmeline could speak to her on the subject of Delamere, as the least emotion might have been of the most fatal consequence; and tho' she earnestly wished he might not have been invited to stay, she was obliged to let it take its course. She left her friend's room no more that evening; and gave her whole thoughts and attention to keeping her quiet and administering her medicines, which Mrs. Stafford seemed pleased to receive from her hands.

Mr. Stafford was one of those unfortunate characters, who having neither perseverance and regularity to fit them for business, or taste and genius for more refined pursuits, seek, in every casual occurrence or childish amusement, relief against the tedium of life. Tho' married very early, and tho' father of a numerous family, he had thrown away the time and money, which should have provided for them, in collecting baubles, which he had repeatedly possessed and discarded, 'till having exhausted every source that that species of idle folly offered, he had been driven, by the same inability to pursue proper objects, into vices yet more fatal to the repose of his wife, and schemes yet more destructive to the fortune of his family. Married to a woman who was the delight of her friends and the admiration of her acquaintance, surrounded by a lovely and encreasing family, and possessed of every reasonable means of happiness, he dissipated that property, which ought to have secured its continuance, in vague and absurd projects which he neither loved or understood; and his temper growing more irritable in proportion as his difficulties encreased, he sometimes treated his wife with great harshness; and did not seem to think it necessary, even by apparent kindness and attention, to excuse or soften to her his general ill conduct, or his 'battening on the moor' of low and degrading debauchery.

Mrs. Stafford, who had been married to him at fifteen, had long been unconscious of his weakness: and when time and her own excellent understanding pressed the fatal conviction too forcibly upon her, she still, but fruitlessly, attempted to hide from others what she saw too evidently herself.

Fear for the future fate of her children, and regret to find that she had no influence over her husband, together with the knowledge of connections to which she had till a few months before been a stranger, had given to Mrs. Stafford, whose temper was naturally extremely chearful, that air of despondence, and melancholy cast of mind, which Emmeline had remarked with so much concern on their first acquaintance.

To such a man as Mr. Stafford, the arrival of Delamere afforded novelty, and consequently some degree of satisfaction. He took it into his head to be extremely civil to him, and pressed him to continue some time at his house; but Delamere well knew that Emmeline would be made unhappy by his remaining more than one night; as Mr. Stafford entered however so warmly into his interest, he begged of him to recollect whether there was not any house to be let within a few miles of Woodfield.

Mr. Stafford instantly named a hunting seat of Sir Philip Carnaby's, which he said would exactly suit him. Its possessor, whom some disarrangement in his affairs had obliged to go abroad for a few years, had ordered it to be let ready furnished, from year to year.

Delamere went the next morning to the attorney who let it; and making an agreement for it, ordered in all the requisites for his immediate residence; and, till it was ready, accepted Mr. Stafford's invitation to remain at Woodfield.

Emmeline, who confined herself wholly to her friend's apartment, knew nothing of this arrangement 'till it was concluded: and when she heard it, remonstrance and objection were in vain.

The illness of Mrs. Stafford, tho' it did not gain ground, was still very alarming, and called forth, to a painful excess, that lively sympathy which Emmeline felt for those she loved. She continued to attend her with the tenderest assiduity; and after five days painful suspence, had the happiness to find her out of danger, and well enough to hear the relation Emmeline had to make of the involuntary elopement.

Mrs. Stafford advised her immediately to write to Lord Montreville; which her extreme anxiety only had occasioned her so long to delay.

CHAPTER VIII

LORD Montreville and Sir Richard Crofts, after exhausting every mode of enquiry at the end of their journey, without having discovered any traces of the fugitives, returned to London. The uncertainty of what was become of his son, and concern for the fate of Emmeline, made his Lordship more unhappy than he had yet been: and the reception he met with on his return home did not contribute to relieve him; he found that no intelligence had been received of Delamere; and Lady Montreville beset him with complaints and reproaches. The violence of her passions had, for some months, subjected her to fits; and the evasion of her son, and her total ignorance of what was become of him, had kept her in perpetual agony during Lord Montreville's absence. His return after so successless a journey encreased her sufferings, and she was of a temper not to suffer alone, but to inflict on others some part of the pain she felt herself.

Lord Montreville attempted in vain to appease and console her. Nothing but some satisfactory account of Delamere had the least chance of succeeding; and his

Lordship, who now supposed that Delamere and Emmeline were concealed in the neighbourhood of London, determined to persevere in every means of discovering them.

For this purpose he had again recourse to the Crofts'; and Sir Richard and both his sons readily undertook to assist him in his search, and particularly the elder undertook it with the warmest zeal.

This young man inherited all the cunning of his father, together with a coolness of temper which supplied the place of solid understanding and quick parts; since it always gave him time to see where his interest lay, and steadiness to pursue it. By incessant assiduity he had acquired the confidence of Lady Montreville, to whom his attention and attendance were become almost necessary.

Her Ladyship never dreamed that a man of his rank could lift his eyes to either of her daughters, and therefore encouraged his constant attendance on them both; while Crofts was too sensible of the value of such an alliance not to take advantage of the opportunities that were incessantly afforded him.

Lady Montreville had repeatedly declared, that if Delamere married Emmeline all that part of the fortune which she had a right to give away should be the property of her eldest daughter. This was upwards of six thousand pounds a year; and whether this ever happened or not, Crofts knew that what was settled on younger children, which must at all events be divided between the two young ladies, would make either of them a fortune worth all attempts, independent of the connection he would form by it with Lord Montreville, who now began to make a very considerable figure in the political world.

With these views, Crofts had for near two years incessantly applied himself to conciliate the good opinion of the whole family, with so much art that nobody suspected his designs. The slight and contemptuous treatment he had always received from Delamere, he had affected to pass by with the calm magnanimity of a veteran statesman; and emulating the decided conduct and steady indifference of age, rather than yielding to the warmth of temper natural to five and twenty, he was considered as a very rising and promising young man by the grave politicians with whom he associated, and by those of his own age a supercilious and solemn coxcomb.

He had studied the characters of the two Miss Delameres, and found that of the eldest the fittest for his purpose; tho' the person of the youngest, and the pride which encased the heart of the other, would have made a less able politician decide for Augusta. But he saw that the very pride which seemed an impediment to his hopes, might, under proper management, contribute to their success. He saw that she really loved nobody but herself; that her personal vanity was greater than the pride of her rank; and that her heart was certainly on that side assailable. He therefore, by distant hints and sighs, affected concealment; and artful speeches gave her to understand that all his prudence had not been able to defend him from the indiscretion of a hopeless passion.

While he was contented to call it hopeless, Miss Delamere, tho' long partial to Fitz-Edward, could not refuse herself the indulgence of hearing it; and at length grew so accustomed to allow him to talk to her of his unbounded and despairing love, that she found it very disagreeable to be without him.

He saw, that unless a title and great estate crossed his path, his success, tho' it might be slow, was almost certain. But he was obliged to proceed with caution; notwithstanding he would have been very glad to have secured his prize before the return of Delamere to his family threw an obstacle in his way which was the most formidable he had to contend with.

He affected, however, the utmost anxiety to discover him; and recited to Lord Montreville an exhortation he intended to pronounce to him, if he should be fortunate enough to do so.

Nothing could be a greater proof of his Lordship's opinion of Crofts than his entrusting him with a commission, which, if successful, could hardly fail of irritating the fiery and ungovernable temper of Delamere, and driving him into excesses which it would require all the philosophic steadiness of Crofts to support without resentment.

While Sir Richard and his two sons therefore set about the difficult task of finding Delamere, Lord Montreville went himself to Fitz-Edward; but heard that for many days he had not been at his apartments, that he had taken no servants with him, and that they knew not whither he was gone, or when he would return.

Lord Montreville, who had depended more on the information of Fitz-Edward than any other he hoped to obtain, left a note at his lodgings desiring to see him as soon as he came to town, and went back in encreased uneasiness to his own house. But among the numberless letters which lay on his library table, the directions of which he hastily read in a faint hope of news of Delamere, he saw one directed by the hand of Emmeline. He tore it eagerly open — it contained an account of all that had happened, written with such clearness and simplicity as immediately impressed its truth; and it is difficult to say whether Lord Montreville's pleasure at finding his son still unmarried, or his admiration at the greatness of his niece's mind, were the predominant emotion.

When the former sentiment a little subsided, and he had time to reflect on all the heroism of her conduct, he was almost ashamed of the long opposition he had given to his son's passion; and would, if he had not known his wife's prejudices invincible, have acknowledged, that neither the possession of birth or fortune could make any amends to him, who saw and knew how to value the beauty of such a mind as that of Emmeline. The inveterate aversion and insurmountable pride of Lady Montreville, he had no hope of conquering; and she had too much in her power, to suffer his Lordship to think of Delamere's losing such a large portion of his inheritance by disobeying her. For these reasons he checked the inclination he felt rising in his own heart to reward and receive his niece, and thought only of taking advantage of her integrity to separate his son from her for ever.

He went with the letter in his hand to Lady Montreville's apartment, where he found Mr. Crofts and the two young ladies.

He read it to them; and when he had finished it, expressed in the warmest terms his approbation of Miss Mowbray's conduct. Lady Montreville testified nothing but satisfaction at what she called 'the foolish boy's escape from ruin,' without having the generosity to applaud *her*, whose integrity was so much the object of admiration.

Possessing neither candour nor generosity herself, she was incapable of loving those qualities in another; and in answer to Lord Montreville's praises of Emmeline, which she heard with reluctance, she was not ashamed to say, that perhaps were the whole truth known, his Lordship would find but little reason to set up his relation's character higher than that of his own children — to which her eldest daughter added — 'Why, to be sure, Madam, there is, as my father says, something very extraordinary in Miss Mowbray's refusing *such a match* — that is, *if* she has no other attachment.'

Augusta Delamere heard all that her father said in commendation of her beloved Emmeline, with eyes suffused with tears, which drew on her the anger of her mother and the malignant sneers of her sister.

The two young ladies however were sent away, while a council was held between Lord and Lady Montreville and Crofts, on what steps it was immediately necessary to take.

Several ideas were started, but none which his Lordship approved. He determined therefore to write to his son; with whose residence at Tylehurst, the house of Sir Philip Carnaby, Emmeline's letter acquainted him; and wait his answer before he proceeded farther.

With this resolution, Lady Montreville was extremely discontented; and proposed, as the only plan on which they could depend, that his Lordship, under pretence of placing her properly, should send Emmeline to France, and there confine her till Delamere, hopeless of regaining her, should consent to marry Miss Otley.

Her Ladyship urged — 'That it could not possibly do the girl any harm; and that very worthy people had not scrupled to commit much more violent actions where their motive was right, tho' less strong, than that which would in this case actuate Lord Montreville, which was,' she said, 'to save the sole remaining heir of a noble house from a degrading and beggarly alliance.'

'Hold! Madam,' cried Lord Montreville, who was extremely displeased at the proposal, and with the speech with which it closed — 'Remember, I beg of you, that when you speak of the Mowbray family, you speak of one very little if at all inferior to your own; nor should you, Lady Montreville, forget, in the heat of your resentment, that you are a woman — a woman too, whose birth should at least give you a liberal mind, and put you above thinking of an action as unfeminine as inhuman. Surely, as a mother who have daughters of your own, you should have some feeling for this young woman, not at all their inferior, but in being born under circumstances for which she is not to blame, and which mark with sufficient unhappiness a life that might otherwise have done as much honour to my family as I hope your daughters will do to yours.'

The slightest contradiction was what Lady Montreville had never been accustomed to bear patiently. The asperity therefore of this speech, and the total rejection of her project, threw her into an agony of passion which ended in an hysteric fit.

Lord Montreville, less moved than usual, committed her to the care of her daughters and women, and continued to talk coolly to Crofts on the subject they were before discussing.

After considering it in every point of view, he determined to leave Delamere at present to his own reflections; only writing to him a calm and expostulatory letter; such as, together with Emmeline's steadiness, on which he now relied with the utmost confidence, might, he thought, effect more than violent measures. His Lordship wrote also to Emmeline, strongly expressing his admiration and regard, and his confidence and esteem encreased her desire to deserve them.

Mrs. Stafford was now nearly recovered; and Delamere settled at his new house, where he always returned at night, tho' he passed almost every day at Woodfield.

His mornings were often occupied in those amusements of which he had been so fond before his passion for Emmeline became the only business of his life; and secure of seeing her continually, and of telling how he loved her, he became more reasonable than he had hitherto been.

The letters, however, which now arrived from Lord Montreville, a little disturbed his felicity. They gave Emmeline an opportunity to exhort him to return to London — to make his peace with his father, and quiet the uneasiness of Lady Montreville, which his Lordship represented as excessive, and as fatal to *her* health as to the peace of the whole family.

Emmeline urged him by every tie of duty and affection to relieve the anxiety of his family, and particularly to attend to the effect his absence and disobedience had on the constitution of his mother, which had long been extremely shaken. But to all her remonstrances, he answered — 'That he would not return, till Lady Montreville would promise never to renew those reflections and reproaches which had driven him from Audley-Hall; and to which he apprehended he should now be more than ever exposed.'

As Emmeline could not pretend to procure such an engagement from her Ladyship, all she could do was to inform Lord Montreville of his objection, and to leave it to him to make terms between Delamere and his mother.

Near a month had now elapsed since Emmeline's arrival at Woodfield; and the returning serenity of her mind had restored to her countenance all its bloom and brilliancy. She had indeed no other uneasiness than what arose from her anxiety to procure quiet to her Uncle's family, and from her observations on the encreasing melancholy of Mrs. Stafford, for which she knew too well how to account.

Even this, however, often appeared alleviated by her presence, and forgotten in her conversation; and she rejoiced in the power of affording a temporary relief to the sorrows of one whom she so truly loved.

This calm was interrupted by Elkerton, by whom the affront he had received at Staines, from Delamere, had not been forgotten, tho' he by no means relished the thoughts of resenting it in the way his friend Jackman, and all who heard of it, proposed.

To risk his life and all his finery, seemed a most cruel condition; but Jackman protested there was no other by which he could retrieve his honour. And his friend at whose house he was, on the borders of Hampshire, who had been an officer in the military service of the East India Company, and had acquired a princely fortune, felt himself inspired with all the punctilios of a soldier, and declared to Elkerton that if he put up with this affront no man of honour could hereafter speak to him.

Poor Elkerton, who in the article of fighting, as well as many others, extremely resembled *'le Bourgeois Gentilhomme,'* made all the evasions in his power; while his *soi disant* friends, who enjoyed his distress, persisted in pushing him on to demand satisfaction of Delamere; but after long debates, he determined first to ask him for an apology. There was, he thought, some hope of obtaining it; if not, he could only in the last extremity have recourse to the desperate expedient of a challenge. He wrote therefore a letter to Delamere, requesting, in the civilest and mildest terms, an apology for his behaviour at Staines; and sent it by a servant; as it was not more than twenty miles from the house where he was, to that Mr. Delamere had taken.

Delamere returned a contemptuous refusal; but neither mentioned the letter to Emmeline, nor thought again about its writer.

The unfortunate Elkerton, who reproached incessantly his evil stars for having thrown this hot-headed boy in his way, could not conceal from his friends the unaccommodating answer he had received to his pacific overture; and it was agreed that Elkerton must either determine to fight him, or be excluded from good company for ever. The challenge, therefore, penned by the Asiatic hero, was copied with a trembling hand by Elkerton; and Jackman, who had offered to be his second, set out with him for the town near Tylehurst.

On their arrival, Jackman took a post-chaise to carry the billet to Delamere, leaving the terrified Elkerton to settle all his affairs, both temporal and spiritual, against the next morning, when Delamere was appointed to meet him on a heath near the town, at seven o'clock.

Jackman found Delamere with Fitz-Edward, who had arrived there that day. He delivered his letter, and Delamere immediately answered it by saying he would not fail to attend the appointment, with his friend Colonel Fitz-Edward.

During Jackman's absence, Elkerton tried to argue himself into a state of mind fit for the undertaking of the next day. But he found no arguments gave him any sort of satisfaction, save two; one was, that as most disputes ended with firing a brace of pistols in the air, the probability was, that he should be as fortunate as others — the second, that if the worst should happen, he should at least make a paragraph worth some hazard: and that whether he killed Delamere, or fell himself, an affair of honour with a young man of his rank would extremely contribute to his fame.

Neither of these reflections however had force enough to prevent his heartily wishing there was no necessity to employ them; and he contrived to make such a bustle with his servant about his pistols, and sent forth so many enquiries for an able surgeon, that it was known immediately at the inn where he was, that the gentleman was come to fight young Squire Delamere.

In a country town, such intelligence soon gained ground; and before Jackman's return, every shop in it had settled the place and manner of the combat.

One of Mr. Stafford's servants was at the inn, which was also the post house; where the landlady failed not to tell him what a bloody-minded man was in the next room. The servant, who like all people of his station delighted in the wonderful and the terrible, collected all the particulars; which he retailed on his arrival at home, with every exaggeration his invention would lend him.

CHAPTER IX

THE maid who waited on Emmeline had no sooner heard these particulars, than conceiving her to be more interested in the fate of Delamere than any other person, she ran up to tell her of it; and tho' she had not retained the name of Elkerton perfectly, Emmeline, who instantly recollected the adventure at Staines, saw the truth at once; and was terrified at the impending event to a degree that made her for a moment incapable of reflection.

To be, however remotely, or however innocently, the cause of any man's hazarding his life, was shocking to all her feelings. But to suppose that Lord Montreville might be made by her means the most wretched of human beings, by the loss of an only and beloved son, was an idea which froze her blood.

Her regard for Delamere, which was the affection of a sister somewhat heightened perhaps by his persevering preference of herself, her friendship for Augusta, and her anxiety for the peace of his whole family, added to her general tenderness of heart, all cooperated to distress her on this occasion. As soon as she could recollect what was best to be done, she sought Mr. Stafford, to whom she related what she had heard, which the servant who had brought the intelligence repeated before him.

Mr. Stafford, at Emmeline's earnest request, set out for the house of Delamere, who had not that day been at Woodfield because he expected Fitz-Edward. Mr. Stafford delivered to him a pressing entreaty from Emmeline that he would forbear to meet Elkerton, or at least delay it 'till she could speak to him; but Delamere shewing Stafford the letter he had received, desired him to go back and make Emmeline easy as well as he could since to comply with her request was entirely out of his power. To the necessity of his meeting Elkerton, Stafford assented; and returned home to relate the little success of his embassy, while the terror and alarm of Emmeline were only encreased by his visit.

Such was her anxiety, that she would have gone herself to Tylehurst, if Mrs. Stafford had not represented to her that it would be certainly improper, and probably ineffectual.

She passed a sleepless night, tormenting herself with a thousand imaginary modes of misery which might arise from the meeting of the next day. But while she continued to form and reject projects for preventing it, seven o'clock passed, and the *rencontre* ended without bloodshed; the cautious valour of Elkerton having been So loud, that a magistrate who lived in the town, and who was well known to Lord Montreville, had heard of it, and, with a party of constables, had followed Elkerton at some distance. They concealed themselves, by the justice's order, in a gravel-pit near the place of combat, and there saw the ground already possessed by Delamere and Fitz-Edward.

The trembling challenger, with a face as pale as if Delamere's pistol had already done its worst, followed by Jackman, on whose undaunted countenance he cast a rueful and imploring look, then rode slowly up, punctual to the time.

The usual ceremonies passed, Elkerton's blood seemed to be all gone to his heart, to encourage it to be stout; and his knees, which trembled most piteously, appeared to resent the desertion. He cast round the heath a hopeless look — no succour approached! The ground was measured; each took their post; and his trembling encreased so violently, that Delamere apprehended very little from a pistol in so unsteady a hand. But had he apprehended more, he was of a temper to receive it, unshrinkingly. The moment to fire now arrived; and Elkerton, while cocking his pistol, saw the *posse* rise out of the gravel-pit; but he was too far gone to be sensible of the seasonable relief; therefore, without knowing what he was about, he fired his pistol before they could seize his arm, and then stood like a statue, nearly insensible of the happiness of his deliverance.

The justice advancing himself on horseback, now put both the gentlemen under arrest: and Elkerton seeing himself at length safe for the present, thought he might venture to insist on standing Mr. Delamere's fire. The more the worthy justice opposed it, the more vehement he grew: but Delamere, who despised him too much to be really angry with him, went off the field, telling Elkerton that any other time, when there were fewer witnesses, he would give him what further satisfaction he might require. He gave his honour to the justice that he would trouble himself no farther about the affair; and Elkerton having given Jackman's bail for his present pacific intentions, was suffered to go also.

He returned to the house of his East Indian friend, exulting secretly in his escape, and openly in his valour, to which latter Jackman did not bear testimony so warmly as he thought friendship required. Determined, however, to lose no part of the glory which he thought he had dearly purchased by being frightened out of his wits, he wrote, in the form of a letter, a most tremendous account of the duel to the daily papers, in which he described all its imaginary horrors, and ended with asserting very roundly, that 'Mr. Elkerton had the misfortune dangerously to wound the Hon. Frederic Delamere; and, when this account came away, there were no hopes of his recovery.'

Having secured himself a fame, at least, for two or three days, he set out for London to enjoy it; never reflecting on any other consequences than those most flattering to his ridiculous vanity. He knew he should be talked of; and by representing what had *not* happened, have a fair opportunity of telling what *had*, in his own way.

When Emmeline, who had never ceased walking about and listening, saw Delamere and Fitz-Edward riding quietly across the lawn which led to the house, she ran eagerly down to meet them; but the idea that Elkerton might possibly be killed checked her joy; and when they came up to her, breathless agitation prevented her asking what she wanted to know. Delamere, who saw her so pale and terrified, threw himself instantly off his horse and caught her in his arms.

'Has no harm happened, Mr. Delamere?'

'None in the world, my Emmeline. Nobody is hurt so much as you are; tho' poor Elkerton was almost as much frightened. Come, pray compose yourself — you have not yet the glory to boast of having a life lost about you.'

'Heaven forbid that I ever should!' answered she — 'I am grateful that there has been no mischief! — Oh! if I could describe what I have suffered, surely you would never terrify me so again.'

She could not restrain her tears. Delamere led her into the house; where, while Mrs. Stafford gave her hartshorn and water, Delamere, at her request, related exactly what had happened: and having given Emmeline his honour that he would think no more of the affair if Elkerton did not, the tranquility of the house seemed to be restored, and Delamere and Fitz-Edward were invited to dinner; where great alteration in the looks of the latter, was remarked by both the ladies. Nor was it in looks only that Fitz-Edward was extremely changed. —His chearfulness was quite gone; he appeared to be ineffectually struggling with some unconquerable uneasiness; and tho' his soft and insinuating manners were the same, he no longer sought, by a thousand agreeable sallies and lively anecdotes, to entertain; or whatever attempt he made was so evidently forced, that it lost its success. Remarkable for his temperance at table, for which he had often endured the ridicule of his companions, he now seemed to fly to the bottle, against his inclination, as if in hopes to procure himself a temporary supply of spirits.

Every day after that on which Emmeline and Mrs. Stafford made this remark, its justice was more evident.

While Delamere was in the fields, Fitz-Edward would sit whole mornings with Mrs. Stafford and Emmeline, leaning on their worktable, or looking over Emmeline, busied with her pencil. Had his marked attention to Mrs. Stafford continued, she would have seen his behaviour with great alarm; but he no longer paid her those oblique yet expressive compliments of which he used to be so lavish. It seemed, as if occupied by some other object, he still admired and revered her, and wished to make her the confidant of the sorrow that oppressed him. If they were accidentally alone, he appeared on the point of telling her;

then suddenly checking himself, he changed the discourse, or abruptly left her; and as he was a man whom it was impossible to know without receiving some impressions in his favour, she felt, as well as Emmeline, a pity for him, which they wished to be justified in feeling, by hearing that whatever was the cause of his unhappiness, he had not brought it on himself by any crime that would make their regard for him blameable. — For Emmeline, tho' she knew that it was with no good design he had contributed to Lord Montreville's getting her off, yet could not persuade herself to hate him for it, when he not only humbly solicited her forgiveness, but protested that he was truly rejoiced, as well as astonished at her steadiness and good conduct; and would be so far from encouraging any such attempt for the future, that he would be the first to call Delamere to an account, could he suppose he harboured intentions which he now considered as ungenerous and criminal.

These declarations had made his peace both with Emmeline and her friend; and his languid and sentimental conversation, tho' it made him less entertaining, did not make him less interesting to either of them.

Mr. Stafford, ever in pursuit of some wild scheme, was now gone for a few days into another county, to make himself acquainted with the process of manuring land with old wigs — a mode of agriculture on which Mr. Headly had lately written a treatise so convincing, that Mr. Stafford was determined to adopt it on his own farm as soon as a sufficient number of wigs could be procured for the purpose.

During this absence, and on the fourth day after Elkerton's exploit, a stormy morning had driven Delamere from the fields; who went into Mrs. Stafford's dressing-room, where he found Fitz-Edward reading Cecilia to Mrs. Stafford and Miss Mowbray while they sat at work.

Mrs. Stafford had her two little boys at her feet; and when Delamere appeared, she desired him to take a chair quietly, and not disturb so sober a party. But he had not been seated five minutes, before the children, who were extremely fond of him, crept to him, and he began to play with them and to make such a noise, that Mrs. Stafford laughingly threatened to send all the riotous boys into the nursery together — when at that moment Millefleur, who had some time before come down to attend his master, entered the room with a letter which he said came express from Berkley-square.

Delamere saw that his father's hand had almost illegibly directed it. He opened it in fearful haste, and read these words —

'Before this meets you, your mother will probably be no more. A paragraph in the newspaper, in which you are said to have been killed in a duel, threw her into convulsions. I satisfied myself of your safety by seeing the man with whom you fought, but your mother is incapable of hearing it. Unhappy boy! if you would see her alive, come away instantly.

MONTREVILLE.'

Berkley-square, Feb 29.

It is impossible to say whether the consternation of Emmeline or that of Delamere was the greatest. By the dreadful idea of having occasioned his mother's death, every other was for a moment absorbed. He flew without speaking down stairs, and into the stable where he had left his horse; but the groom had carried the horse to his own stables, supposing his master would stay 'till night. Without recollecting that he might take one of Mr. Stafford's, he ran back into the room where Emmeline was weeping in the arms of her friend, and clasping her wildly to his bosom, he exclaimed — 'Farewell, Emmeline! Farewell, perhaps, for ever! If I lose my mother I shall never forgive *myself;* and shall be a wretch unworthy of *you.* Dearest Mrs. Stafford! take care I beseech you of her, whatever becomes of me.'

Having said this, he ran away again without his hat, and darted across the lawn towards his own house, meaning to go thither on foot; but Fitz-Edward, with more presence of mind, was directing two of Mr. Stafford's horses to be saddled, with which he soon overtook Delamere; and proceeding together to the town, they got into a post-chaise, and went as expeditiously as four horses could take them, towards London.

Equally impetuous in all his feelings, his grief at the supposed misfortune was as violent as it could have been had he been sure that the worst had already happened. He now remembered, with infinite self-reproach, how much uneasiness and distress he had occasioned to Lady Montreville since he left her in November at Audley-Hall without taking leave — and recollecting all her tenderness and affection for him from the earliest dawn of his memory; her solicitude in his sickness, when she had attended him herself and given up her rest and health to contribute to his; her partial fondness, which saw merit even in his errors; her perpetual and ardent anxiety for what she believed would secure his happiness — he set in opposition to it his own neglect, impatience, and disobedience; and called himself an unnatural and ungrateful monster.

Fitz-Edward could hardly restrain his extravagant ravings during the journey; which having performed as expeditiously as possible, they arrived in Berkley-square; where, when the porter opened the door to them, Delamere had not courage to ask how his mother did; but on Fitz-Edward's enquiry, the porter told them she was alive, and not worse.

Relieved by this account, Delamere sent to his father to know if he might wait upon him.

His Lordship answered — 'That he would only see Colonel Fitz-Edward; but that Delamere might come in, to wait 'till his mother's physicians arrived.'

Lord Montreville was indeed so irritated against Delamere by all the trouble and anxiety he had suffered on his account, that he determined to shew his resentment; and in this resolution he was encouraged by Sir Richard Crofts, who represented to him that his mother's danger, and his father's displeasure, might together work upon his mind, and induce him to renounce an attachment which occasioned to them both so much unhappiness.

It was in this hope that his Lordship refused to see his son; and while Fitz-Edward went to him, Delamere was shewn into another room, where his youngest sister immediately came to him.

She received him with rapture mingled with tears; and related to him the nature of his mother's illness, which had seized her two days before, on her unfortunately taking up a newspaper from the breakfast-table, where it was very confidently said that he was mortally wounded in a duel with a person named Elkerton, of Portland-Place. That Lord Montreville had luckily had a letter from Fitz-Edward the day before, (whom he had forgiven the part he took in regard to Emmeline on no other condition than that he should go down to him, and give his Lordship an account of his conduct) and that therefore he was less alarmed, tho' very much hurried by the paragraph.

He had, however, gone to Elkerton's house, where he found him very composedly receiving the enquiries of his friends, and where he insisted on hearing exactly what had happened.

His Lordship immediately returned to his wife; but the convulsions had arisen to so alarming an height, that she was no longer capable of hearing him; and she had ever since continued to have, at very short intervals, such dreadful fits, as had entirely contracted her left side, and left very little hope of her recovery.

Delamere was extremely shocked at this account; and after waiting some time, Fitz-Edward came to him, and told him that his father was extremely angry, and absolutely refused to see him or hear his apology, unless he would first give his honour that if Lady Montreville should survive the illness his indiscreet rashness had brought upon her, he would, as soon as she was out of danger, go abroad, and remain there till he should obtain forgiveness for his past errors and leave to return.

The heart of Delamere was accessible only by the avenues of affection and kindness; compulsion and threats only made him more resolutely persist in any favourite project. Sir Richard Crofts therefore, who had advised this measure, shewed but little knowledge of his temper, and never was more mistaken in his politics.

Delamere no sooner heard the message, than he knew with whom it originated; and full of indignation at finding his father governed by a man for whom he felt only aversion and contempt, he answered, with great asperity — 'That he came thither not to solicit any favour, but to see his mother. That he would not be dictated to by the Crofts; but would remain in town 'till he knew whether his mother desired to see him; and be ready to wait on his father when he would vouchsafe to treat him as his son.'

He then shook hands with Fitz-Edward, kissed his sister, and walked out of the house, in spite of their united endeavours to detain him. All they could obtain of him was his consent to go to Fitz-Edward's lodgings, as he had none of his own ready; from whence he sent constantly every hour to enquire after Lady Montreville.

CHAPTER X

EMMELINE, in the mean time, remained in great uneasiness at Woodfield. Delamere, on his first arrival in town, wrote a short and confused note; by which she only learned that Lady Montreville was alive. After some days she received the following letter from Augusta Delamere.

'I will now try, my dearest Emmeline, to give you an account of what has passed here since my brother's arrival.

'My mother is happily better; knows every body, and speaks more distinctly; her fits return less frequently; and upon the whole, the physicians give us hopes of her recovery, but very little that she will ever be restored to the use of the arm which is contracted.

'On Friday, in an interval of her fits, Sir Hugh Cathcart and Dr. Gardner, her physicians, proposed that she should see my brother, of whose being living nothing we could any of us say could convince her. She repeated to Dr. Gardner, who staid with her after the other went, that she was deceived.

'He assured her that she was deceived in nothing but in her sudden and unhappy prepossession; for that Mr. Delamere had never been in the least danger, and was actually in perfect health.

' 'He is alive!' ' cried my mother, mournfully — 'I thank God he is alive; but he knows my illness, and I do not see him — Ah! it is too certain I have lost my son!' '

' 'You have not been able to see him, my dear madam; but he came up as soon as he heard of your situation, and now waits your commands at Colonel Fitz-Edward's lodgings. — Do you wish to see him?' '

' 'I do! I do wish to see him! — Oh! let him come!' '

'The agitation of her mind, however, brought on almost instantly a return of the disorder; and before my brother's arrival, she was insensible.

'Her distorted features; her hands contracted, her eyes glazed and fixed, her livid complexion, and the agonizing expression of her countenance, were at their height when Delamere was desired to go into the room: my father believed that the sight of his mother in such a situation could not but affect the feelings of her son.

'It did indeed affect him! He stood a moment looking at her in silent terror; then, as if suddenly recollecting that he had been the cause of this dreadful alteration, he turned away, clasped his hand% together, and burst into tears.

'My mother neither saw him or heard his loud sobs. My sister looked at him reproachfully; and apparently to escape from her, he came to me, and taking my hand, kissed it, and asked how long this melancholy scene would last?

'The physician, who heard the question, said the fit was going off. It did so in a few minutes. She sighed deeply; and seeing the doctor still sitting by her, she asked if he would still perform his promise, and let her see her son?

‘At these words, Delamere stepped forward, and threw himself on his knees by the bed side. He wept aloud; and eagerly kissed his mother’s hands, which he bathed in tears.

‘She looked at him with an expression to which no description can do justice; but unable to speak, she seemed struggling to explain herself; and the physician, fearful of such agitation, said — ‘ ‘There, madam, is Mr. Delamere; not only alive, but willing, I am persuaded, to give you, in regard to his future conduct, any assurances that you require to tranquillise your mind.’ ’

‘ ‘No!’ ’ said she, sighing — ‘ ‘that Delamere is living, I thank heaven! — but for the rest — I have no hopes.’ ’

‘At this moment my Lord entered — ‘ ‘You see, Sir,’ ’ said he sternly to Delamere, whom he had not seen since his arrival in London — ‘ ‘you see to what extremity your madness has reduced your mother.’ ’

‘Delamere, still on his knees, looked sorrowfully up, as if to enquire what reparation he could make?

‘My father, appearing to understand the question, said — ‘ ‘If you would not be indeed a parricide, shew Lady Montreville that you have a sense of your errors, and will give her no farther uneasiness.’ ’

‘ ‘Do, Frederic,’ ’ cried my sister.

‘ ‘In what way, Sir?’ ’ said my brother, very mournfully.

‘ ‘Tell her you will consent to fulfil all her wishes.’ ’

‘ ‘Sir,’ ’ said Delamere firmly, ‘ ‘if to sacrifice my own life would restore my mother’s, I would not hesitate; but if what your Lordship means relates to Miss Otley, it is absolutely out of my power.’ ’

‘ ‘He is already married, I doubt not,’ ’ sighed my mother.

‘ ‘Upon my soul I am not.’ ’

‘ ‘Come, come,’ ’ cried Dr. Gardner, ‘ ‘this is going a great deal too far; your Ladyship is but just convinced your son is living, and my Lord here is already talking of other matters. Tell me, madam — what do you wish Mr. Delamere to say?' '

' 'That he will not marry,' ' eagerly interrupted my father, ' 'but with his mother's consent and mine.' '

' 'I will not, my Lord,' ' said Delamere, sighing.

' 'That as soon as Lady Montreville is well enough to allow you to leave her, you will go abroad for a twelvemonth or longer if I shall judge it expedient.' '

' 'I will promise *that,* if your Lordship makes a point of it — if my mother insists upon it. — But, my Lord, if at the end of that time Emmeline Mowbray is still single — my Lord, you do not expect unconditional submission — I shall then in my turn hope that you and my mother will make no farther opposition to my wishes.' '

'My father, who expected no concession from Delamere, had at first asked of him more than he intended to insist on, and now appeared eager to close with the first terms he could obtain. Accepting therefore a delay, instead of renunciation, he said — ' 'Well, Delamere, if at the end of a twelvemonth you still insist on marrying Miss Mowbray, I will not oppose it. Lady Montreville, you hear what your son engages for; do you agree to the terms?' '

'My mother said, very faintly — ' 'Yes.' '

'The promise was repeated on both sides before the physician and Fitz-Edward, who came in at the latter part of this scene. My mother seemed reluctantly to accede; complained of extreme faintness; and the scene beginning to grow fatiguing to her, my brother offered to retire. She gave him her hand, which he kissed, and at her desire consented to return to the apartments here which he used to occupy. My mother had that evening another attack; tho' it was much less severe. But as the contraction does not give way to any remedies yet used, the physicians propose sending her to Bath as soon as she is able to bear the journey.

'Thus, my dearest Emmeline, I have punctually related all you appear so anxious to know, on which I leave you to reflect. My mother now sees my brother every day; but he has desired that nothing may be said of the past; and their conversations are short and melancholy. Fitz-Edward has left London; and Frederic told me, last night, that as soon as the physicians pronounce my mother entirely out of danger, he shall go down to you. Ah! my lovely friend! what a trial will his be! But I know *you* will encourage and support him in the task, however painful, of fulfilling the promise he has given; and my father, who praises you incessantly, says he is *sure* of it.

Adieu! my dear Miss Mowbray!
your affectionate and attached,
AUGUSTA DELAMERE.'

Berkley-square, March 3.

A few days after the receipt of this letter, Delamere went down to Tylehurst. Dejection was visibly marked in his air and countenance; and all that Emmeline could say to strengthen his resolution, served only to make him feel greater reluctance. To quit her for twelve months, to leave her exposed to the solicitation of rivals who would not fail to surround her, and to hazard losing her for ever, seemed so terrible to his imagination, that the nearer the period of his promised departure grew, the more impossible he thought it to depart.

His ardent imagination seemed to be employed only in figuring the variety of circumstances which might in that interval arise to separate them for ever; and he magnified these possibilities, till he persuaded himself that nothing but a private marriage could secure her. As he saw how anxious she was that he should strictly adhere to the promises he had given his father, he thought that he might induce her to consent to this expedient, as the only one by which he could reconcile his duty and his love. He therefore took an opportunity, when he had by the bitterness of his complaints softened her into tears, to entreat, to implore her to consent to marry him before he went. He urged, that as Lord and Lady Montreville had both consented to their union at the end of the year, if he remained in the same mind, it made in fact no difference to *them;* because he was very sure that his inclinations would not change, and no doubt *could* arise but from herself. If therefore she determined then to be his, she might as well consent to become so immediately as to hazard the difficulties which might arise to their marriage hereafter.

Emmeline, tho' extremely affected by his sorrow, had still resolution enough to treat this argument as feeble sophistry, unworthy of him and of herself; and positively to refuse her consent to an engagement which militated against all her assurances to Lord Montreville.

This decisive rejection of a plan, to which, from the tender pity she testified, he believed he should persuade her to assent, threw him into one of those transports of agonizing passion which he could neither conceal or contend with. He wept; he raved like a madman. He swore he would return to his father and revoke his promise; and the endeavours of Mrs. Stafford and Emmeline to calm his mind seemed only to encrease the emotions with which it was torn.

After having exhausted every mode of persuasion in vain, he was obliged to relinquish the hope of a secret marriage, and to attempt to obtain another concession, in which he at length succeeded. He told Emmeline, that if she had no wish to quit him entirely, but really meant to reward his long and ardent affection, she could not object to bind herself to become his wife immediately on his return to England.

Emmeline made every objection she could to this request. But she only objected; for she saw him so hurt, that she had not the resolution to wound him anew by a positive refusal. Mrs. Stafford too, moved by his grief and despair, no longer supported her in her reserve; and as *their* steadiness seemed to give way *his* eagerness and importunity encreased, till they allowed him to draw up a promise in these words — 'At the end of the term prescribed by Lord Montreville, Emmeline Mowbray hereby promises to become the wife of Frederic Delamere.'

This, Emmeline signed with a reluctant and trembling hand; for tho' she had an habitual friendship and affection for Delamere, and preferred him to all the men she had yet seen, she thought this not strictly right; and felt a pain and repugnance to its performance, which made her more unhappy the longer she reflected on it.

On Delamere, however, it had a contrary effect. Tho' he still continued greatly depressed at the thoughts of their approaching separation, he yet assumed some degree of courage to bear it: and when the day arrived, he bid her adieu without relapsing into those agonies he had suffered before at the mere idea of it.

He carried with him a miniature picture of her, and entreated her to answer his letters; which, on the footing they now were, she could not refuse to promise. He then tore himself from her, and went to take leave of his mother, who still continued ill at Bath; and from thence to London, to bid farewel to his father; after which, Fitz-Edward accompanied him as far as Harwich, where he embarked for Holland.

As he had before been the usual tour of France and Italy, he purposed passing the summer in visiting Germany, and the winter at Vienna; and early in the spring to set out thro' France on his way home, where he purposed being on the 20th of March, when the year which he had promised his father to pass abroad would expire.

Lord Montreville, by obtaining this delay thought there was every probability that his attachment to Emmeline would be conquered. And his Lordship, as well as Lady Montreville, determined to try in the interval to procure for Emmeline some unexceptionable marriage which it would not be possible for her to refuse. They imagined, therefore, that their uneasiness on this head was over: and Lady Montreville, whose mind was greatly relieved by the persuasion, was long since out of all danger from the fits which had so severely attacked her; but the contraction of her joints which they had occasioned, was still so painful and obstinate, that the physicians seemed to apprehend it might be necessary to send her Ladyship to the waters of Barege.

In the mean time, Lord Montreville had obtained a post in administration which encreased his income and his power. Sir Richard Crofts possessed a lucrative employment in the same department; and his eldest son was become extremely necessary, from his assiduity and attention to business, and more than ever a favourite with all Lord Montreville's family, with whom he almost entirely lived.

A lurking *penchant* for Fitz-Edward, which had grown up from her earliest recollection almost insensibly in the bosom of Miss Delamere, had been long chilled by his evident neglect and indifference: she now fancied she hated him, and really preferred Crofts, every way inferior as he was.

While the want of high birth and title, which she had been taught to consider as absolutely requisite to happiness, made her repress every tendency to a serious engagement, she was extremely gratified by his flattery; and when among other young women (from whom he affected not to be able to stifle his unhappy passion,) she was frequently told how much he was in love with her, she was accustomed to answer — 'Ah! poor fellow; so he is, and I heartily pity him.'

But while Lord and Lady Montreville thought Crofts's attendance on their daughters quite without consequence, he and his father insinuated an intended connection between him and one of them, with so much art, that tho' it never reached the ears of the family it was universally believed in the world.

A young nobleman who had passed the greater part of his life in the army, where he had lately signalized himself by his bravery and conduct, now returned to England on being promoted to a regiment; and having some business to transact with Lord Montreville in his official capacity, he was invited to the house, and greatly admired both the Miss Delameres, whose parties he now joined at Bath.

Crofts soon afterwards obtaining a short respite from his political engagement, went thither also; and tho' Miss Delamere really thought Lord Westhaven quite unexceptionable, she had been so habituated to behave particularly to Crofts, that she could not now alter it, or perhaps was not conscious of the familiar footing on which she allowed him to be with her.

Lord Westhaven, who had at first hesitated between the sprightly dignity of the elder sister, and the soft and more bewitching graces of the younger, no sooner saw the conduct of Miss Delamere towards Crofts, than his doubts were at an end. Her faults of temper had been hitherto concealed from him, and he believed her heart as good as her sister's; indeed, according to the sentimental turn her discourse frequently took, he might have supposed it more refined and sublime. But when he observed her behaviour to Crofts, he thought that she must either be secretly engaged to him, or be a decided coquet. Turning therefore all his attention to Augusta, he soon found that her temper was as truly good as her person was interesting, and that the too great timidity of her manner was solely owing to her being continually checked by her mother's partiality to her sister.

A very short study of her character convinced him she was exactly the woman calculated to make him happy. He told her so; and found her by no means averse to his making the same declaration to her father and mother.

Lord Montreville received it with pleasure; and preliminaries were soon settled. In about six weeks, Lord Westhaven and Miss Augusta Delamere were married at Bath, to the infinite satisfaction of all parties except Miss Delamere; who could not be very well pleased with the preference shewn her younger sister by a man whose morals, person, and fortune, were all superior to what even her own high spirit had taught her to expect in a husband.

Crofts, tho' he saw all apprehensions of having Lord Westhaven for a rival were at an end, could not help fearing that so advantageous a match for the younger, might make the elder more unwilling to accept a simple commoner with a fortune greatly inferior.

The removal, however, of Lady Westhaven gave him more frequent opportunities to urge his passion. Lady Montreville was now going to Barege, Bath having been found less serviceable than was at first hoped for; and Delamere was written to to meet her Ladyship and her eldest daughter at Paris, in order to accompany them thither.

Peace having been in the interim established, Lord Westhaven found he should return no more to his regiment, and purposed with his wife to attend Lady Montreville part of the way, and then to go into Switzerland, where his mother's family resided, who had been of that country.

Lady Westhaven was extremely gratified by this scheme; not only because she was delighted to wait on her mother, but because she hoped it would help to dissipate a lurking uneasiness which hung over the spirits of her Lord, and which he told her was owing to the uncertain and distressing situation of a beloved sister. But whenever the subject was mentioned, he expressed so much unhappiness, that his wife had not yet had resolution to enquire into the nature of her misfortunes, and only knew in general that she was unfortunately married.

CHAPTER XI

EMMELINE had now lost her lover, at least for some time; and one of her friends too was gone where she could seldom hear of her. These deprivations attached her more closely than ever to Mrs. Stafford. Mr. Stafford was gone to town; and except now and then a short and melancholy visit from Fitz-Edward, to whom Delamere had lent his house at Tylehurst, they saw nobody; for all the neighbouring families were in London. They found not only society but happiness together enough to compensate for almost every other; and passed their time in a way particularly adapted to the taste of both.

Adjoining to the estate where Mrs. Stafford resided, a tract of forest land, formerly a chase and now the property of a collegiate body, deeply indents the arable ground beyond it, and fringes the feet of the green downs which rise above it. This part of the country is called Woodbury Forest; and the deep shade of the beech trees with which it is covered, is broken by wild and uncultured glens; where, among the broom, hawthorn and birch of the waste, a few scattered cottages have been built upon sufferance by the poor for the convenience of fewel, so amply afforded by the surrounding woods. These humble and obscure cabbins are known only to the sportsman and the woodcutter; for no road whatever leads through the forest: and only such romantic wanderers as Mrs. Stafford and Emmeline, were conscious of the beautiful walks which might be found among these natural shrubberies and solitary shades. The two friends were enjoying the softness of a beautiful April morning in these woods, when, in passing near one of the cottages, they saw, at a low casement half obscured by the pendant trees, a person sitting, whose dress and air seemed very unlike those of the usual inhabitants of such a place. She was intent on a paper, over which she leaned in a melancholy posture; but on seeing the two ladies approach, she started up and immediately disappeared.

Tho' the distance at which they saw her, and the obscurity of the window, prevented their distinguishing the features of the stranger, they saw that she was young, and they fancied she was beautiful. The same idea instantly occurred to Mrs. Stafford and Emmeline; that it was some unfortunate young woman, whom Mr. Stafford had met with and had concealed there. Something of the same sort had happened once before, and Mrs. Stafford's anxiety and curiosity were both awakened by this incident. Tho' the latter was a passion she never indulged where its object was the business of others, she could not repress it where it was excited by suspicion of a circumstance which so nearly concerned herself.

Nor could she conceal from Emmeline her fears on this occasion; and Emmeline, tho' unwilling to encrease them, yet knew enough of her husband's conduct to believe they were too well founded.

Mrs. Stafford had been accustomed to buy poultry of the woman who lived at this cottage, and therefore went in, in hopes of finding some vestige of the person they had seen, which might lead to an enquiry. But they found nothing but the usual humble furniture and few conveniences of such an house; and Mrs. Stafford forbore to enquire, lest the person she had seen might be alarmed and take more effectual means of concealment. But unable to rest, and growing every moment more desirous to know the truth, and to know it before her husband, whom she expected in a few days, returned, she arose very early the next morning, and, accompanied by Emmeline, went to the cottage in the forest.

The man who inhabited it was already gone out to his work, and the woman to a neighbouring town to buy necessaries for her family. The door was open; and the ladies received this intelligence from three little children who were playing before it.

They entered the low, smoky room, usually inhabited by the family. And Mrs. Stafford, with a beating heart, determining to be satisfied, opened a door which led from it, into that, at the window of which she knew the stranger had appeared; and which the people of the house dignified with the appellation of their parlour.

In this room, on the brick floor, and surrounded by bare walls, stood a bed, which seemed to have been brought thither for the accommodation of some person who had not been accustomed to such an apartment.

Mrs. Stafford saw, sleeping in it, a very young woman, pale, but extremely beautiful; and her hand, of uncommon delicacy, lay on the white quilt — A sight, which gave her pain for herself, and pity for the unfortunate person before her, affected her so much, that having stood a moment in astonishment, she stepped back to the place where Emmeline sat, and burst into tears.

The noise, however trifling, brought from above stairs a person evidently a lady's maid, of very creditable appearance, who came down hastily into the room where Mrs. Stafford and Emmeline were, saying, as she descended the stairs — 'I am coming immediately, my Lady.' But at the sight of two strangers, she stopped in great confusion; and at the same moment her mistress called to her.

She hastened, without speaking, to attend the summons; and shut the door after her. After remaining a few moments, she came out again, and asked Mrs. Stafford if she wanted the woman of the house?

To which Mrs. Stafford, determined whatever it cost her to know the truth, said — 'No — my business is with your lady.'

The woman now appeared more confused than before; and said, hesitatingly — 'I — I — my lady — I fancy you are mistaken, madam.'

'Go in, however, and let your mistress know that Mrs. Stafford desires to speak to her.'

The maid reluctantly and hesitatingly went in, and after staying some time, came back.

'My mistress, Madam, says she has not the pleasure of knowing you; and being ill, and in bed, she hopes you will excuse her if she desires you will acquaint her with your business by me.'

'No,' replied Mrs. Stafford, 'I must see her myself. Tell her my business is of consequence to us both, and that I will wait till it is convenient to her to speak to me.'

With this message the maid went back, with looks of great consternation, to her mistress. They fancied they heard somebody sigh and weep extremely. The maid came out once or twice and carried back water and hartshorn.

At length, after waiting near half an hour, the door opened, and the stranger appeared, leaning on the arm of her woman. She wore a long, white muslin morning gown, and a large muslin cap almost concealed her face; her dark hair seemed to escape from under it, to form a decided contrast to the extreme whiteness of her skin; and her long eye lashes hid her eyes, which were cast down, and which bore the marks of recent tears. If it were possible to personify languor and dejection, it could not be done more expressively than by representing her form, her air, her complexion, and the mournful cast of her very beautiful countenance.

She slowly approached Mrs. Stafford, lifted up her melancholy eyes to Emmeline, and attempted to speak.

'I am at a loss to know, ladies,' said she, 'what can be your' — But unable to finish the sentence, she sat down, and seemed ready to faint. The maid held her smelling bottle for her.

'I waited on you, Madam,' said Mrs. Stafford, 'supposing you were acquainted — too well acquainted — with my name and business.'

'No, upon my honour,' said the young person, 'I cannot even guess.'

'You are very young,' said Mrs. Stafford, 'and, I fear, very unfortunate. Be assured I wish not either to reproach or insult you; but only to try if you cannot be prevailed upon to quit a manner of life, which surely, to a person of your appearance, must be dreadful.'

'It is indeed dreadful!' sighed the young woman — 'nor is it the least dreadful part of it that I am exposed to this.'

She now fell into an agony of tears; which affected both Mrs. Stafford and Emmeline so much, that forgetting their fears and suspicions, they both endeavoured tenderly to console her. Having in some measure succeeded, and Mrs. Stafford having summoned resolution to tell her what were her apprehensions, the stranger saw that to give her a simple detail of her real situation was the only method she had to satisfy her doubts, and to secure her compassion and secresy; for which reason she determined to do it; and Mrs. Stafford, whose countenance was all ingenuousness as well as her heart, assured her she should never repent her confidence; while Emmeline, whose looks and voice were equally soothing and engaging to the unhappy, expressed the tenderest interest in the fate of a young creature who seemed but little older than herself, and to have been thrown from a very different sphere into her present obscure and uncomfortable manner of life.

The stranger would have attempted to relate her history to them immediately; but her maid, a steady woman of three or four and thirty, told her that she was certainly unable then, and begged the ladies not to insist upon it till the evening, or the next day; adding — 'My Lady has been very poorly indeed all this week, and is continually fainting away; and you see, ladies, how much she has been frightened this morning, and I am sure she will not be able to go through it.'

To the probability of this observation, the two friends assented; and the young lady naming the next morning to gratify their curiosity, they left her, Mrs. Stafford first offering her any thing her house afforded. To which she replied, that at present she was tolerably well supplied, and only conjured them to observe the strictest secresy, without which, she said, she was undone.

At the appointed time they returned; equally eager to hear, and, if possible, to relieve, the sorrows of this young person, for whom they could not help being interested, tho' they yet knew not how far she deserved their pity.

She had prepared her own little room as well as it would admit of to receive them, and sat waiting their arrival with some degree of composure. They contemplated with concern the ruins of eminent beauty even in early youth, and saw an expression of helpless sorrow and incurable unhappiness, which had greatly injured the original lustre and beauty of her eyes and countenance. A heavy languor hung on her whole frame. She tried to smile; but it was a smile of anguish; and their looks seemed to distress and pain her. Mrs. Stafford and Emmeline, to relieve her, took out their work; and when they were seated at it, she hesitated — then sighed and hesitated again — and at length seemed to enter on her story with desperate and painful resolution, as if to get quickly and at once thro' a task which, however necessary, was extremely distressing. She began in a low and plaintive voice; and frequently stopped to summon courage to continue, while she wiped away the tears that slowly fell from her eyes.

'I cannot believe I shall ever repent the confidence I am about to place in you. My heart assures me I shall not. Perhaps I may find that pity I dare no longer solicit from my own family; perhaps — but I must hasten to tell you my melancholy story, before its recollection again overwhelms me. Yet my fate has nothing in it very singular; numbers have been victims of the same calamity, but some have been more easily forgiven than I shall be. — Some are better able to bear infamy, and be reconciled to disgrace.

'My father, the late Earl of Westhaven, during the life of my grandfather, married, while he was making the tour of Europe, a very beautiful and amiable woman, the daughter of a man of rank in Switzerland; who having lost his life in the French service, had left a family without any provision, except for the eldest son. My grandfather, extremely disobliged by this marriage, made a will by which he gave to his only daughter every part of his extensive property, except what was entailed, and which went with the title; with this reserve, that his grandson should claim and inherit the whole, whenever he became Lord Westhaven. By this will, he disinherited my father for his life; and tho' he survived my father's marriage five years, and knew he had three children, the two younger of whom must be inevitably impoverished by such a disposition, he obstinately refused to alter the will he made under the first impulse of resentment, and died before his son could prevail upon him, by means of their general friends, to withdraw the maledictions with which he had loaded him.

'His death, not only hurt my father in his feelings, but irreparably in his fortune. His sister, who was married to a Scottish nobleman, took possession of estates to the amount of fifteen thousand a year; and all that remained to my father, to support his rank and his encreasing family, was little more than three thousand; and even that income he had considerably diminished, by taking up money, which he was obliged to do while my grandfather lived, for the actual maintenance of his family.

'These unhappy circumstances, while they injured the health and spirits of my father, diminished not his tenderness for his wife, whom he loved with unabated passion.

'To retrench as much as possible, he retired with her and his three children to an estate, which being attached to the title, belonged to him in Cumberland; in hopes of being able to live on the income he had left, and to clear off the burden with which he had been compelled to load his paternal estates. But a slow fever, the effect of sorrow, had seized on my mother, then far advanced in her pregnancy with me; my father, solicitous to save her in whom all his happiness was centred, sent to London for the best advice to attend her. But their assistance was vain; the fever encreased upon her, and she died three weeks after my birth, leaving my father deprived of every thing that could make life valuable in his estimation. He gave himself up to a despair equal to the violence of his love, and would probably have fallen a victim to it, had not the servants sent to Mr. Thirston, who had been his tutor, and for whom he had the greatest friendship and respect. This excellent man represented to him that it was his duty to live for the children of his deplored Adelina; and he consented to try to live.

'It was long before he could bear to see any of us; particularly me, whom he beheld with a mixture of tenderness and regret. The gloomy solitude in which he lived, where every object reminded him of her whose smiles had rendered it a paradise, was ill calculated to meliorate his affliction; but he could not be persuaded, for some months, to leave it, or could he be diverted from going every evening to visit the spot where lay the relicts of his Adelina.

'At length Mr. Thirston prevailed on him to go abroad. But he could not determine to leave my elder brother, then about five years old, of whom he was passionately fond. They embarked for Naples; and he remained abroad five years; while my sister, my brother William, and myself, were left at Kensington, under the care of a female relation, and received such instruction as our ages admitted.

'My father returned to England only to place his eldest son at Eton. Finding no relief from the sorrow which perpetually preyed on him, but in continual change of place, he soon afterwards went again abroad, and wandered over Europe for almost seven years longer, returning once or twice to England in that interval to satisfy himself of our health and the progress of our education.

'When he last returned, my elder brother, then near eighteen, desired to be allowed to go into the army. My father reluctantly consented; and the regiment into which he purchased was soon after ordered abroad. The grief the departure of his son gave him, was somewhat relieved by seeing his elder daughter advantageously disposed of in marriage to the eldest son of an Irish peer. The beauty of Lady Camilla was so conspicuous, and her manners so charming, that though entirely without fortune, the family of her husband could not object to the marriage. She went to Ireland with her Lord; and it was long before I saw her again.

'My brother William, who had always been designed for the navy, left me also for a three years station in the Mediterranean; and I was now always alone with my governess and my old relation, whose temper, soured by disappointment and not naturally chearful, made her a very unpleasant companion for a girl of fourteen. I learned, from masters who attended me from London, all the usual accomplishments; but of the world I knew nothing, and impatiently waited for the time when I should be sixteen; for then the Dutchess of B—, who had kindly undertaken to introduce my sister into company, had promised that she would afford me also her countenance. I remember she smiled, and told me that as I was not less pretty than Lady Camilla, I might probably have as good fortune, if I was but as accomplished. To be accomplished, therefore, I endeavoured with all my power; but the time seemed insupportably long, before this essay was to be made. It was relieved, tho' mournfully, by frequent visits from my father; who was accustomed to sit whole hours looking at me, while his tears bore witness to the great resemblance I had to my mother. My voice too, particularly when we conversed in French, frequently made him start, as if he again heard that which he had never ceased to remember and to regret. He would then fondly press me to his heart, and call me his poor orphan girl, the image of his lost Adelina!

'Tho' my mother had been now dead above fifteen years, his passion for her memory seemed not at all abated. He had, by a long residence abroad, paid off the debts with which he had incumbered his income, but could do no more; and the expences necessary for young men of my brothers' rank pressed hardly upon him. Ever since his return to England, his friends had entreated him to attempt, by marrying a woman of fortune, to repair the deficiency of his own; representing to him, that to provide for the children of his Adelina, would be a better proof of his affection to her memory than indulging a vain and useless regret.

'He had however long escaped from their importunity by objecting, on some pretence or other, to all the great fortunes which were pointed out to him — his heart rejected with abhorrence every idea of a second marriage. But my brothers every day required a larger supply of money to support them as their birth demanded; and to their interest my father at length determined to sacrifice the remainder of a life, which had on his own account no longer any value. The heiress of a rich grocer in the city was soon discovered by his assiduous friends, who was reputed to be possessed of two hundred thousand pounds. On closer enquiry, the sum was found to be very little if at all exaggerated by fame. Miss Jobson, with a tall, meagre person, a countenance bordering on the horrible, and armed with two round black eyes which she fancied beautiful, had seen her fortieth year pass, while she attended on her papa, in Leadenhall-street, or was dragged by two sleek coach horses to and from Hornsey. Rich as her father was, he would not part with any thing while he lived; and, by the assistance of two maiden sisters, had so guarded his daughter from the dangerous attacks of Irishmen and younger brothers, that she had reached that mature period without hearing the soothing voice of flattery, to which she was extremely disposed to listen. My father, yet in middle age, and with a person remarkably fine, would have been greatly to her taste if he could have gratified, with a better grace, her love of admiration. But his friends undertook to court her for him; and his title still more successfully pleaded in his favour. She made some objection to his having a family; but as I alone remained at home, she at length agreed to undertake to be at once a mother-in-law and a Countess. While this treaty was going on, and settlements and jewels preparing, I was taken several times to wait on Miss Jobson: but it was easy to see I had not the good fortune to please her.

'I was but just turned of fifteen, was full of gaiety and vivacity, and possessed those personal advantages, which, if *she* ever had any share of them, were long since faded. She seemed conscious that the splendour of her first appearance would be eclipsed by the unadorned simplicity of mine; and she hated me because it was not in my power to be old and ugly. Giddy as I then was, nothing but respect for my father prevented my repaying with ridicule, the supercilious style in which she usually treated me. Her vulgar manners, and awkward atempts to imitate those of people of fashion, excited my perpetual mirth; and as her dislike of me daily encreased, I am afraid I did not always conceal the contempt I felt in return. Miss Jobson chose to pass some time at Tunbridge previous to her marriage. Thither my father followed her; and I went with him, eager to make my first appearance in public, and to see whether the prophecies of the Duchess would be fulfilled.

'This experiment was made in a party from Tunbridge to Lewes Races where I had the delight of dancing for the first time in public, and of seeing the high and old fashioned little head of Miss Jobson, who affected to do something which she thought was dancing also, almost at the end of the set, while I, as an Earl's daughter, was nearly at the top. Had I been ever accustomed to appear in public, these distinctions would have been too familiar to have given me any pleasure; but now they were enchanting; and, added to the universal admiration I excited, intoxicated me with vanity. My partner, who had been introduced to me by a man of high rank the moment I entered the room, was a gentleman from the West of England, who was just of age, and entered into the possession of a fortune of eight thousand a year.

'Mr. Trelawny (for that was his name) followed us to Tunbridge, and frequently danced with me afterwards. Educated in obscurity, and without any prospect of the fortune to which he succeeded by a series of improbable events, this young man had suddenly emerged into life. He was tolerably handsome; but had a heavy, unmeaning countenance, and was quite unformed. Several men of fashion, however, were kind enough to undertake to initiate him into a good style of living; and for every thing that bore the name of fashion and ton, he seemed to have a violent attachment. To that, I owed his unfortunate prepossession in my favour. — I was admired and followed by men whom he had been taught to consider as the arbiters of elegance, and supreme judges of beauty and fashion; but they could only admire — they could not afford to marry an indigent woman of quality; and they told Trelawny that they envied him the power of pleasing himself. — So Trelawny was talked to about me, till he believed he was in love. In this persuasion he procured a statement of his fortune to be shewn to my father, by one of his friends, and made an offer to lay it at my feet; an offer which, tho' my father would have been extremely glad to have me accept, he answered by referring Mr. Trelawny to me.

'I suspected no such thing; but with the thoughtless inattention of sixteen, remembered little of the fine things which were said to me by Trelawny at the last ball. While I was busied in inventing a new *chapeau* for the next, at which I intended to do more than usual execution, my father introduced Mr. Trelawny, and left the room. I concluded he was come to engage me for the evening, and felt disposed to refuse him out of pure coquetry; when, with an infinite number of blushes, and after several efforts, he made me in due form an offer of his heart and fortune. I had never thought of any thing so serious as matrimony; and indeed was but just out of the nursery, where I had never been told it was necessary to think at all. I did not very well know what to say to my admirer; and after the first speech, which I believe he had learned by heart, he knew almost as little what to say to me; and he was not sorry when I, in a great fright, referred him to my father, merely because I knew not myself what answer to give him. Our conversation ended, and he went to find my father, while I, for the first time in my life, began to reflect on my prospects, and to consider whether I preferred marrying Mr. Trelawny to living with Miss Jobson. To Miss Jobson, I had a decided aversion; for Mr. Trelawny, I felt neither love or hatred. My mind was not made up on the subject, when my father came to me: he had seen Trelawny, and expressed himself greatly pleased with the prudence and propriety of my answer.

' 'My Adelina knows,' continued he, 'that the happiness of my children is the only wish I have on earth; and I may tell her, too, that my solicitude for her exceeds all my other cares — solicitude, which will be at an end if I can see her in the protection of a man of honour and fortune. If therefore, my love, you really do not disapprove this young man, whose fortune is splendid, and of whose character I have received the most favourable accounts, I shall have a weight removed from my mind, and enjoy all the tranquility I can hope for on this side of the grave.

' 'You know how soon I am to marry Miss Jobson. A mother-in-law is seldom beloved. I may die, and leave you unprovided for; for you know, Adelina, the circumstances into which your grandfather's will has thrown me. Our dear Charles, whenever he inherits my title, will repossess the fortune of my ancestors, and will, I am sure, act generously by you and William; but such a dependance, if not precarious, is painful; and by accepting the proposal of Mr. Trelawny, all my apprehensions will be at an end, and my Adelina secure of that affluence to which her merit as well as her birth entitles her. But powerful as these considerations are, let them not influence you if you feel any reluctance to the match. Were they infinitely stronger, I will never again name them, if in doing so I hazard persuading my daughter to a step which may render her for ever unhappy.' '

'Tho' I was very far from feeling for Mr. Trelawny that decided preference which would in other circumstances have induced me to accept his hand, yet I found my father so desirous of my being settled, that as I had no aversion to the man, I could not resolve to disappoint him. Perhaps the prospect of escaping from the power of my mother-in-law, and of being mistress of an affluent fortune instead of living in mortifying dependance on her, might have too much influence on my heart. My father, however, obtained without any difficulty my consent to close with Mr. Trelawny's proposals. We all went to London, where Lord Westhaven married Miss Jobson, and the settlements were preparing by which Mr. Trelawny secured to me a jointure as great as I could have expected if my fortune had been equal to my rank.

'As the new Lady Westhaven was so soon to be relieved from the presence of a daughter she did not love, she behaved to me with tolerable civility. Occupied with her rank, she seemed to have infinite delight in displaying it to her city acquaintance. Her Ladyship thought a coronet so delightful an ornament, that the meanest utensils in her house were adorned with it; and she wore it woven or worked on all her cloaths, in the vain hope perhaps of counteracting the repelling effect of an hideous countenance, a discordant voice, and a manner more vulgar than either. I saw with concern that my father was not consoled by the possession of her great fortune, for the mortification of having given the name and place of his adored Adelina to a woman so unlike her in mind and person. He was seldom well; seldomer at home; and seemed to have no other delight than in hearing from his two sons and from his eldest daughter; and when we were alone, he told me that to see me married would also give him pleasure; but he appeared, I thought, less anxious for the match than when it was first proposed. The preparations, however, went on, and in six weeks were compleated.

'In that interval, I had seen Trelawny almost every day. He always seemed very good humoured, and was certainly very thoughtless. He loved me, or fancied he loved me, extremely; but I sometimes suspected that it was rather in compliance with the taste of others than his own; and that a favourite hunter or a famous pointer were very likely to rival me. My father sometimes laughed at his boyish fondness for such things, and the importance he annexed to them; and sometimes I thought he looked grave and hurt at observing it.

'For my own part, I saw his follies; but none that I did not equally perceive in the conduct of other young men. Tho' I had no absolute partiality to him, I was totally indifferent to every other man. I married him, therefore; and gave away my person before I knew I had an heart.

'We went immediately into Cornwall, to an old fashioned but magnificent family seat; where I was received by Mr. Trelawny's sister, a woman some years older than he was, and who had brought him up. The coarse conversation of this woman, which consisted entirely of details of family economy; and the stupidity of her husband and a booby son of fourteen, were but ill calculated to render my retirement pleasing. Having laughed and wondered once at the uncouth figures and obsolete notions of Mr. Trelawny's Cornish cousins, who hastened, in their best cloaths, to congratulate him, from places whose barbarous names I could not pronounce —and having twice entertained the voters of two boroughs which belonged to the family; I had exhausted all the delights of Cornwall, and prevailed on him to return to a country where I could see a few beings like myself.

'When I came back into the world, I was surrounded by a croud of idle people, whose admiration flattered the vanity of Trelawny more than it did mine; for I became accustomed to adulation, and it lost its charms with its novelty. Trelawny was continually with young men of fashion, who called themselves his friends; and who besides doing him the kindness to advise and instruct him in the disposal of his fortune, would have relieved him from the affections of his wife, if he had ever possessed them. They made love to *me,* with as little scruple as they borrowed money of *him;* and told me that neglect on the part of my husband, well deserved to be repaid with infidelity on mine: but I felt for these shallow libertines only disgust and contempt; and received their professions with so much coldness, that they left me, in search of some other giddy creature, who might not, by ill-timed prudery, belie the promise of early coquetry. It was yet however very much the fashion to admire me; and my husband seemed still to take some delight in hearing and reading in the daily papers that Lady Adelina Trelawny was the most elegant figure at Court, or that every beauty at the Opera was eclipsed on *her* entrance. The eagerness and avidity with which I had entered, from the confinement of the nursery, to a life of continual dissipation, was now considerably abated. I continued it from habit, and because I knew not how to employ my time otherwise; but I felt a dreary vacuity in my heart; and amid splendour and admiration was unhappy.

'The return of my elder brother from his first campaign in America, was the only real pleasure I had long felt. He is perhaps one of the most elegant and accomplished young men of his time; but to be elegant and accomplished is his least praise — His solid understanding, and his excellent heart, are an honour to his country and to human nature. That quick sense of humour, and that strictness of principle, which now make my greatest terror, give a peculiar lustre and dignity to his character. My father received him with that delight a father only can feel; and saw and gloried with all a father's pride, in a successor worthy of his ancestors.

'My brother, who had always loved me extremely, tho' we had been very little together, took up his abode at my house while he staid in England. Trelawny seemed to feel a sort of awe before him, which made him endeavour to hide his vices if not his weakness, while he remained with us. He was more attentive to me than he had long been. My brother hoped I was happy; and tho' Trelawny was a man whose conversation afforded him no pleasure, he behaved to him with every appearance of friendship and regard. He was soon however to return to his regiment; and my father, who had been in a declining state of health ever since his second marriage, appeared to grow worse as the period of separation approached. He seemed to have waited only for this beloved son to close his eyes; for a few days before he was again to take leave, my father found his end very rapidly approaching.

'Perfectly conscious of it, he settled all his affairs; and made a provision for me and my brother William out of the money of the present Lady Westhaven, which the marriage articles gave him a right to dispose of after her Ladyship's death if he left no children by her; and recommended us both to his eldest son.

' 'You will act nobly by our dear William,' said he; 'I have no doubt of it; but above all, remember my poor Adelina. Camilla is happily married. Tell her I die blessing her, and her children! But Adelina — my unfortunate Adelina is herself but a child, and her husband is very young and thoughtless. Watch over her honour and her repose, for the sake of your father and that dear woman she so much resembles, your sainted mother.' '

'I was in the room, in an agony of sorrow. He called me to him. ' 'My daughter,' said he, in a feeble voice, 'remember that the honour of your family — of your brothers — is in your hands — and remember it is sacred. — Endeavour to deserve the happiness of being sister to such brothers, and daughter to such a mother as yours was!'

'I was unable to answer. I could only kiss his convulsed hands; which I eagerly did, as if to tell him that I promised all he expected of me. My own heart, which then made the vow, now perpetually reproaches me with having kept it so ill!

'A few hours afterwards, my father died. My brother, unable to announce to me the melancholy tidings, took my hand in silence, and led me out of the house, which was now Lady Westhaven's. He had only a few days to stay in England, which he employed in paying the last mournful duties to his father; and then embarked again for America, leaving his affairs to be settled by my sister's husband, Lord Clancarryl, to whom he wrote to come over from Ireland; for my brother William was now stationed in the West Indies, where he obtained the command of a man of war; and my brother Westhaven knew, that to leave any material business to Trelawny, was to leave it to ignorance and imbecility.

'In my husband, I had neither a friend or a companion — I had not even a protector; for except when he was under the restraint of my brother's presence, he was hardly ever at home. Sometimes he was gone on tours to distant counties to attend races or hunts, to which he belonged; and sometimes to France, where he was embarked in gaming associations with Englishmen who lived only to disgrace their name. Left to pass my life as the wife of such a man as Trelawny, I felt my brother's departure as the deprivation of all I loved. But the arrival of my sister and her husband relieved me. I had not seen them for some years; and was delighted to meet my sister happy with a man so worthy and respectable as Lord Clancarryl.

'He took possession on behalf of my brother of the estate my aunt was now obliged to resign; and as my sister was impatient to return to Ireland, where she had left her children, they pressed me extremely to go thither with them. Trelawny was gone out on one of his rambles; but I wrote to him and obtained his consent — indeed he long since ceased to trouble himself about me.

'I attended my sister therefore to Lough Carryl; on the beautiful banks of which her Lord had built an house, which possessing as much magnificence as was proper to their rank, was yet contrived with an attention to all the comforts of domestic retirement. Here Lady Clancarryl chose to reside the whole year; and my Lord never left it but to attend to business of Parliament at Dublin.

'His tender attention to his wife; his ardent, yet regulated fondness for his children; the peace and order which reigned in his house; the delightful and easy society he sometimes collected in it, and the chearful confidence we enjoyed in quiet family parties when without company; made me feel with bitterness and regret the difference between my sister's lot and mine. *Her* husband made it the whole business of his life to fulfill every duty of his rank, *mine* seemed only solicitous to degrade himself below his. One was improving his fortune by well regulated economy; the other dissipating his among gamesters and pick-pockets. The conversation of Lord Clancarryl was sensible, refined, and improving; Trelawny's consisted either in tiresome details of adventures among jockies, pedigrees of horses, or scandalous and silly anecdotes about persons of whom nobody wished to hear; or he sunk into sullen silence, yawned, and shewed how very little relish he had for any other discourse.

'When I married him, I knew not to what I had condemned myself. As his character gradually discovered itself, my reason also encreased; and now, when I had an opportunity of comparing him to such a man as Lord Clancarryl, I felt all the horrors of my destiny! and beheld, with a dread from which my feeble heart recoiled, a long, long prospect of life before me — without attachment, without friendship, without love.

'I remained two months in Ireland; and heard nothing of Trelawny, 'till a match having been made on the Curragh of Kildare, on which he had a large bet depending, he came over to be present at it; and I heard with regret that I was to return with him. While he remained in Ireland, his disgusting manners, and continual intoxication, extremely displeased Lord Clancarryl; and I lived in perpetual uneasiness. A few days before we were to embark for England, George Fitz-Edward, his Lordship's younger brother, came from the north of Ireland, where he had been with his regiment, to Lough Carryl; but it was only a passing visit to his family — he was going to England, and we were to sail in the same pacquet.'

At the mention of George Fitz-Edward, Lady Adelina grew more distressed than she had yet been in the course of her narrative. Mrs. Stafford and Emmeline testified signs of surprize. She observed it; and asked if they knew him? Mrs. Stafford answered, they had some acquaintance with him; and Emmeline remarked that she either never heard or had forgotten that his father's second title was Clancarryl.

His very name seemed to affect Lady Adelina so much, and she appeared so exhausted by having spoken so long, that tho' she told them she had but little to add to her mournful story, they insisted upon her permitting them to release her till the evening, when they would attend her again.

CHAPTER XII

THEY found Lady Adelina in better spirits in the evening than they had hoped for — She seemed to have been arguing herself into the composure necessary to go on with her story.

'As you have some acquaintance with George Fitz-Edward, I need not describe his person or his manner; nor how decided a contrast they must form with those of such a man as him to whom I was unhappily united. This contrast, in spite of all my endeavours, was perpetually before my eyes — I thought Fitz-Edward, who was agreeable as his brother, had a heart as good; and *my* heart involuntarily made the comparison between what I was, and what I might have been, if my fate had reserved me for Fitz-Edward.

'We embarked — It was about the autumnal equinox; and before we had sailed two leagues, the wind suddenly changing, blew from the opposite quarter, and then from every quarter by turns. As I was always subject to sickness in the cabin, I had lain down on the deck, on a piece of sail-cloth, and wrapped in my *pelisse;* and Fitz-Edward sat by me. But when the wind grew so violent that it was necessary every moment to shift the sails, I, who was totally insensible, was in the way of the sailors. Fitz-Edward carried me down in his arms; and having often heard me express an abhorrence to the close beds in the cabin, by the help of my own maid he accommodated me with one on the floor; where he continued to watch over me, without attending to his own danger, tho' he heard the master of the pacquet express his apprehensions that we should be driven back on the bar, and beat to pieces.

'Trelawny, in whom self-preservation was generally alive, whatever became of his other feelings, had passed so jovial an evening before he departed, that he was perfectly unconscious of his own danger. After struggling some hours to return into the bay, it was with difficulty accomplished about five in the morning. Fitz-Edward, with the tenderest solicitude, saw me safe on shore, whither Trelawny was also brought. But far from being rejoiced at our narrow escape, he cursed his ill luck, which he said had raised this confounded storm only to prevent his returning in time to see Clytemnestra got into proper order for the October meeting.

'I was so ill the next day, thro' the fear and fatigue I had undergone, that I was absolutely unable to go on board. But nothing that related to me could detain Trelawny, who embarked again as soon as the pacquet was refitted, and after some grumbling at my being too ill to go, left me to follow him by the next conveyance, and recommended me with great coolness to the care of Fitz-Edward.

'We staid only two days after him. Fitz-Edward, as well during the passage as on our journey to London, behaved to me with the tenderness of a brother; and I fancied my partiality concealed from him, because I tried to conceal it. If he saw it, he shewed no disposition to take advantage of it, and I therefore thought I might fearlessly indulge it.

'When I arrived at my house in town, I found that Trelawny was absent, and had left a letter for me desiring me to go down to a house he had not long before purchased in Hampshire, as a hunting seat. Without enquiring his reasons, I obeyed him. I took a melancholy leave of Fitz-Edward, and went into Hampshire; where, as Trelawny was not there, I betook myself to my books, and I fear to thinking too much of Fitz-Edward.

'After I had been there about a fortnight, I was surprized by a visit from the object of my indiscreet contemplations. He looked distressed and unhappy; and his first conversation seemed to be preparing me for some ill news. I was dreadfully alarmed, and enquired eagerly for my sister? — her husband? — her children? —

' 'I hope, and believe they are well,' answered he. 'I have letters of a very late date from my brother.' '

' 'Oh God!' cried I, in an agony (for his countenance still assured me something very bad had happened) 'Lord Westhaven — my brother, my dear brother!' '

' 'Is well too, I hope — at least I assure you I know nothing to the contrary.' '

' 'Is it news from Jamaica then? Has there been an engagement? There has, I know, and my brother William is killed.' '

' 'No, upon my honour,' replied Fitz-Edward, 'had Godolphin been killed, I, who love him better than any man breathing, could not have brought the intelligence — But my dear Lady Adelina, are there then no other misfortunes but those which arise from the death of friends?' '

‘ ‘None,’ answered I, ‘but what I could very well bear. Tell me, therefore, I conjure you tell me, and keep me no longer in suspence — I can hear any thing since I have nothing to apprehend for the lives of those I love.’ ’

‘ ‘Well then,’ answered he, ‘I will tell you. — I fear things are very bad with Mr. Trelawny. It is said that all the estate not entailed, is already gone; and that he has even sold his life interest in the rest. All his effects at the town house are seized; and I am afraid the same thing will in a few hours happen here. I came therefore, lovely Lady Adelina, to intreat you to put yourself under my protection, and to quit this house, where it will soon be so improper for you to remain.’

‘I enquired after the unhappy Trelawny? He told me he had left him intoxicated at a gaming house in St. James’s-street; that he had told him he was coming down to me, to which he had consented, tho’ Fitz-Edward said he much doubted whether he knew what he was saying.

‘Fitz-Edward then advised me to pack up every thing I wished to preserve, and immediately to depart; for he feared that persons were already on the road to seize the furniture and effects in execution.

‘ ‘Gracious heaven!’ cried I, ‘what can I do? — Whither can I go!’ ’

‘ ‘Trust yourself with me,’ cried Fitz-Edward — ‘dear, injured Lady Adelina.’ ’

‘ ‘Let me rather,’ answered I, ‘go down to Trelawny Park.’

‘ ‘Alas!’ said he, ‘the same ruin will there overtake you. Be assured Mr. Trelawny’s creditors will equally attach his property there. You know too, that by the sale of his boroughs he has lost his seat in parliament, and that therefore his person will not be safe. He must himself go abroad.’ ’

'Doubting, and uncertain what I ought to do, I could determine on nothing. Fitz-Edward proposed my going to Mr. Percival's, who had married one of his sisters. They are at Bath, said he; but the house and servants are at my disposal, and it is only five and twenty miles from hence. Hardly knowing what I did, I consented to this proposal; and taking my jewels and some valuable plate with me, I set out in a post chaise with Fitz-Edward, leaving my maid to follow me the next day, and give me an account whether our fears were verified.

'They were but too well founded. Four hours after I had left the house, the sheriff's officers entered it — Information which encreased my uneasiness for the fate of the unfortunate Trelawny; in hopes of alleviating whose miseries I would myself have gone to London, but Fitz-Edward would not suffer me. He said it was more than probable that my husband was already in France; that if he was yet in England, he had no house in which to receive me, and would feel more embarrassed than relieved by my presence. But as I continued to express great uneasiness to know what was become of him, he offered to go to London and bring me some certain intelligence.

'At the end of a week, which appeared insupportably long, he returned, and told me that with some difficulty he had discovered my unhappy husband at the house of one of his friends, where he was concealed, and where he had lost at picquet more than half the ready money he could command. That with some difficulty he had convinced him of the danger as well as folly of remaining in such a place; and had accompanied him to Dover, whence he had seen him sail for France.

'I told Fitz-Edward that I would instantly give up as much of my settlement as would enable Trelawny to live in affluence, till his affairs could be arranged; but he protested that he would not suffer me to take any measure of that sort, till I had the advice of *his* brother; or, till one of my own returned to England.

' 'Do you know,' said he, at the end of this conversation — 'Do you know, Lady Adelina, that I envy Trelawny his misfortunes, since they excite such generous pity. — Good God! of what tenderness, of what affection would not such a heart be capable, if' —

'Fitz-Edward had seldom hazarded an observation of this sort, tho' his eyes had told me a thousand times that he internally made them. He could convey into half a sentence more than others could express by the most elaborate speeches. Alas! I listened to him with too much pleasure; for my treacherous heart had already said more than his insidious eloquence.

'I wrote to Lord Clancarryl, entreating him to come over. He assured me he would do so, the moment he could leave my sister, who was very near her time; but that in the interim his brother George would obey all my commands, and render me every service he could himself do if present.

'Thrown, therefore, wholly into the power of Fitz-Edward; loving him but too well; and seeing him every hour busied in serving me — I will not accuse him of art; I had myself too little to hide from him the fatal secret of my heart; I could not summon resolution to fly from him, till my error was irretrievable — till I found myself made compleatly miserable by the consciousness of guilt.

'After remaining there about a fortnight, I left the house of Mr. Percival, and took a small lodging in the neighbourhood of Cavendish-square. Fitz-Edward saw me every day. — I met him indeed with tears and confusion; but if any accident prevented his coming, or if he even absented himself at my own request, the anguish I felt till I again saw him convinced me that it was no longer in my power to live without him.

'Trelawny had given me no directions for my conduct; nor had he even written to me, 'till he had occasion for money. He then desired me to send him five hundred guineas — a sum I had no immediate means of raising, but by selling some of my jewels. This I would have immediately done; but Fitz-Edward, who would not hear of it, brought me the money in a few hours, and undertook to remit it, together with a letter from me, to the unfortunate man for whom it was designed.

'He tried too — ah, how vainly! — to persuade me, that in acting thus I had done more than my duty to such an husband. His sophistry, aided by my own wishes to believe him, could not quiet the incessant reproaches with which my conscience pursued me — I remembered my father's dying injunctions. I remembered the inflexible notions of honour inherited by both my brothers, and I trembled at the severe account to which I might be called. I could now no longer flatter myself that my error would be concealed, since of its consequences I could not doubt; and while I suffered all the terrors of remorse and apprehension, Lord Clancarryl came over.

'In order to take measures towards settling Trelawny's affairs, it was necessary to send for his sister, who had a bond for five thousand pounds, which claim was prior to every other. This woman, whom it was extremely disagreeable to me to meet, lamented with vulgar clamour her brother's misfortunes; which she said could never have happened if he had not been so unlucky as to get quality notions into his head. I know not what at first raised her suspicions; but I saw that she very narrowly observed Fitz-

Edward; and sneeringly said that it was *very lucky* indeed for me to have such a friend, and *quite kind* in the colonel to take so much trouble. She made herself thoroughly acquainted with all that related to her brother, from the time of our parting in Ireland; and I found that she had attempted to bribe my servant to give her an account of my conduct; in which tho' she had failed of success, she had found that Fitz-Edward had been constantly with me. His attendance was indeed less remarkable when Lord Clancarryl, his brother, was also present; but Mrs. Bancraft, determined to believe ill of me, suffered not this circumstance to have any weight, and hinted her suspicions of our attachment in terms so little guarded, that it was with the utmost difficulty I could prevail on Fitz-Edward not to resent her impertinence.

'Lord Clancarryl despised this vulgar and disgusting woman too much to attend to the inuendos he heard; and far from suspecting my unhappy weakness, he continued to lay me under new obligations to Fitz-Edward by employing him almost incessantly in the arrangement of Trelawny's affairs.

'On looking over the will of that relation, who had bequeathed to Mr. Trelawny the great fortune he had possessed, I discovered the reason of Mrs. Bancraft's attentive curiosity in regard to me – if he died without heirs, above six thousand a year was to descend to her son, who was to take the name. He had been now married above two years, and his bloated and unhealthy appearance (the effect of excessive drinking) indicated short life; and had made her for some time look forward to the succession of the entailed estate as an event almost certain for her son. This sufficiently explained her conduct, and encreased all my apprehensions; for I found that avarice would stimulate malice into that continued watchfulness which I could not now undergo without the loss of my fame and my peace.

'All things being settled by Lord Clancarryl in the best manner he could dispose them for Mr. Trelawny, his Lordship pressed me to go with him to Ireland; but conscious that I should carry only disgrace and sorrow into the happy and respectable family of my sister, I refused, under pretence of waiting to hear again from Trelawny before I took any resolution as to my future residence.

'His Lordship therefore left me, having obtained my promise to go over to Lough Carryl in the spring. Fitz-Edward continued to see me almost every day, attempting by the tenderest assiduity to soothe and tranquillize my mind. But time, which alleviates all other evils, only encreased mine; and they were now become almost insupportable.

'After long deliberation, I saw no way to escape the disgrace which was about to overwhelm me, but hiding myself from my own family and from all the world. I determined to keep my retreat secret, even from Fitz-Edward himself; and to punish myself for my fatal attachment by tearing myself for ever from its object. Could I have supported the contempt of the world, to which it was evidently the interest of Mrs. Bancraft to expose me, I could not bear the most distant idea of the danger to which the life of Fitz-Edward would be liable from the resentment of my brothers. That he might perish by the hand of Lord Westhaven or Captain Godolphin, or that one of those dear brothers might fall by his, was a suggestion so horrid, and yet so probable, that it was for ever before me; and I hastened to fly into obscurity, in the hope, that if my error is concealed till I am myself in the grave, my brothers may forgive me, and not attempt to wash out the offence in the blood of the surviving offender.

'To remain, and to die here unknown, is all I now dare to wish for. My servant having formerly known the woman who inhabits this cottage, contrived to have a few necesaries sent hither without observation; I have made it worth the while of the people to be secret; and as they know not my name, I had little apprehension of being discovered.

'I took no leave of Fitz-Edward; nor have I written to him since. I lament the pain my sudden absence must give him; but am determined to see him no more. Should my child live—'

Lady Adelina was now altogether unable to proceed, and fell into an agony of distress which greatly affected her auditors. Mrs. Stafford and Emmeline said every thing they could think of to console her, and soften the horror she seemed to feel for her unhappy indiscretion. But she listened in listless despondence to their discourse, and answered, that to be reconciled to guilt, and habituated to disgrace, was to be sunk in the last abyss of infamy.

They left her not, however, till they saw her rather more tranquil; and till Mrs. Stafford had prevailed upon her to accept of some books, which she hoped might amuse her mind, and detach it awhile from the sad subject of its mournful contemplations. These she promised to convey to the cottage in a way that could create no suspicion. And relieved of her own apprehensions, yet full of concern for the fair unhappy mourner (to whom neither she or Emmeline had given the least intimation of Fitz-Edward's frequent residence in that country,) they returned to Woodfield, impressed with the most earnest solicitude to soften the calamities they had just heard related, tho' to cure them was impossible.

END OF THE SECOND VOLUME

VOLUME III

CHAPTER I

WHENEVER Mrs. Stafford and Emmeline were afterwards alone, they could think and speak of nothing but Lady Adelina. The misfortunes in which an unhappy marriage had involved her, her friendless youth, her lovely figure, the settled sorrow and deep regret that she seemed to feel for the error into which her too great sensibility of heart had betrayed her, engaged their tenderest pity, and made them both anxious to give her all the consolation and assistance she was now capable of receiving.

When they considered the uncertainty of her remaining long concealed where she was, and the probability that Fitz-Edward himself might discover her, they saw the necessity of her removal from Woodbury Forest. But it was a proposal they could not yet make — nor had they yet recollected any place where she might be more secure.

Emmeline, who felt herself particularly interested by her misfortunes, and who was more pleased with her conversation the oftener she conversed with her, seldom failed of seeing her every day: but Mrs. Stafford, more apprehensive of observation, could not so frequently visit her; and the precaution of both redoubled, when Mrs. Ashwood, Miss Galton, and the two Miss Ashwoods, arrived at Woodfield, where they declared an intention of staying the months of June and July.

Thither also, soon after, came the younger Mr. Crofts, who had made an acquaintance with Mr. Stafford in London with the hope of obtaining an invitation, which he eagerly accepted.

Sir Richard Crofts, in the ambition of making a family, had determined to give every advantage to his eldest son, which might authorise him to look up to those alliances that would, he hoped, make his own obscurity forgotten. From the first dawn of his fortune, he had considered Mr. Crofts as its general heir; and had very plainly told his younger son, that a place under government, which he had procured for him, of about three hundred a year, must be his only dependance; till he should possess two thousand pounds, all the provision he intended making for him at his death — as he meant not to diminish, by a more equal division, the patrimony of his brother. He recommended to him therefore to remedy this deficiency of fortune, by looking out for an affluent wife.

Nature had not eminently qualified him for success in such a project; for his person was short, thick, and ill made, and his face composed of large broad features, two dim grey eyes, and a complexion of a dull sallow white. A vain attempt to look like a gentleman, served only to render the means of his figure more remarkable; and the qualities of his heart and understanding were but little calculated to make his personal imperfections forgotten. His heart was selfish, narrow, unfeeling, and at once mean and proud; his understanding beneath mediocrity; and his conversation consisted of quaint scraps of something that he supposed was wit, or at least very like it. And even such attempts to be entertaining, poor as they were, he retailed from the office where he passed the greatest part of his time, and for a subaltern employment in which, his education had been barely such as fitted him. But ignorant as he was, and devoid of every estimable accomplishment, he had an infinite deal of that inferior kind of policy called cunning; and being accustomed to consider his establishment as depending wholly on himself, he had acquired a habit of sacrificing every sentiment and every passion to that one purpose; and would adopt the opinions, and submit to the caprices of others, whenever he thought they could promote it. He had learned the obsequious attention, the indefatigable industry, the humble adulation which is necessary for the under departments of political business: and while such acquisitions gave him hopes of rising in that line, they failed not to contribute to his success in another. He would walk from the extremity of Westminster to Wapping, to smuggle a set of china or of quadrille boxes, for the mother or aunt of an heiress; and would, with great temper, suffer the old ladies to take advantage of him at cards, while he ogled the young ones. Which, together with his being always ready to perform for them petty services, and to flatter them without scruple, had obtained for him the character of 'one of the best creatures breathing.' But whatever favour these various recommendations obtained for him for a time, from the elderly ladies, he lost his ground when his views were discovered; and tho' he had received what he fancied encouragement from two or three young women of fortune on their first emerging from the nursery, yet they had no sooner acquired an handsomer or richer lover, than 'the best creature breathing' was discarded.

He was not however discouraged; and meeting with Mrs. Ashwood at a rout at Lady Montreville's, he was told by Miss Delamere, who was extremely diverted with her airs of elegance, that she was a rich widow who wanted a husband. He enquired into the circumstances of her fortune; and being assured she possessed such an income as would make him easy, he thought some little advantage she had over him in point of age no diminution of her attractions, and found it convenient to fall immediately in love. She listened to him with complaisance; and soon discovered 'that he was not so plain as at first he appeared to be' — soon afterwards, 'that he was rather handsome, and vastly sensible and agreeable.' After which, he made a rapid progress in her heart; and it was concerted between them that he should follow her to Woodfield.

Emmeline and Mrs. Stafford were wearied to death with the party. But the former forbore to complain, and the latter was forced to submit, and to smile, while anguish was frequently at her heart.

Mrs. Ashwood talked of nothing but fashionable parties and fashionable people, to whom her acquaintance with Lord Montreville's family had introduced her; and she now seldom deigned to name an untitled acquaintance — while Crofts hung on her long narratives with affected admiration; and the two elder of her three daughters, who were all in training to be beauties, aped their mother in vanity and impertinence.

The eldest Miss Ashwood, now about fourteen, was an insupportable torment to Emmeline, as she had taken it into her head to form, with her, a sentimental friendship. She had learned all the cant of sentiment from novels; and her mama's lovers had extremely edified her in teaching her to express it. She talked perpetually of delicate embarrassments and exquisite sensibilities, and had probably a lover, as she extremely wanted a confidant; a post which Emmeline with some difficulty declined. — Of 'the sweet novels' she had read, she just understood as much as made her long to become the heroine of such an history herself, and she wanted somebody to listen to her hopes of being so. But Emmeline shrunk from her advances, and repaid her fondness with general and cool civility; tho' Mrs. Ashwood, who loved rather to listen to Crofts than to attend to her daughters, continually promoted the intimacy in hopes that she would take them off her own hands, and allow them to be the companions of her walks.

This, Emmeline was obliged studiously to evade, as such companions would entirely have prevented her seeing Lady Adelina; and by repeated excuses she not only irritated the curiosity of Mrs. Ashwood and Miss Galton, but gave the former an additional cause of dislike to that which she had already conceived; inasmuch as she was younger, handsomer, and more admired than herself.

Emmeline received frequent letters from Delamere, as warm and passionate as his personal professions. He told her, that as his mother's health was greatly amended, he intended soon to visit those parts of France with which he was yet unacquainted; and should pass some time in the Northern Provinces, from whence he entreated her to allow him to come only for a few days to England to see her — an indulgence which he said would enable him to bear with more tranquility the remaining months of his exile.

Tho' now accustomed to consider him as her husband, Emmeline resolutely refused to consent to this breach of his engagement to his father. She had lately seen in her friends, Mrs. Stafford and Lady Adelina, two melancholy instances of the frequent unhappiness of very early marriages; and she had no inclination to hazard her own happiness in hopes of proving an exception. She wished, therefore, rather to delay her union with Delamere two or three years; but to him she never dared hint at such a delay. A clandestine interview it was, however, in her power to decline; and she answered his request by entreating him not to think of such a journey; and represented to him that he could not expect Lord Montreville would finally adhere to his promises, if he himself was careless of fulfilling the conditions on which his Lordship had insisted. Having thus, as she supposed, prevented Delamere from offending his father, and without any immediate uneasiness on her own account, she gave up her mind to the solicitude she could not help feeling for Lady Adelina. This occupied almost all her time when she was alone; and gave her, when in company, an air of absence and reserve.

Tho' Mrs. Ashwood so much encouraged the attention of James Crofts, she had not forgotten Fitz-Edward, whom she had vainly sought at Lady Montreville's, in hopes of renewing an acquaintance which had in its commencement offered her so much satisfaction.

Fitz-Edward had been amused with her absurdity at the moment, but had never thought of her afterwards; nor would he then have bestowed so much time on a woman to him entirely indifferent, had not he been thrown in her way by his desire to befriend Delamere with Emmeline, on one of those days when Lady Adelina insisted on his leaving her, to avoid the appearance of his passing with her all this time. Happy in successful love, his gaiety then knew no bounds; and his agreeable flattery, his lively conversation, his fashionable manners, and his handsome person, had not since been absent from the memory of Mrs. Ashwood. His being sometimes at the house he had borrowed of Delamere, near Woodfield, was one of the principal inducements to her to go thither. She indulged sanguine hopes of securing such a conquest; and evaded giving to Crofts a positive answer, till she had made another essay on the heart of the Colonel.

He came, however, so seldom to Woodfield, that Mrs. Stafford had seen him there only once since her meeting Lady Adelina; and then he appeared to be under encreased dejection, for which she knew now, how to account.

Emmeline had given Mrs. Stafford so indifferent an account of Lady Adelina one evening, that she determined the next morning to see her. She therefore went immediately after breakfast, on pretence of visiting a poor family who had applied to her for assistance; when as Mrs. Ashwood, Miss Galton and Emmeline, were sitting together, Colonel Fitz-Edward was announced.

He came down to Tylehurst only the evening before; and not knowing there was company at Woodfield, rode over to pass an hour with the two friends, to whom he had frequently been tempted to communicate the source of his melancholy.

Whether it was owing to the consciousness of Lady Adelina's mournful story that arose in the mind of Emmeline, or whether seeing Fitz-Edward again in company with Mrs. Ashwood renewed the memory of what had befallen her when they last met, she blushed deeply the moment she beheld him, and arose from her chair confusion; then sat down and took out her work, which she had hastily put up; and trying to recover herself, grew still more confused, and trembled and blushed again.

Mrs. Ashwood was in the mean time overwhelming Fitz-Edward with compliments and kind looks, which he answered with the distant civility of a slight acquaintance; and taking a chair close to Emmeline, enquired if she was not well?

She answered that she was perfectly well; and attempted to introduce general conversation. But Fitz-Edward was attentive only to her; and Mrs. Ashwood, extremely piqued at his distant manner, meditated an excuse to get Emmeline out of the room, in hopes of obtaining more notice.

Fitz-Edward, however, having talked apart with Miss Mowbray a short time, arose and took leave, having by his manner convinced Mrs. Ashwood of what she reluctantly believed, that some later attachment had obliterated the impression she had made at their first interview.

'I never saw such a figure in my life,' cried she, 'as Mr. Fitz-Edward. Mercy on me! — he is grown *so* thin, and *so* sallow!'

'And *so* stupid,' interrupted Miss Galton. 'He is in love I fancy.'

Emmeline blushed again; and Mrs. Ashwood casting a malicious look at her, said — 'Oh! yes — he doubtless is in love. To men of his gay turn you know it makes no difference, whether a person be actually married or *engaged*.'

Emmeline, uncertain of the meaning of this sarcasm, and unwilling to be provoked to make a tart reply, which she felt herself ready to do, put up her work and left the room.

While she went in search of Mrs. Stafford, to enquire after Lady Adelina, and to relate the conversation that had passed between her and Fitz-Edward, Mrs. Ashwood and Miss Galton were indulging their natural malignity. Tho' well apprized of Emmeline's engagement to Delamere, yet they hesitated not to impute her confusion, and Fitz-Edward's behaviour, to a passion between them. They believed, that while her elopement with Delamere had beyond retreat entangled her with him, and while his fortune and future title tempted her to marry him, her heart was in possession of Fitz-Edward; and that Delamere was the dupe of his mistress and his friend.

This idea, which could not have occurred to a woman who was not herself capable of all the perfidy it implied, grew immediately familiar with the imagination of Mrs. Ashwood, and embittered the sense of her own disappointment.

Miss Galton, who hated Emmeline more if possible than Mrs. Ashwood, irritated her suspicions by remarks of her own. She observed 'that it was very extraordinary Miss Mowbray should walk out so early in a morning, and so studiously avoid taking any body with her — and that unless she had appointments to which she desired no witness, it was very singular she should chuse to ramble about by herself.'

From these observations, and her evident confusion on seeing him, they concluded that she had daily assignations with Fitz-Edward. They agreed, that it would be no more than common justice to inform Mr. Delamere of their discovery; and this they determined to do as soon as they had certain proofs to produce, with which they concluded a very little trouble and attention would furnish them.

James Crofts, whose success was now indisputable, since of the handsome Colonel there were no hopes, was let into the secret of their suspicions; and readily undertook to assist in detecting the intrigue, for which he assured them he had particular talents. While, therefore, Mrs. Ashwood, Miss Galton, and James Crofts, were preparing to undermine the peace and character of the innocent ingenuous Emmeline, she and Mrs. Stafford were meditating how to be useful to the unhappy Lady Adelina. They became every day more interested and more apprehensive for the fate of that devoted young woman, whose health seemed to be such as made it very improbable she should survive the birth of her child. Her spirits, too, were so depressed, that they could not prevail on her to think of her own safety, or to allow them to make any overtures to her family; but, in calm and hopeless languor, she seemed resigned to the horrors of her destiny, and determined to die unlamented and unknown.

Her elder brother, Lord Westhaven, had returned from abroad almost immediately after her concealment. His enquiries on his first arrival in England had only informed him of the embarrassment of Trelawny's affairs, and the inconvenience to which his sister had consequently been exposed; and that after staying some time in England, to settle things as well as she could, she had disappeared, and every body believed was gone to her husband. His Lordship's acquaintance and marriage with Augusta Delamere, almost immediately succeeded; but while it was depending, he was astonished to hear from Lord and Lady Clancarryl that Lady Adelina had never written to them before her departure. He went in search of Fitz-Edward; but could never meet him at home or obtain from his servants any direction where to find him. Fitz-Edward, indeed, purposely avoided him, and had left no address at his lodgings in town, or at Tylehurst.

Lord Westhaven then wrote to Trelawny, but obtained no answer; and growing daily more alarmed at the uncertainty he was in about Lady Adelina, he determined to go, as soon as he was married, to

Switzerland; being persuaded that tho' some accident had prevented his receiving her letters, she had found an asylum there, amongst his mother's relations.

Fitz-Edward, with anxiety even more poignant, had sought her with as little success. After the morning when she discharged her lodgings, and left them in an hackney coach with her maid, he could never, with all his unwearied researches, discover any traces of her.

He knew she was not gone to Trelawny; and dreading every thing from her determined sorrow, he passed his whole time between painful and fruitless conjectures, and the tormenting apprehension of hearing of some fatal event. Incessantly reproaching himself for being the betrayer of his trust, and the ruin of a lovely and amiable woman, he gave himself up to regret and despondence. The gay Fitz-Edward, so lately the envy and admiration of the fashionable world, was lost to society, his friends, and himself.

He passed much of his time at Tylehurst; because he could there indulge, without interruption, his melancholy reflections, and only saw Mrs. Stafford and Emmeline, in whose soft and sensible conversation he found a transient alleviation of his sorrow — sorrow which now grew too severe to be longer concealed, and which he resolved to take the earliest opportunity of acknowledging, in hopes of engaging the pity of his fair friends — perhaps their assistance in discovering the unhappy fugitive who caused it.

From Lady Adelina, they had most carefully concealed, that his residence was so near the obscure abode she had chosen. Fatal as he had been to her peace, and conscientiously as she had abstained from naming him after their first conversation, they knew that she still fondly loved him, and that her fears for his safety had assisted her sense of rectitude when she determined to tear herself from him. But were she again to meet him, they feared she would either relapse into her formal fatal affection, or conquer it by an effort, which in her precarious state of health might prove immediately fatal.

The request which Fitz-Edward had made to Emmeline, that he might be allowed to see her and Mrs. Stafford together, without any other person being present, they both wished to evade; dreading least they should by their countenances betray the knowledge they had of his unhappy story, and the interest they took in its catastrophe.

They hoped, therefore, to escape hearing his confession till Lady Adelina should be removed — and to remove her became indispensibly necessary, as Emmeline was convinced she was watched in her visits to the cottage.

Twice she had met James Crofts within half a quarter of a mile of the cottage; and at another time discovered, just as she was about to enter it, that the Miss Ashwoods had followed her almost to the door; which she therefore forbore to enter. These circumstances made both her and Mrs. Stafford solicitous to have Lady Adelina placed in greater security; and, added to Emmeline's uneasiness for her, was the unpleasant situation in which she found herself.

Observed with malicious vigilance by Mrs. Ashwood, James Crofts, Miss Galton, and the two Misses, she felt as awkward as if she really had some secret of her own to hide; and with all the purity and even heroism of virtue, learned the uneasy sensation which ever attends mystery and concealment. The hours which used to pass tranquilly and rationally with Mrs. Stafford, were now dedicated to people whose conversation made her no amends; and if she retired to her own room, it failed not to excite sneers and suspicions. She saw Mrs. Stafford struggling with dejection which she had no power to dissipate or relieve, and obliged to enter into frequent parties of what is called pleasure, tho' to her it gave only fatigue and disgust, to gratify Mrs. Ashwood, who hated all society but a crowd. James Crofts, indeed, helped to keep her in good humour by his excessive adulation; and chiefly by assuring her, that by any man of the least taste, the baby face of Emmeline could be considered only as a foil to her more mature charms, and that her fine dark eyes eclipsed all the eyes in the world. He protested too against Emmeline for affecting knowledge — 'It is,' said he, 'a maxim of my father's — and my father is no bad judge — that for a woman to affect literature is the most horrid of all absurdities; and for a woman to know any thing of business, is detestable!'

Mrs. Ashwood laid by her dictionary, determined for the future to spell her own way without it.

Besides the powerful intervention of flattery, James Crofts had another not less successful method of winning the lady's favour. He told her that his brother, who had long cherished a passion in which he was at length likely to be disappointed, was in that case determined never to marry; that he was in an ill state of health; and if he died without posterity, the estate and title of his father would descend to himself.

The elder Crofts, very desirous of seeing a brother established who might otherwise be burthensome or inconvenient to him, suggested this finesse; and secured its belief by writing frequent and melancholy accounts of his own ill health — an artifice by which he promoted at once his brother's views and his own. He affected the valetudinarian so happily, and complained so much of the ill effect that constant application to business had on his constitution, that nobody doubted of the reality of his sickness. He took care that Miss Delamere should receive an account of it, which he knew she would consider as the consequence of his despairing love; and when he had interested her vanity and of course her compassion, he contrived to obtain leave of absence for three months from the duties of his office, in order to go abroad for the recovery of his health. He hastened to Barege; and soon found means to re-establish himself in the favour of Miss Delamere; from which, absence, and large draughts of flattery dispensed with French adroitness, had a little displaced him. This stratagem put his brother James on so fair a footing with the widow, that he thought her fortune would be secured before she could discover it to be only a stratagem, and that her lover was still likely to continue a younger brother.

James Crofts seeing the necessity of dispatch, became so importunate, that Mrs. Ashwood, despairing of Fitz-Edward, and believing she might not again meet with a man so near a title, for which she had a violent inclination, was prevailed on to promise she would make him happy as soon as she returned to her own house.

It was now the end of June; and Lady Adelina, whose situation grew very critical, had at length yielded to the entreaties of her two friends, and agreed to go wherever they thought she could obtain assistance and concealment in the approaching hour.

Mrs. Stafford and Emmeline, after long and frequent reflections and consultations on the subject, concluded that no situation would be so proper as Bath. In a place resorted to by all sorts of people, less enquiry is excited than in a provincial town, where strangers are objects of curiosity to its idle inhabitants. To Bath, therefore, it was determined Lady Adelina should go. But when the time of her journey, and her arrangements there, came to be discussed, she expressed so much terror least she should be known, so much anguish at leaving those to whose tender pity she was so greatly indebted, and such melancholy conviction that she should not survive, that the sensible heart of Emmeline could not behold without sharing her agonies; nor was Mrs. Stafford less affected. When they returned home after this interview, Emmeline was pursued by the image of the poor unhappy Adelina. But to give, to the wretched, only barren sympathy, was not in her nature, where more effectual relief was in her power. She thought, that if by her presence she could alleviate the anguish, and soothe the sorrows of the fair mourner, perhaps save her character and her life, and be the means of restoring her to her family, she should perform an action gratifying to her own heart, and acceptable to heaven. The more she reflected on it, the more anxious she became to execute it — and she at length named it to Mrs. Stafford.

Mrs. Stafford, tho' aware of the numberless objections which might have been made to such a plan, could not resolve strenuously to oppose it. She felt infinite compassion for Lady Adelina; but could herself do little to assist her, as her time was not her own and her absence must have been accounted for; but Emmeline was liable to no restraint; and would not only be meritoriously employed in befriending the unhappy, but would escape from the society at Woodfield, which became every day more disagreeable to her. These considerations, particularly the benevolent one of saving an unhappy young woman, over-balanced, in the mind of Mrs. Stafford, the objection that might be made to her accompanying a person under the unfortunate and discreditable circumstances of Lady Adelina; and her heart, too expansive to be closed by the cold hand of prudery against the sighs of weakness or misfortune, assured her that she was right. She knew that Emmeline was of a character to pity, but not to imitate, the erroneous conduct of her friend; and she believed that the reputation of Lady Adelina Trelawny might be rescued from reproach, without communicating any part of its blemish to the spotless purity of Emmeline Mowbray.

CHAPTER II

AS soon as Emmeline had persuaded herself of the propriety of this plan and obtained Mrs. Stafford's concurrence, she hinted her intentions to Lady Adelina; who received the intimation with such transports of gratitude and delight, that Emmeline, confirmed in her resolution, no longer suffered a doubt of its propriety to arise; and, with the participation of Mrs. Stafford only, prepared for her journey, which was to take place in ten days.

Mrs. Stafford also employed a person on whom she could rely; to receive the money due to Lady Adelina from her husband's estate. But of this her Ladyship demanded only half, leaving the rest for Trelawny. The attorney in whose hands Trelawny's affairs were placed by Lord Westhaven, was extremely anxious to discover, from the person employed by Mrs. Stafford, from whence he obtained the order signed by Lady Adelina; and obliged him to attend several days before he would pay it, in hopes, by persuasions or artful questions, to draw the secret from him. He met, at the attorney's chambers, an officer who had made of him the same enquiry, and had followed him home, and since frequently importuned him — intelligence, which convinced Mrs. Stafford that Lady Adelina must soon be discovered, (as they concluded the officer was Fitz-Edward,) and made both her and Emmeline hasten the day of her departure.

About a quarter of a mile from Woodfield, and at the extremity of the lawn which surrounded it, was a copse in which the accumulated waters of a trout stream formed a beautiful tho' not extensive piece of water, shaded on every side by a natural wood. Mrs. Stafford, who had particular pleasure in the place, had planted flowering shrubs and caused walks to be cut through it; and on the edge of water built a seat of reeds and thatch, which was furnished with a table and a few garden chairs. Thither Emmeline repaired whenever she could disengage herself from company. Solitude was to her always a luxury; and particularly desirable now, when her anxiety for Lady Adelina, and preparations for their approaching departure, made her wish to avoid the malicious observations of Mrs. Ashwood, the forward intrusion of her daughters, and the inquisitive civilities of James Crofts. She had now only one day to remain at Woodfield, before that fixed for their setting out; and being altogether unwilling to encounter the fatigue of such an engagement so immediately previous to her journey, she declined being of the party to dine at the house of a neighbouring gentleman; who, on the occasion of his son's coming of age, was to give a ball and *fete champètre* to a very large company.

Mrs. Ashwood, seeing Emmeline averse, took it into her head to press her extremely to go with them; and finding she still refused, said — 'it was monstrous rude, and that she was sure no young person would decline partaking such an entertainment if she had not some *very particular* reason.'

Emmeline, teized and provoked out of her usual calmness, answered 'That whatever might be her reasons, she was fortunately accountable to nobody for them.'

Mrs. Ashwood, provoked in her turn, made some very rude replies, which Emmeline, not to irritate her farther, left the room without answering; and as soon as the carriages drove from the door, she dined alone, and then desiring one of the servants to carry her harp into the summer-house in the copse, she walked thither with her music books, and soon lost the little chagrin which Mrs. Ashwood's ill-breeding had given her.

Fitz-Edward, who arrived in the country the preceding evening, after another fruitless search for Lady Adelina, walked over to Woodfield, in hopes, as it was early in the afternoon, that he might obtain, in the course of it, some conversation with Mrs. Stafford and Emmeline. On arriving, he met the servant who had attended Emmeline to the copse, and was by him directed thither. As he approached the seat, he heard her singing a plaintive air, which seemed in unison with his heart. She started at the sight of him — Mrs. Ashwood's suspicions immediately occurred to her, and at the same moment the real motive which had made him seek this interview. She blushed, and looked uneasy; but the innocence and integrity of her heart presently restored her composure, and when Fitz-Edward asked if she would allow him half an hour of her time, she answered — 'certainly.'

He sat down by her, dejectedly and in silence. She was about to put aside her harp, but he desired her to repeat the air she was singing.

'It is sweetly soothing,' said he, 'and reminds me of happier days when I first heard it; while you sing it, I may perhaps acquire resolution to tell you what may oblige you to discard me from your acquaintance. It does indeed require resolution to hazard such a misfortune.'

Emmeline, not knowing how to answer, immediately began the air. The thoughts which agitated her bosom while she sung, made her voice yet more tender and pathetic. She saw the eyes of Fitz-Edward fill with tears; and as soon as she ceased he said —

'Tell me, Miss Mowbray — what does the man deserve, who being entrusted with the confidence of a young and beautiful woman — beautiful, even as Emmeline herself, and as highly accomplished — has betrayed the sacred trust; and has been the occasion — oh God! — of what misery may I not have been the occasion!

'Pardon me,' continued he — 'I am afraid my despair frightens you — I will endeavour to command myself.

Emmeline found she could not escape hearing the story, and endeavoured not to betray by her countenance that she already knew it.

Fitz-Edward went on —

'When first I knew you, I was a decided libertine. Yourself and Mrs. Stafford, lovely as I thought you both, would have been equally the object of my designs, if Delamere's passion for you, and the reserved conduct of Mrs. Stafford, had not made me doubt succeeding with either. But for your charming friend my heart long retained its partiality; nor would it ever have felt for her that pure and disinterested friendship which is now in regard to her its only sentiment, had not the object of my present regret and anguish been thrown in my way.

'To you, Miss Mowbray, I scruple not to speak of this beloved and lamented woman; tho' her name is sacred with me, and has never yet been mentioned united with dishonour.

'The connection between our families first introduced me to her acquaintance. In her person she was exquisitely lovely, and her manners were as enchanting as her form. The sprightly gaiety of unsuspecting inexperience, was, I thought, sometimes checked by an involuntary sentiment of regret at the sacrifice she had made, by marrying a man every way unworthy of her; except by that fortune to which she was indifferent, and of which he was hastening to divest himself.

'I had never seen Mr. Trelawny; and knew him for some time only from report. But when he came to Lough Carryl, my pity for her, encreased in proportion to the envy and indignation with which I beheld the insensible and intemperate husband — incapable of feeling for her, any other sentiment, than what she might equally have inspired in the lowest of mankind.

'Her unaffected simplicity; her gentle confidence in my protection during a voyage in which her ill-assorted mate left her entirely to my care; made me rather consider her as my sister than as an object of seduction. I resolved to be the guardian rather than the betrayer of her honour — and I long kept my resolution.'

Fitz-Edward then proceeded to relate the circumstances that attended the ruin of Trelawny's fortune; and that Lady Adelina was left to struggle with innumerable difficulties, unassisted but by himself, to whom Lord Clancarryl had delegated the task of treating with Trelawny's sister and creditors.

'Her gratitude,' continued he, 'for the little assistance I was able to give her, was boundless; and as pity had already taught me to love her with more ardour than her beauty only, captivating as it is, would have inspired; gratitude led her too easily into tender sentiments for me. I am not a presuming coxcomb; but she was infinitely too artless to conceal her partiality; and neither her misfortunes, or her being the sister of my friend Godolphin, protected her against the libertinism of my principles.'

He went on to relate the deep melancholy that seized Lady Adelina; and his own terror and remorse when he found her one morning gone from her lodgings, where she had left no direction; and from her proceeding it was evident she designed to conceal herself from his enquiries.

'God knows,' pursued he, 'what is now become of her! — perhaps, when most in need of tenderness and attention, she is thrown destitute and friendless among strangers, and will perish in indigence and obscurity. Unused to encounter the slightest hardship, her delicate frame, and still more sensible mind, will sink under those to which her situation will expose her — perhaps I shall be doubly a murderer!'

He stopped, from inability to proceed — Emmeline, in tears, continued silent.

Struggling to conquer his emotion and recover his voice, Fitz-Edward at length continued —

'While I was suffering all the misery which my apprehension for her fate inflicted, her younger brother, William Godolphin, returned from the West Indies, where he has been three years stationed. I was the first person he visited in town; but I was not at my lodgings there. Before I returned from Tylehurst, he had informed himself of all the circumstances of Trelawny's embarrassments, and his sister's absence. He found letters from Lord Westhaven, and from my brother, Lord Clancarryl; who knowing he would about that time return to England, conjured him to assist in the attempt of discovering Lady Adelina; of whose motives for concealing herself from her family they were entirely ignorant, while it filled them with uneasiness and astonishment. As soon as I went back to London, Godolphin, of whose arrival I was ignorant, came to me. He embraced me, and thanked me for my friendship and attention to his unfortunate Adelina — I think if he had held his sword to my heart it would have hurt me less!

'He implored me to help his search after his lost sister, and again said how greatly he was obliged to me — while I, conscious how little I deserved his gratitude, felt like a coward and an assassin, and shrunk from the manly confidence of my friend.

'Since our first meeting, I have seen him several times, and ever with new anguish. I have loved Godolphin from my earliest remembrance; and have known him from a boy to have the best heart and the noblest spirit under heaven. Equally incapable of deserving or bearing dishonour, Godolphin will behold me with contempt; which tho' I deserve, I cannot endure. He must call me to an account; and the hope of perishing by his hand is the only one I now cherish. Yet unable to shock him by divulging the fatal secret, I have hitherto concealed it, and my concealment he must impute to motives base, infamous, and pusillanimous. I can bear such reflections no longer — I will go to town to-morrow, explain his sister's situation to him, and let him take the only reparation I can now make him.'

Emmeline shuddering at this resolution, could not conceal how greatly it affected her.

'Generous and lovely Miss Mowbray! pardon me for having thus moved your gentle nature; and allow me, since I see you pity me, to request of you and Mrs. Stafford a favour which will probably be the last trouble the unhappy Fitz-Edward will give you.

'It may happen that Lady Adelina may hereafter be discovered —tho' I know not how to hope it. But if your generous pity should interest you in the fate of that unhappy, forlorn young woman, yours and Mrs. Stafford's protection might yet perhaps save her; and such interposition would be worthy of hearts like yours. As the event of a meeting between me and Godolphin is uncertain, shall I entreat you, my lovely friend, to take charge of this paper. It contains a will, by which the child of Lady Adelina will be entitled to all I die possessed of. It is enough, if the unfortunate infant survives, to place it above indigence. Lord Clancarryl will not dispute the disposition of my fortune; and to your care, and that of Mrs. Stafford, I have left it in trust, and I have entreated you to befriend the poor little one, who will probably be an orphan — but desolate and abandoned it will not be, if its innocence and unhappiness interest you to grant my request. Delamere will not object to your goodness being so exerted; and you will not teach it, generous, gentle as you are! to hold in abhorrence the memory of its father. This is all I can now do. Farewell! dearest Miss Mowbray! — Heaven give you happiness, *ma douce amie!* Farewell!'

These last words, in which Fitz-Edward repeated the name by which he was accustomed to address Emmeline, quite overcame her. He was hastening away, while, hardly able to speak, she yet made an effort to stop him. The interview he was about to seek was what Lady Adelina so greatly dreaded. Yet Emmeline dared not urge to him how fatal it would be to her; she knew not what to say, least she should discover the secret with which she was entrusted; but in breathless agitation caught his hand as he turned to leave her, crying —

'Hear me, Fitz-Edward! One moment hear me! Do not go to meet Captain Godolphin. I conjure, I implore you do not!'

She found it impossible to proceed. Her eyes were still eagerly fixed on his face; she still held his hand; while he, supposing her extreme emotion arose from the compassionate tenderness of her nature, found the steadiness of his despair softened by the soothing voice of pity, and throwing himself on his knees, he laid his head on one of the chairs, and wept like a woman.

Emmeline, who now hoped to persuade him not to execute the resolution he had formed, said — 'I will take the paper you have given me, Fitz-Edward, and will most religiously fulfil all your request in it to the utmost extent of my power. But in return for my giving you this promise, I must insist' —

At this moment James Crofts stood before them.

Emmeline, shocked and amazed at his appearance, roused Fitz-Edward by a sudden exclamation.

He started up, and said fiercely to Crofts — 'Well, Sir! — have you any commands here?'

'Commands, Sir,' answered Crofts, somewhat alarmed by the tone in which this question was put — 'I have no commands to be sure Sir but, but, I came Sir, just to enquire after Miss Mowbray. I did not mean to intrude.'

'Then, Sir,' returned the Colonel, 'I beg you will leave us.'

'Oh! certainly, Sir,' cried Crofts, trying to regain his courage and assume an air of raillery — 'certainly — I would not for the world interrupt you. My business indeed is not at all material — only a compliment to Miss Mowbray — yours,' added he sneeringly, 'is, I see, of more consequence.'

'Look ye, Mr. Crofts,' sharply answered Fitz-Edward — 'You are to make no impertinent comments. Miss Mowbray is mistress of her actions. She is in my particular protection on behalf of my friend Delamere, and I shall consider the slightest failure of respect to her as an insult to me. Sir, if you have nothing more to say you will be so good as to leave us.'

There was something so hostile in the manner in which Fitz-Edward delivered this speech, that James Crofts, more at home in the cabinet than the field, thought he might as well avoid another injunction to depart; and quietly submit to the present, rather than provoke farther resentment from the formidable soldier. He therefore, looking most cadaverously, made one of his jerking bows, and said, with something he intended for a smile —

'Well, well, good folks, I'll leave you to your *tête à tête*, and hasten back to my engagement. Every body regrets Miss Mowbray's absence from the ball; and the partner that was provided for her is ready to hang himself.'

An impatient look, darted from Fitz-Edward, stopped farther effusion of impertinence, and he only added — 'Servant! servant!' and walked away.

Fitz-Edward, then turning towards Emmeline, saw her pale and faint.

'Why, my dear Miss Mowbray, do you suffer this man's folly to affect you? Your looks really terrify me!'

'Oh! he was sent on purpose,' cried Emmeline — 'Mrs. Ashwood has lately often hinted to me, that whatever are my engagements to Delamere I was much more partial to you. She has watched me for some time; and now, on my refusing to accompany them to the ball, concluded I had an appointment, and sent Crofts back to see.'

'If I thought so,' sternly answered Fitz-Edward, 'I would instantly overtake him, and I believe I could oblige him to secresy.'

'No, for heaven's sake don't!' said Emmeline — 'for heaven's sake do not think of it! I care not what they conjecture — leave them to their malice — Crofts is not worth your anger. But Fitz-Edward, let us return to what we were talking of. Will you promise me to delay going to London — to delay seeing Mr. Godolphin until — in short, will you give me your honour to remain at Tylehurst a week, without taking any measures to inform Godolphin of what you have told me? I will, at the end of that time, either release you from your promise, or give you unanswerable reasons why you should relinquish the design of meeting him at all.'

Fitz-Edward, however amazed at the earnestness she expressed to obtain this promise, gave it. He had no suspicion of Emmeline's having any knowledge of Lady Adelina; and accounted for the deep interest she seemed to take in preventing an interview, by recollecting the universal tenderness and humanity of her character. He assured her he would not leave Tylehurst 'till the expiration of the time she had named. He conjured her not to suffer any impertinence from Crofts on the subject of their being seen together, but to awe him into silence by resentment. Emmeline now desired him to leave her. But she still seemed under such an hurry of spirits, that he insisted on being allowed to attend her to the door of the house, where, renewing his thanks for the compassionate attention she had afforded him, and entreating her to compose herself, he left her.

Emmeline, intending to go to her own room, went first into the drawing room to deposit her music book. She had hardly done so, when she heard a man's step, and turning beheld Crofts open the door, which he immediately shut after him.

'I thought, Sir,' said Emmeline, 'you had been gone back to your company.'

'No, not yet, my fair Emmeline. I wanted first to beg your pardon for having disturbed so snug a party. Ah! sly little prude — who would think that you, who always seem so cold and so cruel, made an excuse only to stay at home to meet Fitz-Edward? But it is not fair, little dear, that all your kindness should be for him, while you will scarce give any other body a civil look. Now I have met with you I swear I'll have a kiss too.'

Emmeline, terrified to death at his approaching her with this speech, flew to the bell, which she rang with so much violence that the rope broke from the crank.

'Now,' cried Crofts, 'if nobody hears, you are more than ever in my power.'

'Heaven forbid!' shrieked Emmeline, in an agony of fear. 'Let me go, Mr. Crofts, this moment.'

She would have rushed towards the door but he stood with his arms extended before it.

'You did not run thus — you did not scream thus, when Fitz-Edward, the fortunate Fitz-Edward, was on his knees before you. Then, you could weep and sigh too, and look so sweetly on him. But come — you see I know so much that it will be your interest, little dear, to make me your friend.'

'Rather let me apply to fiends and furies for friendship! hateful, detestable wretch! by what right do you insult and detain me?'

'Oh! these theatricals are really very sublime!' cried he, seizing both her hands, which he violently grasped.

She shrieked aloud, and fruitlessly struggled to break from him, when the footsteps of somebody near the door obliged him to let her go. She darted instantly away, and in the hall met one of the maids.

'Lord, Miss,' cried the servant, 'did you ring? I've been all over the house to see what bell it was.'

Emmeline, without answering, flew to her own room. The maid followed her: but desirous of being left alone, she assured the girl that nothing was the matter; that she was merely tired by a long walk; and desiring a glass of water, tried to compose and recollect herself; while Crofts unobserved returned to the house where the *fete* was given with time enough to dress and dance with Mrs. Ashwood.

It was at her desire, that immediately after dinner Crofts had left the company under pretence of executing a commission with which she easily furnished him; but his real orders were to discover the motives of Emmeline's refusal to be of the party. This he executed beyond his expectation. It was no longer to be doubted that very good intelligence subsisted between Emmeline and Fitz-Edward, since he had been found on his knees before her; while she, earnestly yet kindly speaking, hung over him with tears in her eyes. Knowing that Emmeline was absolutely engaged to Delamere, he was persuaded that Fitz-Edward was master of her heart; and that the tears and emotion to which he had been witness, were occasioned by the impossibility of her giving him her hand. He knew Fitz-Edward's character too well to suppose he could be insensible of the lady's kindness; and possessing himself a mind gross and depraved, he did not hesitate to believe all the ill his own base and illiberal spirit suggested.

Tho,' interested hypocrite as he was, he made every other passion subservient to the gratification of his avarice, Crofts had not coldly beheld the youth and beauty of Emmeline; he had, however, carefully forborne to shew that he admired her, and would probably never have betrayed what must ruin him for ever with Mrs. Ashwood, had not the conviction of her partiality to Fitz-Edward inspired him with the infamous hope of frightening her into some kindness for himself, by threatening to betray her stolen interview with her supposed lover.

The scorn and horror with which Emmeline repulsed him served only to mortify his self love, and provoke his hatred towards her and the man whom he believed she favoured; and with the inveterate and cowardly malignity of which his heart was particularly susceptible, he determined to do all in his power to ruin them both.

CHAPTER III

SUCH was the horror and detestation which Emmeline felt for Crofts, that she could not bear the thoughts of seeing him again. But as she feared Mrs. Stafford might resent his behaviour, and by that means embroil herself with the vain and insolent Mrs. Ashwood, with whom she knew Stafford was obliged to keep on a fair footing, she determined to say as little as she could of his impertinence to Mrs. Stafford, but to withdraw from the house without again exposing herself to meet him. As soon as she saw her the next morning, she related all that had passed between Fitz-Edward and herself; and after a long consultation they agreed that to prevent his seeing Godolphin was absolutely necessary; and that no other means of doing so offered, but Mrs. Stafford's relating to him the real circumstances and situation of Lady Adelina, as soon as she could be removed from her present abode and precautions taken to prevent his discovering her. This, Mrs. Stafford undertook to do immediately after their departure. It was to take place on the next day; and Emmeline, with the concurrence of her friend, determined that she would take no leave of the party at Woodfield; for tho' the appearance of mystery was extremely disagreeable and distressing to Emmeline, she knew that notice of her intentions would excite enquiries and awaken curiosity very difficult to satisfy; and that it was extremely probable James Crofts might be employed to watch her, and by that means render abortive all her endeavours to preserve the unhappy Lady Adelina.

Relying therefore on the generosity and innocence of her intentions, she chose rather to leave her own actions open to censure which they did not deserve, than to risk an investigation which might be fatal to the interest of her poor friend. She took nothing with her, Mrs. Stafford undertaking every necessary arrangement about her cloaths — and having at night taken a tender leave of this beloved and valuable woman, and promised to write to her constantly and to return as soon as the destiny of Lady Adelina should be decided, they parted.

And Emmeline, arising before the dawn of the following morning, set out alone to Woodbury Forest — a precaution absolutely necessary, to evade the inquisitive watchfulness of James Crofts. She stole softly down stairs, before even the servants were stirring, and opening the door cautiously, felt some degree of terror at being obliged to undertake so long a walk alone at such an hour. But innocence gave her courage, and friendly zeal lent her strength. As she walked on, her fears subsided. She saw the sun rise above the horizon, and her apprehensions were at an end.

As no carriage could approach within three quarters of a mile of the house where Lady Adelina was concealed, they were obliged to walk to the road where Mrs. Stafford had directed a post chaise to wait for them, which she had hired at a distant town, where it was unlikely any enquiry would be made.

Long disuse, as she had hardly ever left the cottage from the moment of her entering it, and the extreme weakness to which she was reduced, made Emmeline greatly fear that Lady Adelina would never be able to reach the place. With her assistance, and that of her Ladyship's woman, slowly and faintly she walked thither; and Emmeline saw her happily placed in the chaise. Every thing had been before settled as to the conveyance of the servant and baggage, and to engage the secresy of the woman with whom she had dwelt, by making her silence sufficiently advantageous; and as they hoped that no traces were left by which they might be followed, the spirits of the fair travellers seemed somewhat to improve as they proceeded on their journey. — Emmeline felt her heart elated with the consciousness of doing good; and from the tender affection and assistance of such a friend, which could be considered only as the benevolence of heaven itself, Lady Adelina drew a favourable omen, and dared entertain a faint hope that her penitence had been accepted.

They arrived without any accident at Bath, the following day; and Emmeline, leaving Lady Adelina at the inn, went out immediately to secure lodgings in a retired part of the town. As soon as it was dark, Lady

Adelina removed thither in a chair; and was announced by Emmeline to be the wife of a Swiss officer, to be herself of Switzerland, and to bear the name of Mrs. St. Laure — while she herself, as she was very little known, continued to pass by her own name in the few transactions which in their very private way of living required her name to be repeated.

When Mrs. Ashwood found that Emmeline had left Woodfield clandestinely and alone, and that Mrs. Stafford evaded giving any account whither she was gone, by saying coldly that she was gone to visit a friend in Surry whom she formerly knew in Wales, all the suspicions she had herself harboured, and Miss Galton encouraged, seemed confirmed. James Crofts had related, not without exaggerations, what he had been witness to in the copse; and it was no longer doubted but that she was gone with Fitz-Edward, which at once accounted for her departure and the sudden and mysterious manner in which it was accomplished. James Crofts had suspicions that his behaviour had hastened it; but he failed not to confirm Mrs. Ashwood in her prepossession that her entanglement with Fitz-Edward was now at a period when it could be no longer concealed — intelligence which was to be conveyed to Delamere.

The elder Crofts, who had been some time with Lady Montreville and her daughter, had named Delamere from time to time in his letters to his brother. The last, mentioned that he was now with his mother and sister, who were at Nice, and who purposed returning to England in about three months. Crofts represented Delamere as still devoted to

Emmeline; and as existing only in the hope of being no longer opposed in his intention of marrying her in March, when the year which he had promised his father to wait expired; but that Lady Montreville, as time wore away, grew more averse to the match, and more desirous of some event which might break it off. Crofts gave his brother a very favourable account of his progress with Miss Delamere; and hinted that if he could be fortunate enough to put an end to Delamere's intended connection, it would so greatly conciliate the favour of Lady Montreville, that he dared hope she would no longer oppose his union with her daughter: and when once they were married, and the prejudices of the mother to an inferior alliance conquered, he had very little doubt of Lord Montreville's forgiveness, and of soon regaining his countenance and friendship.

This account from his brother added another motive to those which already influenced the malignant and illiberal mind of James Crofts to injure the lovely orphan, and he determined to give all his assistance to Mrs. Ashwood in the cruel project of depriving her at once of her character and her lover. In a consultation which he held on this subject with his promised bride and Miss Galton, the ladies agreed that it was perfectly shocking that such a fine young man as Mr. Delamere should be attached to a woman so little sensible of his value as Emmeline; that it had long been evident she was to him indifferent, and it was now too clear that she was partial to another; and that therefore it would be a meritorious action to acquaint him of her intimacy with Fitz-Edward; and it could not be doubted but his knowledge of it would, high spirited as he was, cure him effectually of his ill-placed passion, and restore the tranquillity of his respectable family. Hiding thus the inveterate envy and malice of their hearts under this hypocritical pretence, they next considered how to give the information which was so meritorious. Anonymous letters were expedients to which Miss Galton had before had recourse, and to an anonymous letter they determined to commit the secret of Emmeline's infidelity — while James Crofts, in his letters to his brother, was to corroborate the intelligence it contained, by relating as mere matter of news what had actually and evidently happened, Emmeline's sudden departure from Woodfield.

Delamere, when he saw his mother out of danger at Barege, had returned to the neighbourhood of Paris, where he had lingered some time, in hopes that Emmeline would accede to his request of being allowed to cross the channel for a few days; but her answer, in which she strongly urged the hazard he would incur of giving his father a pretence to withdraw *his* promise, by violating his own, had obliged him, tho' with infinite reluctance, to give up the scheme; and being quite indifferent where he was, if he was still at a distance from her, he had yielded to the solicitations of Lady Montreville, and rejoined her at Nice. There, he now remained; while every thing in England seemed to contribute to assist the designs of those who wished to disengage him from his passion for Emmeline.

The day after Emmeline's departure with Lady Adelina, Fitz-Edward went to Woodfield; and hearing that Miss Mowbray had suddenly left it, was thrown into the utmost astonishment — astonishment which Mrs. Ashwood and Miss Galton observed to each other was the finest piece of acting they had ever seen.

The whole party were together when he was introduced — a circumstance Mrs. Stafford would willingly have avoided, as it was absolutely necessary for her to speak to him alone; and determined to do so, whatever construction the malignity of her sister-in-law might put upon it, she said —

'I have long promised you, Colonel, a sight of the two pieces of drawing which Miss Mowbray and I have finished as companions. They are now framed; and if you will come with me into my dressing-room you shall see them.'

As the rest of the company had frequently seen these drawings, there was no pretence for their following Mrs. Stafford; who, accompanied by the Colonel, went to her dressing-room.

A conference thus evidently sought by Mrs. Stafford, excited the eager and painful curiosity of the party in the parlour.

'Now would I give the world,' cried Mrs. Ashwood, 'to know what is going forward.'

'Is it not possible to listen?' enquired Crofts, equal to any meanness that might gratify the malevolence of another or his own.

'Yes,' replied Mrs. Ashwood, 'if one could get into the closet next the dressing-room without being perceived, which can only be done by passing thro' the nursery. If indeed the nursery maids and children are out, it is easy enough.'

'They are out, mama, I assure you,' cried Miss Ashwood, 'for I saw them myself go across the lawn since I've been at breakfast. Do, pray let us go and listen — I long of all things to know what my aunt Stafford can have to say to that sly-looking Colonel.'

'No, no, child,' said her mother, 'I shall not send you, indeed — but Crofts, do you think we should be able to make it out?'

'Egad,' answered he, 'I'll try — for depend upon it the mischief will out. It will be rare, to have such a pretty tale to tell Mr. Delamere of his demure-looking little dear. — I'll venture.'

Mrs. Ashwood then shewing him the way, he went on tip toe up stairs, and concealing himself in a light closet which was divided from the dressing room only by lath and plaister, he lent an attentive ear to the dialogue that was passing.

It happened, however, that the window near which Mrs. Stafford and Fitz-Edward were sitting was exactly opposite to that side of the room to which Crofts' hiding-place communicated; and tho' the room was not large, yet the distance, the partition, and the low voice in which both parties spoke, made it impossible for him to distinguish more than broken sentences. From Mrs. Stafford he heard — 'Could not longer be concealed — in all probability may now remain unknown — the child, I will myself attend to.' From Fitz-Edward, he could only catch indistinct sounds; his voice appearing to be lost in his emotion. But he seemed to be thanking Mrs. Stafford, and lamenting his own unhappiness. His last speech, in which his powers of utterance were returned, was — 'Nothing can ever erase the impression of your angelic goodness, best and loveliest of friends! —oh, continue it, I beseech you, to those for whom only I am solicitous, and forgive all the trouble I have given you!'

He then hurried away. Mrs. Stafford, after remaining alone a moment as if to compose herself, went back to the parlour, and Crofts, who thought he had heard enough, tho' he wished to have heard all, slunk from his closet and walked into the garden; where being soon afterwards joined by Mrs. Ashwood and Miss Galton, he, by relating the broken and disjointed discourse he had been witness to, left not a doubt remaining of the cause of Emmeline's precipitate retreat from Woodfield.

And perhaps minds more candid than theirs — minds untainted with the odious and hateful envy which ulcerated theirs, might, from the circumstances that attended her going and Fitz-Edward's behaviour, have conceived disadvantageous ideas of her conduct. But such was the uneasiness with which Mrs. Ashwood ever beheld superior merit, and such the universal delight which Miss Galton took in defamation, that had none of those circumstances existed, they would with equal malignity have studied to ruin the reputation of Emmeline; and probably with equal success — for against such attacks, innocence, however it may console its possessor, is too frequently a feeble and inadequate defence!

While the confederates, exulting in the certainty of Emmeline's ruin, were manufacturing the letter which was to alarm the jealous and irascible spirit of Delamere, Fitz-Edward, (from whom Mrs. Stafford, before she would tell him any thing, had extorted a promise that he would enquire no farther than what she chose to relate to him,) was relieved from insupportable anguish by hearing that Lady Adelina was in safe hands; but he lamented in bitterness of soul the despondency and affliction to which Mrs. Stafford had told him she entirely resigned herself. He knew not that Emmeline was with her, whatever he might suspect; and Mrs. Stafford had protested to him, that if he made any attempt to discover the residence of Lady Adelina, or persisted in meeting her brother, she would immediately relinquish all concern in the affair, and no longer interest herself in what his rashness would inevitably render desperate.

He solemnly assured her he would take no measures without her knowledge; and remained at Tylehurst, secluded from every body, and waiting in fearful and anxious solicitude to hear of Lady Adelina by Mrs. Stafford.

Delamere, (still at Nice with his mother,) who with different sources of uneasiness thought the days and weeks insupportably long in which he lived only in the hope of seeing Emmeline at the end of six months, was roused from his involuntary resignation by the following letter, written in a hand perfectly unknown to him.

'Sir,

'A friend to your worthy and noble family writes this; which is meant to serve you, and to undeceive you in regard to Miss Mowbray — who, without any gratitude for the high honour you intend her, is certainly too partial to another person. She is now gone from Woodfield to escape observation; and none but Mrs. Stafford is let into the secret of where she is. You will judge what end it is to answer; but certainly none that bodes you good. One would have supposed that the Colonel's being very often her attendant at Woodfield might have made her stay there agreeable enough; but perhaps (for I do not aver it) the young lady has some particular reasons for wishing to have private lodgings. No doubt the Colonel is a man of gallantry; but his friendship to you is rather more questionable. The writer of this having very little knowledge of the parties, can have no other motive than the love of justice, and being sorry to see deceit and falsehood practised on a young gentleman who deserves better, and who has a respectful tho' unknown friend in

Y.Z.'

London, July 22, 17—.

This infamous scroll had no sooner been perused by Delamere, than fury flashed from his eyes, and anguish seized his heart. But the moment the suddenness of his passion gave way to reflection, the tumult of his mind subsided, and he thought it must be an artifice of his mother's to separate him from Emmeline. The longer he considered her inveterate antipathy to his marriage, the more he was convinced that this artifice, unworthy as it was, she was capable of conceiving, and, by means of the Crofts, executing, if she hoped by it to put an eternal conclusion to his affection. He at length so entirely adopted this idea, that determining 'to be revenged and love her better for it,' and to settle the matter very peremptorily with the Crofts' if they had been found to interfere, he obtained a tolerable command over his temper and his features, and joined Lady Montreville and Miss Delamere, whom he found reading letters which they also had received from England. His mother asked slightly after his; and, in a few moments, Mr. Crofts arrived, asking, with his usual assiduity, after the health of Lord Montreville and that of such friends as usually wrote to her Ladyship? She answered his enquiries — and then desired to hear what news Sir Richard or his other correspondents had sent him?

'My father's letters,' said he, 'contain little more than an order to purchase some particular sort of wine which he is very circumstantial, as usual, in telling me how to forward safely. He adds, indeed, that he can allow my absence no longer than until the 20th of September.' — He sighed, and looked tenderly at Miss Delamere.

'I have no other letters,' continued he, 'but one from James.'

'And does he tell you no news?' asked Lady Montreville.

'Nothing,' answered Crofts, carelessly, 'but gossip, which I believe would not entertain your Ladyship.'

'Oh, why should you fancy that,' returned she — 'you know I love to hear news, tho' about people I never saw or ever wish to see.'

'James has been at Mr. Stafford's at Woodfield,' said he, 'where your Ladyship has certainly no acquaintance.'

'At Woodfield, Sir?' cried Delamere, unable to express his anxiety — 'at Woodfield! — And what does he say of Woodfield?'

'I don't recollect any thing very particular,' answered Crofts, carelessly — 'I believe I put the letter into my pocket.' He took it out.

'Read it to us Crofts' — said Miss Delamere.

— 'I have lately passed a very agreeable month at Woodfield. We were a large party in the house. Among other pleasant circumstances, during my stay there, was a ball and *fete champètre*, given by Mr. Conway on his son's coming of age. It was elegant, and well conducted beyond any entertainment of the sort I ever saw. There were forty couple, and a great number of very pretty women; but it was agreed on all hands that Miss Mowbray would have eclipsed them all, who unluckily declined going. She left Woodfield a day or two afterwards.'

Delamere's countenance changed. — Crofts, as if looking for some other news in his letter, hesitated, then smiled, and went on. —

'The gossip Fame has made a match for me with Mrs. Ashwood. I wish she may be right. In some other of her stories I really think her wrong, so I will not be the means of their circulation.'

'The rest,' said Crofts, putting up the letter, 'is only about my father's new purchases and other family affairs.'

Delamere, who, in spite of his suspicions of Crofts' treachery, could not hear this corroboration of his anonymous letter without a renewal of all his fears, left the room in doubt, suspence and wretchedness.

The seeds of jealousy and mistrust thus skilfully sown, could hardly fail of taking root in an heart so full of sensibility, and a temper so irritable as his. Again he read over his anonymous letter, and compared it with the intelligence which seemed accidentally communicated by Crofts; and with a fearful kind of enquiry compared the date and circumstances. He dared hardly trust his mind with the import of this investigation; and found nothing on which to rest his hope, but that it might be a concerted plan between his mother and Crofts.

His heart alternately swelling between the indignation such a supposition created and shrinking with horror from the idea of perfidy on the part of Emmeline, kept him in such a state of mind that he could hardly be said to possess his reason. But when he remembered how often his extreme vivacity had betrayed him into error, and hazarded his losing for ever all he held valuable on earth, he tried to subdue the acuteness of his feelings, and to support at least without betraying it, the anguish which oppressed him, till the next pacquet from England, when it was possible a letter from Emmeline herself might dissipate his doubts. Resolutely however resolving to call Crofts to a serious account, if he found him accessary to a calumny so dark and diabolical.

When the next post from England arrived, he saw, among the letters which were delivered to him, one directed by the hand of Emmeline. He flew to his own room, and with trembling hands broke the seal.

It was short, and he fancied unusually cold. Towards its close, she mentioned that she was going to Bath for a few weeks with a friend, and as she did not know where she should lodge, thought he had better not write till she was again fixed at Woodfield.

That she should go to Bath in July, with a nameless friend, and quit so abruptly her beloved Mrs. Stafford — that she should apparently wish to evade his letters, and make her actual residence a secret — were a cloud of circumstances calculated to persuade him that some mystery involved her conduct; a mystery which the fatal letter served too evidently to explain.

As if fire had been laid to the train of combustibles which had, since the receipt of it, been accumulating in the bosom of Delamere, his furious and uncontroulable spirit now burst forth. A temporary delirium seized him; he stamped round the room, and ran to his pistols, which fortunately were not charged. The noise he made brought Millefleur into the room, whom he instantly caught by the collar, and shaking him violently, cried —

'Scoundrel! — why are not these pistols loaded?'

'*Eh! eh! Monsieur!*' exclaimed Millefleur, almost strangled — *que voudriez vous? — vos pistolets! — Mon Dieu! que voudriez vous avec vos pistolets?*'

'Shoot you perhaps, you blockhead!' raved Delamere, pushing furiously from him the trembling valet — then snatching up the pistols, he half kicked, half pushed him out of the room, and throwing them after him, ordered him to clean and load them: after which he locked the door, and threw himself upon the bed.

The resolution he had made in his cooler moments, never again to yield to such impetuous transports of passion, was now forgotten. He could not conquer, he could not even mitigate the tumultuous anguish which had seized him; but seemed rather to call to his remembrance all that might justify its excess.

He remembered how positively Emmeline had forbidden his returning to England, tho' all he asked was to be allowed to see her for a few hours. He recollected her long and invincible coldness; her resolute adherence to the promise she need not have given; and forgetting all the symptoms which he had before fondly believed he had discovered of her returning his affection, he exaggerated every circumstance that indicated indifference, and magnified them into sighs of absolute aversion.

Tho' he could not forget that Fitz-Edward had assisted him in carrying Emmeline away, and had on all occasions promoted his interest with her, that recollection did not at all weaken the probability of his present attachment; for such was Delamere's opinion of Fitz-Edward's principles, that he believed he was capable of the most dishonourable views on the mistress, or even on the wife of his friend. He tortured his imagination almost to madness, by remembering numberless little incidents, which, tho' almost unattended to at the time, now seemed to bring the cruellest conviction of their intelligence — particularly that on the night he had taken Emmeline from Clapham, Fitz-Edward was found there; tho' neither his father or himself, who had repeatedly sent to his lodgings, could either find him at home or get any direction where to meet with him. Almost all his late letters too had been dated from Tylehurst, where it was certain he had passed the greatest part of the summer. — Fitz-Edward, fond of society, and courted by the most brilliant circles, shut himself up in a country house, distant from all his connections. And to what could such an extraordinary change be owing, if not to his attachment to Emmeline Mowbray?

Irritated by these recollections, he gave himself up to all the dreadful torments of jealousy — jealousy even to madness; and he felt this corrosive passion in all its extravagance. It was violent in proportion to his love and his pride, and more insupportably painful in proportion to its novelty; for except once at Swansea, when he had fancied that Emmeline in her flight was accompanied by Fitz-Edward, he had never felt it before; however they might serve him as a pretence, Rochely and Elkerton were both too contemptible to excite it.

The night approached; and without having regained any share of composure, he had at length determined to quit Nice the next day, that his mother and Crofts might not be gratified with the sight of his despair, and triumph in the detected perfidy of Emmeline.

Lady Montreville and her daughter were out when the letters arrived; and he now apprehended that when they returned Millefleur might alarm them by an account of his frantic behaviour, and that they would guess it to have been occasioned by his letters from England. Starting up, therefore, he called the poor fellow to him, who was not yet recovered from his former terrifying menaces; and who approached, trembling, the table where Delamere sat; his dress disordered, his eyes flashing fire, and his lips pale and quivering.

'Come here, Sir!' sternly cried he.

Millefleur sprung close to the table.

'Have you cleaned and loaded my pistols?'

'Monsieur — je, je m'occupais je, je — Monsieur, ils sont —'

'Fool, of what are you afraid? — what does the confounded *poltron* tremble for?'

'Mais Monsieur — c'est que — que — mais Monsieur, je ne scais!'

'Tenez, Mr. Millefleur!' said Delamere sharply — 'Remember what I am going to say. Something has happened to vex me, and I shall go out to-morrow for a few days, or perhaps I may go to England. My mother is to know nothing of it, but what I shall myself tell her; therefore at your peril speak of what has happened this evening, or of my intentions for to-morrow. Come up immediately, and put my things into my portmanteaus, and put my fire arms in order. I shall take you with me. David need not be prepared till to-morrow. I shall go on horseback and shall want him also. The least failure on your part of executing these orders, you will find very inconvenient — you know I will not be trifled with.'

Millefleur, frightened to death at the looks and voice of his master, dared not disobey; and Delamere employing him in putting up his cloaths till after Lady Montreville came in, was, he thought, secure in his secresy. He then made an effort, tho' a successless one, to hide the anguish that devoured him; and went down to supper. He found, that besides their constant attendant Crofts, his mother and sister were accompanied by two other English gentlemen, and a French man of fashion and his sister, who, full of the vivacity and gaiety of their country, kept up a lively conversation with Miss Delamere and the Englishmen. But Delamere hardly spoke — his eyes were wild and inflamed — his cheeks flushed — and deep sighs seemed involuntarily to burst from his heart. Lady Montreville observed him, and then said —

'Surely, Frederic, you are not well?'

'Not very well,' said he; 'but I am otherwise merely from the intolerable heat. I have had the head-ache all day.'

'The head-ache!' exclaimed his mother — 'Why then do you not go to bed?'

'No,' answered he, 'I am better up. Since the heat is abated, I am in less pain. I will take a walk by the fine moon that I see is rising, and be back again presently — and to-morrow,' continued he — 'to-morrow, I shall go northward for a month. I cannot stay under this burning atmosphere.'

Then desiring the company not to move on his account, he arose from the table and hastened away.

'Do, my good Crofts,' said Lady Montreville — 'do follow Frederic —he frightens me to death — he is certainly very ill.'

Crofts hesitated a moment, being in truth afraid to interfere with Delamere's ramble while he was in a humour so gloomy; but on her Ladyship's repeating her request, dared not shew his reluctance. He went out therefore under pretence of following him; while the party present, seeing Lady Montreville's distress, almost immediately departed.

Crofts walked on without much desire to fulfill his commission; for Delamere, whenever he was obliged to associate with him, treated him generally with coldness, and sometimes rudely. There was, however, very little probability of his overtaking him; for

Delamere had walked or rather run to a considerable distance from the street where his mother lived, and then wandering farther into the fields, had thrown himself upon the grass, and had forgotten every thing but Emmeline —'Emmeline and Fitz-Edward gone together! — the mistress on whom he had so fondly doated! — the friend whom he had so implicitly trusted!' These cruel images, drest in every form most fatal to his peace, tormented him, and the agony of disappointed passion seemed to have affected his brain. Deep groans forced their way from his oppressed heart — he cursed his existence, and seemed resolutely bent, in the gloominess of his despair, to shake it off and free himself from sufferings so intolerable.

To the first effusions of his phrenzy, a sullen calm, more alarming, succeeded. He fixed his eyes on the moon which shone above him, but had no idea of what he saw, or where he was; his breath was short, his hands clenched; he seemed as if, having lost the power of complaint, he was unable to express the pain that convulsed his whole frame.

While he continued in this situation, a favourite little spaniel of his mother's, of which he had from a boy been fond, ran up to him and licked his hands and face. The caresses of an animal he had so long remembered, touched some chord of the heart that vibrated to softer emotions than those which had for the last three hours possessed him — he burst into tears.

'Felix!' said he, sobbing, 'poor Felix!'

The dog, rejoicing to be noticed, ran barking round him; and presently afterwards, with hurried steps, came Miss Delamere, leaning on the arm of Crofts.

'My God!' exclaimed she, almost screaming, 'here he is! Oh Frederic, you have so terrified my mother! and Mr. Crofts has been two hours in search of you. Had it not been for the dog, we should not now have found you. Mr. Crofts has returned twice to the house without you.'

'Mr. Crofts may return then a third time,' said Delamere, 'and cease to give himself such unnecessary trouble.'

'But you will come with us, brother? — Surely you will now come home?'

'At my leisure,' replied he, sternly — 'Lady Montreville need be under no apprehensions about me. I shall be at home presently. But I will not be importuned! I will not be watched and followed! and above all, I will not have a governor!'

So saying, he turned from them and walked another way; while they, seeing him so impracticable, could only return to report what they had seen to Lady Montreville. Delamere, however, who had taken another way, entered the house at the same moment.

Lady Montreville had strictly questioned Millefleur as to the cause of his master's disorder; and the poor fellow, who dared not relate the curious passion into which he had fallen on reading his letter, trembled, prevaricated, stammered, and looked so white, that her Ladyship, more alarmed, fancied she knew not what; and full of terror, had sent out Crofts a second time, and the servants different ways, in search of her son. At length Crofts returning the second time without success, Miss Delamere went with him herself; and the dog following her, led her to her brother. But before their return, Lady Montreville's apprehensions had arisen to such an height, that a return of her fits seemed to threaten her, and with difficulty was she brought to her senses when she saw him before her; and when he, moved by the keenness of her sorrow at his imaginary danger, assured her, in answer to her repeated enquiries, that he was merely affected by the heat; that he had no material complaint, and should be quite well and in his usual spirits when he returned from the excursion he proposed going upon the next day. Then, being somewhat appeased, his mother suffered him to retire; and called her counsellor, Mr. Crofts, to debate whether in such a frame of mind she ought to allow the absence of Delamere? Crofts advised her by all means to let him go. He suspected indeed that the anonymous letter had occasioned all the wild behaviour he had been witness to, and thought it very likely that Delamere might be going to England. But he knew that James Crofts and his fair associates were prepared for the completion of their project if he did; and his absence was, on account of Crofts' own affairs, particularly desirable.

For these reasons, he represented to Lady Montreville that opposition would only irritate and inflame her son, without inducing him to stay. He departed, therefore, the next morning, without any impediment on the part of his mother; but was yet undecided whither to go. While Crofts, no longer thwarted by his observation, or humbled by his haughty disdain, managed matters so well, that in spite of the pride of noble blood, in spite of her reluctance to marry a commoner, he conquered and silenced all the scruples and objections of Miss Delamere; and a young English clergyman, a friend of his, coming to Nice, as both he and Crofts declared, *by the merest accident in the world*, just about that time, Crofts obtained her consent to a private marriage; and his friend took especial care that no form might be wanting, to enable him legally to claim his bride, on their return to England.

CHAPTER IV

EMMELINE had now been near a month at Bath, whence she had not written to Delamere. She had seldom done so oftener than once in six or eight weeks; and no reason subsisted at present for a more frequent correspondence.

Far from having any idea that he would think her temporary removal extraordinary, she had not attempted to conceal it from him; and of his jealousy of Fitz-Edward she had not the remotest suspicion. For tho' Mrs. Ashwood's hints, and the behaviour of James Crofts, had left no doubt of their ill opinion of her, yet she never supposed them capable of an attempt to impress the same idea on the mind of Delamere; and had no notion of the variety of motives which made the whole family of the Crofts, with which Mrs. Ashwood was now connected, solicitous to perpetuate the evil by propagating the scandalous story they had themselves invented.

Unconscious therefore of the anguish which preyed upon the heart of her unhappy lover, Emmeline gave her whole attention to Lady Adelina, and she saw with infinite concern the encreasing weakness of her frame; with still greater pain she observed, that by suffering her mind to dwell continually on her unhappy situation, it was no longer able to exert the powers it possessed; and that, sunk in hopeless despondence, her intellects were frequently deranged. Amid these alienations of reason, she was still gentle, amiable and interesting; and as they were yet short and slight, Emmeline flattered herself, that the opiates which her physician (in consequence of the restless and anxious nights Lady Adelina had for some time passed) found it absolutely necessary to administer, might have partly if not entirely occasioned this alarming symptom.

Still, however, the busy imagination of Emmeline perpetually represented to her impending sorrow, and her terror hourly encreased. She figured to herself the decided phrenzy, or the death of her poor friend; and unable to conquer apprehensions which she was yet compelled to conceal, she lived in a continual effort to appear chearful, and to soothe the wounded mind of the sufferer, by consolatory conversation; while she watched her with an attention so sedulous and so painful, that only the excellence of her heart, which persuaded her she was engaged in a task truly laudable, could have supported her thro' such anxiety and fatigue.

She was, however, very desirous that as Mr. Godolphin was now in England he might be acquainted with his sister's calamitous and precarious situation; and she gently hinted to Lady Adelina, how great a probability she thought there was, that such a man as her brother was represented to be, would in her sorrow and her suffering forget her error.

But by the most distant idea of such an interview, she found Lady Adelina so violently affected, that she dared not again urge it; and was compelled, in fearful apprehension, to await the hour which would probably give the fair penitent to that grave, where she seemed to wish her disgrace and affliction might be forgotten.

To describe the anxiety of Emmeline when that period arrived, is impossible; or the mingled emotions of sorrow and satisfaction, pleasure and pity, with which she beheld the lovely and unfortunate infant whose birth she had so long desired, yet so greatly dreaded.

Lady Adelina had, till then, wished to die. She saw her child — and wished to live. — The physical people who attended her, gave hopes that she might. — Supported by the tender friendship of Emmeline, and animated by maternal fondness, she determined to attempt it.

Emmeline, now full of apprehension, now indulging feeble hopes, prayed fervently for her recovery; and zealously and indefatigably attended her with more than her former solicitude. For three days, her hopes gradually grew stronger; when on the evening of the third, as she was sitting alone by the side of the bed where Lady Adelina had fallen into a quiet sleep, she suddenly heard a sort of bustle in the next room; and before she could rise to put an end to it, a gentleman to whom she was a stranger, walked hastily into that where she was. On seeing her, he started and said —

'I beg your pardon, Madam — but I was informed that here I might find Lady Adelina Trelawny.'

The name of Trelawny, thus suddenly and loudly pronounced, awakened Lady Adelina. She started up — undrew the curtain — and fixing her eyes with a look of terrified astonishment on the stranger, she exclaimed, faintly — 'Oh! my brother! — my brother William!' then sunk back on her pillow, to all appearance lifeless.

Mr. Godolphin now springing forward, caught the cold and insensible hand which had opened the curtain; and throwing himself on his knees, cried —

'Adelina! my love! are you ill? — have I then terrified and alarmed you? Speak to me — dear Adelina — speak to me!'

Emmeline, whose immediate astonishment at his presence had been lost in terror for his sister, had flown out of the room for the attendants, and now returning, cried —

'You have killed her, Sir! — She is certainly dead! — Oh, my God! the sudden alarm, the sudden sight of you, has destroyed her!'

'I am afraid it has!' exclaimed Godolphin wildly, and hardly knowing what he said — 'I am indeed afraid it has! My poor sister — my unhappy, devoted Adelina! — have I then found you only to destroy you? But perhaps,' continued he, after a moment's pause, during which Emmeline and the nurse were chafing the hands and temples of the dying patient — 'perhaps she may recover. Send instantly for advice — run — fly — let me go myself for assistance.'

He would now have run out of the room; but Emmeline, whose admirable presence of mind this sudden scene of terror had not conquered, stopped him.

'Stay, Sir,' said she, 'I beseech you, stay. You know not whither to go. I will instantly send those who do.'

She then left the room, and ordered a servant to fetch the physician; for she dreaded least Mr. Godolphin should discover the real name and quality of the patient to those to whom he might apply; and on returning to the bed side, where Lady Adelina still lay without any signs of existence, and by which her brother still knelt in speechless agony, her fears were again alive, least when the medical gentlemen arrived, his grief and desperation should betray the secret to them. While her first apprehension was for the life of her friend, these secondary considerations were yet extremely alarming — for she knew, that should Lady Adelina recover, her life would be for ever embittered, if not again endangered, by the discovery which seemed impending and almost inevitable.

The women who were about her having now applied every remedy they could think of without success, began loudly to lament themselves. Emmeline, commanding her own anguish, besought them to stifle theirs, and not to give way to fruitless exclamations while there was yet hope, but to continue their endeavours to recover their lady. Then addressing herself to Mr. Godolphin, she roused him from the stupor of grief in which he had fallen, while he gazed with an impassioned and agonizing look on the pale countenance of his sister.

'Pardon me, Sir,' said she, 'if I entreat you to go down stairs and await the arrival of the advice I have sent for. Should my poor friend recover, your presence may renew and encrease the alarm of her spirits, and embarrass her returning recollection; and should she not recover, you had better hear such mournful tidings in any place rather than this.'

'Oh! if I *do* hear them,' answerd he, wildly, 'it matters little where. But I *will* withdraw, Madam, since you seem to desire it.'

He had hardly seen Emmeline before. He now turned his eyes mournfully upon her — 'It is, I presume, Miss Mowbray,' said he, 'who thus, with an angel's tenderness in an angel's form, would spare the sorrows of a stranger?'

Emmeline, unable to speak, led the way down to the parlour, and Godolphin silently followed her.

'Go back,' said he, tremulously, as soon as they reached the room — 'go back to my sister; your tender assiduity may do more for her than the people about her. Your voice, your looks, will soothe and tranquillize her, should she awaken from her long insensibility. Ah! tell her, her brother came only to rescue her from the misery of her unworthy lot — Tell her his affection, his brotherly affection, hopes to give her consolation; and restore her — if it may yet be — to her repose. But go, dearest Miss Mowbray go! — somebody comes in — perhaps the physician.'

Emmeline now opening the parlour door, found it to be indeed the physician she expected; and with a fearful heart she followed him, informing him, as they went up stairs, that the sudden appearance of Mrs. St. Laure's brother, whom she had not seen for two or three years, had thrown her into a fainting fit, from which not all their endeavours had recovered her.

He remonstrated vehemently against the extreme indiscretion of such an interview. Emmeline, who knew not by what strange chain of circumstances it had been brought about, had nothing to reply.

So feeble were the appearances of remaining life, that the physician could pronounce nothing certainly in regard to his patient. He gave, however, directions to her attendants; but after every application had been used, all that could be said was, that she was not actually dead. As soon as the physician had written his prescription and retired, Emmeline recollected the painful state of suspence in which she had left Mr. Godolphin, and trying to recover courage to go thro' the painful scene before her, she went down to him.

As she opened the door, he met her.

'I have seen the doctor,' said he, in a broken and hurried voice — 'and from his account I am convinced Adelina is dying.'

'I hope not,' faintly answered Emmeline. 'There is yet a possibility, tho' I fear no great probability of her recovery.'

'My Adelina!' resumed he, walking about the room — 'my Adelina! for whose sake I so anxiously wished to return to England — Gracious God! I am come too late to assist her! Some strange mystery surely hangs over her! Long lost to all her friends, I find her here dying! The sight of me, instead of relieving her sorrow seems to have accelerated her dissolution! And you, Madam, to whose goodness she appears to be so greatly indebted — may I ask by what fortunate circumstance, lost and obscure as she has been, she has acquired such a friend?'

Emmeline, shuddering at the apprehension of enquiries she found it impossible to answer, was wholly at a loss how to reply to this. She knew not of what Mr. Godolphin was informed — of what he was ignorant; and dreaded to say too much, or to be detected in a false representation. She therefore, agitated and hesitating, gravely said —

'It is not now a time, Sir, to ask any thing relative to Lady Adelina. I am myself too ill to enter into conversation; and wish, as you have been yourself greatly affected, that you would now retire, and endeavour to make yourself as easy as you can. To-morrow may, perhaps, afford us more chearful prospects — or at least this cruel suspense will be over, and the dear sufferer at peace.'

She sobbed, and turned away. Godolphin, rising, said in a faultering voice —

'Yes, I will go! since my stay can only encrease the pain of that generous and sensible heart. I will go — but not to rest! — I cannot rest! But do you try, most amiable creature! to obtain some repose — Try, I beseech you, to recover your spirits, which have been so greatly hurried.'

He knew not what he said; and was hastening out of the room, when Emmeline, recollecting how ardently Lady Adelina had desired the concealment of her name and family, stopped him as he was quitting her.

'Yet one thing, Captain Godolphin, allow me to entreat of you?'

'What can I refuse you?' answered he, returning.

'Only — are you known at Bath?'

'Probably I may. It is above three years since I was in England, and much longer since I have been here. But undoubtedly some one or other will know me.'

'Then do indulge me in one request. See as few people as you can; and if you accidentally meet any of your friends, do not say that Lady Adelina is here.'

'Not meet any one if I can avoid it! — and if I do, not speak of my sister! And why is all this? — why this concealment, this mystery? —why —'

Emmeline, absolutely overcome, sat down without speaking. Godolphin, seeing her uneasiness, said —

'But I will not distress you, Madam, by farther questions. Your commands shall be sufficient. I will stifle my anxiety and obey you.' Then bowing respectfully, he added — 'To-morrow, at as early an hour as I dare hope for admittance, I shall be at the door. Heaven bless and reward the fair and gentle Miss Mowbray — and may it have mercy on my poor Adelina!' — He sighed deeply, and left the house.

Lady Adelina, tho' not so entirely insensible, was yet but little amended. But as what alteration there was, was for the better, Emmeline endeavoured to recall her own agitated and dissipated spirits. The extraordinary scene which had just passed, was still present to her imagination; the last words of Godolphin, still vibrated in her ears. 'Fair and gentle Miss Mowbray!' repeated she. 'He knows my name; yet seems ignorant of every thing that relates to his sister!'

Her astonishment at this circumstance was succeeded by reflecting on the unpleasant task she must have if Mr. Godolphin should again enquire into her first acquaintance with his sister. To relate to him the melancholy story she had heard, would, she found, be an undertaking to which she was wholly unequal; and she was equally averse to the invention of a plausible falsehood. From this painful apprehension she meditated how to extricate herself; but the longer she thought of it, the more she despaired of it. The terrors, of such a conversation hourly augmented; and wholly and for ever to escape from it, she sometimes det-ermined to write. But from executing that design, was with-held by considering that if Godolphin was of a fiery and impetuous temper, he would probably, without reflection or delay, fly to vengeance, and precipitate every evil which Lady Adelina dreaded.

After having exhausted every idea on the subject, she could think of nothing on which her imagination could rest, but to send to Mrs. Stafford, acquaint her with the danger of Lady Adelina, and conjure her if possible to come to her. This she knew she would do unless some singular circumstance in her own family prevented her attention to her friends.

Resolved to embrace therefore this hope, she dispatched an hasty billet by an express to Woodfield; and then betook herself to a bed on the floor, which she had ordered to be placed by the side of that where Lady Adelina, in happy tho' dangerous insensibility, still seemed to repose almost in the arms of death.

Emmeline could not, however, obtain even a momentary forgetfulness. Tho' she could not repent her attention to the unhappy Lady Adelina, she was yet sensible of her indiscretion in having put herself into the situation she was now in; the cruel, unfeeling world would, she feared, condemn her; and of its reflections she could not think without pain. But her heart, her generous sympathizing heart, more than acquitted — it repaid her.

Towards the middle of the night, Lady Adelina, who had made two or three faint efforts to speak, sighed, and again in faint murmurs attempted to explain herself. Emmeline started up and eagerly listened; and in a low whisper heard her ask for her child.

Emmeline ordered it instantly to be brought; and those eyes which had so lately seemed closed for ever, were opened in search of this beloved object; then, as if satisfied in beholding it living and well, they closed again, while she imprinted a kiss on its little hand. She then asked for Emmeline; who, delighted with this apparent amendment, prevailed on her to take what had been ordered for her. She appeared still better in a few moments, but was yet extremely languid.

'I have had a dreadful dream, my Emmeline,' said she, at length — 'a long and dreadful dream! But it is gone — you are here; my poor little boy too is well; and this alarming vision will I hope haunt me no more.'

Emmeline, who feared that the dream was indeed a reality, exhorted her to think only of her recovery; of which, added she cheerfully, we have no longer any doubt.

'Comfortable and consoling angel!' sighed Lady Adelina — 'your presence is surely safety. Do not leave me!'

Emmeline promised not to quit the room; and elate with hopes of her friend's speedy restoration to health, fell herself into a tranquil and refreshing slumber.

On awakening the next morning, she found Lady Adelina much better; but still, whenever she spoke, dwelling on her supposed dream, and sometimes talking with that incoherence which had for some weeks before so greatly alarmed her. Her own dread of meeting Godolphin was by no means lessened; and to prevent an immediate interview, she dispatched to him a note.

'Sir,

'I am happy in having it in my power to assure you that our dear patient is much better. But as uninterrupted tranquillity is absolutely necessary, that, and other considerations, induce me to beg you will forbear coming hither to day. You may depend on having hourly intelligence, and that we shall be desirous of the pleasure of seeing you when the safety of my friend admits it.

I have the honour to be, Sir,
your most humble servant,
EMMELINE MOWBRAY.'

Sept. 20, 17—.

To this note, Mr. Godolphin answered —

'If Miss Mowbray will only allow me to wait on her for one moment in the parlour, I will not again trespass on her time till I have her own permission.
W.G.'

This request, Emmeline was obliged, with whatever reluctance, to comply with. She therefore sent a verbal acquiescence; and repaired to the bed-side of Lady Adelina, who had asked for her.

'Will you pardon my folly, my dear Emmeline,' said she languidly — 'but I cannot be easy till I have told you what a strange idea has seized me. I seemed, last night, I know not at what time, to be suddenly awakened by a voice which loudly repeated the name of Trelawny. Startled by the sound, I thought I undrew the curtain, and saw my brother William, who stood looking angrily on me. I felt greatly terrified; and growing extremely sick, I lost the vision. But now again its recollection harrasses my imagination; and the image of my brother, sterner, and with a ruder aspect than he was wont to wear, still seems present before me. Oh! he was accustomed to be all goodness and gentleness, and to love his poor Adelina. But now he too will throw me from him — he too will detest and despise me — Or perhaps,' continued she, after a short pause — 'perhaps he is dead. I am not superstitious — but this dream pursues me.'

Emmeline, who had hoped that the very terror of this sudden interview had obliterated its remembrance, said every thing she thought likely to quiet her mind, and to persuade her that the uneasy images represented in her imperfect slumbers were merely the effect of her weakness and perturbed spirits.

The impression, however, was too strong to be effaced by arguments. It still hung heavy on her heart, irritated the fever which had before been only slight, and deprived her almost entirely of sleep; or if she slept, she again fancied herself awakened by her brother, angrily repeating the name of Trelawny.

Sometimes, starting in terror from these feverish dreams, she called on her brother to pardon and pity her; sometimes in piercing accents deplored his death, and sometimes besought him to spare Fitz-Edward. These incoherences were particularly distressing; as names were often heard by the attendants which Emmeline hoped to have concealed; and it was hardly possible longer to deceive the physician and apothecary who attended her.

With an uneasy heart, and a countenance pensively expressive of its feelings, she went down to receive Captain Godolphin in the parlour.

'I fear, Miss Mowbray,' said he, as soon as they were seated, 'you will think me too ready to take advantage of your goodness. But there is that appearance of candour and compassion about you, that I determined rather to trust to your goodness for pardon, than to remain longer in a state of suspense about my sister, which I have already found most insupportable. In the note you honoured me with to-day you say she is better. Is she then out of danger? Has she proper advice?'

'She has the best advice, Sir. I cannot, however, say that she is out of danger, but' — She hesitated, and knew not how to proceed.

'But — you hope, rather than believe, she will recover,' cried Godolphin eagerly.

'I both hope and believe it. Mr. Godolphin, you yesterday did me the honour to suppose that I had been fortunate enough to be of some service to Lady Adelina; suffer me to take advantage of a supposition so flattering, and to claim a sort of right to ask in my turn a favour.'

'Surely I shall consider it as an honour to receive, and as happiness to obey, any command of Miss Mowbray's.'

'Promise me then to observe the same silence in regard to your sister as I asked of you last night. Trust me with her safety, and believe it will not be neglected. But you must neither speak of her to others, or question me about her.'

'Good God! from whence can arise the necessity for these precautions! What dreadful obscurity surrounds her! What am I to fear? What am I to suppose?'

'You will not, then,' said Emmeline, gravely — 'you will not oblige me, by desisting from all questions 'till this trifling restraint can be taken off?'

'I will, I do promise to be guided wholly by you; and to bear, however difficult it may be, the suspense, the frightful suspense in which I must remain. Tell me, however, that Adelina is not in immediate danger.' But, added he, as if recollecting himself, 'may I not apply for information on that head to her physician?'

'Not for the world!' answered Emmeline, with unguarded quickness — 'not for the world!'

'Not for the world!' — repeated Godolphin, with an accent of astonishment. 'Heaven and earth! But I have promised to ask nothing — I must obey and will now release you, Madam.'

Godolphin then took his leave; and Emmeline, whose heart had throbbed violently throughout this dialogue, sat down alone to compose and recollect herself. She saw, that to keep Godolphin many days ignorant of the truth would be impossible: and from the eager anxiety of his questions, she feared that all the horrors Lady Adelina's troubled imagination had represented would be realized —apprehensions, which seemed armed with new terror since she had seen and conversed with this William Godolphin, of whose excellent heart and noble spirit she had before heard so much both from Lady Adelina and Fitz-Edward, and whose appearance seemed to confirm the favourable impression those accounts had given her.

Godolphin, who was now about five and twenty, had passed the greatest part of his life at sea. The various climates he had visited had deprived his complextion of much of its English freshness; but his face was animated by dark eyes full of intelligence and spirit; his hair, generally carelessly dressed, was remarkably fine, and his person tall, light, and graceful, yet so commanding, that whoever saw him immediately and involuntarily felt their admiration mingled with respect. His whole figure was such as brought to the mind ideas of the race of heroes from which he was descended; his voice was particularly grateful to the ear, and his address appeared to Emmeline to be a fortunate compound of the insinuating softness of Fitz-Edward with the fire and vivacity of Delamere. Of this, however, she could inadequately judge, as he was now under such depression of spirits: and however pleasing he appeared, Emmeline, who conceived herself absolutely engaged to Delamere, thought of him only as the brother of Lady Adelina; yet insensibly she felt herself more than ever interested for the event of his hearing how little Fitz-Edward had deserved the warm friendship he had felt for him. And her thoughts dwelling perpetually on that subject, magnified the painful circumstances of the approaching ecclaircissement; while her fears for Lady Adelina's life, who continued to languish in a low fever with frequent delirium, so harrassed and oppressed her, that her own health was visibly affected. But without attending to it, she passed all her hours in anxiously watching the turns of Lady Adelina's disorder; or, when she could for a moment escape, in giving vent to her full heart by weeping over the little infant, whose birth, so similar to her own, seemed to render it to her a more interesting and affecting object. She lamented the evils to which it might be exposed; tho' of a sex which would prevent its encountering the same species of sorrow as that which had embittered her own life. Of her friendless and desolate situation, she was never more sensible than now. She felt herself more unhappy than she had ever yet been; and would probably have sunk under her extreme uneasiness, had not the arrival of Mrs. Stafford, at the end of three days, relieved her from many of her fears and apprehensions.

CHAPTER V

MRS. Stafford no sooner heard from Emmeline that Godolphin was yet ignorant of the true reason of Lady Adelina's concealment, than she saw the necessity of immediately explaining it; and this task, however painful, she without hesitation undertook.

He was therefore summoned to their lodgings by a note from Emmeline, who on his arrival introduced him to Mrs. Stafford, and left them together; when, with as much tenderness as possible, and mingling with the mortifying detail many representations of the necessity there was for his conquering his resentment, she at length concluded it; watching anxiously the changes in Godolphin's countenance, which sometimes expressed only pity and affection for his sister, sometimes rage and indignation against Fitz-Edward.

Both the brothers of Lady Adelina had been accustomed to consider her with a particular fondness. The unfortunate circumstance of her losing her mother immediately after her birth, seemed to have given her a melancholy title to their tenderness; and the resemblance she bore to that dear mother, whom they both remembered, and on whose memory their father dwelt with undiminished regret, endeared her to them still more. To these united claims on the heart and the protection of William Godolphin, another was added equally forcible, in a letter written by his father with the trembling hand of anxious solicitude, when he felt himself dying, and when, looking back with lingering affection on the children of her whom he hoped soon to rejoin, he saw with anguish his youngest daughter liable from her situation to deviate into indiscretion, and surrounded by the numberless dangers which attend on a young and beautiful woman, whose husband has neither talents to attach her affections or judgment to direct her actions. Lord Westhaven, conscious of her hazardous circumstances, and feeling in his last moments the keenest anguish, in knowing that his mistaken care had exposed her to them, hoped, by interesting both her brothers to watch over her, that he should obviate the dangers he apprehended. He had therefore, in all their conversations, recommended her to his eldest son; and as he was not happy enough to embrace the younger before he died, had addressed to him a last letter on the same subject.

Such were the powerful ties that bound Mr. Godolphin to love and defend Lady Adelina with more than a brother's fondness. Hastening therefore to obey the dying injunctions of his father, and in the hope of rendering the life of his beloved sister, if not happy, at least honourable and contented, he had heard, that she had clandestinely absented herself from her family, and after a long search had found her abandoned to remorse and despair; her reputation blasted; her health ruined; her intellects disordered; and all by the perfidy of a man, in whom he, from long friendship, and his sister, from family connection, had placed unbounded confidence.

Tho' Godolphin had one of the best tempers in the world — a temper which the roughness of those among whom he lived had only served to soften and humanize, and which was immovable by the usual accidents that ruffle others, yet he had also in a great excess all those keen feelings, which fill a heart of extreme sensibility; added to a courage, that in the hour of danger had been proved to be as cool as it was undaunted. Of him might be said what was the glorious praise of immortal Bayard — that he was 'sans peur et sans reproche' (without fear and without reproach;) and educated with a high sense of honour himself, as well as possessing a heart calculated to enjoy, and a hand to defend, the unblemished dignity of his family, all his passions were roused and awakened by the injury it had sustained from Fitz-Edward, and he beheld him as a monster whom it was infamy to forgive. Hardly therefore had Mrs. Stafford concluded her distressing recital, than, as if commanding himself by a violent effort, he thanked her warmly yet incoherently for her unexampled goodness to his sister, recommended her still to her generous care, and the friendship of Miss Mowbray, and without any threat against Fitz-Edward, or even a comment on what he had heard, arose to depart. But Mrs. Stafford, more alarmed by this determined tho' quiet resentment and by the expression of his countenance than if he had burst into exclamations and menaces, perceived that the crisis was now come when he must either be persuaded to conquer his just resentment, or by giving it way destroy, while he attempted to revenge, the fame of his sister.

She besought him therefore to sit down a moment; and when he had done so, she told him, that if he really thought himself under any obligations to Miss Mowbray or to her for the services they had been so fortunate as to render Lady Adelina, his making all they had been doing ineffectual, would be a most mortifying return; and such must be the case, if he rashly flew to seek vengeance on Fitz-Edward: 'for that you have such a design,' continued she, 'I have no doubt; allow me, however, to suppose that I have, by doing your sister some good offices, acquired a right to speak of her affairs.'

'Surely,' answered Mr. Godolphin, 'you have; and surely I must hear with respect and attention, tho' possibly not with conviction, every opinion with which you may honour me.'

She then represented to him, with all the force of reason, how little he could remedy the evil by hazarding his own life or by taking that of Fitz-Edward.

'At present,' continued she, 'the secret is known only to me, Miss Mowbray, and Lady Adelina's woman; if it is farther exposed, the heirs of Mr. Trelawny, who are so deeply interested, will undoubtedly take measures to prove that the infant has no just claim to the estate they so eagerly expect. Mr. Trelawny's sister has already entertained suspicions, which the least additional information would give her grounds to pursue, and the whole affair must then inevitably become public. Surely this consideration alone should determine you — why then need I urge others equally evident and equally forcible.'

Godolphin acknowledged that there was much of truth in the arguments she used; but denied that any consideration should influence him to forgive the man who had thus basely and ungenerously betrayed the confidence of his family.

'However,' added he again, checking the heat into which he feared a longer conversation on this subject might betray him — 'I have not yet, Madam, absolutely formed the resolution of which you seem so apprehensive; and am indeed too cruelly hurt to be able to talk longer on the subject. Suffer me therefore once more to bid you a good day!'

But the encreasing gloom of his countenance, and forced calm of his manner, appeared to be symptoms so unfavourable, that Mrs. Stafford thought there was no hope of being able to prevent an immediate and fatal meeting between him and Fitz-Edward but by engaging him in a promise at least to delay it; this she attempted by the most earnest arguments, and the most pressing persuasions; but all she could obtain was an assurance that he would remain at Bath 'till the next day, and see her again in the evening.

In the mean time the delirium of Lady Adelina, (which had recurred at intervals ever since the transient sight she had of her brother) more frequently, and with more alarming symptoms, returned; and the fever which had at first threatened the loss of her life, now seemed to be fixing on her brain, and to menace, by a total deprivation of reason reducing her to a condition to which death itself must be preferable. She still, even in her wildest wanderings, knew Emmeline, and still caressed her little boy; but much of her time passed in incoherent and rambling discourse; in which she talked of Fitz-Edward and her brother William, and held with them both imaginary dialogues. Sometimes she deprecated the wrath of her elder brother: and then her disordered fancy ran to the younger; to him from whom she had, in her early life, found pity and protection in all her little sorrows.

Mrs. Stafford thought it too hazardous to let her again see her brother, while her intellects were thus disarranged; as she trembled lest she should start into actual madness. But it was absolutely necessary to do something; not only because Mr. Godolphin's impatience made every delay dangerous, but because it was hardly possible to keep the secret from the physicians and attendants, who had already heard much more than they ought to have known.

She determined, therefore, after consulting with Emmeline, to introduce Godolphin into the room adjoining to that where Lady Adelina now sat some hours every day in an easy chair. The affecting insanity of his unhappy sister, and the mournful and pathetic entreaties she frequently used, were likely, in the opinion of the fair friends, to effectuate more than their most earnest persuasions; and prevail on him to drop all thoughts of that resentment, which could not cure but might encrease her calamities.

Mrs. Stafford had heard from him, that he gained information as to the place of his sister's residence from the mother of Lady Adelina's woman; who being the reduced widow of a clergyman, resided in the Bishop's alms-houses at Bromley, where her daughter frequently sent her such assistance as her own œconomy, or the bounty of her lady, enabled her to supply. A few weeks before, she had sent her a note for ten pounds; and not apprehending that an enquiry would be made of her, had desired her to acknowledge the receipt of it, and direct to her at Bath, where she said her lady was with a Miss Mowbray.

Lady Clancarryl, among many expedients to recover traces of her sister, had at length recollected this widow, and had desired Mr. Godolphin to make immediate enquiry of her.

He had hastened therefore to Bromley, and easily found the poor woman, who was paralytic and almost childish. Her letters were read for her by one of her neighbours; a person, who, being present at the arrival of Mr. Godolphin, immediately found that something was to be got; and busily put into his hands the very letter which had enclosed the note, and which contained the direction.

He eagerly copied the address; and leaving a handsome present for the use of the old widow, he delayed not a moment to set out for Bath, where he soon found the house, and where he had enquired for Lady Adelina Trelawny.

The servant of the house who opened the door assured him no such person was there. He supposed that for some reason or other she was denied; and insisting on being allowed to go up stairs, had entered the room in the abrupt manner which had so greatly alarmed his sister.

In hopes of counteracting the fatal effects of the discovery which had unavoidably followed this interview, Godolphin was, on his return in the afternoon, introduced into the dining-room, which opened into Lady Adelina's bed-chamber. The door was a-jar; the partition thin; and Mrs. Stafford was pretty well assured that the poor patient would be heard distinctly. Godolphin came in, pale from the conflict of his mind; and all his features expressed anger and sorrow, with which he seemed vainly struggling. He bowed, and sat down in silence.

Mrs. Stafford only was in the room; and as soon as he was seated, said, in a low voice, yet with forced chearfulness —

'Well, Sir, I hope that Miss Mowbray and myself have prevailed on you to drop at present every other design than the truly generous one of healing the wounded heart of our fair unfortunate friend.'

'And shall he who has wounded it,' slowly and sternly replied Godolphin — 'shall he who has wounded it so basely, escape me?'

At this instant Lady Adelina, who had been some time silent, exclaimed hastily — 'Oh! spare him! my dear brother! and spare your poor Adelina! who will not trouble — who will not disgrace you long!'

'Where is she?' said Godolphin, starting — 'Good God! what is it I hear?'

'Your unhappy sister,' answered Mrs. Stafford; 'whom the idea of your determined vengeance has already driven to distraction.'

Again Lady Adelina spoke. Her brother listened in breathless anguish.

'Ah! William! — and are *you* grown cruel? You, on whom I depended for pity and protection?'

'Surely,' said he, 'surely she knows I am here?'

'No,' answered Mrs. Stafford, 'she knows nothing. But this fear has incessantly pursued her; and since she saw you she dwells more frequently on it, tho' her erring memory sometimes wanders to other objects.'

'It is very true, my Lord!' cried Lady Adelina, with affected calmness, her thoughts wavering again towards Lord Westhaven — 'It is all very true! I have deserved all your reproaches! I am ready to make all the atonement I can! Then you will both of you, my brothers, be satisfied — for William has told me that if I die he should be content, for then all might be forgotten.' She ended with a deep sigh; and Godolphin, wildly starting from his seat, said —

'This is too much! you cannot expect me to bear this! — let me go to her!'

'Would you go then,' answered Mrs. Stafford, 'to confirm her fears and to drive her to deeper desperation? If you see her, it must be to soothe and comfort her; to assure her of your forgiveness, and that you will bury your resentment against — '

'Accursed! doubly accursed be the infamous villain who has driven her to this! And must I bear it tamely! Oh! injured memory of my father! — oh! my poor, undone sister!' He walked about the room; the tears ran from his eyes; and Mrs. Stafford, fearing that his hurried step and deep sobs would be heard by Lady Adelina, determined to bring the scene to a crisis and not to lose the influence she hoped she had gained on his mind. She therefore went into the other room, and shutting the door, advanced with a smile towards the lovely lunatic.

'What will you say, my dear Adelina, if I bring you the best news you can possibly hear?'

'News!' repeated Lady Adelina, looking at her with eyes which too plainly denoted her unsettled mind — 'News! — Ah! dear Madam! I know very well that all the world is happy but me; and if you are happy, I am very glad; but as to *me* — Do you indeed think it is reasonable I should part with him?'

'With whom?' said Mrs. Stafford.

'Why, one condition which they insist upon is, that I should give up my poor little one to them, and never ask to see him again. William was the most urgent for this — William, who used to be so good, so gentle, so compassionate to every body! Alas! he is now more cruel and relentless than the rest!'

'So far from it,' said Mrs. Stafford, 'your brother William loves you as much as ever; he will come and tell you so himself if you will only be composed, and talk less strangely.'

'To see me!' exclaimed she, as if suddenly recovering her recollection — 'Oh! when? — where? — how?'

But again it forsook her; and she continued —

'Ah! he comes perhaps to tell me of the blood he has spilt, and to load me with reproaches for having obliged him to destroy a friend whom he once loved. If that is indeed so, why let him come and plunge another dagger in this poor heart, which has always loved him!'

She was silent a moment, and then languidly went on —

'I thought some time since that I saw him, and Miss Mowbray was with him; but it was only a dream, for I know he is in Jamaica: and when he does come home, he will harden his heart against me — he will be my judge, and sternly will he judge me — he will forget that he is my brother!'

'Never! my poor Adelina,' cried Godolphin, rushing into the room, 'never can I forget that I am your brother — never can I cease to feel for you compassion and tenderness.'

He would have taken her in his arms; but struck by the dreadful alteration that appeared in her face and figure, he stopt short, and looking at her with silent horror, seemed incapable of uttering what he felt.

She knew him; but could neither speak or shed a tear for some moments. At length, she held out to him her emaciated hand.

'It is *indeed* William!' said she. 'He seems, too, very sorry for me. My dear brother, do you then pardon and pity the poor Adelina?'

'Both! both!' answered Godolphin, sobbing, and seating himself by her. He threw his arms round her, and her pale cheek rested on his bosom, while her eyes were fixed on his face.

'Stay!' exclaimed she, after a momentary pause, and disengaging herself suddenly from him — 'Stay! I have yet another question, if I dared ask it! Do you know all? and have you no blood to answer for, on my account? Will you assure me you will not seek it?'

'For mercy's sake!' said Mrs. Stafford, 'satisfy her, Mr. Godolphin —satisfy her at once — you see to what is owing this alienation of her reason.'

'No,' reassumed the afflicted Adelina, 'you need not answer me; I see you cannot — will not forgive — '

'Name him not, Adelina!' sternly and quickly answered he — 'my soul recoils at this idea! I cannot, I will not promise any thing!'

At this period, Emmeline, who was unwilling to trust the servants at such a moment, entered with the infant of Lady Adelina sleeping in her arms.

'See,' said Mrs. Stafford, 'a little unfortunate creature, whose innocence must surely plead forcibly to you: he comes to join our intreaties to you to spare his mother!'

Emmeline laid the infant in the lap of Lady Adelina, who was yet unable to shed a tear. Godolphin beheld it with mingled horror and pity; but the latter sentiment seemed to predominate; and Emmeline, whose voice was calculated to go to the heart, began to try its influence; and imploring him to be calm, and to promise his sister an eternal oblivion of the past, she urged every argument that should convince him of its necessity, and every motive that could affect his reason or his compassion.

He gazed on her with reverence and admiration while she spoke, and seemed greatly affected by what she said. Animated by the hope of success, her eyes were lightened up with new brilliancy, and her glowing cheeks and expressive features became more than ever attractive. A convulsive laugh from Lady Adelina interrupted her, and drew the attention of Godolphin entirely to his sister. Emmeline, who saw her reason again forsaking her, took the sleeping baby from her lap. She had hardly done so, before, trying to rise from the chair, she shrieked aloud — for again the image of Fitz-Edward, dying by the hand of her brother, was before her.

'See!' cried she, 'see! there he lies! — he is already expiring! yet William forgives him not! What? would you strike him again? now! while he is dying? — Go! cruel, cruel brother!' attempting to put Godolphin from her — 'Go! — Oh! touch me not with those polluted hands, they are stained with human blood!' A convulsive shudder and a deep sigh seemed to exhaust all her remaining strength, and she fell back in her chair, pale and faint; and with fixed, unmeaning eyes, appeared no longer conscious even of the terrors which pursued her.

But the look of incurable anguish which her features wore; the wild import of her words; and the sight of the unfortunate child, who seemed born only to share her wretchedness; could not long be beheld unmoved by a heart like Godolphin's, which possessed all that tenderness that distinguishes the truly brave. Again he threw his arms round his sister, and sobbing, said —

'Hear me, Adelina — hear me and be tranquil! I will promise to be guided by your excellent friends — I will do nothing that shall give pain to them or to you!'

'Thank God!' exclaimed Emmeline, 'that you at last hear reason! Remember this promise is given to us all.'

'It is,' answered Godolphin; 'but try to make poor Adelina sensible of it.' She no longer understood any thing; but with her eyes shut, and her hands clasped in each other, was at least quiet.

'I cannot bear it!' continued Godolphin — 'I must go for a few moments to recover myself!' He then left the room, desiring Emmeline to comfort and compose his sister, who soon afterwards asked hastily what was become of him?

Emmeline, pleased to find she had a clear recollection of his having been with her, now told her that he had most solemnly assured them he would think no more of seeking Fitz-Edward on account of this unhappy affair. As she seemed still, in fearful apprehension, to doubt the reality of this promise, Godolphin, who was only in the next room with Mrs. Stafford, returned, and assured her of his pity, his forbearance and his forgiveness.

After some farther efforts on the part of Emmeline, and protestations on that of Godolphin, tears, which had been long denied to Lady Adelina, came to her relief. She wept, caressed her infant, and blessed and thanked her brother and her friends. When capable of recollection, she knew that towards those whom he had once pardoned, he was incapable of reproach or unkindness; and her mind, eased of the fears which had so long harrassed it, seemed to be recovering its tone. Still, however, the sense of her own incurable unhappiness, her own irretrievable unworthiness, and the disgrace of having sullied the honour of her family, and given pain to such a brother, overwhelmed her with grief and confusion; while her reason, as it at intervals returned, served only to shew her the abyss into which she had fallen: and she sometimes even regretted those hours of forgetfulness, when she possessed not the power of steady reflection, and when the sad reality was obliterated by wild and imaginary horrors.

CHAPTER VI

SOME few days elapsed before there was any great alteration for the better in Lady Adelina. But the incessant attention of her friends, the soothing pity of her brother, and the skill of her physician, slowly conquered the lurking fever which had so long hung about her; and her intellects, tho' still disordered at times, were more collected, and gave reason to hope that she would soon entirely recover.

In the meantime Captain Godolphin communicated to Mrs. Stafford the resolution he had taken about his sister. He said that she should renounce for ever all claim on the Trelawny estate, except only the stipend settled on her as a consideration for the fortune she was to receive at the death of the dowager Lady Westhaven, and which was only three hundred a year; a sum which he thought made her but a paltry and inadequate compensation for having passed two years in the society of such a man as Trelawny.

He added, that he had a house in the Isle of Wight (almost all the patrimony his father had been able to give him,) where, as his ship was now out of commission, he proposed residing himself; and whither he should insist upon Lady Adelina's retiring, without any future attempt to see or correspond with Fitz-Edward.

As to the child, he asked if Mrs. Stafford would have the goodness to see that it was taken care of at some cottage in her neighbourhood, 'till he could adjust matters with the Trelawny family, and put an end to all those fears which might tempt them to enquire into its birth; after which he said he would take it to his own house, and call it a son of his own; a precaution that would throw an obscurity over the truth which would hardly ever be removed, when none were particularly interested to remove it.

These designs he desired Mrs. Stafford to communicate to Lady Adelina; and as she was obliged to return home in two days, she took the earliest opportunity of doing so.

To these conditions her brother offered, Lady Adelina thought herself most happy to consent. The little boy was immediately baptized by the name of William Godolphin, and his unfortunate mother now began to flatter herself that her disastrous history might he concealed even from her elder brother, Lord Westhaven; of whose indignation and resentment she had ever the most alarming apprehensions. But while the hope of escaping them by her brother William's generous compassion, gave to her heavy sorrows some alleviation, they were renewed with extreme poignancy, by the approaching separation from her inestimable friends. Mrs. Stafford could no longer delay her return to her family; and Emmeline, who now saw Lady Adelina out of danger and in the protection of her brother, was desirous of accompanying her back to Woodfield.

Lady Adelina ineffectually tried to bear this early departure with some degree of fortitude and resolution. Nor was it *her* heart alone that felt desolate and unhappy at its approach — that of her brother, had received an impression from the mental and personal perfections of Emmeline, which being at first deep, had soon become indelible; and ignorant of her engagement, he had indulged it till he found it no longer possible for him to forbear making her the first object of his life, and that the value of his existence depended wholly on her.

Emmeline was yet quite unconscious of this: but Mrs. Stafford had seen it almost from the first moment of her seeing Godolphin. In their frequent conversation, she observed that the very name of Emmeline had the power of fascination; that he was never weary of hearing her praises; that whenever he thought himself unobserved, his eyes were in pursuit of her; while fondly gazing on her face, he seemed to drink deep draughts of intoxicating passion.

Mrs. Stafford, who knew what ardent and fatal love, such excellence of person and understanding might produce in a heart susceptible of all their power, was alarmed for the happiness of this amiable man; and with regret saw him nourishing an affection which she thought must be entirely hopeless.

These apprehensions, every hour's observation encreased. Yet Mrs. Stafford determined not to communicate them to Emmeline; but to put an end to the flattering delusion which led on Godolphin to indulge his passion, by telling him, as soon as possible, of the engagement Emmeline had formed with Mr. Delamere.

Accident soon furnished her with an opportunity. While they were all sitting together after dinner, a packet of letters was brought in, and among others which were forwarded to Mrs. Stafford from Woodfield, was one for Emmeline.

Mrs. Stafford gave it to her, saying — 'From France, by the post mark?'

Emmeline replied that it was. She changed colour as she opened it.

'From Mr. Delamere?' enquired Mrs. Stafford.

'No,' answered she, 'it is from Lady Westhaven. Your brother and her Ladyship are well,' continued she, addressing herself to Mr. Godolphin, 'and are at Paris; where they propose staying 'till Lady Montreville and Miss Delamere join them as they come to England.'

'And when are they expected?' said Godolphin.

'In about a month,' replied Emmeline. 'But Lord and Lady Westhaven do not propose to return 'till next spring — they only pass a few days all together at Paris.'

'And where is Mr. Delamere wandering to?' significantly and smilingly asked Mrs. Stafford.

'Lady Westhaven says only,' answered Emmeline, blushing and casting down her eyes, 'that he has left Lady Montreville, and is, they believe, gone to Geneva.'

'However,' reassumed Mrs. Stafford, 'we shall undoubtedly see him in England in March.'

Emmeline, in still greater embarrassment, answered two or three other questions which Godolphin asked her about his brother, and soon after left the room.

Godolphin, who saw there was something relative to Delamere with which he was unacquainted, had a confused idea immediately occur to him of his attachment: and the pain it gave him was so acute, that he wished at once to know whether it was well founded.

'Why does Mr. Delamere certainly return in March?' said he, addressing himself to Mrs. Stafford, 'rather than with his mother?'

'To fulfil his engagement,' gravely and coldly replied she.

'Of what nature is it?' asked he.

Mrs. Stafford then related the history of Delamere's long and violent passion for Emmeline; and the reluctant consent he had wrung from Lord and Lady Montreville, together with the promise obtained from Miss Mowbray.

While Mrs. Stafford was making this recital, she saw, by the variations of Godolphin's countenance, that she had too truly guessed the state of his heart. Expressive as his features were, it was not in his power to conceal what he felt in being convinced that he had irrecoverably fixed his affections on a woman who was the destined wife of another: and awaking from the soft visions which Hope had offered, to certain despondence, he found himself too cruelly hurt to be able to continue the conversation; and after a few faint efforts, which only betrayed his internal anguish, he hurried away.

Such, however, was the opinion Mrs. Stafford conceived of his honour and understanding, that she had no apprehension that he would attempt imparting to the heart of Emmeline any portion of that pain with which his own was penetrated; and she hoped that absence and reflection, together with the conviction of its being hopeless, would conquer this infant passion before it could gather strength wholly to ruin his repose.

She was glad that their departure was so near; and hastened it as much as possible. The short interval was passed in mournful silence on the part of Godolphin — on that of Lady Adelina, in tears and regret; while Emmeline, who was herself sensible of great pain in the approaching parting, struggled to appear chearful; and Mrs. Stafford attempted, tho' without much success, to reconcile them all to a separation which was become as necessary as it was inevitable.

At length the hired coach in which they were to return to Woodfield was at the door.

Lady Adelina, unable to speak to either of them, brought her little boy in her arms, and passionately kissing him, gave him into those of Emmeline. Then taking a hand of each of her friends, she pressed them to her throbbing heart, and hastened to conceal the violence of her sorrow in her own room.

Godolphin approached to take leave. He kissed the hand of Mrs. Stafford, and inarticulately expressed his thanks for her goodness to his sister.

'I know,' continued he, 'I need not recommend to you this poor infant: the same generosity which prompted you to save his mother, will effectually plead for him, and secure for him your protection 'till I can take him to that of his own family. And you, Miss Mowbray,' said he, turning to Emmeline and taking her hand — 'most amiable, loveliest of human creatures! where shall I find words to thank you as I ought?'

His emotion was too great for utterance. Emmeline felt it but too sensibly; and hastening into the coach to hide how much she was herself affected, she could only say —

'All happiness attend you, Sir! Remind Lady Adelina of my hopes of soon hearing from her.'

Mrs. Stafford being then seated, and the servant who had been hired to attend the infant following her, the coach drove from the door. Godolphin pursued it with his eyes to the end of the street; and then, as if deprived of all that made life desirable, he gave himself up to languor and despondence, afraid of examining his own heart, least his reason should condemn an inclination, which, however hopeless, he could not resolve to conquer.

But while he found charms in the indulgence of his unhappy love, he determined never to disturb the peace of its object. But rather to suffer in silence, than to give pain to a heart so generous and sensible as hers, merely for the melancholy pleasure of knowing that she pitied him.

As soon as Lady Adelina could bear the journey, they departed together to his house in the Isle of Wight; where he left her, and went in search of Mrs. Bancraft, the sister of Trelawny, of whom he enquired where Trelawny himself might be found.

This woman, apprehensive that he meditated a reconciliation between her brother and his wife, which it was so much her interest to prevent, refused for some time to give him the information he desired. Having however at length convinced her that he had no wish to renew a union which had been productive only of misery to his sister, she told him that Mr. Trelawny was returned to England, and lived at a house hired in the name of her husband, a few miles from London.

There Godolphin sought him; and found the unhappy man sunk into a state of perpetual and unconscious intoxication; in which Bancraft, the husband of his sister, encouraged him, foreseeing that it must soon end in his son's being possessed of an income, to which the meanness of his own origin, and former condition, made him look forward with anxious avidity.

It was difficult to make Trelawny, sinking into ideotism, comprehend either who Godolphin was, or the purport of his business. But Bancraft, more alive to his own interest, presently understood, that on condition of his entering into bonds of separation, Lady Adelina would relinquish the greater part of her claim on the Trelawny estate; and he undertook to have the deeds signed as soon as they could be drawn up. In a few days therefore Godolphin saw Trelawny's part of them compleated; and returned to Lady Adelina, satisfied in having released her from an engagement, which, since he had seen Trelawny, had rendered her in his eyes an object of tenderer pity; and in having acquitted himself according to his strict sense of honour, by causing her to relinquish all the advantages Trelawny's fortune offered, except those to which she had an absolute right.

This affair being adjusted, he again resigned himself to the mournful but pleasing contemplations which had occupied him ever since he had heard of Emmeline's engagement. While Lady Adelina, whose intellects were now restored, but who was lost in profound melancholy, saw too evidently the state of her brother's heart; and could not but lament that his tenderness for her had been the means of involving him in a passion, which the great merit of its object, and his own sensibility, convinced her must be incurable.

The letters of Emmeline were the only consolation she was capable of receiving. They gave her favourable accounts of her child, and of the continued affection of her inestimable friends. Whenever one of these letters was brought, Godolphin eagerly watched her while she was reading it; and then, faultering and impatient, asked if all were well; and if Mr. Delamere was yet returned? She sometimes gave him the letters to peruse; after which he generally fell into long absence, broken only by deep drawn and involuntary sighs — symptoms which Lady Adelina knew too well to doubt of the cause.

In the mean time Mrs. Stafford and Emmeline visited every day their innocent charge, who passed for the child of one of Emmeline's friends gone to the West Indies. Emmeline insensibly grew so fond of him, that she was uneasy if any accident prevented her daily visit; and her friend sometimes laughingly reproached her with the robbery little William committed on her time.

When they were alone, their conversation frequently turned on Lady Adelina and her brother. The subject, tho' melancholy, was ever a favourite with them both; and perhaps the more so because it led them to mournful reflections — for Mrs. Stafford was unhappy, and Emmeline was not gay; nor were her spirits greatly heightened by finding that in spite of herself she thought as much of the brother as the sister, and with a degree of softness and complacency which could not be favourable to her happiness.

When she first discovered in Godolphin those admirable qualities of heart and understanding which he so eminently possessed, she asked herself whether she might indulge the admiration they excited without prejudice to him whom she considered as her husband? And she fancied that she might safely give him that esteem, which his tenderness to his unhappy sister, the softness of his manners, the elegance of his mind, and the generosity of his heart, could hardly fail of extorting from the most indifferent observer.

But insensibly his idea obtruded itself more frequently on her imagination; and she determined to attempt to forget him, and no longer to allow any partiality to rob Delamere of that pure and sincere attachment with which he would expect her to meet him at the altar. It was now long since she had heard from him; but she accounted for it by supposing that he was rambling about, and she knew that letters were frequently lost.

It was at this time something more than two years since they had first met at Mowbray Castle, and in a few weeks Delamere would complete his twenty-first year — a period to which Lord Montreville had long looked forward with anxious solicitude. And now he could not but think with bitterness that his son would not be present to animate the joy of his dependants at this period; but was kept in another country, in the vain hope of extinguishing a passion which could not be indulged without rendering abortive all the pains his Lordship had taken to restore his family to the eminent rank it had formerly borne in his country.

To Sir Richard Crofts, his sons had communicated the success of those plans, by which they had sown, in the irritable mind of Delamere, jealousy and mistrust of Emmeline; and he failed not to animate and encourage their endeavours, while he used his power over the mind of Lord Montreville to limit the bounty and lessen the affection his Lordship was disposed to shew her as the daughter of his brother.

She received regularly her quarterly payment, but she received no more; and instead of hearing, on those occasions, from Lord Montreville himself, she had twice only a methodical letter from Maddox, the London steward.

This might, however, be merely accidental; and Emmeline was far from supposing that her uncle was estranged from her; nor could she guess that the malice of Mrs. Ashwood, and the artifices of the Crofts', had occasioned that estrangement.

Lord Montreville rather connived at than participated in their ungenerous proceedings; and as if fearful of trusting his own ideas of integrity with a plan which so evidently militated against them, he was determined to take advantage of their endeavours, without enquiring too minutely into their justice or candour. Sir Richard had assured him that Mr.

Delamere was in a great measure weaned from his attachment; and that Mr. Crofts was almost sure, that if their meeting could be prevented for a few months longer, there would be nothing more to fear from this long and unfortunate prepossession.

Crofts himself, who had at length torn himself from his bride to pave the way for his being received by her family as her husband, soon appeared, and confirmed all this. He told Lord Montreville that Delamere had conceived suspicions of Emmeline's conduct, (tho' he knew not from what cause) that had at first excited the most uneasy jealousy, but which had at length subsided with his love; that he had regained his spirits; and, when he left his mother and sister, seemed resolved to make a vigorous effort to expel from his mind a passion he was ashamed of having so long indulged.

In saying all this, Crofts rather attended to what his Lordship wished to hear, than to what was really the truth. He knew that a meeting between Delamere and Emmeline would probably at once explain all the unworthy artifices which had been used to divide them, and render those artifices abortive. He therefore told Lord Montreville, that to prevent all probability of a relapse, it would be advisable to remove Emmeline to some place where Delamere could not meet her: and his Lordship, forgetting at once all the obligations he owed her, thought only of following this advice.

Embarrassed, however, himself with public business, he was unable to give to these domestic politics all the attention which they demanded. He threw himself more than ever into the power of the

Crofts', to whose policy he left it to contrive the means, between the months of November and March, of raising an invincible barrier between his son and his niece.

Tho' Delamere's being of age encreased the difficulties of this undertaking, Crofts having no scruples about the methods he was to pursue, had no doubt of accomplishing his end: and to stimulate his endeavours, he needed only the particular advantages which would accrue to himself from the pardon and reception which he hoped to obtain from Lord Montreville and his family.

Every engine therefore that ambition, avarice, malice and cunning could employ, was now put in motion against the character and the peace of the unprotected and unsuspicious Emmeline.

In conscious innocence and unsullied purity, she dreamed not that she had an enemy on earth; for of Mrs. Ashwood, now Mrs. James Crofts, she only remembered that she had once been obliged to her. The little, malicious envy which had given her some pain at the time it was shewn, she now no longer recollected; and tho' she always continued to dislike James Crofts, yet his impertinence she had forgiven, and had written in the usual form to congratulate them both on their marriage.

Of Lord Montreville, she heard nothing; but imputing his silence to his frequent change of place, she conceived no anger against him on that account; and still felt herself bound to keep from her mind, as much as possible, the intrusive image of Godolphin.

CHAPTER VII

WHATEVER resolution Emmeline might form to drive from her heart those dangerous partialities which would be fatal to her repose, she found it impossible to be accomplished while Lady Adelina's frequent letters spoke only of the generous tenderness and excellent qualities of her brother. Of what else, indeed, could she speak, in a solitude where his goodness made all her consolation and his conversation all her pleasure? where he dedicated to her all his time, and thought of procuring for her every alleviation to her retirement which books and domestic amusements afforded? while he taught her still to respect herself; and by his unwearied friendship convincing her that she had still much to lose, made her life receive in her own eyes a value it would otherwise have lost; and prevented her relapsing into that unhappy state of self-condemnation which makes the sufferer careless of the future. He thought, that situated as she was, solitude was her only choice; but to render it as happy as her circumstances allowed, was his continual care: and tho' oppressive sorrow still lay heavy on her heart; tho' it still ached with tenderness and regret towards an object whom she had sworn to think of, to speak of no more; her gratitude and affection towards her brother were as lively, as if its acute feelings had never felt the benumbing hand of despair.

In the total sequestration from the world in which she lived, she had no other topic to dwell upon than her brother, and she gave it all its force. Perfectly acquainted, however, with Emmeline's engagements, she never ventured to mention the passion which she was too well assured Godolphin felt; but she still, almost unknown to herself, cherished a lurking hope that her connection with Delamere might he dissolved, and that her lovely friend was destined to bless her beloved brother.

This distant hope was warm enough to animate her pen in his praise; and Emmeline, tho' every letter she received made on her mind a deeper impression of the merit of Godolphin, yet found such painful pleasure in reading them, that she was unhappy if at the usual periods they did not regularly arrive.

She tried to persuade herself, that the satisfaction she felt in reading these letters arose purely from the delight natural to every uncorrupted mind in contemplating a character honourable to human nature. But accustomed to examine narrowly her own heart, she could not long impose upon herself; and notwithstanding all her endeavour to stifle it, she still found the idea of Godolphin mixing itself with all her thoughts, and embittering the prospect of her certain marriage with Delamere.

In the answers Emmeline gave her friend, she related whatever she thought likely to amuse the fair recluse; gave a regular account of her little charge; but avoided punctiliously the least mention of Fitz-Edward.

Fitz-Edward had received from Mrs. Stafford an account of all that had passed at Bath, except the pains which had been taken to prevent any meeting between him and Godolphin. But notwithstanding her cautious silence on that head, Fitz-Edward, who knew Godolphin well, could hardly be persuaded not to insist on his taking his chance of depriving him of a life which he said he had deserved to lose, and could little brook being supposed to hold on courtesy. Nothing but his consideration for the unhappy Lady Adelina prevented his pursuing the sanguinary projects that agitated his mind. To her peace he owed it to conquer them: and while he was yet struggling against that sense of honour which impelled him to give Godolphin imaginary reparation, by allowing him an opportunity of putting an end to *his* existence or losing his own, his brother, Lord Clancarryl, wrote to desire his attendance in Ireland on some family business of importance; a summons, which after some hesitation, Mrs. Stafford and Miss Mowbray prevailed with him to obey.

Before he went, his eager and affecting entreaties prevailed on Mrs. Stafford to let him see his son, whom he embraced with an ardour of affection of which the fair friends believed so gay and fashionable a man incapable.

The errors of Fitz-Edward, however, were not those of the heart. Among the dissipation of fashion and the indulgences of libertinism, his heart was still sensible, and his integrity retrievable. He felt, therefore, with great keenness, the injury he had done Lady Adelina; and desirous of making all the reparation he could to the infant, he again placed in the hands of Emmeline, a will by which he made it his heir, and recommended to it the protection of Godolphin, whom he besought to consider as his nephew, the son of a man he had once loved, and who had dearly paid for having forfeited all claim to his friendship. When he was departed, nothing seemed likely to interrupt the tranquillity of Emmeline but her encreasing apprehensions for Mrs. Stafford and her children. The derangement of Stafford's affairs, and his wife's unavailing efforts to ward off the ruin which he seemed obstinately bent on incurring, were every day more visible: while his capricious and unreasonable temper, and a strange opinion of his own sagacity, which would never allow him to own himself in the wrong, made him seek to load his wife with the blame of those misfortunes which he had voluntarily sought, and now as obdurately refused to avoid while it was yet in his power.

Mrs. Stafford, who saw too plainly that the destruction of their fortune which she had so long dreaded was now with hasty strides advancing, yet endeavoured to convince him of his infatuation; but he still improved his house and garden, still schemed away all the money he could raise or gain credit for, and still repaid with rudeness and insult her anxious solicitude to save him.

In Emmeline, she ever found pity and tenderness; but pity and tenderness was all she had to bestow.

The affairs of Stafford required interest and money; and Emmeline could command neither. Lord Montreville now took no other notice of her, than to remit her quarterly stipend by the hands of his steward; and tho' he had promised to double it, that promise yet remained unfulfilled.

It was at this time near the end of November, and the mornings were cold and gloomy: but Emmeline, however delicate in her frame, had a constitution which had not, by early and false indulgences, been unfitted for the duties of life; and to personal inconvenience she was always indifferent when the service of those she loved engaged her to brave fatigue or cold. She therefore still continued her morning visit to Woodbury Forest, where she generally past an hour with little William; and in his improving features and interesting smiles, loved to trace his resemblance to his mother. Lady Adelina was very like her brother; and the little boy was not the less tenderly caressed for the similitude she saw to them both.

The appearance of rain had one morning detained her at home later than usual. She went, however, about eleven o'clock; and was busied in playing with the infant, who began now to know her, and was therefore more attractive, when, while she yet held him in her arms, she heard the woman of the house, who was in the outward room, suddenly exclaim — 'Indeed Sir you cannot go in — pray — I beg your honour!' There was hardly time for Emmeline to feel surprize at this bustle, before the door opened, and Delamere stood before her! In his countenance was an expression compounded of rage, fierceness and despair, which extorted from Emmeline an involuntary shriek! Unable to arise, she remained motionless in her chair, clasping the baby to her bosom: Delamere seemed trying to stifle his anger in contempt; vengeance, disdain, and pride, were struggling for superiority: while with his eyes sternly turned upon Emmeline, and smiling indignantly, he exclaimed — 'Till I *saw* this — ' inarticulately and tremulously he spoke — 'till I *saw* this, all the evidence they brought me was insufficient to cure my blind attachment. But now — oh! infamy — madness — damnation! It *is* then possible — It *is* then true! But what is it to me? Torn — torn for ever from this outraged heart — never, never shall this sight blast me again! But what?' continued he, speaking with more quickness, 'what? for Fitz-Edward! for the infamous plunderer of his friend's happiness! However, Madam, on you I intrude no longer. Oh! lost — lost — wretched!' —He could not go on; but in the speechless agony of contending passions he leaned his head against the frame of the door near which he stood, and gazed wildly on Emmeline; who, pale as death, and trembling like a leaf; still sat before him unable to recall her scattered spirits.

He waited a moment, gasping for breath, and as if he had still some feeble expectation of hearing her speak. But the child which she held in her arms was like a basilisk to his sight, and made in his opinion all vindication impossible. Again conviction appeared to drive him to desperation; and looking in a frantic manner round the room, as if entirely bereft of reason, he dashed his hands furiously against his head, and running, or rather flying out of the house, he immediately disappeared.

In terror and astonishment, Emmeline remained immovable and speechless. She almost doubted whether this was any other than a fearful dream, 'till the woman of the house, and the maid who attended on the child, ran into the room frightened — 'Lord! Madam,' cried the woman, 'what is the matter with the young gentleman?'

'I know not,' answered Emmeline, faintly — 'I know not! Where is he now?'

'He's run away into the wood again like any mad,' answered the woman.

'And from whence,' enquired Emmeline, 'did he come?'

'Why, Miss,' said she, 'I was a going out cross our garden to hang out my cloaths; so up a comes to a hedge side, an a says — Good woman, pray be'nt here a lady here as comes from Woodfield? one Miss Mowbray? — I thought how he looked oddish as 'twere about the eyes; but howsever thinking no harm, I says yes. So he runs up to the door, and I called to un, to say as I'd come in and let you know; but before I could get thro' the wicket, whisk he was in the kitchen; then I tried agin to stop un, but I were as good try to stop the wind.'

The agitation and uneasiness of Emmeline encreased rather than subsided. She looked so pale, and with so much difficulty drew her breath, that the women were alarmed least she should faint: and one of them persuaded her to swallow something, while the other ran out to see if the person who had so terrified her was yet in sight. But no traces of him were visible: and after a few moments, Emmeline recalling her presence of mind, and feeling proudly conscious of her own innocence and integrity, recovered in some degree her spirits and resolution.

That Delamere should be in England did not greatly astonish tho' it grieved her; but that he should have conceived such strange suspicions of her and Fitz-Edward, equally surprized and distressed her; since, had she an opportunity of undeceiving him, which he did not seem willing to allow her, she could not relate the truth but by betraying the confidence of her unfortunate friend, and embittering that life she had incurred such hazards to preserve. As soon as she had apparently recovered from the shock of this abrupt intrusion, she was desirous of returning to Woodfield; anxious to know if Delamere had been there, or by what means he had been enabled to find her at the cottage in the forest. The women, who fancied the gentleman they had seen was a lunatic who might lay in wait to hurt her on her way home, would not suffer her to set out 'till they had called a woodcutter from the forest to accompany her. Then, slowly and with difficulty, she returned home; where she heard from Mrs. Stafford that Delamere had neither been there or sent thither. This information encreased her wonder and her disquiet. She related to Mrs. Stafford the distressing interview of the morning; who, having seen frequent instances of those excesses of which Delamere was capable, heard the relation with concern and apprehension.

CHAPTER VIII

SOME days were passed by Emmeline in painful conjectures on what measures Delamere would take, and in uncertainty what she ought to do herself. Sometimes she thought of writing to Lord Montreville: but against that Mrs. Stafford remonstrated; representing, that as she was undoubtedly the injured person, in having been insulted by suspicions so unworthy, she should leave it wholly to Delamere to discover and recant his error; which, if he refused on cooler reflection to do, she would be fortunate in escaping from an engagement with a man who had so little command of his own temper, so little reliance on her principles, as to be driven on a mere suspicion into rudeness and insult.

Greatly mortified at finding it possible for Delamere to think so injuriously of her, and depressed by a thousand uneasy apprehensions, she yielded implicitly to the counsel of her friend. But of her counsel and consolation she was now on the point of being deprived: Stafford, who had been some time in

London, sent an express to fetch his wife thither a few days after the interview between Emmeline and Delamere. His affairs were now growing desperate: James Crofts demanded immediate payment of a sum of money belonging to his wife, that was left her by her father, and which she had 'till now suffered to remain in the hands of her brother. Stafford had made no provision to pay it: his boundless profusion had dissipated all the ready money he could command; and this claim of his sister's, which James Crofts seemed determined to urge, would he knew be the signal for every other creditor to beset him with demands he had no means of discharging.

Tho' Mrs. Stafford had long tho' vainly implored him to stop in his wild career, and had represented to him all the evils which were now about to overtake him, she could not see their near approach without an attempt again to rescue him. And he was accustomed in every difficulty to have recourse to her; tho' while he felt none, he scorned and even resented her efforts to keep them at a distance. He now fancied that her application might prevail on James Crofts to drop a suit he had commenced against him: she hastily therefore set out for London; leaving Emmeline the care of her children; who promised, by the utmost attention to them, to obviate part of the inconvenience of such a journey.

It was unhappily, however, not only inconvenient but fruitless. Mr. and Mrs. James Crofts were inexorable. The suit was tried; Stafford was cast; and nothing remained for him but either to pay the money or to be exposed to the hazard of losing his property and his liberty. His conduct had so much injured his credit, that to borrow, it was impossible. Mrs. Stafford attempted therefore to divest herself of part of her own fortune to assist him with the money: but her trustees were not to be moved; and nothing but despair seemed darkening round the head of the unfortunate Stafford.

Mrs. Stafford saw too evidently that to be in the power of James Crofts, was to trust to avarice, meanness and malignity; and she trembled to reflect that her husband was now wholly at his mercy. The additional motives he had to use that power rigorously she knew not: she was ignorant that the business had so eagerly been pushed to a crisis, not merely by the avidity of James Crofts to possess the money, but also by the directions of Sir Richard, who hoped by this means to drive the family with whom Emmeline resided to another country; where Delamere might find access to her so difficult, that he might never have an opportunity of explaining the cause of his estrangement, or of hearing her vindication.

It was now that Mrs. Stafford remembered the frequent offers of service which she had repeatedly received from Lord Montreville; and to him she determined to apply. She hoped that he might be induced to influence the Crofts' family to give Mr. Stafford time, and to desist from the violence and precipitation with which they pursued him. She even fancied that his Lordship would be glad of an opportunity so easily to realize those offers he had so liberally made; and full of these expectations, she prepared to become a solicitress for favours to a statesman. She felt humbled and mortified at the cruel necessity that compelled her to it; but her children's interest conquering her reluctance, she addressed a letter to Lord Montreville, and received a very polite answer, in which he desired the honour of seeing her at two o'clock the following day; an hour, when he said he should be entirely disengaged. She might as well, however, have attended at his levee; for tho' punctual to the hour when he was to be disengaged, she found two rooms adjoining to that where his Lordship was, occupied by a variety of figures; some of whose faces, were faces of negociation and equality, but more, whose expression of fearful suspence marked them for those of petitioners and dependants. Those of the former description were separately called to an audience; and each, after a longer or shorter stay, retired; while Mrs. Stafford, tho' with an heart but ill at ease for observation, could not help fancying she discerned in their looks the success of their respective treaties.

As soon as these gentlemen were all departed, Mrs. Stafford, who had already waited almost three hours, was introduced into the study; where, with many gracious bows and smiling apologies, Lord Montreville received her.

Sir Richard Crofts had that morning warmly represented to his Lordship the necessity of the Staffords going abroad and taking Emmeline with them. Lord Montreville knew that Delamere was returned, and was embroiled with Emmeline; he was therefore eager enough to follow the advice which appeared so necessary, and to promote any plan which might prevent a renewal of the attachment. He enquired not into the cause of this estrangement, satisfied with its effect; and had secretly determined to give Mrs. Stafford no assistance in the endeavours she was using to keep her family from dispersion and distress.

But statesman as he was, he could not entirely forget that he *once* felt as other men; and he could not hear, without some emotion, the melancholy description that Mrs. Stafford gave of the impending ruin of her family and all its fearful consequences: which she did with so much clear simplicity, yet with so much proper dignity, that he found his resolution shaken; and recollecting *that he had a conscience*, was about to ask it by what right he assumed the power of rendering an innocent family wandering exiles, merely to save himself from a supposed possible inconvenience.

But while every lingering principle of goodness and generosity was rising in the bosom of his Lordship to assist the suit of Mrs. Stafford, a servant entered hastily and announced the Duke of N——. His Grace of course waited not in the anti-room, but was immediately introduced.

Lord Montreville then civilly apologized to Mrs. Stafford for being unable to conclude the business; adding, that if she would see Sir Richard Crofts the next day, he would take care it should be settled to her satisfaction. She withdrew with a heavy heart; and feeling infinite reluctance in the proposed application to Sir Richard Crofts, she employed the whole afternoon in attempting to move, in favour of her husband, some of those friends who had formerly professed the most unbounded and disinterested friendship for him and his family.

Of many of these, the doors were shut against her; others affected the utmost concern, and lamented that their little power and limited fortunes did not allow them to assist in repairing the misfortunes they deplored: some told her how long they had foreseen Mr. Stafford's embarrassments, and how destructive building and scheming were to a moderate fortune; while others made vague proffers of inadequate services, which on farther conversation she found they never intended to perform if unluckily she had accepted their offers. In all, she saw too plainly that they looked on Mr. Stafford's affairs as desperate; and in their coldness and studied civility, already felt all the misery and mortification of reduced circumstances.

With encreased anguish, she was now compelled to go, on the following day, to Sir Richard Crofts; whom she knew only from Emmeline's description.

He also, in imitation of his patron, had his anti-chamber filled with soliciting faces. She waited not quite so long, indeed, for an audience, but with infinitely less patience. At length, however, she was shewn into the apartment where Sir Richard transacted business.

Bloated prosperity was in his figure, supercilious scorn in his eyes: he rose half off his seat, and slightly inclined his head on her entrance.

'Madam, your servant — please sit down.'

'I waited on you, Sir Richard, to — '

'I beg your pardon, Madam. But as I am perfectly acquainted, and informed, and aware of the business, there is no occasion or necessity to give you the trouble to repeat, and dwell upon, and explain it. It is not, I find, convenient, or suitable, or commodious, for Mr. Stafford to pay to my son James who had married his (Mr. Stafford's) sister, that part, and proportion, and residue, of her fortune, which her father at his death gave, bequeathed, and left to her.'

'It is not only inconvenient, Sir,' answered Mrs. Stafford, 'but impossible, I fear, for him to do it immediately; and this is what I wished to speak to you upon.'

'I am aware, and informed, and apprized, Madam, of what you would say. I am sorry it is as you say so inconvenient, and impracticable, and impossible. However, Madam, my way in these cases is to go very plainly, and straitly, and directly to the point; therefore I will chalk out, and describe, and point out to you a line of conduct, which if you chuse to follow, and adopt, and pursue, it appears to me that all may be adjusted, settled, and put to rights.'

'You will oblige me, Sir Richard, by doing so.'

'Well then, it is this — As it appears, and is evident, and visible, that you have not the money in question, you must immediately sell, and dispose of, and make into money, your house and effects in Dorsetshire, and after paying, and satisfying, and discharging the debt to my son James, you must (as I understand your husband is besides deeply in debt,) withdraw, retire, and remove to France, or to Normandy, or Switzerland, or some cheap country, 'till your affairs come round, and are retrieved, and accommodated and adjusted.'

'This we might have done, Sir Richard, without troubling you with the present application.'

'No, Madam, you might *not.* I assure you I have talked, and reasoned, and argued some time with Mr. James Crofts, before I could induce, and prevail upon, and dispose him to wait, and remain, and continue unpaid, until this arrangement and disposition could take place. He wants the money, Madam, for a particular purpose; and tho' from my heart I grieve, and lament, and deplore the necessity of the measure, I do assure you, Madam, nothing else will give you any chance of winding up, compleating, and terminating the business before us. You will therefore, Madam, think, and consider, and reflect on its necessity, and give your final answer to my son James, who will wait for it only 'till to-morrow morning.'

He then rang his bell; and saying he had an appointment with Lord Montreville, who must already have waited for him, he made a cold bow and hastened out of the room.

CHAPTER IX

MRS. Stafford now saw that nothing remained but to follow her husband to a prison, or prevail on him to go to the Continent while she attempted anew to settle his affairs.

Obstinate even in despair, she had the utmost difficulty to convince him of the necessity of this measure; and would never, perhaps, have done it, if the more persuasive argument of a writ, taken out by James Crofts, had not driven him to embrace it rather than go into confinement.

Mrs. Stafford with difficulty procured money to furnish him for his journey, and saw him depart for Dover; while she herself returned to Emmeline, who had passed the three weeks of her absence in great uneasiness. No news had been received of Delamere; and she now believed, that of the promise he had forced from her he meant not to avail himself; yet did not relinquish it; but in proud and sullen resentment, disdained even to enquire whether he had justly harboured anger against her. She wished to have withdrawn a promise she could no longer think of without pain and regret; but she found Mrs. Stafford so unhappy, that she could not resolve to oppress her by complaints; and after some struggles with herself, determined to let the matter take its course.

Willingly, however, she consented to accompany her friend to France; where Mrs. Stafford, at her husband's request, now determined to go with her family. She had found an opulent tradesman in a neighbouring town, who engaged, on receiving a mortgage on the estate, and ten per cent. interest, (which he so managed as to evade the appearance of usury,) to let her have the money to pay Mr. Crofts, and a farther sum for the support of her family: and having got a tenant for the house, and satisfied as many of the clamorous creditors as she could, she prepared, with a heavy heart, to quit her abode, with Emmeline and her infant family.

As it was necessary that little William should be sent to the Isle of Wight before their departure, Emmeline wrote to fix a day at the distance of a month, on which she desired Lady Adelina to send some careful person for him. But ten days before the expiration of that period, letters came from Mr. Stafford, in which he directed his wife, who intended to embark at Brighthelmstone and land at Dieppe, to change her route, and sail from Southampton to Havre. He also desired her to hasten her journey: and as every thing was now put on the best footing the time would allow, Mrs. Stafford immediately complied; and with her own unfortunate family, Emmeline, and little William, (whom they now meant to carry themselves to Lady Adelina) they left Woodfield.

The pain of quitting, probably for ever, a favourite abode, which she feared would at length be torn from her children by the rapacity of the law, and the fatigue of travelling with infant children, under such circumstances, almost overcame the resolution and spirits of Mrs. Stafford. Emmeline, ever reasonable, gentle, and consoling, was her principal support; and on the evening of the second day they arrived at Southampton.

While Emmeline almost forgot in her attention to her friend her own uncertain and unpleasant state, Delamere remained in Norfolk, where he had hid himself from the enquiries of his father, and from the importunities of his mother, who was now, with her eldest daughter, settled again in Berkley-square. Here he nourished inveterate resentment against Fitz-Edward: and finding it impossible to forget Emmeline, he continued to think of her as much as ever, but with indignation, jealousy and rage.

He had, immediately on receiving, as he believed, a confirmation of all those imposed suspicions with which the Crofts' had so artfully inspired him, resolved to demand satisfaction of Fitz-Edward; and hearing on enquiry that he was in Ireland, but his return immediately expected, he waited with eager and restless uneasiness till the person whom he had commissioned to inform him of his return should send notice that he was again in London.

Week after week, however, passed away. He still heard, that tho' expected hourly, Fitz-Edward arrived not. Time, far from softening the asperity with which his thoughts dwelt on this supposed rival, seemed only to irritate and inflame his resentment; and ingenious in tormenting himself, he now added new anguish to that which corroded his heart, by supposing that Emmeline, aware of the danger which threatened her lover from the vengeance of his injured friend, had written to him to prevent his return. This idea was confirmed, when the agent whom he employed to watch the return of Fitz-Edward at length informed him that he had obtained leave of absence from his regiment, now in England, and was to pass the remainder of the winter with Lord and Lady Clancarryl.

The fury of his passions seemed to be suspended, while with gloomy satisfaction he looked forward to a speedy retribution: but now, when no immediate prospect offered of meeting the author of his calamities, they tormented him with new violence. Emmeline and Fitz-Edward haunted his dreams; Emmeline and Fitz-Edward were ever present to his imagination; he figured to himself his happy rival possessed of the tenderness and attachment of that gentle and sensible heart. The anguish these images inflicted affected his health; and while every day, as it passed, brought nothing to alleviate his despair, he became more and more convinced that the happiness of his life was blasted for ever; and growing impatient of life itself, determined to go to Ireland and insist on an opportunity of losing it, or of taking that of the man who had made it an insupportable burthen.

He set out therefore, attended only by Millefleur, and gave Lord Montreville no notice of his intention 'till he reached Holyhead; from thence he wrote to his Lordship to say that he had received an invitation to visit some friends at Dublin, and that he should continue about a month in Ireland. His pride prompted him to do this; least his father, on hearing of his absence, should suppose that he was weak enough to seek a reconciliation with Emmeline, whose name he now never mentioned, being persuaded that his Lordship knew how ill she had repaid an affection, which, tho' he could not divest himself of, he was now ashamed to acknowledge.

Lord Montreville, happy to find he had really quitted her, was extremely glad of this seasonable journey; which, as the Crofts' assured him Emmeline was on the point of leaving England, would, he thought, prevent his enquiring whither she was gone, and by introducing him into a new set of acquaintance, turn his thoughts to other objects and perfect his cure.

While Delamere then was travelling to Ireland in pursuit of Fitz-Edward, Mrs. Stafford and Emmeline left Southampton on a visit to Lady Adelina in the Isle of Wight; being desirous of delivering little William into the arms of his mother and his uncle. Tho' it was now almost the end of January, they embarked in an open boat, with the servant who waited on the child; but being detained 'till almost noon on account of the tide, it was evening before they reached a village on the shore, three miles beyond Cowes, where they were to land.

On arriving there, they found that the house of Captain Godolphin was situated two miles farther. Mrs. Stafford, ever attentive and considerate, was afraid that the sight of the child so unexpectedly, might overpower the spirits of Lady Adelina, and cause speculation among the servants which it was absolutely necessary to avoid. Emmeline therefore undertook to walk forward, attended by a boy in the village, who was to shew her the way, and apprize Lady Adelina of the visitor she was to expect.

Pleasure, in spite of herself, flowed in her bosom at the idea of again meeting Godolphin; tho' she knew not that he had conceived for her the most pure and ardent passion that was ever inspired by a lovely and deserving object.

He had long since found that his heart was irrecoverably gone. But tho' he struggled not against his passion, he loved too truly to indulge it at the expence of Emmeline; and had therefore determined to avoid her, and not to embitter *her* life with the painful conviction that their acquaintance had destroyed the happiness of *his*. For this reason he did not intend going himself to fetch his nephew from Woodbury Forest, but had given a careful servant directions to go thither in a few days after that when Emmeline herself prevented the necessity of the journey.

Her walk lay along the high rocks that bounded the coast; and it was almost dark before she entered a small lawn surrounded with a plantation, in which the house of Godolphin was situated. About half an acre of ground lay between it and the cliff, which was beat by the swelling waves of the channel. The ground on the other side rose more suddenly; and a wood which covered the hill behind it, seemed to embosom the house, and take off that look of bleakness and desolation which often renders a situation so near the sea unpleasant except in the warmest months of Summer. A sand walk lead round the lawn. Emmeline followed it, and it brought her close to the windows of a parlour. They were still open; she looked in; and saw, by the light of the fire, for there were no candles in the room, Godolphin sitting alone. He leaned on a book, which there was not light enough to read; scattered papers lay round him, and a pen and ink were on the table.

Emmeline could not forbear looking at him a moment before she approached the door. She could as little command her curiosity to know on what he was thus deeply thinking. The boy who was with her ran round to the kitchen, and sent up a servant to open the door; who immediately throwing open that of the parlour, said — 'A lady, Sir!'

Godolphin starting from his reverie, arose, and unexpectedly beheld the subject of it.

His astonishment at this visit, was such as hardly left him the power to express the pleasure with which that astonishment was mingled. 'Miss Mowbray!' exclaimed he — 'It is indeed Miss Mowbray?'

For a moment he surveyed her in silent extasy, then congratulated himself upon his unhoped for good fortune; and answering her enquiries about Lady Adelina, he suddenly seemed to recollect the papers which lay on the table, hurried them into a drawer, and again returning to Emmeline, told her how happy he was to see her look so well. He thought indeed that he had never seen her so infinitely lovely. The sharpness of the air during her walk had heightened the glow of her complexion; her eyes betrayed, by their soft and timid glances, the partiality of which she was hardly yet conscious; she trembled, without knowing why; and could hardly recover her composure, while Godolphin, who would trust no other person to deliver the message, ran eagerly up stairs to acquaint Lady Adelina. 'My sister,' cried he, immediately returning, 'will be with you instantly; a slight pain in her head has kept her on the bed almost all day. But to what do we owe the happiness of seeing you here, when we thought you on the point of sailing for France by another route?'

Emmeline then hastily explained the change in their plan; adding, gravely 'You will have another visitor, who cannot fail of being welcome both to you and Lady Adelina. Mrs. Stafford stays with him at the village, while she desired me to come on to prepare you for his reception, and to know how you will have him introduced?'

'As my child,' answered Godolphin. 'My servants are already prepared to expect such an addition to my family. Ever amiable, ever lovely Miss Mowbray!' continued he, with looks that encreased her confusion — 'what obligation does not our little boy — do we not all owe you?'

At this moment Lady Adelina, who had been obliged to wait some moments to recover herself from the joyful surprize into which the news of Emmeline's arrival had thrown her, ran into the room, and embracing with transport her lovely friend, sighed; but unable to weep, sat down, and could only kiss her hands with such wild expressions of rapture, that Emmeline was alarmed least it should have any ill effect on her intellects, or on a frame ever extremely delicate; and which now had, from her having long indulged incurable sorrow, assumed an appearance of such languor and weakness, that Emmeline with extreme concern looked on her as on a beautiful shadow whom she probably beheld for the last time.

She stood a moment pensively gazing on her face. Godolphin said gently to his sister, who still held the hand of Emmeline — 'Adelina, my love, recollect yourself — you keep Miss Mowbray standing.'

'What is yet more material,' answered Emmeline, smiling, 'is, that you keep me from writing a note to Mrs. Stafford, which the boy who waits here is to take back to her.'

Godolphin answered that he would go himself to Mrs. Stafford, and instantly departed; while Emmeline began to talk to Lady Adelina of the immediate arrival of her child. She at length succeeded in getting her to speak of him, and to weep extremely; after which, she grew more composed, and her full heart seemed relieved by talking of her brother.

Her words, tho' faint, and broken by the emotion she felt, yet forcibly conveyed to the heart of Emmeline impressions of that uncommon worth they described.

'Never,' said she, 'can I be sufficiently grateful to heaven for having given me such a brother. 'Tis not in words, my Emmeline, to do him justice! He is all that is noble minded and generous. Tho' from the loss of his vivacity and charming spirits, I know too well how deeply my unworthy conduct has wounded him; tho' I know, that by having sullied the fair name of our family, and otherwise, I have been the unhappy cause of injuring his peace, yet never has a reproach or an unkind word escaped him. Pensive, yet always kind; melancholy, and at times visibly unhappy; yet ever gentle, considerate, and attentive to me; always ready to blame himself for yielding to that despondence which he cannot without an effort conquer; trying to alleviate the anguish of *my* mind by subduing that which frequently preys on his own; and now burying the memory of my fault in compassion to my affliction, he adopts my child, and allows me without a blush to embrace the dear infant, for whom I dare not otherwise shew the tenderness I feel.'

Emmeline, affected by this eulogium, to which her heart warmly assented, was silent.

'There is,' reassured Lady Adelina, 'but one being on earth who resembles him: — it is my Emmeline! If ever two creatures eminently excelled the rest of their species, it is my friend and my brother!'

Something throbbed at the heart of Emmeline at these words, into which she was afraid to enquire: her engagement to Delamere, yet uncancelled, lay like a weight upon it; and seemed to impress the idea of her doing wrong while she thus listened on the praises of another; and felt that she listened with too much pleasure! She asked herself, however, whether it was possible to be insensible of the merit of Godolphin? Yet conscious that she had already thought of it too much, she wished to change the topic of discourse — But Lady Adelina still pursued it.

'Lord Westhaven,' said she, 'my elder brother, is indeed a most respectable and excellent man. Equally with my brother William, he inherits from my father, integrity, generosity and nobleness of mind, together with a regularity of morals and conduct, unusual in so young a man even in any rank of life, and remarkable in him, who has passed almost all his in the army. But he is, tho' not yet thirty, much older than I am, and has almost always been absent from me; those who know him better, have told me, that with as many other good qualities as William, he has less softness of temper; and being almost tree from error himself, makes less allowance for the weakness of others. Such, however, has been the management of my younger brother, that the elder knows not the truth of my circumstances — he does not even suspect them. You may very possibly see him and Lady Westhaven abroad. I know I need not caution my Emmeline — she will be careful of the peace of her poor friend.'

Emmeline soon satisfied Lady Adelina on that head, who then asked when she heard of Delamere?

This question Emmeline had foreseen: but having predetermined not to distress her unfortunate friend, by telling her into what difficulties her attendance on her and her child had led her, and being shocked to own herself the subject of suspicions so injurious as those Delamere had dared to harbour, she calmly answered that Delamere was returned to England, but that she had seen him only for a few moments.

'And did he not object,' enquired Lady Adelina, 'to your quitting England, since he is himself returned to it?'

Emmeline, who could not directly answer this question, evaded it by saying—

'My absence or my presence you know cannot hasten the period, 'till the arrival of which our marriage cannot take place — *if* it ever takes place at all.'

'*If* it ever takes place at all?' repeated Lady Adelina — 'Does then any doubt remain of it?'

'An affair of that sort,' replied Emmeline, assuming as much unconcern as she could, 'is always doubtful where so many clashing interests and opposite wishes are to be reconciled, and where so very young a man as Mr. Delamere is to decide.'

'Do you suspect that he wavers then?' very earnestly asked Lady Adelina, fixing her eyes on the blushing face of Emmeline.

'I really am not sure,' answered she — 'you know my promise, reluctantly given, was only conditional. I am far from being anxious to anticipate by firmer engagements the certainty of its being fulfilled; much better contented I should be, if he yet took a few years longer to consider of it. You, Lady Adelina,' continued she, smiling, 'are surely no advocate for early marriages; and Mrs. Stafford is greatly averse to them. You must therefore suppose that what my two friends have found inimical to their happiness, I cannot consider as being likely to constitute mine.'

This speech had the effect Emmeline intended. It brought back the thoughts of Lady Adelina from the uncertainties of her friend to her own actual sorrows. She sighed deeply.

'You say truly,' said she. '*I* have no reason to wish those I love may precipitately form indissoluble engagements; nor *do* I wish it. Would to God *I* had not been the victim of an hasty and unhappy marriage; or that I had been the *only* victim. Emmeline,' added she, lowering her voice, now hardly audible, 'Emmeline, *may* I ask? — where is — spare me the repetition of a name I have solemnly vowed never to utter — you understand me?'

'I do,' answered Emmeline, gravely. 'He has been in Ireland; but is now I suppose in London, as the time he told me he should pass there has long since elapsed. I heard he was to return no more to Tylehurst, and that Mr. Delamere had given up the house there; but of this I know nothing from themselves. The person you enquire after, I have seen only once, and that for half an hour. Mrs. Stafford can tell you more, if you wish to hear it.'

'Ah! pardon my wretched weakness, Emmeline! I know I ought to conquer it! But I cannot help wishing — I cannot help being anxious to hear of him! Yet would I conceal from every one but you that the recollection of this unhappy man never a moment leaves me. Tell me, my angelic friend! for you I may ask and be forgiven — has he seen his son?'

'He has; and was extremely affected. But dear Lady Adelina, do not, I beseech you, enquire into the particulars of the interview. Try, my beloved friend, to divest yourself of these painful recollections —ah! try to recover your peace, and preserve your life, for the sake of our dear little William and those friends who love you.'

The unhappy Adelina, who notwithstanding all her efforts, was devoured by an incurable affection for a man whom she had sworn to banish from her heart for ever, and whose name her brother would not suffer her to pronounce, now gave way to an agony of passion which she could indulge only before Emmeline; and so violently was she affected by regret and despair, that her friend trembled least her reason should again forsake its seat. She tried, by soothing and tenderness, to appease this sudden effusion of grief; and had hardly restored her to some degree of composure, before Mrs. Stafford entered the room and embraced most cordially Lady Adelina, while Godolphin followed her with the little boy in his arms. In contemplating the beauty of his nephew, he had forgotten the misery of which his birth had been the occasion; for with all the humanity of a brave man, Godolphin possessed a softness of heart, which the helpless innocence of the son, and the repentant sorrow of the mother, melted into more than feminine tenderness. He carried the child to his sister, and put it into her arms —

'Take him, my Adelina!' said he — 'take our dear boy: and while you embrace and bless him, you will feel all you owe to those who have preserved him.'

Lady Adelina did indeed feel such complicated sensations that she was unable to utter a word. She could only press the little boy to her heart and bedew his face with tears. Her affecting silence and pale countenance alarmed both Mrs. Stafford and Emmeline; and the former, willing to give her thoughts a new turn, said —

'You do not suppose, my dear friends, that we intend to go back to Southampton to night? so I hope you will give us some supper and beds in this hospitable island.'

Godolphin, who had been too much enchanted to think before, immediately saw that the meaning of Mrs. Stafford's solicitude was merely to call the thoughts of his sister from herself to her guests; he seconded therefore this intention, by desiring Lady Adelina to give proper orders about the apartments for her friends; and to take his little boy to that which had been prepared for his reception. The three ladies therefore withdrew with the child; where Lady Adelina soon recovered some degree of serenity, and was able to sit at table while they supped.

Had Mrs. Stafford been before unsuspicious of the passion of Godolphin for Emmeline, she would have been convinced of it during the course of this evening. His voice, his countenance, his manner, evidently betrayed it; and whenever the eyes of Emmeline were turned to any other object, his were fixed on her face, with looks so expressive of tender admiration, yet tempered by a kind of hopeless dejection, that the most uninterested observer could hardly have mistaken his thoughts.

But it was not her face, however interesting; or her form, however graceful; that rivetted the chains of Godolphin. He had seen many faces more regularly beautiful, and many figures equally elegant, with indifference: he had heard, with coldness, the finest sentiments uttered by the fairest mouths; and had listened to the brilliant sallies of fashionable wit, with contempt. In Emmeline, he discovered a native dignity of soul, an enlarged and generous heart, a comprehensive and cultivated understanding, a temper at once soft and lively, with morals the most pure, and manners simple, undesigning and ingenuous. To these solid perfections, genius had added all the lighter graces; and nature, a form which, enchanting as it must ever have been, seemed to receive irresistible charms from the soul by which it was informed.

All his philosophy could not prevent his being sensible of the attractions of such a woman; nor was his resolution sufficiently strong to enable him to struggle against their influence, even when he found he had nothing to hope. But yielding to the painful delight of loving her, he persuaded himself that tho' he could not conquer he could conceal it; and that while she was ignorant of his passion it could be injurious only to himself.

His absence and silence during supper was broken only by his natural politeness. After it concluded, they drew round the fire; and the three ladies entered into one of those interesting conversations that are so pleasant where mutual confidence and esteem reign among the party.

Godolphin continued silent; and insensibly fell into a train of thought the most dangerous to that appearance of indifference which he believed he could observe. Looking at Emmeline as she talked to his sister, and remembering all the friendship she had shewn her, hearing the sound of her voice and the elegance of her expressions, he began insensibly to consider how blessed he *might* have been, had he known her before her hand was promised and her affections given to the fortunate Delamere.

'Had it but been *my* lot!' said he to himself— 'had it been *my* lot! — ah, what happiness, after the fatigues and dangers of my profession, to return to this place which I love so much, and to be received by such a friend — such a mistress — such a wife as she will make!' He indulged these ideas, 'till absolutely lost in them, he was unconscious of every thing but their impression, and starting up, he struck his hands together and cried —

'Merciful heaven! — and can it then never be?'

Alarmed at the suddenness of an exclamation so causeless, Lady Adelina looked terrified and her friends amazed.

'What brother? — what are you speaking of?' enquired she.

'I beg your pardon,' said Godolphin, instantly recollecting himself, and blushing for this unguarded sally — 'I beg your pardon. I was thinking of some business I have to settle; but I do not deserve to be forgiven for suffering my mind in such company to dwell on any thing but the pleasure I enjoy; and for yielding to a foolish custom I have acquired of uttering aloud whatever is immediately in my mind; an habit,' added he, smiling, 'that has grown upon me by living so much alone. Since Lady Adelina is now fixed with me, I hope I shall cease to speak and think like an hermit, and be again humanized. Adelina, my love, you look fatigued.'

'Ah!' replied she, 'of what fatigue can I be sensible when with those who I most love and value; and from whom, to-morrow — to-morrow I must part!'

'I doubt that extremely,' said Godolphin, trying to carry the conversation entirely from his own strange behaviour. 'If I have any skill in the weather, to-morrow will bring a gale of wind, which will opportunely make prisoners of our two fair friends for another day.'

'How infinitely,' cried Lady Adelina, 'shall I be obliged to it.'

The rising of the wind during the whole evening had made Godolphin's conjecture highly probable. Mrs. Stafford, impatient to return to her children, whom she never willingly left wholly in the care of servants, heard its encreasing violence with regret. Emmeline tried to do so too; but she could not prevail on herself to lament a circumstance likely to keep her another day with Lady Adelina and her little boy. She wanted too to see a little of this beautiful island, of which she had heard so much; and found several other reasons for wishing to remain, without allowing herself to suppose that Godolphin had on these wishes the smallest influence.

CHAPTER X

EARLY the next morning, Emmeline arose; and looking towards the sea, saw a still encreasing tempest gathering visibly over it. She wandered over the house; which tho' not large was chearful and elegant, and she fancied every thing in it bore testimony to the taste and temper of its master. The garden charmed her still more; surrounded by copse-wood and ever-greens, and which seemed equally adapted to use and pleasure. The country behind it, tho' divested of its foliage and verdure, appeared more beautiful than any she had seen since she left Wales; and with uncommon avidity she enjoyed, even amid the heavy gloom of an impending storm, the great magnificent spectacle afforded by the sea. By reminding her of her early pleasures at Mowbray Castle, it brought back a thousand half-obliterated and agreeable, tho' melancholy images to her mind; while its grandeur gratified her taste for the sublime.

As she was indulging these contemplations, the wind suddenly blew with astonishing violence; and before Mrs. Stafford arose, the sea was become so tempestuous and impracticable, that eagerly as he wished to return to her children she could not think of braving it.

Godolphin had seen Emmeline wandering along the cliff, and had resolutely denied himself the pleasure of joining her; for from what had passed the evening before, he began to doubt his own power to forbear speaking to her of the subject that filled his heart.

They now met at breakfast; and Emmeline was charmed with her walk, tho' she had been driven from it by the turbulence of the weather, which by this time had arisen to an hurricane. When their breakfast ended, Mrs. Stafford followed Lady Adelina, who wanted to consult her on something that related to the little boy; Godolphin went out to give some orders; and Emmeline retired to a bow window which looked towards the sea.

Could she have divested her mind of its apprehensions that what formed for her a magnificent and sublime scene brought shipwreck and destruction to many others, she would have been highly pleased with a sight of the ocean in its present tremendous state. Lost in contemplating the awful spectacle, she did not see or hear Godolphin; who imagining she had left the room with his sister, had returned, and with his arms crossed, and his eyes fixed on her face, stood on the other side of the window like a statue.

The gust grew more vehement, and deafened her with its fury; while the mountainous waves it had raised, burst thundering against the rocks and seemed to shake their very foundation. Emmeline, at the picture her imagination drew of their united powers of desolation, shuddered involuntarily and sighed.

'What disturbs Miss Mowbray?' said Godolphin.

Emmeline, unwilling to acknowledge that she had been so extremely absent as not to know he was in the room, answered, without expressing her surprize to see him there — 'I was thinking how fatal this storm which we are contemplating, may be to the fortunes and probably the lives of thousands.'

'The gale,' returned Godolphin, 'is heavy, but by no means of such fatal power as you apprehend. I have been at sea in several infinitely more violent, and shall probably be in many others.'

'I hope not,' answered Emmeline, without knowing what she said — 'Surely you do not mean it?'

'A professional man,' said he, smiling, and flattered by the eagerness with which she spoke, 'has, you know, no will of his own. I certainly should not seek danger; but it is not possible in such service as ours to avoid it.'

'Why then do you not quit it?'

'If I intended to give you a high idea of my *prudence*, I should say, because I am a younger brother. But to speak honestly, that is not my only motive; my fortune, limited as it is, is enough for all my wishes, and will probably suffice for any I shall *now* ever form; but a man of my age ought not surely to waste in torpid idleness, or trifling dissipation, time that may be usefully employed. Besides, I love the profession to which I have been brought up, and, by engaging in which, I owe a life to my country if ever it should be called for.'

'God forbid it ever should!' said Emmeline, with quickness; 'for then,' continued she, hesitating and blushing, 'what would poor Lady Adelina do? and what would become of my dear little boy?'

Godolphin, charmed yet pained by this artless expression of sensibility, and thrown almost off his guard by the idea of not being wholly indifferent to her, answered mournfully — 'To them, indeed, my life may be of some value; but to myself it is of none. Ah, Miss Mowbray! it might have been worth preserving had I — But wherefore presume I to trouble you on a subject so hopeless? I know not what has tempted me to intrude on your thoughts the incoherences of a mind ill at ease. Pardon me — and suffer not my folly to deprive me of the happiness of being your friend, which is all I will ever pretend to.'

He turned away, and hastened out of the room; leaving Emmeline in such confusion that it was not 'till Mrs. Stafford came to call her to Lady Adelina's dressing-room, that she remembered where she was, and the necessity of recollecting her scattered thoughts. When they met at dinner, she could not encounter the eyes of Godolphin without the deepest blushes: Lady Adelina, given wholly up to the idea of their approaching separation, and Mrs. Stafford, occupied by uneasiness of her own, did not attend to the singularity of her manner.

The latter had never beheld such a tempest as was now raging; and she could not look towards the sea, whose high and foaming billows were breaking so near them, without shivering at the terrifying recollection, that in a very few hours her children, all she held dear on earth, would be exposed to this capricious and furious element. Tho' of the steadiest resolution in any trial that merely regarded herself, she was a coward when these dear objects of her fondness were in question; and she could not help expressing to Mr. Godolphin some part of her apprehensions.

'As I have gained some credit,' answered he, 'for my sagacity in foreseeing the gale, I might perhaps as well not hazard the loss of it, by another prophecy, for which you, Lady Adelina, will not thank me. — It will be fine, I am afraid, to-morrow.'

'And the following day we embark for France,' said Mrs. Stafford; 'how providential that we could not sail yesterday!'

'Your heart fails you, my dear Mrs. Stafford,' replied Godolphin, 'and I do not wonder at it. But I will tell you what you shall allow me to do: I will attend you to-morrow to Southampton, where in the character of a veteran seaman I will direct your departure, (as the whole pacquet is yours) according to the appearance of the weather; and to indulge me still farther, you shall suffer me to see you landed at Havre. Adelina, I know, will be wretched 'till she hears you are safe on the other side; and will therefore willingly spare me to bring her such intelligence; and give me at the same time a fortunate opportunity of being useful to you.'

Mrs. Stafford, secretly rejoiced at a proposal which would secure them a protector and as much safety as depended on human skill, could not conceal her wish to assent to it; tho' she expressed great reluctance to give him so much trouble.

Godolphin then consulted the eyes of Emmeline, which on meeting his were cast down; but he could not find that they expressed any displeasure at his offer: he therefore assured Mrs. Stafford that he should consider it as a pleasurable scheme with a party to whom he was indifferent; 'but when,' added he, 'it gives me the means of being of the least use to you, to Miss Mowbray, and your children, I shall find in it not only pleasure but happiness. Alas! how poorly it will repay the twentieth part of the obligation we owe you!'

It was settled therefore that Mr. Godolphin was to cross the channel with them. Again Emmeline tried to be sorry, and again found herself incapable of feeling any thing but satisfaction in hearing that he would be yet longer with them.

During the rest of the evening, he tried to assume a degree of chearfulness; and did in some measure feel it in the prospect of this farther temporary indulgence.

Lady Adelina, unable to conceal her concern, drooped without any effort to imitate him; and when they parted for the night, could not help deploring in terms of piercing regret their approaching separation.

The assurances Godolphin had given them of a favourable morning were fulfilled. They found that tho' there was yet a considerable swell, the wind had subsided entirely, and that they might safely cross to Southampton. The boat that was to convey them was ready; and Emmeline could not take leave of Lady Adelina without sharing the anguish which she could not mitigate. They embraced silently and in tears; and Emmeline pressed to her heart the little boy, to whom she was tenderly attached.

Godolphin was a silent spectator of this melancholy farewel. The softness of Emmeline's heart was to him her greatest charm, and he could hardly help repeating, in the words of Louis XIV — 'She has so much sensibility that it must be an exquisite pleasure to be beloved by her!'

He sighed in remembering that such could not be his happiness; then wishing to shorten a scene which so violently affected the unsettled spirits of Lady Adelina, he would have led Mrs. Stafford and Emmeline away; but Lady Adelina insisted on following them to the shore; smiled thro' her tears; and promised to behave better. Silently they walked to the sea-side. Mrs. Stafford hastily embracing her, was handed into the boat by Godolphin; who then advancing with forced gaiety to Emmeline, about whom his sister still fondly hung, said — 'Come, come, I must have no more adieus — as if you were never to meet again.'

'Ah! who can tell,' answered Lady Adelina, 'that we ever shall!'

Emmeline spoke not; but kissing the hand of her weeping friend, gave her own to Godolphin; while Lady Adelina, resting on the arm of her woman, and overwhelmed with sorrow, suffered the boat to depart.

It rowed swiftly away; favoured by the tide. Lady Adelina remained on the shore as long as she could distinguish it; and then slowly and reluctantly returned to solitude and tears; while her two friends, attended by her brother, landed safely at Southampton, where he busied himself in settling every thing for their departure the next morning in the pacquet which they had hired, and which now lay ready to receive them.

During their passage to Havre, which was short and prosperous, the attention of Godolphin was equally divided between Mrs. Stafford, her children, and Emmeline. But when he assisted the latter to leave the vessel, he could not forbear pressing her to his heart, while in a deep sigh he bade adieu to the happiness of being with her; for he concluded she would not long remain single, and after she was married he determined never more to trust himself with the dangerous pleasure of beholding her.

He had never mentioned the name of Delamere; and knew not that he was returned to England. Having once been assured of her engagement, he was unable to enquire into the circumstances of what had destroyed his happiness. He knew they were to be married in March, and that Delamere had promised to remain on the Continent 'till that period. He doubted not, therefore, but that Emmeline, in compliance with the entreaties of her lover, had consented to accompany Mrs. Stafford to France, and by her presence to charm away the months that yet intervened; after which he supposed they would be immediately united.

Notwithstanding some remarks he had made on the interest she seemed to take in regard to himself, he imputed it merely to her general sensibility and to his relationship to Lady Adelina. He supposed that Delamere possessed her heart; and tho' it was the only possession on earth that would give him any chance of happiness, he envied this happy lover without hating him. He could not blame him for loving her, who was in his own opinion irresistible; nor for having used the opportunity his good fortune had given him of winning her affections. The longer he conversed with her, the more he was convinced that Delamere, in being as he believed master of that heart, was the most fortunate of human beings. But tho' he had not resolution enough to refuse himself the melancholy yet pleasing gratification of contemplating perfections which he thought could never be his, and tho' he could not help sometimes betraying the fondness which that indulgence hourly encreased, he never seriously meditated supplanting the happy Delamere. He did not think that to attempt it was honourable; and his integrity would have prevented the trial, had he supposed it possible to succeed.

Mrs. Stafford had at first seen with concern that Godolphin, whom she sincerely esteemed, was nourishing for her friend a passion which could only serve to make him unhappy. But she now saw its progress rather with pleasure than regret. She was piqued at the groundless jealousy and rash injustice of Delamere towards Emmeline: and disappointed and disgusted at Lord Montreville's conduct towards herself; sickening at the little sincerity of the latter, and doubtful of the temper of the former, she feared that if the alliance took place, her friend would find less happiness than splendour: and she looked with partial eyes on Godolphin; who in morals, manners, and temper, was equally unexceptionable, and whose fortune, tho' inferior to his birth, was yet enough for happiness in that style of life which she knew better calculated for the temper and taste of Emmeline than the parade and grandeur she might share with Delamere.

Godolphin had no parents to accept her with disdainful and cold acquiescence — no sister to treat her with supercilious condescension. — But all his family, tho' of a rank superior to that of Delamere, would receive her with transport, and treat her with the respect and affection she deserved.

Mrs. Stafford, however, spoke not to Emmeline of this revolution in her sentiments, but chose rather to let the affair take its course than to be in any degree answerable for its consequences.

The hour in which Godolphin was to leave them now approached. Unable to determine on bidding Emmeline farewel, he could still have lingered with her, and would have gone on with them to Rouen, where Stafford waited their arrival: but this, Mrs. Stafford was compelled to decline; fearing least this extraordinary attention in a stranger should induce her husband to make enquiry into their first acquaintance, and by that means lead to discoveries which could not fail of being injurious to Lady Adelina.

Of all that related to her, he was at present ignorant. He had been told, that the infant which his wife and Miss Mowbray so often visited, was the son of an acquaintance of the latter; who being obliged soon after its birth to go to the West Indies, had sent it to Bath to Emmeline, who had undertaken to overlook the nurse to whose care it was committed.

Into a circumstance which offered neither a scheme to occupy his mind, or money to purchase his pleasures, Stafford thought it not then worth his while farther to enquire; but now, in a country of which he understood not the language, and detached from his usual pursuits, Mrs. Stafford knew not what strange suspicions the assiduity of Godolphin might excite in a head so oddly constructed; and without explaining her reasons to Godolphin, she said enough to convince him that he must, with whatever reluctance, leave the lovely travellers at Havre.

He busied himself, however, in adjusting every thing for the safety of their journey; and being in the course of their preparations left alone with Emmeline in a room of the hotel, he could not forbear using the last opportunity he was likely to have of speaking to her —

'Has Miss Mowbray any commands to Lady Adelina?'

'My most affectionate love!' answered Emmeline, 'my truest remembrance! And tell her, that the moment I am settled I will give her an account of my situation, and of all that happens worth her knowing.'

'We shall hear then,' said he, forcing a melancholy smile, 'we shall hear when you meet the fortunate, the happy Mr. Delamere.'

'Lady Adelina,' blushingly replied Emmeline, 'will certainly know it if I should meet him; but nothing is at present more improbable.'

' 'Tis now,' reassumed Godolphin, 'the last week of January — February — March — ah! how soon March will come! Tell me, how long in that month may Adelina direct to Miss Mowbray?'

'Mr. Delamere, Sir,' said Emmeline, gravely, 'is not now in France.'

'But may he not immediately return thither from Geneva or any other place? Is my sister, Lady Westhaven, to be present at the ceremony?'

'The ceremony,' answered she, half angry and half vexed, 'may perhaps never take place.'

The awkwardness of her situation in regard to Delamere arose forcibly to her mind, and something lay very heavy at her heart. She tried to check the tears which were filling her eyes, least they should be imputed to a very different cause; but the effort she made to conquer her feelings rendered them more acute. She took out a handkerchief to wipe away these involuntary betrayers of her emotion, and sitting down, audibly sobbed.

Godolphin had asked these questions, in that sort of desperate resolution which a person exerts who determines to know, in the hope of being able to endure, the worst that can befal him. But he was now shocked at the distress they had occasioned, and unable to bear the sight of her tears.

'Pardon me,' cried he, 'pardon me, most lovely, most amiable Emmeline! — oh! pardon me for having given a moment's pain to that soft and sensible bosom. Had I suspected that a reference to an event towards which I supposed you looked forward with pleasure could thus affect you, I had not presumed to name it. Whenever it happens,' added he, after a short pause — 'whenever it happens, Delamere will be the most enviable of human beings: and may you, Madam, be as happy as you are truly deserving of happiness!'

He dared not trust his voice with another word: but under pretence of fetching a glass of water left the room, and having recovered himself, quickly returned and offered it to Emmeline, again apologizing for having offended her.

She took the glass from him; and faintly smiling thro' her tears, said in the gentlest accents — 'I am not offended — I am only low spirited. Tired by the voyage, and shrinking from the fatigue of a long journey, yet you talk to me of a journey for life, on which I may never set out in the company you mention — and still more probably never undertake at all.'

The entrance of Mrs. Stafford, who came to entreat some directions from Godolphin, prevented the continuance of this critical conversation; in which, whatever the words imported in regard to Delamere, he found but little hope for himself. He attributed what Emmeline had said to mere evasion, and her concern to some little accidental neglect on the part of her lover which had excited her displeasure. Ignorant of the jealousy Delamere had conceived from the misrepresentation of the Crofts', which the solicitude of Emmeline for the infant of Lady Adelina had so immediately matured, he had not the most distant idea of the truth; nor suspected that the passion of Delamere for Emmeline, which he knew had within a few weeks been acknowledged without hesitation, and received with encouragement, was now become to him a source of insupportable torment; that she had left England without bidding him adieu, or even informing him that she was gone.

The two chaises were now ready; and Godolphin having placed in the first, Mrs. Stafford and her younger children, approached Emmeline to lead her to the second, in which she was to accompany the elder. He stopped a moment as they were quitting the room, and said — 'I cannot, Miss Mowbray, bid you adieu till you say you forgive me for the impertinence of my questions.'

'For impertinence?' answered Emmeline, giving him her hand — 'I cannot forgive you, because I know not that you have been guilty of it. Before I go, however, allow me to thank you most sincerely for the protection you have afforded us.'

'And not one word,' cried he, 'not one parting good wish to your little *protégé* — to my poor William?'

'Ah! I send him a thousand!' answered Emmeline.

'And one last kiss, which I will carry him.' She suffered him to salute her; and then he hastily led her to the chaise; and, as he put her in, said very solemnly — 'Let me repeat my wishes, Madam, that wheresoever you are, you may enjoy felicity — felicity which I shall never again know; and that Mr. Delamere — the fortunate Delamere —may be as sensible of your value as —'

Emmeline, to avoid hearing this sentence concluded, bade the chaise proceed. It instantly did so with all the velocity a French postillion could give it; and hardly allowed her to observe the mournful countenance and desponding air with which Godolphin bowed to her, as she, waving her hand, again bade him adieu!

The travellers arrived in due time safe at Rouen; where Mrs. Stafford found that her husband had been prevented meeting her, by the necessity he fancied himself under to watch the early nests of his Canary birds, of which he had now made a large collection, and whose encrease he attended to with greater solicitude than the arrival of his family. Mrs. Stafford saw with an eye of hopeless regret a new source of expence and absurdity opened; but knowing that complaints were more likely to produce anger and resentment in his mind, than any alteration in his conduct, she was obliged to conceal her chagrin, and to take possession of the gloomy chateau which her husband had chosen for her residence, about six miles from Rouen; while Emmeline, with her usual equality of temper, tried to reconcile herself to her new abode, and to share and relieve the fatigue and uneasiness of her friend. She found the activity she was for this purpose compelled to exert, assuaged and diverted that pain which she now could no longer hope to conquer, tho' she had not yet had the courage to ascertain, by a narrow examination of her heart in regard to Godolphin, that it would be removed no more.

On the evening after he had bade her adieu, Godolphin embarked in the pacquet which was on its departure to England. The weather, tho' cold, was calm; and he sat down on the deck, where, after they had got a few leagues from France, all was profoundly quiet. Only the man at the helm and one sailor were awake on board. The vessel glided thro' the expanse of water; while the soul of Godolphin fled back to Emmeline, and dwelt with lingering fondness on the object of all its affection.

CHAPTER XI

EMMELINE having thus quitted England, and Delamere appearing no longer to think of her, the Crofts', who had brought about an event so desirable for Lord Montreville, thought it time to claim the reward of such eminent service.

Miss Delamere, in meeting Lady Westhaven at Paris, had severely felt all the difference of their situation; and as she had repented of her clandestine union almost as soon as she had formed it, the comparison between her sister's husband and her own had embittered her temper, never very good, and made her return to England with reluctance; where she knew that she could not long evade acknowledging her marriage, and taking the inferior and humiliating name of *Mrs. Crofts.*

To avoid returning was however not in her power; nor could she prevail on Crofts to delay a declaration which must be attended with circumstances, to her most mortifying and unpleasant. But impatient to demand a daughter of Lord Montreville as his wife, and still more impatient to receive twelve thousand pounds, which was hers independant of her father, he would hear of no delay; and the present opportunity of conciliating Lord and Lady Montreville, was in the opinion of all the Crofts family not to be neglected.

Sir Richard undertook to disclose the affair to Lord Montreville, and to parry the first effusions of his Lordship's anger by a very common, yet generally successful stratagem, that of affecting to be angry first, and drowning by his own clamours the complaints of the party really injured.

For this purpose, he waited early one morning on Lord Montreville, and with a countenance where scornful superiority was dismissed for pusillanimous dejection, he began. —

'My Lord — when I reflect and consider and remember the innumerable, invaluable and extraordinary favours, kindnesses and obligations I owe your Lordship, my heart bleeds — and I lament and deplore and regret that it is my lot to announce and declare and discover what will I fear give infinite concern and distress and uneasiness to you — and my Lord — '

'What is all this, Sir Richard?' cried Lord Montreville, hastily interrupting him. — 'Is Delamere married?'

'Heaven forbid!' answered the hypocritical Crofts. — 'Bad, and unwelcome, and painful as what I have to say is, it does not amount to arise to that misfortune and calamity.'

'Whatever is it Sir,' said his Lordship impatiently, 'let me hear it at once. — Is it a dismission from my office?'

'Never, I hope!' replied Sir Richard. 'At least, for many years to come, may this country not know and feel and be sensible of such a loss, deprivation and defection. My Lord, my present concern is of a very different nature; and I do assure and protest to your Lordship that no time nor intreaties nor persuasion will erase and obliterate and wipe away from my mind, the injury and prejudice the parties have done *me*, by thus — '

'Keep me no longer in suspense!' almost angrily cried Lord Montreville.

'Mr. Crofts, my Lord; Mr. Crofts is, I find, married —'

'To *my* daughter, Sir Richard. — Is it not so?'

'He is indeed, my Lord! and from this moment I disclaim, and renounce and protest against him; for my Lord —'

Sir Richard continued his harangue, to which Lord Montreville did not seem to attend. He was a moment silent, and then said —

'I have been more to blame than the parties. — I might have foreseen this. But I thought Fanny's pride a sufficient defence against an inferior alliance. Pray Sir, does Lady Montreville know of this marriage?'

Sir Richard then related all that his son had told him; interlarding his account with every circumstance that might induce his Lordship to believe he was himself entirely ignorant of the intrigue. Lord Montreville, however, knew too much of mankind in general, and of the Crofts' in particular, to give implicit credit to this artful recital. But Sir Richard was now become so necessary to him, and they had so many secrets in common of great consequence to the political reputation of both, that he could not determine to break with him. He considered too that resentment could not unmarry his daughter; that the lineal honours of his family could not be affected by her marriage; and that he owed the Crofts' some favour for having counteracted the indiscretion of Delamere. Determining therefore, after a short struggle, to sacrifice his pride to his politics, he dismissed Sir Richard with infinitely less appearance of resentment than he expected; and after long contention with the furious and irascible pride of his wife, prevailed upon her to let her daughter depart without her malediction. She would not see Crofts, or pardon her daughter; protesting that she never could be reconciled to a child of hers who bore such an appellation as that of '*Mrs. Crofts*.' Soon afterwards, however, the Marquisate which Lord Montreville had been so long promised was to be granted him. But his wife could not bear, that by assuming a title which had belonged to the Mowbray family, (a point he particularly wished to obtain) he should drop or render secondary those honours which he derived from *her* ancestors. Wearied by her persecution, and accustomed to yield to her importunity, he at length gratified her, by relinquishing the name he wished to bear, and taking the title of Marquis of Montreville, while his son assumed that of Viscount Delamere. This circumstance seemed more than any other to reconcile Lady Montreville to her eldest daughter, whose surname she could evade under the more satisfactory appellation of Lady Frances. She was now therefore admitted to her mother's presence; Crofts received an haughty and reluctant pardon; and some degree of tranquillity was restored to the noble house of Mowbray-Delamere; while the Crofts', more elated and consequential than before, behaved as if they had inherited and deserved the fortune and splendour that surrounded them: and the table, the buildings, the furniture of Sir Richard, vied in expence and magnificence with those of the most affluent of the nobility.

Lord Delamere, to whom the acquisition of a title could offer nothing in mitigation of the anguish inflicted by disappointed love, was now at Dublin; where, immediately on his arrival, he had enquired for Colonel Fitz-Edward at the house of his brother, Lord Clancarryl.

As the family were in the country, and only a servant in it, he could not for some days obtain the information he wanted. He heard, however, that Lord Clancarryl was very soon expected, and for his arrival he determined to wait. In this interval of suspense, he heard from a correspondent in England, that Miss Mowbray had not only disappeared from Woodfield, but had actually quitted England; and was gone no one knew precisely whither; but it was generally supposed to be France.

Tho' he had sworn in bitterness of heart to drive for ever from it this perfidious and fatal beauty, it seemed as if forgetting his resolution, he had in this intelligence received a new injury. He still fancied that she should have told him of her design to quit England, without recollecting that he had given her no opportunity to speak to him at all.

Again he felt his anger towards Fitz-Edward animated almost to madness; and again impatiently sought to hasten a meeting when he might discuss with him all the mischief he had sustained.

Lord Clancarryl coming for a few days to Dublin, found there letters from Lord Montreville, in which his Lordship bespoke for his son the acquaintance of the Clancarryl family. Desirous of shewing every attention to a young man so nearly connected with his wife's family, by the marriage of her brother, Lord Westhaven, to his youngest sister, and related also to himself, Lord Clancarryl immediately sought Delamere; and was surprized to find, that instead of receiving his advances with warmth or even with politeness, he hardly returned them with common civility and seemed to attend to nothing that was said. The first pause in the conversation, however, Delamere took advantage of to enquire after Colonel Fitz-Edward.

'My brother,' answered Lord Clancarryl, 'left us only three days ago.'

'For London, my Lord?'

'No; he is gone with two other friends on a kind of pleasurable tour. — They hired a sloop at Cork to take them to France.'

'To France!' exclaimed Delamere — 'Mr. Fitz-Edward gone to France?'

'Yes,' replied Lord Clancarryl, somewhat wondering at the surprize Delamere expressed — 'and I promoted the plan as much as I could; for poor George is, I am afraid, in a bad state of health; his looks and his spirits are not what they used to be. Chearful company, and this little tour, may I hope restore them. But how happens it that he knew not, Sir, of your return? He was persuaded you were still abroad; and expressed some pleasure at the thoughts of meeting you when you least expected it.'

'No, no, my Lord,' cried Delamere, in a voice rendered almost inarticulate by contending passions — 'his hope was not to meet *me*. He is gone with far other designs.'

'What designs, Lord Delamere?' gravely asked Lord Clancarryl.

'My Lord,' answered Delamere, recollecting himself, 'I mean not to trouble you on this matter. I have some business to adjust with Mr. Fitz-Edward; and since he is not here, have only to request of your Lordship information when he returns, or whither a letter may follow him?'

'Sir,' returned Lord Clancarryl with great gravity, 'I believe I can answer for Colonel Fitz-Edward's readiness to settle *any business* you may desire to adjust with him; and I wish, since there is *business* between ye, that I could name the time when you are likely to meet him. All, however, I can decidedly say is, that he intends going to Paris, but that his stay in France will not exceed five or six weeks in the whole; and that such letters as I may have occasion to send, are to be addressed to the care of Monsieur de Guisnon, banker, at Paris.'

Delamere having received this intelligence, took a cold leave; and Lord Clancarryl, who had before heard much of his impetuous temper and defective education, was piqued at his distant manner, and returned to his house in the country without making any farther effort to cultivate his friendship.

Debating whether he should follow Fitz-Edward to France or wait his return to Ireland, Delamere remained, torn with jealousy and distracted by delay. He was convinced beyond a doubt, that Fitz-Edward had met Emmeline in France by her own appointment. 'But let them not,' cried he — 'let them not hope to escape me! Let them not suppose I will relinquish my purpose 'till I have punished their infamy or cease to feel it! — Oh, Emmeline! Emmeline! is it for this I pursued — for this I won thee!'

The violence of those emotions he felt after Lord Clancarryl's departure, subsided only because he had no one to listen to, no one to answer him. He determined, as Lord Clancarryl seemed so certain of his brother's return in the course of six weeks, to wait in Ireland 'till the end of that period, since there was but little probability of his meeting him if he pursued him to France. He concluded that wherever Emmeline was, Fitz-Edward might be found also; but the residence of Emmeline he knew not, nor could he bear a moment to think that he might see them together.

The violence of his resentment, far from declining, seemed to resist all the checks its gratification received, and to burn with accumulated fury. His nights brought only tormenting dreams; his days only a repetition of unavailing anguish.

He had several acquaintance among young men of fashion at Dublin. With them he sometimes associated; and tried to forget his uneasiness in the pleasures of the table; and sometimes he shunned them entirely, and shut himself up to indulge his disquiet.

In the mean time, Lady Clancarryl was extremely mortified at the account her husband gave her of Delamere's behaviour. She knew that her brother, Lord Westhaven, would be highly gratified by any attention shewn to the family of his wife; particularly to a brother to whom Lady Westhaven was so much attached. She therefore entreated her Lord to overlook Delamere's petulance, and renew the invitation he had given him to Lough Carryl. But his Lordship, disgusted with the reception he had before met with, laughed, and desired her to try whether *her* civilities would be more graciously accepted. Lady Clancarryl therefore took the trouble to go herself to Dublin: where she so pressingly insisted on Delamere's passing a fortnight with them, that he could not evade the invitation without declaring his animosity against Fitz-Edward, and his resolution to demand satisfaction — a declaration which could not fail of rendering his purpose abortive. He returned, therefore, to Lough Carryl with her Ladyship; meaning to stay only a few days, and feeling hurt at being thus compelled to become the inmate of a family into which he might so soon carry grief and resentment.

Godolphin, after his return to the Isle of Wight, abandoned himself more than ever to the indulgence of his passion. He soothed yet encreased his melancholy by poetry and music; and Lady Adelina for some time contributed to nourish feelings too much in unison with her own. He now no longer affected to conceal from her his attachment to her lovely friend; but to her only it was known. Her voice, and exquisite taste, he loved to employ in singing the verses he made; and he would sit hours by her *piano forté* to hear repeated one of the many sonnets he had written on her who occupied all his thoughts.

SONNET

When welcome slumber sets my spirit free
Forth to fictitious happiness it flies,
And where Elysian bowers of bliss arise
I seem, my Emmeline — to meet with thee!

Ah! Fancy then, dissolving human ties,
Gives me the wishes of my soul to see;
Tears of fond pity fill thy softened eyes;
In heavenly harmony — our hearts agree.

Alas! these joys are mine in dreams alone,
When cruel Reason abdicates her throne!
Her harsh return condemns me to complain
Thro' life unpitied, unrelieved, unknown.
And, as the dear delusions leave my brain,
She bids the truth recur — with aggravated pain.

But Lady Adelina herself at length grew uneasy at beholding the progress of this unhappy passion. His mind seemed to have lost all its strength, and to be incapable of making even an effort to shake off an affection which his honour would not allow him to attempt rendering successful. His spirits, affected by the listless solitude in which he lived, were sunk into hopeless despondence; and his sister was every day more alarmed, not only for his peace but for his life.

She therefore tried to make him determine to quit her, for a short abode in London; but to do that he absolutely refused. Lord Clancarryl had long pressed him to go to Ireland: he had not seen his eldest sister for some years; and ardently wished to embrace her and her children. But Fitz-Edward was at her house; and to meet was impossible. Lady Clancarryl, deceived by a plausible story, which had been framed to account for Lady Adelina's absence, was, as well as her Lord, entirely ignorant of the share Fitz-Edward had in it: they believed it to have been occasioned by her antipathy to Trelawny, and her fear lest her relations should insist on her again residing with him; and it was necessary that nothing should be said to undeceive them.

Godolphin had therefore been obliged to form several excuses to account for his declining the pressing invitations he received; and he found that his eldest sister was already much hurt by his apparent neglect. In one of her last letters, she mentioned that Fitz-Edward was gone to France; and Lady Adelina pointed out to Godolphin several passages which convinced him he had given pain by his long absence to his beloved Camilla, and prevailed upon him to go to Ireland. He arrived therefore at Lough Carryl two days after his sister had returned thither with Lord Delamere.

CHAPTER XII

MR. Godolphin was extremely surprized to find, in Ireland, Delamere, the happy Delamere! who he supposed had long since been with Emmeline, waiting the fortunate hour that was to unite them for ever. A very few weeks now remained of the year which he had promised to remain unmarried; yet instead of his being ready to attend his bride to England, to claim in the face of the world his father's consent, he was lingering in another country, where he appeared to have come only to indulge dejection; for he frequently fled from society, and when he was in it, forgot himself in gloomy reveries.

Nobody knew why he came to Ireland, unless to satisfy a curiosity of which nothing appeared to remain; yet he still continued there; and as Lord and Lady Clancarryl were now used to his singular humour, they never enquired into its cause; while he, flattered by the regard of two persons so amiable and respectable, suffered not his enmity to Fitz-Edward to interfere with the satisfaction he sometimes took in their society; tho' he oftener past the day almost entirely alone. Godolphin could not repress the anxious curiosity he felt, to know what, at this period, could separate lovers whose union appeared so certain. But this curiosity he had no means of satisfying. Lady Clancarryl had heard nothing of his engagement, or any hint of his approaching marriage; and tho' he was on all other topics, when he entered at all into conversation, remarkably open and unguarded, he spoke not, in company, of any thing that related to himself.

He seemed, however, to seek a closer intimacy with Godolphin, of whose excellent character he had often heard, and whose appearance and conversation confirmed all that had been reported in his favour. Godolphin neither courted him or evaded his advances; but could not help looking with astonishment on a man, who on the point of being the husband of the most lovely woman on earth, could saunter in a country where he appeared to have neither attachments or satisfaction. Sometimes he almost ventured to hope that their engagement was dissolved: but then recollecting that Lady Adelina had assured him the promise of Emmeline was still uncancelled, he checked so flattering an illusion, and returned again to uncertainty and despondence.

On the third day after Godolphin's arrival, Delamere, who intended to go back to Dublin the following morning save one, joined Lady Clancarryl and her brother in the drawing-room immediately after dinner.

Godolphin, on account of the expected return of Fitz-Edward, had determined to make only a short stay at Lough Carryl. He wished to carry with him to his own house, portraits of his sister and her children; and was expressing to her this wish — 'I should like to have them,' said he, 'in a large miniature; the same size as one I have of Adelina.'

'Have you then a portrait of Adelina,' enquired Lady Clancarryl, 'and have not yet shewn it me?'

'I have,' answered Godolphin; 'but my sister likes not that it should be seen. It is very like her *now*; but has little resemblance to her former pictures. This is painted by a young lady, her friend.' He then took it out of his pocket, and gave it to Lady Clancarryl.

'And is Adelina so thin and pale,' asked her Ladyship, 'as she is here represented?'

'More so,' answered Godolphin.

'She is then greatly changed. — Yet the eyes and features, and the whole air of the countenance, I should immediately have acknowledged.' Continuing to look pensively at the picture, she added, "Tis charmingly coloured; and might represent a very lovely and penitent Magdalen. The black veil; and tearful eye, are beautifully touched. But why did you indulge her in this melancholy taste?'

Godolphin, excessively hurt at this speech, answered mournfully — 'Poor Adelina, you know, has had little reason to be gay.'

Delamere, who during this conversation seemed lost in his own reflections, now suddenly advanced, and desired Lady Clancarryl would favour him with a sight of the picture. He took it to a candle; and looking steadily on it, was struck with the lightness of the drawing, which extremely resembled the portraits

Emmeline was accustomed to make; tho' this was more highly finished than any he had yet seen of hers.

Without being able to account for his idea, since nothing was more likely than that the drawing of two persons might resemble each other, he looked at the back of the picture, which was of gold; and in the centre a small oval crystal contained the words *Em. Mowbray*, in hair, and under it the name of *Adelina Trelawny.* It was indeed a memorial of Emmeline's affection to her friend; and the name was in her own hair; — a circumstance that made it as dear to Godolphin as the likeness it bore to his sister: and the whole was rendered in his eyes inestimable, by its being painted by herself. Delamere, astonished and pained he knew not why, determined to hear from Godolphin himself the name of the paintress: returning it to him, he said — 'A lady, you say, Sir, drew it. May I ask her name?'

Godolphin, now first aware of the indiscretion he had committed, and flattering himself that the chrystal had not been inspected, answered with an affectation of pleasantry — 'Oh! I believe it is a secret between my sister and her friend which I have no right to reveal; and to tell you the truth I teized Adelina to give me the picture, and obtained it only on condition of not shewing it.'

Delamere, who had so often sworn to forget her, still fancied he had a right to be exclusively acquainted with all that related to Emmeline. He felt himself piqued by this evasion, and answered somewhat quickly — 'I know the drawing, Sir; it is done by Miss Mowbray.'

Godolphin was then compelled to answer 'that it was.'

'I envy Miss Mowbray her charming talent,' cried Lady Clancarryl. 'Pray who is Miss Mowbray?'

'A relation of Lord Delamere's,' answered Godolphin; 'and a most lovely and amiable young woman.'

Delamere, whose varying countenance ill seconded his attempt to appear indifferent on this subject, now grew pale, now red.

'Are you acquainted then with Miss Mowbray, Sir?' said he to Godolphin.

'I have seen her,' replied Godolphin, 'with my sister, Lady Adelina Trelawny.'

He then hurried the discourse to some other topic; being unwilling to answer any other questions that related either to his sister or her friend.

But Delamere, whose wounds bled afresh at the name of Emmeline, and who could not resist enquiring after her of a person who had so lately seen her, took the earliest opportunity of seeking Godolphin to renew this discourse.

They met therefore the following morning in the breakfast parlour; and Delamere suddenly turning the conversation from the topics of the day, said — 'You are, I find, acquainted with Miss Mowbray. You may perhaps know that she is not only a relation of mine, but that I *was* particularly interested in whatever related to her.'

Godolphin, whose heart fluttered so as almost to deprive him of speech, answered very gravely — 'I have heard so from Mrs. Stafford.'

'Then you know, perhaps — But you are undoubtedly well acquainted with Colonel Fitz-Edward?'

'Certainly,' replied Godolphin. 'He was one of my most intimate friends.'

'Then, Sir,' cried Delamere, losing all temper, 'one of your most intimate friends is a villain!'

Godolphin, shocked at an expression which gave him reason to apprehend Lady Adelina's story was known, answered with great emotion — 'You will be so good, my Lord, as to explain that assertion; which, whatever may be its truth, is very extraordinary when made thus abruptly to me.'

'You are a man of honour, Mr. Godolphin, and I will not conceal from you the cruel injuries I have sustained from Fitz-Edward, nor that I wait here only to have an opportunity of telling him that I bear them not tamely.' He then related, in terms equally warm and bitter, the supposed alienation of Emmeline's affections by the artifices of Fitz-Edward, enumerated all the imaginary proofs with which the invidious artifices of the Crofts' had furnished him, and concluded by asserting, that he had himself seen, in the arms of Emmeline, a living witness of her ruin, and the perfidy of his faithless friend.

To this detail, including as it did the real history of his sister under the false colours in which the Crofts' had drest it to mislead Delamere and destroy Emmeline, Godolphin listened with sensations impossible to be described. He could not hear without horror the character of Emmeline thus cruelly blasted; yet her vindication he could not undertake without revealing to a stranger the unhappy story of Lady

Adelina, which he had with infinite difficulty concealed even from his own family.

The fiery and impatient spirit of Delamere blazing forth in menace and invective, gave Godolphin time to collect his thoughts; and he almost immediately determined, whatever it cost him, to clear up the reputation of Emmeline.

Tho' he saw, that to explain the whole affair must put the character of his sister, which he had been so solicitous to preserve, into the power of an inconsiderate young man, yet he thought he might trust to the honour and humanity of Delamere to keep the secret; and however mortifying such a measure appeared, his justice as well as his love would not allow him to suffer the innocent Emmeline to remain under an imputation which she had incurred only by her generous and disinterested intentions to the weakness and misfortunes of another.

But resolutely as he bore the pain of these reflections, he shrunk from others with which they were mingled: he foresaw, that as soon as the jealousy of Delamere was by his information removed; his love, which seemed to be as passionate as ever, would prompt him to seek a reconciliation: his repentance would probably be followed by Emmeline's forgiveness and their immediate union.

Farewel then for ever to all the hopes he had nourished since his unexpected meeting with Delamere! — Farewel to every expectation of happiness for ever!

But tho' in relinquishing these delightful visions he relinquished all that gave a value to life, so truly did he love and revere her, that to have the spotless purity of her name sullied even by a doubt seemed an insupportable injustice to himself; and his affection was of a nature too noble to owe its success to a misrepresentation injurious to its object. That the compassion which had saved his sister, should be the cause of her having suffered from the malicious malice of the Crofts' and the rash jealousy of Delamere, redoubled all his concern; and he was so much agitated and hurt, that without farther consideration he was on the point of relating the truth instantly, had not the entry of Lord Clancarryl for that time put an end to their discourse: from this resolution, formed in the integrity of his upright heart, nothing could long divert him; yet he reflected, as soon as he was alone, on the violent and ungovernable passions which seemed to render Delamere, unguided by reason and incapable of hearing it. He was apprehensive that the discovery, if made to him at Lough Carryl, might influence him to say or do something that might discover to Lady Clancarryl the unhappy story of her sister; and he thought it better to delay the explanation 'till he could follow Delamere to Dublin, which he determined to do in a few days after he left Lough Carryl.

This interval gave him time to feel all the pain of the sacrifice he was about to make. Nor could all his strength of mind, and firmness of honour, prevent his reluctance or cure his anguish.

He was about to restore to the arms of his rival, the only woman he had ever really loved; and whom he adored with the most ardent passion, at the very moment that his honour compelled him to remove the impediments to her marriage with another.

Sometimes he thought that he might at least indulge himself in the melancholy pleasure of relating to her in a letter what he had done, as soon as the explanation should be made: but even this gratification he at length determined to refuse himself.

'If she loves Delamere,' said he, 'she will perhaps rejoice in the effect and forget the cause. If she has, as I have sometimes dared to hope, some friendship and esteem for the less fortunate Godolphin, why should I wound a heart so full of sensibility by relating the conflicts of my soul and the passion I have vainly indulged?'

A latent hope, however, almost unknown, at least unacknowledged, lingered in his heart. It *was* possible that Emmeline, resenting the injurious suspicions and rash accusations of Delamere, might refuse to fulfil her engagement. But whenever this feeble hope in spite of himself arose, he remembered her soft and forgiving temper, her strict adherence to her word on other occasions, and it faded in conviction that she would pardon her repentant lover when he threw himself on her mercy; and not evade a promise so solemnly given, which he learned from Delamere himself had never been cancelled.

Delamere now returned to Dublin; and in a few days Godolphin followed him: but on enquiring at his lodgings, he heard that he was gone out of town for some days with some of his friends on a party of pleasure. Godolphin left a letter for him desiring to see him immediately on his return; and then again resigned himself to the painful delight of thinking of Emmeline, and to the conscious satisfaction of becoming the vindicator and protector of her honour even unknown to herself.

Emmeline, in the mean time, unhappy in the unhappiness of those she loved, and by no means flattered by the prospect of dependance thro' life, of which Lord Montreville now made her see all the dreariness and desolation, by the careless and irregular manner in which even her small quarterly stipend was remitted to her, yet exerted all her fortitude to support the spirits of Mrs. Stafford. Calm in the possession of conscious innocence, and rich in native integrity and nobleness of nature, she was, tho' far from happy herself, enabled to mitigate the sorrows of others. Nor was her residence, (otherwise disagreeable and forlorn enough,) entirely without its advantages: it afforded her time and opportunity to render herself perfectly mistress of the language of the country; of which she had before only a slight knowledge. To the study of languages, her mind so successfully applied itself, that she very soon spoke and wrote French with the correctness not only of a native, but of a native well educated.

While she thus suffered banishment in consequence of the successful intrigues of the Crofts family, they enjoyed all the advantages of their prosperous duplicity; at least they enjoyed all the satisfaction that arises from accumulating wealth and an ostentatious display of it. Sir Richard, by the political knowledge his place afforded him, had been enabled (by means of trusty agents) to carry on such successful traffic in the stocks, that he now saw himself possessed of wealth greater than his most sanguine hopes had ever presented to his imagination. But as his fortune enlarged, his spirit seemed to contract in regard to every thing that did not administer to his pride or his appetite. In the luxuries of the table, his house, his gardens, he expended immense sums; and the astonished world saw, with envy and indignation, wealth, which seemed to be ill-gotten, as profusely squandered: but dead to every generous and truly liberal sentiment, these expences were confined only to himself; and in regard to others he still nourished the sordid prejudices and narrow sentiments with which he set out in life — a needy adventurer, trusting to cunning and industry for scanty and precarious bread. Mr. Crofts, who had received twelve thousand pounds with his wife, (whose clandestine marriage had prevented its being secured in settlement,) used it, as his father directed, in gaming in the stocks, with equal avidity and equal success. Lady Frances, in having married beneath herself, had yet relinquished none of the privileges of high birth: she played deep, dressed in the extremity of expence, and was celebrated for the whimsical splendor of her equipages and the brilliancy of her assemblies. Her husband loved money almost as well as the fame acquired by these fashionable displays of her Ladyship's taste; but on the slightest hint of disapprobation, he was awed into silence by her scornful indignation; and with asperity bade to observe, that tho' the daughter of the Marquis of Montreville had so far forgotten her rank as to marry the son of Crofts the attorney, she would allow nobody else to forget that she was still the daughter of the Marquis of Montreville.

This right honourable eloquence subdued the plebeian spirit of Crofts; while he was also compelled to submit patiently, lest Lord Montreville should be offended and withhold the fortune he farther expected to receive. Lady Frances therefore pursued the most extravagant career of dissipation unchecked. She was young, handsome and vain; and saw every day new occasion to lament having thrown herself away on Crofts; and as she could not now release herself from him, she seemed determined to render him at least a fashionable husband.

Mrs. James Crofts trod as nearly as she could in the footsteps of Lady Frances; whose name she seemed to take exquisite pleasure in repeating, tho' its illustrious possessor scarce deigned to treat her with common civility; and never on any account admitted her to any thing but her most private parties, with a few dependants and persons who found the way to her favour by adulation. Mrs. James Crofts however consoled herself for the slights she received from Lady Frances, by parading in all inferior companies with the names of her high and illustrious relations: and she employed the same tradespeople; laid out with them as much money; and paid them better than Lady Frances herself. —

Her chariot and job horses were discarded for a fashionable coach; her house at Clapham, for an elegant town residence. She tried to hide the approaches of age, by rouge; and dress and amusements effectually kept off the approaches of thought; her husband, slowly yet certainly was creeping up the hill of preferment; her daughters were certainly growing more beautiful and accomplished than their mother; and Mrs. James Crofts fancied she was happy.

CHAPTER XIII

IT was now early in May; and in the blooming orchards and extensive beech woods of Normandy, Emmeline found much to admire and something to lament.

The Seine, winding thro' the vale and bringing numberless ships and vessels to Rouen, surrounded by hills fringed with forests, the property of the crown, and extending even to that of Arques, formed a rich and entertaining scene. But however beautiful the outline, the landscape still appeared ill finished: dark and ruinous hovels, inhabited by peasants frequently suffering the extremes of poverty; half cultivated fields, wanting the variegated enclosures that divide the lands in England; and trees often reduced to bare poles to supply the inhabitants with fewel, made her recollect with regret the more luxuriant and happy features of her native country.

The earth, however, covered with grass and flowers, offered her minute objects on which she delighted to dwell; but she dared not here wander as in England far from home: the women of the villages, who in this country are robust and masculine, often followed her with abuse for being English; and yet oftener the villagers clattered after her in their sabots, and addressed her by the name of *la belle Demoiselle Anglaise*, with a rudeness and familiarity that at once alarmed and disgusted her.

The long avenue of fir and beech which led to the chateau, and the *parterre*, *potagerie*, and *verger* behind it, were therefore the scenes of her morning and evening walks. She felt a pensive pleasure in retracing the lonely rambles she used to take at the same season at Mowbray Castle; and memory bringing before her the events of the two years and an half which had elapsed since she left it, offered nothing that did not renew her regret at having bid its solitary shades and unfrequented rocks adieu!

The idea of Godolphin still obtruded itself continually on her mind: nor could all her resolution prevent its obtruding with pleasure, tho' she perpetually condemned herself for allowing it to recur to her at all. Lady Adelina, in her two or three last letters, had not mentioned him farther than to say he was in Ireland; and Emmeline was ashamed of suffering her thoughts to dwell on a man, whose preference for her seemed uncertain and perhaps accidental, since he had neither absolutely declared himself when present or sought to engage her favour when absent; and tho' she was now fully persuaded that of Delamere she should hear no more as a lover, yet while her promise remained in his hands uncancelled, she fancied herself culpable in indulging a partiality for another.

Nor could she reflect on the jealousy which had tortured Delamere, and the pain he must have suffered in tearing her from his heart, without mingling with her resentment some degree of pity and sorrow.

She was one afternoon sitting at an open window of the chateau, revolving in her mind these reflections, when raising her eyes at a sudden noise, she saw driving along the avenue that led to it, an English post chaise and four, preceded by a valet de chambre, and followed by two livery servants.

To those who are driven by misfortune to seek a melancholy asylum in a foreign country, there is an inconceivable delight in beholding whatever forcibly brings back to the memory, the comforts and conveniences of their own: Emmeline, who had for many weeks seen only the boors of the curé of the village, gazed at English servants and English horses with as much avidity as if she beheld such an equipage for the first time.

Instantly however her wonder was converted into pleasure. — Lady Westhaven was assisted out of the chaise by a gentleman, whose likeness to Godolphin convinced the fluttering heart of Emmeline that it was her Lord; and eagerly enquiring for Miss Mowbray, she was immediately in her arms.

As soon as the joy (in which Mrs. Stafford partook,) of this unexpected meeting had a little subsided, Lady Westhaven related, that hearing by a letter they had received at Paris from Mr. Godolphin, that Emmeline was with Mrs. Stafford in or near Rouen, she had entreated Lord Westhaven to make a journey to see her.

'And I assure you Emmeline,' added she, 'I had no great difficulty to persuade him. His own curiosity went as far as my inclination; for he has long wished to see this dangerous Emmeline; who began by turning the head of *my* brother, and now I believe has turned the more sage one of *his* — for Godolphin's letters have been filled only with your praises.'

Emmeline, who had changed colour at the beginning of this speech, blushed more deeply at its conclusion. Involuntary pleasure penetrated her heart to hear that Godolphin had praised her. But it was immediately checked. Lady Westhaven seemed to know nothing of Delamere's desertion; of the history of Lady Adelina she was undoubtedly ignorant. How could Emmeline account for one without revealing the other? This reflection overwhelmed her with confusion, and she hardly heard the affectionate expressions with which Lady Westhaven testified her satisfaction at meeting her.

'I trust, my Lord,' said her Ladyship, 'that the partiality which I foresee you will feel for my fair cousin for her own sake, will not be a little encreased by our resemblance. — Tell me, do you think us so very much alike?'

'I never,' answered he, 'saw a stronger family likeness between sisters. Our lovely cousin has somewhat the advantage of you in height.'

'And in complexion, my Lord, notwithstanding the improvements I have learned to make to mine in France.'

'*I* should not,' answered his Lordship smiling, 'have ventured such a remark. I was merely going to add that you have the same features as Miss Mowbray, with darker hair and eyes; if however our charming Emmeline has a form less attractive, I have heard enough of her to be convinced that her understanding and her heart justify all that Lord Delamere or Mr. Godolphin have said of her.'

Lady Westhaven then expressed her wonder that she had heard nothing of Delamere for some months. — 'And it is most astonishing to me,' said she to Emmeline, 'that the month of March should elapse without *your* hearing of him.'

The distress of Emmeline now redoubled; and became so evident, that Lady Westhaven, convinced there was something relative to her brother of which she was ignorant, desired her to go with her into another room.

Incapable of falsehood, and detesting concealment, yet equally unwilling to ruin the reputation of the unhappy Adelina with her brother's wife, and having no authority to divulge a secret entrusted to her by her friend, Emmeline now felt the cruellest conflict. All she could determine was, to tell Lady Westhaven in general terms that Lord Delamere had undoubtedly altered his intentions with regard to her, and that the affair was, she believed, entirely and for ever at an end.

However anxious her Ladyship was to know from what strange cause such a change of sentiments proceeded, she found Emmeline so extremely hurt that she forbore at present to press the explanation. Full of concern, she was returning to the company, having desired Emmeline to remain and compose herself; when, as she was leaving the room, she said —

'But I forgot, my dear Emmeline, to ask you where you first became acquainted with Mr. Godolphin?'

Again deep blushes dyed the cheeks of the fair orphan; for this question led directly to those circumstances she could not relate.

'I knew him,' answered she, faultering as she spoke, 'at Bath.'

'And *is* he,' enquired Lady Westhaven, 'so *very* charming as his brother and his family represent him?'

'He is indeed very agreeable,' replied she — 'very much so. Extremely pleasant in his manner, and in his person very like Lord Westhaven.'

'He never told us how he first became acquainted with *you*; and to tell you the truth Emmeline, if I had not thought, indeed known, that you was engaged to Lord Delamere, I should have thought Godolphin your lover.'

This speech did not serve to hasten the composure Emmeline was trying to regain. She attempted to laugh it off; but succeeded so ill, that Lady Westhaven rejoined her Lord and Mr. and Mrs. Stafford, full of uneasy conjectures; and Emmeline, with a still more heavy heart, soon after followed her.

The pressing and earnest invitation of Mrs. Stafford, induced her guests to promise her their company for some days. But Lady Westhaven was so astonished at her brother's desertion of Emmeline, and so desirous of accounting for it without finding occasion to impute cruelty and caprice to him, or imprudence and levity to Emmeline, that she took the earliest opportunity of asking Mrs. Stafford, with whom she knew Miss Mowbray had no secrets, to explain to her the cause of an event so contrary to her expectations.

Mrs. Stafford had heard from Emmeline the embarrassment into which the questions of Lady Westhaven had thrown her; and with great difficulty at length persuaded her, that she owed it to her own character and her own peace to suffer her Ladyship to be acquainted with the truth: that she could run no risk in telling her what, for the sake of her Lord (whose happiness might be disturbed, and whose life hazarded by its knowledge) she certainly would not reveal. Besides which motives to secresy, the gentleness and humanity of Lady Westhaven would, Mrs. Stafford said, be alone sufficient to secure Lady Adelina from any possible ill consequences by her being made acquainted with the unhappy story.

These arguments wrung from Emmeline a reluctant acquiescence: and Mrs. Stafford related to Lady Westhaven those events which had been followed by Delamere's jealousy and their separation.

The love and regard, which on her first knowledge of Emmeline Lady Westhaven had conceived for her, and which her admirable qualities had ever since encreased, was now raised to enthusiasm. She knew not (for Mrs. Stafford and Emmeline were themselves ignorant) of the artful misrepresentations with which the Crofts' had poisoned the mind of her brother; and was therefore astonished at his suspicions and grieved at his rashness. She immediately proposed writing to him; but this design both her friends besought her for the present to relinquish. Emmeline assured her that she had so long considered the affair as totally at an end, that she could not now regret it; or if she felt any regret, it was merely in resigning the hope of being received into a family of which Lady Westhaven was a part. Her Ladyship could not however believe that Emmeline was really indifferent to her brother; and accounted for her present coldness by supposing her piqued and offended at his behaviour, for which she had so much reason.

Anxious therefore to reconcile them, she still continued desirous of writing to Delamere. And so much did her affectionate heart dwell on the happiness she should have in re-uniting her brother and her friend, that only the difficulty which there seemed to be in vindicating Emmeline without injuring Lady Adelina, withheld her; and she promised to delay writing 'till means could be found to clear up the reputation of the one without ruining that of the other.

Lord Westhaven had, during his stay, learnt from Mrs. Stafford the circumstances that had driven her and her family abroad; and had heard them with a sincere wish to alleviate the inconveniences that oppressed a woman whose manners and conduct convinced him she deserved a better fate. Unwilling however to hold out to her hopes that he was not sure he should be able to fulfil, he contented himself with procuring from Emmeline general information of the state of their affairs, and silently meditated the noble project of doing good, as soon as it should be in his power.

Her children, for whose sake only she seemed to be willing to support with patience her unfortunate lot, were objects particularly interesting to Lord Westhaven; and for the boys he thought he might, on his return to England, assist in providing. To their father, consoling himself in trifling follies and dirty intrigues for his misfortunes, it seemed more difficult to be serviceable.

While these benevolent purposes engaged his attention, Lady Westhaven reflected with regret on her approaching departure, which must divide her from Emmeline, whom she seemed now to love with redoubled affection. His Lordship, ever solicitous to gratify her, proposed that Emmeline should go with them into Switzerland with the Baron de St. Alpin, his Lordship's uncle; who, after a life passed in the service of France, now prepared to retire to his native country.

The Baron had seen his nephew at Paris. He had embraced with transport the son of a beloved sister, and insisted on his and Lady Westhaven's going back with him to his estate in the Païs de Vaud, as soon as he should have the happiness of being rejoined by his only son, the Chevalier de Bellozane, who was expected with his regiment from Martinique. Lord Westhaven, on his first visit to the paternal house of his mother, had found there only one of her sisters, who, with the Baron, were the last survivors of a numerous family. He could not therefore resist his uncle's earnest entreaties to accompany him hack; and Lady Westhaven, who was charmed with the manners of the respectable veteran and interested by his affection for her Lord, readily consented to delay her return to England for three months and to cross France once more to attend him.

To have Emmeline her companion in such a journey seemed to offer all that could render it charming. But how could she ask her to quit Mrs. Stafford, to whom she had been so much obliged; and who, in her present melancholy solitude, seemed more than ever to need her consolatory friendship?

Her Ladyship however ventured to mention it to Emmeline; who answered, that tho' nothing in the world would give her more pleasure than being with such friends, she could not, without a breach of duty which it was impossible to think of, quit Mrs. Stafford, to whom she was bound by gratitude as well as by affection.

Lord Westhaven acquiesced in the justice of this objection, but undertook to remove it by rendering the situation of her friend such as would make a short absence on both sides more supportable.

He therefore in his next conversation with Stafford represented the inconvenience of a house so far from a town, and how much better his family would be situated nearer the metropolis. He concluded by offering him a house he had himself hired at St. Germains; which he said he should be obliged to Mrs. Stafford and her family if they would occupy 'till his return from Switzerland. And that no objection might arise as to expence, he added, that considering himself as Miss Mowbray's banker, he had furnished her with five hundred pounds, with which she was desirous of repaying some part of the many obligations she owed Mr. and Mrs. Stafford.

Mrs. Stafford, who saw immediately all the advantages that might arise to Emmeline from her residence with Lady Westhaven, had on the slightest hint been warmly an advocate for her going., However reluctant to part with her, she suffered not her own gratifications to impede the interest of her fair charge. But she could not prevail on Emmeline to yield to her entreaties, 'till Lord Westhaven having settled every thing for the removal of the family to St. Germains, she was convinced that Mrs. Stafford would be in a pleasant and advantageous situation; and that she ought, even for the sake of her and her children, whom Lord Westhaven had so much the power of serving, to yield to an arrangement which would so much oblige him.

The chateau they inhabited was ready furnished; their cloaths were easily removed; and the Staffords and their children set out at the same time with Lord Westhaven, his wife, and Emmeline; who having seen them settled at St. Germains greatly to the satisfaction of Mrs. Stafford, went on to Paris; where, in about a week, they were joined by the Baron de St. Alpin, and the Chevalier de Bellozane.

CHAPTER XIV

THE Baron de St. Alpin was a venerable soldier, near sixty, in whom the natural roughness of his country was polished by a long residence among the French. He was extremely good humoured and chearful, and passionately fond of the Chevalier de Bellozane, who was the youngest of three sons, the two elder of whom had fallen in the field. The military ardour however of the Baron had not been buried with them; and he still entrusted the sole survivor of his house, and the last support of his hopes, in the same service.

With infinite satisfaction he embraced this beloved son on his return from Martinique, and with exultation presented him to his nephew, to Lady Westhaven, and Miss Mowbray. The Baron was indeed persuaded that he was the most accomplished young man in France, and had no notion that every body did not behold him with the same eyes.

Bellozane was tall, well made, and handsome; his face, and yet more, his figure, bore some resemblance to the Godolphin family; his manners were elegant, his air military, his vivacity excessive, and he was something of a coxcomb, but not more than is thought becoming of men of his profession in France at two and twenty.

Having lived always in the army or in fashionable circles at Paris, he had conceived no advantageous ideas of his own country, where he had not been since his childhood. His father now retiring thither himself, had obtained a long leave of absence for him that he might go also; but Bellozane would willingly have dispensed with the journey, which the Baron pressed with so much vehemence, that he had hardly time to modernize his appearance after his American campaigns; a point which was to him of serious importance.

He had therefore with reluctance looked forward to their journey over the Alps. But as soon as his father (who had met him at Port L'Orient on his landing) introduced him at Paris to his English relations and to Emmeline, the journey seemed not only to have lost its horrors, but to become a delightful party of pleasure, and he was happy to make the fourth in the post-coach in which Lady Westhaven, Emmeline, and her Ladyship's woman, travelled; Lord Westhaven and the Baron following in a post-chaise.

Nothing could exceed the happiness of the Baron, nor the gaiety of his son. Lord Westhaven and his wife, tho' they talked about it less, were not less pleased with their friends and their expedition; while Emmeline appeared restored to her former chearfulness, because she saw that they wished to see her chearful: but whenever she was a moment alone, involuntary sighs fled towards England; and when she remembered how far she must be from Lady Adelina, from little William, in short, from Godolphin, how could she help thinking of them with concern?

During the day, however, the Chevalier gave her no time for reflection. He waited on her with the most assiduous attention, watched her looks to prevent her slightest wishes, talked to her incessantly, besought her to teach him English, and told her all he had seen in his travels, and much that he had done. A Frenchman talks without hesitation of himself, and the Chevalier was quite a Frenchman.

Too polite however for exclusive adulation, Lady Westhaven shared all his flattery; and her real character being now unrepressed by the severity of her mother, she, all gaiety and good humour, was extremely amused with the extravagant gallantry of the Chevalier and at Emmeline's amazement, who having been little used to the manners of the French, was sometimes alarmed and sometimes vexed at the warmth of his address and the admiration which he professed towards them both.

Lady Westhaven assured her that such conversation was so usual that nobody ever thought of being offended at it; and that Bellozane was probably so much used to apply the figures of speech, which she thought so extraordinary, to every woman he saw, that he perhaps knew not himself, and certainly never thought of, what he was saying.

Emmeline therefore heard from him repeatedly what would from an Englishman have been considered as an absolute declaration of love, without any other answer than seeming inattention, and flying as soon as possible to some other topic.

In the progress of their journey these common place speeches and this desultory gallantry was gradually exchanged for a deportment more respectful. He besought Emmeline very seriously to give him an opportunity of speaking to her apart; which she with the utmost difficulty evaded. His extreme gaiety forsook him — the poor Chevalier was in love.

It was in vain he communicated his malady to *la belle cousine*, (as he usually called Lady Westhaven); *la belle cousine* only laughed at him, and told him he had according to his own account been so often in love, that this additional penchant could not possibly hurt him, and would merely serve to prevent what he owned he had so much dreaded, being '*ennuyé a la mort*' at St. Alpin.

When he found the inexorable Lady Westhaven refused seriously to attend to him, he applied with new ardour to Emmeline herself, to whom his importunity began to be distressing, as she forsaw in his addresses only a repetition of the persecution she had suffered from the fiery and impetuous Delamere. Still, however, she was often obliged to hear him. She could hear him only with coldness; which he was far from taking as discouragement. As she did not love to think *herself engaged*, she could not use that plea, or even name an engagement which she believed might now never be claimed by *him* to whom it was given. All therefore she could say was, that she had no thoughts of marrying. An answer, which however frequently repeated, Bellozane determined to think favourable; and Emmeline knew not how to treat with peremptory rudeness the cousin of Lord Westhaven and of Captain Godolphin.

But whatever diminution of her ease and tranquillity she might suffer or apprehend from the growing attachment of this young man, the journey was attended with so many pleasant circumstances, that all parties were desirous that it might be lengthened.

The extreme eagerness with which the Baron de St. Alpin had wished to revisit his estate, gave way to the pleasures he found in travelling in such society; and as Lady Westhaven had never been farther south than Lyons, and Emmeline had never seen the Southern Provinces at all, it was determined on their arrival at that city to proceed to the shore of the Mediterranean before they went into Switzerland.

It was the finest season of the year and the loveliest weather imaginable. The party consulted therefore only pleasure on their way. Sometimes they went on no more than a single stage in a day, and employed the rest in viewing any place in its neighbourhood worth their curiosity. They often left their carriages to walk, to saunter, to dine on the grass on provisions they had brought with them; and whenever a beautiful view or uncommon scene presented themselves, they stopped to admire them; and Bellozane drew sketches, which were put into Emmeline's *port feuille.*

As they were travelling between Marseilles and Toulon they entered a road bounded on each side by mountainous rocks, which sometimes receding, left between them small but richly cultivated vallies; and in other parts so nearly met each other, as to leave little more room than sufficed for the carriage to pass; while the turnings of the road were so angular and abrupt, that it seemed every moment to be carrying them into the bosom of the rock. Thro' this defile, as it was quite shady, they agreed to walk.

In some places huge masses impended over them, of varied form and colour, without any vegetation but scattered mosses; in others, aromatic plants and low shrubs; the lavender, the thyme, the rosemary, the mountain sage, fringed the steep craggs, while a neighbouring aclivity was shaded with the taller growth of holly, phillyrea, and ever-green oak; and the next covered with the glowing purple of the Mediterranean heath. The summits of almost all, crowned with groves of fir, larch, and pine.

Emmeline in silent admiration beheld this beautiful and singular scene; and with the pleasure it gave her, a soft and melancholy sensation was mingled. She wanted to be alone in this delightful place, or with some one who could share, who could understand the satisfaction she felt. She knew nobody but Godolphin who had taste and enthusiasm enough to enjoy it.

Insensibly she left Lady Westhaven and the Chevalier behind her; and passing his Lordship and the Baron, who were deeply engaged in a discourse about the military operations of the past war, she walked on with some quickness. Intent on the romantic wildness of the cliffs with which she was surrounded, and her mind associating with these objects the idea of him on whom it now perpetually dwelt, she had brought Godolphin before her, and was imagining what he would have said had he been with her; with what warmth he would enjoy, with what taste and spirit point out, the beauty of scenes so enchanting!

She had now left her companions at some distance; yet as she heard their voices swell in the breeze along the defile, she felt no apprehension. In the narrowest part of it, where she saw only steep craggs and the sky, which their bending tops hardly admitted, she was stopped by a transparent stream, which bursting suddenly with some violence out of the rock, is received into a small reservoir of stone and then carried away in stone channels to a village at some distance.

While Emmeline stood contemplating this beautiful spring, she beheld, in an excavation in the rock close to it, two persons sitting on a bench, which had been rudely cut for the passenger to rest. One of them appeared to be a man about fifty; he wore a short, light coloured coat, a waistcoat that had once been of embroidered velvet; from his head, which was covered first with a red thrum night-cap, and then with a small hat, bound with tarnished lace, depended an immense *queüe*; his face, tho' thin and of a mahogena darkness, seemed to express penetration and good humour; and Emmeline, who had at first been a little startled, was no longer under alarm; when he, on perceiving her near the entrance of the cavern, flew nimbly out of it, bowed to the ground, and pulling off most politely his thrum night-cap, enquired — '*Si Mademoiselle voudrez bien se reposer?*" (if the young lady would please to sit down?).

Emmeline thanked him, and advanced towards the bench; from which a girl about seventeen, very brown but very pretty, had on her approach arisen, and put up into a kind of wallet the remains of the provisions they had been eating, which were only fruit and black bread. As soon as the old Frenchman perceived that Emmeline intended to sit down, he sprung before her, brushed down the seat with his cap, and then making several profound bows, assured '*Mademoiselle qu'elle pourroit s'asseoir sans incommodite.*' (that she might sit down without inconvenience).

The young woman, dressed like the *paisannes* of the country, was modestly retiring; but Emmeline desired her to remain; and entering into conversation with her, found she was the daughter of the assiduous old Frenchman, and that he was going with her to Toulon in hopes of procuring her a service.

The Baron and Lord Westhaven now approached, and laughingly reproached Emmeline for having deserted them. She told them she was enchanted with the seat she had found, and should wait there for the Chevalier and Lady Westhaven.

'I am only grieved,' said she, 'that I have disturbed from their humble supper these good people.'

The two gentlemen then spoke to the old Frenchman; whose countenance had something of keen intelligence and humble civility which prejudiced both in his favour.

'*Je vois bien*,' said he, addressing himself to Lord Westhaven — '*je vois bien que j'ai l'honneur de parler a un Milor Anglais.*' (I perceive I have the honour to speak to an English nobleman).

'*Eh! comment?*' answered his Lordship — '*comment? tu connois donc bien les Anglais?*' (How? Are you then well acquainted with the English?).

'*Oh oui! — j'ai passé a leur service une partie de ma jeunesse. — Ils sont les meilleur maitres —* ' (I passed part of my youth in their service. — They are the best masters in the world).

'*Parle tu Anglais, mon ami?*' (Do you speak English, my friend?).

'Yes Milor, I speak little English. '*Mais,*' continued he, relapsing into the volubility of his own language — *Mais il y'a à peu pres dix neuf ans, depuis que mon maitre — mon pauvre maitre mouroit dans mes bras; helas! — s'i avoit vecu — car il etoit tout jean — j'aurois passé ma vie entiere avez lui — j'aurois retournez avec lui en Angleterre — Ah c'est un païs charmant que cette Angloterre.*' (It is almost nineteen years, since my master — my poor master, died in my arms; had he lived, for he was quite a young man, I should have passed my life with him — I should have returned with him to England — Ah! That England is a charming country!).

'You have been there then?'

He answered that he had been three times; and should have been happy had it pleased heaven to have ended his days there.

'The praise you bestow on our country, my friend,' said Lord Westhaven, 'is worth at least this piece *de six francs*, and the beauty *de cette jolie enfant,*' (of this pretty maid) added he, turning towards the little *paisanne*, 'is interesting enough to induce me to enquire whether such a gift may not serve to purchase *quelques petites amplettes a la ville.*' (some little necessaries, bargains, at the neighbouring town). He presented the young woman with another crown.

The old Frenchman seemed ready to thank his Lordship with his tears.

Without solicitation or ceremony, seeing that the gentlemen were disposed to listen to him, he began to relate his 'short and simple' story.

Lady Westhaven and the Chevalier now arrived: but she sat down by Emmeline, and desired the old man to continue whatever he was saying.

'He has been praising our country,' said Lord Westhaven, 'and in return I am willing to hear the history of himself, which he seems very desirous of relating.'

'I was in the army,' said he, 'as we all are; 'till being taken with a pleurisy at Calais, and rendered long incapable of duty, I got my discharge, and hired myself as a travelling valet to a Milor Anglais. With him (he was the best master in the world) I lived six years. I went with him to England when he came to his estate, and five years afterwards came back with him to France. He met with a misfortune in losing *une dame tres amiable*, and never was quite well afterwards. To drive away trouble, *pour se dissiper*, he went among a set of his own countrymen, and I believe *le chagrin*, and living too freely, gave him a terrible fever. *Une fievre ardente lui saisit a Milan, ses compagnons apparemment n'aimoit gueres les malades;*' (a burning fever seized him at Milan; his companions seemed to have but little affection for the sick;) for nobody came near him except a young surgeon who arrived there by accident, and hearing that an Englishman of fashion lay ill, charitably visited him. But it was too late: he had already been eleven days under the hands of an Italian physician, and when the English gentleman saw him he said he had only a few hours to live.

'He sat by him, however. But my poor master was senseless; 'till about an hour before he died he recovered his recollection.

'He ordered me to bring him two little boxes, which he always carried with him, and charged me to go to England with his body, and deliver those boxes to a person he named. He bade me give one of his watches, which was a very rich one, to his brother, and told *me* to keep the other in memory of my master.

'Then he spoke to the stranger — "Sir," said he, "since you have the humanity to interest yourself for a person unknown to you, have the goodness to see that my servant is suffered to execute what I have directed, and put your seal on my effects. The money I have about me, my cloaths, and my common watch, I have given him. He knows what farther I would have done; I told him on the second day of my illness. Baptist — you remember — "

'He tried to say something more; but in a few moments he died in my arms.

'With the assistance of the young English surgeon, I arranged every thing as my master directed. I went with his corps to England, and received a large present from his brother, whom, however, I did not see, because he was not in London. Then I returned to France.'

'Since you loved England so much,' enquired the Baron, '*puisque vous aimiez tant cet païs pourquoi ne pas y' rester?*' (why not stay there?).

'*Ah, Monsieur! j'etois riche; et je brulez de partager mes richesse avez une jolie fille dont j'etois eperdument amoureux.*' (Ah, Sir! I was rich, and I longed eagerly to share my riches with a pretty young woman with whom I was distractedly in love).

'*Eh Bien?*'

'I married her, Monsieur; and for about two years we were the happiest people on earth. But we were very thoughtless. *Je ne scais comment cela se faisoit, mes espece Anglais, qui je croyais inepuisable se dissiperent peu a peu, et enfin il falloit songer a quelque provision pour ma femme et mes deux petites filles.*' (I know not how it happened, my English money, which I thought inexhaustible, diminished by little and little; and at length it was necessary to think what I was to do for my wife and my two little girls).

'I returned therefore into the Limosin, of which province I was a native; but some of my family were dead, and the rest had neither power or inclination to assist their poor relations. The seigneur of the village had bought a post at Paris, and was about to quit his chateau. He heard I was honest; and therefore, tho' he had very little to lose, he put me into it. I worked in the garden, and raised enough, with the little wages we had, to keep us. My wife learned to work, and my two little girls were healthy and happy.

'*Oui Messieurs, nous etions pauvre a la verité! mais nous etions tres contents.*" (Yes, gentlemen, we were indeed poor, but we were very, very happy) 'till about eight months ago; and then an epidemical distemper broke out in the village, and carried off my wife and my eldest daughter.

'*Oh, Therese! et toi ma petite Suzette, je te pleurs; encore amerement je te pleurs.*' (Oh! Theresa! — and you, my poor Suzette, I lament ye! — bitterly I still deplore your loss!).

The poor Frenchman turned away and wept bitterly.

'Je scais bien,' continued he — *'je scais bien qu'il faut s'accoutumer a les souffrances.'* (I know well — I know, that we must learn to suffer). We might still have lived on, Madelon and me, at our ruinous chateau; but the possessor of it dying, his son sent us notice that he should pull it down (indeed it must soon have fallen) and ordered us to quit it.

'Ainsi me voila, Messieurs, a cinquante ans, sans pain. Mais pour cela je ne m'embarrasse pas; si je pourrois bien placer ma pauvre Madelon tout ira bien!' (So here I am, gentlemen, at fifty years old, without bread to eat. But it is not that which troubles me — if I could get a comfortable place for my poor Madelon, all would be well!)

There was in this relation a touching simplicity which drew tears from Lady Westhaven and Emmeline. The whole party became interested for the father and the daughter, who had wept silently while he was relating their story.

'Can nothing be done for these poor creatures?' said Lady Westhaven.

'Certainly we will assist them,' answered her Lord. — 'But let us enquire how we can best do it. *Tu t'appelles?'* (Your name?) continued he, speaking to the Frenchman.

'Baptiste La Fere — mais mon nomme de guerre, et de condition fut toujours Le Limosin.' (Baptiste La Fere. But the name under which I served as a soldier and as a servant is Le Limosin).

'Dites moi donc, (tell me then) *Monsieur Le Limosin,'* said his Lordship, 'what hopes have you of placing your daughter at Toulon?'

'Alas! Milor, but little. I know nobody there but an old relation of my poor wife's, who is *Touriere* at a convent; and if I cannot get a service for Madelon, I must give the good abbess a little money to take her till I can do something better for her.'

'And where do you expect to get money?'

'*Tenez, mon Seigneur*,' answered he, pulling a watch out of his pocket, '*ayez la bonté d'examiner cet montre* (See my Lord; have the goodness to look at this watch). It is an English watch. Gold; and in a gold case. I have been offered a great deal of money for it; but in all my poverty, in all my distresses, I have contrived to keep it because it was the last gift of my dear master. But now, my poor Madelon must be thought of, and if it must be so, I will sell it and pay for her staying in the convent.'

'You shall not do that, my friend,' replied Lord Westhaven, still holding the watch in his hand.

It had a cypher, H.C.M., and a crest engraved on it.

'H.C.M,' said his Lordship, 'and the Mowbray crest! Pray what was your master's name?'

'*Milor Moubray*,' answered Le Limosin.

'*Comment? Milor Mowbray?*'

'*Oui Milor — regardez s'il vous plait. Voila son chiffre, Henri-Charles Moubray — et voila le cimier du famille.*' (Yes, my Lord, be so good as to observe. There is his cypher, H. C. M., and there the family crest).

Emmeline, who no longer doubted but this was her father's servant, was so much affected, that Lady Westhaven, apprehending she would faint, called for assistance; and the Chevalier, who during this conversation had attended only to her, snatched up the beechen cup out of which Le Limosin and

Madelon had been drinking, and which still stood on the ground, and flying with it to the spring, brought it instantly back filled with water; while Lady Westhaven bathed her temples and held to her her salts. She soon recovered; and then speaking in a faint voice to his Lordship, said — 'My Lord, this is the servant in whose arms my poor father expired. Do allow me to intercede with your Lordship for him and for his daughter; but let him not know, to-night at least, who I am. I cannot again bear a circumstantial detail about my father.'

Lord Westhaven now led Le Limosin out of the cave; told him he had determined, as he had known his master's family, to take him into his own service, and that Lady Westhaven would provide for his daughter. At this intelligence the poor fellow grew almost frantic. He would have thrown himself at the feet of his benefactor had he not been prevented; then flew back to fetch his Madelon, that she might join in prayers and benedictions; and hardly could Lord Westhaven persuade him to be tranquil enough to understand the orders he gave him, which were, to hire some kind of conveyance at the next village to carry his daughter to Toulon; where he gave him a direction to find his English benefactor the next day.

It was now late; and the party hastened to leave this romantic spot, which had been marked by so singular a meeting. On their arrival at Toulon, they equipped, and sent away before them to St. Alpin, Le Limosin and Madelon, the latter of whom Lady Westhaven took entirely to wait on Emmeline.

The soft heart and tender spirits of Emmeline had not yet recovered the detail she had heard of her father's death. A pensive melancholy hung over her; which the Chevalier, nothing doubting his own perfections, hoped was owing to a growing affection for himself. But it had several sources of which he had no suspicion; and it made the remaining three weeks of their tour appear tedious to Emmeline; who languished to be at St. Alpin, where she hoped to find letters from Mrs. Stafford and from Lady Adelina. She thought it an age since she had heard from the latter; and secretly but anxiously indulged an hope of meeting a large pacquet, which might contain some intelligence of Godolphin.

END OF THE THIRD VOLUME

VOLUME IV

CHAPTER I

THE Chateau de St. Alpin was a gloomy and antique building, but in habitable repair. The only constant resident in it for some years had been the Demoiselle de St. Alpin, now about five and forty; whose whole attention had been given to keeping it in order, and collecting, in the garden, variety of plants, in which she took singular pleasure. Detached from the world, and with no other relations than her brother and her nephews, whom she was seldom likely to see, she found in this innocent and amusing pursuit a resource against the tedium of life. Her manners, tho' simple, were mild and engaging; and her heart perfectly good and benevolent. With her, therefore, Emmeline was extremely pleased; and the country in which her residence was situated, was so beautiful, that accustomed to form her ideas of magnificent scenery from the first impressions that her mind had received in Wales, Emmeline acknowledged that her eye was here perfectly satisfied.

With her heart it was far otherwise. On her arrival at St. Alpin, she found letters from Lady Adelina enclosed in others from Mrs. Stafford. Lady Adelina gave such an account of her own health as convinced Emmeline it was not improved since she left England. Of Mr. Godolphin she only said, that he was returned from Ireland, but had staid with her only a few hours, and was then obliged to go on business to London, where his continuance was uncertain.

Mrs. Stafford gave of herself and her family a more pleasing account. She said she had hopes that the readjustment of Mr. Stafford's affairs would soon allow of their return to England; and as it might possibly happen on very short notice, and before Emmeline could rejoin them, she had sent, by a family who were travelling to Geneva, and who readily undertook the care of it, a large box which contained some of her cloaths and the caskets which belonged to her, which had been long left at Mrs. Ashwood's after Emmeline's precipitate departure from her house with Delamere, and which, on Mrs. Ashwood's marriage and removal, she had sent with a cold note (addressed to Miss Mowbray) to the person who negociated Mr. Stafford's business in London.

Their lengthened journey had so much broken in on the time allotted to their tour, that Lord and Lady Westhaven purposed staying only a month at St. Alpin. The Baron, who had equal pride and pleasure in the company of his nephew, endeavoured by every means in his power to make that time pass agreeably; and felt great satisfaction in shewing to the few neighbours who were within fifteen miles of his chateau, that he had, in an English nobleman of such rank and merit, so near a relation.

He had observed very early the growing passion of his son for Miss Mowbray. He was assured that she returned it; for he never supposed it possible that any woman could behold the Chevalier with indifference.

He had heard from Lord Westhaven that Emmeline was the daughter of a man of fashion, but was by the circumstances of her birth excluded from any share of his fortune, and entirely dependant on the favour of the Marquis of Montreville. The old Baron, charmed himself with her person and her manners, rather approved than opposed the wishes of his son; and however convenient it might have been to have seen him married to a woman of fortune, he was disposed to rejoice at his inclining to marry at all; and convinced that with Emmeline he must be happy, thought he might dispense with being rich. The Chevalier, confident of success, and believing that Emmeline had meant by her timid refusals only encouragement, grew so extremely importunate, that she was sometimes on the point of declaring to him her real situation.

But from this she was deterred by the apprehension that he would apply to Lord Delamere for the relinquishment of her promise; and should he obtain it, consider himself as having a claim to the hand his Lordship resigned.

This was an hope, which whatever his vanity might have suggested, she never meant to give him; yet she had the mortification to find that all her rejections, however repeated, were considered by the Chevalier as words of course. It was in vain she assured him that besides her disinclination to change her situation by marriage at all, she had other forcible objections; that she should never think of passing her life out of England; that not only their country, but their manners, their ideas on a thousand subjects, so materially differed as to make every other reason of her refusal unnecessary.

When she seriously urged thus much, he usually answered that he would then reside in England; that he would accommodate his manner of living to her pleasure; and that as to the ideas which had displeased her, he would never again offend her with their repetition.

Emmeline had indeed been extremely hurt and disgusted at that levity of principle on the most serious subjects which the Chevalier avowed without reserve, and for which he appeared to value himself. 'Tho' brought up a Calvinist, he had as he owned always conformed to the mode of worship and ceremonies of the Catholics while he was among them; and usually added, that had he served amid the Turks or the Jews, he should have done the same, as a matter of great indifference.

The Baron, whose life had been more active than contemplative, was unaccustomed to consider these matters deeply. And as every thing Bellozane advanced had with him great authority, he was struck with his lively arguments; and whatever might be their solidity, could not help admiring the wit of the Chevalier, whom he sometimes encouraged to dispute with Lord Westhaven. The religion of Lord Westhaven was as steady and unaffected as his morals were excellent; and he entered willingly into these dialogues with Bellozane, in hopes of convincing him that infidelity was by no means necessary to the character of a soldier; and that he was unlikely to serve well the country to which he belonged, or for which he fought, who began by insulting his God.

He found however that the young man had imbibed these lessons so early, and fancied them so much the marks of a superior and penetrating mind, that he could make no impression by rational argument. Bellozane usually answered by a sprightly quotation from some French author, and his Lordship soon declined the conversation, believing that if sickness and sorrow did not supercede so slow a cure, time at least would convince him of his folly.

But such was the effect of this sort of discourse on Emmeline, that had Bellozane been in other respects unexceptionable, and had her heart been free from any other impression, she would never have listened to him as a lover.

From his own account of himself in other respects, Emmeline had gathered enough to believe that he was profligate and immoral. But as she could not appear to detect these errors without allowing him to suppose her interested in his forsaking them, she generally heard him in silence; and only when pressed to name her objections stated his loose opinions as one in her mind very material.

To this he again repeated, that his opinions he would correct; his residence should be settled by herself. — 'Had she any objections to his person?' enquired he, as he proudly surveyed it in the long old fashioned glass which ornamented the *sal a manger.*'

Emmeline, blushing from the conscious recollection of the resemblance it bore in height and air to that of Godolphin, answered faulteringly — 'That to his person there could be no objection.'

'To his fortune?'

'It was undoubtedly more than situated as she was she could expect.'

'To his family?'

'It was a family whose alliance must confer honour.'

'What then?' vehemently continued the Chevalier — 'What then, charming Emmeline, occasions this long reserve, this barbarous coldness? Since you can form no decided objection; since you have undoubtedly allowed me to hope; why do you thus cruelly prolong my sufferings? Surely you do not, you cannot mean finally to refuse and desert me, after having permitted me so long to speak to you of my passion?'

'It is with some justice,' gravely and coldly answered Emmeline — 'I own it is with some justice that you impute to me the appearance of coquetry; because I have listened with too much patience, (tho' certainly never with approbation,) to your discourse on this subject. But be assured that whatever I have said, tho' perhaps with insufficient firmness, I now repeat, in the hope that you will understand it as my unalterable resolution — The honour you are so obliging as to offer me, I *never* can accept; and I beg you will forbear to urge me farther on a subject to which I never can give any other answer.'

This dialogue, which happened on the second day of her residence at St. Alpin, and the first moment he could find her alone, did not seem to discourage the Chevalier. He observed her narrowly: the country round St. Alpin, which, as well as the place itself, he thought '*triste et insupportable*,' seemed to delight and attract her. He saw her not only enduring but even fond of his aunt and her plants, which were to him, '*les sujets du monde les plus facheaux*.' (the most wearisome, or to use the cant of the times the most *boring* subjects in the world) — His excessive vanity made him persist in believing that she could not admire such a place but thro' some latent partiality to its master; nor seek the company and esteem of his aunt, but for the sake of her nephew.

These remarks, and a conviction formed on his own self-love and on the experience of his Parisian conquests, made him disregard her refusal and persecute her incessantly with his love. Lord Westhaven saw her uneasiness; but knew not how to relieve her without offending the Baron and the

Chevalier, or divulging circumstances of which he did not think himself at liberty without her permission to speak.

Lady Westhaven, to whom Emmeline was obliged to complain of the importunity of Bellozane, repeatedly but very fruitlessly remonstrated with him. What she had at first ridiculed, now gave her pain; and anxious as she was to reconcile her brother to her friend, from whom she thought only his warmth of temper and a misunderstanding had divided him, she wished to shorten as much as possible their stay at St. Alpin.

Her own situation too made her very anxious to return to England; and she was impatient to see Lord Delamere, to explain to him all the mystery of Emmeline's conduct; a detail which she could not venture by the post, tho' she had written to him from Lyons, intreating him to suspend all opinion in regard to Miss Mowbray's conduct 'till she should see him.

This letter never reached the hands of Lord Delamere, and therefore was not answered to St. Alpin; whither his sister had desired him to direct, and where she now grew very uneasy at not hearing from him.

Le Limosin and his Madelon had arrived at St. Alpin some time before their noble patrons, with whose goodness they were elated to excess. Le Limosin himself, assiduous to do every thing for every body, flew about as if he was about twenty. His particular province was to attend with Lady Westhaven's English servant on her Ladyship and Miss Mowbray; and Madelon was directed to wait on the latter as her *fille de chambre*.

Emmeline, with painful solicitude for which she could hardly account, wished to hear from Le Limosin those particulars of her father of which he was so well able to inform her. He had served, too, her mother; whose name she had hardly ever heard repeated, and of whom, before witnesses, she dared not enquire.

Lord Westhaven had not yet explained to him to what he principally owed the extraordinary kindness he had met with. He knew not that the lady on whom he had the honour to wait was the daughter of the master to whom he had been so much obliged.

The first days that Lord and Lady Westhaven and Emmeline had passed with the Baron, had been engaged by company or in parties which he made to shew the views of the surrounding country to his English guests. The Chevalier never suffered Emmeline to be absent from these excursions, nor when at home allowed her to be a moment out of his company. If she sought refuge in the chamber of Mrs. St. Alpin, he followed her; if she went with her to her plants, thither also came Bellozane; and having acquired from his aunt's books a few physical and botanical terms, affected to desire information, which the old Lady, highly pleased with his desire of improvement in her favourite studies, gave him with great simplicity.

Lord Westhaven grew apprehensive that the jaunts of pleasure which the Baron continued to propose would be too fatigueing for his wife. And as they were now to go on a visit to one of St. Alpin's old military friends, who resided at the distance of fifteen miles, and where they were to remain all night, he prevailed on her to stay at home, where Emmeline also desired to be left.

Bellozane, detesting a party which the ladies were not to enliven, made some efforts to be excused also; but he found his declining to go would so much chagrin and disappoint his father, that, with whatever reluctance, he was obliged to set out with him.

Lady Westhaven, who was a good deal indisposed, went to lie down in her own room; whither Emmeline attended her, and finding she was disposed to sleep, left her. Mrs. St. Alpin was busied in her garden; and Emmeline, delighted with an opportunity of being alone, retired to her room to write to Mrs. Stafford. She had not proceeded far in her letter, when a servant informed her that the messenger who had been sent to Geneva for her box was returned with it. She desired that it might be brought up. Madelon came to assist her in opening it, and then left her.

She took out the cloaths and linen, and then the two embroidered caskets, which she put on the table before her, and gazed at with melancholy pleasure, as silent memorials of her parents. They brought also to her mind the recollection of Mrs. Carey, and many of her infantine pains and pleasures at Mowbray Castle, where she remembered first to have remarked them in a drawer belonging to that good woman; to which, tho' it was generally locked, she had occasionally sent her little charge when she was herself confined to her chair.

One of them she had began to inspect at Clapham, and perused some of the letters it contained. They were from her grandmother, Mrs. Mowbray, to her father; and were filled with reproaches so warm and severe, and such pointed censures of his conduct in regard to Miss Stavordale, her mother, to whom one letter yet more bitter was addressed, that after reading three of them, Emmeline believed that the further inspection of the casket was likely to produce for her only unavailing regret.

Still however she would then have continued it, painful as it was, but had been interrupted by the sudden entrance of Lord Montreville, who came to enquire after his son. The sight of Mr. Mowbray's picture, which she had taken out, created in the breast of his Lordship a momentary tenderness for his niece. She had since always worn that picture about her; but the papers, by which she had been too much affected after that interview farther to peruse, she had again secured in the caskets; and being almost immediately afterwards taken by Delamere on her involuntary journey to Stevenage, from whence she returned no more to Clapham, she had not since had them in her possession.

Her mind in this interval had acquired greater strength; and she at length wished to know those particulars of her mother's fate, into which she had hitherto forborne thro' timidity to enquire. Being now therefore alone, and having these repositories once more in her hands, she resolutely inspected them.

The first contained some twenty letters. Some were those she had before seen, and others followed them equally severe. They seemed in sullen resentment to have been preserved; and Emmeline could not but reflect with pain on the anger and asperity in which they were written; on the remorse and uneasiness with which they must have been read.

The second casket seemed also to hold letters. On opening it, Emmeline found they were part of the correspondence between her father and mother during the early part of their acquaintance, when, tho' they sometimes resided in the same house, the vigilant observation of Mrs. Mowbray very seldom allowed them to converse.

Among these, were several pieces of poetry, elegant and affecting. After having read which, Emmeline imagined she had seen all the box contained, a few loosely folded papers only remaining; but on opening one of these, what was her astonishment to find in it two certificates of her mother's marriage; one under the hand of a Catholic priest, by whom she had been married immediately on their arrival at Dunkirk; the other signed a few days before the birth of Emmeline by an English clergyman, who had again performed the ceremony in the chapel of the English Ambassador at Paris.

That the memory of her mother should thus be free from reproach; that the conduct of her father, which had hitherto appeared cruel and unjust, should be vindicated from every aspersion; and that she should herself be restored to that place in society from which she seemed to be excluded for ever; was altogether such unexpected, such incredible happiness, as made her almost doubtful of the evidence of her senses. Ignorant as she was of the usual form of such papers, yet the care with which these seemed to be executed left her little doubt of their regularity. One other folded paper yet remained unread. Trembling she opened it. It was written in her father's hand and endorsed

MEMORANDUM

'The harshness with which my mother and her family have treated Miss Stavordale, for a supposed crime, has forced her to put herself under my protection. Miss Stavordale is now my wife; but of this I shall not inform my family, conceiving myself accountable no longer to persons capable of so much rashness and injustice. Least any thing however should happen before I can make a will in due form, I hereby acknowledge Emmeline Stavordale (now Mowbray) as my wife; and her child, whether a son or a daughter, heir to my estate. My brother being possessed of a very large fortune, both by his late marriage and the gifts of his mother's family, will hardly dispute the claim of such child to my paternal estate.

'(This is a duplicate of a paper sent to Francis Williamson, my steward at Mowbray Castle.) Signed by me at Paris in presence of two witnesses, this fifteenth of March 17—.

HENRY CHARLES MOWBRAY.

Witnessed by
ROBERT WALLACE,
BAPTISTE LA FERE, (dit Le Limosin.)'

This, which was the same date as the last certificate, confirmed every claim which they both gave Emmeline to her name and fortune. A change of circumstances so sudden; her apprehensions that the Marquis of Montreville, who she thought must have long known, should dispute her legitimacy, and her wonder at the concealment which Mr. Williamson and Mrs. Carey seemed passively to have suffered; which together with a thousand other sensations crouded at once into her mind, so greatly affected her, that feeling herself grow sick, she was obliged to call Madelon, who being at work in an adjoining room, ran in, and seeing her lady look extremely pale, and hearing her speak with difficulty, she threw open the window, fetched her some water, and then without waiting to see their effects she flew away to call Mrs. St. Alpin; who presently appeared, followed by her maid carrying a large case which was filled with bottles of various distillations from every aromatic and pungent herb her garden or the adjacent mountains afforded.

Emmeline, hardly knowing what she did, was compelled to swallow a glass full of one of these cordials; which Mrs. St. Alpin assured her was '*excellente pour les vapeurs*.' It almost deprived her of breath, but recalled her astonished spirits; and having with great difficulty prevailed on her kindly-busy hostess to leave her, she locked up her papers, and threw herself on the bed; where, having directed Madelon to draw the curtains and retire, she tried to compose her mind, and to consider what steps she ought to take in consequence of this extraordinary discovery.

CHAPTER II

CONVINCED of the noble and disinterested nature of Lord Westhaven, Emmeline thought she ought immediately on his return to shew him the papers she had found, and entreat him to examine, for farther particulars, Le Limosin, who seemed providentially to have been thrown in her way on purpose to elucidate her history.

After having formed this resolution, her mind was at liberty for other reflections. Delamere returned to it: his unjust suspicions; his haughty reproaches; his long, indignant anger, which vouchsafed not even to solicit an explanation; she involuntarily compared with the gentleness, the generosity of Godolphin; with his candid temper, his warm affections, his tender heart. And with pain she remembered, that unless Delamere would relinquish the fatal promise she had given him, she could not shew the preference which she feared she must ever feel for him. Sometimes she thought of asking Lord Westhaven to apply to Delamere for her release. But how could she venture on a measure which might involve in such difficulties, Lady Adelina, and engage Lord Westhaven in an enquiry fatal to his repose and that of his whole family? How could she, by this application, counteract the wishes of Lady Westhaven, who anxiously hoped to re-unite her brother and her friend; and who desired ardently to be in England, that she might explain herself, to Delamere, all the circumstances that had injured Emmeline in his opinion; which she thought she could easily do without hazarding any of the evils that might follow from an inconsiderate disclosure of the occurrences he had misunderstood.

Uneasily ruminating on the painful uncertainty of her situation and the difficulties which every way surrounded her, she continued alone; 'till Lady Westhaven, alarmed at hearing she had been ill, sent her woman to enquire after and know if she might herself come to her? Emmeline, to relieve at once her friendly solicitude, arose and went to her apartment; where she made light of her sickness, and endeavoured to assume as much chearfulness as possible. — 'Till she had seen Lord Westhaven, she determined not to mention to her Ladyship the discovery of the morning; feeling that there would be great indelicacy in eagerly divulging to her a secret by which she must tacitly accuse the Marquis of Montreville of having thus long detained from its legal owner the Mowbray estate; and of having brought up in indigence and obscurity, the daughter of his brother, while conscious of her claim to education and affluence.

Struggling therefore to subdue the remaining tumult of her spirits, she rejoined her friend. They passed the afternoon tranquilly with Mrs. St. Alpin; and about eleven o'clock the following morning, Lord Westhaven, the Baron, and the Chevalier, returned.

Emmeline took the earliest opportunity of telling Lord Westhaven than she wished to speak to him alone. There was no way of escaping from the Chevalier but by his Lordship's openly declaring that he wanted a private conference with his fair cousin, whom he led into the garden. Bellozane, who hoped that his earnest solicitations had prevailed on Lord Westhaven to befriend his love, was glad to see them walk out together, while he watched them from a window.

Emmeline put into her pocket the two certificates and the memorandum written by her father. Without explanation or comment, she gave them, as soon as they were at a little distance from the house, to Lord Westhaven.

He read them twice over in silence; then looking with astonishment at Emmeline, he asked her from whence she had these papers?

'They were enclosed, my Lord,' answered she 'in two little boxes or caskets which were left to me among other things by my father's nurse; who becoming the housekeeper at Mowbray Castle, brought me up. They afterwards long remained at the house of Mrs. James Crofts, with whom you know I resided; on her removal after her marriage, they were sent, together with some of my cloaths, to Mrs. Stafford's agent in London; from whence she lately received them; and having an opportunity of sending them to Geneva by a family travelling thither, she forwarded them to me, and I found them yesterday in the trunk brought by the messenger which you know the Baron sent thither on purpose.'

Again Lord Westhaven read the papers; and after pausing a moment said —

'There is no doubt, there can be none, of the authenticity of these papers, nor of your consequent claim to the Mowbray estate. Surely,' added he, again pausing — 'surely it is most extraordinary that Lord Montreville should have suffered the true circumstances of your birth to remain thus long unexplained. Most cruel! most ungenerous! to possess himself of a property to which he must know he had no right! Your father's memorandum says that he had forwarded a duplicate of it to Francis Williamson; do you know whether that person is yet living?'

'He is dead, my Lord. He died in consequence of an accident at Mowbray Castle, where he was many years steward.'

'He must however have had sufficient time to give Lord Montreville every information as to his master's marriage, even if his Lordship knew it not, as he probably did, by other means. Yet from a man of honour — from Lord Montreville — such conduct is most unworthy. I can hardly conceive it possible that he should be guilty of such concealment.'

'Surely, my Lord, it *is* possible,' said the candid and ingenuous Emmeline — 'surely it is possible that my uncle might, by some accident, (for which without knowing more we cannot account) have been kept in ignorance of my mother's real situation. For your satisfaction and mine, before we say more on this subject, would it not be well to hear what Le Limosin, who was I suppose present both at my mother's marriage and at my father's death, has to relate?'

To this proposal Lord Westhaven agreed. The *sal a compagnie* was usually vacant at this time of day. Thither they went together, and sent for Le Limosin; who loved talking so much that nothing was more easy than to make him tell all he remembered, and even minutely describe every scene at which he had been present.

'Le Limosin,' said Lord Westhaven, as soon as he came into the room, 'I was much pleased and interested with the account you gave me when I first met you, of the English master whom you call *Milor Mowbray*. I know his family well. Tell me, does this picture resemble him?'

His Lordship shewed him a portrait of Mr. Mowbray which had been drawn at Paris.

Le Limosin looked a moment at it — the tears came into his eyes.

'*O oui — oui, mi Lor! — je me rapepelle bien ce portrait! — Ah! quel resemblance! Quelques mois avant sa mort tel etoit mon pauvre maitre! Ah!*' added he, giving back, with a sigh, the picture to Lord Westhaven — '*cela me fend le coeur!*' (O yes, my Lord; I recollect well this picture. What a likeness! Such, a few months before he died, was my poor master! Alas! It cuts me to the heart).

'Now then,' reassumed Lord Westhaven, 'look, Le Limosin, at that.' He put before him the resemblance of Emmeline's mother, which had been painted at the same time.

'*Eh! pardi oui — voila — voila Madame! le charmante femme, dont la perte couta la vie a mon maitre. Helas! — je m'en souviens bien du jour que je vis pour la premiere fois cette aimable dame. Elle n'avoit qu'environ quatorze a quintze ans. Ah! qu'elle etoit pour lors, gaï; espiegle, folatre, et si belle! — si belle!*' (Ah! Hah! Yes, there is, sure enough, my Lady. The charming woman whose loss cost my master his life. Alas! How well I recollect the first day I saw this amiable lady; she was then only between fourteen and fifteen; and at that time so gay, so full of frolic and vivacity, and so very, very pretty!).

'Tell me,' said Lord Westhaven, 'all you remember of her.'

'I remember her, my Lord,' said Le Limosin, speaking still in French, 'I remember her from the first of my going to England with Milor Mowbray. She lived then with Madame Mowbray; and the servants told me, that being a distant relation to an orphan, Madame had taken her and intended to give her a fortune. Milor Mowbray, when he first returned from his travels, used to live for two or three months together with Madame his mother; but she was strict and severe, and used frequently to reproach him with his gaieties — *il etoit un peu libertin Milor, comme sont a l'ordinaire les jeunes seigneurs de sa nation* (He was a little free, my Lord; as the young noblemen of his country usually are). He admired Mademoiselle Stavordale as a beautiful child, and used to romp with her; but as she grew older, Madame Mowbray was dissatisfied with him for taking so much notice of her, and would oblige her to live always up in Madame's dressing room, so that my master could hardly ever see her. Madame, however, told my master one day, that tho' Mademoiselle Stavordale had no fortune, she would not object to his marrying her in a year or two if he was then in the same mind. But my master was in turn offended. He said he would not be dictated to, nor told whether he should marry or remain single. *Madame etoit forte brusque — elle piquoit Monsieur par un reponse un peu vive* (Madame was very hasty; she irritated my master by a sharp answer) — and they had a violent disagreement; in consequence of which he quitted her house, and only went now and then afterwards to see her quite in form. Some months afterwards he called me to him; and as I was dressing him he asked me if I had no female friend among his mother's servants. 'Baptiste,' said he, 'I cannot get the Demoiselle Stavordale out of my head. — *J'aime a la folie cette fille mais pour le mariage, je ne suis pas trop sur, que je m'acquitterai bien, en promissant de l'aimer pour la vie. — Je veux aussi qu'elle m'aime sans que l'interet y'entre pour quelque chose. — Puisque Madame ma mere s'amuse a me guetter, je voudrois bien la tromper; je scais que tu est habile — ne pourra tu pas nous menager une petite tete a tete?'* (I love that girl to madness; but as to marrying her I am not quite sure I should acquit myself well were I to promise that I would love her for ever. I desire too that interest may have nothing to do with her affection for me. As my mother amuses herself with watching me, I long to deceive her. You are a clever fellow; cannot you contrive for us a private meeting?) *'Milor, je faisois mon possible — et enfin — par la bonté et l'honeteté — d'une fille qui servoit Madame — je vins heureusement about — Quelque jour apres — Monsieur enleva la belle Stavordale tant en depit — qu'en amour.'* (My Lord, I did my best; and at last by the goodness and civility of a young woman who waited on Madame, I happily accomplished it. Some days after which, my master carried off the fair Stavordale, as much thro' revenge as love).

At this recital, Emmeline found herself cruelly hurt; but Lord Westhaven besought her to command herself, and Le Limosin went on.

'To avoid the rage and reproaches of Madame Mowbray, which it was likely would be very loud, my master took Mademoiselle Stavordale immediately abroad. We landed at Dunkirk; but the young lady was so unhappy at the step she had taken, *elle pleuroit, elle se desoloit, elle s'abandonna a le desepoir — enfin, tant elle faisoit,* (she wept, she lamented, she gave herself up to despair) that Monsieur sent for a priest, and they were married. Soon afterwards my lady was likely to bring Monsieur an heir. *Ah! qu'ils etoient pour lors heureux* (Ah! May they be happy). But their happiness was interrupted by the death of my master's mother, Madame Mowbray, who had never forgiven him, and who disposed of all her money that was in her own power to his brother. My poor lady took this sadly to heart. She reproached herself with being the cause of my master's losing such a fortune. He said he had yet enough; and tried to console my lady. Still, still it hung on her spirits; and she could not bear to think that Madame Mowbray, who had brought her up, and had been kind to her when she had no other friend, should have died in anger with her. I believe my master was sorry then that he had not reconciled himself with his mother, as my lady often begged and entreated that he would; but it was now too late; and he said his brother had used him unkindly, and had certainly helped to irritate his mother against him; and he would not write to him tho' my lady often desired and prayed that he would. As she grew near her time, she was more and more out of spirits, and my master finding her uneasy because they had not been married by an English priest, had the ceremony performed again in the chapel of the English Ambassador. My master could not however make her forget her concern for the death of his mother; and she was always melancholy, as if she had foreseen how little a time she had herself to live. Alas! she brought my master a daughter, and died in three hours!'

'If I were to live a thousand years,' continued Le Limosin, 'I should never forget my poor master's distraction when he heard she was dead. It was with great difficulty that even with the assistance of his English servants I could prevent his destroying himself in the phrenzy of his grief. I dared not leave him a moment. He heard nothing we said to him; he heeded not the questions I asked him about the child; and at last I was forced to send an express to Mr. Oxenden, his friend, who was at some distance from Paris. He came; and by the help of another English gentleman they forced him out of the house while the body of my mistress was removed to be carried to England. He was so near madness, that his friends were afraid of his relapsing, even after he grew better, if they asked him many questions about it. So they gave me orders as to her funeral; and after about a fortnight he came back to the house where the child was, attended by his two friends.

'It was an heart-piercing sight, Milor, to see him weep over the little baby as it lay in the arms of its nurse. After some time he called me, and told me that he should not be easy, unless he was sure his little girl would be taken proper care of; that he had no friend in France to whom he chose to entrust her; and therefore ordered me to go with the nurse to England, and directed Therése, my mistress's fille de chambre, to go also, that the child might be well attended. He told me that he should perhaps quit Paris before I could get back; in which case he would leave directions where I should follow him. Then he kissed his little girl, and his two friends tore him away. I immediately proceeded to England as he directed, with the nurse, and Therése, and we carried the infant to the Chateau de Mowbray. The French nurse could speak no English, and could not be prevailed upon to stay above two days. Therése too longed to get back to France; and we immediately returned to Paris, where I found a letter from my master, ordering me to follow him into Italy.

'At Milan, Milor, I rejoined him. He looked very ill; and complained of feeling himself indisposed. But still he went out; and I believe drank too much with his English friends. The third or fourth day after I got there he came home from a party which he had made out of town with them about ten o'clock in the morning, and told me he had a violent pain in his head. He went up into his room. "I am strangely disordered, Baptiste," said he, as he put his hand to his temples — "perhaps it may go off; but if it should grow worse, as I am afraid it will, remember that you take those two little boxes in which I keep my papers to

England, and deliver them to my steward at Mowbray Castle. I have already written to him about my daughter." Then almost shrieking with the acute pain which darted into his head, he cried — "I cannot talk, nor can I now write to my brother as I think I ought to do about my child. But send, send for a notary, and when I am a little easier I will dictate a will."

'Milor, I sent for the notary, but he waited all day in the anti-room to no purpose. My poor master was never again easy enough to see him — never again able to dictate a will. He grew more and more delirious, and continued to complain of his head, his head! Alas! he did not even know me, till about an hour before his death.'

Emmeline, whose tears had almost choaked her during the greatest part of this narration, now said to Lord Westhaven —

'My Lord, do not let him repeat the scene of my father's death; I am not now able to bear it.'

'Well, Le Limosin,' said his Lordship, 'this young lady, who is the daughter of your master; the same whom you helped to carry, an infant, to Mowbray Castle, will soon have it in her power to reward your fidelity and attachment to her father.'

Le Limosin now threw himself on his knees in a transport of joy and acknowledgment. Lord Westhaven, fearing that his raptures might quite overcome the disturbed spirits of his fair mistress, desired her to give him her hand to kiss; which she did, and trying, but ineffectually, to smile thro' her tears, was led by his Lordship into her own room. He told her that at present he wished to conceal from Lady Westhaven the discovery they had made. 'For tho' I am convinced,' added he, 'that for your sake she will rejoice in it, she will be hurt at the extraordinary conduct of her father, and harrass herself with conjectures about it and apologies for it, which I wish to spare her in her present state.'

Emmeline assured him she would observe a strict silence; and he left her to give to Le Limosin a charge of secresy. He then retired to his room, and wrote to Lord Montreville, stating the simple fact, and enclosing copies of the certificates; and after shewing his letter to Emmeline, sent it off to England.

Emmeline now went out to walk, in hopes of recovering her composure and being able to appear at dinner without betraying by her countenance that any thing extraordinary had been the subject of her conversation with Lord Westhaven. The Chevalier, however, was soon at her side. And still flattering himself that his Lordship had undertaken to plead his cause, he addressed her with all the confidence of a man sure of success.

Emmeline was very little disposed to listen to him; and with a greater appearance of chagrin and impatience than she had yet shewn, repeated to him her determination not to marry. He still declared himself sure of her relenting; and added, that unless she had designed finally to hear him favourably she would never have allowed him so repeatedly to press his attachment. This speech, which indirectly accused her of coquetry, encreased her vexation. But the persevering Chevalier was not to be repressed. He told her that he had projected a party of pleasure on the lake the next day, in which he intended to include a visit to the Rocks of Meillerie.

'It is classic ground, Mademoiselle,' said he, 'and is fitted to love and despair. Ah! will you not there hear me? Will you still inhumanly smile; will you still look so gentle, while your heart is harder than the rocks we shall see — colder than the snow that crowns them! — an heart on which even the pen of fire which Rousseau held would make no impression!'

He held her hands during this rhapsody. She could not therefore immediately escape. But on the appearance of a servant, who announced the dinner's being ready, she coldly disengaged herself and went into the house.

CHAPTER III

THE agitation she had undergone in the morning, affected both the spirits and the looks of Emmeline; and when, immediately after dinner, Bellozane proposed the party of pleasure he had projected for the next day, Lady Westhaven answered — 'As for me I shall on my own account make no objection, but I cannot equally answer for our fair cousin — Emmeline, my love, you seem ill. I cannot imagine, my Lord, what you have been saying to her?'

'I have been advising her,' answered Lord Westhaven, 'to go into a convent; and her looks are merely looks of penitence for all the mischief she has done. She determines to take the veil, and to do no more.'

Emmeline, tho' hardly able to bear even this friendly raillery, turned it off with a melancholy smile. The party was agreed upon; the Baron went out to give orders for preparing the provisions they were to take with them, and the Chevalier to see that the boat was in a proper state for the expedition and give the boatmen notice.

Lady Westhaven then began talking of England, and expressed her astonishment at having heard nothing from thence for above six weeks. While Lord Westhaven was attempting to account for this failure of intelligence, which he saw gave his wife more concern than she expressed, a servant brought in several large pacquets of letters, which he said the messenger who was usually sent to the post town, had that moment brought in.

His Lordship, eagerly surveying the address of each, gave to Emmeline one for her; which opening, she found came from Mrs. Stafford, and enclosed another.

St. Germains, June 6.

'My dearest Emmeline will forgive me if I write only a line in the envelope, to account for the long detention of the enclosed letter. It has, by some mistake of Mr. La Fosse, been kept at Rouen instead of being forwarded to St. Germains; and appears to have passed thro' numberless hands. I hope you will get it safe; tho' my being at Paris when it *did* arrive here has made it yet a week lat'r. By the next post I shall write more fully, and therefore will now only tell you we are well, and that I am ever, with the truest attachment, your

C. STAFFORD.'

Emmeline now saw by the seal and the address that the second letter was from Lord Montreville. It appeared to have been written in great haste; and as she unfolded it, infinite was her amazement to find, instead of a remittance, which about this time she expected, the promise she had given Delamere, torn in two pieces and put into a blank paper.

The astonishment and agitation she felt at this sight, hardly left her power to read the letter which she held.

Berkley-square, May 5, 17—

'Dear Miss Mowbray,

'My son, Lord Delamere, convinced at length of the impropriety of a marriage so unwelcome to his family, allows me to release you from the promise which he obtained. I do myself the pleasure to enclose it, and shall be glad to hear you receive it safe by an early post. My Lord Delamere assures me that you hold no promise of the like nature from him. If he is in this matter forgetful, I doubt not but that you will return it on receipt of this.

'Maddox informs me that he shall in a few days forward to you the payment due: to which I beg leave to add, that if you have occasion for fifty or an hundred pounds more, during your stay on the continent, you may draw on Maddox to that amount. With sincere wishes for your health and happiness, I am, dear Miss Mowbray, your obedient and faithful humble servant,

MONTREVILLE.'

Tho' joy was, in the heart of Emmeline, the predominant emotion, she yet felt some degree of pique and resentment involuntarily arise against Lord Montreville and his son; and tho' the renunciation of the latter was what she had secretly wished ever since she had discovered the capricious violence of Delamere and the merit of Godolphin, the cold and barely civil stile in which his father had acquainted her with it, seemed at once to shock, mortify, and relieve her.

After having considered a moment the contents of her own letters, she cast her eyes towards Lady Westhaven, whose countenance expressed great emotion; while her Lord, sternly and displeased ran over his, and then put them into his pocket.

'What say *your* letters from England, my fairest cousin?' said he, advancing and trying to shake off his chagrin.

'Will you do me the honour to peruse them, my Lord?' said she, half smiling. — 'They will not take you up much time.'

He read them. 'It is a settled thing then I find. Lady Westhaven, yours are, I presume, from Berkley-square?'

'They are,' answered she. — 'Never,' and she took out her handkerchief — 'never have I received any less welcome!'

She gave one from Lady Frances Crofts to his Lordship, in which, with many details of her own affairs, was this sentence —

'Before this, you have heard from my father or my mother that Lord Delamere has entirely recovered the use of his reason, and accepts of Miss Otley with her immense fortune. This change was brought about suddenly. It was settled in Norfolk, immediately after Lord Delamere's return from Ireland. I congratulate you and Lord W. on an event which I conclude must to both of you be pleasing. I have seen none of the family for near three weeks, as they are gone back into Norfolk; only my brother called for a moment, and seemed to be greatly hurried; by which, as well as from other circumstances, I conclude that preparations are making for the wedding immediately.'
May 18.

Lady Westhaven, who saw all hopes of being allied to the friend of her heart for ever at an end — who believed that she had always cherished an affection for her brother, and who supposed that in consequence of his desertion she was left in mortifying dependance on Lord Montreville, was infinitely hurt at this information. The letter from her father to Emmeline confirmed all her apprehensions. There was a freezing civility in the style, which gave no hopes of his alleviating by generosity and kindness the pain which her Ladyship concluded Emmeline must feel; while Lord Westhaven, knowing that to her whom he thus insulted with the distant offer of fifty or an hundred pounds, he really was accountable for the income of an estate of four thousand five hundred a year, for near nineteen years, and that he still withheld that estate from her, could hardly contain his indignation even before his wife; whom he loved too well not to wish to conceal from her the ill opinion he could not help conceiving of her father.

Emmeline, who was far from feeling that degree of pain which Lady Westhaven concluded must penetrate her heart, was yet unwilling to shew that she actually received with pleasure (tho' somewhat allayed by Lord Montreville's coldness) an emancipation from her engagement. Of her partiality to Godolphin, her friend had no idea; for Emmeline, too conscious of it to be able to converse about him without fearing to betray herself, had studiously avoided talking of him after their first meeting; and she now imagined that Lady Westhaven, passionately fond of her brother as she was, would think her indifference affected thro' pique; and carried too far, if she did not receive the intelligence of their eternal separation with some degree of concern. These thoughts gave her an air of vexation and embarrassment which would have saved her the trouble of dissimulation had she been an adept in its practice. Extremely harrassed and out of spirits before, tears now, in spite of her internal satisfaction, and perhaps partly arising from it, filled her eyes; while Lady Westhaven, who was greatly more hurt, exclaimed —

'My brother then marries Miss Otley! After all I have heard him say, I thought it impossible!'

'He will however, I doubt not, be happy,' answered Emmeline. 'The satisfaction of having made Lord and Lady Montreville completely happy, must greatly contribute to his being so himself.'

'Heaven grant it!' replied Lady Westhaven. 'Poor Frederic! he throws away an invaluable blessing! Whether he will, in any other, find consolation, I greatly doubt. But however changed his heart may he, my dearest Emmeline,' added she, tenderly embracing her, 'I think I can venture to assure you that those of Lord Westhaven and your Augusta, will, towards you, ever be the same.'

Emmeline now wished to put an end to a conversation which Lady Westhaven seemed hardly able to support; and she languished herself to be alone. Forcing therefore a smile, tho' the tears still fell from her eyes, she said — 'My dear friends, tho' I expected this long ago, yet I beg you to consider that being but a woman, and of course vain, my pride is a little wounded, and I must recollect all your kindnesses, to put me in good humour again with myself. Do not let the Chevalier follow me; for I am not disposed to hear any thing this evening, after these sweetest and most consoling assurances of your inestimable friendship. Therefore I shall take Madelon with me, and go for a walk.'

She then left the room, Lady Westhaven not attempting to detain her; and her Lord, vexed to see his gentle Augusta thus uneasy, remained with her, pointing out to her the fairest prospects of establishment for her beloved Emmeline; tho' he thought the present an improper opportunity to open to her his knowledge of those circumstances in her friend's fortune, which, without such conspicuous merit, could hardly fail of obtaining it.

To go to a great distance from the house, alone, Emmeline had not the courage; and to stay near it, subjected her to the intrusion and importunity of the Chevalier. She therefore determined, to take Madelon, whose presence would be some protection without any interruption to her thoughts. She had wished, ever since her arrival at St. Alpin, to visit alone the borders of the lake of Geneva. Madelon alert and sprightly, undertook to shew her the pleasant way, and led her thro' a narrow path crossing a hill covered with broom and coppice wood, into a dark and gloomy wood of fir, cypress, and chesnut, that extended to the edge of the water; from which it was in some places separated by rocks pointing out into the lake, while in others the trees grew almost in the water, and dipped their extremities in the limpid waves beneath them.

Madelon informed Emmeline that this was the place where the servants of the castle assembled to dance of an holyday, in the shade; and where boats usually landed that came from the other side of the lake.

The scene, softened into more pensive beauty by the approach of a warm and serene evening, had every thing in it that could charm and soothe the mind of the lovely orphan. But her internal feelings were at this time too acute to suffer her to attend to outward circumstances. She wished only for tranquillity and silence, to collect her thoughts; and bidding Madelon find herself a seat, she went a few yards into the wood, and sat down in the long grass, where even Madelon might not remark her.

The events of the two last days appeared to be visions rather than realities. From being an indigent dependant on the bounty of a relation, whose caprice or avarice might leave her entirely destitute, she was at once found to be heiress to an extensive property. From being bound down to marry, if he pleased, a man for whom she felt only sisterly regard, and who had thrown her from him in the violence of unreasonable jealousy and gloomy suspicion, she was now at liberty to indulge the affections she had so long vainly resisted, and to think, without present self-accusation, or the danger of future repentance, of Godolphin. In imagination, she already beheld him avowing that tenderness which he had before generously struggled to conceal. She saw him, who she believed would have taken her *without* fortune, receiving in her estate the means of bestowing happiness, and the power of indulging his liberal and noble spirit. She saw the tender, unhappy Adelina, reconciled to life in contemplating the felicity of her dear William; and Lord Westhaven, to whom she was so much obliged, glorying in the good fortune of a brother so deservedly beloved; while still calling her excellent and lovely friend Augusta by the endearing appellation of sister, she saw her forget, in the happiness of Godolphin, the concern she had felt for Delamere.

From this delicious dream of future bliss, she was awakened somewhat suddenly by Madelon; who running towards her, told her that a boat, in which there appeared to be several men, was pointing to land just where she had been sitting. Emmeline, wearied as she was with the Chevalier's gallantry, immediately supposed it to be him, and she knew he was out on the lake. She therefore advanced a step or two to look. It was so nearly dark that she could only distinguish a man standing in the boat, whose figure appeared to be that of Bellozane, and taking Madelon by the arm, she hastily struck into the wood, to avoid him by returning to St. Alpin before he should perceive her.

She had hardly walked twenty paces, when she heard the boat put on shore, and two or three persons leap out of it. Still hoping, however, to get thro' the wood before Bellozane could overtake her, she almost ran with Madelon. But somebody seemed to pursue them. Her cloaths were white; and she knew, that notwithstanding the evening was so far shut in, and the path obscured by trees, she must yet he distinguished gliding between their branches. The persons behind gained upon her, and her pace quickened as her alarm encreased; for she now apprehended something yet more disagreeable than being overtaken by Bellozane. Suddenly she heard — *'Arretez, arretez, Mesdames! de grace di tes moi si vous etes de la famille du Baron de St. Alpin?'* (Stay, stay a moment, ladies! Have the goodness to tell me whether you belong to the family of the Baron de St. Alpin?).

The first word of this sentence stopped the flying Emmeline, and fixed her to the spot where she stood. It was the voice of Godolphin — Godolphin himself was before her!

The suddenness of his appearance quite overcame her, breathless as she was before from haste and fear; and finding that to support herself was impossible, she staggered towards a tree which grew on the edge of the path, but would have fallen if Godolphin had not caught her in his arms.

He did this merely from the impulse of his natural gallantry and good nature. What were his transports, when he found that the fugitive whom he had undesignedly alarmed by asking a direction to St. Alpin, was his adored Emmeline; and that the lovely object whose idea, since their first meeting, had never a moment been absent from it, he now pressed to his throbbing heart? Instantly terrified, however, to find her speechless and almost insensible, he ordered the servant who followed him to run back for some water; and seating her gently on the ground, he threw himself down by her and supported her; while Madelon, wringing her hands called on her *aimable*, her *belle maitresse*; and was too much frightened to give her any assistance.

Before the man returned with the water, her recollection was restored, and she said, faintly — 'Mr. Godolphin! Is it possible?'

'Loveliest Miss Mowbray, how thoughtlessly have I alarmed you! — Can you forgive me?'

'Ah!' cried she, disengaging herself from his support — 'how came you here, and from whence?'

Godolphin, without considering, and almost without knowing what he said, replied — 'I come from Lord Delamere.'

'From Lord Delamere!' exclaimed she, in amazement. 'Is he not in London then? — is he not married?'

'No; I overtook him at Besançon; where he lies ill — very ill!'

'Ill!' repeated Emmeline. — 'Ill, and at Besançon! — merciful heaven!'

She now again relapsed almost into insensibility: for at the mention of Godolphin's having overtaken him, and having left him ill, a thousand terrific and frightful images crouded into her mind; but the predominant idea was, that it was on her account they had met, and that Delamere's illness was a wound in consequence of that meeting.

That such an imagination should possess her, Godolphin had no means of knowing. He therefore very naturally concluded that the violent sorrow which she expressed, on hearing of Delamere's illness, arose from her love towards him; and, in such a conclusion, he found the ruin of those hopes he had of late fondly cherished.

'Happy, happy Delamere!' said he, sighing to himself. — 'Her first affections were his, and never will any secondary tenderness supersede that early impression. Alas! his rejection of her, has not been able to efface it — For me, there is nothing to hope! and while I thus hold her to my heart, I have lost her for ever! I came not hither, however, solely on my own account, but rather to save from pain, her and those she loves. 'Tis not then of myself I am to think.'

While these reflections passed thro' his mind, he remained silent; and Emmeline concluded that his silence was owing to the truth of her conjecture. The grief of Lady Westhaven for her brother, the despair of Lord Montreville for his son, presented themselves to her mind; and the contemptuous return of her promise, which a few hours before she thought of with resentment, was now forgotten in regret for his illness and pity for his sufferings.

'Ah!' cried she, trying to rise, 'what shall I say to Lady Westhaven? — How disclose to her such intelligence as this?'

'It was to prevent her hearing it abruptly,' said Godolphin, 'that I carne myself, rather than sent by a messenger or a letter, such distressing information.'

So strongly had the idea of a duel between them taken possession of the mind of Emmeline, that she had no courage to ask particulars of his illness; and shuddering with horror at the supposition that the hand Godolphin held out to assist her was stained with the blood of the unfortunate Delamere, she drew hers hastily and almost involuntarily from him; and taking again Madelon's arm, attempted to hasten towards home.

But the scene of anguish and terror which she must there encounter with Lady Westhaven, the distress and vexation of her Lord, and the misery of believing that Godolphin had made himself for ever hateful to all her own family, and that if her cousin died she could never again behold him but with regret and anguish, were altogether reflections so overwhelming, and so much more than her harassed spirits were able to sustain, that after tottering about fifty yards, she was compelled to stop, and gasping for breath, to accept the offered assistance of Godolphin. Strongly prepossessed with the idea of her affection for Delamere, he languidly and mournfully lent it. He had no longer courage to speak to her; yet wished to take measures for preventing Lady Westhaven's being suddenly alarmed by his appearance; and he feared, that not his appearance only, but his countenance, would tell her that he came not thither to impart tidings of happiness.

It was now quite dark; and the slow pace in which only Emmeline could walk, had not yet carried them through the wood. The agitation of Emmeline encreased: she wished, yet dreaded to know the particulars of Delamere's situation; and unable to summons courage to enquire into it, she proceeded mournfully along, almost borne by Godolphin and Madelon; who understanding nothing of what had been said, and not knowing who the gentleman was who had thus frightened her mistress, was herself almost as much in dismay.

After a long pause, Emmeline, in faultering accents, asked 'if the situation of Lord Delamere was absolutely desperate?'

'I hope and believe not,' said Godolphin. 'When I left him, at least there were hopes of a favourable issue.'

'Ah! wherefore did you leave him? Why not stay at least to see the event?'

'Because he so earnestly desired that his sister might know of his situation, and that I only might acquaint her with it and press her to go to him.'

'She will need no entreaties. Poor, poor Delamere!' — sighing deeply, Emmeline again became silent.

They were to mount a small hill, which was between the wood they had left and the grounds immediately surrounding St. Alpin, which was extremely steep and rugged. Before she reached the top, she was quite exhausted.

'I believe,' said she, I must again rest before I can proceed.'

She sat down on a bank formed by the roots of the trees which sustained the earth, on the edge of the narrow path.

Godolphin, excessively alarmed at her weakness and dejection, which he still attributed to the anguish she felt for Delamere, sat by her, hardly daring to breathe himself, while he listened to her short respiration, and fancied he heard the violent palpitation of her heart.

'And how long do you think,' said she, again recurring to Delamere — 'how long may he linger before the event will be known?'

'I really hope, and I think I am not too sanguine, that the fever will have left him before we see him again.'

'The fever!' repeated Emmeline — 'has he a fever then?'

'Yes,' replied Godolphin — 'I thought I told you that a fever was his complaint. But had you not better, my dear Madam, think a little of yourself! Ill as you appear to be, I see not how you are to get home unless you will suffer me to go on and procure some kind of conveyance for you.'

'I shall do very well,' answered she, 'as I am, if you will only tell me about Lord Delamere. He has only a fever?'

'And is it not enough,' said Godolphin. 'Tho', were I Lord Delamere, I should think an illness that called forth in my favour the charming sensibility of Miss Mowbray, the happiest event of my life.'

Having said this, he fell into a profound silence. The certainty of her affection for Delamere, deprived him of all spirits when he most wanted to exert them. Yet it was necessary to take some measures for introducing himself at St. Alpin without alarming Lady Westhaven, and to consider how he was to account to his brother for Delamere's estrangement from Emmeline; and while he canvassed these and many other perplexities, Emmeline, who was relieved from the most distressing of her apprehensions, and dared not for the world reveal what those apprehensions had been, in some degree recovered herself; and growing anxious for Lady Westhaven, said she believed she could now walk home.

As she was about to arise with an intention to attempt it, they heard the sound of approaching voices, and almost immediately lights appeared above the hill, while 'Mademoiselle! — Miss Mowbray! — Madelon! — Madelon!' was frequently and loudly repeated by the persons who carried them.

'The Baron and Lord Westhaven,' said Emmeline, 'alarmed at my being out so late, have sent persons in search of me.'

Her conjecture was right. In a moment the Chevalier, with a flambeau in his hand, was before them; who, when he found Emmeline sitting in such a place, supported by a young man whom he had never before seen, was at once amazed and displeased. There was no time for explanation. Lord Westhaven immediately followed him; and after stopping a moment to consider whether the figure of

Godolphin which rose before him was not an illusion, he flew eagerly into his arms.

The manly eyes of both the brothers were filled with tears. Lord Westhaven had not seen Godolphin for four years; and, since their last parting, they had lost their father. After a short pause, his Lordship introduced Godolphin to Bellozane; and then taking the cold and trembling hand of Emmeline, who leaned languidly on Madelon, he said —

'And you, my lovely cousin, for whose safety we have been above an hour in the cruellest alarm, where did you find William, and by what extraordinary chance are ye here together?'

Emmeline with great difficulty found voice enough to explain their accidental meeting. And Bellozane observing her apparent faintness, said — 'you seem, Mademoiselle, to be extremely fatigued. Pray allow me the honour of giving you my arm.'

'If you please,' said she, in a low voice. And supposing that Godolphin would be glad to have some conversation with his brother, she accepted his assistance and proceeded.

This preference, however, of Bellozane, Godolphin imputed to her coldness or dislike towards himself; and so struck was he with the cruel idea, that it was not without an effort he recollected himself enough to relate to his brother, as they walked, all that it was necessary for him to know. Lord Westhaven, anxious for a life so precious to his wife and her family as was that of Lord Delamere, determined immediately to go to him. At present it was necessary to reveal as tenderly as possible his situation to his sister, Lady Westhaven; and first to dissipate the uneasiness she had suffered from the long absence of Emmeline.

CHAPTER IV

LORD Westhaven first entered the room where his wife was, whose alarming apprehensions at Emmeline's long stay were by this time extreme.

'Our Emmeline is returned, my love,' said he, 'and has met with no accident.'

Lady Westhaven eagerly embracing her, reproached her tenderly for her long absence. But then observing how pale she looked, and the fatigue and oppression she seemed to suffer, her Ladyship said —

'Surely you have been frightened — or are you ill? You look so faint!'

'She is a little surprized,' interrupted Lord Westhaven, seeing her still unable to answer for herself. 'She has brought us a visitor whom we did not expect. My brother Godolphin landed just as she was returning home.'

At this intelligence Lady Westhaven could express only pleasure. She had never seen Godolphin, who was now introduced, and received with every token of regard by her Ladyship, as well as by the Baron and Mrs. St. Alpin; who beheld with pleasure another son of their sister, and beheld him an honour to their family.

Bellozane, however, saw his arrival with less satisfaction. He remembered that Emmeline had been, as she had told him, well acquainted with Godolphin in England; and recollected that whenever he had been spoken of, she had always done justice to his merit, yet rather evaded than sought the conversation. Her extraordinary agitation on his arrival, which was such as disabled her from walking home, seemed much greater than could have been created by the sight of a mere acquaintance; his figure was so uncommonly handsome, his countenance so interesting, and his address such a fortunate mixture of dignity and softness, that Bellozane, vain as he was, could not but acknowledge his personal merit; and began to fear that the coldness and insensibility of Emmeline, which he had, till now, supposed perseverance would vanquish, were less occasioned by her affected blindness to his own perfections, than by her prepossession in favour of another.

Whatever internal displeasure this idea of rivalry gave the Chevalier, he overwhelmed Godolphin with professions of regard and esteem, not the less warm for being wholly insincere.

But Godolphin, who saw, in the encreasing dejection of Emmeline, only a confirmation of her attachment to Delamere, drooped in hopeless despondence. Emmeline, unable to support herself, retired early to her room; and Godolphin, complaining of fatigue, was conducted to his by Bellozane; while Lord Westhaven meditated how to disclose to his wife, without too much distressing her, the illness of her brother. He thought, that as she had suffered a good deal of vexation in the course of the day, as well as terror at Emmeline's absence at so late an hour in the evening, he would defer till the next morning this unwelcome intelligence. As soon, however, as she was retired, he communicated to his uncle and aunt the situation of Lord Delamere, and the necessity there was for their quitting St. Alpin the next day, to attend him; an account which they both heard with sincere regret. Mrs. St. Alpin heartily wished Lord Delamere was with her, being persuaded she could immediately cure him with remedies of her own preparing; while the Baron expressed his vexation and regret to find the visit of his nephews so much shortened.

Lord Westhaven went to his own apartment in great uneasiness. He heard from his brother, that Lord Delamere, repenting of his renunciation of Emmeline, was coming to St. Alpin, when illness stopped him at Besançon. He knew not how to act about her; who, heiress to a large fortune, was of so much more consequence than she had been hitherto supposed. He had a long contention in view with Lord Montreville; and was now likely to be embarrassed with the passion of Delamere, if he recovered, (who would certainly expect his influence over Emmeline to be exerted to obtain his pardon); or if the event of his illness should prove fatal, he dreaded the anguish of Lady Westhaven and the despair of the whole family.

He was besides hurt at that melancholy and unhappy appearance, so unlike his former manners, which he had observed in Godolphin; and for which, ignorant of his passion for Emmeline, he knew not how to account. His short conversation with him had cleared up no part of the mystery which he could not but perceive hung about the affairs of Lady Adelina; and he only knew enough to discover that something remained which it would probably pain him to know thoroughly.

The pillow of Emmeline also was strewn with thorns. For tho' the sharpest of them was removed, by having heard that Delamere was ill without having suffered from the event of any dispute in which he might on her account have engaged, she was extremely unhappy that he had, in pursuit of her, come to France, which she now concluded must be the case, and sorry for the disquiet which she foresaw must arise from his indisposition and his love.

She was sure that Lady Westhaven would immediately fly to her brother. And in that event how was she herself to act?

Could she suffer her generous, her tender friend, to whom she was so much obliged, to encounter alone all the fatigue and anxiety to which the sickness and danger of this beloved brother would probably expose her? Yet could she submit to the appearance of seeking a man who had so lately renounced her for ever, with coldness, contempt, and insult? If she went not with Lady Westhaven, she had no choice but that of travelling across France alone, to rejoin Mrs. Stafford; since she could not remain with propriety a moment at St. Alpin, with the Chevalier de Bellozane; whose addresses she never meant to encourage, and whose importunate passion persecuted and distressed her. Godolphin too! — whither would Godolphin go? Could she go where he was, and conceal her partiality? or could she, by accompanying him to Besançon, plunge another dagger in the heart of Delamere, and shew him, not only that he had lost that portion of her regard he had once possessed, but that all her love was now given to another?

That she was most partial to Godolphin, she could no longer attempt to conceal from herself. The moment her fears that he had met Delamere hostilely were removed, all her tenderness for him returned with new force. She again saw all the merit, all the nobleness of his character; but she still tormented herself with uneasy conjectures as to the cause of his journey to Switzerland; and wearied herself with considering how she ought to act, 'till towards morning, when falling, thro' mere fatigue and lassitude, into a short slumber, she saw multiplied and exaggerated, in dreams, the dreadful images which had disturbed her waking; and starting up in terror, determined no more to attempt to sleep. It was now day break; and wrapping herself in her muslin morning gown and cloak, she went down into the garden of Mrs. St. Alpin, where, seated on a bench, under a row of tall walnut trees, which divided it from the vineyard, she leaned her head against one of them; and lost in reflections on the strangeness of her fate, and the pain of her situation, she neither saw or heard any thing around her.

Godolphin, in the anxiety she had expressed for Delamere, believed he saw a confirmation of his fears; which had always been that the early impression he had made on her heart would be immoveable, and that neither his having renounced her or his rash and heedless temper would prevent her continuing to love him. Wretched in this idea, he concluded all hopes of obtaining her regard for ever at an end; while every hour's experience of his own feelings, whether he thought of or saw her, convinced him that his love, however desperate, was incurable. Accustomed to fatigue, all that he had endured the day before could not restore to him that repose which was driven away by these reflections. Almost as soon as he saw it was light, he left his room, and with less interest than he would once have taken in such a survey, wandered over the antique apartments of the paternal house of his mother. He then went down into the garden; and musing rather than observing, passed along the strait walk that went between the walnut trees into the vineyard. At the end of it he turned, and, in coming again towards the house, saw Emmeline sitting on the bench beneath them, who had not seen him the first time he passed her, but who now appeared surprized at his approach.

She had not, however, time to rise before he went up to her, and bowing gravely, enquired how she did after the alarm he had been so unfortunate as to give her the evening before?

'I fear,' said he, seating himself by her, 'that Miss Mowbray is yet indisposed from her late walk and my inconsiderate address to her. I know not how to forgive myself for my indiscretion, since it has distressed you.'

'Such intelligence as I had the misfortune of hearing, Sir, of the brother of Lady Westhaven — a brother so dear to her — could hardly fail of affecting me. I should have been concerned had a stranger been so circumstanced; but when —'

'Ah! Madam,' interrupted Godolphin, 'you need not repeat all the claims which give the fortunate Delamere a right to your favour. But do not suffer yourself, on his account, to be so extremely alarmed. I hope the danger is by no means so great as to make his recovery hopeless. Since of those we love, the most minute account is not tedious, and since it may, perhaps, alleviate your apprehensions for his safety, will you allow me to relate all I know of his illness? It will engage me, perhaps, in a detail of our first acquaintance, and carry me back to circumstances which I would wish to forget; if your gratification was not in my mind a consideration superior to every other.'

Emmeline, trembling, yet wishing to hear all, could not refuse. She bowed in silence; and Godolphin considering that as an assent, reassumed his discourse.

'Soon after I had the happiness of seeing you last, my wish to embrace Lady Clancarryl and her family (from whose house I had been long obliged to absent myself because Mr. Fitz-Edward was with them) carried me to Ireland; and to my astonishment I there met Lord Delamere.

'The relationship between their families, made my sister anxiously invite him to Lough Carryl. Thither reluctantly he came; and an accident informed him that I had the good fortune, by means of Lady Adelina Trelawny, to be known to you.

'He did me the honour to shew me particular attention; and the morning after he found I had the happiness of being acquainted with Miss Mowbray, he took occasion, when we were alone, to ask me, abruptly, whether I knew Colonel Fitz-Edward? I answered that I certainly did, by the connection in our families; and that he was *once* my most intimate friend.

'He then unreservedly, and with vehemence said, that Fitz-Edward was a villain! Astonished and hurt at an assertion which (how true soever it might be) I thought alluded to that unhappy affair which I hoped was a secret, I eagerly asked an explanation. But judge, Miss Mowbray, of the astonishment, the pain, with which I heard him impute to *you* the error of my unfortunate Adelina — when I saw him take out three anonymous letters, one of which I found had hastened his return from France, purporting that Fitz-Edward had availed himself of his absence to win your affections, that he had taken, of those affections, the most ungenerous advantage, and that on going to a place named (which I remembered to be the house where my little William was nursed,) he might himself see an unequivocal proof of your fatal attachment and Fitz-Edward's perfidy.

'When I had read these odious letters, and listened to several circumstances he related, which confirmed in his apprehension the truth of the assertions they contained, he went on to inform me, that following this cruel information, he had seen you with the infant in your arms; had bitterly reproached you, and then had quitted you for ever! — But as he could not rest without trying to punish the infamous conduct of Fitz-Edward, he had pursued him to Ireland, where, instead of finding him, he heard that he was gone to France, undoubtedly to meet you, by your own appointment; but as Lord Clancarryl still expected him back, he determined to wait a little longer, in hopes of an opportunity of discussing with him the subjects of complaint he had related.

'Tho' I immediately saw what I ought to do, astonishment for a moment kept me silent, and in that moment we were interrupted.

'This delay however unwelcome, gave me time for reflection. Lord Delamere was to go the same day from Lough Carryl to Dublin. I resolved to follow him thither, and relate the whole truth; since I would by no means suffer your generous and exalted friendship for my sister to stain the lovely purity of a character which only the malice of fiends could delight in blasting, only the blind and infatuated rashness of jealousy a moment believe capable of blemish! Many reasons induced me, however, to delay this necessary explanation 'till I saw him at his own lodgings. Thither I followed him, two days after he departed from Lough Carryl. But on enquiry for him, was surprized and mortified to find that he had received letters from England which had induced him immediately to return thither, and that he had sailed in the packet for Holyhead the day after his arrival at Dublin.'

Emmeline, astonished at the malice which appeared to have been exerted against her, remained silent; but in such tremor, that it was with difficulty she continued to hear him.

'I now, therefore, relinquished all thoughts of returning to the house of my sister, and followed him by the first conveyance that offered, greatly apprehending, that if the letters he had received gave him notice of Fitz-Edward's return to London, my interposition would be too late to prevent their meeting. I knew the hasty and inconsiderate Delamere would, without explanation, so conduct himself towards Fitz-Edward, that neither his spirit or his profession would permit him to bear; and that if they met, the consequence must, to one of them, be fatal. I was impatient too to rescue your name, Madam, from the unmerited aspersions which it bore. But when I arrived in London, and hastened to Berkley-square, I heard that Lord and Lady Montreville, together with Lady Frances Crofts, her husband and Lord Delamere, had gone all together to Audley Hall, immediately after his return from Ireland. Thither, therefore, I went also.'

'Generous, considerate Godolphin!' sighed Emmeline to herself.

'Tho' related, by my brother's marriage, to the family of the Marquis of Montreville, I was a stranger to every member of it but Lord Delamere. He was gone to dine out; and in the rest of the family I observed an air of happiness and triumph, which Lord Montreville informed me was occasioned by the marriage which was intended soon to take place between his son and Miss Otley; whose immense fortune, and near relationship to his mother's family, had made such a marriage particularly desirable. I was glad to hear he was likely to be happy; but it was not therefore the less necessary to clear up the error into which he had fallen. On his coming home, he appeared pleased and surprized to see me; but I saw in his looks none of that satisfaction which was so evident in those of the rest of the house.

'As soon as we were alone, he said to me — "You see me, Mr. Godolphin, at length taken in the toils. Immediately after leaving Lough Carryl, I received a letter from a person in London, whom I had employed for that purpose, which informed me that he heard, at the office of the agent to Fitz-Edward's regiment, that he was certainly to be in town in a few days. He named, indeed, the exact time; and I, who imagined that pains had been taken to keep us from meeting, determined to return to England instantly, that he might not again avoid me. On reaching London, however, I found that the intelligence I had received was wholly unfounded, and originated in the mistake of a clerk in the agent's office. None knew where Fitz-Edward was, or when he would return; and though I wrote to enquire at Rouen, where I imagined the residence of Miss Mowbray might induce him to remain, I have yet had no answer. The entreaties and tears of my mother prevailed on me to come down hither; and reckless of what becomes of me, since Emmeline is undoubtedly lost to me for ever, I have yielded to the remonstrance of my father and the prayers of my mother, and have consented to marry a woman whom I cannot love. Let not Fitz-Edward, however, imagine," (vehemently and fiercely he spoke) "that he is with impunity to escape; and that tho' my vengeance may be delayed, I can *forgive* the man who has basely robbed me of her whom I *could* love — whom I *did* love — even to madness!"

'I own to you, Madam, that when I found this unfortunate young man had put into his father's hands the promise you had given him, and that it was returned to you, I felt at once pity for him, and — hope for myself, which, 'till then, I had never dared to indulge.'

Godolphin had never been thus explicit before. Pale as death, and deprived of the power as well as of the inclination to interrupt him, Emmeline awaited, in breathless silence, the close of this extraordinary narrative.

'It was now,' reassumed he, 'my turn to speak. And trusting to his honour for his silence about my unhappy sister, I revealed to him the whole truth. I at once cleared your character from unjust blame, and, I hope, did justice to those exalted virtues to which I owe so much. I will not shock your gentle and generous bosom with a relation of the wild phrenzy, the agonies of regret and repentance, into which this relation threw Lord Delamere. Concerned at the confusion his reproaches and his anguish had occasioned to the whole family, I lamented that I could not explain to *them* what I had said to *him*, which had produced so sudden a change in his sentiments about you; but to such women as the Marchioness of Montreville and her daughter, I could not relate the unhappiness of my poor Adelina; and Delamere steadily refused to tell them how he became convinced of your innocence, and the wicked arts which had been used to mislead him; which he openly imputed to the family of the Crofts'; against whom his fiery and vindictive spirit turned all the rage it had till now cherished against Fitz-Edward.

'The Marquis, tho' extremely hurt, had yet candour enough to own, that if I was convinced that the causes of complaint which his son had against you were ill founded, I had done well in removing them. Yet I saw that he wished I had been less anxious for the vindication of innocence; and he beheld, with an uneasy and suspicious eye, what he thought officious interference in the affairs of his family. I observed, too, that he believed when the influence that he supposed I had over the mind of Lord Delamere was removed, he should be able to bring him back to his engagements with Miss Otley, which had, I found, been hurried on with the utmost precipitation.

The ladies, who had at first overwhelmed me with civilities, now appeared so angry, that notwithstanding Lord Delamere's entreaties that I would stay with him till he could determine how to act, I immediately returned to London; and from thence, after passing a week with Adelina, whom I had only seen for a few hours since my return from Ireland, I set out for St. Alpin.'

'But Lord Delamere, Sir?' said Emmeline, inarticulately.

'Alas! Madam,' dejectedly continued Godolphin, 'I mean not to entertain you on what relates to myself; but to hasten to that which I farther have to say of the fortunate Delamere! I waited a few days at Southampton for a wind; and then landed at Havre, proceeded to St. Germains, where Mrs. Stafford's last letters had informed Adelina she was settled. I knew, too, that you were gone with my brother and Lady Westhaven to St. Alpin. Mrs. Stafford had only the day before forwarded to you Lord Montreville's letter, which, by one from his Lordship to herself, she knew contained the promise you had given Lord Delamere. She said, that this renunciation would give you no pain. She made me hope that your heart was not irrevocably his. Ah! why did I suffer such illusions to lead me on to this conviction! But pray forgive me, lovely Miss Mowbray! I am still talking of myself. From St. Germains I made as much haste as possible to Besançon. I rode post; and, just as I got off my horse at the hotel, was accosted by a French servant, whom I knew belonged to Lord Delamere.

'The man expressed great joy at seeing me, and besought me to go with him to his master, who, he said, had, thro' fatigue and the heat of the weather, been seized with a fever, and was unable to proceed to St. Alpin, whither he was going.

'I was extremely concerned at his journey; and, I hope, not so selfish as to be unmoved by his illness. I found, indeed, his fever very high, but greatly irritated and encreased by his impatience. As soon as he saw me, he told me that he was hurrying to St. Alpin, in hopes of obtaining your pardon; that he had broke off his engagement with Miss Otley, and never would return to England till he carried you thither as his wife.

"I am now well enough to go on, indeed Godolphin," added he, "and if I can but see her! — "

'I was by no means of opinion that he was in a condition to travel. His fever encreased; after I left him in the evening, he grew delirious; and Millefleur, terrified, came to call me to him. I sat up with him for the rest of the night; and being accustomed to attend invariably to the illness of men on ship board, I thought I might venture, from my experience, to direct a change in the method which the physician he had sent for pursued. In a few hours he grew better, and the delirium left him; but he was then convinced that he was too weak to proceed on his journey.

'He knew I was coming hither, and he entreated me to hasten my departure. "Go, my good friend," said he — "send Augusta to me. She will bring with her the generous, the forgiving angel, whom my rash folly has dared to injure!

She will behold my penitence; and, if her pardon can be obtained, it will restore me to life; but if I cannot see them — if I linger many days longer in suspence, my illness must be fatal!"

'As I really did not think him in great danger, and saw every proper care was now taken of him, I determined to come on; not only because I wished to save Lady Westhaven the pain of hearing of his illness by any other means, but because —'

He was proceeding, when a deep and convulsive sigh from Emmeline made him look in her face, from which he had hitherto kept his eyes, (unable to bear the varying expressions it had shewn of what he thought her concern for Delamere.) He now beheld her, quite pale, motionless, and to all appearance lifeless. Her sense of what she owed to the generosity of Godolphin; her concern for Delamere; and the dread of those contending passions which she foresaw would embitter her future life, added to the sleepless night and fatigueing day she had passed, had totally overcome her. Godolphin flew for assistance. The servants were by this time up, and ran to her. Among the first of them was Le Limosin, who expressed infinite anxiety and concern for her, and assiduously exerted himself in carrying her into the house; where she soon recovered, begged Godolphin's pardon for the trouble she had given, and was going to her own room, led by Madelon, when Bellozane suddenly appeared, and offered his assistance, which Emmeline faintly declining, moved on.

Godolphin, who could not bear to leave her in such a state, walked slowly by her, tho' she had refused his arm. The expression of his countenance, while his eyes were eagerly fixed on her face, would have informed any one less interested than Bellozane, of what passed in his heart, and the Chevalier surveyed him with looks of angry observation, which did not escape Emmeline, ill as she was. On arriving, therefore, at the foot of the staircase, she besought, in English, Godolphin to leave her, which he instantly did. She then told the Chevalier that she would by no means trouble him to attend her farther; and he, satisfied that no preference was shewn to his cousin, at least in this instance, bowed, and returned with him into the room where they usually assembled in a morning, and where they found Lord Westhaven.

CHAPTER V

HIS Lordship told them that Lady Westhaven had been less alarmed at the account he had given her of Delamere than he had apprehended; and that she was preparing to begin their journey towards him immediately after breakfast.

'I must send,' continued he, 'Miss Mowbray to her; who is, I understand, already up and walking.'

Bellozane then informed his Lordship of what he knew of Emmeline. But Godolphin was silent: he dared not trust himself with speaking much of her; he dared not relate her illness, lest the cause of it should be enquired into. 'Does Miss Mowbray go with my sister?' asked he.

'That I know not,' replied Lord Westhaven. 'Augusta will very reluctantly go without her. Yet her situation in regard to Lord Delamere is such' — He ceased speaking; looked embarrassed; and, soon after, the Chevalier quitting the room, before whom civility would not allow them to converse long in English, and to whom his Lordship thought he had no right to reveal the real situation of Emmeline, while it yet remained unknown to others, he related to his brother the circumstances of the discovery that had been made of her birth, and of her consequent claim to the Mowbray estate.

Godolphin, who would, from the obscurest indigence, have chosen her in preference to all other women, heard this account with pleasure, only as supposing that independance might be grateful to her sensibility, and affluence favourable to the liberality of her spirit. But the satisfaction he derived from these reflections, was embittered and nearly destroyed, when he considered, that her acquiring so large a fortune would make her alliance eagerly sought by the very persons who had before scorned and rejected her; and that all the family would unite in persuading her to forgive Delamere, the more especially as this would be the only means to keep in it the Mowbray estate, and to preclude the necessity of refunding the income which had been received for so many years, and which now amounted to a great sum of money. When the pressing instances of all her own family, and particularly of Lady Westhaven, whom she so tenderly loved, were added to the affection he believed she had invariably felt for Delamere, he thought it impossible that her pride, however it might have been piqued by the desertion of her lover, could make any effort against a renewal of her engagement; and his own hopes, which he had never cherished till he was convinced Delamere had given her up, and which had been weakened by her apparent affection for him, were by this last event again so nearly annihilated, that, no longer conscious he retained any, he fancied himself condemned still to love, serve, and adore the object of his passion, without making any effort to secure its success, or being permitted to appear otherwise than as her friend. He was vexed that he had been unguardedly explicit, in telling her that he had ever indulged those hopes at all; since he now feared it would be the means of depriving her conversation and her manner, when they were together, of that charming frankness, of which, tho' it rivetted his chains and encreased his torments, he could not bear to be deprived. Melancholy and desponding, he continued long silent after Lord Westhaven ceased speaking. Suddenly, however, awakening from his reverie, he said — 'Does your Lordship think Miss Mowbray *ought* to go to meet Lord Delamere?'

'Upon my word I know not how to advise: my wife is miserable without her, and fancies the sight of her will immediately restore Delamere. On the other hand, I believe Emmeline herself will with reluctance take a step that will perhaps, appear like forcing herself into the notice of a man from whom she has received an affront which it is hardly in female nature to forgive.'

They were now interrupted by Bellozane, who flew about the house in evident uneasiness and confusion. He did not yet know how Emmeline was to be disposed of: he saw that Lord Westhaven was himself uncertain of it; and he had been applying for information to Le Limosin and Madelon, who had yet received no orders to prepare for her departure.

While Emmeline had created in the bosoms of others so much anxiety, she was herself tortured with the cruellest uncertainty. Unable to resolve how she ought to act, she had yet determined on nothing, when Lady Westhaven sent for her, who, as soon as she entered the room, said — 'My dear Emmeline, are you not preparing for our journey?'

'How can I, dearest Madam how can I, with any propriety, go where Lord Delamere is? After the separation which has now so decidedly and irrevocably taken place between us, shall I intrude again on his Lordship's sight?

and solicit a return of that regard with which I most sincerely wish he had forborne to honour of me?'

'You are piqued, my lovely friend; and I own with great reason. But Mr. Godolphin has undoubtedly told you that poor Frederic is truly penitent; that he has taken this journey merely to deprecate your just anger and to solicit his pardon. Will my Emmeline, generous and gentle as she is to others, be inexorable only to him? Besides, my sweet coz, pray consider a moment, what else can you do? You certainly would not wish to stay here? Surely you would not travel alone to St. Germains. And let me add my own hopes that you will not quit me now, when poor Frederic's illness, and my own precarious health, make your company not merely pleasant but necessary.'

'That is indeed a consideration which must have great force with me. When Lady Westhaven commands, how shall I disobey, even tho' to obey be directly contrary to my judgment and my wishes?'

'Commands, my dear friend,' very gravely, and with an air of chagrin, said her Ladyship, 'are neither for me to give or for you to receive. Certainly if you are so determined against going with me, I must submit. But I did not indeed think that Emmeline, however the brother may have offended her, would thus have resented it to the sister.'

'I should be a monster, Lady Westhaven,' (hardly was she able to restrain her tears as she spoke,) — 'was I a moment capable of forgetting all I owe you. But do you really think I *ought* again to put myself in the way of Lord Delamere — again to renew all the family contention which his very unfortunate partiality for me has already occasioned; and again to hazard being repulsed with contempt by the Marquis, and still more probably by the Marchioness of Montreville? My lot has hitherto been humble: I have learned to submit to it, if not without regret, at least with calmness and resignation; yet pardon me if I say, that however unhappy my fortune, there is still something due to myself; and if I again make myself liable to the humiliation of being *refused*, I shall feel that I am degraded in mind, as much as I have been in circumstances, and lost to that proper pride to which innocence and rectitude has in the lowest indigence a right, and which cannot be relinquished but with the loss of virtue.'

The spirit which Emmeline thought herself obliged to exert, was immediately lost in softness and in sorrow when she beheld Lady Westhaven in tears; who, sobbing, said — 'Go then, Miss Mowbray! — Go, my dear Emmeline! (for dear you must ever be to me) leave *me* to be unhappy and poor Frederic to die.'

'Hear me, my dear Madam!' answered she with quickness — 'If to *you* I can be of the least use, I will hesitate no longer; but let it then be understood that I go *with* you, and by no means *to* Lord Delamere.'

'It shall be so understood — be assured, my love, it shall! You will not, then, leave me? — You will see my poor brother?'

'My best, my dearest friend,' replied Emmeline, collecting all her fortitude, 'hear me without resentment explain to you at once the real situation of my heart in regard to Lord Delamere. I feel for him the truest concern; I feel it for him even to a painful excess; and I have an affection for him, a sisterly affection for him, which I really believe is little inferior to your own. But I will not deceive you; nor, since I am to meet him, will I suffer him to entertain hopes that it is impossible for me to fulfil. To be considered as the friend, as the sister of Lord Delamere, is one of the first wishes my heart now forms — against ever being his wife, I am resolutely determined.'

'Impossible! — Surely you cannot have made such a resolution?'

'I have indeed! — Nor will any consideration on earth induce me from that determination to recede.'

'And is it anger and resentment only have raised in your heart this decided enmity to my poor bother? Or is it, that any other —'

Emmeline, whose colourless cheeks were suffused with a deep blush at this speech, hastily interrupted it. —

'Whatever, dear Lady Westhaven, are my motives for the decision, it is irrevocable; as Lord Delamere's sister, I shall be honoured, if I am allowed to consider myself. — As such, if my going with you to Besançon will give you a day's — an hour's satisfaction, I go.'

'Get ready then, my love. But indeed, cruel girl, if such is your resolution it were better to leave you here, than take you only to shew Lord Delamere all he has lost, while you deprive him of all hopes of regaining you. But I will yet flatter myself you do not mean all this. — "At lovers' perjuries they say Jove laughs." — And those of my fair cousin will be forgiven, should she break her angry vow and receive her poor penitent. Come, let us hasten to begin our journey to him; for tho' that dear Godolphin, whom I shall love as long as I live,' (ah! thought Emmeline, and so shall I) 'assures me he does not think him in any danger, my heart will sadly ache till I see him myself.'

Emmeline then left her to put up her cloaths and prepare for a journey to which she was determined solely by the pressing instances of Lady Westhaven. To herself she foresaw only uneasiness and embarrassment; and even found a degree of cruelty in permitting Lord Delamere to feed, by her consenting to attend him, those hopes to which she now could never accede, unless by condemning herself to the most wretched of all lots — that of marrying one man while her love was another's. The late narrative which she had heard from Godolphin, encreased her affection for him, and took from her every wish to oppose its progress; and tho' she was thus compelled to see Delamere, she determined not to deceive him, but to tell him ingenuously that he had lost all that tenderness which her friendship and long acquaintance with him would have induced her to cherish, had not his own conduct destroyed it —

But it was hardly less necessary to own to him part of the truth, than to conceal the rest. Should he suspect that Godolphin was his rival, and a rival fondly favoured, she knew that his pride, his jealousy, his resentment, would hurry him into excesses more dreadful, than any that had yet followed his impetuous love or his unbridled passions.

The apprehensions that he must, if they were long together, discover it, were more severely distressing than any she had yet felt; and she resolved, both now and when they reached Besançon, to keep the strictest guard on her words and looks; and to prevent if possible her real sentiments being known to Delamere, to Lady Westhaven, and to Godolphin himself.

So painful and so difficult appeared the dissimulation necessary for that end; and so contrary did she feel it to her nature, that she was withheld only by her love to Lady Westhaven from flying to England with Mrs. Stafford; and should she be restored to her estate, she thought that the only chance she had of tranquillity would be to hide herself from Delamere, whom she at once pitied and dreaded, and from Godolphin, whom she tenderly loved, in the silence and seclusion of Mowbray Castle.

Her embarrassment and uneasiness were encreased, when, on her joining Lord and Lady Westhaven, whose carriages and baggage were now ready, she found that the Chevalier de Bellozane had insisted on escorting them; an offer which they had no pretence to refuse. On her taking leave of the Baron, he very warmly and openly recommended his son to her favour; and Mrs. St. Alpin, who was very fond of her, repeated her wishes that she would listen to her nephew; and both with unfeigned concern saw their English visitors depart. Captain Godolphin had a place in his brother's chaise; Madelon occupied that which on the former journey was filled by Bellozane in the coach, the Chevalier now proceeding on horseback.

During the journey, Emmeline was low and dejected; from which she was sometimes roused by impatient enquiries and fearful apprehensions which darted into her mind, of what was to happen at the end of it. Every thing he observed, confirmed Godolphin in his persuasion that her heart was wholly Delamere's: her behaviour to himself was civil, but even studiously distant; while the unreserved and ardent addresses of Bellozane, who made no mystery of his pretensions, she repulsed with yet more coldness and severity: and tho' towards Lord and Lady Westhaven the sweetness of her manners was yet preserved, she seemed overwhelmed with sadness, and her vivacity was quite lost.

As soon as they reached Besançon, Lord Westhaven directed the carriages to stop at another hotel, while he went with his brother to that where Lord Delamere was. At the door, they met Millefleur; who, overjoyed to see them, related, that since Mr. Godolphin left his master the violence of his impatience had occasioned a severe relapse, in which, according to the orders Mr. Godolphin had given, the surgeons had bled and blistered him; that he was now again better, but very weak; yet so extremely ungovernable and self-willed, that the French people who attended him could do nothing with him, and that his English footmen, and Millefleur himself, were forced to be constantly in his room to prevent his leaving it or committing some other excess that might again irritate the fever and bring on alarming symptoms. They hastened to him; and found not only that his fever still hung on him, tho' with less violence, but that he was also extremely emaciated; and that only his youth had supported him thro' so severe an illness, or could now enable him to struggle with its effects.

The moment they entered the room, he enquired after his sister and Emmeline; and hearing the latter was actually come, he protested he would instantly go to her.

Lord Westhaven and Godolphin resolutely opposed so indiscreet a plan: the former, by his undeviating rectitude of mind and excellent sense, had acquired a greater ascendant over Delamere than any of his family had before possessed; and to the latter he thought himself so much obliged, that he could not refuse to attend to him. He consented therefore at length to remain where he was; and Lord Westhaven hastened back to his wife, whom he led immediately to her brother.

She embraced him with many tears; and was at first greatly shocked at his altered countenance and reduced figure. But as Lord Westhaven and Godolphin both assured her there was no longer any danger if he would consent to be governed, she was soothed into hope of his speedy recovery and soon became tolerably composed.

As Lord Westhaven and Godolphin soon left them alone, he began to talk to his sister of Emmeline. He told her, that when he had been undeceived by Mr. Godolphin, and the scandalous artifices discovered which had raised in his mind such injurious suspicions, he had declared to Lord and Lady Montreville his resolution to proceed no farther in the treaty which they had hurried on with Miss Otley, and had solicited their consent, to his renewing and fulfilling that, which he had before entered into with Miss Mowbray; but that his mother, with more anger and acrimony than ever, had strongly opposed his wishes; and that his father had forbidden him, on pain of his everlasting displeasure, ever again to think of Emmeline.

After having for some time, he said, combated their inveterate prejudice, he had left them abruptly, and set out with his three servants for St. Alpin, (where Godolphin informed him Emmeline was to be,) when a fever, owing to heat and fatigue, seized and confined him where he now was.

'Ah, tell me, my sister, what hopes are there that Emmeline will pardon me? May I dare enquire whether she is yet to be moved in my favour?'

Lady Westhaven, who during their journey could perceive no symptoms that her resolution was likely to give way, dared not feed him with false hopes; yet unwilling to depress him by saying all she feared, she told him that Emmeline was greatly and with justice offended; but that all he could at present do, was to take care of his health. She entreated him to consider the consequence of another relapse, which might be brought on by his eagerness and emotion; and then conjuring him to keep all he knew of Lady Adelina a secret from Lord Westhaven (the necessity of which he already had heard from Godolphin) she left him and returned to Emmeline.

To avoid the importunity of Bellozane, and the melancholy looks of Godolphin, which affected her with the tenderest sorrow, she had retired to a bed chamber, where she waited the return of Lady Westhaven with impatience.

Her solicitude for Delamere was very great; and her heart greatly lightened when she found that even his tender and apprehensive sister did not think him in any immediate danger, and believed that a few days would put him out of hazard even of a relapse.

She now again thought, that since Lady Westhaven had nothing to fear for his life, her presence would be less necessary; and her mind, the longer it thought of Mowbray Castle, adhering with more fondness to her plan of flying thither, she considered how she might obtain in a few days Lady Westhaven's consent to the preliminary measure of quitting Besançon.

CHAPTER VI

WHILE the heiress of Mowbray Castle meditated how to escape thither from the embarrassed and uneasy situation in which she now was; and while she fancied that in retirement she might conceal, if she could not conquer, her affection for Godolphin, (tho' in fact she only languished for an opportunity of thinking of him perpetually without observation), Lady Westhaven laid in wait for an occasion to try whether the ruined health and altered looks of her brother, would not move, in his favour, her tender and sensible friend.

While Delamere kept his chamber, Emmeline easily evaded an interview; but when, after three or four days, he was well enough to leave it, it was no longer possible for her to escape seeing him. However Godolphin thought himself obliged to bury in silence his unfortunate passion, he could not divest himself of that painful curiosity which urged him to observe the behaviour of Emmeline on their first meeting. Bellozane had discovered on what footing Lord Delamere had formerly been; and he dreaded a renewal of that preference she had given her lover, to which his proud heart could ill bear to submit, tho' he could himself make no progress in her favour. Tho' Lady Westhaven had entreated her to see Delamere alone, she had refused; assigning as a reason that as he could never again be to her any other than a friend, nothing could possibly pass which her other friends might not hear. Delamere was obliged therefore to brook the hard conditions of seeing her as an indifferent person, or not seeing her at all. But tho' she was immoveably determined against receiving him again as a lover, she had not been able to steel her heart against his melancholy appearance; his palid countenance, his emaciated form, extremely affected her. And when he approached her, bowed with a dejected air, and offered to take her hand — her haughtiness, her resentment forsook her — she trembling gave it, expressed in incoherent words her satisfaction at seeing him better, and betrayed so much emotion, that Godolphin, who with a beating heart narrowly observed her, saw, as he believed, undoubted proof of her love; and symptoms of her approaching forgiveness.

Delamere, who, whenever he was near her, ceased to remember that any other being existed; would, notwithstanding the presence of so many witnesses, have implored her pardon and her pity; but the moment he began to speak on that subject, she told him, with as much resolution as she could command, that the subject was to her so very disagreeable, as would oblige her to withdraw if he persisted introducing it.

While his looks expressed how greatly he was hurt by her coldness, those of Godolphin testified equal dejection. For however she might repress the hopes of his rival by words of refusal and resentment, he thought her countenance gave more unequivocal intelligence of the real state of her heart.

Bellozane, as proud, as little used to controul and disappointment, and with more personal vanity than Lord Delamere, beheld with anger and mortification the pity and regard which Emmeline shewed for her cousin; and ceasing to be jealous of Godolphin, he saw every thing to apprehend from the rank, the fortune, the figure of Delamere — from family connection, which would engage her to listen to him — from ambition, which his title would gratify — from her tenderness to Lady Westhaven, and from the return of that affection which she had, as he supposed, once felt for Lord Delamere himself.

But the more invincible the obstacles which he saw rising, appeared, the more satisfaction he thought there would be in conquering them. And to yield up his pretensions, on the first appearance of a formidable rival, was contrary to his enterprising spirit and his ideas of that glory, which he equally coveted in the service of the fair and of the French King.

With these sentiments of each other, the restraint and mistrust of every party impeded general or chearful conversation. Godolphin soon left the room, to commune with his own uneasy thoughts in a solitary walk; Lord Westhaven would then have taken out Bellozane, in order to give Lord Delamere an opportunity of being alone with his sister and Emmeline. But he was determined not to understand hints on that subject; and when his Lordship asked him to take an afternoon's walk, found means to refuse it. Afraid of leaving two such combustible spirits together, Lord Westhaven, to the great relief of Emmeline, staid with them till Delamere retired for the night.

But the behaviour of Bellozane to Emmeline, which was very particular, as if he wished it to be noticed, had extremely alarmed Delamere; and whenever they afterwards met, they surveyed each other with such haughty reserve, and their conversation bordered so nearly on hostility and defiance, that Emmeline, who expected every hour to see their animosity blaze out in a challenge, could support her uneasiness about it no longer; and sending early to speak to Lord Westhaven on the beginning of the second week of their stay, she represented to him her fears, and entreated him to prevail on the Chevalier to leave them and return to St. Alpin.

'I have attempted it already,' said he, 'but with so little success, that if I press it any farther I must quarrel with him myself. I know perfectly well that your fears have too much foundation; and that if we can neither separate or tranquillise these unquiet spirits, we shall have some disagreeable affair happen between them. I know nothing that can be done but your accepting at once your penitent cousin.'

'No, my Lord,' answered she, with an air of chagrin, 'that I will not do! I most ardently wish Lord Delamere well, and would do any thing to make him happy — except sacrificing my own happiness, and acting in opposition to my conscience.'

'Why, my dear Emmeline, how is this? You had once, surely, an affection for Delamere; and his offence against you, however great, admits of considerable alleviation. Consider all the pains that were taken to disunite you, and the importunity he suffered from his family. Surely, when you are convinced of his repentance you should restore him to your favour; and however you may be superior to considerations of fortune and rank, yet when they unite in a man otherwise unexceptionable they should have some weight.'

'They have none with me, upon my honour, my Lord. And since we have got upon this topic, I will be very explicit — I am determined on no account to marry Lord Delamere. But that I may give no room to charge me with caprice or coquetry (since your Lordship believes I once had so great a regard for him), or with that unforgiving temper which I see you are disposed to accuse me of, it is my fixed intention, if I obtain, by your Lordship's generous interposition, the Mowbray estate, to retire to Mowbray Castle, and never to marry at all.'

Lord Westhaven, at the solemnity and gravity with which she pronounced these words, began to laugh so immoderately, and to treat her resolution with ridicule so pointed, that he first made her almost angry, and then obliged her to laugh too. At length, however, she prevailed on him again to listen to her apprehensions about Delamere and Bellozane.

'Do not, my Lord, rally me so cruelly; but for Heaven's sake, before it is too late, prevent any more meetings between these two rash and turbulent young men. Why should the Chevalier de Bellozane stay here?'

'Because it is his pleasure. I do assure you seriously, my dear Miss Mowbray, that I have almost every day since we came hither attempted to send my fiery cousin back to St. Alpin. But my anxiety has only piqued him; and he determines more resolutely to stay because he sees my motive for wishing him gone. He is exactly the character which I have somewhere seen described by a French poet. — A young man who,

> 'leger impetueux,
> De soi meme rempli, jaloux, presomptueux,
> Bouillant dans ses passions; cedant a ses caprices;

Pour un peu de valeur, se passoit de tous ses vices.'

(Volatile — impetuous —
Full of himself — jealous — presumptuous —
Fiery in his passions; yielding to every caprice;
And who believes some courage an apology for all his vices.)

'Yet, among all his faults, poor Bellozane has some good qualities; and I am really sorry for this strange perseverance in an hopeless pursuit, because it prevents my asking him to England. I give you my honour, Emmeline,' continued his Lordship, in a more serious tone, 'that I have repeatedly represented to him the improbability of his success; but he answers that you have never positively dismissed him by avowing your preference to another; that he knows your engagement with Lord Delamere is dissolved, and that he considers himself at liberty to pursue you till you have decidedly chosen, or even till you are actually married. Nay, I doubt whether your being married would make any difference in the attentions of this eccentric and presuming Frenchman, for I do not consider Bellozane as a Swiss.'

'Well, but my dear Lord, if the Chevalier will persist in staying, I must determine to go. I see not that my remaining here will be attended with any good effects. It may possibly be the cause of infinite uneasiness to Lady Westhaven. Do, therefore, prevail upon her to let me go alone to St. Germains. When I am gone, Lord Delamere will think more of getting well than of forcing me into a new engagement. He will then soon be able to travel; and the Chevalier de Bellozane will return quietly to the Baron.'

'Why to speak ingenuously, Emmeline, it *does* appear to me that it were on every account more proper for you to be in England. Thither I wish you could hasten, before it will be possible for Lord Delamere, or indeed for my wife, who must travel slowly, to get thither. I do not know whether your travelling with us will be strictly proper, on other accounts; but if it were, it would be rendered uneasy to you by the company of these two mad headed boys; for Bellozane I am sure intends, if you accompany us, to go also.'

'What objection is there then to my setting out immediately for St. Germains, with Le Limosin and Madelon, if Lady Westhaven would but consent to it?'

'I can easily convince her of the necessity of it; but I foresee another objection that has escaped you.'

'What is that, my Lord?'

'That Bellozane will follow you.'

'Surely he will not attempt it?'

'Indeed I apprehend he will. I have no manner of influence over him; and he is here connected with a set of military men, who are the likeliest people in the world to encourage such an enterprize — and if at last this Paris should carry off our fair Helen!' —

'Nay, but my Lord do not ridicule my distress.'

'Well then, I will most seriously and gravely counsel you: and my advice is, that you set out as soon as you can get ready, and that my brother Godolphin escort you.'

Emmeline was conscious that she too much wished such an escort; yet fearing that her preference of him would engage Godolphin in a quarrel with Bellozane or Lord Delamere, perhaps with both, she answered, while the deepest blush dyed her cheeks —

'No, my Lord, I cannot — I mean not — I should be sorry to give Captain Godolphin the trouble of such a journey and I beg you not to think of it — '

'I shall speak to him of it, however.'

'I beg, my Lord — I intreat that you will not.'

'Here he is — and we will discuss the matter with him now.' Godolphin at this moment entered the room; and Lord Westhaven relating plainly all Emmeline's fears, and her wishes to put an end to them by quitting Besançon, added the proposal he had made, that Godolphin should take care of her till she joined Mrs. Stafford.

Tho' Godolphin saw in her apprehensions for the safety of Delamere, only a conviction of her tender regard for him, and considered his own attachment as every way desperate; yet he could not refuse himself, when it was thus offered him, the pleasure of being with her — the exquisite tho' painful delight of being useful to her. He therefore eagerly expressed the readiness, the happiness, with which he should undertake so precious a charge.

Emmeline, fearful of betraying her real sentiments, overacted the civil coldness with which she thought it necessary to refuse this offer. Godolphin, mortified and vexed at her manner as much as at her denial, ceased to press his services; and Lord Westhaven, who wondered what could be her objection, since of the honour and propriety of Godolphin's conduct he knew she could not doubt, seemed hurt at her rejection of his brother's friendly intention of waiting on her; and dropping the conversation, went away with Godolphin.

She saw that her conduct inevitably impressed on the mind of the latter a conviction of her returning regard for Delamere; and she feared that to Lord Westhaven it might appear to be the effect of vanity and coquetry.

'Perhaps he will think me,' said she, 'so vain as to suppose that Godolphin has also designs, and that therefore I decline his attendance; and coquet enough to wish for the pursuit of these men, whom I only affect to shun, and for that reason prefer going alone, to accepting the protection of his brother. Yet as *I* know the sentiments of Godolphin, which it appears Lord Westhaven does not, surely I had better suffer his ill opinion of me, than encourage Godolphin's hopes; which, till Delamere can be diverted from prosecuting his unwelcome addresses, will inevitably involve him in a dispute, and such a dispute as I cannot bear to think of.'

Uncertain what to do, another day passed; and on the following morning, while she waited for Lady Westhaven, she was addressed by Godolphin, who calmly and gravely enquired if she would honour him with any commands for England?

'Are you going then, Sir, before my Lord and Lady?'

'I am going, Madam, immediately.'

'By way of Paris?'

'Yes, Madam, to Havre; whence I shall get the quickest to Southampton, and to the Isle of Wight. I am uneasy at the entire solitude to which my absence condemns Adelina.'

'You have heard no unfavourable news, I hope, of Lady Adelina or your little boy?'

'None. But I am impatient to return to them.'

'As you are going immediately, Sir,' said Emmeline (making an effort to conquer a pain she felt rising in her bosom) 'I will not detain you by writing to Lady Adelina. Perhaps as it is possible — as I hope'—

She stopped. Godolphin looked anxious to hear what was possible, what she hoped.

'As I shall so soon, so very soon be in England, perhaps we may meet,' reassumed she, speaking very quick 'possibly I may have the happiness of seeing her Ladyship and dear little William.'

'To meet *you*,' replied Godolphin, very solemnly, 'Adelina shall leave her solitude; for certainly a journey to see her in it will hardly be undertaken by *Lady Delamere*.'

He then in the same tone wished her health and happiness till he saw her again, and left her.

He was no sooner gone, than she felt disposed to follow him and apologize for her having so coldly refused his offers of protection. Pride and timidity prevented her; but they could not stop her tears, which she was obliged to conceal by hurrying to her own room. Lady Westhaven soon after sent for her to a late breakfast: she found Lord Delamere there; but heard that Godolphin was gone.

Soon after breakfast, Lady Westhaven and her brother, (who could not yet obtain a clear intermission of the fever which hung about him, and who continued extremely weak,) went out together for an airing; and Lord Westhaven, unusually grave, was left reading in the room with Emmeline.

He laid down his book. 'So,' said he, 'William is flown away from us.'

It was a topic on which Emmeline did not care to trust her voice.

'I wish you could have determined to have gone with him.'

'I wish, my Lord, I could have reconciled it to my ideas of propriety; since certainly I should have been happy and safe in such an escort; and since, without any at all, I must, in a day or two, go.'

'I believe it will be best. Lord Delamere is no better; and Bellozane has no thought of leaving us entirely, tho' his military friends take up so much of his time that he is luckily less with Delamere. Lord Delamere has again, Miss Mowbray, been imploring me to apply to you. He wishes you only to hear him. He complains that you fly from him, and will not give him an opportunity of entering on his justification.'

'I am extremely concerned at Lord Delamere's unhappiness. But I must repeat that I require of his Lordship no justification; that I most sincerely forgive him if he supposes he has injured me; but that as to any proposals such as he once honoured me with, I am absolutely resolved never to listen to them; and I entreat him to believe that any future application on the subject must be entirely fruitless.'

'Poor young man!' said Lord Westhaven. 'However you must consent to see him alone, and tell him so yourself; for from me he will not believe you so very inflexible — so very cruel.'

'I am inflexible, my Lord, but surely not cruel. The greatest cruelty of which I could be guilty, either to Lord Delamere or myself, would be to accept his offers, feeling as I feel, and thinking as I think.'

'I do not know how we shall get him to England, or what will be done with him when he is there.'

'He will do well, my Lord. Doubt it not.'

'Upon my honour I *do* doubt it! It is to me astonishing that a young man so volatile, so high-spirited as Delamere, should be capable of an attachment at once so violent and so steady.'

'Steady! — Has your Lordship forgotten Miss Otley?'

'His wavering then was, you well know, owing to some evil impressions he had received of you; which, tho' he refuses to tell me the particulars, he assures me were conveyed and confirmed with so much art, that a more dispassionate and cooler lover would have believed them without enquiry. How then can you wonder at *his* petulant and eager spirit seizing on probable circumstances, which his jealousy and apprehension immediately converted into conviction? As soon as he knew these suspicions were groundless, did he not fly to implore your pardon; and hasten, even at the hazard of his life, to find and appease you? Such is the present situation of his mind and of his health, that I very seriously assure you I doubt whether he will survive your total rejection.'

Emmeline, unable to answer this speech gravely, without betraying the very great concern it gave her, assumed a levity she did not feel.

'Your Lordship,' said she, 'is disposed to think thus, from the warm and vehement manner in which Lord Delamere is accustomed to express himself. If he is really unhappy, I am very sorry; but I am persuaded time, and the more fortunate alliance which he is solicited to form, will effect a cure. Don't think me unfeeling if I answer your melancholy prophecy in the words of Rosalind —

'Men have died from time to time, and worms have eaten them — but not for love.'

She then ran away, and losing all her forced spirits the moment she was alone, gave way to tears. She fancied they flowed entirely for the unhappiness of poor Delamere, and for her uncertain situation. But tho' the former uneasiness deeply affected her sensible heart, many of the tears she shed were because Godolphin was gone, and she knew not when she should again see him.

Godolphin, repining and wretched, pursued his way to Paris. He thought that Emmeline's coldness and reserve were meant to put an end to any hopes he might have entertained; and that her reconciliation and marriage with Lord Delamere must inevitably take place as soon as she had, by her dissimulated cruelty, punished him for his rashness and his errors. His daily observation confirmed him in this opinion: he saw, that in place of her candid and ingenuous manners, a studied conduct was adopted, which concealed her real sentiments — sentiments which he concluded to be all in favour of Delamere. And finding that he could not divest himself of his passion for her, he thought that it was a weakness, if not a crime, to indulge it in her presence, while it imposed on himself an insupportable torment; and that, by quitting her, he should at least conceal his hopeless attachment, and save himself the misery of seeing her actually married to Lord Delamere. He determined, therefore, to tear himself away; and to punish himself for the premature expectations with which he had begun his journey to St. Alpin, by shutting himself up at East Cliff (his house in the Isle of Wight) and refusing himself the sight of her, of whom it would be sufficient misery to think, when she had given herself to her favoured and fortunate lover.

Full of these reflections, Godolphin continued his road, intending to take the passage boat at Havre. But at the hotel he frequented at Paris, he met a gentleman of his acquaintance who was going the next day to England by way of Calais; and as he had his own post chaise, and only his valet with him, he told Godolphin that if he would take a place in his chaise he would send his servant post. This offer Godolphin accepted; and altering his original design, went with his friend to Calais to cross to England.

CHAPTER VII

IT was now impossible for Emmeline to avoid a conversation with Lord Delamere, which his sister urged her so earnestly to allow him. Bellozane was, by the French officers, with whom he principally lived, engaged out for two days; and Lord and Lady Westhaven easily found opportunity to leave Emmeline with Delamere.

He was no sooner alone in her presence, than he threw himself on his knees before her — 'Will you,' cried he, 'Ah! will you still refuse to hear and to forgive me? Have I offended beyond all hopes of pardon?'

'No, my Lord. — I do most readily and truly forgive every offence, whether real or imaginary, that you believe you have committed against me.'

'You forgive me — But to what purpose? — Only to plunge me yet deeper into wretchedness. You forgive me — but you despise, you throw me from you for ever. Ah! rather continue to be angry, than distract me by a pardon so cold and careless!'

'If your Lordship will be calm — if you will rise, and hear me with temper, I will be very explicit with you; but while you yield to these extravagant transports, I cannot explain all I wish you to understand; and must indeed beg to be released from a conversation so painful to me, and to you so prejudicial.'

Delamere rose and took a chair.

'I need not, Sir,' said Emmeline, collecting all her courage, 'recall to your memory the time so lately passed, when I engaged to become yours, if at the expiration of a certain period Lord and Lady Montreville consented, and you still remained disposed to bestow on me the honour of your name.'

'What am I to expect,' cried Delamere, eagerly interrupting her — 'Ah! what am I to expect from a preface so cold and cruel? You have indeed no occasion to recall to my memory those days when I was allowed to look forward to that happiness, which now, thro' the villainy of others, and my own madness and ideotism, I have lost. But, Madam, it must not, it cannot be so easily relinquished! By heaven I will not give you up! — and if but for a moment I thought — '

'You seemed just now, Sir, disposed to hear me with patience. Since, however, you cannot even for a few minutes forbear these starts of passion, I really am unequal to the task of staying with you.'

She would then have hastened away; but Delamere forcibly detained her, again protested he would be calm, and again she went on.

'At that time, I will own to you, that without any prepossession, almost without a wish either to accept or decline the very high honour you offered me, I was content to engage myself to be your wife; because you said such an engagement would make *you* happy, and because I then knew not that it would render *me* otherwise.'

'Was you even then thus indifferent? Had I no place in your heart, Madam, when you would have given me your hand?'

'Yes, Sir — you had then the place I now willingly restore to you. I esteemed you; I looked upon you with a sisterly affection; and had I married you, it would have been rather to have made you happy, than because I had any wish to form other ties than those by which our relationship and early acquaintance had connected us.'

'Ah! my angelic Emmeline! it will still make me happy! Let the reasons which then influenced you, again plead for me; and forget, O! forget all that has passed since my headlong folly urged me to insult and forsake you!'

'Alas! my Lord, that is not in my power! You have cancelled the engagements that subsisted between us; and, as I understand, have actually formed others more indissoluble, with a lady of high rank and of immense fortune — one whose alliance is as anxiously courted by your family, as mine is despised. Can your Lordship again fly from your promises? Can you quit at pleasure the affluent and high-born heiress as you quitted the deserted and solitary orphan?'

'Cursed, cursed cruelty!' exclaimed Delamere, speaking thro' his shut teeth — 'But go on, Madam! I deserve your severity, and must bear your reproaches! Yet surely you know that but for the machinations of those execrable Crofts', I should never have acted as I did — you know, that however destitute of fortune chance had made you, I preferred you to all those who might have brought me wealth!'

'I acknowledge your generosity, Sir, and on that head meant not to reproach. I merely intended to represent to you what you seem to have forgotten — that were I disposed to restore you the hand you so lately renounced, you could not take it; since Miss Otley will certainly not relinquish the claim you have given her to your regard.'

'You are misinformed. — I am under no engagement to Miss Otley. — I am not by heaven! by all that is sacred!'

'Were not all preparations for your marriage in great forwardness, Sir, when you left England? and must not your consent have been previously obtained before Lord Montreville would have made them? However, to put an end to all uncertainty, I must tell you, my Lord, with a sincerity which will probably be displeasing to you, that my affections —'

'Are no longer in your own power!' cried he, hastily interrupting her — 'Speak, Madam — is it not so?'

'I did not say that, Sir. I was going to assure you that I now find it impossible to command them — impossible to feel for you that preference, without which I should think myself extremely culpable were I to give you my hand.'

'I understand you, Madam! You give that preference to another. The Chevalier de Bellozane has succeeded to your affections. He has doubtless made good use of the opportunities he has had to conciliate your favour; but before he carries his good fortune farther, he must discuss with me the right by which he pretends to it.'

'Whether he has or has not a right to pretend to my regard, Sir,' said Emmeline, with great spirit, 'this causeless jealousy, so immediately after you have been convinced of the fallacy of your supposition in regard to another person, convinces me, that had I unfortunately given you an exclusive claim to my friendship and affection, my whole life would have been embittered by suspicion, jealousy, and caprice. Recollect, my Lord, that I have said nothing of the Chevalier de Bellozane, nor have you the least reason to believe I have for him those sentiments you are pleased to impute to me.'

'But can I doubt it!' exclaimed Delamere, rising, and walking in an agony — 'Can I doubt it, when I have heard you disclaim me for ever! — when you have told me your affections are no longer in your power!'

'No, Sir; my meaning was, what I now repeat — that as my near relation, as my friend, as the brother of Lady Westhaven, I shall ever esteem and regard you; but that I cannot command now in your favour those sentiments which should induce me to accept of you as my husband. What is past cannot be recalled; and tho' I am most truly concerned to see you unhappy, my determination is fixed and I must abide by it.'

'Death and hell!' cried the agonized Delamere — 'It is all over then! You utterly disclaim me, and hardly think it worth while to conceal from me for whose sake I am disclaimed!'

Emmeline was terrified to find that he still persisted in imputing her estrangement from him to her partiality for Bellozane; foreseeing that he would immediately fly to him, and that all she apprehended must follow.

'I beg, I entreat, Lord Delamere, that you will understand that I give no preference to Mr. de Bellozane. I will not only assure you of that, but I disclaim all intention of marriage whatever! Suffer me, my Lord, to entreat that you will endeavour to calm your mind and regain your health. Reflect on the cruel uncertainty in which you have left the Marquis and the Marchioness; reflect on the uneasy situation in which you keep Lord and Lady Westhaven, and on the great injury you do yourself; and resolutely attempt, in the certainty of succeeding, to divest yourself of a fatal partiality, which has hitherto produced only misery to you and to your family.'

'Oh! most certainly, most certainly!' cried Delamere, almost choaked with passion — 'I shall undoubtedly make all these wise reflections; and after having gone thro' a proper course of them, shall, possibly, with great composure, see you in the arms of that presumptuous coxcomb — that vain, supercilious Frenchman! — that detested Bellozane! No, Madam! no! you may certainly give yourself to him, but assure yourself I live not to see it!'

He flew out of the room at these words, tho' she attempted to stop and to appease him. Her heart bled at the wounds she had yet thought it necessary to inflict; and she was at once grieved and terrified at his menacing and abrupt departure. She immediately went herself after Lord Westhaven, to intreat him to keep Bellozane and Delamere apart. His Lordship was much disturbed at what had passed, which Emmeline faithfully related to him: Bellozane was still out of town; and Lord Westhaven, who now apprehended that on Delamere's meeting him he would immediately insult him, said he would consider what could be done to prevent their seeing each other 'till Delamere became more reasonable. On enquiry, he found that the Chevalier was certainly engaged with his companions 'till the next day. He therefore came back to Emmeline about an hour after he had left her, and told her that he thought it best for her to set out that afternoon on her way to St. Germains.

'You will by this means make it difficult for Bellozane to overtake you, if he should attempt it; and when he sees you have actually fled from Delamere, he will be little disposed to quarrel with him, and will perhaps go home. As to Delamere, his sister and I must manage him as well as we can; which will be the easier, as he is, within this half hour, gone to bed in a violent access of fever. Indeed, in the perturbation of mind he now suffers, there is no probability of his speedy amendment; for as fast as he regains strength, his violent passions throw his frame again into disorder. — But perhaps when he knows you are actually in England, he may try to acquire, by keeping himself quiet, that share of health which alone can enable him to follow you.'

Emmeline, eagerly embracing this advice, which she found had the concurrence of Lady Westhaven, prepared instantly for her departure; and embracing tenderly her two excellent friends, who hoped soon to follow her, and who had desired her to come to them to reside as soon as they were settled in London, where they had no house at present, she got into a chaise, with Madelon, and attended by Le Limosin, who was proudly elated at being thus '*l'homme de confience*' to Mademoiselle Mowbray she left Besançon; her heart deeply impressed with a sense of Delamere's sufferings, and with an earnest wish for the restoration of his peace.

Tho' Godolphin had been gone four days, and went post, so that she knew he must be at Paris long before her, she could not, as she proceeded on her journey, help fancying that some accident might have stopped him, and that she might overtake him. She knew not whether she hoped or feared such an encounter. But the disappointed air with which she left every post house where she had occasion to stop for horses, plainly evinced that she rather desired than dreaded it. She felt all the absurdity and ridicule of expecting to see him; yet still she looked out after him; and he was the object she sought when she cast her eyes round her at the several stages.

Without overtaking him, or being herself overtaken by Bellozane, she arrived in safety and in the usual time at Paris, and immediately went on to St. Germains; Le Limousin being so well acquainted with travelling, that she had no trouble nor alarm during her journey.

When she got to St. Germains, she was received with transport by Mrs. Stafford and her family. She found her about to depart, in two days, for England, where there was a prospect of settling her husband's affairs; and she had undertaken to go alone over, in hopes of adjusting them for his speedy return; while he had agreed to remain with the children 'till he heard the success of her endeavours. Great was the satisfaction of Mrs. Stafford to find that Emmeline would accompany her to England; with yet more pleasure did she peruse those documents which convinced her that her fair friend went to claim, with an absolute certainty of success, her large paternal fortune.

Lord Westhaven had given her a long letter to the Marquis of Montreville, to whom he desired she would immediately address herself; and he had also written to an eminent lawyer, his friend, into whose hands he directed her immediately to put the papers that related to her birth, and by no means to trust them with any other person.

With money, also, Lord Westhaven had amply furnished her; and she proposed taking lodgings in London, 'till she could settle her affairs with Lord Montreville; and then to go to Mowbray Castle.

On the second day after her reaching St. Germains, she began her journey to Calais with Mrs. Stafford, attended by Le Limosin and Madelon. When they arrived there, they heard that a passage boat would sail about nine o'clock in the evening; but on sending Le Limosin to speak to the master, they learned that there were already more cabin passengers than there was room to accommodate, and that therefore two ladies might find it inconvenient.

As the evening, however, was calm, and the wind favourable, and as the two fair travellers were impatient to be in England, they determined to go on board. It was near ten o'clock before the vessel got under way; and before two they were assured they should be at Dover. They therefore hesitated not to pass that time in chairs on the deck, wrapped in their cloaks; and would have preferred doing so, to the heat and closeness of the cabin, had there been room for them in it.

By eleven o'clock, every thing insensibly grew quiet on board. The passengers were gone to their beds, the vessel moved calmly, and with very little wind, over a gently swelling sea; and the silence was only broken by the waves rising against its side, or by the steersman, who now and then spoke to another sailor, that slowly traversed the deck with measured pace.

The night was dark; a declining moon only broke thro' the heavy clouds of the horizon with a feeble and distant light. There was a solemnity in the scene at once melancholy and pleasing. Mrs. Stafford and Emmeline both felt it. They were silent; and each lost in her own reflections; nor did they attend to a slight interruption of the stillness that reigned on board, made by a passenger who came from below, muffled in a great coat. He spoke in a low voice to the man at the helm, and then sat down on the gunwale, with his back towards the ladies; after which all was again quiet.

In a few minutes a deep sigh was uttered by this passenger; and then, after a short pause, the two friends were astonished to hear, in a voice low, but extremely expressive, these lines, addressed to Night.

SONNET

I love thee, mournful sober-suited Night,
When the faint Moon, yet lingering in her wane
And veil'd in clouds, with pale uncertain light
Hangs o'er the waters of the restless main.

In deep depression sunk, the enfeebled mind
Will to the deaf, cold elements complain,
And tell the embosom'd grief, however vain,
To sullen surges and the viewless wind.

Tho' no repose on thy dark breast I find,
I still enjoy thee — chearless as thou art;
For in thy quiet gloom, the exhausted heart,
Is calm, tho' wretched hopeless, yet resign'd.
While, to the winds and waves, its sorrows given,
May reach — tho' lost on earth — the ear of heaven!

'Surely,' said Mrs. Stafford in a whisper, 'it is a voice I know.'

'Surely,' repeated the heart of Emmeline, for she could not speak, 'it is the voice of Godolphin!'

'Do you,' reassumed Mrs. Stafford — 'do you not recollect the voice?'

'Yes,' replied Emmeline, 'I think — I believe — I rather fancy it is — Mr. Godolphin.'

'Shall I speak to him?' asked Mrs. Stafford, 'or are you disposed to hear more poetry? He has no notion who are his auditors.'

'As you please,' said Emmeline.

Again the person sighed, and repeated with more warmth —

> 'And reach, tho' lost on earth — the ear of heaven!'

'Yes — if *she* is happy, they will indeed be heard! Ah! that cruel *if* — *if* she is happy! and can I bear to doubt it, yet leave her to the experiment!'

There now remained no doubt but that the stranger was Godolphin; and Emmeline as little hesitated to believe herself the subject of his thoughts and of his Muse.

'Why do *you* not speak to him, Emmeline?' said Mrs. Stafford archly.

'I cannot, indeed.'

'I must speak then, myself;' and raising her voice; she said —'Mr. Godolphin, is it not?'

'Who is so good as to recollect me?' cried he, rising and looking round him. It was very dark; but he could just distinguish that two ladies were there.

Mrs. Stafford gave him her hand, saying — 'Have you then forgotten your friends?'

He snatched her hand, and carried it to his lips.

'There is another hand for you,' said she, pointing to Emmeline — 'but you must be at the trouble of taking it.'

'That I shall be most delighted to do. But who is it? Surely it cannot be Miss Mowbray, that allows me such happiness?'

'Have you, in one little week,' said the faultering Emmeline, 'occasion to ask that question?'

'Not now I hear that voice,' answered Godolphin in the most animated tone — 'Not when I hold this lovely hand. But whence comes it that I find you, Madam, here? or how does it happen that you have left my brother and sister, and the happy Delamere?' He seemed to have recollected, after his first transport at meeting her, that he was thus warmly addressing *her* who was probably only going to England to prepare for her union with his rival.

'Do not be so unreasonable,' said Mrs. Stafford, 'as to expect Miss Mowbray should answer all these questions. But find a seat; and let us hear some account of yourself. You have also to make your peace with me for not seeing me in your way.'

Godolphin threw himself on the deck at their feet.

'I find a seat here,' said he, 'which I should prefer to a throne. As to an account of myself, it is soon given. I met a friend, whose company induced me to come to Calais rather than travel thro' Normandy; and the haste he was in made it impossible for me to stop him. Miss Mowbray had refused to give me any commission for you; and I had nothing to say to you that would have given you any pleasure. I was, therefore, unwilling to trouble you merely with a passing enquiry.'

'But whence comes it that you sail only to-night, if your friend was so much hurried?'

'He went four days ago; but I — I was kept — I was detained at Calais.'

Emmeline felt a strange curiosity to know what could have detained him; but dared not ask such a question.

They then talked of Lord and Lady Westhaven.

'Lord Delamere is, I conclude, much better?' said Godolphin.

'When I took leave of Lord and Lady Westhaven,' coldly answered Emmeline, 'I did not think him much better than when we first saw him. His servant said he was almost as ill as when you, Sir, with friendship so uncommon, attended him.'

'Call it not uncommon, Madam! — It was an office I would have performed, not only for any Englishman in another country, but I hope for any human being in any country, who had needed it. Should I then allow you to suppose there was any great merit in my rendering a slight service to the brother of Lady Westhaven; and who is besides *dear to one* to whom I owe obligations so infinite.'

The stress he laid on these words left Emmeline no doubt of his meaning. She was, however, vexed and half angry that he persisted in believing her so entirely attached to Delamere; and, for the first time she had ventured to think steadily on the subject, meditated how to undeceive him. Yet when she reflected on the character of Delamere; and remembered that his father would now claim an authority to controul her actions — that one would think himself at liberty to call any man to an account who addressed her, and the other to refuse his consent to any other marriage than that which would be now so advantageous to the family — she saw only inquietude to herself, and hazard to the life so dear to her, should she suffer the passion of Godolphin openly to be avowed.

'Is it not remarkable,' said Mrs. Stafford, 'that you should voluntarily have conducted us to France, and by chance escort us home?'

'Yes,' answered Godolphin. — 'And a chance so fortunate for me I should think portended some good, was I sanguine, and had I any faith in omens.'

'Are you going immediately to London?'

'Immediately.'

'And from thence to East Cliff?'

'I believe I shall be obliged to stay in town a week or ten days. — But my continuance there shall be longer, if you or Miss Mowbray will employ me.'

The night now grew cold; and the dew fell so heavily, that Mrs. Stafford expressed her apprehensions that Emmeline would find some ill effects from it, and advised her to go down.

'Oh! no,' said Godolphin, with uncommon anxiety in his manner — 'do not go down. There are so many passengers in the cabin, and it is so close, that you will find it extremely disagreeable. It will not now be half an hour before we see the lights of Dover; and we shall presently be on shore.'

Emmeline, who really apprehended little from cold, acquiesced; and they continued to converse on general topics 'till they landed.

Godolphin saw them on shore immediately, and attended them to the inn. He then told them he must go back to see after the baggage, and left them hastily. They ordered a slight refreshment; and when it was brought in, Emmeline said — 'Shall we not wait for Mr. Godolphin?'

'The Gentleman is come in, Madam,' said the waiter, 'with another lady, and is assisting her up stairs. Would you please I should call him?'

Emmeline felt, without knowing the nature of the sensation, involuntary curiosity and involuntary uneasiness.

'No, do not call him,' said Mrs. Stafford — 'I suppose he will be here immediately. But send the French servant to us.'

Le Limosin attending, she gave him some requisite orders, and then again enquired for Captain Godolphin.

Le Limosin answered, that he was gone to assist a lady to her room, who had been very ill during the passage.

'Of which nation is she, Le Limosin?'

'I am ignorant of that, Madam, as I have not heard her speak. *Monsieur Le Capitaine* is very sorry for her, and has attended her the whole way, only the little time he was upon deck.'

'Is she a young lady?' enquired Mrs. Stafford.

'Yes, very young and pretty.'

The curiosity of Mrs. Stafford was now, in spite of herself, awakened. And the long stay Godolphin made, gave to Emmeline such acute uneasiness, as she had never felt before. It is extraordinary surely, said she to herself, that he should be thus anxious about an acquaintance made in a pacquet boat.

She grew more and more disturbed at his absence; and was hardly able to conceal her vexation from Mrs. Stafford, while she was ashamed of discovering it even to herself. In about ten minutes, which had appeared to her above an hour, Godolphin came in, apologised, without accounting, for his stay, and while they made all together a slight repast, enquired how they intended to proceed to London and at what time.

On hearing that they thought of setting out about noon, in a chaise, he proposed their taking a post coach; 'and then,' added he, 'you may suffer me to occupy the fourth place.' To this Mrs. Stafford willingly agreed; and Emmeline, glad to find that at least he did not intend waiting on his pacquet boat acquaintance to London, retired with somewhat less uneasiness than she had felt on her first hearing that he had brought such an acquaintance on shore.

After a few hours' sleep, the fair travellers arose to continue their journey. They heard that Mr. Godolphin had long left his room, and was at breakfast with the lady whom he had been so careful of the preceding morning. At this intelligence Emmeline felt all her anxiety revive; and when he came into the room where they were to speak to them, hardly could she command herself to answer him without betraying her emotion.

'Miss Mowbray is fatigued with her voyage,' said he, tenderly approaching her — 'The night air I am afraid has affected her health?'

'No, Sir;' coldly and faintly answered Emmeline.

'How is the young lady you was so good as to assist on shore, Sir?' said Mrs. Stafford. 'I understand she was ill.'

Godolphin blushed; and replied, with some little embarrassment, 'she is better, Madam, I thank you.'

'So,' thought Emmeline, 'he makes then no mystery of having an interest in this lady.'

'Are you acquainted with her?' enquired Mrs. Stafford.

'Yes.'

Politeness would not admit of another question: yet it was impossible to help wishing to ask it. Godolphin, however, turned the discourse, and soon afterwards went out. Emmeline felt ready to cry, yet knew not for what, and dreaded to ask herself whether she had not admitted into her heart the tormenting passion of jealousy.

'Why should I be displeased,' said she. Why should I be unhappy? Mr. Godolphin believes me attached to Delamere, and he ceased to think of me, wherefore should I lament that he thinks of another; or what right have I to enquire into his actions — what right have I to blame them?'

The post coach was now ready. Emmeline, attended by Madelon, Mrs. Stafford, and Godolphin, got into it, and a lively and animated conversation was carried on between the two latter. Emmeline, in the approaching interview with her uncle, and in the wretchedness of Delamere, which she never ceased to lament, had employment enough for her thoughts; but in spite of herself they flew perpetually from those subjects to the acquaintance which Captain Godolphin had brought with him from Calais.

CHAPTER VIII

WHEN they arrived at Canterbury, the ladies were shewn into a parlour, where Godolphin did not join them for near half an hour. Emmeline had accounted for her lowness of spirits by her dread of meeting her uncle on such terms as they were likely to meet; but Mrs. Stafford knew the human heart too well to be ignorant that here was another and a concealed source of that melancholy which overwhelmed her. It was in vain she had attempted to dissemble. It was, to her friend, evident, that her compassion, her good wishes, were Delamere's, but that her heart was wholly Godolphin's, and was now pierced with the poignant thorns of new-born jealousy and anxious mistrust.

While they waited together the return of Godolphin, Mrs. Stafford said — 'I fancy that post chaise that passed us about half an hour ago, contained Mr. Godolphin's *acquaintance*.'

'Did it? Why do you think so?'

'Because he looked after it so earnestly; and there seemed to be only a young woman in it.'

'I did not observe it indeed,' replied Emmeline, with the appearance of carelessness.

'I should like to see her nearer,' continued Mrs. Stafford, with some archness — 'By the glympse I had of her she appeared to be very handsome.'

'Do you think she is a French woman?' enquired Emmeline, still affecting great indifference.

'No, she appeared to be English. But if you please I will enquire of him?'

'I beg you will not,' in an half angry tone, answered Emmeline — 'I am sure it is very immaterial.'

At this moment Godolphin entered; and with looks of uneasiness apologized for his long stay. 'I have an awkward embarrassment,' said he, 'on my hands: a poor young woman, who is wholly a stranger in this country, and whom I have undertaken to conduct to London; but she is so ill that I am afraid she is unfit to go on — Yet how to leave her here I know not.'

'Pray, Sir,' said Emmeline, 'do not let us be any restraint to you. If your presence is necessary to the lady, you had surely better continue with her, than put her to any inconvenience to go on.'

Godolphin, who was at once pleased and pained by the quickness with which she spoke, said — 'I will tell you, my dear Miss Mowbray, very ingenuously, that if I were quite sure the character of this unhappy young woman is such as may entitle her to yours and Mrs. Stafford's protection, I should without scruple have asked it. I know,' continued he, looking distressed, 'how compassionate and good you both are; but I ought not therefore to hazard improperly taxing such generosity and sensibility.'

'Who is this young person, Sir?' asked Mrs. Stafford.

'If it will not tire you I will tell you. On my arrival at Calais this day se'nnight, I found all the pacquet boats on the other side, and was obliged to wait with my friend Cleveland a whole day. As I was sauntering about the streets after dinner, I passed by an Englishman whose face I thought I recollected. The man looked confused, and took off his hat; and I then perfectly remembered him to have been one of the best sailors I had on board in the West Indies, where he received a dangerous wound in the arm.

'I stopped, and asked him by what accident he came to Calais, and why his appearance was no better; for his honest hard features seemed pinched with want, his dress was shabby, his person meagre, and his look dejected.

' 'I am ashamed to tell you, Captain,' said he, 'how I came hither; but in short because I could not live at home. You know I got prize money when I served under your honour. Mayhap I might have managed it better; but howsomdever 'tis gone, and there's an end on't. So as we are all turned adrift in the world, some of my ship mates advised me to try a little matter of smuggling with them, and come over here. I have lived among these Frenchmen now these two months, and can, to be sure, just live; but rot 'em, if I could get any thing to do at home, I wouldn't stay another hour, for I hates 'em all, as your honour very well knows. A lucky voyage or two will put some money mayhap in my way, with this smuggling trade; and then I reckons to cross over home once for all, and so go down to Liverpool to my friends, if any one um be alive yet.' '

'I reproved my acquaintance severely for his proceeding, and told him, that to enable him to go to his friends, I would supply him with money to buy him cloaths, which I found he principally wanted; being ashamed to appear among his relations so ill equipped, after having received a considerable sum in prize money.

'The poor fellow appeared to be very grateful, and assured me that to prove his sincerity he would embark in the same pacquet boat. 'But Lord, Captain,' added he, 'I be'nt the only Englishman who stays in this rascally country agin their will — your honour remembers Lieutenant Stornaway, on board your honour's ship?' '

'Aye, to be sure I do.'

' 'Well; he, poor lad, is got into prison here for debt, and there I reckon he'll die; for nobody that ever gets into one of their confounded jails in this country, ever gets out again.' '

'As I perfectly remembered Stornaway, a gallant and spirited young Scotsman, I was much hurt at this account, and asked if I could be admitted to see him. I found it attended with infinite difficulty, and that I must apply to so many different persons before I could be allowed to see my unfortunate countryman, that the pacquet boat of the next day must sail without me. Cleveland therefore departed; and I, with long attendance on the Commandant and other officers, was at length introduced into the prison. I will not shock you with a description of it, nor with the condition in which I found the poor young man; who seemed to me likely to escape, by death, from the damp and miserable dungeon where he lay, without necessary food, without air, and without hope of relief. He related to me his sorrowful and simple tale. He was brought up to the sea; had no friends able to assist him; and on being discharged, after the peace, had gone, with what money he received, and on half pay, to France, in hopes of being able to live at less expence than in England, and to learn, at the same time, a language so necessary in his profession.

‘ ‘And for some time,’ said he, ‘I did pretty well; till going with one of my countrymen to see a relation of his, who was (tho’ born of Scots parents) brought up as a pensioner in a convent, and a Catholic, I was no longer my own master, and tho’ I knew that it was almost impossible for me to support a wife, I yet rashly married, and have made one of the loveliest young creatures in the world a beggar.

‘ ‘She was totally destitute of fortune; and was afraid her friends, who were but distant relations, and people of rank in Scotland, would insist on her taking the veil, as the most certain and easiest means of providing for her. She had a decided aversion to a monastic life; and poor as I was, (for I did not attempt to deceive her,) hesitated not to quit her convent with me, which it was easy enough to do by the management of her relation, with whom she was allowed to go out. We set out, therefore, together for England. I had about twenty Louis in my pocket, which would have carried us thither comfortably: but calamity overtook us by the way. We travelled in stages and diligences, as we found cheapest; in one of which I imagined my poor girl caught the infection of the small pox, with which she fell ill at Amiens. I attended her with all the agonizing fear of a wretch who sees his only earthly good on the point of being torn from him for ever; and very, very ill she was for many days and nights. Yet her lovely face was spared; and in a month I saw her quite out of danger, but still too weak to travel. As I spared nothing that could contribute to her ease or her recovery, my money was dreadfully diminished, and I had barely enough left to carry me alone to England. But as our credit was yet good, I purposed our living on it till her strength was somewhat re-established, and that I would then go to England, get a supply of money, and return to pay my debts and fetch my wife.

' 'This was the only expedient," said poor Stornaway, 'that I could think of, and perhaps was the very worst I could have adopted; since by this means we insensibly got into debt, and to creditors the most inexorable.

' 'At the end of three weeks, my wife was tolerably well. I divided with her the money I had left, and went off in the night to Calais, flattering myself I should return to her within a fortnight. But so vigilant were those to whom I owed money, and so active the *maréchaussés*, that I was pursued, and thrown, without hesitation and without appeal, into this prison; where my little remaining money, being all exhausted in fees, to save me from even worse treatment, I have now lain near six weeks in the situation in which you see me. As to myself,' continued the poor young man, 'my life has been a life of hardship, and I have learned to hold it as nothing; but when I reflect on what must have been the condition of my Isabel, I own to you, dear Sir, that my fortitude forsakes me, and the blackest despair takes possession of my soul.' '

'I had but little occasion to deliberate,' said Godolphin, continuing his narrative — 'had but little occasion to deliberate. I enquired into the debt. It was a trifle. I blushed to think, that while Englishmen were daily passing thro' the place in pursuit of pleasure, a gentleman, an officer of their nation, languished for such a sum in the horrors of a confinement so dreadful. The debt was easily discharged; and I took the unhappy Stornaway to my lodgings, from whence he was eagerly flying to Amiens, when I was called aside by one of the *maréchaussés*, who desired to speak to me.

' 'Sir,' said the man, 'you have been generous to me, and I will hazard telling you a secret. Orders are coming to stop your friend, whom you have released from prison, for stealing a pensioner out of a convent. Get him off to England immediately, or he will be taken, and perhaps confined for life.' '

'I hastened Stornaway instantly into a boat, and sent him after a pacquet which had just sailed, and which I saw him overtake. He conjured me, in an agony of despair, to enquire for his wife, without whom he said he could not live, and that rather than attempt it, he would return and perish in prison. I promised all he desired; and as soon as I was sure he was safe, I set out post for Amiens, where I found the poor young woman in a situation to which no words can do justice. She had parted with almost every thing for her support; and was overwhelmed by the weight of misfortunes, which, young and inexperienced as she was, she had neither the means to soften or the fortitude to bear. I brought her away to Calais, and embarked with her yesterday, having only staid long enough to furnish her with cloaths, and to recruit her enfeebled frame after her journey. But sea sickness, added to her former ill state of health, has reduced her to a condition of deplorable weakness. She speaks so little English that she is unable to travel alone; and I was in hopes that by her chaise keeping up with the coach, I might have assisted her on the road; but she is now so extremely ill that I am afraid she must remain here.'

During the first part of this short account, Emmeline, charmed more than ever with Godolphin, and ashamed of having for a moment entertained a suspicion to the disadvantage of such a man, sat silent; but at the conclusion of it, her eyes overflowed with tears; she felt something that told her she ought to apologize to him for the error she had been guilty of — tho' of that error he knew nothing; and impelled by an involuntary impulse, she held out her hand to him. — Dear, generous, noble-minded Godolphin! was uttered by her heart, but her lips only echoed, the last word.

'Godolphin!' said she, 'let us go to this poor young creature — let us see her ourselves.'

'Certainly we will,' cried Mrs. Stafford; 'and indeed, Sir, you ought to have told us before, that we might sooner have offered all the assistance in our power.'

'I was afraid,' answered he. 'I knew not whether I might not be deceived in the character of Mrs. Stornaway; and dared not intrude upon you, lest it should be found that the object merited not your good offices.'

'But she is in distress!' said Emmeline — 'she is a stranger! — and shall we hesitate? — '

Godolphin, who found in the tenderness of her address to him, and in the approbation her eyes expressed, a reward as sweet as that which the consciousness of doing good afforded from his own heart; kissed the hand she had given him, in silence, and then went to enquire if the poor young woman could see the ladies. She expressed her joy at being so favoured, and Mrs. Stafford and Emmeline were introduced.

The compassion they expressed, and the assurances they gave her that she would meet her husband in London, and that she should stay with them 'till she did, calmed and composed her; and as her illness was merely owing to fatigue and anxiety, they believed a few hours rest, now her mind was easier, would restore her. Tho' they were impatient to get on to London, they yet hesitated not to remain at Canterbury all night, on the account of this poor stranger. Godolphin, on hearing their determination, warmly thanked them: the heart of Emmeline was at once eased of its inquietude, and impressed with a deeper sense than ever of Godolphin's worth: she gave way, almost for the first time, to her tenderness and esteem, without attempting to check or conceal her sentiments; while Mrs. Stafford, who ardently wished to see her in possession of her estate and married to Godolphin, rejoiced in observing her to be less reserved; and Godolphin himself, hardly believing the happiness he possessed real, forgot all his fears of her attachment to Delamere, and dared again entertain the hopes he had discarded at Besançon — as he thought, for ever.

The next day Mrs. Stornaway was so much recovered that they proceeded in their journey, taking her into the coach with them and directing Madelon to travel in the chaise, accompanied by her father. They arrived early in town; and Godolphin, leaving them at an hotel, went in search of lodgings. He soon found apartments to accommodate them in Bond-street; and thither they immediately went; Mrs. Stafford taking upon herself the protection of the poor forlorn stranger 'till Godolphin could find her husband, on whose behalf he immediately intended to apply for a berth on board some ship in commission. He had given him a direction to his banker, and bid him there leave an address where he might be found in London. The next day he brought the transported Stornaway to his wife; and the gratitude these poor young people expressed to their benefactor, convinced the fair friends that they had deserved his kindness, and that there was no deception in the story the Lieutenant had told them about his wife. Godolphin took a lodging for them in Oxford-street; and gave them money for their support till he could get the young man employed, which his interest and indefatigable friendship soon accomplished.

In the mean time he saw Emmeline every day, and every day he rose in her esteem. Yet still she hesitated to discover to him all she thought of him; and at times was so reserved and so guarded, that Godolphin knew not what to believe. He knew she was above the paltry artifice of coquetry; yet she fearfully avoided being alone with him, and never allowed him an opportunity of asking whether he had any thing to hope from time and assiduity.

'Is he not one of the best creatures in the world?' said Mrs. Stafford, after he left the room, on the second day of their arrival, to go out in the service of the Stornaways.

'Yes.'

'Yes! and is that all the praise you allow to such a man? Is he not a perfect character?'

'As perfect, I suppose, as any of them are.'

'Ah! Emmeline, you are a little hypocrite. It is impossible you can be insensible to the merit of Godolphin; and I wonder you are not in more haste to convince him that you think of him as he deserves.'

'What would you have me do?'

'Marry him.'

'Before I am sure he desires it?' smilingly asked Emmeline.

'You cannot doubt that, tho' you so anxiously repress every attempt he makes to explain himself. Shall I tell you what he has said to me? Shall I tell you what motive carried him to St. Alpin?'

'No — I had rather not hear any thing about it.'

'And why not?'

'Because it is better, for some time, if not for ever, that Godolphin should be ignorant of those favourable thoughts I may have had of him — better that I should cease to entertain them.'

'Why so, pray?'

'Because I dread the mortified pride and furious jealousy of Lord Delamere on one hand; and on the other the authority of my uncle, who, 'till I am of age, will probably neither restore my fortune nor consent to my carrying it out of his family.'

'For those very reasons you should immediately marry Godolphin. When you are actually married, Delamere will reconcile himself to the loss of you. To an inevitable evil, even his haughty and self-willed spirit must submit. And should Lord Montreville give you any trouble about your fortune, who can so easily, so properly oblige him to do you justice, as a man of spirit, of honour, of understanding, who will have a right to insist upon it?'

It was impossible to deny so evident a truth. Yet still Emmeline apprehended the consequence of Delamere's rage and disappointment; and thought that there would be an indelicacy and an impropriety in withdrawing herself from the protection of her own family almost as soon as she could claim it, and that her uncle might make such a step a pretence for new contention and longer wrath. The result, therefore, of all her deliberations ended in a determination neither to engage herself or to marry 'till she was of age; and, 'till then, not even to encourage any lover whatever. By that time, she hoped that Lord Delamere, wearied by an hopeless passion, and convinced of her fixed indifference, would engage in some more successful pursuit. She knew that by that time all affairs between her and Lord Montreville must be adjusted. If the affection of Godolphin was, as she hoped, fixed, and founded on his esteem for her character, he would not love her less at the end of that period, when she should have the power of giving him her estate unincumbered with difficulties and unembarrassed by law suits; and should, she hoped, escape the misery of seeing Delamere's anguish and despair, on which she could not bear to reflect.

She ingenuously explained to Mrs. Stafford her reasons for refusing to receive Godolphin's proposals; in which her friend, tho' she allowed them to be plausible, by no means acquiesced; still insisting upon it, that the kindest thing she could do towards Lord Delamere, as well as the properest in regard to the settlement of her estate, was immediately to accept Godolphin. But Emmeline was not to be convinced; and all she could obtain from Mrs. Stafford was an extorted promise, reluctantly given, that she would not give any advice or encouragement to Godolphin immediately to press his suit. Emmeline, tho' convinced she was right, yet doubted whether she had fortitude enough to persist in the conduct she wished to adopt; if exposed at once to the solicitations of a woman of whose understanding she had an high opinion, and to the ardent supplications of the man she loved.

The day after her arrival in London, she had sent to Berkley-square, and was informed that Lord Montreville and his family were in Norfolk.

Thither therefore she wrote, and enclosed the letter she had brought from Lord Westhaven. Her own was couched in the most modest and dutiful terms, and that of Lord Westhaven was equally mild and reasonable. But they gave only disquiet and concern to the ambitious and avaricious bosom of Lord Montreville. Tho' already tortured by Delamere's absence and illness, and uncertain whether the object of his long solicitude would live to reap the advantage of his accumulated fortunes, he could not think but with pain and reluctance of giving up so large a portion of his annual income: still more unwilling did he feel to refund the produce of the estates for so long a period; and in the immediate emotion of his vexation at receiving Lord Westhaven's first letter, he had sent for Sir Richard Crofts, who, having at the time of Mr. Mowbray's death been entrusted with all the papers and deeds which belonged to him, was the most likely to know whether any were among them that bore testimony to the marriage of Mr. Mowbray and Miss Stavordale.

The fact was, that a very little time before he died, his steward, Williamson, had received the memorandum of which Emmeline had found a copy; and, on the death of his master, had carried it to Sir Richard Crofts; Lord Montreville being then in the North of England. Sir Richard eagerly enquired whether there were any other papers to the like purport. Williamson replied, he believed not; and very thoughtlessly left it in his hands. When, a few days afterwards, he called to know in whose name the business of the Mowbray estate was to be carried on, Sir Richard (then acting as an attorney, and only entering into life) told him that every thing was to be considered as the property of Lord Montreville; because there were many doubts about the marriage of Mr. Mowbray, and great reason to think that the paper in question was written merely with a view to pique and perplex his brother, with whom he was then at variance; but that Lord Montreville would enquire into the business, and certainly do justice to any claims the infant might have on the estate.

Soon after, Williamson applied again to have the paper restored; but Crofts answered, that he should keep it, by order of Lord Montreville; tho' it was of no use; his Lordship having obtained undoubted information that his brother was never married.

Sir Richard had reflected on the great advantage that would accrue to his patron from the possession of this estate; to which, besides its annual income, several boroughs belonged. He thought it was very probable that the little girl, then only a few weeks old, and without a mother or any other than mercenary attendants, might die in her infancy: if she did not, that Lord Montreville might easily provide for her, and that it would be doing his friend a great service, and be highly advantageous to himself, should he conceal the legal claim of the child, even unknown to her uncle, and put him in immediate possession of his paternal estate.

Having again strictly questioned Williamson; repressed his curiosity by law jargon; and frightened him by threats of his Lord's displeasure if he made any effort to prove the legitimacy of Emmeline; he very tranquilly destroyed the paper, and Lord Montreville never knew that such a paper had existed.

Williamson, timid and ignorant of every thing beyond his immediate business, returned in great doubt and uneasiness to Mowbray Castle. When he received the child and the two caskets, he had questioned the Frenchman who brought her and heard an absolute confirmation of the marriage of his master. He then examined the caskets, and found the certificates. But without money or friends, he knew not how to prosecute the claim of the orphan against the power and affluence of Lord Montreville; and after frequent consultations with Mrs. Carey, they agreed that the safest way would be carefully to secure those papers till Emmeline was old enough to find friends; for should they attempt previously to procure justice for her, they might probably lose the papers which proved her birth, as they had already done that which Williamson had delivered to Crofts. As long as Williamson lived, he carefully locked up these caskets. His sudden death prevented him from taking any steps to establish the claim of his orphan mistress; and that of Mrs. Carey two years afterwards, involved the whole affair in obscurity, which made Sir Richard quite easy as to any future discovery.

But as the aggressor never forgives, Sir Richard had conceived against Emmeline the most unmanly and malignant hatred, and had invariably opposed every tendency which he had observed in Lord Montreville to befriend and assist her, for no other reason but that he had already irreparably injured her.

He hoped, that as he had at length divided her from Lord Delamere, and driven her abroad, she would there marry a foreigner, and be farther removed than ever from the family, and from any chance of recovering the property of which he had deprived her: Instead of which, she had, in consequence of going thither, met the very man in whose power it was to prove the marriage of her mother; and, in Lord Westhaven, had found a protector too intelligent and too steady to be discouraged by evasion or chicanery — too powerful and too affluent to be thrown out of the pursuit, either by the enmity it might raise or the expence it might demand.

Nothing could exceed the chagrin of Sir Richard when Lord Montreville put into his hands the first letter he had on this subject from Lord Westhaven. Accustomed, however, to command his countenance, he said, without any apparent emotion, that as no papers in confirmation of the fact alledged had ever existed among those delivered to him on the death of Mr. Mowbray, it was probably some forgery that had imposed on Lord Westhaven.

'I see not how that can be,' answered Lord Montreville. 'It is not likely that Emmeline Mowbray could forge such papers, or should even conceive such an idea.'

'True, my Lord. But your Lordship forgets and overlooks and passes by the long abode and continuance and residence she has made with the Staffords. Mrs. Stafford is, to my certain knowledge and conviction, artful and designing and intrigueing; a woman, my Lord, who affects and pretends and presumes to understand and be competent and equal to business and affairs and concerns with which women should never interfere or meddle or interest themselves. It is clearly and evidently and certainly to the interest and advantage and benefit of this woman, that Miss Mowbray, over whom she has great influence and power and authority, should be established and fixed and settled in affluence, rather than remain and abide and continue where nature and justice and reason have placed her.'

'I own, Sir Richard, I cannot see the thing in this light. However, to do nothing rashly, let us consider how to proceed.'

Sir Richard then, advised him by no means to answer Lord Westhaven's letter, but to wait till he saw his Lordship; as in cases so momentous, it was, he said, always wrong to give any thing in black and white. In a few days afterwards he heard out of Norfolk, (for he had come up from thence to consult with Sir Richard Crofts) that Lord Delamere was ill at Besançon. His precipitate departure had before given him the most poignant concern; and now his fears for his life completed the distress of this unfortunate father. On receiving, however, the second letter from Lord Westhaven, together with that of Emmeline, his apprehensions for the life of his son were removed, and left his mind at liberty to recur again to the impending loss of four thousand five hundred a year, with the unpleasant accompanyment of being obliged to refund above sixty thousand pounds. Again Sir Richard Crofts was sent for, and again he tried to quiet the apprehensions of Lord Montreville. But his attempt to persuade him that the whole might be a deception originating with the Staffords, obtained not a moment's attention. He knew Stafford himself was weak, ignorant, and indolent, and would neither have had sagacity to think of or courage to execute such a design; and that Mrs. Stafford should imagine and perform it seemed equally improbable. He was perfectly aware that Lord Westhaven had a thorough acquaintance with business, and was of all men on earth the most unlikely to enter warmly into such an affair, (against the interest too of the family into which he had married) unless he was very sure of having very good grounds for his interference.

But tho' Sir Richard could not prevail on him to disbelieve the whole of the story, he saw that his Lordship thought with great reluctance of the necessity he should be under of relinquishing the whole of the fortune. He now therefore recommended it to him to remain quiet, at least 'till Lord Westhaven came to England; to send an answer to Miss Mowbray that meant nothing; and to gain time for farther enquiries. These enquiries he himself undertook; and leaving Lord Montreville in a political fit of the gout, he returned from Audley Hall to London, and bent all his thoughts to the accomplishment of his design; which was, to get the original papers out of the hands of Emmeline, and to bribe Le Limosin to go back to France.

While these things were passing in England, Lord Delamere (whose rage and indignation at Emmeline's departure the authority of Lord Westhaven could hardly restrain) had learned from his brother-in-law the real circumstances of the birth of his cousin, and he heard them with the greatest satisfaction. He now thought it certain that his father would press his marriage as eagerly as he had before opposed it; and that so great an obstacle being removed, and Emmeline wholly in the power of his family, she would be easily brought to forgive him and to comply with the united wishes of all her relations.

In this hope, and being assured by Lord Westhaven that Bellozane was actually returned into Switzerland without any design of following Emmeline, (who had been induced, he said, to leave Besançon purely to avoid him) he consented to attempt attaining a better command over his temper, on which the re-establishment of has health depended; and after about ten days, was able to travel. Lord and Lady Westhaven, therefore, at the end of that time, slowly began with him their journey to England.

CHAPTER IX

EMMELINE had now been almost a week in London; and Mrs. Stafford, with the assistance of Godolphin, had succeeded so much better than she expected, in the arrangement of some of those affairs in which she apprehended the most difficulty, that very little remained for her to do before she should be enabled to return to France (where her husband was to sign some papers to secure his safety); and that little depended on James Crofts, who seemed to be making artificial delay, and trying to give her all the trouble and perplexity in his power.

He had, however, another motive than merely to harrass and distress her. His father had employed him to deal with Le Limosin; well knowing that there was nothing so base and degrading that he would not undertake where his interest was in question; and Sir Richard had promised him a considerable addition to his fortune if he had address enough to prevent so capital a sum as Emmeline claimed from being deducted from that of the family to whom his brother was allied; and from whence he had expectations, which could not but suffer from such a diminution of its wealth and interest.

The tediousness therefore that the Crofts' created promised still to detain Emmeline in London; and her uncle's letter, which coldly and hardly with civility deferred any conference on her affairs till the arrival of Lord Westhaven, convinced her that from his tenderness she had nothing, from his justice, little to hope.

Godolphin was very anxious to be allowed personally to apply to him on the claim of his niece. But this Emmeline positively refused. She would not even allow Mr. Newton, the lawyer to whom Lord Westhaven had recommended her, and in whose hands her papers were safely deposited, to write officially to Lord Montreville; but determined to wait quietly the return of Lord Westhaven himself, on whom she knew neither the anger of her uncle, or the artifices of Sir Richard, would make any impression; while his Lordship's interference could not be imputed to such motives as might possibly be thought to influence Godolphin, or would it give her the appearance of proceeding undutifully and harshly against Lord Montreville, which appearances she might be liable to, should she hastily institute a suit against him.

She grew, however, very uneasy at the determined attendance of Godolphin, whose presence she knew was so necessary to poor Lady Adelina. She saw that he was anxious about his sister, yet could not determine to tear himself from her, and to insist upon his returning to Lady Adelina, would be to assume a right, to which, on the footing they were, she declined pretending. She failed not, however, every day to represent to him the long solitude in which Lady Adelina had been left, and to read to him parts of her letters which breathed only sorrow and depression.

Whenever this happened, Godolphin heard her with concern, and promised to set out the next day; but still something was to be done for the service of Emmeline, and still he could not bear to resign the delight he had now so long enjoyed of seeing her every day, and of indulging those hopes she had tacitly allowed him to entertain.

Mrs. Stafford, notwithstanding her promise to Emmeline, had not been able to forbear discovering to him part of the truth. Yet when he reflected on the advantages Delamere had over him in fortune, in rank, in the influence his family connection and his former engagement might give him, he trembled least, if he should be himself absent when Lord Delamere arrived, her tender and timid spirit would yield to the sorrow of her lover and the authority of her family; and that almost in despite of herself, he might lose her for ever. While he yet lingered, and continued to promise that he would go to the Isle of Wight, the eight first days of their stay in town glided away. Early in the morning of the ninth, Godolphin entered the room where Mrs. Stafford and Emmeline were at breakfast.

'I must now indeed,' said he, 'lose no time in going to Adelina. I am to day informed that Mr. Trelawny is dead.'

'Shall we then see Lady Adelina in town?' eagerly asked Emmeline, who could not affect any concern at the death of such a man.

'I apprehend not,' replied Godolphin. 'Whatever business there may be to settle with the Bancrafts, I am sure will be more proper for me than for her. To them I must now go, at Putney; and only came to inform you, Madam,' addressing himself to Mrs. Stafford, 'of the reason of my sudden absence.'

'Shall you return again to London, Sir, before you proceed into Hampshire?'

'Not unless you or Miss Mowbray will allow me to suppose that to either of you my return may be in any way serviceable.'

Mrs. Stafford assured him she had nothing to trouble him upon which required such immediate attention. Emmeline then attempted to make an answer of the same kind. But tho' she had for some days wished him to go, she could not see him on the point of departing without being sensible of the anguish his absence would occasion her; and instead of speaking distinctly her thanks, she only murmured something, and was so near bursting into tears, that fearing to expose herself, she was hurrying out of the room.

'No message — no letter — not one kind word,' said he, gently detaining her, 'to poor Adelina? Nothing to your little *protégé*?'

'My — love to them both, Sir?'

'And will you not write to my sister?'

'By the post,' said Emmeline, struggling to get from him to conceal her emotion.

He then kissed her hand, and suffered her to go. While the explanation Mrs. Stafford gave of her real feelings, elated him to rapture, in which he departed, protesting that nothing should prevent his return, to follow the good fortune which he now believed might be his, as soon as he could adjust his sister's business with her husband's relations.

Mrs. Stafford recommended it to him to bring Lady Adelina to London with him, as the affection Emmeline had for her would inevitably give her great influence. Godolphin, in answer to this advice, only shook his head; and Mrs. Stafford remained uncertain of his intentions to follow it.

A few days now elapsed without any extraordinary occurrence. Emmeline thought less of the impending restoration of her fortune (for its restoration Mr. Newton assured her he had no doubt), than of him with whom she hoped to share it. She impatiently longed to hear from Lady Adelina that he was with her: and sometimes her mind dwelt with painful solicitude on Lady Westhaven and Delamere, for whose health and safety she was truly anxious, and of whom she had received no account since her arrival in London.

As she was performing the promise she had made to Godolphin of writing to Lady Adelina by an early post, Le Limosin announced Mr. James Crofts; who immediately entered the room with his usual jerking and familiar walk. Emmeline, who incapable as she was of hating any body, yet felt towards him a disgust almost amounting to hatred, receiving him with the coldest reserve, and Mrs. Stafford with no more civility than was requisite to prevent his alledging her rudeness and impatience as reasons for not settling the business on which she concluded he came.

He began with general conversation; and when Mrs. Stafford, impatient to have done with him, introduced that which went more immediately to the adjustment of the affair she wished to settle, he told her, that being extremely unwilling to discuss a matter of business with a *lady*, and apprehensive of giving offence to one for whom he and his dear Mrs. Crofts had so sincere a regard, he had determined to leave all the concerns yet between them to his attorney; a man of strict honour and probity, to whom he would give her a direction, and to whom it would be better for *her* attorney to apply, than that they should themselves enter on a topic whereon it was probable they might differ.

Mrs. Stafford, vexed at his dissimulation and finesse, again pressed him to come to a conclusion without the interference of lawyers. But he again repeated the set speech he had formed on the occasion; and then addressing himself to Emmeline, asked smilingly, and affecting all interest in her welfare, 'whether the information he had received was true?'

'What information, Sir?'

'That Miss Mowbray has the most authentic claim to the estate of her late father.'

'It is by no means an established claim, Sir; and such as you must excuse me if I decline talking of.'

'I am told you have papers that put it out of dispute. If you would favour me with a sight of them, perhaps I could give you some insight into the proceedings you should commence; and I am sure my I friendship and regard would make any service I could do you a real satisfaction to myself.'

'I thank you, Sir, for your professions. The papers in question are the hands of Mr. Newton of Lincolns Inn. If he will allow you to see them I have no objection.'

'You intend then,' said James Crofts, unable entirely to conceal his chagrin — 'you intend to begin a suit with my Lord Montreville?'

'By no means, Sir. I am persuaded there will be no necessity for it. But as you have just referred Mrs. Stafford to a lawyer, I must beg leave to say, that if you have any questions to ask you must apply to mine.'

James Crofts, quite disconcerted notwithstanding his presumptuous assurance, was not ready with an answer; and Emmeline, who doubted not that he was sent by his father to gain what intelligence he could, was so provoked, that not conceiving herself obliged to preserve the appearance of civility to a man she despised, she left him in possession of the room, from whence Mrs. Stafford had a few moments before departed. He therefore was obliged to withdraw; having found his attempt to shake the integrity of Le Limosin as fruitless as that he had made to get sight of the papers.

He had not long been gone, when a servant brought to Emmeline the following note. —

> 'I have heard you are in town with Mrs. Stafford, and beg leave to wait on you. Do not, *ma douce amie*, refuse to grant me this favour. Besides the happiness of seeing you and your friend, I have another very particular reason for soliciting you to grant such an indulgence to
>
> GEORGE FITZ-EDWARD.
>
> 'I write this from a neighbouring coffee-house, where I expect your answer.'

Emmeline immediately carried this billet to Mrs. Stafford; who told her there was no reason why she should refuse the request it contained. She therefore wrote a card of compliment to Colonel Fitz-Edward, signifying that she should be glad to see him.

In a few moments Fitz-Edward appeared; and Emmeline, tho' aware of his arrival, could not receive him without confusion and emotion. Nor could she without pity behold his altered countenance and manner, so different from what they were when she first saw the gay and gallant Fitz-Edward at Mowbray Castle. He began by expressing, with great appearance of sincerity, his joy at seeing her; enquired after Lord Delamere, and mentioned his astonishment at what he had heard — that Delamere had so repeatedly enquired after him, and signified such a wish to see him, yet had never written to him to explain his business.

Emmeline, who knew well on what he had so earnestly desired to meet him, blushed, but did not think it necessary to clear up a subject which Godolphin's explanation to Delamere had rendered no longer alarming.

'You know, perhaps,' said Fitz-Edward, 'that Mr. Trelawny is dead.'

'I do.'

'And your fair unhappy friend? — May I now — (or is it still a crime?,) enquire after her?'

'She is, I believe, well,' answered Emmeline, 'and remains at the house of her brother.'

'Tell me, Miss Mowbray — will she after a proper time refuse, do you think, her consent to see me? will *you*, my lovely friend, undertake to plead for me? will you and Mrs. Stafford, who know with what solicitude I sought her, with what anguish I deplored her loss, intercede on my behalf? — you, who know how fondly my heart has been devoted to her from the moment of our fatal parting?'

'I can undertake nothing of this kind, Sir. The fate of Lady Adelina depends, I apprehend, on her brothers. To them I think you should apply.'

'And why not to herself? Is she not now at liberty? And when destiny has at length broken the cruel chains with which she was loaded, will she voluntarily bind herself with others hardly more supportable? If she refers me to her brothers, I must despair: — the cold-hearted Lord Westhaven, the inflexible and rigid Godolphin, will make it a mistaken point of honour to divide us for ever!'

'You cannot suppose, Sir, that *I* shall undertake to influence Lady Adelina to measures disapproved by her family. I know not that Lord Westhaven is cold and unfeeling as you describe him: on the contrary, I believe he unites one of the best heads and warmest hearts. If your request is proper, you certainly risk nothing by referring it to him.'

Of Godolphin she spoke not; fearful of betraying to the penetrating and observing Fitz-Edward how little he answered in her idea the character of unfeeling and severe.

'I know not what to do,' said Fitz-Edward. 'Should I address myself to her brothers without success, I am undone; since I well know that from their decision there will be no appeal. I cannot live without her, Emmeline — indeed I cannot; and in the hope only of what has lately happened, have I dragged on till now a reluctant existence. Once, and but once, I dared write to her. But her brother returned the letter. She suffered him cruelly to return it, in a cover in which he informed me, "that the peace and honour of Lady Adelina Trelawny made it necessary for her to forget that such a man existed as Colonel Fitz-Edward." Godolphin,' continued he — 'Godolphin may carry this too far; he may oblige me to remind him that there is more than one way in which his inexorable punctilio may be satisfied.'

'Certainly,' cried Emmeline, in great agitation, which she vainly struggled to conceal, 'there is no method more likely to convince Lady Adelina of your tenderness for her, than that you hint at; and if you should be fortunate enough to destroy a brother to whom she owes every thing, your triumph will be complete.'

'I cannot indeed. I am not likely to see her; and if I were, this is a subject on which nothing shall induce me to influence her.'

Mrs. Stafford, who had been detained in another room by a person who came to her upon business, now joined them;

and Fitz-Edward without hesitation repeated to her what he had been saying to Emmeline.

'I do not think indeed, Colonel, that Miss Mowbray can interfere; and I am of her opinion, that as soon as such proposals as you intend to make are proper, you should address them to her brothers.'

'Mr. Godolphin, Madam, treats me in a way which only my tenderness, my love for his sister, induces me to bear. I have met him accidentally, and he passes rudely by me. I sent a gentleman to him to desire an amicable interview. He answered, that as we could not meet as friends, he must be excused from seeing me at all. Had I been as rash, as cruel as he seems to be, I should then have noticed, in the way it demanded, such a message: but conscious that I had already injured him, I bore with his petulance and his asperity. I love Godolphin,' continued he — 'from our boyish days I have loved and respected him. I know the nobleness of his nature, and I can make great allowances for the impatience of injured honour. But will he not carry it too far, if now that his sister is released from her detested marriage he still persists in dividing us?'

'You are not sure,' said Mrs. Stafford, 'that he will do so. Have patience at least till the time is elapsed when you may try the experiment. In the interim I will consider what ought to be done.'

'My ever excellent, ever amiable friend!' exclaimed Fitz-Edward warmly — 'how much do I owe you already! Ah! add yet to those obligations the restoration of Adelina, and I shall be indebted to you for more than life. As to you, my sweet marble-hearted Emmeline, I heartily pray that all your coldness both towards me and poor Delamere may be revenged by your feeling, on behalf of him, all the pain you have inflicted.'

Alas! thought Emmeline, your wicked wish is already accomplished, tho' not in favour of poor Delamere.

Fitz-Edward then obtained permission to wait on them again; tho' Mrs. Stafford very candidly told him, that after Captain Godolphin came to town, she begged he would forbear coming in when he heard of his being there.

'We will try,' said she, 'to conciliate matters between you, so that ye may meet in peace; and till then pray forbear to meet at all.'

Fitz-Edward, flattering himself that Mrs. Stafford would interest herself for him, and that Emmeline, however reserved, would be rather his friend than his enemy, departed in rather better spirits; and left the fair friends to debate on the means of preventing what was very likely to happen — a difference of the most alarming kind between him and Godolphin, should the latter persist in refusing him permission to address, at a proper season, Lady Adelina.

The long delays that seemed likely to arise before her own business would be adjusted with Lord Montreville; the fiery and impatient spirits with which it appeared to be her lot to contend; the vexation to which she saw Mrs. Stafford subjected by the sordid and cruel conduct of the Crofts' towards her; and lastly, her encreasing disquietude about Godolphin, whom she feared to encourage, yet was equally unwilling and unable to repulse; oppressed her spirits, and made her stay in London very disagreeable to her. She had never before been in it for more than a night or two; and at this time of the year (it was the beginning of October) the melancholy, deserted houses in the fashionable streets, and the languor that appeared in the countenances of those who were obliged to be in town, offered no amusement or variety to compensate for the loss of the pure air she had been accustomed to breathe, or for the beautiful and interesting landscapes which she remembered to have enjoyed in Autumn at Mowbray Castle; where she so much languished to be, that she sometimes thought, if her uncle would resign it and the estate immediately around, to her, she could be content to leave him in possession of the rest of that fortune he coveted with so much avidity.

CHAPTER X

A FEW days longer passed, and Emmeline yet heard nothing of the return of Lord and Lady Westhaven; a circumstance at which she grew extremely uneasy. Not only as it gave her reason to fear for the health of Lord Delamere, for whom she was very anxious; but for that of Lady Westhaven, whom she so tenderly loved.

She observed too, with concern, that under pretence of waiting the arrival of his son and his son in law, Lord Montreville delayed all advances towards a settlement; and that Mrs. Stafford, wearied by the duplicity and chicanery of the Crofts', and miserable in being detained so long from her children, grew quite disheartened, and was prevented only by her affection for Emmeline from returning to France and abandoning all hopes of an accommodation which every day seemed more difficult and more distant.

The arrival of Lord Westhaven was on her account particularly desirable, as he had promised Emmeline to make a point of assisting her; and on his assurances she knew it was safe to rely, since they were neither made to give himself an air of importance, nor meant to quiet the trouble of present importunity, by holding out the prospect of future advantage never thought of more.

Nothing, however, could be done to hasten this important arrival; and the fair friends, tho' uneasy and impatient, were obliged to submit. But from the restlessness of daily suspence, they were roused by two letters; which brought in its place only poignant concern. That to Mrs. Stafford was from her husband; who, tho' he had neither relish for her conversation nor respect for her virtues, was yet dissatisfied without her; and even while she was wholly occupied in serving him, tormented her with murmurs and suspicions. He scrupled not to hint, 'that as she was with her beloved Miss Mowbray, she forgot her duty to her family; and that as she had been now gone near a month, he thought it quite long enough, not only to have done the business she undertook, but to have enjoyed as much pleasure as was in her situation reasonable. He therefore expected her to return to France, and supposed that she had settled every thing to facilitate his coming back to England.' The unreasonable expectations, and ungrateful suspicions, which this letter contained, overwhelmed her with mortification. To return without having finished the business on which she came, would be to expose herself to insult and reproach; yet to stay longer, without a probability of succeeding by her stay, would only occasion an aggravation of his ill humour, and probably a worse reception when she rejoined him.

The letter to Emmeline was from Lady Adelina, and ran thus. —

East Cliff; Oct. 16.

'Godolphin, my Emmeline, is at length returned to your unhappy friend, who has passed many, many melancholy days since he left her. My dear brother appears not only in better health, but in better spirits than when he went from hence. Ought I then to repine? when I see him, and when he tells me that you are well; and that affluence, and with it, I hope, happiness will be yours? The very name of happiness and of Adelina should not come in the same page! Ah! never must they any where meet again. Pardon me for thus recurring to myself: but the mournful topic will intrude! Unhappy Trelawny! he had not quite compleated his twenty-fifth year. Tho' I never either loved or esteemed him, and tho' to my early and hasty marriage I owe all the misery of my life, his death has something shocking in it. My weak spirits, which have of late been unusually deranged, are sadly affected by it. Yet surely in regard to him I have little to reproach myself. Did he not abandon me to my destiny? did he not plunge headlong into follies from which he resented even an effort to save him? Alas! unless I could have given him that understanding which nature had denied him, my solicitude must ever have been vain! It is some alleviation, too, to my concern, to reflect, that as much of his honour as depended on me, has not, by the breath of public fame, been sullied. And I try to persuade myself, that since his life was useful to nobody, and had long been, from intemperance, burthensome to himself, I should not suffer his death to dwell so heavily upon me. Yet in spite of every effort to shake off the melancholy which devours me, it encreases upon me; and to you I may say, for you will hear and pity me, that there exists not at this moment so complete a wretch as your Adelina!

'To my brother William, all gentle and generous as he is, I cannot complain. It were ingratitude to let him see how little all his tenderness avails towards reconciling me to myself; towards healing the wounds of my depressed spirit, and quieting the murmurs of this feeble heart. Yet methinks to have a friend, in whose compassionate bosom I might pour out its weakness and its sorrows, would mitigate the extreme severity of those sufferings which are now more than I can bear.

'Where have I on earth such a friend but in my Emmeline? And will she refuse to come to me? Ah! wherefore should she refuse it? I shall be alone; for Godolphin is obliged to go immediately to London to settle all the business I shall now ever have with the family of Trelawny, and put it on such a footing as may preclude the necessity of my ever meeting any of them hereafter. He tells me that your affairs advance nothing till Lord Westhaven's return; and that our dear Mrs. Stafford talks of being obliged to go back to her family. If she must do so, you will not stay in London alone; and where is your company so fondly desired, where can you have such an opportunity of exercising your generous goodness, as in coming hither? Our little boy — do you not long to embrace him? Ah! lovely as he is, why dare I not indulge all the pleasure and all the pride I might feel in seeing him; and wherefore must anguish so keen mingle with tenderness so delicious!

'Ah! my friend, come to me, I entreat, I implore you! The reasons why I cannot see London, are of late multiplied rather than removed, and I can only have the happiness of embracing you here. Hesitate not to oblige me then; for I every hour wish more and more ardently to see you. When

I awake from my imperfect slumbers, your presence is the first desire of my heart: I figure you to myself as I wander forth on my solitary walks. And when I do sleep, the image of my angelic friend, consolatory and gentle, makes me some amends for visions less pleasant, that disturb it.

'Ah! let me not see you in dreams alone; for above all I want you — "when I am alone with poor Adelina." Come, O come; and if it be possible — save me — from myself!

A.T.'

The melancholy tenor of this letter greatly affected Emmeline. She wished almost as eagerly as her friend to be with her. But how could she determine to become an inmate at the house of Godolphin, even tho' he was himself to be absent from it? She communicated, however, Lady Adelina's request to Mrs. Stafford, who could see no objection to any plan which might promote the interest of Godolphin. She represented therefore to Emmeline how very disagreeable it would be to her to be left alone in town, when she should herself be obliged to leave her, as must now soon happen. That there was, in fact, no very proper asylum for her but the house of her uncle, which he seemed not at all disposed to offer her. But that to Lady Adelina's proposal there could be no reasonable objection, especially as Godolphin was not to be there.

Emmeline yet hesitated; till another letter from Stafford, more harsh and unreasonable than the first, obliged her friend to fix on the following Thursday for her departure; the absurd impatience of her husband thus defeating its own purpose; and Emmeline, partly influenced by her persuasions, and yet more by her own wishes, determined at length to fix the same time for beginning her journey to the Isle of Wight.

There was yet two days to intervene; and Mrs. Stafford was obliged to employ the first of them in the city, among lawyers and creditors of her husband. From scenes so irksome she readily allowed Miss Mowbray to excuse herself; who therefore remained at home, and was engaged in looking over some poems she had purchased, when she heard a rap at the door, and the voice of Godolphin on the stairs enquiring of Le Limosin for Mrs. Stafford. Le Limosin told him that she was from home, but that Mademoiselle Mowbray was in the dining room. He sent up to know if he might be admitted. Emmeline had no pretence of refusing him, and receiving him with a mixture of confusion and pleasure, which she ineffectually attempted to hide under the ordinary forms of civility.

The eyes of Godolphin were animated by the delight of beholding her. But when she enquired after Lady Adelina, as she almost immediately did, they assumed a more melancholy expression.

'Adelina is far from being well,' said he. 'Has she not written to you?'

'She has.'

'And has she not preferred a request to you?'

'Yes.'

'What answer do you mean to give it? Will you refuse once more to bless and relieve, by your presence, my unhappy sister?'

'I do not know,' said Emmeline, deeply blushing, 'that I ought, (especially without the concurrence of my uncle,) to consent; yet to contribute to the satisfaction of Lady Adelina — to give her any degree of happiness — what is there I can refuse?'

'Adorable, angelic goodness!' eagerly cried Godolphin. 'Best, as well as loveliest of human creatures! You go then?'

'I intend beginning my journey on Thursday.'

'And you will allow me to see you safe thither?'

'There can surely be no occasion to give you that trouble, Sir,' said Emmeline apprehensively; 'nor ought you to think of it, since Lady Adelina's affairs certainly require your attendance in London.'

'They do; but not so immediately as to prevent my attending you to East Cliff. If you will suffer me to do that, I promise instantly to return.'

'No. I go only attended by my servants or go not at all.'

Godolphin was mortified to find her so determined. And easily discouraged from those hopes which he had indulged rather from the flattering prospects offered to him by Mrs. Stafford than presumption founded on his own remarks, he now again felt all his apprehensions renewed of her latent affection for Delamere. The acute anguish to which those ideas exposed him, and their frequent return, determined him now to attempt knowing at once, whether he had or had not that place in Emmeline's heart which Mrs. Stafford had assured him he had long possessed.

Sitting down near her, therefore, he said, gravely — 'As I may not, Miss Mowbray, soon have again the happiness I now enjoy, will you allow me to address you on a subject which you must long have known to be nearest my heart; but on which you have so anxiously avoided every explanation I have attempted, that I fear intruding too much on your complaisance if I enter upon it?'

Emmeline found she could not avoid hearing him; and sat silent, heart violently beating. Godolphin went on. —

'From the first moment I beheld you, my heart was yours. I attempted, indeed, at the beginning of our acquaintance — ah! how vainly attempted! — to conquer a passion which I believed was rendered hopeless by your prior engagement. While I supposed you the promised wife of Lord Delamere, I concealed, as well as I was able, my sufferings, and never offended you with an hint of their severity. Had you married him, I think I could have carried them in silence to the grave. Those ties, however, Lord Delamere himself broke; and I then thought myself at liberty to solicit your favour. It was for that purpose I took the road to St. Alpin, when the unhappy Delamere stopped me at Besançon.

'When I afterwards related to you his illness; the sorrow, the lively and generous sorrow, you expressed for him, and the cold and reserved manner in which you received me, made me still believe, that tho' he had relinquished your hand he yet possessed your heart. I saw it with anguish, and continued silent. All that passed at Besançon confirmed me in this opinion. I determined to tear myself away, and again conceal in solitude a passion, which, while I felt it to be incurable, I feared was hopeless. Accident, however, detaining me at Calais, again threw me in your way; and I heard, that far from having renewed your engagement with Lord Delamere, you had left him to avoid his eager importunity. Dare I add — that then, my pity for him was lost in the hopes I presumed to form for myself; and studiously as you have avoided giving me an opportunity of speaking to you, I have yet ventured to flatter myself that you beheld not with anger or scorn, my ardent, my fond attachment.'

From the beginning of this speech to its conclusion, the encreasing confusion of Emmeline deprived her of all power of answering it. With deepened blushes, and averted eyes, she at first sought for refuge in affecting to be intent on the netting she drew from her work box; but having spoiled a whole row, her trembling hands could no longer go on with it; and as totally her tongue refused to utter the answer, which, by the pause he made, she concluded Godolphin expected. After a moment, however, he went on.

'I have by no means encouraged visions so delightful, without a severe alloy of fear and mistrust. Frequently, your coldness, your unkindness, gives me again to despondence; and every lovely prospect I had suffered my imagination to draw, is lost in clouds and darkness. Yet I am convinced you do not intend to torture me; and that from Miss Mowbray I may expect that candour, that explicit conduct, of which common minds are incapable. Tell me then, dearest and loveliest Emmeline, may I venture to hope that tender bosom is not wholly insensible? Will you hear me with patience, and even with pity?'

'What, Sir, can I say?' faulteringly asked Emmeline. 'I am in a great measure dependant, at least for some time, on Lord Montreville; and till I am of age, have determined to hear nothing on the subject on which you are pleased to address me.'

'Admitting it to be so,' answered Godolphin, 'give me but an hope to live upon till then!'

'I will not deny, Sir,' said Emmeline still more faintly, 'I will not deny that my esteem for your character — my — my —'

'Oh! speak!' exclaimed Godolphin eagerly — 'speak, and tell me that —'

At this moment, Le Limosin hastily came into the room, and said — '*Mademoiselle, le Chevalier de Bellozane demande permission de vous parler.*'

Godolphin, vexed at the interruption, and embarrassed at the arrival of the Chevalier, said hastily — 'You will not see him?'

'How can I refuse him?' answered she; 'perhaps he comes with some intelligence of your brother — of my dear Lady Westhaven.'

By this time the Chevalier was in the room. Emmeline received him with anxious and confused looks, arising entirely from her apprehensions about Lady Westhaven and Lord Delamere; but the vanity of Bellozane saw in it only a struggle between her real sentiments and her affectation of concealment. She almost instantly, however, enquired after her friends.

'I left them,' said Bellozane, 'almost as soon as you did, and went (because I wanted money and my father wanted to see me,) back to St. Alpin, where I staid almost a fortnight; and having obtained a necessary recruit of cash, I set off for Paris; where (my leave of absence being to expire in another month) I was forced to make interest to obtain a longer permission, in order to throw myself, lovely Miss Mowbray, at your feet, and to pass the winter in the delights of London, which they tell me I shall like better than Paris.'

Emmeline, disgusted at his presumption and volatility, enquired if he knew nothing since of Lord and Lady Westhaven.

'Oh, yes,' said he, 'I saw them all at Paris, and asked them if they had any commands to you? But I could get nothing from my good cousin but sage advice, and from Lady Westhaven only cold looks and half sentences; and as to poor Delamere, I knew he was too much afraid of my success to be in a better temper with me than the other two; so we had but little conversation.'

'But they are well, Sir?'

'No; Delamere has been detained all this time by illness, at different places. He was better when I saw him; but Lady

Westhaven was herself ill, and my cousin was, in looks, the most rueful of the three.'

'But, Sir, when may they be expected in England?'

'That I cannot tell. The last time I saw Lord Westhaven was above a week before I left Paris; and then he said he knew not when his wife would be well enough to begin their journey, but he hoped within a fortnight.'

'Good God!' thought Emmeline, 'what can have prevented his writing to me all this time?'

Godolphin, after the first compliments passed with the Chevalier, had been quite silent. He now, however, asked some questions about his brother; by which he found, that in consequence of endeavouring to discourage Bellozane's voyage to England, Lord Westhaven had offended him, and that a coldness had taken place between them. Bellozane had ceased to consider Godolphin as a rival, when he beheld Lord Delamere in that light; and was now rather pleased to meet him, knowing that his introduction into good company would greatly be promoted by means of such a relation.

'Do you know,' said the Chevalier, addressing himself to Emmeline, 'that I have had some trouble my fair friend, to find you?'

'And how,' enquired Godolphin, 'did you accomplish it?'

'Why my Lord Westhaven, to whom I applied at Paris, protested that he did not know; so remembering the name of le Marquis de Montreville, I wrote to him to know where I might wait on Mademoiselle Mowbray. Monseigneur le Marquis being at his country house, did not immediately answer my letter. At length I had a card from him, which he had the complaisance to send by a gentleman, un Monsieur — Monsieur *Croff* who invited me to his house, and introduced me to Milady *Croff*, his wife, who is daughter to

Milor Montreville. *Mon Dieu! que cette femme la, est vive, aimable; qu'elle a l'air du monde, et de la bonne compagnie.*' (How lively and agreeable she is — how much she has the air of a woman of fashion and of the world.)

'You think Lady Frances Crofts, then, handsomer than her sister?' asked Godolphin.

'*Mais non — elle n'est pas peut-etre si belle — mais elle a cependant un certain air. Enfin — je le trouve charmante.*' (Not so handsome perhaps, but there is a something — in short, I think her charming.)

Godolphin then continuing to question him, found that the Crofts' had invited Bellozane with an intention of getting from him the purpose of his journey, and what his business was with Emmeline; and finding that it was his gallantry only brought him over, and that he knew nothing of the late Mr. Mowbray's affairs, had no longer made any attempt to oppose his seeing her.

Godolphin, tho' he believed Emmeline not only indifferent but averse to him, was yet much disquieted at finding she was likely again to be exposed to his importunities. He trembled least if he discovered her intentions of going to East Cliff, he should follow her thither; for which his relationship to Lady Adelina would furnish him with a pretence; and desirous of getting him away as soon as possible, he asked if he would dine with him at his lodgings.

Bellozane answered that he was already engaged to Mr. Crofts; and then turning to Emmeline, offered to take her hand; and enquired whether she had a softer heart than when she left Besançon?

Emmeline drew away her hand; and very gravely entreated him to say no more on a subject already so frequently discussed, and on which her sentiments must ever be the same. Bellozane gaily protested that he had been too long a soldier to be easily repulsed. That he would wait on her the next day, and doubted not but he should find her more favourably disposed. '*Je reviendrai demain vous offrir encore mon hommage. Adieu! nympthe belle et cruelle. La chaine que je porte fera toute ma gloire.*' (I shall come again to-morrow to offer my homage. Adieu! Fair, cruel nymph! I place my glory in wearing your chains.) He then snatched her hand, which in spite of her efforts he kissed, and with his usual gaiety went away, accompanied by Godolphin.

Hardly had Emmeline time to recollect her dissipated spirits after the warm and serious address of Godolphin, and to feel vexation and disgust at the presumptuous forwardness of Bellozane, from which she apprehended much future trouble, before a note was brought from Mrs. Stafford, to inform her, that after waiting some hours at the house of the attorney she employed, the people who were to meet her had disappointed her, and that there was no prospect of her getting her business done 'till a late hour in the evening; she therefore desired Emmeline to dine without her, and not to expect her till ten or eleven at night.

As it was now between four and five, she ordered up her dinner, and was sitting down to it alone, when Godolphin again entered the room. Vexation was marked in his countenance: he seemed hurried; and having apologized for again interrupting her, tho' he did not account for his return, he sat down.

'Surely,' cried Emmeline, alarmed, 'you have heard nothing unpleasant from France?'

'Nothing, upon my honour,' answered he. 'The account the Chevalier gives is indeed far from satisfactory, yet I am persuaded there is nothing particularly amiss, or we should have heard.'

'It is that consideration only which has made me tolerably easy. Yet it is strange I have no letter from Lady Westhaven. Will you dine with me?' added Emmeline. It was indeed hardly possible to avoid asking him, as Le Limosin at that moment brought up the dinner.

'Where is Mrs. Stafford?' said he.

'Detained in the city.'

'And you dine alone, and will allow me the happiness of dining with you?'

'Certainly,' replied Emmeline, blushing, 'if you will favour me with your company.'

Godolphin then placed himself at the end of the table; and in the pleasure of being with her, thus unmarked by others, and considering her invitation as an assurance that his declaration of the morning was favourably received, he forgot the chagrin which hung upon him at his first entrance, and thought only of the means by which he might perpetuate the happiness he now possessed.

Emmeline tried to shake off, in common conversation, her extreme embarrassment. But when dinner was over, and Le Limosin left the room, in whose presence she felt a sort of protection, she foresaw that she must again hear Godolphin, and that it would be almost impossible to evade answering him.

She now repented of having asked him to dine with her; then blamed herself for the reserve and coldness with which she had almost always treated a man, who, deserving all her affections, had so long possessed them.

But the idea of poor Delamere — of his sadness, his despair, arose before her, and was succeeded by yet more frightful images of the consequences that might follow his frantic passions. And impressed at once with pity and terror, she again resolved to keep, if it were possible, the true state of her heart from the knowledge of Godolphin.

'I have seldom seen one of my relations with so little pleasure,' said he, after the servant had withdrawn, 'as I to-day met my volatile cousin de Bellozane. I hoped he would have persecuted you no farther with a passion to which I think you are not disposed to listen.'

'I certainly never intend it.'

'Pardon me then, dearest Miss Mowbray, if I solicit leave to renew the conversation his abrupt entrance broke off. You had the goodness to say you had some esteem for my character — Ah! tell me, if on that esteem I may presume to build those hopes which alone can give value to the rest of my life?'

Emmeline, who saw he expected an answer, attempted to speak; but the half-formed words died away on her lips. It was not thus she was used to receive the addresses of Delamere; her heart then left her reason and her resolution at liberty, but now the violence of its sensations deprived her of all power of uttering sentiments foreign to it, or concealing those it really felt.

Godolphin drew from this charming confusion a favourable omen. — 'You hear me not with anger, lovely Emmeline!' cried he — 'You allow me, then, to hope?'

'I can only repeat, Sir,' said Emmeline, in a voice hardly audible, that until I am of age, I have resolved to hear nothing on this subject.'

'And why not? Are you not now nearly as independant as you will be then?'

'Alas!' said Emmeline, 'I am indeed! — for my uncle concerns not himself about me, and it is doubtful whether he will do me even the justice to acknowledge me.'

'He must, he shall!' replied Godolphin warmly — 'Ah! entrust me with your interest; let me, in the character of the fortunate man whom you allow to hope for your favour — let me apply to him for justice.'

'That any one should make such an application, except Lord Westhaven, is what I greatly wish to avoid. I shall most reluctantly appeal to the interference of friends; and still more to that of *law*. The last is, you know, very uncertain. And instead of the heiress to the estate of my father, as I have lately been taught to believe myself, I may be found still to be the poor destitute orphan, so long dependant on the bounty of my uncle.'

'And as such,' cried Godolphin, greatly animated, 'you will be dearer to me than my existence! Yes! Emmeline; whether you are mistress of thousands, or friendless, portionless and deserted, your power over this heart is equally absolute — equally fixed! Ah! suffer not any consideration that relates to the uncertainty of your situation, to delay a moment the permission you must, you will give me, to avow my long and ardent passion?'

'It must not be, Mr. Godolphin!' (and tears filled her eyes as she spoke) 'Indeed it must not be! It is not now *possible*, at least it is very improper, for me to listen to you. Ah! do not then press it. I have indeed already suffered you to say too much on such a topic.'

Godolphin then renewed his warm entreaties that he might be permitted openly to profess himself her lover: but she still evaded giving way to them, by declaring that 'till she was of age she would not marry. 'Had I no other objections,' continued she, 'the singularity of my circumstances is alone sufficient to determine me. I cannot think of accepting the honour you offer me, while my very *name* is in some degree doubtful; it would, I own, mortify me to take any advantage of your generosity; and should I fail of obtaining from Lord Montreville that to which I am now believed to have a claim, his Lordship, irritated at the attempt, will probably withdraw what he has hitherto allowed me — scanty support, and occasional protection.'

'Find protection with your lover, with your husband!' exclaimed he — 'And may that happy husband, that adoring lover, be Godolphin! May Adelina forget her own calamities in contemplating the felicity of her brother; and may her beauteous, her benevolent friend, become her sister indeed, as she has long been the sister of her heart?'

'You will oblige me, Sir,' said Emmeline, feeling that notwithstanding all her attempts to conceal it the truth trembled in her eyes and faultered in her accents — 'you will oblige me if you say no more of this.'

'I will obey you, if you will only tell me I may hope.'

'How can I say so, Sir, when so long a time must intervene before I shall think of fixing myself for life.'

'Yet surely you know, the generous, the candid Miss Mowbray knows, whether her devoted Godolphin is agreeable to her, or whether, if every obstacle which exists in her timid imagination were removed, he would be judged wholly unworthy of pretending to the honour of her hand?'

'Certainly not unworthy,' tremblingly said Emmeline.

'Let me then, thus encouraged, go farther — and ask if I have a place in your esteem?'

'Do not ask me — indeed I cannot tell — Nay I beg, I entreat,' added she, trying to disengage her hands from him, 'that you will desist — do not force me to leave you.'

'Ah! talk not, think not of leaving me; think rather of confirming those fortunate presages I draw from this lovely timidity. I cannot go till I know your thoughts of me — till I know what place I hold in that soft bosom.'

'I think of you as an excellent brother; as a generous and disinterested friend; for such I have found you; as a man of great good sense, of noble principles, of exalted honour!'

'As one then,' said Godolphin, vehemently interrupting her, 'not unworthy of being entrusted with your happiness; who may hope to be honoured with a deposit so inestimable, as the confidence and tenderness of that gentle and generous heart?'

'I do indeed think very highly of you. — I cannot, if I would, deny it.'

'And you allow me, then, to go instantly to Lord Montreville?'

'Oh! no! no! — surely nothing I have said implied such a consent.'

Godolphin, however, was still pressing; and at length brought her to confess, with blushes, and even with tears, her early and long partiality for him, and her resolution either to be his, or die unmarried. She found, indeed, all attempts to dissimulate, vain: the reserve she had forced herself to assume, gave way to her natural frankness; and having once been induced to make such an acknowledgment of the state of her heart, she determined to have no longer any secrets concealed from him who was its master.

She therefore candidly told him how great was her compassion for Lord Delamere, and how severe her apprehension of his rage, resentment and despair.

He allowed the force of the first; but as to the other, he would not suppose it a reason for delaying her marriage.

'Poor Delamere,' said he, 'is of a temper which opposition and difficulty renders more eager and more obstinate. Yet when you are for ever out of his reach; as the obstacle will become invincible, he must yield to necessity.

While you remain single, he will still hope. The greatest kindness, therefore, that you can do him, will be to convince him that he has nothing to expect from you; and put an end at once to the uncertainty which tortures him.'

'To drive him to despair? Ah! I know so well the dreadful force of his passions, and the excesses he is capable of committing when under their influence, that I dare not, I positively will not, risk it. I love Delamere as my brother; I love him for the resemblance he is said to bear to my father. I pity him for the errors which the natural impetuosity of his temper, inflamed by the unbounded indulgence of his mother, continually leads him into; and the misfortunes these causes are so frequently inflicting on him; and should his fatal inclination for me, be the means of bringing on himself and on his family yet other miseries, I should never forgive myself; or him by whose means they were incurred.'

'From me, at least, you have nothing of that sort to apprehend: I truly pity Delamere; I feel what it must be to have relinquished the woman he loves; and to find her lost to his hopes, while his passion is unabated: — be assured my compassion for him will induce me rather to soothe his unhappiness than to insult him with an ostentatious display of my enviable fortune. Yet if you suffer me to believe my attachment not disagreeable to you, how shall I wholly conceal it? how appear as not *daring* to avow that, which is the glory and happiness of my life? and by your being supposed disengaged and indifferent, see you exposed to the importunities of an infinite number of suitors, who, however inconsequential they may be to you, will torment *me*. I do not know that I have much of jealousy in my nature; yet I cannot tell how I shall bear to see Delamere presuming again on your former friendship for him —

Even the volatile and thoughtless Bellozane has the power to make me uneasy, when I see him so persuaded of his own merit, and so confident of success.'

'While you assert that you are but little disposed to jealousy, you are persuading me that you are extremely prone to it. You know Bellozane can never have the smallest interest in my heart. But as to Delamere, I am decided against inflaming his irritable passions, by encouraging an avowed rival, tho' I will do all I can by other means, to discourage him. The only condition on which I will continue to see you is, that you appear no otherwise interested about me, than as the favoured friend of your sister, your brother, and Lady Westhaven. Press me, therefore, no farther on the subject, and let us now part.'

'Tell me, first, whether your journey remains fixed for Thursday? — whether you still hold your generous resolution of going to Adelina?'

'I do. But I must insist on going alone.'

'And if Bellozane should enquire whither you are going? You see nothing prevents his following you; and to follow you to East Cliff, he will, you know, have sufficient excuse. Emmeline, I cannot bear it! — there is a presumption in his manner, which offends and shocks me; and which, however you may dislike it, it may not always be in your power to repress!'

'Surely he need not know that I am going thither.'

It was now, therefore, agreed between them that if Bellozane called upon her the next day, as he said he intended, she should be denied to him; and that early on the following morning, which was Thursday, she should set out for East Cliff, attended by Madelon and Le Limosin.

This arrangement was hardly made when Mrs. Stafford returned, weary and exhausted from the unpleasant party with which she had passed the day.

With Emmeline's permission (who left the room that she might not hear it) Godolphin related to Mrs. Stafford the conversation they had held. It was the only information which had any power to raise her depressed spirits; and as soon as Emmeline rejoined them, she added her entreaties to those of Godolphin. They urged her to conquer immediately all those scruples which divided her from him to whom she had given her heart; and to put herself into such protection as must at once obviate all the difficulties she apprehended. But Emmeline still adhered to her resolution of remaining single, if not 'till she was of age, at least till her affairs with her uncle were adjusted, and 'till she saw the unhappy Delamere restored to health and tranquillity. But notwithstanding this delay, Godolphin, assured of possessing her affection, left her with an heart which was even oppressed with the excess of its own happiness.

CHAPTER XI

EMMELINE seemed to be happier since she had confessed to Godolphin his influence over her mind, and since she had made him in some measure the director of her actions. She hoped that she might conceal her partiality 'till she had nothing to fear from Delamere; at present she was sure he had no suspicion that Godolphin was his rival; and she flattered herself, that on his return to England, the conviction of her coldness would by degrees wean him away from his attachment, and that he would learn to consider her only as his sister.

These pleasing hopes, however, were insufficient to balance the concern she felt for Mrs. Stafford; who having long struggled against the calamities, now seemed on the point of sinking under their pressure, and of determining to attend, in despondent resignation, the end of her unmerited sufferings.

Emmeline attempted to re-animate her, by repeating all the promises of Lord Westhaven, on whose word she had the most perfect reliance. She assured her, that the moment her own affairs were settled, her first care should be the re-establishment of those of her beloved friend. For some time the oppressed spirits of Mrs. Stafford would only allow her to answer with her tears these generous assurances. At length she said —

'It is to you, my Emmeline, I could perhaps learn to be indebted without being humbled; for you have an heart which receives while it confers an obligation. But think what it is for one, born with a right to affluence and educated in its expectation, with feelings keen from nature, and made yet keener by refinement, to be compelled, as I have been, to solicit favours, pecuniary favours, from persons who have no feeling at all — from the shifting, paltry-spirited James Crofts, forbearance from the claim of debts; from the callous-hearted and selfish politician, his father, pity and assistance; from Rochely, who has no ideas but of getting or saving money, to ask the loan of it! and to bear with humility a rude refusal. I have endured the brutal unkindness of hardened avarice, the dirty chicane of law, exercised by the most contemptible of beings; I have been forced to attempt softening the tradesman and the mechanic, and to suffer every degree of humiliation which the insolence of sudden prosperity or the insensible coolness of the determined money dealer, could inflict. Actual poverty, I think, I could have better born;

> 'I should have found, in some place of my soul,
> A drop of patience!'

But ineffectual attempts to ward it off by such degradation I can no longer submit to. While Mr. Stafford, for whom I have encountered it all, is not only unaffected by the poignant mortifications which torture me; but receives my efforts to serve him, if successful, only as a duty — if unsuccessful, he considers my failure as a fault; and loads me with reproach, with invective, with contempt! — others have, in their husbands, protectors and friends; mine, not only throws on me the burthen of affairs which he has himself embroiled, but adds to their weight by cruelty and oppression. Such complicated and incurable misery must overwhelm me, and then — what will become of my children?'

Penetrated with pity and sorrow, Emmeline listened, in tears, to this strong but too faithful picture of the situation of her unfortunate friend; and with difficulty said, in a voice of the tenderest pity —

'Yet a little patience and surely things will mend. It cannot be very long, before I shall either be in high affluence or reduced to my former dependance; perhaps to actual indigence. Of these events, I hope the former is the most probable: but be it as it may, you and your children will be equally dear to me. — If I am rich, my house, my fortune shall be yours — if I am poor, I will live with you, and we will work together. But for such resources as the pencil or the needle may afford us, we shall, I think, have no occasion. You, my dear friend, will continue to exert yourself for your children; Lord Westhaven is greatly interested for you; and all will yet be well.'

'I am afraid not,' replied Mrs. Stafford. 'Among the various misfortunes of life, there are some that admit of no cure; some, which even the tender and generous friendship of my Emmeline can but palliate. Of that nature, I fear, are many of mine. My past life has been almost all bitterness; God only knows what the remainder of it may be, but

'Shadows, clouds, and darkness, rest upon it.'

'Ah! give not up your mind to these gloomy thoughts,' said Emmeline. 'Setting aside all hopes I have of being able, without the assistance of any one, to clear those prospects, I have a firm dependance on Lord Westhaven, and am sure I shall yet see you happy.'

'Never, I believe, in this world!' dejectedly answered Mrs. Stafford. 'But why should I distress you, my best Emmeline, with a repetition of my hopeless sorrows; why cannot I now refrain, as I have hitherto done, from taxing with my complaints your lively sensibility?' She then began to talk of their journey for the next day, for which every thing was now ready. It would have been very agreeable to Emmeline could Mrs. Stafford have gone by Southampton, and have accompanied her for a few days to East Cliff; but she said, that besides her suffering so much at sea, which made the long passage to France very dreadful to her, she had already, in a letter to her husband, fixed to go by Calais; and as he might either send or come to meet her on that road, he might be offended if she took the other: besides these reasons, she had yet another in the chance the Calais road afforded of meeting Lord and Lady Westhaven. The two last arguments were unanswerable: Emmeline relinquished the project of their going together; and they passed the rest of the day in the last preparations for their separate journeys. In the course of it, Bellozane called twice, but was not admitted. Godolphin was allowed to sup with them; and early the next morning came again to see them set out. They parted on all sides with tears and reluctance — Emmeline, with Madelon in the chaise with her, and Le Limosin on horseback, took the road to Southampton, and Mrs. Stafford pursued her melancholy journey to Dover.

Emmeline arrived at Southampton late the same evening, where she slept; and the next morning landed on the Isle of Wight.

It was a clear and mild day, towards the end of October; and she walked, attended by her servants, to East Cliff. As she approached the door of Godolphin's house, her heart beat quick; a thousand tender recollections arose that related to its beloved master, and some mournful apprehensions for the fate of its present lovely and unhappy inhabitant.

The maid who had so long waited on Lady Adelina opened the door, and expressed the utmost delight at seeing Emmeline. 'Ah! dearest Madam!' said she, 'how good it is in you to come to my lady! Now, I hope, both her health and her spirits will be better. But the joy of knowing you are here, will overcome her, unless I inform her of it with caution; for tho' she rather expected you, I know it will be extreme.'

Barret then ran to execute this welcome commission, and in a few moments Lady Adelina, supported by her, walked into the room, holding in her hand little William, and fell, almost insensible, into the arms of her friend.

The expression of her countenance, faded as it was, where a gleam of exquisite pleasure seemed to lighten up the soft features which had long sunk under the blighting hand of sorrow; her weeds, forming so striking a contrast to the fairness of her transparent skin; and the lovely child, now about fourteen months old, which hung on her arm; made her altogether appear to Emmeline the most interesting, the most affecting figure, she had ever seen. Neither of them could speak. Lady Adelina murmured something, and she fondly pressed Emmeline to her heart; but it was not till its oppression was relieved by tears, that she could distinctly thank her for coming. Emmeline, with equal marks of tenderness, embraced the mother and caressed the son, whose infantine beauty would have charmed her had he been the child of a stranger. After a little, they grew more composed; and Emmeline, while Lady Adelina in the most melting accents spoke of her brother William, and enquired tenderly after her elder brother and his wife, had time to contemplate her lovely but palid face; from which the faint glow of transient pleasure, the animated vivacity of momentary rapture, was gone; and a languor so great seemed to hang over her, such pensive and settled melancholy had taken possession of her features, that Emmeline could hardly divest herself of the idea of immediate danger; and fancied that she was come thither only to see the beauteous mourner sink into the grave. She trembled to think on the consequence which, in such a state of health, might arise from the conflict she would probably have to undergo in regard to Fitz-Edward. Emmeline herself dared not name him to Godolphin in their long conference. It was a subject, on which (however slightly touched) he had always expressed such painful sensibility, that she could not resolve to enter upon it with him. Yet she foresaw, that on Lord Westhaven's arrival either a general explanation must take place, or that his Lordship would accept, for his sister, the offer of Fitz-Edward, to which there would be in his eyes, (while he yet remained ignorant of their former unfortunate acquaintance,) no possible objection. She supposed that Lord and Lady Clancarryl, equally ignorant of that error (which had been partly owing to their own confidence in Fitz-Edward) would press Lady Adelina to accept him; and that Godolphin must either consent to forgive, and receive him as his brother, or give such reasons for opposing his alliance with Lady Adelina, as would probably destroy the peace of his family and the fragile existence of his sister. Sometimes, she thought that his inflexible honour would yield, and induce him to bury the past in oblivion. But then she recollected all the indignation he had but lately expressed against Fitz-Edward, and doubted, with fearful apprehension, the event.

The first day passed without that mutual and unreserved confidence being absolutely established, which the lovely friends longed to repose in each other. Lady Adelina languished to enquire after, to talk of Fitz-Edward, yet dared not trust herself with his name; and Emmeline, tho' well assured that the knowledge of those terms which she was now on with Godolphin would give infinite pleasure to his sister, yet had not courage to reveal that truth which her conscious heart secretly enjoyed. Affected with her friend's depression, and unwilling to keep her up late, she complained of fatigue soon in the evening, and retired to her own room. She there dismissed Madelon, and bade her, as soon as Mrs. Barret came from her lady's apartment, let her know that she desired to speak to her.

She wished to enquire of this faithful servant her opinion of her lady's health. And as soon as she came to her, expressed her fears about it in terms equally anxious and tender.

'Ah! Madam,' said Barret, 'all you observe as to my lady is but too just; and what I go thro' about her, (especially when the Captain is not here) I am sure no tongue can tell. Sometimes, Ma'am, when I have left her of a night, and she tells me she is going to bed, I hear her walk about the room talking; then she goes to the bed (for I have looked thro' the key hole) where Master Godolphin sleeps, and looks at him, and bursts into tears and laments herself over him, and again begins to walk about the room, and speaks as it were to herself; and at other times, she will open the window, and leaning her head on her two hands, sit and look at the clouds and the stars; and sighs so deeply, and so often, that it makes my heart quite ache to hear her. The child was very ill once with a tooth fever, while the Captain was gone to France; and then indeed I thought my poor lady would have been quite, quite gone in her head again; for she talked *so* wildly of what she would do if he died, and said such things, as almost frightened me to death. We sent to Winchester for a physician; and before he could come, for you know, Ma'am, what a long way 'tis to send, she grew so impatient, and had terrified herself into such agonies, that when the doctor did come, he said she was in a great deal the most danger of the two. Thank God, Master Godolphin soon got well; but it was a long time before my lady was quiet herself again; and since that, Ma'am, she will hardly suffer Master out of her sight at all; but makes either his own maid or me sit in the room to attend upon him while she reads or writes. When she walks out, she generally orders one of us to take him with her; and only goes out alone after he is in bed of a night. Then, indeed, she stays out long enough; and tho' you see, Ma'am, how sadly she looks, she never seems to care at all about her own health, but does things that really would kill a strong person.'

'What then does she do?' enquired Emmeline.

'Why, Ma'am, quite late sometimes of a night, when every body else is asleep, she will go away by herself perhaps to that wood you see there, or down to the sea shore; and she orders me to let nobody follow her. Quite of cold nights this Autumn, when the wind blew, and the sea made a noise so loud and dismal, she has staid there whole hours by herself; only I ventured to disobey her so far as to see that no harm came to her. But three or four times, Ma'am, she remained so long that I concluded she must catch her death. At last, I bethought me of getting one of the maids to go and tell her Master was awake; and I have got her to come in by that means out of the wind and the cold. Then, Ma'am, she seems to take pleasure in nothing but sorrow and melancholy. The books she reads are so sad, that sometime, when her own eyes are tired and she makes me read them to her, I get quite horrible thoughts in my head. But my lady, instead of trying, as I do, to shake them off, will go directly to her music, and play such mournful tunes, that it really quite overcomes me, as I am at work in another room. At other times she goes and writes verses about her own unhappiness. How is it possible, Ma'am, that with such ways of passing her time, my lady, always so delicate as she was in health, should be well?: for my part I only wonder she is not quite dead.'

'But how do you know, Barret, that your lady employs herself in writing verses about her own unhappiness?'

'Dear, Ma'am, I have found them about every where. When the Captain is absent, my lady is indifferent where she leaves them. Sometimes four or five sheets lay open on the table in her little dressing room, and sometimes upon her music.'

Emmeline was too certain that such were the occupations of her poor friend. During the short time they had been together, Lady Adelina had shewn her some work; and as she took it out of her drawer, she drew out some papers with it.

'I do but little work,' said she. 'I find even embroidery does not serve to call off my thoughts sufficiently from myself. I read a good deal in books of mere amusement, for of serious application I am incapable; and here is another specimen of my method of employing myself, which perhaps you will not think a remedy for melancholy thoughts.'

She put a written paper into Emmeline's hand, who was about to open it; but Lady Adelina added, with a pensive smile, 'do not read it now; rather keep it till you are alone.'

This paper Emmeline took out to peruse as soon as she had dismissed Barret. Her heart bled as she ran over this testimony of the anguish and despondence which preyed on the heart of Lady Adelina. It was an

ODE TO DESPAIR

Thou spectre of terrific mien,
Lord of the hopeless heart and hollow eye,
In whose fierce train each form is seen
That drives sick Reason to insanity!
I woo thee with unusual prayer,
'Grim visaged, comfortless Despair!'
Approach; in me a willing victim find,
Who seeks thine iron sway — and calls thee kind!

Ah! hide for ever from my sight
The faithless flatterer Hope — whose pencil, gay,
Portrays some vision of delight,
Then bids the fairy tablet fade away;
While in dire contrast, to mine eyes
Thy phantoms, yet more hideous, rise,
And Memory draws, from Pleasure's wither'd flower,
Corrosives for the heart — of fatal power!

I bid the traitor Love, adieu!
Who to this fond, believing bosom came,

A guest insidious and untrue,
With Pity's soothing voice — in Friendship's name;
The wounds *he* gave, nor Time shall cure,
Nor Reason teach me to endure.
And to that breast mild Patience pleads in vain,
Which feels the curse — of meriting its pain.
Yet not to me, tremendous power!
Thy worst of spirit-wounding pangs impart,
With which, in dark conviction's hour,
Thou strik'st the guilty unrepentant heart!
But of Illusion long the sport,
That dreary, tranquil gloom I court
Where my past errors I may still deplore
And dream of long-lost happiness no more!

To thee I give this tortured breast,
Where Hope arises but to foster pain;
Ah! lull its agonies to rest!
Ah! let me never be deceiv'd again!
But callous, in thy deep repose
Behold, in long array, the woes
Of the dread future, calm and undismay'd,
Till I may claim the hope — that shall not fade!

The feelings of a mind which could dictate such an address, appeared to Emmeline so greatly to be lamented, and so unlikely to be relieved, that the tender and painful compassion she had ever been sensible of for her unhappy friend, was if possible augmented. Full of ideas almost as mournful as those by which they had been inspired, she went to bed, but not to tranquil sleep. Her spirits, worn by her journey, and oppressed by her concern for Lady

Adelina, were yet busy; and instead of the uneasy images which had pursued her while she waked, they represented to her others yet more terrifying. She beheld, in her dreams, Godolphin wildly seeking vengeance of Fitz-Edward for the death of his sister. Then, instead of Fitz-Edward, Lord Delamere appeared to be the object of his wrath, and mutual fury seemed to animate them against the lives of each other. To them, her uncle, in all the phrenzy of grief and despair, succeeded; overwhelmed her with reproaches for the loss of his only son, and tore her violently away from Godolphin, who in vain pursued her.

These horrid visions returned so often, drest in new forms of terror, that Emmeline, having long resisted the impression they made upon her, could at length bear them no longer; but shaking off all disposition to indulge sleep on such terms, she arose from her bed, and wrapping herself up in her night gown, went to the window. The dawn did not yet appear; but she sat down by the window, of which she had opened the shutter to watch its welcome approach.

The morning, for it was between three and four, was mild; the declining stars were obscured by no cloud, and served to shew dimly the objects in the garden beneath her. She softly opened the sash; listened to the low, hollow murmur of the sea; and surveyed the lawn and the hill behind it, which, by the faint and uncertain light, she could just discern. All breathed a certain solemn and melancholy stillness calculated to inspire horror. Emmeline's blood ran cold; yet innocence like hers really fears nothing if free from the prejudices of superstition. She endeavoured to conquer the disagreeable sensations she felt, and to shake off the effects of her dreams; but the silence, and the gloominess of the scene, assisted but little her efforts, and she cast an eye of solicitude towards the Eastern horizon, and wished for the return of the sun.

In this disposition of mind, she was at once amazed and alarmed, by seeing the figure of a man, tall and thin, wrapped in a long horseman's coat, as if on purpose to disguise him, force himself out from between the shrubs which bounded one part of the lawn. He looked not towards the windows; but with folded arms, and his hat over his eyes, was poring on the ground, while with slow steps he crossed the lawn and came immediately under the windows of the house.

When she first perceived him, she had started back from that where she sat; but tho' greatly surprized, she could not forbear watching him: on longer observing his figure, she fancied it was that of a gentleman; and by his slow walk and manner he did not appear to have any design to attack the house. Her presence of mind never forsook her unless where her heart was greatly affected; and she had now courage enough to determine that she would still continue for some moments to observe him, and would not alarm the servants till she saw reason to believe he had ill intentions. She sat therefore quite still; and saw, that instead of making any attempt to enter the house, he traversed the whole side of it next the lawn, with a measured and solemn pace, several times; then stopped a moment, again went to the end, and slowly returned; and having continued to do so near an hour, he crossed the grass, and disappeared among the shrubs from whence he had issued.

Had not Emmeline been very sure that she not only heard his footsteps distinctly as he passed over a gravel walk in his way, but even heard him breathe hard and short, as if agitated or fatigued, she would almost have persuaded herself that it was a phantom raised by her disordered spirits. The longer she reflected on it, the more incomprehensible it seemed, that a man should, at such an hour, make such an excursion, apparently to so little purpose. That it was with a dishonest design there seemed no likelihood, as he made no effort to force his way into the house, which he might easily have done; and had he come on a clandestine visit to any of the servants, he would probably have had some signal by which his confederates would have been informed of his approach. But he seemed rather fearful of disturbing the sleeping inhabitants; his step was slow and light; and on perceiving the first rays of the morning, he 'started like a guilty thing,' and swiftly stepped away to his concealment.

Emmeline continued some time at the window after his disappearance, believing he might return. But it soon grew quite light: the gardener appeared at his work; and she was then convinced that he would for that time come no more.

So extraordinary a circumstance, however, dwelt on her mind; nor could she entirely divest herself of alarm. A strange and confused idea that this visitor might be some one not unknown to her, crossed her mind. His height answered almost equally to that of Bellozane, Godolphin, and Fitz-Edward. The latter, indeed, was rather the tallest, and to him she thought the figure bore the greatest resemblance. Yet he had taken leave of her ten days before she left London, and told her he was going down to Mr. Percival's, in Berkshire; where, as he was very anxious to hear of Lady Adelina, he had desired Mrs. Stafford to write to him; (who had done so, and had received an answer of thanks dated from thence before the departure of Emmeline from London). That Fitz-Edward, therefore, should be the person, seemed improbable; yet it was hardly less so that a night ruffian should be on foot so long, without any attempt to execute mischief, or even the appearance of examining how it might be perpetrated. After long consideration, she determined, that lest the first conjecture should be true, she would speak to nobody of the stranger she had seen; but would watch another night, before she either terrified Lady Adelina with the apprehension of robbers, or gave rise to conjectures in her and the servants of yet more disquieting tendency. Having taken this resolution, and argued herself out of all those fears for her personal safety which might have enfeebled a less rational mind, she met Lady Adelina at breakfast with her usual ease, and almost with her usual chearfulness: but she was pale, and her eyes were heavy: Lady Adelina remarked it with concern; but Emmeline, making light of it, imputed it intirely to the fatigue of her journey; and when their breakfast was finished, proposed a walk. To this her friend assented; and while she went to give some orders, and to fetch the crape veil in which she usually wrapped herself, (for even her dress partook something of the mournful cast of her mind), Emmeline, already equipped, went into the lawn, and saw plainly where the stranger had made his way thro' the thick shrubs, and where the flexible branches of a young larch were twisted away, a laurel broken, and that some deciduous trees behind them had lost all their lower leaves; which, having sustained the first frosts, fell on the slightest violence. She marked the place with her eye; and determined to observe whether, if he came again, it was from thence.

Emmeline now desired that Madelon might come with them to wait on little William, rather than his own maid; as she understood English so ill, that she would be no interruption to their discourse. They then walked arm in arm together towards the sea; and there Lady Adelina, who now enjoyed the opportunity she had so long languished for, opened to her sympathizing friend the sorrows of an heart struggling vainly with a passion she condemned, and sinking under ineffectual efforts to vindicate her honour and eradicate her love.

She knew not that Fitz-Edward had ever written to her. Godolphin, well acquainted with his hand, had kept the letter from her. She knew not that he had applied to Emmeline: and tho' she had torn herself from him, and had vowed never again to write to him, to name him, to hear from him, she involuntarily felt disposed to accuse him of neglect, of ingratitude, of cruelty, for having never attempted to write to her or see her; and added the poignant anguish of jealousy to the dreary horrors of despair. That Fitz-Edward was for ever lost to her, she seemed to be convinced; yet that he should forget her, or attach himself to another, seemed a torment so entirely insupportable, that when her mind dwelt upon it, as it perpetually did, her reason was inadequate to the pain it inflicted; and when she touched on that subject, Emmeline too evidently saw symptoms of that derangement of intellect to which she had once before been a melancholy witness.

With a mind thus unsettled, and a heart thus oppressed, the consequences of touching on the application of Fitz-Edward to herself, might, as Emmeline believed, have the most alarming effect on Lady Adelina. And she dared not therefore name it unless she had the concurrence of Godolphin. She only attempted to soothe and tranquillize her mind, without giving her those assurances of his undiminished attachment, which, she thought, might in the event only encrease her anguish, if her brother remained inflexible. On the other hand, she forbore to remonstrate with her on the necessity there might be to forget him; being too well convinced that the arguments which were to enforce that doctrine, would be useless, and perhaps appear cruel, to a heart so deeply wounded as was that of the luckless, lovely Adelina.

But in pouring her sorrows into the bosom of her friend she appeared to find consolation. The tender pity of Emmeline was a balm to her wounded mind; and growing more composed, she began to discourse on the singular discovery Emmeline had made, and to enter with some interest into the affairs depending between her and the Marquis of Montreville; and by questions, aided by the natural frankness of Emmeline, at length became acquainted with the happy prospects, which, tho' distant, opened to Godolphin.

This was the only information that seemed to have the power of suspending for a moment the weight of those afflictions which Lady Adelina suffered. 'My brother then,' cried she — 'my dear Godolphin, will be happy! And you, my most amiable friend, will constitute, while you share his felicity. Ah! fortunate, thrice fortunate for ye both, was the hour of your meeting; for heaven and nature surely designed ye for each other! Fortunate, too, were those circumstances which divided my Emmeline from Delamere, before indissoluble bonds enchained you for ever. Had it been otherwise; had *your* guardian angel slumbered as *mine did*; you too, all lovely and deserving as you are, would have been condemned to the bitterest of all lots, and might have discovered all the excellence and worth of Godolphin, when your duty and your honour allowed you no eyes but for Delamere. *Your* destiny is more happy — yet not happier than you deserve. Ah! may it quickly be fixed unalterably; and long, very long, may it endure! So shall your Adelina, for the little while she drags on a reluctant existence, have something on which to lean for the alleviation of her sorrows; and when she shall interrupt your felicity no longer by the sight of cureless calamity, she will, in full confidence, entrust the sole tie she has on earth, the dear and innocent victim of her fatal weakness, to the compassionate bosoms of Godolphin and his Emmeline!'

The tremulous voice and singular manner in which Lady Adelina uttered these words, made Emmeline tremble. She now tried to divert the attention of her poor friend, from dwelling too earnestly either on her own wretchedness or the promised felicity of her brother: but, as if exhausted by the mingled emotions of pain and pleasure, she soon afterwards fell into a deep silence; scarce attending to what was said; and after a long pause, she suddenly called to Madelon, in whose arms her little boy had fallen asleep, and looking at him earnestly a moment, took him from the maid, and carried him towards the house. Emmeline, more and more convinced of her partial intellectual derangement, followed her, dreading lest she should see it encrease, without the power of applying any remedy. Before Lady Adelina reached the gate, which opened from the cliffs to the lawn, she was fatigued by her lovely burthen and forced to stop. Emmeline would then have taken him; but she said 'No!' and sitting down on the ground, held him in her lap, till Barret, who had seen her from a window, came out and took him from her; to which, as to a thing usual, she consented, and then walked calmly home with Emmeline, who, extremely discomposed by the wildness of her manner, was fearful of again introducing any interesting topic, lest she should again touch those fine chords which were untuned in the mind of her unhappy friend; and which seemed occasionally to vibrate with an acuteness that threatened the ruin of the whole fabric. Barret, who afterwards came to assist her in dressing, told her, that within the last six weeks her lady had often been subject to long fits of absence, sometimes of tears; which generally ended in her snatching the child eagerly to her, kissing him with the wildest fondness, and that after having kept him with her some time, and wept extremely, she usually became rational and composed for the rest of the day.

CHAPTER XII

WHEN Emmeline met Lady Adelina at dinner, she had the satisfaction to find her quite tranquil and easy. As the afternoon proved uncommonly fine, and Emmeline was never weary of contemplating the scenery which surrounded them, she willingly consented to Lady Adelina's proposal of another ramble; that she might see some beautiful cliffs, a little farther from the house than she had yet been. There, she was pleased to find, that her fair friend seemed to call off her mind from its usual painful occupations to Admire the charms, which on one side a very lovely country, and on the other an extensive sea view, offered to their sight.

'You cannot imagine, my Emmeline,' said she, 'how exquisitely beautiful the prospect is from the point of these rocks where we stand, in the midst of summer; now the sun, more distant, gives it a less glowing and rich lustre, and reflects not his warm rays on the sea, and on the white cliffs that hang over it. Here it was, that indulging that melancholy for which I have too much reason, I made, while my brother was absent last summer, some lines, which, if it was pleasant to repeat one's own poetry, I would read to you, as descriptive at once of the scene, and the state of mind in which I surveyed it.'

Emmeline now earnestly pressing her to gratify the curiosity she had thus raised, at length prevailed upon her to repeat the following

Far on the sands, the low, retiring tide,
In distant murmurs hardly seems to flow,
And o'er the world of waters, blue and wide
The sighing summer wind, forgets to blow.

As sinks the day star in the rosy West,
The silent wave, with rich reflection glows;
Alas! can tranquil nature give *me* rest,
Or scenes of beauty, soothe me to repose?

Can the soft lustre of the sleeping main,
You radient heaven; or all creation's charms,
'Erase the written troubles of the brain,'
Which Memory tortures, and which Guilt alarms?
Or bid a bosom transient quiet prove,
That bleeds with vain remorse, and unextinguish'd love!

The 'season and the scene' were brought by this description full on the mind of Emmeline; yet she almost immediately repented having pressed Adelina to repeat to her what seemed to have led her again into her usual tract of sad reflection. She fell, as usual, into one of her reveries, and as they walked homewards said very little. The rest of the evening, however, passed in a sort of mournful tranquillity — Adelina seemed to feel encreasing pleasure as she gazed on her friend; and remembering all her goodness, reflected on the happiness of her brother. But this satisfaction was not of that kind which seeks to express itself in words; and Emmeline, sensible of great anxiety for her and Godolphin, (who would, she knew, be cruelly hurt by the relapse which he feared threatened his sister) and busied in no pleasant conjectures about the person whom she had seen in the lawn, was in no spirits for conversation. Nor did her thoughts, when they wandered to other objects from those immediately before her, bring home much to appease her anxiety. That nothing had yet been heard of Lord and Lady Westhaven, was extremely disquieting. She knew not that the Marquis of Montreville had received a letter for her under cover to him; and that having sent it to Mr. Crofts in another, in order to be forwarded to her, the latter had exercised his political talents, and supposing it related to her claims on Lord Montreville, and probably contained instructions for pursuing them, and that therefore his Lordship would be but little concerned if it never reached the place of its destination, he had very composedly put it into the fire; and undertook, should it be enquired for, to account for its failure without suffering the name of Lord Montreville to be called in question.

The Marquis, tho' his conscience had been so long under the direction of Sir Richard Crofts that it ought to have acquired insensibility as callous as his own, yet found it sometimes a very troublesome companion; and it often spoke to him so severely on the subject of his niece, that he was more than once on the point of writing to her, to say he was ready to make her the retribution to which his heart told him she had the clearest pretensions, and which his fears whispered that a court of justice would certainly render her.

These qualms and these fears, would inevitably have produced a restoration of the Mowbray estate to its owner, had they not been counteracted by the influence of the Marchioness of Montreville and Sir Richard Crofts. The Marchioness, now in declining health, felt all the inefficacy of riches, and all the fallacy of ambition; yet could she not determine to relinquish one, or to own that the other had but little power to confer happiness. That Emmeline Mowbray, whom she had despised and rejected, should suddenly become heiress to a large fortune, and that of that fortune her own children should be deprived; that Lord Westhaven should be the instrument to assist her in this hateful transition, and should interfere for this obscure orphan, against the interest of the illustrious family into which he had married; stung her to the soul, and irritated the natural asperity of her temper, already soured by the repeated defection of Delamere, and her own continual ill health, till it was grown insupportable to others, and injurious to herself; since it aggravated all her complaints, and put it out of the power of medicine to relieve her.

Rather than encrease these maladies by opposition, his Lordship was content to yield to delay. And while her haughtiness and violence withheld him on one hand from settling with his niece, Sir Richard assailed him on the other with cool and plausible arguments; and together they obliged him to have recourse to such expedients as gained time, without his having much hope that he could finally detain the property of his late brother from his daughter, who seemed likely to establish her right to its possession.

At once to indulge his avarice and quiet his conscience, he would willingly have consented to pay her a considerable portion, and to leave her right to the whole undecided; but of such an accommodation there seemed no probability, unless he could win over Lord Westhaven to his interest. He thought, however, that there could be little doubt of his re-uniting the Mowbray estate with his own, by promoting the marriage between Emmeline and Lord Delamere, which he had hitherto so strenuously opposed. But this, he knew, must be the last resort; not only because he was ashamed so immediately to avow a change of opinion in regard to Emmeline, which could have happened only from her change of circumstances, but because the dislike which Lady Montreville had originally conceived towards her, now amounted to the most determined and inveterate hatred.

Bent on conversing fully with Lord Westhaven before he took any measures whatever either to detain or to restore the estate, the Marquis was desirous of seeing him immediately on his arrival in England, and to precede any conversation he might hold with Emmeline. For this reason he kept back all information that related to his son-in-law's return; and tho' he knew that the indisposition of Lord Delamere and his sister had kept Lord Westhaven at Paris almost three weeks, and that they were travelling only twenty miles a day, from thence to Calais, he had withheld even this intelligence from the anxious Emmeline.

Lady Frances Crofts, never feeling any great disposition to filial piety, and having lost, in the giddy career of dissipation, the little sensibility she ever possessed, was soon tired of attending on her mother at Audley Hall. The fretful impatience or irksome lassitude which devoured a mind without resources, and weary of itself, in the melancholy gloom of a sick chamber, soon disgusted and fatigued her; she therefore left Audley Hall in October, and after staying ten days or a fortnight in Burlington-street, where she made an acquaintance with Bellozane, she went to pass the months that yet intervened before it was fashionable to appear in London, at a villa near Richmond; which she had taken in the summer, and fitted up with every ornament luxury could invent or money purchase. She retired not thither, however, to court the sylvan deities: a set of friends of both sexes attended her. Bellozane was very handsome, very lively, very much a man of fashion: Lady Frances, who thought him no bad addition to her train, invited him also. Bellozane became the life of the party; and was soon so much at his ease in the family, and so great a favourite with her Ladyship, at a very early period of their acquaintance, that only her high rank there exempted her from those censures, which, in a less elevated condition, would have fallen on her, from the grave and sagacious personages who are so good as to take upon them the regulation of the world.

Crofts, detained by his office in London, heard more than gave him any pleasure. But like a wise and cautious husband, he forebore to complain. Besides the fear of his wife, which was no inconsiderable motive to silence, he had the additional fear of the martial and fierce-looking French soldier before his eyes; who talked, in very bad English, of such encounters and exploits as made the cold-blooded politician shudder.

When, on Friday evenings, after the business of his office was over, he went down to Richmond, he now always found there this foreign Adonis; and beheld him with mingled hatred and horror, tho' he concealed both under the appearance of cringing and servile complaisance. And when Lady Frances compared the narrow-spirited and mean-looking Crofts, with the handsome, animated, gallant Bellozane, the poor husband felt all the disadvantages of the comparison, and as certainly suffered for it. Scorning to dissimulate with a man whom she thought infinitely too fortunate in being allied to her on any terms, and superior to the censures of a world, the greater part of whom she considered as beings of another species from the daughter of the Marquis of Montreville, her Ladyship grew every day fonder of the Chevalier, and less solicitous to conceal her partiality. She found, too, her vanity and inordinate self love gratified, in believing that this elegant foreigner did justice to her superior attractions, and had been won by them, from that inclination for Emmeline which had brought him to England. A conquest snatched from *her*, whom she had always considered at once with envy and contempt, was doubly delightful; and Bellozane, with all the volatility of his adopted country, saw nothing disloyal or improper in returning the kind attentions of Lady Frances, *en attendant* the arrival of Emmeline; with whom he was a good deal piqued for her having left London so abruptly without informing him whither she was gone. He still preferred her to every other person; but he was not therefore insensible to the kindness, or blind to the charms of Lady Frances; who was really very handsome; and who, with a great portion of the beauty inherited by the Mowbray family, possessed the Juno-like air as well as the high spirit of her mother. In aid of these natural advantages, every refinement of art was exhausted; and by those who preferred its dazzling effects to the interesting and graceful simplicity of unadorned beauty, Lady Frances, dressed for the opera, might have been esteemed more charming, than Emmeline in her modest muslin night gown; or than the pensive Madona, which, in her widow's dress, was represented by Lady Adelina.

These two friends, after having passed a calm afternoon together, retired early to their respective apartments. Emmeline, who had a repeating watch, given her by Lord

Westhaven, wound it up carefully; and having bolted her chamber door, lay down for a few hours; being sure that the anxiety she felt would awaken her before the return of that on which the stranger had appeared the preceding night. Fatigue and long watching closed her eyes; but her slumber was imperfect; and suddenly awaking at some fancied noise, she pressed her repeater and found it was half past three o'clock.

This was about the time on which the man had appeared the night before; and tho' she felt some fear, she had yet more curiosity to know whether he came again. She arose softly, therefore, and went to the window, which she did not venture to open. But she had no occasion to look towards the shrubbery to watch the coming of the stranger; he was already traversing the length of the house, dressed as before; and with his arms folded, and his head bent towards the ground, he slowly moved in the same pensive attitude.

Emmeline, tho' now impressed with deeper astonishment, summoned resolution narrowly to observe his air and figure. Had not his hat concealed his face, the obscurity would not have allowed her to examine his features. But tho' the great coat he wore considerably altered the outline of his person, she still thought she discerned the form of Fitz-Edward. His height and his walk confirmed this idea; and the longer she observed him, the more she was persuaded it was Fitz-Edward himself. This conviction was not unaccompanied by terror. She wished to speak to him; and to represent the indiscretion, the madness of his thus risking the reputation of Lady Adelina; and his own life or that of one of her brothers; while the very idea of Godolphin's resentment and danger filled her mind with the most alarming apprehensions. She determined then to open the window and speak to him: yet if it should not be Fitz-Edward? At length she had collected the courage necessary; and knowing that tho' the whole family was yet fast asleep she could easily rouse them, if the person to whom she spoke should not be known to her, and gave her any reason for alarm, she was on the point of lifting up the sash, when the stranger put an end to her deliberations by hastily walking away to his former covert among the shrubs; and she saw him no more.

Emmeline, wearied alike with watchfulness and uneasiness, now went to bed; having at length determined to keep Barret (on whose silence and discretion she could rely) with her the next night; and when the Colonel appeared (for the Colonel she was sure it was) to send her to him, or at least make her witness to what she should herself say to him from the window. The anxiety of her mind made her very low on the early part of the next day; and Lady Adelina was still more so. They dined, however, early; and as the evening was clear, and they had not been out in the morning, Lady Adelina proposed their taking a short walk to the top of the hill behind the house, which commanded a glorious view that Emmeline had not seen; but as it was cold, they agreed to leave little William at home. The grounds of Godolphin behind the house, consisted only of a small paddock, divided from the kitchen garden by a dwarf wall; and the copse, which partly cloathed the hill, and thro' which a footpath went to a village about two miles beyond it. The woody ground ceasing about half way up, opened to a down which commanded the view. They stood admiring it a few moments; and then Emmeline, who could not for an instant help reflecting on what she had seen for two nights, felt something like alarm at being so far from the house.

She complained therefore that it was cold; and the evening (at this season very short) was already shutting in.

The wind blew chill and hollow among the half stripped trees, as they passed thro' the wood; and the dead leaves rustled in the blast. 'Twas such a night as Ossian might describe. Emmeline recollected the visionary beings with which his poems abound, and involuntarily she shuddered. At the gate that opened into the lawn, Lady Adelina stopped as if she was tired. She was talking of something Godolphin had done; and Emmeline, who on that subject was never weary of hearing her, turned round, and they both leaned for a moment against the gate, looking up the wood walk from which they had just descended. The veil of Lady Adelina was over her face; but Emmeline, less wrapped up, suddenly saw the figure which had before visited the garden, descending, in exactly the same posture, down the pathway, which was rather steep. He seemed unknowingly to follow it, without looking up; and was soon so near them, that Emmeline, losing at once her presence of mind, clasped her hands, and exclaimed — 'Good God! who is this?'

'What?' said Lady Adelina, looking towards him.

By this time he was within six paces of the gate; and sprung forward at the very moment that she knew him, and fell senseless on the ground.

Emmeline, unable to save her, was in a situation but little better. Fitz-Edward, for it was really himself, knelt down by her, and lifted her up. But she was without any appearance of life; and he, who had no intention of rushing thus abruptly into her presence, was too much agitated to be able to speak.

'Ah! why would you do this, Sir?' said Emmeline in a tremulous voice. 'What can I do with her?' added she.

'Merciful Heaven, what can be done? How *could* you be so cruel, so inconsiderate?'

'Don't talk to me,' said he — 'don't reproach me! I am not able to bear it! I suffer too much already! Have you no salts? Have you nothing to give her?'

Emmeline now with trembling hands searched her pockets for a bottle of salts which she sometimes carried. She luckily had it; and, in another pocket, some Hungary water, with which she bathed the temples of her friend, who still lay apparently dead.

She remained some moments in that situation; and Emmeline had time to reflect, which she did with the utmost perturbation, on what would be the consequence of this interview when she recovered her recollection. She dreaded lest the sight of Fitz-Edward should totally unsettle her reason. She dreaded lest Godolphin should know he had clandestinely been there; and she concluded it were better to persuade him to leave them before the senses of Lady Adelina returned.

'How fearfully long she continues in this fainting fit,' cried she, 'and yet do I dread seeing her recover from it.'

'You dread it! — and why dread it?'

'Indeed I do. When her recollection returns, it may yet be worse; you know not how nearly gone her intellects have at times been, and the least emotion may render her for ever a lunatic.'

'It is the cruelty of her brother,' sternly replied Fitz-Edward, 'that has driven her to this. His rigid conduct has overwhelmed her spirits and broken her heart. But now, since we have met, we part not till I hear from herself whether she prefers driving me to desperation, or quitting, in the character I can now offer her, the cold and barbarous Godolphin.'

'Do not, ah! pray do not attempt to speak to her now. Let me try to get her home; and when she is better able to see you, indeed I will send to you.'

'Can you then suppose I will leave her? But perhaps she is already gone! She seems to be dead — quite dead and cold!'

Nothing but terror now lent Emmeline strength to continue chafing her temples and her hands. In another moment or two the blood began to circulate; and soon after, with a deep sigh, Lady Adelina opened her eyes.

'For pity's sake,' said Emmeline in a low voice — 'for pity's sake do not speak to her.' Then addressing herself to her, she said — 'Lady Adelina, are you better?'

'Yes.'

'Do you think I can assist you home?'

'She shall not be hurried,' said Fitz-Edward.

'Ah! save me! save me!' exclaimed she, faintly shrieking — 'save me!' and clasping her arms round Emmeline, she attempted to rise.

'Am I then grown so hateful to you,' said Fitz-Edward, as he assisted and supported her — 'that for one poor moment you will not allow me to approach you? Will no penitence, no sufferings obtain your pity?'

'Take me away, Emmeline!' cried she, in a hurried manner — 'ah! take me quick away! Godolphin will come, he will come indeed. — Let us go home — go home before he finds us here!'

'It is as I said!' exclaimed Fitz-Edward: 'her brother has terrified her into madness. But —'

Emmeline, now making an effort to escape falling into a condition as deplorable as was her friend's, said, with some firmness — 'Mr. Fitz-Edward, I must entreat you to say nothing about her brother. It is a topic of all others least likely to restore her.'

Adelina still clung to her; and putting away Fitz-Edward with her hand, laid her head on the shoulder of Emmeline, who said — 'I fancy you can walk. Shall we go towards home?'

Lady Adelina, without speaking, and still motioning with her hand to Fitz-Edward to leave her, moved on. But so enfeebled was she, that in the very attempt she had again nearly fallen; Emmeline being infinitely too much frightened to lend her much assistance.

'She cannot walk,' cried Fitz-Edward, 'yet will not let me support her. Will you, Miss Mowbray, accept my arm; perhaps it may enable you to guide better the faultering steps of your friend.'

Emmeline thought that at all events it was better to get her into the house; and therefore taking, in silence, the arm that Fitz-Edward offered her, she proceeded across the lawn. Lady Adelina appeared to exert herself. She quickened her pace a little; and they were soon at a small gate, which opened in a wire fence near the house to keep the cattle immediately from the windows. Here Emmeline determined to make another effort on Fitz-Edward to persuade him to leave them.

'Now,' said she, 'we shall do very well. Had you not better quit us?'

He seemed disposed to obey; when Mrs. Barret, who had seen them from the door, where she had been watching the return of her lady, advanced hastily towards them, and said to Emmeline — 'Dear Ma'am, I am so glad you and my lady are come in! The Captain is quite frightened at your being out so late.'

'The Captain!' exclaimed Emmeline.

'Yes, Ma'am, the Captain has been come in about two minutes; he is but just seeing Master Godolphin, and then was coming out to meet you.'

'Take hold of your lady, Barret,' cried Emmeline. Barret ran forward. But Lady Adelina (whom the terror of her brother's return at such a moment had again entirely overcome), was already lifeless in the arms of Fitz-Edward; and Emmeline, whose first idea was to go in and prevent Godolphin from coming out to meet them, could get no farther than the door; where, breathless and almost senseless, she was only prevented from falling by leaning against one of the pillars.

'Your lady is in a fainting fit, Mrs. Barret,' said Fitz-Edward; 'pray assist her.'

The woman at once knew his voice, and saw the situation of her lady; and terrified both by the one and the other, screamed aloud. Godolphin, caressing his nephew in the parlour, heard not the shriek; but a footman who was crossing the hall ran out; and flying by Emmeline, ran to the group beyond her; where, as Mrs. Barret still wildly called for help for Lady Adelina, he proposed to Fitz-Edward to carry her ladyship into the house, which they together immediately did.

This was what Emmeline most dreaded. But there was no time for remonstrance. As they passed her at the door, she put her hand upon Fitz-Edward's arm, and cried — 'Oh! stop! for God's sake stop!'

'Why stop?' said he. 'No! nothing shall now detain me; I am determined, and *must* go on!' She saw, indeed, that Godolphin's being in the house only made him more obstinately bent to enter it.

The door of the parlour now opened; and Godolphin saw, with astonishment inexpressible, his sister, to all appearance dead, in the arms of Fitz-Edward; and Emmeline, as pale and almost as lifeless, following her; who silently, and with fixed eyes, sat down near the door.

'What can be the meaning of this?' exclaimed Godolphin. 'Miss Mowbray! — my Emmeline! — my Adelina!'

The child, with whom Godolphin had been at play, reached out his little arms to Lady Adelina, whom they had placed on a sopha. Godolphin sat him down upon it; and not knowing where to fix his own attention, he looked wildly, first at his sister, and then at Emmeline; when Fitz-Edward, totally regardless of him, knelt by the side of Lady Adelina, and surveyed her and the little boy with an expression impossible to be described.

'For mercy's sake tell me,' said Godolphin, as he took the cold and trembling hands of Emmeline in his — 'for mercy's sake tell me what all this means? Is my sister, my poor Adelina dead?'

'I hope not!'

'You are yourself almost terrified to death. Your hands tremble. Tell me, I conjure you tell me, what you have met with, and to what is owing the extraordinary appearance of Mr. Fitz-Edward here?'

'That, or any farther enquiry Mr. Godolphin has to make, which may relate to me,' said Fitz-Edward sternly, 'I shall be ready at any other time to answer; but now it appears more necessary to attend to this dear injured creature!'

'Injured, Sir!' cried Godolphin, turning angrily towards him — 'Do you come hither to tell me your crimes, or to triumph in their consequence?'

'Oh! for the love of heaven!' said Emmeline, with all the strength she could collect, 'let this proceed no farther. Consider,' added she, lowering her voice, 'the servants are in the room. Reflect on the consequence of what you say.'

'Let every body but Barret go out,' said Godolphin aloud.

The child, whose usual hour of going to rest was already past, had crept up to his mother, heedless of the people who surrounded her, and had dropped asleep on her bosom.

'Should I take Master, Sir?' enquired the nursery maid of Godolphin.

'Leave him!' answered he, fiercely.

Excess of terror now operated to restore, in some measure, to Emmeline the presence of mind it had deprived her of. She found it absolutely necessary to exert herself; and advancing towards Lady Adelina, by whose side Fitz-Edward still knelt, she took one of her hands — 'I hope,' said she to Barret, 'your lady is coming to; she is less pale, and her pulse is returning. Colonel Fitz-Edward, would it not be better for you now to leave us?'

'I must first speak to Adelina.'

'Impossible! you cannot speak to her to-night.'

'Nor can I leave her, Madam, unless she herself dismisses me. — Leave her, thus weak and languid, to meet perhaps on my account reproach and unkindness!'

'Reproach and unkindness! Mr. Fitz-Edward,' said Godolphin, in a passionate tone — 'Reproach and unkindness! Do me the favour to say from whom you apprehend she may receive such treatment?'

'From the cruel and unrelenting brother, who has persisted in wishing to divide us, even after heaven itself has removed the barrier between us.'

'Sir,' replied Godolphin, with a stern calmness — 'in this house, and in Miss Mowbray's presence, *you* may say any thing with impunity, and *I* may bear this language even from the faithless destroyer of my sister.'

Fitz-Edward now starting from his knees, looked the defiance he was about to utter, when Lady Adelina drew a deep and loud sigh, and Barret exclaimed — 'For God's sake, gentlemen, do not go on with these high words. My lady is coming to; but this sort of discourse will throw her again into her fits worse than ever. Pray let me entreat of you both to be pacified.'

'I insist upon it,' said Emmeline, 'that you are calm, or it will not be in my power to stay. I must leave you, indeed I must, Mr. Godolphin! if you would not see me expire with terror, and entirely kill your sister, you must be cool.' She was indeed again deprived nearly of her breath and recollection by the fear of their instantly flying to extremities.

Lady Adelina now opened her eyes and looked round her. But there was wildness and horror in them; and she seemed rather to see the objects, than to have any idea of who were with her.

The child, however, was always present to her. 'My dear boy here?' cried she, faintly; 'poor fellow, he is asleep!'

'Shall I take him from you, Ma'am?' asked her woman.

'Oh! no! I will put him to bed myself.' She then again reposed her head as if fatigued, and sighed. ''Twas all,' said she, 'long foreseen. But destiny, they say, must be fulfilled, and fate will have its way. I wish I had not been the cause of his death, however.'

'Of whose death, dear Madam?' said Barret. 'Nobody is dead; nobody indeed.'

'Did I not hear him groan, and see him die? did not he tell me, I know not what, of my Lord Westhaven? I shall remember it all distinctly to-morrow!'

She now rested again, profoundly sighing; and Emmeline beckoning to Fitz-Edward and Godolphin, took them to the other end of the room, where the arm of the sopha she reclined on concealed them from her view. 'Pray,' said she, addressing herself to them both, 'pray leave her.' Then recollecting that she dared not trust them together, she added — 'No, don't both go at once. But indeed it is absolutely necessary to have her kept quite quiet and got to bed as soon as possible.'

'I believe it is,' answered Godolphin. 'Poor Adelina! her dreadful malady is returned.'

'It is indeed,' said Emmeline. 'I have seen it too evidently approaching for some days; and this last shock' — she stopped, and repented she had said so much.

'Mr. Fitz-Edward,' cried Godolphin, 'will you walk with me in another room?'

'Certainly.'

'Oh! no! no!' exclaimed Emmeline with quickness.

They were going out together; but taking an arm of each, she eagerly repeated 'oh! no! no! not together!'

The imagination of Lady Adelina was now totally disordered. She had risen; and carrying the child in her arms, walked towards her brother, who in traversing the apartment with uneasy steps was by this time near the door; while Fitz-Edward was at the other end of the room, where Emmeline was trying to persuade him to quit the house.

Lady Adelina, supported by her maid, and trembling under the weight of the infant she clasped to her bosom, stepped along as quickly as her weakness would allow; and putting her hand on Godolphin's arm, she cried, in a slow and tremulous manner — 'Stay, William! I have something to say to you before you go. Lord Westhaven, you know, is coming; and you have promised that he shall not kill me. I may however die; and I rather believe I shall; for since this last sight I am strangely ill. You and Emmeline will take care of my poor boy, will ye not? Had Fitz-Edward lived — nay do not look so angry, for now he cannot offend you — had poor Fitz-Edward lived, he would perhaps have taken him. But now, I must depend on Emmeline, who has promised to be good to him. They say she will have a great fortune too, and therefore I need not fear that you will find my child burthensome.'

'Burthensome!' cried Godolphin. 'Good God, Adelina!'

'Well! well! be not offended. Only you know, when people come to have a family of their own, the child of another may be reckoned an incumbrance. I know that now you love my William dearly; but then, you know, it will be another thing.'

'Gracious heaven!' exclaimed Godolphin, 'what can have made her talk in this manner?'

'Reason in madness!' said Fitz-Edward, advancing towards her. 'Her son, however, shall be an incumbrance to nobody.'

Emmeline now grasping his hand, implored him not to speak to her. Lady Adelina neither heard nor noticed him: but again addressing herself to her brother, said, with a mournful sigh — And now, since I have told you what was upon my mind, I will go put my little boy to bed. Good night to you dear William! You and Miss Mowbray will remember! — ' She then walked out of the room, and calmly took the way to her own, attended by her maid.

Emmeline, not daring to leave together these two ardent spirits irritated against each other, remained, trembling, with them; hoping by her presence to prevent their animosity from blazing forth, and to prevail upon them to part. They both continued for some time to traverse the room in gloomy silence. At length Fitz-Edward stopped, and said —'At what hour to-morrow, Sir, may I have the honour of some conversation with you?'

'At whatever hour you please, Sir — the earlier, however, the more agreeable.'

'At seven o'clock, Sir, I will be with you.'

'If you please; at that hour I will be ready to receive your commands.'

Fitz-Edward then took his hat, and bowing to Emmeline, wished her a good night, and left the room. Starting from her chair, she followed him into the hall, and shut the parlour door after her.

'Fitz-Edward,' cried she, detaining him, and speaking in an half whisper — 'Fitz-Edward, hear me! Do you design to kill me?'

'To kill you?' replied he. 'No surely.'

'Then do not go till you have heard me.'

'It is unpleasant to me to stay in Godolphin's house after what has just passed. But as you please.'

She led him into a little breakfast room; and regardless of being without light, shut the door.

'Tell me,' said she, 'before I die with terror — tell me with what intention you come to-morrow?'

'Simply to have a positive answer from Mr. Godolphin, if he will, together with his brother, allow me, when the usual mourning is over, to address their sister with proposals of marriage; which in fact they have no right to prevent. And if Mr. Godolphin refuses —'

'What, if he refuses?'

'I shall take my son into my own care, and wait till Lady Adelina will herself exert that freedom which is now hers.'

'Godolphin doats on the child. Nothing, I am persuaded, will induce him to part with it.'

'Not part with it? He must, nay he shall!'

'Pray be calm — pray be quiet. Stay yet a few months — a few weeks.'

'Not a day! Not an hour!'

'Good God! what can be done? Mischief will inevitably happen!'

'I am sorry,' replied Fitz-Edward, 'that you are thus made uneasy. But I cannot recede; and my life has not been pleasant enough lately to make me very solicitous about the event of my explanation with Mr. Godolphin. Conscious, however, that he has some reason to complain of me, I do not wish to increase it. I mean to keep my temper, if I can: but if he suffers his to pass the bounds which one gentleman must observe towards another, I shall not consider myself as the aggressor, or as answerable for the consequences.

'But why, oh! why would you come hither? Wherefore traverse the garden of a night, and suffer appearances to be so much against you, and what is yet worse, against Lady Adelina?'

'Who told you I have done so — Godolphin?'

'No. He was, you well know, absent. But I saw you myself; with terror I saw you, and meditated how to speak to you alone, when our unhappy meeting in the wood this evening put an end to all my contrivances.'

'Yet I had no intention of terrifying you, or of abruptly rushing into the presence of Adelina. It is true, that for some nights past I have walked under the window where she and my child sleep: for I could not sleep; and it was a sort of melancholy enjoyment to me to be near the spot which held all I have dear on earth. As I pass at the ale house where I lodge as a person hiding in this island from the pursuit of creditors, my desire of concealment did not appear extraordinary. I have often lingered among the rocks and copses, and seen Adelina and my child with you. Last night I came out in the dusk, and was approaching, to conceal myself near the house, in hopes, that as you love walking late, and alone, I might have found an opportunity of speaking to you, and of concerting with you the means of introducing myself to her without too great an alarm.'

'Would to heaven you had! But now, since all this has happened, consent to put off this meeting with Godolphin. Do not meet, at least, to-morrow! I entreat that you will not.'

'On all subjects but this,' said he, as he opened the door — 'on all subjects but this, Miss Mowbray knows she may command me. But this is a point from which I cannot, without infamy, recede; and in which she must forgive me, if all my veneration and esteem for her goodness and tenderness does not induce me to desist.'

He then went into the hall; and by the lamp which burnt there, opened himself the door into the garden, and hastily walked away. While the trembling and harrassed Emmeline, finding him inflexible, went back to Godolphin, with very little hopes that she should, with him, have better success.

CHAPTER XIII

ON entering the room, Emmeline sat down without speaking.

'How is Adelina, my dearest Miss Mowbray?'

'I know not.'

'You have not, then, been with her?'

'No.'

'Were it not best to enquire after her?'

'Certainly. I will go immediately.'

'But come to me again — I have much to say to you.'

Emmeline then went up stairs. She found that the composing medicine, which Barret had been directed to keep always by her, had been liberally administered; and that her lady was got into bed, and was already asleep. Barret sat by her. Deep sighs and convulsive catchings marked the extreme agitation of her spirits after she was no longer conscious of it herself. With this account Emmeline returned, in great uneasiness, to Godolphin.

'I thank Heaven,' said he, 'that she is at least for some moments insensible of pain! Now, my Emmeline, for surely I may be allowed to say *my* Emmeline, sit down and try to compose yourself. I cannot bear to see you thus pale and trembling.'

He led her to a seat, and placed himself by her; gazing with extreme concern on her face, palid as it was and expressive only of sorrow and anxiety.

'Whence is it,' said she, after a pause of some moments, 'that I see you here? Did I not come hither on the assurance you gave me that you would long be detained in or near London by the business of your sister?'

'I certainly did say so. But I could not then foresee what happened on the Sunday after you left London.'

'Has, then, any thing happened?'

'The return of Lord and Lady Westhaven, with Lord Delamere.'

'Are they all well?'

'Tolerably so. But my brother is very anxious to see Adelina; and expects you with little less solicitude. He could not think of giving Lady Westhaven the trouble of such a journey; nor could he now leave her without being unhappy. I therefore, at his pressing request, came myself to fetch you both to London.'

'And do you mean that we should begin our journey to-morrow?'

'I *meant* it, certainly, till the events of this evening made me doubtful how far my sister herself may be in a situation to bear change of place and variety of objects; or being able, whether she may chuse to leave to me the direction of her actions.'

'Ah! impute not to Lady Adelina the meeting with Fitz-Edward; it was entirely accidental; its suddenness overcame her, and threw her into the way in which you saw her.'

'And what has a man to answer for, who thus comes to insult his victim, and to rob her of the little tranquillity time may have restored to her?'

'Indeed I think you injure poor Fitz-Edward. Fondly attached to your sister, he has no other wish or hope than to be allowed to address her when the time for her mourning for Mr. Trelawny is expired. For this permission he intended to apply to you: but the severity with which you ever received his advances discouraged him; and he then, in the hope of hearing that such an application would not be rendered ineffectual by her own refusal, and languishing to see his son, came hither; not with any intention of forcing himself abruptly into the presence of Lady Adelina, but to see *me* and induce me to intercede with her for an interview. Accident threw us in his way; your sister fell senseless on the ground; and when she did recover, endeavoured to avoid him: but she was too weak to walk home without other assistance than mine, and I was compelled to accept for her, that which Fitz-Edward offered. On hearing from Barret that you was returned, the terror which has ever pursued her, lest you and Fitz-Edward should meet as enemies, again overcame her, and occasioned the scene you must, with so much astonishment, have beheld.'

'Has Adelina had any previous knowledge of the proposals Fitz-Edward intends to make?'

'None, I believe, in the world.'

'Do you know whether they have ever corresponded?'

'I am convinced they have not.'

'There are objections, in my mind, *insuperable* objections, to this alliance. These, however, I must talk over with the Colonel himself.'

'Not *hostilely*, I hope. Surely you have too much regard for the unhappy Adelina, to give way now to any resentment you may have conceived against him; or if *that* does not influence you, think of what *I* must suffer.' She knew not what she had said; hardly what she intended to say.

'Enchanting softness!' exclaimed Godolphin in a transport — 'Is then the safety of Godolphin so dear to that angelic bosom?'

'You know it but too well. But if *my* quiet is equally dear to *you*, promise me that if this meeting to-morrow *must* take place, you will receive Fitz-Edward with civility, and hear him with patience. Remember on how many accounts this is necessary. Remember how many expressions there are which his profession will not allow him to hear without resentment, that must end in blood. Yours is *no common* cause of enmity; none of those trifling quarrels which daily send modern beaux into the field. Your characters are both high as military men, and as gentlemen; and your former intimacy must, I know, impress more deeply on the mind of each the injury or offence that either suppose they receive. Be careful then, Godolphin; promise me you will be careful!'

'Ah! lovely Emmeline! more lovely from this generous tenderness than from your other exquisite perfections; can I be insensible of the value of a life for which *you* interest yourself? and shall I suffer any other consideration to come in competition with your peace?'

'You promise me then?'

'To be calm with Fitz-Edward, I do. And while I remember his offence (for can I forget while I suffer from it?) I will also recollect, that *you*, who have also suffered on the same account, think him worthy of compassion; and I will try to conquer, at least to stifle, my resentment. But what shall we do with Adelina?'

'That must depend on her situation in the morning. I have greatly apprehended an unhappy turn in her intellects ever since my first coming. The death of Trelawny, far from appearing to have relieved her by removing the impediment to her union with Fitz-Edward, seems rather to have rendered her more wretched. Continually agitated by contending passions, she was long unhappy, in the supposition that Fitz-Edward had obeyed her when she desired him to forget her. Since Trelawny's decease, as she has more fearlessly allowed her thoughts to dwell on him, she has suffered all the anxiety of expecting to hear from him, and all the bitterness of disappointment. And I could plainly perceive, that she was still debating with herself, whether, if he *did* apply to her, she should accept him, or by a violent effort of heroism determine to see him no more. This conflict is yet to come. Judge whether, in the frame of mind in which you see her, she is equal to it; and whether any additional terror for you and for him will not quite undo her. Alas! far from aggravating, by pursuing your resentment, anguish so poignant, try rather to soothe her sorrows and assist her determination. And whatever that determination may be, when it is once made she may perhaps be restored to health and to tranquillity.'

'Indeed I will do all you dictate, my loveliest friend! Surely I should ill deserve the generosity you have shewn to me, were I incapable of feeling for others, and particularly for my sister. But wherefore that air of defiance which Fitz-Edward thought it necessary to assume? He seemed to come more disposed to *insult* than to conciliate the family of Lady Adelina.'

'Alas! do you make no allowance for the perturbed situation of his mind, when he saw the woman he adores to all appearance dead, and for the first time beheld the poor little boy? He looked upon you as one who desires to tear from him for ever these beloved objects; and forgetting that he was the aggressor, thought only of the injury which he supposed you intended.'

'There is, indeed, some apology for the asperity of his manner; and perhaps I was in some measure to blame. Generous, candid, considerate Emmeline! how does your excellent heart teach you to excuse those weaknesses you do not feel, and to pity and to forgive errors which your own perfect mind makes it impossible for you to commit! Ah! how heavily is your tenderness perpetually taxed: *here*, it is suffering from the sight of Adelina — in town, it will have another object in the unfortunate Delamere.'

'Did you not tell me he was in tolerable health?'

'Alas! what is bodily health when the mind is ill at ease? The anxiety of Delamere to see you, to hear his destiny from yourself, is uneasy even to me, who feel my own exquisite happiness in knowing what that destiny must be. I look with even painful commiseration on this singular young man. Yet from passions so violent, and obstinacy so invincible, I must have rejoiced that Miss Mowbray has escaped; even tho' her preference of the fortunate Godolphin had not rendered his lot the most happy that a human being can possess.'

'Since you are so good,' said Emmeline faintly, for she was quite exhausted, 'to compassionate the situation of mind of Delamere, you will, I think, see the humanity of concealing from him — that —' She could find no term that she liked, to express her meaning, and stopped.

'That he has a fortunate rival?' said Godolphin. 'No, dearest Emmeline, I hope I am incapable of such a triumph! 'Till poor Delamere is more at ease, I am content to enjoy the happiness of knowing your favourable opinion, without wishing, by an insulting display of it, to convince him he has for ever

'Thrown a pearl away richer than all his tribe!'

'Yet I am sure you will think it still more cruel to give him hope. I will tell you all my weakness. While I see you here, all benignity and goodness to me, I feel for Lord Delamere infinite pity; but were you to receive him with your usual sweetness, to give him many of those enchanting smiles, and to look at him with those soft eyes, as if you tenderly felt his sorrows, I am not sure whether the most unreasonable jealousy would not possess me, and whether I should not hate him as much as I now wish him well.'

'That were to be indeed unreasonable, and to act very inconsistently with your natural candour and humanity. I will not think so ill of you as to believe you. You know I must of course often see Lord Delamere: but after the avowal you have extorted from me, surely I need not repeat that I shall see him only as my friend.'

Godolphin then kissed her hands in rapture; and for a few moments forgot even his concern for Lady Adelina. Emmeline now wished to break off the conversation; and he at length allowed her to leave him. After having enquired of Barret after her mistress, who was happily in a calmer sleep, she retired to her own room, where she hoped to have a few hours of repose: but notwithstanding the promises of Godolphin, she felt as the hour of the morning approached on which he was to meet Fitz-Edward, that anxiety chased away sleep, and again made her suffer the cruellest suspense.

The heart of Godolphin, glowing with the liveliest sense of his own happiness, yet felt with great keenness the unfortunate situation of his sister. He began to doubt whether he had any right to perpetuate her wretchedness; and whether it were not better to leave it to herself to decide in regard to Fitz-Edward. The delicacy of his honour made him see an infinity of objections to their marriage, which to common minds might appear chimerical and romantic. To that part of his own family who were yet ignorant of her former indiscretion, as he could not urge his reasons, his opposition of Fitz-Edward must seem capricious and unjust. Lord Westhaven must therefore either be told that which had hitherto with so much pains been concealed from him, or he must determine to refer Fitz-Edward entirely to Lady Adelina herself; and on this, after long deliberation, he fixed.

Exactly as the clock struck seven, Fitz-Edward was at the door; and was introduced into Godolphin's study, who was already up and waiting for him. Emmeline, still full of apprehension, had arisen before six, and hearing Lady Adelina was still asleep, had gone down stairs, and waited with a palpitating heart in the breakfast room.

She was glad to distinguish, at their first meeting, the usual salutations of the morning. She listened; but tho' the rest of the house was profoundly silent, she could not hear their conversation or even the tone in which it was carried on. It was not, however, loud, and she drew from thence a favourable omen. Near two hours passed, during which breakfast was carried in to them; and as the servant passed backwards and forwards, she heard parts of sentences which assured her that then, at least, they were conversing on indifferent subjects.

Now, therefore, the agitation of her spirits began to subside; and she dared even to hope that this meeting would prove the means of reconciliation, rather than of producing those fatal effects she had dreaded.

In about a quarter of an hour, however, after they had finished their breakfast, they went out and crossed the lawn together. Then again her heart failed her; and without knowing exactly what she intended, she took the little boy, whom the maid had just brought to her, and walked as quickly as possible after them. Before she could overtake them, they had reached the gate; and in turning to shut it after him, Godolphin saw her, and both together came hastily back to meet her. At the same moment, the child putting out his hands to Godolphin, called him papa! as he had been used to do; and Fitz-Edward, snatching him up, kissed him tenderly, while his eyes were filled with tears.

Godolphin took the hand of Emmeline. 'Why this terror? why this haste?' said he, observing her to be almost breathless.

'I thought — I imagined — I was afraid —' answered she, not knowing what she said.

'Be not alarmed,' said Godolphin — 'We go together as friends.'

'And Godolphin,' interrupted Fitz-Edward, 'is again the same noble minded Godolphin I once knew, and have always loved.'

'Let us say then,' cried Emmeline, 'no more of the past. Let us look forward only to the future.'

'And the happiness of that future, at least as far as it relates to me, depends, dearest Miss Mowbray, on you.'

'On me!'

'Godolphin wishes me not now to see his sister. I have acquiesced. He wishes me even to refrain from seeing her till she has been six months a widow. With this, also, I have complied. But as it is not in my power to remain thus long in a suspence so agonizing as that I now endure, he allows me to write to her, and refers wholly to herself my hopes and my despair. Ah! generous, lovely Emmeline! *you* can influence the mind of your friend. When she is calm, give her the letter I will send to you; and if you would save me from a life of lingering anguish to which death is preferable, procure for me a favourable answer.'

Emmeline could not refuse a request made by Fitz-Edward which Godolphin seemed not to oppose. She therefore acquiesced; and saw him, after he had again tenderly caressed the child, depart with Godolphin, who desired her to return to the house, in order to await Lady Adelina's rising; where he would soon join her. With an heart lightened of half the concern she had felt on this melancholy subject, she now went to the apartment of her poor friend, who was just awakened from the stupor rather than the sleep into which the soporifics she had taken had thrown her. With an heavy and reluctant eye she looked round her, as if hopeless of seeing the image now always present to her imagination. Emmeline approached her with the child. She seemed happy to see them; and desiring her to sit down by the bed side, said — 'Tell me truly what has happened? Have I taken any medicine that has confused my head, or how happens it that I appear to have been in a long and most uneasy dream? Wild and half formed images still seem to float before my eyes; and when I attempt to make them distinct, I am but the more bewildered and uneasy.'

'Think not about it, then, till the heaviness you complain of is gone off.'

'Tell me, Emmeline, have I really only dreamed, or was a stranger here yesterday? I thought, that suddenly I saw Fitz-Edward, thin, pale, emaciated, looking as if he were unhappy; and then, as it has of late often happened, I lost at once all traces of him; and in his place Godolphin came, and I know not what else; it is all confusion and terror!'

Emmeline now considered a moment; and then concluded that it would be better to relate distinctly to her, since she now seemed capable of hearing it, all that had really passed the preceding evening, than to let her fatigue her mind by conjectures, and enfeeble it by fears. She therefore gave her a concise detail of what had happened; from the accidental meeting with Fitz-Edward, to the parting she had herself just had with him in the garden. She carefully watched the countenance of Lady Adelina while she was speaking; and saw with pleasure, that tho' excessively agitated, she melted into tears, and heard, with a calmer joy than she had dared to hope, the certainty of Fitz-Edward's tender attachment, and the unhoped for reconciliation between him and her brother. Having indulged her tears some time, she tenderly pressed the hand of Emmeline, and said, in a faint voice, that she found herself unable to rise and meet Godolphin till she had recovered a little more strength of mind, and that she wished to be left alone. Emmeline, rejoiced to find her so tranquil, left her, and rejoined Godolphin, who was by this time returned; and who read, in the animated countenance of Emmeline, that she had favourable news to relate to him of his sister.

While they enjoyed together the prospect of Lady Adelina's return to health and peace, of which they had both despaired, the natural chearfulness of Emmeline, which anxiety and affection had so long obscured, seemed in some degree to return; and feeling that she loved Godolphin better than ever, for that generous placability of spirit he had shewn to the repentant Fitz-Edward, she no longer attempted to conceal her tenderness, or withhold her confidence from her deserving lover. They breakfasted together; and afterwards, as Lady Adelina still wished to be alone, they walked over the little estate which lay round the house, and Emmeline allowed him to talk of the improvements he meditated when she should become its mistress. The pleasure, however, which lightened in her eyes, and glowed in her bosom, was checked and diminished when the image of Delamere, in jealousy and despair, intruded itself. And she could look forward to no future happiness for herself, undashed with sorrow, while he remained in a state of mind so deplorable. When they returned into the house, Barret brought to Godolphin the following note. —

> 'Dearest and most generous Godolphin! I find myself unequal to the task of *speaking* on what has passed within these last twenty four hours. I wish still to see you. But let our conversation turn wholly on Lord Westhaven, of whom I am anxious to hear; and spare me, for the present, on the subject which now blinds with tears your weak but grateful and affectionate
>
> ADELINA.'

Godolphin now assured her, by Emmeline, that he would mention nothing that should give her a moment's pain, and that she should herself lead the conversation.

He soon after went up to her and Emmeline, in her dressing room; and found her still calm, tho' very low and languid. The name of Fitz-Edward was carefully avoided. But in the short time they were together, Godolphin observed that the eyes of Lady Adelina seemed, on the entrance of any one into the room, fearfully and anxiously to examine whether they brought the letter she had been taught to expect from Fitz-Edward. It was easy to see that she deeply meditated on the answer which she must give; and that she felt an internal struggle, which Godolphin feared might again unsettle her understanding. She was too faint to sit up long; and desirous of being left entirely alone, Godolphin had for the rest of the day the happiness of entertaining Emmeline apart. He failed not to avail himself of it; and drew from her a confession of her partiality towards him, even from the first day of their acquaintance; and long before she dared trust her heart to enquire into the nature of those sentiments with which it was impressed.

Late in the evening, a messenger arrived with the expected letter from Fitz-Edward. To convince Godolphin of the perfect integrity with which he acted, he sent him a copy of it; adding, that he was then on his road to London, where he should await, in painful solicitude, the decision of Lady Adelina. It was determined that Emmeline should give her the letter the next morning; and that if after reading it she retained the same languid composure which she had before shewn, they should go in the evening to Southampton, and from thence proceed the following day to London, where Lord and Lady Westhaven so anxiously expected their arrival.

When Emmeline delivered the letter, Lady Adelina turned pale, and trembled. She left her to read it; and on returning to her in about half an hour, Emmeline found her drowned in tears. She seemed altogether unwilling to speak of the contents of the letter; but assured Emmeline that she was very well able to undertake the journey her brother proposed, and she believed it would be rather useful than prejudicial to her. 'As to the letter,' added she, with a deep sigh, 'it will not for some days be in my power to answer it.'

Every thing was, by the diligence of Godolphin, soon prepared for their departure. Lady Adelina, her little boy, Emmeline and Godolphin, attended by their servants, went the same evening to Southampton; from whence they began their journey the next day; and resting one night at Farnham, arrived early on the following at the house Lord Westhaven had taken in Grosvenor-street.

CHAPTER XIV

THE transports with which Lord Westhaven received his sister, were considerably checked by her melancholy air and faded form. The beauty and vivacity which she possessed when he last saw her, were quite gone, tho' she was now only in her twenty second year; and tears and sighs were the only language by which she could express the pleasure she felt at again seeing him. Imputing, however, this dejection entirely on her late unfortunate marriage, his Lordship expressed rather sorrow than wonder. He admired the little boy, whom he believed to be the son of Godolphin; and he met Emmeline with that unreserved and generous kindness he had ever shewn her.

Lady Westhaven, with the truest pleasure, again embraced the friend of her heart; and with delight Emmeline met her; but it was soon abated by the sanguine hopes she expressed that nothing would now long delay the happiness of Lord Delamere.

'My Emmeline,' said she, 'will now be indeed my sister! Lord Montreville and my mother can no longer oppose a marriage so extremely advantageous to their son. *She* will forgive them for their long blindness; and pardoning poor Delamere for the involuntary error into which he was forced, will constitute the happiness of him and of his family.'

To this, Emmeline could answer that she had not the least intention of marrying. Lady Westhaven laughed at that assertion. And she foresaw a persecution preparing for her, on behalf of Delamere, which was likely to give her greater uneasiness than she had yet suffered from any event of her life.

Lord Westhaven, as soon as they grew a little composed, took an opportunity of leaving the rest of the party; and went into his dressing room, where he sent for Emmeline.

'Well, my lovely cousin,' said he, when she was seated, 'I have seen Lord Montreville on your business. I cannot say that his Lordship received me with pleasure. But some allowances must be made for a man who loves money, on finding himself obliged to relinquish so large an estate, and to refund so large a sum as he holds of yours.'

'I hope, however, you, my Lord, have had no dispute on my account with the Marquis?'

'Oh! none in the world. What he *thought*, I had no business to enquire; what he said, was not much; as he committed the arguments against you to Sir Richard Crofts, who talked very long, and, as far as I know, very learnedly. He spoke like a lawyer and a politician. I cut the matter short, by telling him that I should attend to nothing but from an honest man and a gentleman.'

'That was severe, my Lord.'

'Oh! he did not feel it. Wrapped in his own self-sufficiency, and too rich to recollect the necessity of being honest, he still persisted in trying to persuade me that nothing should be done in regard to restoring your estate 'till all the deeds had been examined; as be had his doubts whether, allowing your father's marriage to be established, great part of the landed property is not entailed on the heirs male. In short, he only seemed desirous of gaining time and giving trouble. But the first, I was determined not to allow him; and to shorten the second, I took Mr. Newton with me the next day, and desired Sir Richard, if he could prove any entail, to produce his proofs. For that, he had an evasion ready — he had not had *time* to examine the deeds; which I find are all in his hands. *We*, however, were better prepared. Mr. Newton produced the papers that authenticate your birth; he offered to bring a witness who was present when Mr. Mowbray was married to Miss Stavordale; nay even the clergyman who performed the ceremony at Paris, and who is found to be actually living in Westmoreland. The hand writing of your father is easily proved; and Mr. Newton, summing up briefly all the corroborating testimonies that exist of your right to the Mowbray estate, concluded by telling Lord Montreville, that at the end of two days he should wait upon his Lordship for his determination, whether he would dispute it in a court of law or settle it amicably with me on behalf of his niece. Newton then left us; and I desired your uncle to allow me a few moments private conversation; which, as he could not refuse it, obliged old Crofts, and that formal blockhead his son, to leave us alone together. I then represented to him how greatly his character must suffer should the affair become public. That tho' I believed myself he was really ignorant of the circumstances which gave you, from the moment of your father's death, an undoubted claim to the whole of his fortune, yet that the world will not believe it; but will consider him as a man so cruelly insatiable, so shamefully unjust, as to take advantage of a defenceless orphan to accumulate riches he did not want, and had no right to enjoy. I added, that if notwithstanding he chose to go into court, he must excuse me if I forgot the near connection I had with him, and appeared publicly as the assertor of your claim, and of course as his enemy.

'The Marquis seemed very much hurt at the peremptory style in which I thought myself obliged to speak. He declined giving any positive answer; saying, only, that he must consult his wife and his son. What the former said, I know not; but the latter, generous in his nature, and adoring *you*, protested to his father that he would himself, as your next nearest relation, join in the suit against him, if the estate was not immediately given up. This spirited resolution of Lord Delamere, and the opinions of several eminent lawyers whom Sir Richard was sent to consult, at length brought Lord Montreville to a resolution before the expiration of the two days; and last night I received a letter from him, to say that he would, on Monday next, account with you, and put you in possession of your estate; the management of which, however, and the care of your person, he should reserve to himself 'till you were of age.'

'Good God!' exclaimed Emmeline; trembling, 'am I to meet my uncle on Monday on this business?'

'Yes; and wherefore are you terrified?'

'At the idea of his anger — his hatred; and of being compelled to live with the Marchioness, who always disliked me, and now must detest me.'

Lord Westhaven then assured her that he would be there to support her spirits. That her uncle, whatever might be his feelings, would not express them by rudeness and asperity; but would more probably be desirous of shewing kindness and seeking reconciliation. Yet that it was improbable he should propose her residing with Lady

Montreville; 'whose present state of health,' said he, 'makes her incapable of leaving her room, and for whose life the most serious apprehensions are entertained by her physicians.'

Emmeline, thus reassured by Lord Westhaven on that subject, and extremely glad to hear there would be no necessity for proceedings at law against her uncle, returned with some chearfulness to the company; where it was not encreased by the entrance of Lord Delamere, which happened soon afterwards.

The very ill state of health indicated by his appearance, extremely hurt her. Nor was she less affected by his address to her, so expressive of the deepest anguish and regret. She could not bear to receive him with haughtiness and coldness; but mildly, and with smiles, returned the questions he put to her on common subjects. His chagrin seemed to wear off; and hope, which Emmeline as little wished to give, again reanimated in some degree his melancholy countenance.

The next day, and again the next, he came to Lord Westhaven's; but Emmeline cautiously avoided any conversation with him to which the whole company were not witnesses. Godolphin too was there: her behaviour to him was the same; and she would suffer neither to treat her with any degree of particularity. Godolphin, who knew her reason for being reserved towards *him*, was content; and Delamere, who suspected now how dangerous a rival he had, was compelled, to remain on the footing only of a relation; still hoping that time and perseverance might restore him to the happiness he had lost.

Monday now arrived, and Emmeline was to wait on her uncle in Berkley-square. At twelve o'clock Lord Westhaven was ready. Emmeline was led by him into the coach. They took up Mr. Newton in Lincoln's-inn; and then went to their rendezvous. Emmeline trembled as Lord Westhaven took her up stairs: she remembered the terror she had once before suffered in the same house; and when she entered the drawing-room, could hardly support herself.

The Marquis, Sir Richard Crofts, his eldest son, and Lord Delamere, with two stewards and a lawyer, were already there. Lord Montreville coldly and gravely returned his niece's compliments; Sir Richard malignantly eyed her from the corners of his eyes, obscured by fat; and Crofts put on a look of pompous sagacity and consequential knowledge; while Lord Delamere, who would willingly have parted with the whole of his paternal fortune rather than with her, seemed eager only to see a business concluded by which she was to receive benefit.

The lawyer in a set speech opened the business, and expatiated largely on Lord Montreville's great generosity.

Lord Westhaven looked over the accounts: they appeared to have been made out right. The title deeds of the estate were then produced; the usual forms gone thro'; and papers signed, which put Emmeline in possession of them. All passed with much silence and solemnity: Lord Montreville said very little; and ineffectually struggled to conceal the extreme reluctance with which he made this resignation. When the business was completed, Emmeline advanced to kiss the hand of her uncle: he saluted her; but without any appearance of affection; and coldly enquired how she intended to dispose of herself?

'I propose, my Lord, wholly to refer myself to your Lordship as to my present residence, or any other part of my conduct in which you will honour me with your advice.'

'I am sorry, Miss Mowbray, that the ill state of health of the Marchioness prevents my having the pleasure of your company here. However my daughter, Lady Westhaven, will of course be happy to have you remain with her till you have fixed on some plan of life, or till you are of age.'

'Not only till Miss Mowbray is of age, my Lord, but ever, both Lady Westhaven and myself should be gratified by having her with us,' said Lord Westhaven.

To this no answer was given; and a long silence ensued. Emmeline felt distressed; and at length said — 'I believe, my Lord, Lady Westhaven will expect us.'

They then rose; and taking a formal leave of the Marquis, were allowed to leave the room. Lord Delamere, however, took Emmeline's hand, and as he led her to the coach implored her to indulge him with one moment's conversation at any hour when they might not be interrupted. But with great firmness, yet with great sweetness, she told him that she must be forgiven if she adhered to a resolution she had made to give no audience on the topic he wished to speak upon, for many months to come.

'Almost two years!' exclaimed he — 'almost two long years must I wait, without knowing whether, at the end of that time, you will hear and pity me! Ah! can you, Emmeline, persist in such cruelty?'

'A good morning to your Lordship,' said she, as she got into the coach.

'Will you dine with us, Delamere?' asked Lord Westhaven.

'Yes; and will go home with you now, and dress in Grosvenor-street.' He then gave some orders to his servants, and stepped into the coach.

'I never was less disposed in my life,' said he, 'to rejoin a party, than I am to go back to those grave personages up stairs: it is with the utmost difficulty I command my temper to meet those Crofts' on the most necessary business. My blood boils, my soul recoils at them!'

'Pooh, pooh!' cried Lord Westhaven, 'you are always taking unreasonable aversions. Your blood is always boiling at some body or other. I tell you, the Crofts' are good, necessary, plodding people. Not too refined, perhaps, in points of honour, nor too strict in those of honesty; but excellent at the main chance, as you may see by what they have done for themselves.'

Delamere then uttered against them a dreadful execration, and went on to describe the whole family with great severity and with great truth, 'till he at length talked himself into a violent passion; and Lord Westhaven with difficulty brought him to be calm by the time they had set down Mr. Newton and stopped at his own door. At the same instant Lord Westhaven's coach arrived there, a splendid chariot, most elegantly decorated, came up also. Delamere, struck with its brilliancy, examined the arms and saw his own: looking into it, he changed countenance, and said to Lord Westhaven — 'Upon my word! Crofts' wife and your Swiss relation, de Bellozane!'

'Crofts' wife?'

'Aye. I mean the woman who was once Fanny Delamere, my sister.'

'Come, Delamere, forget these heartburnings, and remember that she is your sister still.'

'I should be glad to know (if it were worth my while to enquire) what business Bellozane has with *her*?'

By this time they were in the house, where Lady Frances and the Chevalier arrived also.

Lord Westhaven met them with his usual politeness; but Delamere only slightly touched his hat to Bellozane, and sternly saluted his sister with 'your servant, Lady Frances

Crofts!' He then passed them, and went into Lord Westhaven's dressing room; while her Ladyship, regardless of his displeasure, and affecting the utmost gaity, talked and laughed with Lord Westhaven as she went up stairs. Emmeline followed them, listening to the whispered compliments of Bellozane with great coldness; and Lady Frances, entering with a fashionable flounce the drawing room where her sister was, cried — 'Well child! how are you? I beg your pardon for not coming to enquire after you sooner: but I have had such crouds of company at Belleville Lodge, that it was impossible to escape. And here's this animal here, this relation of your Lord's, really haunts me; so I was forced at last to bring him with me.' This speech was accompanied by a significant smile directed at Bellozane.

Lady Westhaven, checked by such an address from flying into the arms of her sister, now expressed, without any great warmth, that she was glad to see her. Something like general conversation was attempted. But Lady Frances, who hoped to hide, under the affectation of extravagant spirits, the envy and mortification with which she contemplated the superior happiness of her sister, soon engrossed the discourse entirely. She talked only of men of the first rank, or of *beaux esprits* their associates, who had been down in parties to Belleville Lodge (the name she had given to her villa near Richmond); and she repeated compliments which both the Lords and the wits had made to her figure and her understanding. When she seemed almost to have exhausted this interesting topic, Lady Westhaven said, as if merely for the sake of saying something — 'Mr. Crofts has been so obliging as to call here twice since we came to London; but unluckily was not let in. Pray how does he do?'

'Mr. Crofts? Oh! I know very little of him. At this time of the year we never meet. *He* lives, you know, in Burlington-street, and *I* live at Belleville; and if he comes thither, as he sometimes does of a Friday or Saturday, he finds me too much engaged to know whether he is there or not. I believe, tho', he is very well; and I think the last time I saw him he was nearly as lively, and amusing as he usually is. Don't you think he was, Bellozane?'

'*O! assurement oui,*' replied the Chevalier, sneeringly, '*Monsieur Croff a toujours a beaucoup de vivacité. — C'est un homme fort amusant ce Monsieur Croff.*' (Oh! Certainly, Mr. Crofts is always very sprightly. A most entertaining personage.)

Lady Westhaven, disgusted, shocked, and amazed, had no power to take any share in such a dialogue; and Lady Frances went on.

'Well! but now I assure you, Augusta, I'm going to be most uncommonly good; and am coming, tho' 'tis a terrible heavy undertaking, to pass a whole week, without company, with *mon tres cher Mari*, in Burlington-street. Nay, I will go still farther, and make a family party with you to the play, which I generally detest of all things.'

'That is being really very kind,' said Lady Westhaven. 'But since you are so tenderly disposed towards your own family, would it not be well if you were to enquire after my mother? You know, I suppose, how very ill she is; how much worse 'tis feared she may be?'

'Yes, I shall certainly call,' replied Lady Frances with the utmost *sang froid*, 'before I go home. But as to her illness, you are frightened at nothing: she has only her old complaints.'

'Her old complaints! And are not they enough? If I were in a situation to be useful to her; or even as it is, if Lord

Westhaven would permit me, I should certainly think it my duty constantly to attend her.'

'Probably you might. And it is equally probable that it would be of no use if you did. She has Brackley, and all her own people about her; and no more *could* be done for her, even tho' you were to hazard your *precious* life, or if *I*, (who you know would not risk by it that of an heir to an Earldom) should sacrifice *my* ease and *my* friends to attend her.'

The unfeeling malignity of this speech was so extremely distressing to Lady Westhaven, that she could hardly command her tears.

Lord Westhaven saw her emotion, and said, 'Augusta, my love, your sister is too brilliant for you. You have not acquired that last polish of high life, which quite effaces all other feelings; nor will you, perhaps, ever arrive at it.'

'God forbid that I ever should!' cried Lady Westhaven, unable to conceal her indignation.

'Poor thing!' said Lady Frances, with the most unblushing assurance — 'You have curious ideas of domestic felicity: and it's a thousand pities, that instead of being what you are, destiny had not made you the snug, notable wife of a country parson, with three or four hundred a year — You would have been pure and happy, to drive about in a one horse chaise, make custards, walk tame about the house, and bring the good man a baby every year: but really, you are now quite out of your element.' She then rang the bell for her carriage; which being soon ready, she gaily wished her sister good day, and the Chevalier handed her down stairs; where, as she descended, she said, loud enough to be heard, *'S'il y'a une chose au monde que je deteste plus qu'un notre, c'est la tristesse d'une societé comme celà'* (If there is any thing in the world I utterly detest, 'tis such dismal society as that.)

The Chevalier assented with his lips; but his heart and his wishes were fled towards Emmeline. He was, however, so engaged with her proud and insolent rival, that he no longer dared openly to avow his predilection for her: and Lady Frances seemed so sure of the strength of that attachment which was her disgrace, that she brought him on purpose where Emmeline was, to shew how little she apprehended his defection.

Lord Westhaven, after pausing a second, ran down stairs after them; and just as Bellozane was stepping into the chariot, took him by the arm, and begged to speak to him for two minutes.

He apologized to Lady Frances, and they went together into a room; where Lord Westhaven, with all the warmth which his relationship authorized, remonstrated against his stay in England; represented the expence and uneasiness it must occasion to the good old Baron; and above all, exhorted him to fly immediately from the dangerous society of Lady Frances Crofts.

Bellozane received this advice from his cousin with a very ill grace. He said, that he could not discover why his Lordship assumed an authority over him, or pretended either to blame his past conduct or dictate his future. That he came to England a stranger; brought thither by his honourable passion for Miss Mowbray, which he had a right to pursue; but that Mr. Godolphin, who was his only relation then in England, had either from accident or design shewn him very little attention; while Lady Frances had, with the most winning *honeteté*, invited him to her house, and supplied the want of *that* hospitality which his own family had not afforded him. And that infinitely obliged as he was to her, he should ill brook any reflection on a woman of honour who was his friend.

'But my Lord,' added he, 'if your Lordship will allow me to visit here as Miss Mowbray's favoured lover, I will not only drop the acquaintance of Lady Frances, but will put myself entirely under your Lordship's direction.'

Lord Westhaven, piqued and provoked, answered — 'that he had no power whatever to direct Miss Mowbray; and if he had, should never advise her to receive him. Be assured, Monsieur le Chevalier, that you have no chance of ever being acceptable to her, and you must think no more of her.'

Bellozane, equally impatient of advice and contradiction, burst from him; and went back to Lady Frances in a very ill humour.

Delamere, who had been dressing while his eldest sister remained, now joined Lady Westhaven and Emmeline in the drawing room. Thither also came Lady Adelina; who, during the five days they had been in town had not been well enough till this day to dine below.

She was now languid and faint, and obliged to retire, as soon as the cloth was removed, to her own room. Emmeline attended her; and when they were alone together, she complained of finding herself every day more indisposed. 'The air of London,' said she, 'is not good for my child: I cannot help fancying he droops already. And the noise of a house where there are unavoidably so many visitors, and such a multitude of servants, is too much for my spirits. As Lord Westhaven is desirous of my staying in London till my sister Clancarryl arrives, that we may meet all together after being so many years divided, I will not press my return to East Cliff; but I wish he would allow me to go to some village near London, where I may occasionally enjoy solitude and silence; for I have that upon my heart, Emmeline, that demands both.'

Emmeline communicated her wish to Godolphin the same evening; who undertook to settle it with Lord Westhaven as his sister desired; and the next day Lady Adelina and her little boy removed to Highgate, where her brother had procured her a handsome lodging; and he, quitting those he usually occupied in town, went to reside with her.

After having been there a few days, she sent to Emmeline the following letter, which she desired might be delivered by her own hand.

To the Honourable George Fitz-Edward.

'I have thus long forborne to answer your letter, because I have not 'till now been able to collect that strength of mind which is necessary, when I am to obey the inexorable duty that tears me from you for ever!

'That you yet *love* me well enough to solicit my hand, is I own most soothing and consolatory: but where, Fitz-Edward, is the Lethean cup, without which you cannot *esteem* me? — without which, I cannot esteem myself? No! I am not worthy the honour of being your wife! It is fit my fault be punished — punished by the cruel obligation it lays me under of renouncing the man I love!

'Fitz-Edward, I will not dissemble! I cannot, if I would! My affection for you is become a part of my existence, and can end but in the grave. Under the dread of your infidelity or your danger, my reason was too weak to support me: now that I have no longer any apprehensions of either, my reason is returned — it is returned to shew me all my wretchedness, and to afford me that light by which I must plunge a dagger into my own bosom.

'Had I, however, no objections on my own account, there is one that on another appears insuperable. Were the marriage you solicit to take place, and to be followed by a family, could I bear that my William, the delight and support of my life, should be as an alien in his father's house, and either appear as the son of Godolphin or learn to blush for his mother!

'We must part, Fitz-Edward! Indeed we must! Or if we are obliged to meet, do you at least forget that we ever met before.

'I know that the daughter of Lord Westhaven, in youth, beauty, and innocence, would not have been, however portionless, unworthy of you. But what would you receive in the widow of Trelawny? A mind unsettled by guilt and sorrow; spirits which have lost all relish for felicity; a blemished, if not a ruined reputation, a faded person, and an exhausted heart — exhausted of almost every sentiment but that so fatally predominant; which now forces me to blot my paper with tears, as I write this last farewel!

'Farewel! Most beloved Fitz-Edward! — Ah! Try if it be possible to be happy! Be assured I wish it; even tho' it be necessary for that end to drive from your memory, for ever, the lost

ADELINA TRELAWNY.'

Emmeline, to whom this letter was sent open, could not but approve the sentiments it contained, while her heart bled for the pain it must have cost Lady Adelina, and for that which it must inflict on Fitz-Edward.

When she had dispatched a note to his lodgings, to name an early hour the next day for speaking to him, she went down into the drawing room, where a large party of company were already assembled. Emmeline, to avoid a particular conversation with Lord Delamere, which he incessantly solicited, placed herself near one of the card tables; when, at a late hour of the evening, dressed in the utmost exuberance of fashion, blazing in jewels and blooming in rouge, entered Mrs. James Crofts, followed by the two eldest of her daughters; one, drest in the character of Charlotte in the *Sorrows of Werter*, and the other, as Emma, the nut brown maid. Their air and manner were adapted, as they believed, to the figures of those characters as they appear in the print shops; and their excessive affectation, together with the gaudy appearance of their mama, nearly conquered the gravity of Emmeline and of many others of the company.

While Mrs. Crofts paid her compliments to Lady Westhaven and Emmeline, and gave herself all those airs which she believed put her upon an equality with the circle she was in, the two Misses anxiously watched the impression which they concluded their charms must make on the gentlemen present. Their mama had told them that most likely all of them were Lords, or Lords' sons at least; and the girls were not without hopes, that among them there might be some of that species of men of quality, whom modern novelists describe as being in the habit of carrying forcibly away, beautiful young creatures, with whom perchance they become enamoured, and marrying them in despite of all opposition. They longed above all things to meet with such adventures, and to be carried off by a Lord, or a Baronet at least; whose letters afterwards, to some dear Charles or Harry, could not fail to edify the world. After Mrs. Crofts had displayed her dress, and convinced the company of her being quite in a good style of life; and when her daughters had committed hostilities for near an hour upon the hearts of the gentlemen, they sailed out in the same state as they entered; nor could all Emmeline's good humour prevent her smiling at the satyrical remarks made on them by some of the company; nothing more strongly exciting the ridicule and contempt of people of real fashion than awkward and impotent efforts to imitate them.

The next day, Fitz-Edward attended at the hour Emmeline appointed, and received from her the letter of Lady Adelina, with a degree of anguish which gave great pain to Emmeline and Godolphin. Still, however, he was not quite deprived of hope; but flattered himself that the persuasions of her sister, Lady Clancarryl (who was now every day expected, with her husband and family, to pass the rest of the winter in London) added to those of Lord Westhaven, and the good offices of Emmeline, would together prevail on Lady Adelina to alter a resolution which rendered them both wretched.

Some weeks, however, passed, and she still adhered to it; while the melancholy conversation which Emmeline frequently had with Fitz-Edward, and the importunity and unhappiness of Delamere, deprived her of much of that tranquillity she might otherwise have enjoyed; particularly after the recovery of Lady Westhaven (who presented her Lord with a son), and the arrival of Mrs. Stafford and her family from France.

Lord Westhaven, who held a promise particularly sacred when made to the unfortunate, had procured for Mr. Stafford a lucrative employment in the West Indies. Thither he immediately went; and his wife, whose spirits and health were greatly hurt, was happy to accept the offer Emmeline made her of going down with her children to Mowbray Castle. The Marquis of Montreville had presented his niece with the furniture he had sent thither, being in truth ashamed to charge it; there was therefore every thing necessary; and there Emmeline intended Mrs. Stafford should reside 'till she should be established in some residence agreeable to her; which she intended to fix if possible near her own; and she now felt all the advantages of that fortune, which enabled her to repay the obligations she owed to her earliest friend.

CHAPTER XV

THE rank, and extensive connections of Lady Westhaven, led her unavoidably into a good deal of company; but it was among persons as respectable for their virtues as their station. Emmeline, of course, often accompanied her: but almost all her mornings, and frequently her evenings, were dedicated to Lady Adelina; who hardly saw any body but her, Lady Westhaven, her brothers, and her sister; and never went out but for the air.

Godolphin passed with her much of his time: to the love and pity he had before felt for her, was added veneration and esteem, excited by the heroism of her conduct. At her lodgings, too, he could see Emmeline without the restraint they were under in other places. There, he could talk to her of his love; and there, she consented to hear him.

Lady Westhaven went constantly every morning to visit her mother, who had lately been rather better, and whose health her physicians entertained some hopes of re-establishing. Her own unhappy temper seemed to be the chief impediment to her recovery; her violent passions, unsubdued by sickness and disappointment; and her immeasurable pride, which even the approach of death could not conquer, kept her nerves continually on the stretch; and allowed her no repose of mind, even when her bodily sufferings were suspended. That her favourite project of uniting the only surviving branches of her own family, by the marriage of Lord Delamere to Miss Otley, was now for ever at an end, was a perpetual source of murmuring and discontent. And tho' Emmeline had as splendid a fortune, with a person and a mind infinitely more lovely, her Ladyship could not yet prevail upon herself to desire, that the name for which she felt such proud veneration, and the fortune of her own illustrious ancestors, should be enjoyed, or carried down to posterity by her, who had become the object of her capricious but inveterate dislike.

Emmeline was very glad that the Marchioness thro' prejudice, and her uncle thro' shame, forbore to persecute her in favour of their son: but tho' perfectly aware of the antipathy Lady Montreville entertained towards her, she yet shewed her all the attention she would receive; and would even constantly have waited on her, had she not expressed more pain than pleasure in her presence.

Lady Frances Crofts, by this time fixed in Burlington-street for the winter, called now and then on her mother; but her visits were short and cold. It unfortunately happened, that the Marchioness, whose amusement was now almost solely confined to reading the daily prints, had found in one of them a paragraph evidently pointed at the intimacy subsisting between Lady Frances and the Chevalier de Bellozane, which had long been the topic of public scandal.

Lady Frances called upon her while her mind was under the first impression of this disgraceful circumstance; and she spoke to her daughter of her improper attachment to that young foreigner with more than her usual severity. Lady Frances, far from hearing her remonstrance with calmness, retorted, with rudeness and asperity, what she termed unjust reproaches; and asserted her own right to associate with whom she pleased. The Marchioness grew more enraged, and they parted in great wrath: in consequence of which, Lady Montreville, in the inconsiderate excess of her anger, sent for her husband and her son; and exclaiming with all her natural acrimony against the shameful conduct of Lady Frances, insisted upon their obliging Crofts to separate his wife from her dangerous and improper acquaintance, and forcing her immediately into the country.

Lord Montreville, who had already heard too much of his daughter's general light conduct, and her particular partiality to Bellozane, now saw new evils gathering round him, from which he knew not how to escape. The fiery and impatient Delamere, already irritated against Bellozane for his pretensions to Emmeline, broke forth in menace and invective; and nothing but his father's anguish, and even tears, prevented his flying directly to him to execute that vengeance which his mother had dictated. She herself, in the violence of her passion, had overlooked the consequence of putting this affair into the hands of the inconsiderate and headlong Delamere; but when she saw him thus inflamed, terror for *him*, was added to resentment against her daughter; and altogether produced such an effect on her broken constitution, that in a few days afterwards her complaints returned with great violence, and all remedies proving ineffectual, she expired in less than a fortnight. Lady Westhaven and Emmeline attended on her themselves for the last four or five days; but she was insensible; and knew neither of them. Delamere, very fond of his mother, and whose feelings were painfully acute, suffered for many days the most violent paroxysms of grief; yet it was a considerable alleviation to reflect that he had not finally been the cause of her death. Lord Montreville bore it with more composure; and the softer, tho' deep sorrow of Lady Westhaven, found relief in the constant and tender attention of her Lord, and the sympathy of Emmeline.

Lady Frances Crofts, not insensible to remorse, but resolutely stifling it, affected to hear the news with proper concern, yet as what had been for many months expected. She sent constantly to enquire after her father; and the Marquis hoping that while her mind was softened by such a mournful event his remonstrance might make a deeper impression, determined to go to her; therefore the day after the remains of the Marchioness had been carried to the family vault of the Delameres, he took his chair, and went to Burlington-street.

On entering the house, the servants, who concluded he came to Mr. Crofts, were taking him into those apartments below which their master occupied: but his Lordship told them he must speak to their lady. Her own footman said her Ladyship had given orders to be denied.

'To her father, puppy?' — said Lord Montreville. 'Where is she?'

'In her dressing room, my Lord.'

He then passed alone up stairs — As he went, he heard the voice of laughter and gaiety, and was more shocked than surprized, when, on opening the door, he saw Lady Frances in a morning dishabille, and the Chevalier de Bellozane making her tea. At the entrance of her father thus unexpectedly, she changed colour; but soon assuming her usual assured manner, said she was glad to see his Lordship well enough to come out.

'Dismiss this young man,' said he sternly. 'I must speak to you alone.'

'*Va mon ami*,' cried Lady Frances, with the utmost ease, '*pour quelques moments*.'

Bellozane left the room; and then Lord Montreville, with paternal affection, tried to move her. But she had conquered her feelings; and answered with great calmness — 'That conscious of her own innocence, she was quite indifferent to the opinion of the world. And that tho' she certainly wished to be upon good terms with her own family, yet if any part of it chose to think ill of her, they must do so entirely from prejudice, which it was little worth her while to attempt removing.'

Lord Montreville, now provoked beyond all endurance, gave way to the indignation with which he was inflamed, and denounced his malediction against her, if she did not immediately dismiss Bellozane and regulate her manner of life. She heard him with the most callous insensibility; and let him depart without making any attempt to appease his anger or calm his apprehensions. From her, he went down to Crofts; to whom he forcibly represented the necessity there was for putting an immediate stop to the scandal which the conduct of his wife occasioned. Pusillanimous and mean-spirited, Crofts chose neither to risk his personal safety with the Chevalier, nor the diminution of his fortune by attempting to procure a divorce, which would compel him to return what he loved much better than honour.

He saw many others do extremely well, and mightily respected, whose wives were yet gayer than his own; and convinced that while he had money he should always obtain as much regard as he desired, he rather excused to Lord

Montreville the conduct of Lady Frances than shewed any disposition to resent it. The Marquis left him with contempt, and ordered his chair to Lord Westhaven's. As he went, he could not forbear reflecting on the contrast between his eldest and youngest daughter, and between his eldest daughter and his niece. He grew extremely anxious for Lord Delamere's marriage with Emmeline: sure of finding, in her, an honour to his family, which might console him for his present misfortunes: and he deeply regretted that infatuation which had blinded him to her superior merit, and hazarded losing her for ever. Disgusted already with the Crofts, he remembered that it had been in a great measure owing to them, and he thought of them only with repentance and dislike.

He saw Lord Westhaven alone; and relating to him all that had passed that morning, besought him to consider what could be done to divide Bellozane from Lady Frances Crofts.

Lord Westhaven had seen and heard too much of the intimacy between them. He was extremely hurt that so near a relation of his own should occasion such uneasiness in the family of his wife; but as he had not invited him over, and always discouraged his stay, he had on that head nothing with which to reproach himself. And all he could now do, was, to promise that he would speak again to Bellozane, and write to the Baron de St. Alpin, entreating him to press the return of his son to Switzerland. His Lordship entered warmly into the apprehensions of Lord Montreville; and undertook to use all his influence with Delamere to prevent his running rashly into a quarrel with a young man as passionate and as violent as himself.

Lord Montreville then spoke of Emmeline; and expressed his wishes that the union between her and his son might speedily be accomplished: but on this subject Lord Westhaven gave him very little hopes. Tho' Emmeline had done her utmost to conceal even from Lord and Lady Westhaven the true state of her heart, his Lordship had, in their frequent conferences on her affairs, clearly perceived what were her sentiments. But since they were in favour of his brother, he could not think of attempting to alter them, however sorry for Delamere; and could only determine to observe an absolute neutrality.

He did not communicate to the Marquis all he thought, but told him in general, that Emmeline seemed at present averse to every proposal of marriage, and firm in the resolution she had made, to remain single till she had completed her twenty-first year. Lord Westhaven sent for Bellozane; who had lately been less frequent in his visits at Grosvenor-street, and who seemed to resent the coldness with which his cousins received him, and to have conceived great anger at the reserve and even aversion with which Emmeline treated him. The servant whom his Lordship dispatched with a note to Bellozane, returned in about ten minutes, and said that the Chevalier was gone to Bath. Lord Westhaven now hoped that for some time the intercourse which had given such offence, and occasioned such misery, would be at an end: in the afternoon, however, Crofts came in; and on Lady Westhaven's enquiry after her sister, he told her that she was going that afternoon to Speenhamland in her way to Bath. Conduct, so glaringly improper and unfeeling, a defiance so bold to the opinions of the world and the common decencies of society, extremely hurt both her Ladyship and her Lord. The latter, however, found some satisfaction in reflecting that at least Delamere and Bellozane could not immediately meet.

Above a month now passed with as much tranquillity as the ardent supplications of Delamere to Emmeline would admit. Lord and Lady Clancarryl, with their family, arrived in London to pass the rest of the winter; and Lady Adelina, insensibly won from her retirement by the pleasure of meeting at once her sister and her two brothers, seemed to be in better health, and sometimes in better spirits. As she was now frequently induced to join these charming family parties, she was obliged to see Fitz-Edward among them; and he entertained new hopes that she would at length conquer her scruples and accept his hand: she carefully, however, avoided all conversation with him but in mixed company; and Emmeline being continually with her, they were equally prevented from hearing, with any degree of particularity, Godolphin or Fitz-Edward.

The Marchioness of Montreville had now been dead almost two months; and Lady Westhaven, who from respect to her memory had hitherto forborne to appear in public, was prevailed upon to go to a new play; for the author of which, a nobleman, one of her friends being particularly interested, he prevailed on all the people of fashion and taste whom he knew to attend on the third night of its representation. Lady Westhaven, Lady Clancarryl, and Emmeline, were by his earnest entreaties induced to be among them: but as Lord Westhaven, Lord Clancarryl, Godolphin, and Fitz-Edward, were absent, being gone all together to the seat of the former, in Kent, for a few days, they foresaw but little pleasure in the party; and Lady Westhaven expressed even a reluctance for which she knew not how to account. The eagerness of Lord — to serve his friend at length over-ruled her objections; his Lordship himself and Lord Delamere were to attend them; and they were to be joined by some other ladies there. The stage box had been retained for them; and they proceeded to the playhouse, where they were hardly seated, before Lady Westhaven saw, with infinite mortification and alarm, her sister, Lady Frances Crofts, enter the next box, handed by the Chevalier de Bellozane, and accompanied by a lady, of fashion indeed, but of very equivocal character, with whom she had lately contracted a great intimacy. All attention to the play was now at an end. Incapable of receiving amusement, Lady Westhaven would instantly have returned home; and Emmeline, who saw rage and fierceness in the countenance of Lord Delamere, was equally anxious to do so: but they knew not how to account for such a wish to their party without making their fears public; and while they deliberated how to act, the play went on. Lady Frances, as if quite unconscious of any impropriety in her conduct, spoke to them and to Delamere. They forced themselves to answer her with civility; but her brother, turning from her, darted an angry look at Bellozane, and went to the other side of the house. He from thence watched with indignation the familiar whispers which passed between her and the Chevalier; and reflecting on the recent death of his mother, which had been hastened if not occasioned by this connection; remembering how greatly the sufferings of her last hours had been embittered by it, and recalling to his memory a thousand other causes of anger against Bellozane, he heated his imagination with the review of these injuries, till he raised himself into an agony of passion, which it was soon impossible for him, had he been so disposed, to restrain.

A very few minutes after the play ended, Lady Westhaven, impatient to get away before her sister, beckoned to Delamere; and finding her servants ready, told her party she was too much tired to stay the entertainment, and rose with Emmeline to go. Lord — led her Ladyship, and Delamere took the hand of Emmeline: the two former walked hastily thro' the lobby; but as the two latter followed, they were suddenly stopped by Rochely, who, making one of his solemn bows, advanced close to Emmeline, and with great composure congratulated her in his usual slow and monotonous manner, on her late acquisitions; assured her of his great respect and esteem; and added, that as he understood she would, when she came of age, be possessed of a large sum of money, he flattered himself she would allow him to manage it for her, as Lord Montreville at present did; declaring that nobody could be more attentive to the interest of his customers. The profound gravity with which, in such a place, he made such a request; the sordid meanness of spirit, which could induce a man already so very rich, to solicit custom with the avidity of a mechanic beginning business; and the uncouth and formal figure of the person himself; would have excited in Emmeline ridicule as well as contempt, at any other time: but now, distrest at the delay this meeting occasioned, she hurried over some answer, she hardly knew what, and hastened towards the door. Just, however, before they reached it, Bellozane, with Lady Frances Crofts hanging on his arm, overtook and passed them: the Chevalier slightly touched his hat to Emmeline; and Lady Frances, nodding familiarly, said 'Good night! good night!' Lady Frances and Bellozane went on; and Emmeline, who saw fury in the eyes of Delamere, now wished as much to linger behind as she had before done to hurry forward. But Delamere quickening his pace, overtook them as they descended the steps, and rushed so closely and with so much intended rudeness by Bellozane, that it was with the utmost difficulty he could avoid falling and dragging his fair associate with him. The fiery Frenchman recovering his footing, turned fiercely to Delamere, and asked, in French, what he meant? Lord Delamere, in the same language, replied, that he meant to tell him he was a scoundrel! Instantly a mutual blow was exchanged: the shrieks of Emmeline brought the sentinels; who, together with the croud which immediately gathered, forced them from each other.

Lord — , who had taken care of Lady Westhaven to her coach, alarmed at Emmeline's not joining them, and at the noise he heard, now came back to see what was the matter. He met her, more dead than alive, coming towards him, attended by a stranger; and she had just breath enough to implore him not to think of *her*, but to find Lord Delamere, and try to prevent the fatal consequence of what had just happened.

Leaving her to the care of the gentleman he had found her with, who almost supported her to the coach, his Lordship went forward in quest of Delamere, whom he met with two or three other gentlemen. Bellozane, after stating to them the affront he had received, and giving Lord Delamere a card, had returned back into the lobby with Lady Frances and her friend; from whence it was supposed he had gone out with them across the stage, as Lady Frances appeared in great alarm. Lord — now entreated Delamere to go with him to the coach, where he told him his sister was in the utmost terror for his safety. But enquiring eagerly whether Miss Mowbray was safe with her, and hearing she was, he said he would be in Grosvenor-street to supper, and desired they would go home. Lord — then very warmly remonstrated on the cruelty of terrifying his sister, and insisted on his going with him to the coach: but they were by this time among the croud at the door, where people began to go out fast; and Delamere, whose passions were now inflamed to a degree of madness, broke violently away from his Lordship; and rushing into the street, instantly disappeared. Every attempt which himself, his servants, or some gentlemen who were witness to the transaction, made to find him, being ineffectual, Lord — now returned to the coach, where Lady Westhaven was fainting in the arms of Emmeline; who, equally alarmed, and hardly able to support herself, was trying to assist and console her. Lord — , instead of returning to his own family, now sent a footman to desire they would go home without him; and remaining in Lady Westhaven's carriage, directed it to be driven with the utmost speed to Grosvenor-street. As they went, he attempted to appease the agonizing fears of them both, by persuading them that they might find Lord Delamere at home before them; but they knew too well the ferocity with which he was capable of pursuing his vengeance when it was once awakened; and arrived at home in such disorder, that neither could speak. — The coach, however, no sooner stopped than somebody ran out. They had no power to ask who; but the voice was that of Godolphin; who finding his brother likely to be detained two days longer, and existing only while he could see Emmeline every hour, had returned alone to town, and now waited their arrival from the play. He was astonished at the situation he found them in, as he assisted them out of the carriage. He received, however, a brief account of the cause from Lord — ; while Lady Westhaven, a little recovered by the sight of Godolphin and the hartshorn and water she had taken, found her voice.

'For God's sake! dear Godolphin, lose not a moment, but go after my brother. We dread lest he went immediately in search of Bellozane — Oh! fly! and endeavour to prevent the horrid effects that may be expected from their meeting!'

'Pray go!' said Emmeline. 'Pray go instantly!'

Godolphin needed not entreaty. He took his hat, and ran away directly, without knowing whither to go. He thought, however, that it was possible Delamere might go to Berkley-square, and send from thence an appointment to Bellozane. Thither therefore he hastened; but heard that Lord Delamere had not been at home since he dressed to dine in Grosvenor-street, and that the Marquis was gone to Lord Dornock's, where he was to stay some days; news, which encreased the alarm of Godolphin, who had hoped that his influence might be used to prevent the rashness of his son. He ordered Millefleur, and Delamere's coachman, footmen, and grooms, to run different ways in search of their master, while he went himself to the lodgings of Bellozane. Bellozane, he learnt, came from Bath only that morning, and had dressed at his lodgings, but had not been there since.

He now flew to the house of Lady Frances Crofts. Mr. Crofts was gone down to his father's; and Lady Frances, who had come from Bath the same day, had dined with her friend, and was to be set down by her carriage after supper. Eagerly asking the name of this friend, he was directed to Charlotte-street, Oxford-street; where on hastening he found Lady Frances, who was vainly attempting to conquer the terrors that possessed her. Bellozane, he heard, had procured chairs for her and the lady with her, at the stage door, and had there wished them a good night, tho' they had both intreated of him to go home with them. They added, that they had refused to let him look for their carriage, which was driven off in the croud, lest he should meet with Delamere; but were greatly afraid he had gone back to the avenues of the play-house with that design. Godolphin, however unpromising his search yet appeared, determined not to relinquish it. But while he continued running from place to place, Lady Westhaven and Emmeline sat listening to every noise and terrifying themselves with conjectures the most dreadful. Almost as soon as Godolphin was gone, they had conjured Lord — to go on the same search: but he returned not; and of Godolphin they heard nothing. Even the late hours when fashionable parties break up, now passed by. Every coach that approached made them tremble between hope and fear; but it rolled away to a distance. Another and another passed, and their dreadful suspence still continued. Emmeline would have persuaded Lady Westhaven to go to bed; but nothing could induce her to think of it. She sometimes traversed the room with hurried steps; sometimes sat listening at the window; and sometimes ran out to the stair case, where all the servants except those who had been dispatched in pursuit of Lord Delamere were assembled.

The streets were now quiet; the watch called a quarter past five; and convinced that if something fatal had not happened some body would have returned to them by this time, their terror grew insupportable. A quick rap was now heard at the door. Emmeline flew to the stairs 'Is it Lord Delamere?' 'No, Madam,' replied a servant, 'it is Captain Godolphin.' Afraid of asking, yet unable to bear another moment of suspence, she flew down part of the stairs. Godolphin, with a countenance paler than death, caught her in his arms 'Whither would you go?' cried he, trembling as he spoke.

'Have you found — Delamere?'

'I have.'

'Alive and well?'

'Alive — but — '

'Oh! God! — but what?'

'Wounded, I fear, to death. Keep his sister from knowing it too suddenly.'

That was almost impossible. Lady Westhaven had at first sat down in the drawing room in that breathless agony which precluded the power of enquiry; then losing her weakness in desperation, she ran down, determined to know the worst, and was already on the stairs.

Emmeline, white and faint, leaned on Godolphin — 'Where is he, where is my brother?' cried Lady Westhaven.

Godolphin beckoned to the servants to assist him in getting her up stairs. After a moment, they were all in the drawing room.

'Tell me,' cried she, with an accent and look of despair — 'Tell me for I will know! You have seen my brother; he is killed! I know he is killed!'

'He is alive,' answered Godolphin, hardly bearing to wound her ears with such intelligence as he had to deliver — 'at least he *was* alive when I left him.'

'*Was* alive! He is wounded then — and dying!'

Uttering a faint shriek, Lady Westhaven now sprung towards the door, and protested she would go to him wherever he was. Emmeline clung about her, and besought her to be patient — to be pacified.

'Perhaps,' cried she, 'his situation may not be so desperate. Let us rather enquire what can be done for him, than indulge the extravagance of our own despair.'

'Ah! tell me, then, where? — how?' Lady Westhaven could say no more. Godolphin thought it best to satisfy her.

'I will not relate the first part of my search. It was fruitless. At length I saw a croud before the door of the Bedford. I asked what was the matter? and heard that two gentlemen had fought a duel, by candlelight, with swords;

that one was killed and the other had escaped. This was too much like what I expected to hear: I forced my way into the room. Lord Delamere was bleeding on the ground. Two surgeons were with him. I cleared the room of all but them, and the necessary attendants. I saw him carefully conveyed to bed. I left them with him; and came to tell you. Now I must hasten back to him. I will not flatter you; the surgeons gave me very little — indeed no hope of his life.'

'Oh! my father! my father!' exclaimed Lady Westhaven, 'what will become of him when he hears this?'

'I would go to him,' said Godolphin, 'but that I must return to poor Delamere. What little he said was to request that I would stay with him.'

'Go then,' said Emmeline — 'we must do without you. Let him not miss the comfort of your presence.'

'Yes,' answered he, 'I must indeed go.' Emmeline, leaving Lady Westhaven a moment to her woman, followed him out, and he said to her — 'Try, I conjure you, my Emmeline, to exert yourself for the sake of your poor friend. Keep her as tranquil as you can; and may ye both acquire fortitude to bear what is, I fear, inevitable!'

'Oh! my father!' loudly exclaimed Lady Westhaven, with a dreadful shriek — 'Who shall dare to announce these tidings to you?'

'Send,' continued Godolphin, 'an express to Lord Montreville. He is at Lord Dornock's; and dispatch another to my brother. Pray take care of your own health. It is now impossible for me to stay — the poor languishing Delamere expects me.' He then ran hastily away; and Emmeline, struggling with all her power against her own anguish, was obliged to commit her friend to the care of her servants, while she sat down to write to Lord Montreville. Her letter contained only two lines.

'My dear Lord,

'Your son is very ill. We are much alarmed; and Lady Westhaven begs you will immediately come hither. Do not go to Berkley-square.'

EMMELINE MOWBRAY.'

Grosvenor-street,
April 5th

This note, short as it was, she had the utmost difficulty to make legible. A servant was sent off with it, who was ordered to answer no questions; and in another short and incoherent note she told to Lord Westhaven the melancholy truth, and sent it by express into Kent.

Having thus obeyed Godolphin as well as she could; she returned to Lady Westhaven, who could not be prevailed upon to go to bed, but insisted on being allowed to see her brother. Emmeline, dreadfully terrified by her obstinacy, now sent for the two physicians who usually attended the family. One of them had been taken by Godolphin to Delamere; but the other instantly attended the summons. Every argument he could use failing entirely of effect, he was obliged to administer to her a remedy, which soon acting on her fatigued and exhausted spirits, threw her for a short time into insensibility. While poor Emmeline, who expected soon the arrival of the unhappy father, and who waited with torturing anxiety for news from Godolphin, could not even sit down; but wandered about the house, and walked from room to room, as if change of place could shorten or lessen her dreadful suspence.

No news, however, came from Godolphin. But a little before eight o'clock, the Marquis's chaise stopped at the door.

He got out; asked faulteringly of the servants for his son. Their looks imported sad tidings; but they were ordered to profess ignorance, and it was the excrutiating task allotted to Emmeline to inform this wretched parent that his only son, the pride and support of his life, had fallen; and what made it still more horrid, by the hand of his daughter's paramour. Lord Montreville entered the drawing room; and the wild and pallid looks of his niece struck him with such horror, that he could only pronounce with trembling lips the name of Delamere: and then throwing himself into a chair, seemed to expect she should tell him what he was unable to ask.

She approached him; but words failed her.

'Delamere! — my son!' cried he, in a voice hollow and tremulous.

'He is not dead, my Lord.'

'Not dead! wherefore is it then that you look thus? Oh! what is it I am to know?'

Emmeline then briefly related his situation, as she had heard it from Godolphin. She had only said, that tho' desperately wounded he yet lived, when Lord Montreville, gazing on her with eyes that bespoke the agony of his soul, and seizing her violently by the hand, said — 'Come, then, with me! come with me, now, this instant!'

He then burst out of the room, still taking her with him. She knew not why he wished her to follow; but went, unequal to resistance or enquiry.

His chariot was at the door. They both got in, and just as it was driving away, Millefleur ran up to it.

'Your master? — your master? —' said Lord Montreville.

'Ah! My Lord, he is — yet living!'

'*Yet* living!'

'And Captain Godolphin sent me to see if you was come, in hopes that you might see him.'

'Go on!' cried Lord Montreville, with a degree of fierceness that made Emmeline shudder. The horses flew. He continued in dreadful and gloomy silence, interrupted only by deep groans. Emmeline had no comfort to offer, and dared not speak to him. At length they arrived at the place. The servants assisted their lord to leave the chariot. Just as he got out of it, Dr. Gardner came out; but too much shocked to be able to speak, he waved his hand to say that all was over; and almost instantly, Godolphin, with a countenance most expressive of what he felt, came out to him also.

'My dear Lord, your going up will be of no use; spare yourself so great a shock, and suffer me to attend you home.'

'He is dead then?'

Deep and mournful silence told him it was so.

'I will see him, however,' said he, pushing by those who would have detained him.

'No, no,' cried Emmeline. 'Pray, my Lord! pray, my dear uncle!'

'Uncle!' exclaimed he. 'Have I deserved to be your uncle? But I am punished — dreadfully, dreadfully punished!'

A croud was now gathering; and Godolphin was compelled to let him proceed; while he himself approached Emmeline, who was left half dead in the chariot.

'Ah! attend not to me!' said she. 'Go, I beg of you, with my poor uncle!'

Dreadful was the scene when the miserable father beheld the body of his son. In that bitter anguish which is incapable of tears, he reproached himself for the obstinacy with which, even against his own judgment, he had opposed his marriage with Emmeline. —'Instead of seeing thus my hopes blasted for ever, I might have grown old among his children and the children of my brother's daughter! But I drove her to France; and in consequence of that, the scourge, the dreadful scourge has fallen upon me! I and my house are low in the dust! Weak and wretched infatuation! Dreadful sacrifice to vain and empty ambition; Oh! my poor murdered boy!' Then, after a moment's pause, he turned suddenly to Godolphin, whose manly countenance was covered with tears. 'Tell me, Sir! did he not wish to see his misjudging father? did he leave me nothing — not even his forgiveness?'

'Lord Delamere,' said Godolphin, 'was wounded in the lungs, and every effort to speak threatened his immediate dissolution. He expressed a wish to see you and Miss Mowbray; but said very little else.'

'I brought her, because I knew he must wish to see her. But he will see her no more!' A deep and hollow groan now burst from him: his sorrow began to choak him; and exclamation was at an end; yet struggling a moment with it, he said quickly to Godolphin — 'Do you think he suffered great pain?'

'I believe very little, my Lord.'

'And he had every assistance?'

'He had instantly every assistance that skill could offer. Two surgeons of eminence were at supper with company in the house; and they were with him before I was, which was not ten minutes after the accident. I never left him afterwards, but to run to Lady Westhaven.'

'Excellent young man! you will still, I know, remain with him, and do what *I* cannot do.' He then paused a moment, and his anguish seemed to gather strength — while with a look of deep and gloomy despair he approached the bed;

slowly and sternly invoked the vengeance of heaven on his eldest daughter; and then continued with glazed and motionless eyes to gaze on the body. From this dreadful torpor it was necessary to rouse him, and to remove him from the room. The united efforts of Godolphin and the surgeons, with difficulty effected it. He was however at length placed in the chariot; and with Emmeline, who was more dead than alive, was conveyed to Grosvenor-street. Godolphin, dreading the scene he was to encounter when they got thither, followed them on foot; and assisted Lord Montreville to his chamber, where he entreated the servants not to allow him to see Lady Westhaven, till they were both better able to bear the interview. He then returned to Emmeline; who, quite overcome by excessive terror and fatigue, had hardly strength so speak to him; and unable to support herself longer, retired to bed, where a violent fever seized her; and for near a week she was so alarmingly ill, that Godolphin, in the wildest distraction, believed he saw her snatched from him by the inexorable hands of death. Lady Adelina came to her the evening after Delamere's decease, and never left her bed side while there was the least appearance of danger; Godolphin continued whole days in the little dressing room that adjoined to it; and Fitz-Edward, who insisted on attending him during these hours of torturing suspence, was unavoidably frequently in the presence of Lady Adelina, whose every sentiment was for the time absorbed in her fear for a life so dear to them all.

At length Emmeline, tho' yet too ill to leave her room, was no longer in danger; and Lord Westhaven, who returned instantly to town on hearing the mournful news helped to appease the violent grief of his wife. But on the more settled and silent anguish of her wretched father, his good offices made not the least impression. He seemed to abhor all thoughts of consolation: and when the remains of poor Delamere were carried to be deposited with those of his mother, he shut himself up in total darkness, and refused to admit even Lady Westhaven to participate his sorrows. When she was allowed to pay her duty to him, he conjured her to keep from him the sight of any of the Crofts', and that she would prevent even their name being repeated in his presence. With their visits there was no danger of his Lordship's being offended; for as he had, in consequence of this family calamity, resigned all the places he held, Sir Richard and his two sons were already eagerly paying their court to his successor; and had entered into new views, which formed new political connections, with an avidity which made them equally forgetful of their patron's personal afflictions and of that favour to which they owed their sudden and unmerited elevation. Amidst all the misery which the guilty and scandalous conduct of his wife had brought upon the family of his benefactor, the point on which Mr. Crofts felt the most solicitude, was to know what portion of the Delamere estate was irrevocably settled in equal divisions on the daughters, if the Marquis of Montreville died without a son. The physicians now advised Lord Westhaven to carry the Marquis into the country as soon as possible; where he might enjoy the solitude he so much desired, without being excluded from the air, as he was in town, by being confined entirely to his bed chamber and dressing room. The sight of any of his own seats; places which he had so lavishly embellished for the residence of him who was now no more, he could not yet endure; and Lord Westhaven with some difficulty prevailed upon him to remove to *his* house in Kent. Thither, therefore, the Marquis and Lord Westhaven's family removed, at the end of a fortnight; but Emmeline, tho' pretty well recovered, desired Lady Westhaven not to insist on her being of the party; being convinced, that tho' he tried to see her with fortitude, and to behave to her with tenderness, the sight of her was painful to her uncle, and perpetually brought to his mind his own fatal misconduct in regard to his son.

Lady Westhaven yielded reluctantly to her reasons, and departed without her: but as her health made her immediate departure from London necessary, she went with Lady Adelina to Highgate; who now remained there only for the purpose of taking leave of Lord and Lady Clancarryl, as they were within a fortnight to return to Ireland.

In this interval, they heard that Lady Frances Crofts, infatuated still with her passion for Bellozane, had followed him to Paris, whither he had fled after his fatal encounter with her brother. Bellozane, stung with guilt, and pursued by remorse, hurried from her with detestation; and concealing himself in Switzerland, saw her no more. For some time she continued to live in France in a style the most disgraceful to her family and herself. Nobody dared name her to her unhappy father. But Lord Westhaven at length interposed with Crofts, who, influenced by his authority, and still more by his own desire to lessen her expences, went over, and found no great difficulty in procuring a *lettre de cachet*, which confined her during pleasure to a convent.

CHAPTER XVI

TO fix some plan for her future life, Emmeline now thought absolutely and immediately necessary. To go to Mowbray Castle seemed the properest measure she could adopt; and on that she appeared to determine. But tho' she still meant to adhere to her resolution of remaining single until she became of age, the tender importunity of her lover, the pressing entreaties of her friends, and her own wishes to make them happy, were every hour more powerfully undermining it. Her mind, softened by grief for the death of poor Delamere, and more fondly attached than ever to the generous Godolphin; whose noble qualities that unhappy event had served to call forth anew, was rendered less capable than ever of resisting his prayers; and Delamere, on whose account her determination had been originally made, could now no longer suffer by her breaking it. Still, however, she insisted upon it, that a term little short of what she had named should elapse before her marriage should take place; as a compliment to the memory of her unfortunate lover, and to the deep sorrow of her uncle and Lady Westhaven.

Here, then, she rested her last defence. And when their encreasing solicitations obliged her to consent to shorten the term to three months, Godolphin undertook to make it the particular request of Lord Montreville and his daughter, that their marriage should take place within three weeks. Animated by the hopes of hastening the period, he went himself into Kent; where he pleaded so successfully to Lady Westhaven, that she not only wrote pressingly to Emmeline, but prevailed on the Marquis to give him a letter also; in which, after deploring, in terms expressive of anguish and regret, that unfortunate infatuation which had eventually robbed him of his son, he told her that he had very little more now to wish, dead as he was to the world, than to see her happily married. That the tender attention of the generous Godolphin to that beloved son, in the last hours of his life, had endeared him to him above all other men; that his character, connections and conduct were unexceptionable; and therefore, his Lordship added, that tho' he did not know that he could himself bear to see it, he wished she would not hesitate to complete his happiness; observing, that if she thought it too early after the loss of so near a relation, she might have the ceremony performed with such privacy, that only the respective families need know of its celebration. Emmeline, having now no longer a subterfuge, was obliged to let Godolphin take his own way. He exerted himself so anxiously to get the deeds completed, that before the end of three weeks they were finished. Lord and Lady Clancarryl prolonged their stay on purpose; and they, together with Lady Adelina and Fitz-Edward, were present at the ceremony. When it was over, Lord and Lady Clancarryl took an affectionate leave of the bride and bridegroom, and set out for Ireland, accompanied by Fitz-Edward; who, with the most painful reluctance tearing himself from Lady Adelina by her express desire, was yet allowed to carry with him the hope, that at the end of her mourning she would relent, and accede to the entreaties of all her family.

Godolphin, his Emmeline, his sister and her little boy, took immediately afterwards the road to East Cliff. They continued there the months of May and June; where, about six weeks after their marriage, they were visited by Lord and Lady Westhaven; the latter having never left her father 'till then, and being impatient to return to him, tho' she assured Mrs. Godolpin that he was much calmer and more composed than they had at first expected. In the filial attention of his youngest daughter he found all the consolation his misfortunes would admit of on this side the grave; and Emmeline, who had deeply lamented the lingering and hopeless anguish to which her uncle was condemned, heard with satisfaction that resignation was, however slowly, blunting the anguish he had endured; and that having relinquished for ever all those ambitious pursuits to which he had sacrificed solid happiness, he thought only of rewarding the piety and tenderness of his youngest daughter; and heard of the happiness of his niece with pleasure. When Lord and Lady Westhaven left East Cliff, Mr. and Mrs. Godolphin and Lady Adelina went to Mowbray Castle; where Mrs. Stafford received them with transport, and where they were surrounded by numberless tenants and dependants, who blessed the hour of its restoration to its benevolent and lovely mistress, as well as that which had given her to a man, who had a heart as nobly enlarged, and a spirit generously liberal, as her own.

The comfortable establishment of Mrs. Stafford at Woodfield, was a point which Emmeline had much at heart; and Godolphin, who knew it was now almost her first wish, took his measures with so much success, that it was soon accomplished. Mrs. Stafford, however, at their united request, consented to stay with them while they remained at Mowbray Castle; and Emmeline had the delightful assurances of having made her happy, as well as of having greatly contributed to the restored tranquillity of Lady Adelina.

Mowbray Castle, ever so peculiarly dear to Mrs. Godolphin, and where she was now blessed with her beloved husband and her charming friends, brought however to her mind the mournful remembrance of poor Delamere; and the tears of rapture with which the greatness of her own happiness sometimes filled her eyes, were mingled with those of sorrow for his untimely death. She considered him as the victim of his mother's fatal fondness and his father's ambition; yet that his early death was not immediately owing to his violent passion for her, was a great consolation; and with only the one source of regret which his premature fate occasioned, and which being without remedy yielded inevitably to time; she saw an infinite deal for which to be grateful, and failed not to offer her humble acknowledgments to that Providence, who, from dependance and indigence, had raised her to the highest affluence; given her, in the tenderest of husbands, the best, the most generous and most amiable of men; and had bestowed on her the means and the inclination to deserve, by virtue and beneficence, that heaven, where only she can enjoy more perfect and lasting felicity.

FINIS

www.ingramcontent.com/pod-product-compliance
Lightning Source LLC
Chambersburg PA
CBHW031016030726
47497CB00004B/885

* 9 7 8 0 6 4 5 7 5 1 9 0 1 *